PARADISE COURT
&
AFTER HOURS

Jenny Oldfield was born in Yorkshire in 1949 and studied English at university. She has had stories published in magazines such as *Bella*, *Woman & Home* and *Cosmopolitan*, and has written crime novels, and books for young adults. She lives in Ilkley with her two children.

JENNY OLDFIELD

PARADISE COURT & AFTER HOURS

PAN BOOKS

Paradise Court first published 1995 by Pan Books Ltd
After Hours first published 1996 by Pan Books Ltd

This omnibus edition published 2002 by Pan Books
an imprint of Pan Macmillan Ltd
Pan Macmillan, 20 New Wharf Road, London N1 9RR
Basingstoke and Oxford
Associated companies throughout the world
www.panmacmillan.com

ISBN 0 330 41822 X

1 3 5 7 9 8 6 4 2

A CIP catalogue record for this book is available from
the British Library.

Printed and bound in Great Britain by Mackays of Chatham plc, Kent

PARADISE COURT

Part One

SHAME
November 1913

Chapter One

Tommy O'Hagan waited in the dark alley for a signal from his sister Daisy's dressing room. His worn jacket gave no protection against the swirling November wind. 'Come on, Daisy,' Tommy muttered through chattering teeth. He was starved as well as freezing, and this waiting was getting him down. 'I can't stay here all day!' In the dim, grey light he looked no more than a huddled bag of bones.

At last a shapely hand and wrist emerged through a window and beckoned him. Tommy nipped down to the stage door, Daisy opened it and he slipped in out of the cold afternoon.

'Thanks, Daisy,' he said, though at first he couldn't swear it *was* her under all that muck on her face. Then she spoke.

'Get a move on, Tommy. If they catch you hanging about backstage my name'll be mud!' She propelled him forward by the shoulder. He blundered down a long, cream corridor with open doors to left and right through which he caught the heady impression of feathers, frills, silky dresses and limbs, and the heavy scent of greasepaint and powder. He paused to breathe it all in, but Daisy gave him another hefty push. 'And don't never say I don't do nothing for you!' she cried, shoving him through a narrow door at the far end of the corridor.

Tommy heard it thud shut behind him. The muggy

warmth hit him and he waited for his eyes to get used to the huge, dark auditorium. Better than hanging about the street-corners, he thought. Not that he'd have paid tuppence to see Daisy prancing about up there. But seeing it for free was different. Practicality, not principle, gave Tommy this cast of mind for he'd never in all his fifteen years had the tuppence in his pocket to pay for a ticket.

Daisy hurried back to her crowded dressing room to finish fixing her hair.

Hettie Parsons caught her friend's reflection in the mirror as she pinned a cockade of purple ostrich feathers into her own dark coils. She felt a tiny stab of envy; though she was only twenty-five herself, Daisy's youthful figure seemed to her to be hour-glass perfect. 'Who's it this time, another new gentleman friend?' she asked casually. Her long fingers clipped the head-dress firmly in place. Daisy would be getting into bother one of these days.

Daisy snorted. 'I should say so! No, that was my little brother, Tommy.' She sat alongside Hettie and stole a couple of hairpins. Expertly she wound her long auburn hair into full, soft folds on top of her head.

'You got to be more careful,' Hettie warned. 'One of these days someone's gonna tell Mr Mills and then you're done for.' She'd seen it happen before. If one of the other girls got it in for you, they could easily go telling tales to the manager.

But Daisy just shrugged. 'Here, have one last pull at this lace of mine, will you?' she asked, standing up and turning her back. She breathed in deeply to let Hettie pull the bottom stay holes as tight as they would go.

'If you get much thinner round your waist, you'll vanish,' Hettie warned. But she pulled hard, as requested. Though Daisy's waist was slim, her stays showed the round fullness of her breasts.

'Thanks.' Daisy gave a pert glance at the mirror; chest out, stomach in. Then she went and struggled into her costume, stuffing yards of white petticoat inside the bustled, frilled confection of purple satin and lace.

Up in the gods, Tommy O'Hagan lounged against a brass rail and watched the curtain go up. The lights came on and he squinted down at the stage for a sight of Daisy, but since it was too far for his short-sighted eyes to see he soon gave it up. It was warm and dry, an ideal place for a kip. He slumped in his corner on this, his one shot at luxury, and caught up on some sleep.

Hettie and Daisy stood side by side in the chorus line in their low-cut frocks. They swayed to the music. This wasn't exactly the Alhambra or the Empire, and they weren't Marie Lloyd. So what? They were young and pretty and sang like larks. The Southwark Palace lay open beneath them; row upon row of upturned faces sitting in their plush new velvet seats. They saw the tiers of balconies and boxes, all carved into grapes and cherubs, and painted gold. The heat of the coloured electric lights at their dainty feet and the curling cigarette smoke beyond made them light-headed. They drank in the applause from the galleries. They sang their hearts out before they left the stage to give way to the mother-in-law jokes of Archie Small, resident comic and ladies' man.

Hettie's feet were killing her inside her pointed boots, and her ribcage felt bruised and sore from the rigid whalebone stays. Her own figure was wearing well; still round in the right places, still slender at the waist. Her luxurious, dark, wavy hair was one of her best points. She held her head high, knowing she could still put on a good show against the likes of Daisy O'Hagan and Mr Mills's newer recruits. And she knew her way around better than they did.

Gratefully she eased out of her costume and changed into her street clothes, eager for an hour or two at home with her feet up in front of the fire before they had to come back for the evening show.

A couple of stage-hands came down the corridor, one with a ladder, the other with coils of cable slung over his shoulder. They leaned in at the dressing-room door and winked at the girls.

'Daisy, Daisy, give me your answer do,' they crooned.

Daisy had a sharp retort ready for each of them.

'We going to be here all day?' Hettie asked irritably. Sometimes she wondered why she'd got in with Daisy O'Hagan. After all, she was only a kid of nineteen, new to the halls and too cheeky by half. Though there were only six years between them, Hettie herself was very steady by comparison. Perhaps she felt Daisy needed keeping an eye on. Anyway, she lived close by, just down the court from Hettie, with that ragged family of hers. They shared the same tram ride home.

At last Daisy put on her thin, shabby outdoor coat and she and Hettie stepped through the stage door into the cobbled alleyway and the cold November afternoon. The lamplighters had already been by and brought their small cheer to the main street, so the girls jumped the dark puddles and hurried up there. They soon caught a tram and rode home together past the new Town Hall, across Park Road into the maze of closes and courts just south of London Bridge.

Here they alighted and once again braved the narrow streets.

'Your dad in work just now?' Hettie asked. She buttoned her collar tight and walked quickly past a row of tenements where the gangs hung out.

Daisy shook her head. 'It's been three months since he

lost that last job washing bottles. He says it's women's work and wild horses wouldn't drag him back there again. You should've seen his hands though. Cut to shreds they was by that job.'

'And what you lot living on?' Hettie demanded. She knew Daisy was the oldest in a family of six or seven kids. She'd lost count. With old man O'Hagan out of work, there couldn't be much money coming in.

But Daisy stuck her chin out. 'We manage!'

Hettie stopped on the pavement. 'You'll come in and have a cup of tea then?' she asked kindly.

They stood under the lamp at the corner of Duke Street and Paradise Court. Daisy would carry on into the court to reach her home three floors up in one of the old boarding-houses, where she shared just two rooms with her mother and father and all those brothers and sisters. Hettie would step through the double doors of the Duke of Wellington public house, advertising its fine ales in big gold letters and offering a bright welcome to all the thirsty carmen, dockers, railway workers and builders who lived hereabouts. For Hettie and the Parsons tribe, this was home.

Daisy, pale without her make-up under the gaslight, nodded gratefully. 'Don't mind if I do,' she said grandly, taking up the hem of her skirt and sweeping past a group of young lads lounging on the doorstep.

'S'nice night, Ethel!' one cawed, his Adam's apple working up and down his scraggy throat. He wore a peaked cap, but no neck scarf around his collarless shirt.

'I should shay sho!' Daisy called back, unabashed.

The boy's mates went wild with delight. 'You clicked there,' they shouted in a raucous band. 'She your bird?' and, 'Hey, Smudge just got off!' they cried.

Daisy stepped inside the swing doors of the pub into a room full of mahogany tables and shiny mirrors. There was a strong smell of mingled beer and sawdust. The boys' catcalls drifted through. 'Bleeding monkey parade,' she said, her grin as bright as a button. 'Who do they think they are?'

'Did you see that one with the big belt and the white silk scarf?' Hettie giggled. 'Really loves himself, he does.' But she pulled her face straight when she caught her father's severe eye behind the bar. 'Come through,' she whispered quickly to Daisy. 'Come upstairs and put your feet up.' And she led the way.

Arthur Ogden, lounging against the bar, watched them go and heard the boys' surge of raw laughter outside. He hunched over his porter and beckoned to the landlord, Wilf Parsons, known as Duke. 'That girl of yours still working the halls?' he asked. 'Can't you get her into decent work?'

Carefully Duke dried and polished the glass in his hand. He breathed on it and rubbed it sparkling clean. He wasn't going to rise to Arthur's easy bait. Arthur Ogden was a work-shy wastrel with two kids of his own just growing old enough to begin to cause him a problem or two. Duke would defend his own to the hilt, but he didn't want a scrap. So he went carefully. 'Thought you went about for a bit with a girl from the halls?'

Arthur's dull eyes lit up. 'Did once, and that's the God's honest truth. Lovely looking girl, she was, by the name of Maisie.' He sank into reverie.

'Would that be before or after you hitched up with your Dolly?' Duke put in. Arthur Ogden was all hot air as far as women and work went. Besides, mention of his wife, Dolly, was guaranteed to shut him up.

Where Arthur was small and weedy, Dolly was ample. Where Arthur shirked, she grafted. While Arthur boasted and boozed, Dolly would stand and nod with a grin on her wide face until it cracked in two. 'Arthur Ogden,' she'd yell down the street in perfect good humour whenever she heard of his shenanigans, 'that's sixteen women you've had since we tied the knot to my certain knowledge! And according to you every one a stunner!' And Arthur would have the grace to look at his boots and grunt guiltily. 'It's no wonder you nod off by the fire when you get home nights,' Dolly would tease.

Upstairs, the kettle sat singing on the hob. Daisy O'Hagan warmed her feet by the fire and sighed. 'Didn't see hide nor hair of our Tommy after the show,' she grumbled. 'Cheeky little hooligan, ain't got no manners.' She stretched her long legs luxuriously and hitched her skirt well clear of her slim ankles.

'Leave the poor little blighter alone,' Hettie said. She too settled comfortably in a chair on the far side of the hearth. 'Looks as if he could do with a slap-up supper, he does.' Though things had sometimes been tough at the Duke, what with their mother dying when Sadie was born, and their dad being left to cope, the Parsons kids had never gone short of a good square meal at the end of each day.

Hettie felt sorry for kids like Tommy. You saw them everywhere; without so much as a decent pair of shoes to their name, dressed in jackets three sizes too small, ragged-arsed and skinny. Only last week she'd seen young Tommy, desperate to earn a penny, chasing rats for Annie Wiggin down the bottom of the court. Annie hated rats and was prepared to part with real money to be rid of them. 'I'll give you a penny for a pair!' she declared. 'They've got to be still warm, mind you, and none of that rigid mortis. You bring them to me hanging by their horrible little tails. I don't want no stinking old ones you dug up to try and trick me with! Fresh ones, you hear!' And she'd stumped off into her front room to dust, clean and box the stuffing out of her one easy chair.

Hettie waited until Daisy had finished her mug of tea

and the doorstep wedge of bread and dripping that she'd given her before she made a move away from the cosy fire. She checked her hair in the mirror over the mantelpiece, and smoothed and tucked her lacy white blouse inside the tiny waistband of her skirt. 'Ain't you got no home to go to?' she grumbled softly. There was no sign in the house of either her older sister, Frances, or of young Sadie. 'Well, it's either get yourself off home or help me with the spuds,' she said. She went through to the kitchen to begin making supper for her father and the boys.

Daisy leapt up, scattering crumbs and swigging down the last of her tea. 'Better go.' She winced at the chilblains on her toes as her warmed feet made contact with the Parsons' hearthrug. 'Ma wants me to mind the little ones. Ta for the tea.'

She was already on her way downstairs when she bumped into Robert Parsons.

'Steady on, where's the fire?' he called. He grabbed her round the waist as she half fell against him. 'Or has our Frances been having a swipe at you two lovely girls again?' He grinned and took a second or two longer than he needed to set Daisy back on her feet. 'She's a bit strait-laced, is Frances. Is that why you're in such a rush?'

With the way down blocked by Hettie's brother, Daisy retreated coyly upstairs. 'Frances ain't in. Hettie's cooking supper,' she reported breathlessly. She felt herself colour up under Robert's brazen gaze. His handsome, moustached face was still grinning below her as she backed off. Beyond him, she caught sight of poor Ernie, trailing after.

'And you mean to say you was on your way without so much as saying hello to me and Ernie?' Robert put his arm around her waist again and swept her back into the living room. 'Even knowing how it makes our day?'

Daisy was reduced to blushes and giggles. Robert Parsons overwhelmed her with his teasing, though she was bold enough with other men. He did it to all the girls, but Daisy was half in love with his hazel eyes and bristling dark moustache.

Hettie marched in from the kitchen, knife in hand. 'Robert, you put Daisy down, you hear. You're a rotten flirt and she has to go and help her ma!' She flashed her brother a cross look. 'And, Ernie, I need some help if anyone's to get anything inside their bellies tonight.'

Ernie set off to obey and follow Hettie back into the kitchen, when Robert stuck out an arm to stop him. He winked. 'Here, Ernie, come and say hello to Daisy first.' There was a broad grin on his face as he loosened his stiff collar. He stuck two fingers inside it and unhooked the metal studs. 'Come on, Ernie, don't be shy.'

Daisy blushed and smiled at slow, awkward Ernie. Though he had Robert's sturdy build and wide brown eyes, and was as good-looking as the rest of the Parsons, he had none of their quickness of mind and speech. He moved forward at half speed, darting glances at his older brother. Daisy thrust out a hand. 'Hello, Ernie,' she said in her animated way, and she gave him a brilliant smile.

Ernie took the hand. It was small and slim. He looked up at Daisy's smooth face, at her grey, dark-fringed eyes and thick auburn hair. 'Hello,' he mumbled, wide-eyed and nodding furiously.

'That's right, Ern,' Robert encouraged. He'd rolled back his shirt-sleeves and now slicked back his hair with his fingertips as he watched Ernie's greeting in the mantelpiece mirror. He turned to Daisy. 'Ernie's always going on about you,' he said. 'He thinks you're a dazzler!'

Daisy's glance was suspicious. 'You're having me on,' she said.

'No, honest.' Robert crossed his arms and studied Daisy.

'He does.' And he began to hum, 'He's half crazy, all for the love of you!'

Ernie stood, enthralled.

'Not funny, I don't think!' Hettie yelled from the kitchen.

'Well, bring him along to the show, why don't you?' Daisy suggested. 'I think he'd like that.' She made a move to go.

Robert nodded slowly, still standing his ground. 'Maybe I will,' he agreed.

Hettie emerged from the kitchen threatening dire consequences if Ernie didn't manage to tear himself away from the lovely Daisy, and Robert sent him up to help while he escorted Daisy back downstairs. He parted with her in the public bar. 'Mind how you go,' he said, holding the door with exaggerated courtesy.

'Here, Robert, there's three barrels standing here waiting for you to tap,' Duke called gruffly from behind the bar. 'Never mind the girls, just for once in your life.'

Robert went off grinning to help his father hammer the brass taps into the new barrels. He took up the heavy wooden mallet they kept on the top cellar step and inserted the first tap with a sharp, expert blow. Then he tapped gently at the bung on the top which would let air into the barrel when they began to draw the beer. It was a skilful job, to be done without loss of liquid and without disturbing the sediment newly settled at the bottom of the barrel. Duke watched and grunted with satisfaction as Robert finished the job.

'I only hope it tastes better than the last lot!' Arthur Ogden said sourly, as he slammed his pint pot on the counter for a refill.

Chapter Two

By 1913, Wilf Parsons, known to all his customers as Duke, had run the pub on the corner of Duke Street and Paradise Court for almost a quarter of a century. He'd seen service in India as a farrier, chosen because of his massive build and his long-time knowledge of horses. His own father had driven a hansom cab, and his father before him. Wilf had been brought up to the ring of iron shoes on the cobbled yard below, and he'd sat alongside his father through the dirty black fogs of many a London winter.

At seventeen the strong lad had joined the army for adventure, and left it at twenty-five with the usual conviction that the sun never set on the British Empire. Army service had impressed upon him the values of orderliness over impending chaos, sternness in the face of insurrection, and a belief in polishing, spitting and polishing again against all the combined forces of darkness.

The army had turned him into an upright, impressive young man who didn't question things deeply. But afterwards he sought a situation minus the constant 'yes, sir, no, sir, three bags full, sir' of life in the army. He knew enough to be his own boss now.

First he must find a wife, and through his father's family he was introduced to a girl in service with a Chelsea property owner. She was the cousin of a cousin, named

Patience, and that was her nature too. Pattie, as Wilf called her, was a drudge to the Chelsea family; a tweeny who was as badly treated by the housekeeper and the other servants as she was by the mistress of the house. Up before five each day, she had to clean and lay fires in twelve different rooms before the rest of the household had risen. It was her job to provide hot water for the bedroom pitchers, her job to cart away the lukewarm slops. If a coal scuttle was ever found empty, Pattie felt the housekeeper's stick. She scrubbed and brushed and polished until midnight seven days a week. Bed was a box in a garret.

Duke rescued his Pattie from this slave labour by marrying her. She was just nineteen. He was twenty-six. He found work as a cellarman in a pub in Spitalfields, where his size and muscle came into their own once more. He rolled the great barrels down chutes and up cellar steps with enviable ease, and hoisted the empty ones like toys on to the dray carts. Besides, he never fell sick and he never missed a day through drunkenness, unlike so many in his trade.

While Pattie gave him children to dote on; first Frances, a solemn, round-faced baby with her mother's pale colouring but her father's striking dark eyes; then gurgling, smiling Hettie, so Duke worked his way into the esteem of the pub owner. And when, in 1889, Jess was born, a third daughter and so a cause of disappointment to the burly cellarman, the offer came of a pub of his own.

It meant moving across the water and leaving behind all Pattie's family for new neighbours, new streets. But they went eagerly to set up home above the run-down Duke of Wellington public house at the corner of busy Duke Street and dingy, ramshackle Paradise Court.

Five years on, the family had grown to be as much a part

of the place as the bricks and mortar. Indeed, Wilf had already come to be called 'Duke', and the name had stuck.

When the Parsons moved in with their young family, the Duke itself was one of the old-style beer houses; disreputable home to King Beer and Queen Gin. But the neighbourhood was a warm, closely connected one of men who'd built the underground railways, or who worked the markets and the docks, and women who'd begun to go out to work in the factories and shops. A problem shared was a problem halved, they said. And the Duke was the place to meet and give vent to troubles after work. This was true for the men at least. The women often preferred to stay at home to gossip, or else they chatted on street-corners in fine weather, while their hordes of children played at marbles in the gutter.

Wilf Parsons, or Duke as he now was, wanted to provide a place a notch or two above the standard in the working men's own homes. To that end he painted and spruced the place up with cast-iron tables with glossy mahogany tops. And when money allowed, he lined the walls with beautiful bevelled and etched mirrors and fancy brass brackets for the gaslights. Electricity failed to impress him, however, and he clung for many years to the familiar hiss of gas and the gauzy white mantels.

Meanwhile, Duke's family had increased in size. Robert was born, his pride and joy. The boy was perfect in looks and temperament; impossible to upset and with a ready smile for all the coos and caresses bestowed by his older sisters. Duke felt his heart would burst with pride whenever he took an hour off on a Sunday and walked at the head of his small procession across London Bridge and under the stern white walls of the old Tower.

It almost burst with a more painful emotion before long,

however, when he nearly lost Pattie as she bore him their next child. Never strong, she found the complicated labour was almost too much for her, and poor Ernie himself was damaged in some unseen way; not perfect like Robert.

Duke thanked God that Pattie was spared, and for a time they were careful to have no more children. Then, in a kind of gentle, autumn affection, a baby was conceived. It was another troubled pregnancy, and this time Pattie was too weak and worn out to survive the labour. Sadie, another girl, was born, but her mother died to give her life. Duke almost went under from grief, but his own sister, Florrie, stepped in. She pulled things together, and brought up the children while he worked on behind the bar, steadily serving the drinkers of Duke Street and Paradise Court.

Business never slackened and time lessened the hurt, though it never entirely healed the wound. After Pattie's death a strange thing happened to Duke. As if angry with her for dying, he turned to disliking all women. A mild, slightly amused distrust of their fussy, gossipy ways developed, and he could never rid himself of the suspicion that a woman would, given half the chance, worm her way under your skin and into your affections, where she would not be welcome. There was no place there except for Pattie; Duke was adamant about that. It meant he even kept his own daughters half at bay, as if Frances, Hettie, Jess and Sadie would insinuate themselves and coax and steal away a little part of his heart.

Now with Sadie aged fifteen, the rest were practically off his hands. Frances held down her steady job at Boots the Chemist, Hettie had found herself a good life and income treading the boards. Jess was comfortably in service over in Hackney. Robert used a mixture of brain and brawn to pick up any well-paid work that was going in the docks. And Ernie, poor Ernie was at least happy in his own way. All in all, Duke felt that his motherless family had managed to stay on top.

As for himself, he still cut a fine figure. Nearly sixty, respected up and down Duke Street, and in the court, life dealt him little blows, it was true. But nothing serious, nothing he couldn't manage to shrug off.

Now he looked balefully over the top of the shelf he was wiping down as Annie Wiggin marched through the swing doors. Annie was one of life's little blows.

She came up to the bar in her scuffed, unlaced boots and rapped her jug down. Steadily Duke wrung out the rag he was using. Rattle, rattle went Annie's earthenware jug. 'Ain't no one round here got a pint of porter?' she demanded. She rested her elbows on the bar. 'As if my money's not as good as the next man's!' she declared.

Arthur Ogden shuffled a yard or two further down the bar. Annie's sharp tongue was to be avoided. A couple of other young drinkers looked on in casual amusement.

'Men!' Annie proclaimed again. 'All the bleeding same! All over you when they want something from you! Like bleeding December any other time! Freeze to bleeding death standing waiting for any of them! Here, ain't no one going to serve a person!'

Every tea-time Annie shuffled down Paradise Court in her lost husband's cast-off boots. They were the only things he left behind when he went, telling her he was off to sea on another trip and would be back in two weeks. Two weeks soon stretched to two months, and still the old boots dried and curled at the hearthside. After two years to the day, Annie declared him lost at sea and began a life of her own running a haberdashery stall at the local market. She bought and sold vast yards of virginal white lace, bags of beaded, pearled and silvery buttons that sat in their boxes like buried treasure. Her stall was decked with blue and white and cherry-red ribbons, and it was stocked with hooks, needles, pins, scissors and skewers like a miniature torture chamber. And yet Annie herself trudged everywhere in her faithless husband's boots. 'I fell in the cart good and proper marrying him,' she would grumble. 'Still, it's a gamble you have to take.' And so life went on.

As she stood and rattled her jug in Duke's deaf ears, Hettie swept downstairs and into the pub, on her way out to the evening show. She gave Annie a smile and tutted at her father. 'Here, Annie, pass us your jug,' she volunteered. 'I'll fix you up.'

'And tell your dad from me he's too slow to catch bleeding cold,' Annie moaned. Then she looked critically at Hettie's green velvet coat and matching hat, all adorned with feathers and a kingfisher-blue bird's wing, intact and standing proud of the crown. 'Where you been buying your bits and pieces?' she asked suspiciously, with narrowed eyes.

Hettie kept on smiling as she handed back the full jug. 'From you mostly, course!'

'But not that blue item sticking up there.' Annie pointed an accusing finger. 'You never bought that from me!'

'I said "mostly"!' Hettie answered defiantly. 'As a matter of fact, I got this from Coopers'.'

'Ooh, la-di-da!' Annie shrieked. '"As a metter hof fect . . .!" Go on, tell us what you paid for that bit of dead pigeon, Hettie Parsons!' She made fun of Hettie hobnobbing in the big department store.

'Calm down, Annie.' Hettie came round to the front of the bar and took her by the elbow. 'Got your jug safe? Right then, I'll walk you home. I need to talk to you about some jet buttons I seen on your stall last time I passed.'

'Jet buttons?' Annie heard the words through her disgruntled haze. She allowed herself to be propelled smartly between the swing doors and out on to the street. Through years of practice, the beer stayed in the jug as Annie shuffled down the cobbled street. Hettie steered her past lamp-posts, across the court to one of the houses at the bottom. 'Jet buttons don't come cheap,' she told Hettie as the younger woman opened her front door. 'But I might be able to do something special, seeing as it's you,' she promised.

'Thanks a lot! I'll drop by at the stall some time soon. Night, Annie,' Hettie said good-humouredly. She pulled her collar high, winked at Tommy O'Hagan in residence under a nearby lamp-post and stopped to ask him where Daisy was.

'Gone,' he said darkly. 'Gawd knows where!'

'To work, you ninny!' Hettie told him. It meant she was late, so she set off up the close at a trot, regretting the plumage on the green hat after all, for it caught in the wind and made negotiating the shallow tram step into an art form that a working girl in a hurry could well do without.

At the tram stop Frances descended as her sister, Hettie, got on. The women had only time for a quick hello. 'Something up?' Hettie called through a side window. Frances looked even more serious than usual. And she was late back from work.

'I've been to see Jess,' Frances replied.

'And?' Hettie craned her head sideways. The feathers in her hat flapped furiously. She held it on with one hand as the tram wheels ground, sparked and rattled off.

'Tell you later!' Frances waved. She stood on the pavement in her slim grey jacket. Her fur hat, pulled well down, was practical and warm. Her gloves were good kidskin leather. People would take her for a teacher perhaps, or an officer working for the Relief Board, and they wouldn't notice the attractive symmetry of her oval face, the fine brows, the chestnut tint in her hair. She made herself too severe and plain for that. At twenty-eight, Frances was considered a long-term spinster. She'd put herself on the shelf by choice at first, and now she was stuck there.

No boys called out to her at the corner of Duke Street, and Arthur Ogden felt unaccountably guilty as she came quietly through the public bar. 'Evening, Miss Parsons,' he said politely. Then he picked up his cap and pulled it firmly on to his head. 'Best be on my way,' he called out to Duke.

Frances smiled and went on up.

Blow it, Arthur thought after she'd gone. What am I saying? Time for another one at least! And he took off his cap again.

Robert had told Frances time and again that she was bad for business.

'How can you say that?' she said, alarmed rather than amused. 'I don't say anything! I don't do anything to make you say that, do I?'

'Exactly!' Robert said, grinning. 'You just are, Frances! Respectable, that's what you are!'

'And that's bad for business?' she retorted. 'Well, then, I'm glad!' She would storm off, unable to take Robert's jokes.

Now she went upstairs with a preoccupied look. As she paused at the top step to take off her hat, she sighed. But the sight of Ernie through in the kitchen, his broad back turned, his figure full of studied concentration as he stood at the sink to wash the dishes, filled her with a rush of warm feeling. She went in quickly and gave him a bright hug of greeting. 'Now tell me about your day,' she said. 'While I toast some cheese here at the fire. Go on, Ernie, who have you seen?'

'Daisy,' he said slowly. He sounded unreasonably happy.

'Good. And what have you done?' Frances relaxed as she knelt by the fire. She held a slice of bread and cheese at arm's length on a long toasting fork.

'Brought up three barrels from the cellar with Robert.'

'Good again! And where's Sadie?'

Ernie plodded on through the pile of dirty plates. He was meticulous about the washing up. 'Don't know,' he decided. 'She's not here.'

Frances nodded. The heat began to send her into deep thought. She remembered the note Jess had sent to the chemist's shop the day before yesterday. 'Dear Frances,' it read. 'Come and see me on Saturday afternoon. I need to talk to you. Love from your sister Jess.'

She'd gone along, puzzled and fearful. Jess had been with the Holdens for three years or more, with no trouble, no complaints. Like everyone else, she had to work hard, but that didn't trouble their family. They'd all been brought up to work. No, it couldn't be that. Frances had opened the iron gate and trodden up to the tradesmen's entrance with increasing worry. She rang the bell. Jess herself came flying down the corridor to answer the door. Frances went in, spent ten minutes with her sister, listening hard.

Then, feeling leaden and slow, she'd come back home on the tram. Now she heard her father's heavy footstep on the stair. Ernie still worked quietly and methodically in the kitchen. Duke came in.

'Joxer's behind the bar for ten minutes,' he said. He sighed and sat down. 'Is there any tea up here?' Duke was practically teetotal and never drank beer or spirits when he was working. Ernie heard, came through for the kettle and took it away to fill it at the tap. 'Good boy,' Duke said.

Frances was still crouched by the fire, but the toasting fork lay on the hearth neglected. The firelight caught her face, flickering shadow then warm red light across it. There were glints of red-gold in her light brown hair. 'Dad,' she sighed, then stopped.

Duke sat in the chair behind her. 'Trouble?' he guessed.

She turned and saw the lines on his face, the years of hard work. She could hardly bear to be the bringer of bad news. 'It's Jess,' she said quietly. She'd promised, she reminded herself. She was the oldest sister and she took the family's troubles squarely on her own shoulders. She would have to tell him. She looked up again at the light of the fire flickering over her father's face.

He looked down at her and guessed the truth. 'She hasn't, has she?' he said sadly. There was no need to go into any details; he just knew.

'She has.' Frances nodded.

Duke sat and looked for a long time into the fire. 'And?' he prompted at last.

Frances swallowed hard. 'She wants to know will you take her back?' she said. 'Jess asked me to ask you, can she come home?'

Chapter Three

Duke soon went downstairs again to take over from Joxer at the bar. He had given no definite answer to Frances's anxious question on her sister Jess's behalf.

'Don't rush me,' he said. 'Jess has got herself into this mess. She ain't the first and she definitely won't be the last.' He went straight down and gruffly told the cellarman to get off home. He served beer to his customers in his usual steady way. So, his third and troublesome daughter was in a spot of bother. He wouldn't be pushed into a rash decision, he'd told Frances. Maybe she could come home to have the child, maybe not. But then he thought of the gutter women, clutching ragged bundles to their thin chests, who sold themselves for sixpence to put bread in their little ones' mouths. He saw them down the dingy back courts, white-faced flotsam of the city. No daughter of his must come to that. Duke held a glass up to the light and polished it for a third or fourth time.

'Fill 'er up.' Arthur Ogden was into the slurred phase of his night's drinking. 'Make it 'alf an' 'alf.' He grinned across at Sadie Parsons, who seemed to his bleary gaze to be a golden angel in a halo of gaslight. She stood by the door, having just come in, heralded by a gust of sharp, cold air.

'About time,' Duke called sharply to her. 'Where you been till this time?'

'I been at Maudie's like I said.' Sadie took off the tartan beret perched jauntily on the back of her head, walked over and threw it down on the shiny bar top. She ducked under the counter to join her father amidst the bottles and barrels. 'Remember, I said I was going to Maudie's house.' She gave him a bright, conciliatory peck on the cheek.

'Yes, and missed all the chores,' Duke grumbled. 'Hettie had to make supper with no one around to lend a hand.'

'What about Frances?' Sadie settled unconcerned on to a high stool behind the bar. Her bright, thick hair tumbled in a loose plait to her waist, chestnut brown against her white blouse. She was the prettiest of the Parsons girls, with all the shine of undimmed youth. Her face was a small triangle of pleasing features; dark eyes widely set and heavily lashed, a small, straight nose and soft, full mouth whose pouts and smiles would soon storm the stoutest hearts. And she flitted between school and friends' houses and home with a carelessness that her sister Frances had never had, an innocence long since gone from Hettie's life, and the delicate beauty shared by all the sisters, Jess included. 'I thought Frances would be here,' she repeated. Her father was in a bad mood about something, so she must sit and humour him.

'She had to go to see Jess,' Duke said, short and sharp. 'It's too much to get Hettie to do everything, what with her going out again at night.'

Sadie nodded. 'I'm sorry, Dad, I never thought.'

'You never do, you young ones. That's your trouble. Just you wait till you're finished with school and working in the rope factory down the road. See how you like it.' He grumbled on. The rope factory was his worst threat, but he was serious in his own mind about being stricter with Sadie, to make up for the mistakes he'd made with Jess. Jess had always been headstrong, and look now! If she could get herself into trouble as easy as this, without Sadie's looks, think what might happen to the youngest girl in a year or two!

'I'm not working in no rope factory!' Sadie protested. 'I'm gonna work in a hat shop.' She swung her legs off the stool and landed daintily on the floor.

'Course you are,' Arthur Ogden encouraged. 'Pretty as a picture, she is, Duke. Can't send her to work in no factory.' He hunched over the bar and peered at Sadie. 'Just like my Amy. She's gone into hats!'

'She never!' Sadie went up to him to learn more. Amy Ogden, Arthur's daughter, had been a year or two ahead of her at school. She'd worked for a time on Annie's stall straight after she left, but that meant being out in the cold in all weathers and she didn't take to it. Sadie hadn't heard this latest development. 'Is your Amy in a big store up the West End selling hats?' It was Sadie's own dream come true.

Arthur frowned and shook his head, slopping his beer in the process. 'Not exactly. Dolly found a place for her at Coopers'.'

Coopers' Drapery Stores was at the top end of Duke Street by the railway line. Still, it was one up from a job on the market. Sadie pictured her working with ribbon and lace. She'd be selling those huge, frothy hats you saw in Coopers' big plate-glass windows.

'Dolly works in "Hosiery",' Arthur explained. 'So she got a place for Amy in "Hats".'

'She makes them, does she?' Sadie was still eager to know more about the latest fashions worn by the better off ladies.

Arthur nodded. 'Top hats. My Amy puts the greaseproof band inside to stop the oil on their heads from staining the silk lining. Very posh hats, they are.' He looked pleased with his daughter's achievements and smiled sloppily into his drink. 'Mind you, she works long hours, and it's only seven pence for two dozen hats.'

'It's a job, ain't it?' Duke said. He wiped the stains around Arthur's glass as he kept an eye on the door. Chalky White and his gang had just come in. 'Go up and get something to eat,' he told Sadie. 'And no messing.'

Sadie made a face. She ducked under the counter, too late to avoid the bunch of new customers advancing on the bar.

Chalky White was well known on Duke Street and down the court, where he lived in a squalid corner in one of the cheapest rooms rented out to workmen. In his late twenties, he worked as a warehouseman on Albion Dock, but this was only a front for the many dodgy deals he was involved in. Everyone knew Chalky cheated his way along the waterfront, earned plenty, then blew the money on the clubs and halls. He was over six feet tall, kept fit at Milo's, the local boxing club, and had a reputation for knowing how to handle himself in a fight. He was a flashy dresser and didn't mind spending the easy money on the string of women he went around with. But they didn't like his temper. 'You never know where you are with Chalky,' they said. 'He'd as soon hit you in the gob as give you a kiss.' They quickly dropped him, and afterwards every one had a tale to tell about Chalky's drunken rages. Yet when he was sober and dolled up for a night out, he could be hard to refuse. 'He's got a way with him,' they warned. 'You have to watch out.'

He swaggered in ahead of four or five mates and caught sight of Sadie. 'Oh my, what lucky fellow's walking out with you?' he called with a low whistle. He jostled his pals with his elbows.

Sadie stopped in her tracks. She blushed and looked back at Duke.

'Go on up,' he repeated.

'What's the rush?' Chalky said. He leaned against the door. 'I only want to know who's her beau. It's not one of them little ikeys hanging around out there, is it? You're too good for any of them, you know!'

Sadie blushed a deeper red. 'I'm not walking out with no one,' she said, gathering her dignity. 'And if I was, it wouldn't be with any of them hooligans.'

'Quite right. Like I said, a girl like you can afford to be a bit choosy, can't she, Arthur?'

Chalky got one step bolder, reached out and took Sadie's arm. Then he advanced her with mock gallantry towards the bar, surrounded by his friends. Arthur grabbed his cap and prepared to leave. If there was trouble brewing he wanted to be well clear of it. 'Don't ask me,' he mumbled. There was an inch of beer left in his pint glass. He gulped it down, jammed his cap on his head and called out his farewells. Duke was getting up a head of steam back there behind the bar at the way Chalky was messing his girl about. 'Night all!' He threaded his way to the door between smoky tables. Everyone had a wary eye on the Chalky White gang. They knew Duke wouldn't stand any nonsense.

But as Arthur scuttled out into the street, Robert Parsons came in. Quickly he sized things up, threw his cigarette to the floor and moved in on Chalky. Stockier than the glib warehouseman, but smaller by four or five inches, Robert squared up. Both his hands were clenched into fists, resting at hip height. He thrust out his broad chest and his dark moustache seemed to bristle with anger. White looked down at him, a superior smirk stretched across his thin lips. 'Watch it, boys, I think we got trouble,' he sneered.

Sadie had backed off against the bar into the space afforded by Arthur Ogden's hasty exit. She felt hot tears of shame brim and prick her eyelids. 'Leave off, Robert,' she pleaded. 'He ain't doing no harm.'

'No, and if you'd done as I told you and gone upstairs when you was asked, we could all have been spared this blooming circus!' Duke snapped.

Sadie fled, her cheeks wet.

Duke leaned forward on the bar, his hands spread wide. He didn't mind Robert showing Chalky White who was boss if necessary, but he cast a worried eye over the empty glasses ranged along the bar top. Quickly he removed them to a safe place in the stone sink. Other customers cleared a space around the two men and an air of tense expectation spread through the room. One or two of the boys hanging about on the doorstep crept in to watch the fight.

'That's my little sister,' Robert began slowly. His eyes swivelled from Chalky to the heavy mob ganged up behind him. He'd already clean forgotten his own flirting with Daisy O'Hagan earlier that evening. In his book that was innocent fun, whereas Chalky White was a dirty-minded lout who couldn't even keep his foul mouth and hands off a fifteen-year-old girl. His fists were raised to chest level now, thrust out in front of him. He'd fight the lot of them if he had to.

'You don't say!' Chalky's insulting grin stiffened. He pulled at the white cuffs of his best shirt, then back went his shoulders. He cleared his throat. 'Now look,' he said. 'No point taking this any further, is there?'

A disappointed sigh went round the room like a great barrage balloon beginning to deflate and sag. Chalky's mates backed off. Chalky himself thrust his hands into his trouser pockets. 'I'll give you a fight any time you want, down at Milo's that is. But just now I'm busy and my mind's on other things.' He grinned, still casually twisting the knife. 'And I got all my best clobber on.'

Robert's glance ran over Chalky's grey silk necktie neatly knotted between the peaks of his high white collar. He wore a dark waistcoat fully buttoned, with a fancy gold watch chain slung in two loops across his chest. A long fitted jacket over lighter grey trousers and soft leather shoes completed the outfit. It was best clobber all right. Most East-Enders would never hope to own a suit of clothes like that. If they had one once for their own wedding day, it was in pawn by now and only got out for funerals. Robert snorted in disgust. He turned on his heel. Chin thrust out, he headed straight upstairs to rant at soft-headed Sadie.

Chalky winked at his mates. He turned and leaned on the bar. 'Six pints of best bitter,' he said to Duke, staring him out without flinching. 'And have one for yourself.'

Duke nodded. He drew from the barrel into a jug, then poured the beer with expert ease, giving each pint a good head. His own gaze was steady as he took Chalky's money. 'You lot heading somewhere special?' he asked.

'Up the Palace,' Chalky replied, smooth and easy.

'Best be quick. Show's started.' Duke slammed the coins in the till and turned back. 'They won't let you in if you're late.'

Chalky swatted the air and grinned. 'I'm best pals with Fred Mills, the manager,' he explained. 'He always lets us in, no bother.' He paused. 'Reckon we can still get an eyeful of one of your girls up there without being flattened by your Robert. And very nice too.'

Duke watched the froth from the beer stick to the sides of Chalky's glass as he downed his pint. He stood his ground, like one of the cart-horses his father had driven. Scum like Chalky didn't deserve an answer. He lived like a pig in his filthy room so he could squander all his money on women, booze and clothes. Down any court, in any tenement block, you could find a bad penny. Chalky was that penny in Paradise Court. Only when he finally swaggered out through the doors and tossed a coin to the waiting gang of boys could Duke breathe freely in his own pub.

Dolly Ogden glanced at the clock on the wall as her husband's unsteady footsteps clattered down the passage towards the back kitchen. He fell down the three steps into the room. She didn't look up again until she'd put the finishing touch to the seam on the stocking she was busy with, then she added it to the creamy pile on the table. By this time Arthur had staggered to his feet.

'Gawd's sake, man, stand up!' she said, as Arthur flopped into the wooden rocking-chair she'd just vacated. But she sighed as she assessed his condition and gave up the struggle. Instead, she shook a pair of stockings free of the silky pile, rolled them up from the toes and tucked the top band of one around the whole roll to secure them together. Then she stacked them at the far end of the table for Amy to count.

Amy, at seventeen, found her father's drunkenness more difficult to bear. 'He stinks of the pub!' she whispered, standing with her back to him.

'Yes, and he's your father,' Dolly reminded her.

Amy shook her head fiercely at this lack of logic. She felt a hairpin or two loosen and a broad swathe of blonde hair threaten to fall free. She fixed it back in place. 'How can I ever bring anyone back when he comes home in this condition?' she demanded in a high and mighty tone.

'Why, who do you want to bring back here?' Dolly went to the fire to swing the battered tin kettle on to the hob.

'I'm just saying *if*. *If* I wanted to bring someone home!' Amy said exasperated. She was a younger version of her mother, already slightly plumper than was fashionable, but with a developing sense of her own style and grace. She wore her waist nipped in tight, and made sure that her dark-blue day dress made the most of her full breasts and hips. Her arms, which she considered too heavy, were carefully draped with full, lacy sleeves, but the plumpness showed at her wrists and ankles. Still, her blonde hair was naturally thick and wavy. She didn't need to pad it out with wire frames like some girls did.

'Well, until you do,' Dolly said with raised eyebrows, 'just count these stockings for me and count your blessings while you're at it.' And she went across to bang about at the sink in the corner, rinsing cups, straining out tea-leaves from the cracked brown pot to see if they could be reused once more.

Among the blessings Amy felt she could count were the recent attentions at work of the boss's son, Teddy Cooper. She thought of him now as she stacked up the stockings.

Teddy was always coming and poking his nose into the hatters' workshop. He pretended to check the work, but really he came to stop and chat with some of the better looking girls. 'Hats' was way up in the rear attics above Coopers' shop, up the back stairs and loosely supervised by Bert Buggles, who was as silly as his name suggested.

Bert always had his long, thin nose stuck into the racing papers. He didn't care tuppence what the lads and girls under him got up to, unless Mr Cooper himself stepped up with an especially important order. Then he became suddenly strict in a mincing sort of way. Hat trade was generally poor, and Amy certainly hadn't found the pressure of work too great since she'd come to Coopers' last autumn, unlike her poor mother in 'Hosiery'.

When Teddy Cooper put in his daily appearance in 'Hats', he didn't usually affect Bert's interest in the winner of the Epsom 2.30. The girls were free to spoon with the young man to their hearts' content. And it seemed to her that she, Amy, was his chosen one. He singled her out for special comment, praising her hair and pretty blue eyes. Once he even put an arm around her waist and popped a chocolate from his coat pocket into her surprised mouth. Yesterday he had whispered a promise to take her to the Balham Empire if she was good. She'd never been to the cinematograph.

Amy cast a sideways glance at her sleeping father. She'd already decided to keep quiet about Teddy Cooper, since there was never any risk of having to bring a young gentleman like him home to meet her ma and pa. Still, she'd go out to see *The Perils of Pauline* with him since he'd asked, and she'd have a good time on the quiet. A girl deserved to be given a chance.

It was all right for her brother, Charlie. He was a boy. They'd always thought Charlie would amount to something, right from the start. Now, with his scholarship and his big ideas, they'd been proved right. As for Amy, they thought the hatters was good enough. The local women blessed the ground Mr Jack Cooper trod on for keeping them all in work. Teddy, though, called his old man a pompous prig. Amy stifled a laugh at the memory.

'What's up now?' Dolly asked. She woke Arthur and practically ladled the weak tea down his throat.

'Nothing.' Amy wasn't telling.

'You don't laugh at nothing, leastways not if you're right in the head. Must be something,' Dolly grumbled on. 'Just tell Charlie to come down here a minute, will you. I want him to run up to the Duke to ask how much the old man's put down on the slate tonight. He'll only lie to me if I ask him straight.' She took it all for granted. Arthur would drink. She'd sew stockings. She'd pay for his beer and hope there was money left over to pay for a shoulder of bacon or some sheep's liver a couple of times a week. If not, well, there was no point losing sleep. Dolly's broad face rarely registered emotion, but she laughed uproariously when she got the chance, usually at puny Arthur's expense.

Charlie came down and took on the errand, ungracious as only a fifteen-year-old boy can be. His head hung down, his eyes stared at the dark stone flags. 'You know I hate going up to that place,' he moaned.

'Oh, la-di-da!' Dolly mocked. 'That place, as you call it, is home from home for your pa. And Duke Parsons is a decent sort. Now you get yourself up there and find out how much we owe him, or else!' Her voice rose to a bellow. Charlie scuttled off.

'Ma!' Amy protested as the door slammed shut.

'Well!' Dolly pulled off Arthur's worn-out jacket and slung his inert arm around her broad shoulder. 'What is he when all's said and done? A little stool-arsed jack, that's what! Here, Amy, be a good girl, help me get your pa to bed.' Dolly brooked no argument in her own house. Amy and Charlie did as they were told.

Chapter Four

The gang of boys hanging around the front steps of the Duke was one reason why Charlie loathed this errand. Though he was older than most of them, it was hard to hold his own against the insults they chucked at him. And he usually had to dodge the odd hob-nailed kick.

'Go boil your head!' he muttered. He wrenched himself free from the grasp of a little O'Hagan, no more than nine or ten years old and desperate to rise in the gang's estimation.

The kid tried to link arms with him again.

'Ooh!' the others cried. 'Shall we? Shall we stroll 'cross the Common?'

They swung their hips as girls did, mimicking a woman's walk. 'Get lost!' Charlie yelled. He freed himself and practically fell forward into the passage leading into the bar. Quickly he made his way through the groups of men standing and sitting in the smoke-filled room. 'How much does my pa owe?' he asked. He had to raise his voice and yell over the sound of the pianola playing away in a far corner. The tune broke off before Duke had time to reply.

Duke consulted the slate. 'Well, young man, he downed five pints of Bass and two pints of half and half. Tell your ma she owes nine pence three farthing.' His answer sailed loud and clear across the room. Charlie nodded his thanks. He felt the hairs at the nape of his neck prickle with embarrassment. He would never get used to this. All he could hope now was that the gang outside would be off down the street on a game of knock-down ginger, hammering on the door of some helpless old woman. As long as they found someone else to annoy he didn't care. Stopping in the passage by the door to button his jacket and steel his nerves, he looked up and saw Sadie coming downstairs.

'Hello, Charlie.' She hugged a big cast-iron pan in front of her, but still stepped swift and sure through the door which he held open for her. She wore her tartan beret, a dark coat and a big blue woollen scarf wound high around her neck. Her long plait and short skirts swung as she turned down the street. 'Are you on your way home?' she called back.

Charlie fell in beside her. 'Yes. Where are you taking that?' The gang had melted away; no fear of being kicked and put down in front of Sadie. It was because he stopped at school and studied instead of hopping the wag with the rest. That's why they called him names; he wouldn't join in with the crowd.

Sadie sighed and raised her eyebrows. 'Frances says I have to take it down the court to the O'Hagans. One of the little ones ain't right. I dunno.' Her lace-up boots tapped along the stone pavement. 'It's a pan of broth,' she explained. 'Frances boiled the ham bones with some pearl barley. She says it's good for you when you're feeling under the weather.'

Charlie strode along. He glared at the little O'Hagan kid, who scuttled on ahead of them now, barefoot, heading for home. He was skinny as a whippet in his threadbare rags. 'Must've smelt the broth,' Charlie noted. He stopped by the door of his own terraced house. At least the steps were clean and scrubbed. His ma did her best, not like some.

'You going straight in?' Sadie asked. 'Why not come down with me instead?' She felt she had to be bold with Charlie Ogden. He was too slow to take things up on his own account, with his nose always glued to a book.

Just lately she'd noticed that behind the buttoned-up jacket and serious manner lurked something interesting and attractive. He was a good head taller than she was, with what she called a nice face. His features were fine and regular, unlike most of the lumpy-skinned, misshapen faces of many of the boys at school. She'd decided to set her cap at him.

'No,' Charlie said after a moment's hesitation. He stared at his ma's whitened steps. She made a border down each side with carefully applied donkey-stone. 'Thanks.' He took the three steps at once and disappeared through the door.

'Thanks for nothing!' Sadie huffed. She tip-tapped on down to the end of the court.

'What's that?' Tommy enquired, sniffing the air. He'd appeared from the cellars of the tenement block like a jack-in-the-box. Now he poked his nose at Sadie's pan and lifted the lid with a grimy hand.

She smacked it smartly. 'Leave off, Tommy. It's broth for your sick brother, that's what. Anyhow, what you got there?' She pointed to a big square object sticking out from behind his back.

He side-stepped, angling to get past without showing what he had hidden. But a tiny, pitiful cheeping sound gave his game away. 'Cage birds,' he said, giving himself over to a couple of minutes' delay. Girls went soft over cage birds.

'Oh, Tommy!' Sadie said. Her face lit up. She put the soup down on the black, greasy pavement. 'Let's have a look. Oh, they're pretty. Where did you get 'em?' Inside Tommy's wire cage, with its bent and battered ribs, perched two ruffled larks. Their breasts sagged mournfully, their round, black eyes blinked with shock.

Tommy held up his property for inspection. 'Railway embankment,' he told her proudly. 'I limed 'em myself.'

'Oh.' Sadie's voice was less enthusiastic. 'Poor little mites. But will someone buy them?' She hoped the pathetic things would last the night. Knowing Tommy, he'd have no food to give them.

He nodded. 'I'm off back up the Palace to catch the crowd coming out. There's always a lady there can get her beau to buy her a songbird.'

Sadie sighed and picked up her pan of broth. 'Best of luck then.' She turned and went on her way. He was never short of ideas, but then you had to look out for yourself in a family like that. Funny, she thought, Tommy's the same age as me and Charlie, but you'd never guess it. He had the face of a fifty-year-old stuck on the body of a runty little kid. She was still shaking her head as she climbed the narrow stairs with the broth, up to the top floor of the block. This was what Tommy called home.

Mary and Joe O'Hagan and their family lived in two rooms at number 48 Paradise Court. It was a bleak, bare-fronted tenement of blackened bricks and grimy windows, butted up against a blank stretch of factory wall and facing out on to another identical block across the narrow cobbled street. Their two rooms, a kitchen and a bedroom, lay at the back of the building, shut off from fresh air and sunlight. Down on the ground floor they shared an earth closet with a dozen other families in the block. Up here in the garret, Mary O'Hagan brought in washing and stood at the wooden tub all day and most of the night with her board, her scrubbing brush and soap.

Sadie tapped at the door and went straight in. Joe O'Hagan sat at the bare table, an empty look in his eyes. He was small and thin, with a hangdog bearing, as if kicks were all he ever expected from life, and all he ever got. Beaten down in body and soul, terrible things took place around him. It was as much as he could do each morning to stumble into his worn trousers and button up his frayed shirt. Then he would sit, bent over the table, vacant and listless, while Mary thumped at the washing-board. Meanwhile, Daisy would smarten herself up at the piece of broken mirror propped on the bedroom sill. Tommy would be out early to beg and scrounge, while the little ones swarmed from kitchen to bedroom, and up and down the dark stairs.

Sadie put the broth on the table. 'Frances sent it,' she said quietly. Peering through the door into the bedroom, she saw a small child lying on a bed under an old blanket. 'How is he?' she asked.

Mary came forward. She wiped her red hands on a coarse apron and shook her head. The pan lid rattled as she lifted it to peer inside. Again she said nothing, but took it to the mean fire in the grate and set it to heat there. Sadie bent and lifted a little one from the floor. She set the child against one hip. Another came and tugged at her skirt.

'You heard the tale, did you?' Joe O'Hagan opened his mouth and the flat, Irish voice drifted across the room. The silent, round-eyed children turned curiously towards him. 'I expect that's why you was sent.'

'Joe, Sadie doesn't want to listen to all our moans and groans,' Mary reminded him. 'We're just waiting on the few shillings Daisy gives us each week, then we can fetch the doctor,' she explained.

Sadie nodded uncomfortably. The child in the bed coughed and turned.

'Aye, but I went before the Board today.' Joe insisted on telling the whole story, his peaky face pale and set. 'I've lost three kids to Paradise Court, and I'll be damned before it's a fourth. We need a doctor. So I went before the Board. "My child has to see a doctor," I tell them. "He has the fever bad. He sleeps five to a bed with the other children. Without a doctor I doubt he'll last the weekend."' Joe paused to study the wood grain on the table. '"And have you no money at all coming into the house?" they ask me. "Nothing to pay for the care of your own child?" I explain we're waiting for Daisy's few shillings. They look me up and down. "And have you no better off family to help you?" Where would I have better off family? My three brothers are all in Dublin, and I wish I was too. I've been here fifteen years, in work and out. Why did I come to the Board if it wasn't necessary, I say?' Joe raised his fist and thumped it weakly on to the table. Mary raised her apron to hide her face. Sadie hugged the child.

'So they turn me away at last. "Wait for your daughter to come home tonight with the money you need to pay your own way." One of them marches me out of the office. "And next time you come before us, I advise you to wear a suit," he says. I say to him, if I had a suit, I'd *pawn* it and pay for a doctor myself. I wouldn't go to the likes of him.'

A hush fell on the room as Joe stopped for breath. It was broken by the child coughing and Mary sniffing. 'Daisy will bring us the doctor,' she promised.

'Aye, not those nice bastards over there.' Joe sat, wrapped in misery.

'Joe!' Mary remonstrated. She turned and took the child from Sadie, then went and bent over the pot on the fire. Strands of greying hair fell forward on to her face. With a weary gesture she pushed them back. She was worn out.

'Daisy's a good girl, and she's good to us,' she told Sadie as she stirred the broth.

'Oh aye,' Joe said, hollow-voiced. 'Working in a place like that!'

Sadie left them while Joe issued dire warnings about the consequences of working at the Palace and Mary took a shallow bowl of broth through to her sick child. When she got back to the Duke, she ran straight upstairs to Frances, fell against her shoulder and cried her eyes out. Life was hard down Paradise Court.

Hettie and Daisy came off-stage for the last time that night, just as Archie Small went on for his final session of wisecracks and songs.

'Hello, girls!' He winked as their paths crossed backstage.

'I'm melting!' Daisy gasped. 'Gawd, them lights don't half give off some heat!' She still held the smell of hot dust and metal in her nostrils.

'I'll soon cool you down,' Archie leered. 'Just you wait!'

Daisy glanced at Hettie and mirrored her friend's expression of disgust. 'Ugh!' She gave a little shiver and they ran for the dressing room, jostled by the other girls, crying out their exhaustion.

'Let's have a bit of hush down there,' the stage-manager warned. 'Get yourselves off home before Mr Mills comes and catches you making all that racket.'

'No need to tell us,' Hettie called back. 'You won't see me for dust.' She staggered ahead of Daisy into the room, jockeyed for a chair and fell backwards into it. 'My poor feet!' She moaned. The place was swirling with discarded silk dresses and petticoats, reeking of hot bodies and face powder. The amount of female flesh on view would fill fifty seaside postcards. Hettie bent double to pull off her heeled boots, snagged a nail on her stocking and sent a ladder shooting from ankle to thigh. 'Oh gawd, bang goes my wages!' she cried.

'Come on, Hettie, help me out of this.' Daisy stood over her, demanding help with the tight bodice. 'I gotta get home.'

'That's a turn-up.' Hettie hoisted herself out of the chair to loosen the lace that kept Daisy's waist nipped in so tight. She heard Daisy groan. 'Why, what's the rush?'

'Nothing.'

Both women vanished for a few seconds beneath yards of crimson silk. They emerged, hairstyles miraculously intact. Then they hung the dresses on the rack and scrambled for their street clothes.

'Anyone seen Freddie?' Daisy asked.

'Freddie' was what they called Mr Mills when his back was turned. 'Hasn't he got them wages down here yet?'

'Not bleeding likely,' someone muttered. Greasepaint came off left, right and centre, leaving pale, tired faces in the mirror. 'When did he ever rush down with the wages, you tell me!'

Daisy shrugged herself into her dowdy jacket and set her hat at a sideways angle. She rubbed at her cheeks to encourage a faint pink glow. 'Ready?' she asked Hettie.

'Blimey.' Hettie eyed Daisy. 'I said, where's the fire?'

'Nowhere. Only, I have to get back.'

Hettie vaguely remembered Frances mentioning a little brother ill at home. She knew, too, that Daisy's wage was practically all that kept body and soul together at number 48. Suddenly the rush to get off home made sense. 'Half a tick,' she said. 'And I'll be with you.'

But they were still standing inside the stage door twenty minutes later, waiting for Freddie to show up. Archie Small was already off-stage, pursued by raucous laughter. He bounded down the corridor towards the bunch of girls who were kicking their heels by the door.

'Still here, darling?' He slid up to Daisy and snatched her by the waist. 'Just waiting for Archie.'

Daisy wriggled free. 'Leave off, you horrible little man!'

Archie wore a loud checked suit, with spats and patent leather pumps. His bow-tie nestled against several spare chins, and his waistcoat buttons strained against a large belly. His hair was slicked to one side to conceal a mottled bald patch. 'She only says that because she likes me!' He winked at the other girls.

Daisy jabbed him hard with her elbow.

'Hush, here comes Freddie!' someone warned.

They quietened down as the manager approached, and Archie went off to lounge in an alcove, where he lit up a cigarette. 'Bleeding nuisance!' Daisy muttered to Hettie. She stood anxiously in line to receive her wages.

Fred Mills took his time. He made the most of the power of his position. Tonight he'd brought along some friends to 'meet the girls'. Everyone knew what that meant. Most backed away, sullen and offhand.

'Hettie, I'd like you to meet Mr White.' Mills pressed a few coins into Hettie's palm and drew her forward by the wrist.

Hettie had already recognized Chalky and his gang. Just our luck, she thought, knowing that Daisy was keen to be off. It could mean having to stay behind for a drink at least. She wished she'd taken less care with her outdoor dress. The blue feathers on her hat winked and shone.

'We already met,' Chalky said. 'In fact, we're neighbours, you might say. Hello, Hettie.' He glanced at his pals to measure their approval. 'We was just having a chat with your Robert earlier, wasn't we?' As he turned back to study her, she felt every stitch of her clothing being removed in his mind's eye. But she wouldn't drop her gaze, not for a king's ransom.

'And Daisy!' Chalky oozed the famous charm. He passed a hand through his hair, and when Daisy felt her own hand raised to his lips, she could smell the sickly sweet macassar oil that darkened and slicked down his short cropped style. He hung over her, standing much too close, as bandy-legged Mills passed on down the row of girls. Still, she'd got her wages clutched tight in her other hand.

Jealousy was too strong a word to describe the sensation Archie Small felt when he saw Chalky and his mates ogling fresh-faced Daisy O'Hagan. But he was peeved. He'd set his own mind on that little girl. Anyway, he pushed himself clear of the cold brick wall and strolled towards the group. He approached warily. His difficulty was that Chalky White was a friend of the manager. Even Archie had to mind his p's and q's if he wanted to go on cracking jokes at the Palace alongside the performing Jack Russells and the fez-wearing conjurors. He couldn't risk antagonizing Fred Mills. 'I found us that taxi-cab, girl,' he said, sidling between Daisy and Hettie. 'I got it waiting for us up on the street.'

Chalky's grin tightened. Daisy frowned. Hettie dug her in the ribs. 'Come on!' she whispered. This was their chance to get straight off. Once outside, they could ditch Archie and head for the tram.

'What you girls want with a taxi-cab?' Chalky wheedled. 'We can walk you home, can't we, boys?'

A chorus of agreement followed.

'See. We're even going your way.' Chalky looked down at Archie. 'Run along to your old lady, why don't you? Let a dog see the rabbit.'

Archie felt his forehead break out into a sweat. He clenched his teeth. Daisy was a fool. She'd been slow to catch on and Chalky had got the better of him in full view

43

of all the other girls. Well, she'd be sorry. He backed off in a foul temper, glaring at Hettie as if it were her fault.

Hettie shrugged. Daisy *was* a fool if she thought Chalky White was any better than Archie Small. Hadn't she heard the stories about him?

'Ain't you supposed to get straight back home, so they can fetch the doctor?' she reminded her.

'That's right.' Daisy still met Chalky's bold gaze. 'Another time, maybe.'

But Chalky wouldn't let it drop. He'd made up his mind that Daisy was his girl, for tonight at least. 'Who's sick?' he asked, as he took her by the arm.

'My little brother, Jim. Ma says he's bad.'

'He ain't croaking, is he? Anyhow, what doctor would turn out at this time of night?' Chalky winked at Fred Mills and turned Daisy around towards the door. 'Now just be nice, Daisy girl, and keep a poor man happy!'

The manager glared at Daisy.

She sighed and shrugged. 'Just for half an hour then.'

Little fool, Hettie thought again.

But Chalky paraded Daisy up to the stage door. He winked at Mills again, and glanced back to check that someone else had grabbed Hettie and the pair were following. Hettie found herself on the arm of a small-time crook called Syd Swan, who grinned at her like a lunatic and dragged her along.

Outside, the cold air blasted them. Further up the alley, she saw the tall figure of Chalky White already pressing against Daisy, one arm over her shoulder, the other roaming over her body. He kissed her long and hard. Hettie stared at Syd. 'Don't you try nothing!' she warned, and marched firmly ahead of him up the alley, past the spooning pair.

At least Daisy had the sense to keep up. Two minutes

later, Hettie heard rapid footsteps. Chalky passed by, linked up with Daisy. He sang a cocky little song about taxi-cabs:

> 'To newly wedded couples, it's the best thing that is
> out,
> It fairly beats the hansom cab, without the slightest
> doubt.'

Daisy laughed and ran ahead, like a little flirt. Her laugh showed her even, white teeth and she poked out her pink tongue at Chalky. Hettie looked on as he swung Daisy in the air and landed her again with both hands round her waist.

> 'When driving to the station to go on honeymoon,
> The driver can't look through the top to watch you
> kiss and spoon.'

He sang in a raw voice but Daisy laughed on delightedly. They had to walk all the way home in the drizzling rain through the still crowded streets. 'One last drink,' Chalky said, as the Duke came into view. 'Come on, girls, one last drink never hurt no one.'

Daisy looked doubtful. She glanced down Paradise Court to her black tenement at the bottom. Inside the Duke, the pianola thumped out a tune. Lights glittered through the fancy scrolls and lettering of the etched glass doors.

'I never ask twice,' Chalky said, one hand on the giant brass handle.

'Right you are,' Daisy agreed. She swept in ahead of the rest. 'One last drink!'

She enjoyed all the eyes on her as she flounced up to the bar with Chalky White.

Chapter Five

The pub was crowded out with dockers, carters and market traders all having a fling after a hard week. If you had a few coppers to enjoy yourself you came out. Back home, your old woman would moan on about the cost of this and that, with a long face and a surefire tendency to make it look like your fault if bread had gone up by a farthing a loaf that week. Here at the Duke there was music, a decent place to sit, or the chance to have a knees-up if you felt in the mood. Besides, coming out with your mates was a sign you were getting work, holding your own. It was a bad week if you didn't make it down the Duke on a Saturday night.

The men crowded round the bar. They'd come through another bad year, with more strikes on the docks and down the markets. Nothing had moved through the East End for months as the fruit and veg lay rotting in great piles in the warehouses. You had to live hand to mouth then and your family nearly starved. During August they'd even cut off the water and gas, and then there were hundreds of rats running through the uncollected rubbish.

Now, at the onset of winter, things were better, though union pressure rumbled on and the bosses still didn't give an inch if they could help it. You still queued on the waterfront for your day's work, slipping someone a back-hander for a better chance. But at least the food moved out of the docks now and on to the markets. The dockers, the carters, the stall-holders had backed off from the threatened riots. The system creaked on.

Duke poured pints steadily all night long, with Robert on hand. He relied on this extra help on busy nights; Robert was good for keeping an eye on the barrels and clearing off the empties. He was popular with the customers, many of whom he knew from his dock work. Duke watched him now, mingling with his mates. He shared a joke, throwing his head back to lead the laughter. He was a strong, handsome lad, his foot just on the first rung of life's ladder.

Robert brought two fistfuls of empty glasses to the bar. A cigarette hung from the corner of his mouth, one eye closed against the drifting smoke. 'Watch out, Pa,' he warned. 'Here comes trouble.'

Annie Wiggin had just put in another appearance with some of her fellow stall-holders on the market. They'd gone down the court specially to bang on her door and persuade her out for a natter; four or five skinny women with big voices and loud laughs. Their kids were in bed, minded by the eldest. Their old men were already here, drowning life's sorrows. So they'd donned their bits of finery; their hats decked with ostrich feathers, their long fringed shawls, and they paraded themselves down to the Duke for a bit of a laugh and a singsong. 'Come on, Annie, for gawd's sake. Can't have you moping about all on your own!' They were family women and they took Annie's case to heart. If their man walked out on them, like Annie's husband had done, they wouldn't half give him what for. If they could lay hands on him, of course; which Annie couldn't with hers.

'You're not wearing them old boots again, Annie!' Liz Sargent protested when she answered their knock. 'Them's your working boots!' She glared down at the offending articles; misshapen, boiled, resoled and stitched until they resembled old kippers.

'Them's my only boots,' Annie muttered. 'They was his boots, and I wear 'em in his memory.' She put on a dark jacket which she grabbed from a peg in the gloomy passage. She turned her key in the lock and thrust it down her bodice. 'Well, what we waiting for?' she demanded.

The women made their way back up the court towards the gaslight at the corner. 'What you want to remember him for? That's what I'd like to know.' Liz thought badly of Annie for not putting her best foot forward, so to speak. 'He was a rotten old bugger, so they tell me.'

Annie sighed. 'He was. But he's the cross I have to bear, and these old boots remind me.' She would say no more, but she marched ahead of her spruced-up friends, straight into the public bar.

'Now then, Mrs S.' Duke addressed Liz, deliberately ignoring the bothersome Annie. 'What'll it be?'

The orders went out; a sharp cry for a pint of porter or a drop of gin from each of the market women. If their menfolk were present, they kept well hidden, leaving the women to their own devices. Liz Sargent adjusted a small length of fox fur around her shoulders and grabbed her drink. 'Any rate, I see you put your best hat on to come out with us.' She nodded her approval at the bunches of fake cherries bedecking Annie's black straw boater. 'I suppose that's something.'

'And it ain't even bleeding Sunday!' Annie scowled sarcastically.

'So who died?' Nora Brady winked at Liz.

'No one died. What you mean? This ain't my funeral hat!' Annie glanced at herself in the fancy long mirror behind Duke's broad shoulders. She tucked a wisp of hair behind her ear.

'Who got spliced then?' The women gave wicked, knowing looks.

'Leave off, why don't you? Can't a woman have a bleeding drink?' Poor Annie grew fed up with their teasing and sank her face into a pint of porter.

The women made a great show of leaving her alone. They told Duke to be sure and take good care of her, before they drifted off in pairs to different corners of the room. 'She's all on her ownsome,' they cheeked, thrusting bold faces across the bar at him and pouting their lips. 'Poor lonesome Annie!'

'Silly cows,' Annie grumbled. But she stayed put. If he did but know it, Duke *was* the reason she came in night after night with her earthenware jug, and she didn't care who noticed it.

Underneath the profusion of cherries and regardless of old man Wiggin's boots, Annie wasn't a bad-looking woman. Past her best, it had to be admitted, but sprightly. Well into her forties, her hair had lost none of its auburn tinge, though she hid this good feature by scraping it back from her forehead and twisting it into a tight bun as severe as any workhouse warden's. Her face had a fine, birdlike quality, with rapidly changing expressions. In repose, her eyes were big and dark, the skin tight over her high cheekbones. But seeing herself as the scourge of all errant men had served to fix frown lines on Annie's forehead, and the corners of her mouth were set down. No man alive would have called Annie Wiggin attractive, but a *woman* might stop to look at her and declare she was wearing well, considering.

Duke caught Annie giving him the eye as usual and shuffled off down the bar. He never knew why she bothered, since he gave her not one word of encouragement. 'What'll it be, Annie?' was the longest sentence he'd addressed to her in all the years she'd been patronizing the establishment; through his being married to Pattie and the mourning period after, through her own marriage to Wiggin, who scarpered without paying his bills, and through all the years since he ran off. 'What'll it be, Annie?' he said as he reached for her empty jug in the early evening. 'What'll it be, Annie?' when she called in by herself late at night.

Yet whenever he glanced her way, Annie had her eye on him. He alone of all men must have been excluded from Annie's list of hopeless cases. She sat there rolling her eyes and smiling; an unusual expression for Annie on the whole. If Arthur Ogden attempted so much as a remark on the weather as he passed round the back of Annie's stool, she'd spit at him like a cat. A broad-shouldered navvy lodging in the Ogdens' spare room would feel the lash of her tongue, and she reserved special venom for anyone bearing the look of the sea. They were the happy-go-lucky, often handsome and feckless men who drifted in and out of the tenement rooms, sometimes American, sometimes Polish, with dark walrus moustaches and heavy brows.

Why then in God's name did Annie Wiggin roll her eyes at him? He was Duke Parsons, a decent widower of sixty, weighed down by family care and struggling to keep business afloat during the strikes and troubles. Duke shook his head and backed off in search of Robert, Frances, even Ernie. Anyone would do. He ducked out the back way into the corridor and yelled upstairs. It was Ernie who appeared on the landing, a smile on his face.

'Come on down, son, and give us a hand with the empties,' Duke said. 'It's last orders, so look sharp.'

Ernie nodded and came eagerly down with his flat-footed, heavy gait. He hadn't developed the controlled, springy stride of the average youth. Instead, his legs straddled an invisible ditch, and he thrust them forward like an awkward toddler as he rushed along the corridor into the bar.

Duke grinned and stuck his thumbs in his waistcoat pockets. He was a good son, young Ernie, without a bad bone in his body. But his great, open features made your heart ache in this wicked world.

'Clear the bar for me, Ern,' Duke said, pointing carefully. 'And mind how you go.'

Ernie took each glass between his two large hands as if it was the football cup. He gently deposited them in the sink. Annie sat and watched him. She drank her own glass to the dregs and held it up. 'Here, Ern, take this one from me.' She gave his hand a tiny pat as she handed it over.

But both Annie and Duke noticed the shine go from Ernie's face when his chore took him along the bar towards the corner with the pianola. He'd just lifted another glass when he spotted Daisy with Chalky and his crowd. They were singing their heads off.

Hettie had managed to give Syd Swan the slip and head straight upstairs as they came into the pub. So Daisy stood alone surrounded by young men, head high, face flushed. She'd taken off her coat and wore a blouse as white and thin as any Ernie had ever seen. It was adorned with tucks and frills, and curved in at her tiny waist over a skirt of shiny purple. Ernie sighed as he stared. Somehow he knew he'd never get to sing with Daisy like that, and hold her round her slim waist, no matter how much she smiled and petted him.

Suddenly Chalky broke off singing. He'd noticed Ernie's long, lingering stare. His laughing face narrowed and turned mean as he fixed the boy with a look. Syd's gaze followed. Even Daisy, her throat flushed above the snowy white blouse, stopped singing and put a hand involuntarily to her cheek. Chalky moved a fraction of an inch in Ernie's direction, head on one side, scowling.

'Stop gawping, Ern, for gawd's sake!' Robert broke out of a nearby crowd and seized the glass from his grasp. 'Don't you know you look like a bleeding idiot standing there!' He gave his brother a hefty shove back towards the sink.

Chalky checked his stride, shrugged and turned his attentions back to Daisy.

Robert took a long drag on his cigarette, immediately regretting what he'd just said. There was nothing Ernie could do about it; that was just the way he was, standing there with his mouth open, ogling the girl. He meant nothing by it. But Robert jutted his chin and bounced back Duke's meaningful glare. 'What you looking at, you silly cow?' he muttered at Annie Wiggin as he went past with a handful of empties.

He'd go round in a second and talk to Ern; he'd fix up that trip to the Palace with him. They'd sit together in the plush seats and Ernie would be able to gawp at Daisy to his heart's content. It'd be Robert's treat. After all, the poor kid never went out and it would do him good.

After a few minutes swilling glasses in the sink, Robert had restored himself to good humour. Ernie was plodding around the bar once more, lifting stools on to table tops as gradually customers packed up and went home. Robert stopped for a few words with Walter Davidson on his way out.

'You been down the club lately?' Walter asked. He and Robert sometimes met up at Milo's for a spot of boxing.

Robert nodded. 'I been to see a man about a taxi-cab.' He grinned. 'Wants to sell it. I told him we was interested.'

Walter laughed. 'Blimey, Rob. We're interested all right. Did you tell the geezer we'd have to pay 'im in washers?'

He was a regular at the Duke, spending too much of his meagre wage from Coopers' on beer and cigarettes. Like all the young men round about, he was ambitious to be his own boss. He'd talked often to Robert about the dream of running their own taxi-cab together. Horses were finished in that line of work these days; too messy and slow by far. Both men wanted to be part of the future in the shape of a shiny black, purring automobile. But neither earned more than a pittance; Robert on the docks and Walter in one of Coopers' sweatshops. They were past the boyhood stage of swaggering down the street calling after the birds, but they were still a million miles away from achieving their ambition. Walter thought ruefully of the shilling he'd just squandered pouring beer down his gullet. 'I hope you didn't promise him nothing stupid, Rob.'

'Would I? I said we could pay him bit by bit, on the never-never,' Robert reassured him.

'What did he say?'

'He said we could have the taxi bit by bit an' all; one wheel at a time, with the engine bust up into little pieces.' He winked at his friend.

Walter laughed and went out.

'Silly beggars,' Duke muttered. He'd overheard. 'What you thinking of buying one of them newfangled things for, then? What's wrong with the old hansoms?' He turned on the last, lingering drinkers, including Annie Wiggin. 'Ain't you got no homes to go to?'

Annie fixed her cherry-laden hat further on to her head. 'All right, all right, I'm on my way.' She gave Duke a pert look and shuffled off.

'C'mon, mate,' he grumbled at Chalky White. But he went warily. Chalky had had one too many as usual, and his temper turned nasty when he was drunk.

''E-wants-ter-gerrid-of-us,' the tall, dangerous-looking

man slurred. He leant forward in front of Daisy and grabbed Syd's arm. 'You 'ear?'

Daisy extricated herself from his long reach. 'Well, it's time for me to say ta-ta, at any rate,' she said brightly. As she stood up, Chalky overbalanced and fell. He crashed against Syd, then made a grab at Daisy. As he caught the sleeve of her blouse, it ripped slightly. She turned on him. 'Here, watch what you're about!'

Chalky wasn't too drunk to feel put down by Daisy's cry. 'Very sorry, miss,' he sneered. He launched himself towards her. 'Very sorry, I'm sure.'

Daisy smoothed herself down. 'That's all right.' She tried to meet his gaze, but then looked away and began to search for her coat. There was something about Chalky that made her feel trapped. She wore an uncertain smile as he advanced again, but she felt breathless. 'Gotta go,' she said.

'Not so fast.' He held her by the arm. His hand easily circled her slender forearm. 'You're going my way, any rate.'

'I gotta get back home,' Daisy explained. 'My brother's sick, remember.'

'Aah, poor little mite.' Chalky propelled her out of the pub on to the wet pavement. 'What are you, all of a sudden, bleeding Florence Nightingale?'

'I told you; he needs a doctor!' Daisy felt lousy. The story about Jim was all too true. And she'd been larking around all night instead of getting home to her ma with the money for the doctor. She pictured Jimmy lying under the blanket coughing. She could kill herself for ignoring the poor little thing. Her pa had even been up before the Board; a thing he only did when a kid was at death's door. 'Listen, Chalky, it's true. I gotta go!'

She wrenched herself free and ran off round the corner,

down the straight stretch of unlit cobbles to the far end of the court.

Well, she thought, what difference does an hour or two make? Ma can't fetch a doctor till morning. I'll go up, give her the cash, and she can go straight up Duke Street in the morning.

She was almost sobbing by the time she arrived home. Her attempts to excuse herself had failed. She felt in poor shape as she climbed the dark stairs. She was a wicked, selfish girl with not an ounce of fellow feeling, she told herself. She delved into her pocket for the long-awaited shillings, gritted her teeth and opened the battered, half-rotten door.

Chapter Six

Frances waited for the lull of a Sunday morning in late December before she tackled her father once more about the problem of Jess. This time, he wouldn't be able to claim the distraction of pub work, and he would have had more than enough time to absorb the news. She wanted to play her cards right. Jess needed to be out of that place in Hackney and home with the family before Christmas, when her disgrace would be growing obvious for all to see. That would still give them time to plan ahead.

A pale sun struggled through watery clouds above the grey roofs of Duke Street. Duke stood at an upstairs window, looking down at Dolly Ogden dragging an unwilling Charlie and Amy off to church. She did her best to smarten them up, sending Charlie down the pawn shop on a Saturday tea-time to redeem his Norfolk jacket for Sunday best. Come Monday morning she'd be sending it back, bundled up with her one decent pair of boots and a couple of china dogs from her front-room mantelpiece. That bit of money was vital to see them through the week since Arthur had lost his job at the glass factory. But Dolly was canny; she'd never see them go hungry, and she was bent on putting Charlie through school until his scholarship money ran out. So she sailed up the street to church every Sunday with her kids, one on either side, like a battleship in full regalia, escorted into port by two dutiful tugs.

'Pa,' Frances began in her quiet voice, 'did you hear, they're recruiting for jobs in the Post Office exchange?' She sat in her upright chair by the table, where she kept her sewing basket with its never decreasing pile of socks and stockings for darning. That's how she kept herself busy now, weaving her needle in and out as she sidled into conversation about Jess.

'Listen here, it says I can buy a motor car for only one hundred and thirty-three pounds.' Duke held up his news-paper and pointed to an advertisement. 'One hundred and thirty-three pounds! Rob needs to think again, I say. Taxi-cabs. Motor stables.' He snorted and rubbed the end of his nose with his forefinger, then thrust his large head back between the pages of the paper.

But Frances was not one to be deterred. Her long fingers dipped and bobbed as the needle sped in and out. 'It's women they need to work the switchboards. It'd be a definite step up from tweeny work.' She held her breath and let the idea sink in. 'The Post Office is an up-and-coming job for a woman nowadays.'

'Switchboards.' Duke insisted on missing the point as stubbornly as Frances persisted in making it. 'Telephones. Newfangled nonsense.'

'Now, Pa, telephones are quite common and I'm always on at you to get one for here, you know that. But listen, most women want to come out of service these days. Everyone wants the Post Office jobs and you can't blame them. Look what happens when you stay in service all your life.'

'No need to tell me.' Duke stared stolidly at the advert for the Model T. Then he broke the silence. 'How can you work on a switchboard when you're carrying a babe in arms? That's what you're on about, ain't it? It's Jess. But you tell me how she can have a baby and go working for the Post Office!' He was angry. Frances must be wrong in the head, thinking that Jess could go applying for jobs in her condition, and unmarried.

Frances sighed. 'Look, Pa, Jess is having this baby, we know that. But it ain't the end of the world. It don't have to be. We've got time to think about things, ain't we? First off, she either has the kid, or she don't.'

Duke left his newspaper and came and banged the flat of his hand on the table. The veins in his neck stood out. 'No, you look. The girl's a fool!' he cried. 'Getting herself into this mess!'

'How do you know she had any choice?' Frances looked up at him with her steady gaze. 'From what Jess told me, there wasn't even a by-your-leave.'

'Who was it, that's what I'd like to know?' Duke backed off, stunned.

'The Holdens' son, Gilbert.'

Duke leaned on the table, covering his forehead with one broad hand. Then he breathed deep and stood up straight. If you got a wound in the war, or a kick from a horse, you went and had it cleaned up. A few stitches saw you right. But no one knew how to stitch up this kind of blow.

'Any rate,' Frances went on, 'without the kid she could go about getting a job straight off. If she decides to have it, well, there's plenty of us around here to help her look after it. She can still go out to work and earn her keep.' She kept steadily at her darning. What she wanted was for Duke to take it for granted that Jess would come home, where she belonged. 'That's why I'm telling you, Pa. There's plenty of jobs for women around these days. And the sooner Jess is out of service the better.'

'If there's plenty of jobs around, why's young Amy Ogden sweating away over them top hats in Coopers'?' Duke demanded. 'If there's plenty of jobs, why's our Ett parading herself half-naked in front of them dirty-minded little bleeders at the Palace every night of the week? Tell me that. If there's jobs, why are them poor bleeding women walking the streets out there? Don't talk daft, Frances!'

Duke had raised his voice, but now he halted. That last remark had hit a nerve with him. He turned away, shaking his head. That's what had struck him the night Frances first told him about Jess; what if she ended up like those skeleton-women, clutching her bundle of rags that was really a baby starving to death? He walked to the window to gaze out. Then he took a deep breath. 'Tell her she can come home,' he said.

Frances nodded without showing any reaction. But she was satisfied. She finished off her work, snipped the thread and rolled the socks into a pair. 'I'll go and fetch her this afternoon then.'

Duke's head had sunk to his chest.

'Will you tell the others, Pa?'

'Yes. Go and fetch her home, there's a good girl. Quick as you can.'

Frances went to him, reached up on tiptoe and kissed his lined cheek. She'd been thirteen when her mother passed on. Never since that time had she seen her father look so bad as he did this moment. 'Don't worry, Pa, we'll manage.'

'I'll knock his bleeding head off if I get the chance!' His voice was cracked and hoarse.

She nodded and went to put on her coat and hat. She stepped straight downstairs and out of the house, her heart heavy. She only hoped Jess would be good and co-operative now, since Duke had relented. She'd better realize what it had taken out of the old man; this arrow of disgrace in his respectable heart.

The tram took her up Duke Street, along Bridge Road to Southwark Bridge. Over the river, she stepped out of the cold drizzle down into Cannon Street underground station. She headed north-east to Hackney, feeling the train rattle and shudder, blind to the attractions of Van Houten's Cocoa and Nestle's Milk Chocolate. To outsiders, she was the schoolteacher figure in her high-necked grey costume with its fur collar and matching toque hat. She sat severely, hands crossed over the black leather bag on her knee.

Frances had always been called Frances, never Fran, even within the Parsons family. One look at her told you she warranted the use of her full name if you wished to avoid the risk of receiving one of her somewhat haughty stares. She didn't invite intimacy, with her straight-backed carriage and fastidious manners. She didn't invite suitors either, since she lacked the easy banter of her sister Hettie, or Daisy O'Hagan from down the court.

Her cool appearance might be something she regretted but couldn't do anything to alter. She'd lost her mother at precisely that age when a girl needs some role model in her budding relationships with the opposite sex. She'd no one to turn to when she needed to know the details of how to behave after a man began to show interest. Not a natural flirt, her uncertainty converted at first into shyness, then into a distinct air of reserve. At the age when most girls walked out on the Common or went cycling into the countryside with the boy of their choice, Frances turned to books and study. This was an unusual thing for a girl, even then. She filled her head with novels, with images of Mr E. M. Forster's elegant young ladies touring round Italy or showing up in India to be married. And she turned her back on the Chalky Whites and Syd Swans who drifted in and out of the tenements or who propped up the bar in the pub downstairs.

If she was lonely she didn't show it. Her one disastrous experience in life came after she'd finished with Board School, where she'd won prizes and praise from all around. 'Frances should go and train as a teacher in college,' her own teachers informed Duke. 'She's very able.' But the family was poor, with different expectations. So she submitted to being sent into service much against her will. At seventeen, she wrote home to Hettie in her beautiful copperplate hand that the work for her Mayfair family was dreary and disgusting. She skivvied from dawn till dusk. But worse, the children of the house persistently bullied and cheeked her in front of their parents, much to everyone's amusement. 'There's an old dog called Bob in the house and he's not too bad, I suppose. Otherwise I hate them all, every last one,' she wrote with uncharacteristic bluntness.

By nineteen her heart was set on moving on. She scoured the newspapers for job advertisements, wrote many letters of application, mostly to the biscuit, cardboard-box and glasswork factories in her home borough. But biscuit factories didn't need women with perfect handwriting and scholarly punctuation. She suffered dozens of rejections. Finally, Boots the Chemist announced that it was extending its branches into many East End districts. They did need women clever enough to decipher the illegible scribbles made by doctors on their prescriptions, and fastidious enough to measure and mix small quantities of medicinal substances. Frances wrote off and secured a position.

For the last eight years she'd worked hard to establish herself as an indispensable employee of the pharmacy. The work was repetitive and tiring, but it wasn't demeaning. To have broken out of the degrading cycle imposed on most

East End girls in service was a matter of pride to her. She even went on with her learning, through Workers' Education classes in literature and politics. It set her further apart.

At twenty-eight she had become this serious, subdued woman in grey, sitting beneath the gaudy advertisements in the underground train, staunch in her family loyalty, respected but not popular. Frances would nevertheless rescue Jess from the Holdens and keep the family together. She steeled herself to the task, left the train and emerged up the steps into the cold grey light.

Getting Jess out of the house in Hackney proved straightforward enough. Frances arrived on the Holdens' front doorstep and announced that she'd come to take her sister home.

Mrs Holden, a whalebone-plated woman with a wistful and rather helpless air despite her ample proportions, looked puzzled. She'd just returned from church, and called to her husband for help with this strange request. He came down the stairs past the gilt-framed pictures, across the Turkish rug. Mr Holden was prepared to stand no nonsense.

Before he could say, 'Now look here!' between clenched teeth, Frances stepped in with, 'Your son, Gilbert, has misbehaved towards my sister, Mr Holden, and we want her home to look after her.' She looked him straight in the eye.

The head of the household blustered, the wife looked shocked and faint. But it turned out, when Jess was summoned and the final confrontation took place in the housekeeper's room, that Mr Holden was forced to admit that his wayward son was already a father twice over, in similar circumstances. That Jess was merely an unfortunate third couldn't be denied. Still she had to suffer Mr Holden's unreasonable indignation at her for 'putting herself in Gilbert's way, don't you know!' and tempting him once again off the straight and narrow.

'Hush,' Frances warned Jess, who struggled through her tears to defend her bludgeoned reputation. 'My sister will take her wages and we'll leave without fuss, Mr Holden. We wouldn't want to cause your family any distress just before Christmas, you see. And you can tell your wife that I'm very sorry indeed for her son's behaviour. I trust she'll soon recover her spirits.' Mrs Holden had already been led away upstairs in a state of shock.

Mr Holden, rendered powerless by Frances's cool tactics, handed Jess eight pounds ten shillings; half her annual wage. She went up and packed her small canvas bag while Frances was sent to wait in the back scullery. No one spoke as they took their leave of the house by the servants' door; not the housekeeper who'd seen it coming a mile off, not the cook who'd befriended Jess for a time, and certainly not Gilbert Holden, conspicuous by his absence during the row, but who stood now in his shirt-sleeves looking down on them from an upstairs window. The glass reflected light from the cloud-laden sky as Jess glanced back up.

'Good riddance,' Frances said, hurrying Jess down the path on to the street. 'Now, Jess, you got to know Pa ain't exactly waiting to welcome you with open arms when we get back.' Her voice had relaxed into the East End twang.

Jess nodded. 'What about the rest?'

'Let's wait and see, shall we?' She hurried away, the nasty taste of hypocrisy still in her mouth. 'Oh, it's very nice being shocked and throwing a faint all over the place!' she exclaimed. 'But what's the betting she's back at church with that son of hers, for the nativity service, loving her neighbour and angling for a respectable girl for him to marry!'

'Poor cow, whoever she is,' Jess agreed. 'But don't let's talk about it no more.' She looked straight ahead, shoulders back, walking firmly alongside her eldest sister. 'And there's one more thing, Frances. I don't want to explain nothing about what happened back there, and that's that!'

It hurt too much to remember Gilbert's endless dirty remarks, his hands pawing her at every end and turn, the disgusting behaviour that had led to this disgrace. There was one dark and violent moment that Jess would lock away for ever and never talk about. In those unspeakable seconds, a woman was helpless, friendless and alone. Then she had to carry her own pain and humiliation as best she could. Jess clutched her bag and marched along.

'I don't think Pa could believe it at first.' Frances felt deeply for Duke in all this. They'd descended into the underground on to an almost empty platform.

'Me neither. I sometimes think maybe I'll wake up tomorrow and find the whole thing's been a bad dream.' She grinned at Frances in a brave attempt to lighten the mood.

Frances smiled back. 'Ready?' she asked when they'd negotiated the tram journey and the light traffic of Duke Street.

Jess pulled at the skirt of her dark-blue coat and checked her reflection in the windows of the Duke. 'Ready as I'll ever be,' she announced, stepping upstairs into the lion's den.

'She's here!' Hettie called back into the living room. She'd peeped over the banisters and seen the top of Jess's head coming upstairs. Then she fled into the kitchen.

Sadie sat as instructed at the table with Ernie, stiff and awkward as if they expected visitors she hardly knew. She pulled her long plait in front of one shoulder, then tossed it back again. She bit her lip. 'Sit still, Ern!' she told him. She could hear Jess and Frances pause on the landing before they came in.

Ernie glanced at Robert for his lead. Rob leaned against the mantelpiece smoking a cigarette. Everything was all right then, Ernie thought. He smiled back at Sadie.

So when Jess finally came in, Ernie jumped up as he always did when she came home to visit on her half day off. He went right up to her and hugged her, knocking her hat off. 'Make the tea!' he shouted through to Hettie. 'Jess is here!'

'Watch it, Ern!' Robert jumped nimbly forward to rescue the hat.

'Leave him be, I won't break, you know,' Jess said. 'I'm only having a kid.' She put one arm around Ernie's waist and gave him a cuddle.

'Blimey.' Even Robert had to admire her coolness. 'I thought I was the one who knew my way around the place!' He felt he was seeing a new Jess here. He had expected her to creep back home like a mouse, yet here she was making jokes about the worst thing that could happen to a girl. 'Good for you.' He winked. 'I'll go down and tell Pa you're here.'

Then Hettie came in with a full pot of tea, tears in her eyes, hardly knowing where to look. Jess was the last one she'd expected to be in this mess. It was one thing when a girl at the Palace got into trouble. There was a network, people to tell them what to do next. But not your sister. She thought Jess looked pinched and peaky. They'd worn her out at that horrible place and sent her home in this condition, fit for nothing.

Jess let go of Ernie and went up to Hettie. 'That's a nice blouse you got on, Ett.' She took the pot from her and set it on the hob. 'I like the trimming.'

'I got it from Annie. It's a bit she had left over on the roll,' Hettie said. 'I'll try and get you some next time I'm down the market.' She plumped up a cushion in the easy chair, inviting Jess to sit in it. The 'trouble' was vanishing like Rob's cigarette smoke.

And soon they were having their Sunday afternoon chat; Sadie complaining to Jess that Charlie Ogden was made of stone, despite all her efforts. 'I want him to ask me to walk out with him,' she protested. 'But he's always got his nose stuck in some flamin' book!'

'He must be blind then,' Jess commiserated. Sadie had come to sit at her feet on the hearthrug. 'You getting to look so pretty and all.'

Sadie beamed up at her. 'Do you think so? Here, how do you like *my* new blouse? It's only an old one of Ett's, but we put a bit of extra lace round the neck. What d'you think?'

Without them knowing it, Duke had sidled into the room and taken a cup of tea from Frances. He stood by the door listening to the female chit-chat, watching his grown-up children gathered together; the contented smiles, the pleasant laughter.

His gaze fell on Jess and his mind flew back down the years. A third daughter, the midwife had told him. 'But there, never mind, we can't choose these things.'

When Robert followed on a couple of years after, it was almost as if Duke completely forgot about Jess. With her father's mind absorbed by his son, little Jess missed the fussing and petting he'd lavished on the older girls, and she seemed easy to overlook. He recalled her as a quiet child, without Frances's strong will or Hettie's sparkle. The only clear memory he had of Jess from her early years was that she ran like the wind. She carried home prizes from the running races at school, having beaten all the boys. 'Look, Pa!' She would hold up her spinning-top for him to see.

'Ern, go and give Robert a hand downstairs,' he said gruffly.

Jess started at the sound of his deep voice. The blood rushed to her face as she stood up to face him. Frances edged her forward. 'Go on!'

Jess recalled all the times in her childhood when she'd looked up to her father and tried to please him; how she'd often failed. Then she would hide her hurt by withdrawing into a corner, and he would call that sulking. Well, she'd displeased him now, and no mistake. 'Hello, Pa,' she said quietly, hanging her head.

'Pa?' Sadie jumped in, anxious to fill the gap.

He looked Jess up and down. 'If I could get my hands on him!' he threatened.

'Now, Pa.' Frances laid a hand on his arm. Jess finally met his gaze.

He sighed. 'Well, we'll have to make the best of it,' he said. 'Since it's the season of goodwill.'

They all nodded and smiled.

'Let's make it a Christmas to remember,' Frances suggested. 'A real family gathering.' She and Hettie had been busy baking, and ordering, a turkey, beef and ham. They'd kept their fingers crossed.

'A celebration,' Duke conceded. 'Why not?' He still studied Jess, trying to judge how she would manage the shame of the baby's birth.

Then Daisy came running upstairs, bursting in without knocking to tell them that little Jimmy had been sick again. 'He had a dreadful night, coughing and coughing, and all the little 'uns were whimpering and whining about it. But this time we had the money to help him straight off, thank God. So Ma goes up for Dr Fry and that medicine he gave him did the trick like before. Magic it was!' Her lovely face was all smiles. She'd only just popped in to tell them the news, she said. 'And hello and Happy Christmas, Jess!' She winked and sped off, while they stayed and caught Jess up on all the street news, and the comings and goings down Paradise Court.

Chapter Seven

Amy Ogden sat behind a row of wooden heads stuck on poles arranged along a narrow table. The heads were of various sizes, shiny and featureless, and marked with figures showing measurements for the top hats which the workshop produced. She was one of six women and two men, excluding the supervisor Bert Buggles. As the youngest there, she was the recipient of many of the worst jobs in the lengthy hatting process. Sometimes she moulded the stubborn leather band around the crown of the wooden model, or else she ironed the swansdown forehead pad firmly in position before the lining was attached. Her hands were always chapped, her breathing hindered by the ceaseless steam from the irons.

Strips of russia leather and gauze lay lengthways down the table, while the precious moire silk for the linings was carefully stacked in bolts on a shelf behind.

Despite the luxurious quality of the finished article, conditions in Coopers' sweatshop were grim. The low room with its sloping ceilings and tiny skylights was poorly lit and ventilated, but it was cold none the less. Damp plaster fell away to expose bare brick wall and was never repaired. The place stank of leather and glue.

Only the determined cheerfulness of the women made the place bearable, with the unfortunate Bert providing the main butt of their humour. Today, for instance, in the run-up to Christmas, one of the women had been forced to bring in her youngest infant who was sick with croup. Still under three and hardly able to speak in sentences, the child was dressed up in the supervisor's apron, with a measuring tape around his neck. 'We got ourselves a new gaffer. Let's all take orders from Donald!' they proclaimed. 'We'll get more sense out of 'im, any rate!'

Bert slouched off unmoved by the *coup*, and poor Donald was soon responding to the women's calls; 'Please, Bert, can you 'elp with this gauze vent!' and, 'Look 'ere, Bert, I asked two days back for you to soften up this leather for me!' He would clamber on their knees in his big leather apron, barking his hard, dry cough all over the half-made hats.

In the early afternoon Teddy Cooper paid his routine visit. As usual, he looked as if he had very little to do with the place. His grey Homburg hat was perched on the back of his head, and his immaculate striped bow-tie, his collar and natty tweed suit suggested a day at the races rather than any serious function in office or shop.

Amy glanced up as he came in, and a smile brightened her small, blunt features. In the dull stretch of the day, when her back had begun to ache and her fingers to rub into blisters, a visit from Teddy was a breath of fresh air. Today he brought oranges and a news story from the papers about a famous music-hall star, George Robey, who'd earned one thousand pounds in just one week.

'What'd you do with a thousand a week, Emmy?' he asked the mother of the sick boy.

'I should think I'd died and gone to heaven,' came the caustic reply. Emmy was impervious to his charms.

'Watch this.' Undeterred, Teddy winked and invited Donald to come up close. 'I'm Extraordinary Edward, the famous juggler. Watch!' And he set up a rapid display with the three oranges, flipping them between his hands, behind his back with surprising dexterity. 'Dazzling! Delightful! Delictitious!. . . But chiefly your own!' he declaimed. Everyone shrieked, whistled and clapped. Sam, the leather worker, and Dora the chief moulder each caught an orange from him and whisked them off.

Amy laughed. 'You been practising. I can tell.'

When she looked up at him, her eyes were shining white orbs with blue centres. 'Now that's very observant of you, Amy.' Teddy gave Donald the last orange and came to perch at her section of the table. 'As a matter of fact, I have!'

As he leaned sideways across her station and screened her from view, the others took it as a signal that the show was over. They bowed their heads to their work and Emmy came to draw Donald further off.

Teddy studied Amy's face from close quarters. Her skin was milky white and smooth. The upper lip arched in a full curve, the blue eyes conveyed guilelessness. 'What's a nice girl like you . . .' he began.

'Doin' in a place like this?' she giggled. 'Don't ask me, ask your pa!'

'Hm. What if I ask the governor to look out for a place for you in the shop?' he asked, looping his fingers through a pair of scissors and threatening to snip at one of Amy's blonde curls.

She gasped. 'Would you?'

'Course I would. I can just picture you behind the counter in your little white collar and cuffs; a good-looking girl like you.' The scissors snipped close to Amy's earlobe. She didn't flinch. '"Yes, madam, no, madam, three bags full, madam!"' He replaced the scissors with a flourish. 'I'll ask him straight after Christmas if you like.'

'Really and truly?' Teddy was offering her a dream come true; a move out of this overcrowded, tawdry sweat-shop into the world of mahogany counters and glass display cases where she felt she belonged. 'Will you really?' She stared up at Teddy. He was part of that world in his expensive suit and tie, with his nice voice and manners. He called the severe Mr Cooper 'the governor' and made it seem as if he could do anything. After all, he was the boss's son.

Teddy bent low over Amy to whisper in her ear. 'For you, my dear, anything!' He grinned and sat upright. 'And let's start with that jaunt I promised.'

'What jaunt?' She felt flushed by his boldness in front of the other women, yet at the same time determined not to care. She wanted to lead him on to the point where the job in the shop was a reality. That was all that mattered.

'Our trip to the Empire,' he reminded her. 'How about tonight? Meet me downstairs outside the back entrance, half seven sharp.' He swung his legs off the table and stood up, hands in pockets.

All she had time to do was to nod her head once, then he was off, ruffling Donald's hair, winking at Emmy, humming a tune. He went out of the workshop in fine fettle, down into Hosiery in the basement, to fill up his social diary into the New Year. If only all the girls were as easy to seduce as Amy Ogden, he thought. Unluckily, most of them had their eyes a bit more wide open and they played harder to get; though get them he did in the end.

Amy sat and held her breath. She finished here at half six. She'd have to be off like a shot to get changed and be back for half seven, looking her very best. There wasn't much time. Maybe Bert would let her clock off ten minutes early today. These thoughts swam through her head.

'Where is it this time?' Dora broke into her plans. 'The

Jewel, the Gem or the Empire?' Dora was a tall, masculine-looking woman, very blunt. She knew how the boss's son operated. He only ever took a girl out once, got as far as he could with her, then dropped her. They all knew about it. The only wonder was why his old man never tried to put a stop to it.

Amy stiffened. 'None of your business.'

'"Let me take you away from this horrible place, my darlin'!"' Dora mocked. 'Oh my gawd, Amy, you ain't fell for that line, have you? It's old as the hills!'

'Just watch it,' Emmy advised more kindly. 'Dora's right; don't be a ninny and go falling for it.'

'I won't.' Amy nodded and put on a firmer expression.

'That's right, don't believe a word he says and you'll be fine.' Emmy shifted a bolt of grey silk from the shelf to the table and picked up her scissors. 'It don't stop you from going out and having a good time, just as long as you keep your head screwed on.'

'Just don't say we didn't warn you,' Dora insisted darkly. 'Ask Louise Makins in House'old Appliances. He took her to the Empire last week, I think it was. Ask Louise Makins about his nibs!'

Amy frowned. 'No need. I can look after myself, don't you worry.'

The women gossiped on, growing more ribald about Teddy Cooper's style of courtship. 'He looks a proper gent at first, don't he?' Dora said. 'He talks like a toff and he always gives the girls a bit of a treat first off; a night out at the local fleapit, or a slap-up meal. But they soon find out he's no gent after all.'

'How would you know, Dora Kennedy? He asked you out, has he?' Amy was nettled. She knew for a fact that Teddy would never ask the angular, tall moulder. She was only speaking out of pique, Amy told herself.

'Ask anyone. Ask Louise.' Dora turned to Emmy, hands on hips, determined to undermine Amy's silly vanity. 'You hear what she told me? She says he don't mind where he does it, or who he does it with. And when he does do it, it's over so quick you'd wonder what all the fuss was about.' Dora grinned. 'She says it's about as exciting as posting a letter!'

'She never!' Emmy guffawed. Then she reflected a moment. 'Yes, that'd be right. He's a boss, ain't he? It's always like that with the bosses.'

Amy refused to join in. Teddy Cooper was the only purveyor of bright dreams in her dim, twilit world. The others could say what they liked. She'd hang on to him, come what may.

Ernie Parsons sat beside Robert in the red velvet seats at the Southwark Palace. He was in his own seventh heaven.

Every time the crimson curtains swept down across the stage, he roared himself hoarse and clapped until the last echo had died in the vast, domed auditorium. When they opened again on to the golden stage, he laughed till he cried at the little man with heavy eyebrows who flip-flapped across the boards in his giant boots, performing all manner of acrobatic stilt walks on the tips of their wooden soles. He laughed when Robert laughed at the jokes about mothers-in-law and unpaid rent. But it was Ernie who led the singing when it came to Gilbert the Filbert and Daisy.

This last he sung until his lungs nearly burst. 'Steady on, Ern,' Robert said. He pulled him back in his seat. 'Daisy's coming back on in a bit.' He gave the couple sitting next to him an embarrassed smile, then hid behind a cloud of cigarette smoke tinged pink by the lights that blazed down on to the stage.

Ernie sat back entranced as the creamy-limbed chorus girls finally returned. Here he sat in the midst of thousands of people; the balconies were crammed full, there were men standing shoulder to shoulder at the back, and he alone seemed to have a special link with the girls onstage. One was his sister, one was his friend. It was as if Daisy and Hettie sang specially for him. To him they blew their kisses across their white-gloved palms, to him they curtseyed. The orchestra played, the audience joined in the songs. Ernie couldn't imagine anything better.

'C'mon, Ern,' Robert said when the curtain fell for the last time. 'Let's get round to the stage door and join the queue for the postcard queens.' If he was giving Ernie a treat, he had to do the thing right. They had to end up crowding the stage door, waiting for the chorus girls to emerge. He dragged Ernie up the gangway, nodding hello to a few mates, but not stopping to chat.

Ernie, overwhelmed by the squeaks and thuds of the hinged seats as hundreds of people stood up and stretched their legs, grabbed Robert's coat-tails. His face twitched with alarm.

'Don't do that. You're not a little kid any more!' Robert said sharply. He snatched his jacket free. 'C'mon, you want to see Daisy, don't you?'

Ernie took his courage in both hands and nodded. He put one elbow up as a shield, ducked his head and followed on through the crowd.

At the stage door, Robert thrust his way past a group of twenty or so young men towards a high, narrow window further down the alley; the same window young Tommy had used to signal to Daisy. Seconds later, Hettie came to the door, opened it a crack and let Robert and Ernie in. Then she shut it fast on the noisy gang outside.

'Lucky for you Mr Mills went off early,' she explained.

'So you can come in and wait for us in the warm tonight.' She hurried ahead of them down the corridor into the dressing room. 'Everybody decent?' she sang out. Those who weren't would have time to nip behind the screens.

'More's the pity,' Robert said with a wink. 'Come on, Ern, don't be shy.' He played the man about town with bravado, though on a docker's pay his cheap worsted jacket and clumsily cut waistcoat weren't up to the role. Still, he made up for it with his confident manner and sturdy good looks. All the girls sang out cheerful hellos and smiled kindly at Ernie.

'Hello, Ern. You come to walk us home?' Daisy's muffled voice asked. Her back was to them and her arms raised to fix her hair in the mirror. Then she twisted to look at him, two hairpins clenched between her white teeth.

Ernie nodded hard. 'Yes, please.'

'That's good. You can be my new beau,' she teased. She finished her hair and swept towards Ernie.

'Leave off, Daisy,' Hettie muttered. 'He'll think you mean it.' But she didn't want to spoil Ernie's big night out, so she held her tongue as Daisy ignored her advice and asked Ernie to help her on with her coat and hat. The thrill he felt was spread all over his broad, open face. Who could want to spoil that?

Fully dressed now, Daisy held up her arm, face to face with Ernie. 'C'mon,' she insisted, 'you gotta hook your arm like this, Ern, and I gotta slip mine through the hook, like this, see. That's if we're walking out together!'

Mechanically Ernie did as he was told. Disbelief spread across his face and he turned to Robert.

'You sure Chalky White don't mind?' Robert asked, half serious. He wasn't one to spare her blushes. 'We don't want Ern messing with the likes of Chalky and his gang.'

Daisy coloured up. 'That was ages ago. Anyhow, it ain't none of your business,' she said, with a deft little push against his chest. 'Ready, Ern? Let's go.' She sailed down the corridor with him, out into the cold alley and up past the gaggle of men at the door.

Hettie and Robert followed on. 'That the truth?' he asked. 'She got rid of Chalky?' He watched Daisy carefully from behind.

Hettie sighed. 'That's what she reckons. Says she told him she didn't like the look of him thank you very much.' They reached the main street, still humming with traffic and people.

'They looked pretty flaming friendly down our place that Saturday night.' Robert was taken aback. He knew it was usually Chalky who gave the girls their marching orders.

'You don't know Daisy,' Hettie said with a small frown.

'What you on about? She's only lived down the court ever since I can remember!'

'No. I mean she takes it into her head that she likes some bloke or other, or else she doesn't, and either way she goes at it like a steam engine. I can just picture her telling Chalky to get lost. And look at her now with poor Ern. See what I mean?'

Daisy was showing Ernie how to walk in step, arms entwined around each other's waists.

'Poor Ern, nothing!' Robert said. 'He's enjoying every second of it!'

'But she's putting it on,' Hettie told him. 'She's like that with all the men; it's all an act with Daisy. Show her a man, and she'll make up to him no matter what. Next day it's all over. She blows hot and cold; it'll get her into deep trouble one of these days.'

Robert shrugged. 'Leave off, Ett, she's a big girl now.

What's her game, though? She after someone with plenty of cash, then? Some rich charlie to get her out of that lousy tenement?'

Hettie shook her head. 'Gawd knows. I don't think *she* does.' They walked together in silence. 'I tell you one thing, Rob; she ain't after poor Ern!'

The foursome walked through pools of light past dingy, windswept alleys, and underneath a railway arch as a train thundered overhead.

Amy's rendezvous with the boss's son took place as planned. The fact that she'd never been to the cinema before heightened the thrill of meeting up with Teddy Cooper, who looked dashing as usual.

He was a loose-limbed man, slight but well proportioned, with a small head and fine, almost straw-coloured hair parted neatly to one side. He had his mother's straight, slim features from the Kearney side. The Coopers were smaller, squatter, more pugnacious. Teddy had early learned the value of a smile to bridge those awkward family moments of disapproval. A smile had always melted his mother's soft heart and disarmed even his short-tempered father. Now he used it to good effect with the girls.

'My, you're a bobby dazzler!' he told Amy, linking arms and rushing her up the street to find a taxi.

Amy was gratified. It had been worth the effort of dashing into the Duke on her way home to borrow one of Hettie's best blouses. At seventeen, Amy's own wardrobe was practically non-existent. What she had, her mother pawned anyway. As she sat beside Teddy in the taxi, smelling the brown leather seats, she saw the familiar streets whirl by and almost pinched herself to believe her luck.

The unreality of her evening was reinforced by the incredible magic of the moving picture show. If Teddy was bored by this part of the outing, he managed not to show it, sitting at ease with his arm draped around Amy's soft, round shoulder. The flickering light fell on her upturned face and across the creamy lace on her breasts. She held his hand tight as a train appeared to rush straight at them on the screen, and she marvelled at the actualities that showed the suffragettes rallying at Hyde Park and going on to attack the Houses of Parliament. 'What's it say, Teddy?' she leaned over and whispered. The screen writing was moving on too quickly for her to follow.

'It says, "The fooligans were repulsed by the police with heavy loss of dignity, drapery and millinery!"' he read out in a voice loud enough for others to overhear.

They laughed out loud at the pictures of small, well-dressed women being picked up lock, stock and barrel by burly policemen and carted off to prison. Then the piano struck up the first dramatic chords for the main feature. It began with a flying machine accident and a thrilling rescue from the spars of its flimsy wings. Amy held her breath. Sometimes she had to close her eyes and let Teddy hug her close. These were the thrills of a lifetime, sitting there watching the flickering black and white pictures, casting off dull care.

'Oh, Teddy, that was wonderful!' Amy sat glued to her seat until the last piano chord had died away. She sighed happily and let him raise her and lead her into the aisle. On his arm, being led out of the cinema, she felt very grand to be introduced to a friend of Teddy's as 'Miss Amy Ogden'. Teddy said the man's name was Maurice Leigh.

The man nodded. 'Did you enjoy the picture, Miss Ogden?'

'Oh yes!' She cast an animated glance at Teddy.

'Enjoy it? She missed half of it!' Teddy laughed. 'Half the time she had her head buried inside my jacket!'

'Oh, Teddy, I never!'

'Oh, Teddy, she did! You'd better tell your manager this picture's too strong for the weaker sex, Maurice. It'll have them fainting in the aisles in the more thrilling bits if he's not careful!'

The man grinned back without much amusement. He'd recently transferred to working at the Empire from being deputy manager at the Southwark Palace under Fred Mills. That was where he'd regularly come across Teddy Cooper before; it was one of his man-about-town haunts. Maurice saw moving pictures as the new thing, bound to supersede the old music halls before the decade was out. He first fell under their spell during the short bioscope sequences grudgingly added to the bill by Mr Mills, to follow the novelty acts he booked each week. Wanting to keep up with the times, Maurice moved on to the Balham Empire. 'I'll tell Mr Phillips what you say,' he told Teddy. 'Too much excitement isn't good for the ladies, eh?'

'That's the ticket.' Teddy drew Amy quickly on, out through the glittering foyer. In the street he hailed another taxi. 'Time for a little drink,' he said.

Amy was surprised when he stopped the taxi outside Coopers'. 'I thought you said we was going for a drink?' she queried. A few hundred yards up the street the Duke's bright lights beckoned.

Teddy paid the driver and the cab drove off. He pulled Amy along by the side of the store, past windows full of tan shoes, kid gloves, walking canes with silver handles. 'So I did. A quiet little drink, not a nasty noisy one up at the pub.' He took a key from his pocket and unlocked a tradesmen's door at the back of the shop. 'Courtesy of my old man. He keeps a good drinks cabinet in the office.' He grinned.

Amy grinned back. Teddy had a cheek, taking her up to his old man's office on the first floor, getting out his whisky. She followed, dragging at his coat sleeve as they passed through the department which sold women's costumes. He stopped and let her finger the trimmings on a black velvet costume which would cost weeks of wages to Amy. He fiddled with the change machines as she went and touched costume after costume with her fingertips, sending the small canisters flying along the overhead system of pulleys and fine, taut steel wires. Amy heard their ghostly whir and ping in the dark, empty store.

'C'mon.' Teddy went and pulled her along. 'I need a drink.' He pointed through an archway into the next department. 'See, that's ladies' millinery.'

She had a glimpse of magnificent hats the size of large dinner plates, swathed in net, edged with lace, resplendent with feathers and bows. 'Is that where I'll work, after Christmas, Teddy?' She went close to him and nestled inside his arm against his chest. 'After you've asked your old man?'

He wouldn't have believed her simplicity if he hadn't seen it so often before. He nodded, made more promises and drew her on.

Teddy Cooper didn't expect to expend much more energy on words at this stage of the seduction. He'd offer the girl a strong drink. She'd take it. There'd be surrender in her eyes as he backed her up against the big, flat expanse of his father's desk.

At the last minute Amy struggled, being young and ignorant. It wasn't out of self-respect that she tried to push him off, nor any vestige of honour, but out of sheer panic. She felt Teddy's strong body close against her. It pressed her down and back. There was some fumbling and breathlessness. She tried to scream, but he put one hand over her mouth. Afterwards, she opened her eyes in time to see his face backing off into the dim room, hard and expressionless.

'Get dressed quickly,' he said. He went and wiped the two whisky glasses and placed them back in the cupboard along with the bottle, which he put to the back of the shelf.

Dazed and confused, Amy did as she was told. Sobs rose and racked her throat as she struggled to fasten her blouse. She felt him take her roughly by the arm and send her out of the office. She heard doors lock as they passed from department to department and down the stairs. The magnificent hats taunted her from their stands. Even she now knew they mocked her with Teddy's empty promises.

Only once she dared to glance up at him as he locked the last door and they stood out on the dark, cold street. His face showed nothing at all. Next day in the workshop he wouldn't even bother to acknowledge her.

Chapter Eight

The next day came without blurring Amy's razor-sharp awareness of the horrible scene in Mr Cooper's office. But her sleepless night did allow her to make private adjustments to her hopes and dreams. When Teddy cut her dead at work, she knew for a certainty that she'd never set foot in the hatshop again. Still shocked, she felt a hot surge of anger. Bleeding idiot! she told herself. Bleeding little fool! But Dora's told-you-so looks gradually eased and the women grew kinder as they saw how far she'd fallen off her little pedestal of vanity. They promised not to breathe a word of the affair to Amy's mother, Dolly, when they spotted her trudging up out of the depths of the basement after a hard day's work, and Amy herself decided that her family would never know. If they all kept quiet, at least she would be able to hang on to her job. But if a breath of it got through to old man Cooper, Amy would be out on the street and begging Annie Wiggin for her old job back, for it would be Amy not Teddy who got the blame.

There was one blessing, she told herself; at least she could be sure she hadn't gone and got herself pregnant like Jess Parsons. Everyone knew Jess had been forced to leave her place in Hackney and was hanging around waiting for the nine months to be up. Dress it up how you like, Jess had landed herself in more of a mess than Amy. Frances

Parsons might be forbidding anyone in the family to talk about it, but the gossip was up and down the court, and all along the neighbouring streets.

Christmas came and went at the Duke with plenty of eating and drinking upstairs, and the usual neighbourhood gatherings in the bar below. Jess settled well into the family routine. Her greatest surprise in coming home under these circumstances was her sister Frances's reaction to it all. Frances, whom she considered so proper, talked most matter-of-factly about the possibilities concerning the baby. Would Jess want to go through with the pregnancy, or did she want Frances to talk to the women she knew at the Workers' Education Institute who would have respectable connections in the medical profession? If Jess wanted to go ahead and have the baby, would she then put it up for adoption? There were many middle-class women, childless and pining for a baby, who would give it a good home. All this Frances considered over her pile of mending, or sitting in rare moments with her feet up after a long day in the pharmacy. 'Let's do what we think is best, Jess,' she insisted. 'Let's not get bogged down by all that nonsense about who's to blame and your life being ruined. It's so old hat.'

'Does Pa think I'm ruined, then?' Jess had taken over the cooking since she came back. She was busy peeling enough potatoes to feed a battalion, sleeves rolled back, sharp knife in hand.

Frances put her head to one side. 'Most likely. He was brought up strict, remember, and he's seen some terrible things. Girls being driven out on to the street, men setting out to get drunk and go and ruin a girl's good name. He's lived too long round here to take it well.'

'If it's that bad for him having me round, I can pack my things and go, y'know.' Jess's condition still made her hypersensitive as far as Duke was concerned.

'Don't be soft. We managed to have a good Christmas together, didn't we? Does it look as if he's dying to get rid of you? No, you've got to stay and see it through, whatever you decide.'

'I've already decided.' Jess came in from the kitchen, drying her hands on the apron. She knelt beside the fire and leaned back against her sister's lap. 'I want to keep this baby, Frances.' She said it quietly, with complete conviction.

Frances listened to the tick of the clock and watched the flames flicker in the background.

'I've thought it through a thousand times. I never wanted this baby, and I'd give hundreds of pounds for it never to have happened in the first place.' She paused. When she continued, her rich voice was deliberately flattened out and quiet. 'And before you ask, Frances, I ain't never going to talk about exactly how it happened. Only to say I never did nothing to make it happen, and when it did I fought it like mad, only it didn't make no difference.' She looked up quickly. 'Don't you tell Pa! It wouldn't do any good telling him. That's that. That's all there is to it.'

Frances kept quiet about having told Duke as much, right at the start. 'Why? Why is that all, Jess? There should be a price for him to pay, that's what I think. As it is, he gets away scot-free.'

'Oh yes.' Jess's voice rose a little in scorn. 'Maybe he does. But what do I do about it? Where do I turn? To his ma and pa? You seen them, Frances. All the years I worked for them in that big house, scrubbing and polishing, fetching and carrying. Well, it counted for nothing when it came to protecting their precious little boy!'

Frances had to concede the point. 'It's a crying shame,' she said softly.

Jess took her hand. 'You're right there. Any rate, I'll keep the child, but I still ain't happy about what Pa thinks.' She could take the blame, deal with gossip from people on the fringes of her life, the neighbours up and down Duke Street, but she didn't know if she could stand Duke's anger and hurt. And she was past being able to sit in a corner to sulk.

Frances stroked Jess's bowed head. Her hair curled softly; the only one of the sisters whose hair lifted from her forehead in dark waves. Otherwise she was plainer; less pleasing at first glance according to general opinion. Her cheeks were thinner, her mouth less curved. Her straight brows tapered over deep-set, dark eyes which gave her the look of someone in retreat from the world. Jess's natural look was one of suspicion and withdrawal. In figure she was too spare about the shoulders, and she never allowed her dress to emphasize her natural curves. 'You don't make the best of yourself,' Hettie used to natter. 'Anyone would think you was a proper ugly duckling!' Jess would laugh self-consciously and go on to praise the copper highlights in Hettie's luxurious hair.

The day after their talk, Frances came back from work with some new information for Jess. She knew of a place out in the Kent countryside where Jess could go while her baby was born. Jess heard her race upstairs in unaccustomed haste. 'Oh, Jess!' she cried, flinging her hat down on the chair. 'I got some good news for you. There's a woman I know from night class. She came in the shop today, and guess what! Her sister lives out in the country in a small place, and she says she'd be glad to have you stay with them. They're nice people. And the best of it is, Jess, this woman's been a midwife all these years. Delivering babies is nothing to her!'

Jess stood by the kitchen range, hands covered in flour. She was in the midst of an evening bread-baking session, with Ernie moulding scoops of dough into round shapes on a floured board. The room smelt of fermenting yeast and sugar.

'D'you hear, Jess? I found a place for you to have the baby!'

'Thanks but no thanks,' Jess replied. She ducked her head and carried on kneading dough.

'What do you mean? Think about it. It'll be the middle of summer, it'd be like a holiday for you. Fresh air and sunshine. Jess, think about it, please!' If she stayed here for the birth, if there were complications, Duke wouldn't cope so easily. Besides the benefit of the baby being given a healthy start, there was her father to consider. Going away was easily the best plan, if only stubborn Jess would listen. 'There'd be the hop picking, if you felt up to it. Remember what good fun that was when you was a little tiny kid, Jess, sitting high up on them carts down the narrow lanes.'

'Stop going on about it, Frances, will you. I said thanks but no thanks.' Clouds of flour rose from the board as Ernie passed her the soft round shapes and she kneaded them a second time. 'And while we're at it, Frances, you can stop looking around for work for me an' all. I can do that myself when the time comes.'

Frances stood stock-still in the middle of the room as if Jess had struck her across the face. A look of pain filled her eyes. She'd been making plans for all their sakes, determined to make the best of it. As the oldest sister, that was her responsibility. Besides, she had the right connections.

As soon as Jess saw the impact of her words, she wiped

collect. As far as she knew, she had never made a mistake in the intricate process, and her pills were commended for their perfect roundness.

Between times, she sold pick-me-ups such as Seidlitz Powders or Andrews Liver Salts, and Williams Pink Pills for anaemia. Her customers relied on her knowledge of the proprietary brands and often trusted her advice over any doctor's.

So her daily life went on, full and entirely predictable. One change came about in the evenings, though. She began to take an interest through friends at the Workers' Education Institute in Mrs Pankhurst's campaign to get women the vote. She went to a meeting and heard one of the Pankhurst daughters speak. She liked her ringing tones and call to action. But coming away, outside the hall, she felt it was for other women to act; women with money and good speaking voices and influence with politicians, not for working women like her. Besides, the direct action alarmed her. Frances wasn't one for setting fire to post-boxes or smashing shop windows. Only, she went home and looked at pregnant Jess, and thought how unfair it was for women living in this man's world. It made her feel helpless, watching Jess struggle.

At home, Robert joked his way through chores in the bar, pitting his strength against the thirty-six-gallon barrels as he rolled, tipped and heaved them on to their wooden gantry, alongside Joxer. Fixing them in place with wooden chocks and tapping the bung holes for Duke was his daily task, done in the early hours before he ventured down to the dockside. He held a blue ticket, second in line to the red-ticket men, but ahead of the casuals who turned up on these raw mornings with little hope of work.

The dockers' living was always precarious, but Robert was healthy and often favoured because of his strength and good nature. Only, Chalky White seemed to have developed a grudge against him after the minor row in the pub, and he often put in a bad word with the gaffers, who themselves had to keep Chalky sweet. He knew all the angles and could exert a certain influence over who got work, so Robert's heart would sink whenever he saw Chalky's tall, pale figure in the queue. It was often a sign that he'd be turned away, back to hanging about at home or down at the boxing club.

At twenty-two, and with too much time on his hands, he would drift into pubs further afield, knowing Duke would disapprove of any serious drinking bout on home territory. He'd heard what his pa said about the men who came in at Christmas, slammed their guinea on the bar and ordered drink for as long as the money lasted. This would send them home dead-drunk after five or six separate sessions, while their wives and kids went without. 'A man who can't hold his drink ain't a proper man,' Duke said. 'And that includes knowing when to stop.'

Once or twice during the spring Robert took Ernie back to the Palace to watch Daisy and Hettie do their stage routines. The boy treated it like magic still, but it was beginning to bore Robert. He liked to spend more and more time with the ladies, and though Daisy would flirt gamely with both him and Ernie after the show, she'd begun to lose some of her sparkle. Anyway, they'd known each other for donkey's years. He wanted grown-up, worldly women who knew their way around. Frances could sniff and make comments about that 'type' of woman all she liked; it wouldn't stop him from going out with them and having a good time.

*

Hettie confided her own worries about Daisy to Jess, who kept indoors most of the time these days.

'There's something up with her, and I can't put my finger on it.' She shrugged. 'Why should I worry, that's what I'd like to know?'

'I seen her the other day when you brought her up here. She looks all right to me.' Jess had hold of one end of a sheet, Hettie the other. They were folding laundry.

'No, she's getting thin, losing her looks. And you seen how Robert was acting up to her, same as he always does. She hardly took no notice.'

'Good thing, too. Rotten little flirt.'

'Who, Robert?' Hettie took the folded sheet and smoothed it flat on top of the pile on the table.

Jess laughed. 'Yes, Robert! No, it's Daisy I'm on about, ain't it? It's time she started to behave.'

Hettie had to admit it was true. 'Only I still feel sorry for her, giving over most of her money to keep them kids fed. And she has to keep herself looking decent, too. You have to in our line of work. And she ain't even twenty yet. It ain't much of a life.'

'Better than being in service,' Jess reminded her.

'Sorry, Jess, I never thought.' Hettie took another sheet from the basket and tossed one end to Jess. 'It ain't all a bed of roses up at the Palace, you know.'

'I never said it was.'

'No, but I know that's what people think. Anyway, I seen poor Daisy having a ding-dong battle with Archie Small when I came away last night. They was in the girls' dressing room after the show. Archie was trying it on with Daisy as per usual, and she was pushing him off as quick as ever he came at her. You should've seen his chins wobble whenever she pushed him, never mind his horrible fat belly!'

'Ugh!' Jess shrieked and shook out the sheet with a sharp snap.

Hettie laughed. 'See! And I'd 've done the same if he came pestering me. Only, you can't afford to go making enemies in that place. That's why Daisy had to get in with Chalky White that time.'

'Why?' Placidly Jess folded the last sheet and glanced at her sister.

'Because Freddie wanted her to.'

Jess tutted. 'That ain't right.'

'No, it ain't. And Daisy still gets the silly bleeders round the stage door bringing her chocolates all the time. She's still as popular as ever, but there's something going on with her. Like I said, I can't put my finger on it.'

'She out of her depth? I mean to say, one sweetheart bringing chocolates is nice for a girl. Three or four with chocolates is a headache.' Jess lifted the pile of laundry and made off to the bedrooms. 'Tell her to give one of them to me if he's halfway decent!'

Hettie stifled her laugh as Duke's footsteps came upstairs. At the same time, Sadie shot in from the kitchen. 'Here, you wasn't listening, was you?' Hettie made a grab for her youngest sister.

'No. Listen, he's coming now, Ett! Can you hear? Will you ask him now? You promised!' Sadie tugged at Hettie's arm.

'I never. Any rate, why don't you ask him yourself?'

'Oh, Ett, please! He'll say yes if you ask him!' The undreamt of had happened to Sadie two days before. After school, Charlie Ogden had come up and asked her to go cycling that weekend. Now she needed her pa's permission.

'Pipe down!' Hettie warned.

Duke opened the door. 'Here, what you two up to?' he

93

asked. Sadie had scrambled to the table to sit, but he'd heard her squeaking on to Hettie about something.

Hettie made a great show of clearing her throat. 'Sadie's got a young man!' She came out with it, plain as a pike-staff.

Sadie yelped. 'Oh, Ett, I haven't!'

'Well, then, you won't want to go cycling with him if he don't exist!' She stood, hands on hips, a smile playing round her pretty mouth.

'I do.' Sadie gasped and darted at her. 'Oh, Ett, how could you!' She stopped, pulled her skirt straight and faced her father. 'Pa, can I go cycling on Sunday with Charlie Ogden?' Her face flamed red with embarrassment. She'd kill Hettie after.

Duke brushed the ends of his grey moustache. Hettie could see his own eyes light up in a hidden grin. 'Well, my pet, there's just one thing about that when you stop to think.'

'What, Pa? Charlie's a nice boy. He reads books!' Sadie pleaded.

Duke nodded. 'I dare say he does. But does he own a bicycle?'

She stared hard. 'He'll borrow one!'

'Do *you* own a bicycle?'

'I'll borrow one an' all!'

Duke checked the venue, grumbled about women on bicycles, but he was visibly weakening. Finally, despite his resolution to be strict with Sadie, he agreed. He remembered his own young days, before the army, when he and a gang of pals used to go cycling into the countryside. His youngest daughter was growing up, he realized. They had their share of troubles, but the family was sticking together. That was what mattered to him most of all.

Frances came home as Hettie got ready to go out to

work. She gathered them round the supper table, with Ernie sitting opposite. 'I've got a piece of really good news,' she said, laying her gloves across her lap and leaning forward towards him.

Chapter Nine

At eighteen Ernie had never held down a job. He was willing and strong, but employers would look him up and down and decide against him. They set him against skinnier but brighter lads and weren't to know that Ernie's goodwill was worth more than sharp wit in the fetching and carrying kind of job Ernie wanted to do. So the family had to put up over the years with the general opinion that he was useless in the work sense. Duke could keep him busy in the pub and Ernie seemed happy helping Robert or Joxer to take delivery from the draymen, or to roll the empty barrels up the slope into their carts. But now things were about to change.

'Henshaw's want an errand boy,' Frances announced. 'The last one's gone off hop picking for the summer and they need someone else.'

Henshaw's was a thriving corner shop and eating-house on the edge of the market area up Duke Street. They did good business in the café selling hot pea soup and tea to the traders. The shop had also built up its own profits by running a good delivery service on orders for eggs and bread. Their errand boys were usually much younger than Ernie, Mr Henshaw told Frances, but he knew him as a steady, strong lad and he might be willing to give him a go.

'This last lad has left me in the lurch. You can't get a

steady delivery boy for love nor money,' he said. He'd caught Frances in passing on her way back from work.

'Ernie's steady,' she promised. Mr Henshaw was offering the chance of a lifetime.

'And can he ride a bike?'

'Yes, Robert taught him. He's really very willing, Mr Henshaw. You won't find a more willing lad than Ernie, and he won't let you down like some.'

The shopkeeper, an upstanding Methodist, nodded. 'Can he read the names on the orders, though? We never considered that, did we?'

Frances frowned. 'Ernie can't read, it's true. But his memory's good. You just have to tell him the name and he'll remember it. He knows his numbers. You just show him the house number on the order and he'll remember the rest.'

In the end Henshaw agreed. He and his wife, Bea, were childless after an early tragedy with their only son. The boy had died of scarlet fever and the couple had lost heart. But Henshaw had a soft spot for Ernie Parsons, who was known up and down the street as a gentle giant. Though he was often on the receiving end of the street boys' name-calling and tricks, he was never seen to use his strength to retaliate. He would just stick his fists in his pockets and whistle, cap tilted back, looking straight ahead. And he knew these streets inside out, going up and down to the public baths, the football park, the market stalls.

'Mr Henshaw will set you to work tomorrow morning, Ern, and he'll see how you do. You'll have to be up early and you'll have to look smart. They'll give you an apron at the shop, and they'll show you what to do when you get there.'

Slowly Ernie took it all in. He was going to join the great London workforce. He'd be trusted to run errands and then he'd be paid for doing them. Mr Henshaw would give him a wage at the end of each week.

'Oh, Ern, you'll ride that nice bike with Henshaw's name printed on, and you'll carry all the stuff in that great basket on the front. It'll be smashing.' Hettie was delighted for him.

'Pa?' Ernie turned for advice. If his pa said yes, he'd love to try. But he was afraid that Duke would miss him too much in the pub. What would he do without him? That's what his pa always said.

'I don't know, son. It's a big step.' Duke was worried. He wasn't sure that Frances hadn't overestimated Ernie. If he were to bite off more than he could chew, it could do real damage to the boy. Duke didn't know if even Frances realized how much Ernie relied on slow, clear orders given to him step by step by someone who understood the way his mind worked. 'He's used to me telling him what to do,' he explained.

'But it'd do him good to learn something different, Pa. He can't rely on you for ever!' Frances glanced at Hettie and Jess for support. This was a sore subject for Duke. 'The job will give him a whole new life. It's time he had a go.'

'Frank Henshaw will keep an eye on him, Pa,' Hettie added. 'If you ask me, it's a good idea.' She went up and kissed Ernie on the cheek. 'I gotta go now, Ern. I hope it all works out. See you tomorrow.' She breezed out with a wink at Robert. 'See if you can talk the old man round,' she whispered.

'I don't know.' Duke sat stubbornly at the table, heavy forearms resting on the cloth. 'I don't want Ern to take a knock over it. What if Henshaw decides it ain't working out?'

Solemnly Ernie looked from face to face as the family conference was played out. Sometimes he felt as if he wanted the chance to prove himself like Frances, Jess and Robert said. But other times he just wanted to stay in the bar and help his pa. 'No, I'll stay here!' He put in a comment of his own at last. 'Pa needs me.'

It brought Frances to a full stop. She turned to Duke in mute appeal.

The old man grinned then sighed. 'No, Ern, I reckon you'd best give it a go. I can't keep you here with me for ever, like Frances says.' He stood up and put a hand on his son's shoulder. 'I couldn't sleep for thinking I'd ditched your chances over this. Go ahead, son, do it!'

Ernie sat opposite, looking suddenly down in the mouth.

'No need to take on. I'm not saying I don't need you no more! You can do this little job for Henshaw and you can still come home and help me and Robert with the barrels.' Duke went and gave his shoulder a friendly slap when he saw the boy's face light up again. 'I only hope it's the right thing, son, and I wish you luck.'

Frances was satisfied. Duke would always have to have the last word, of course, and she had to admit he was getting a bit contrary in his old age. He was set in his ways, but not too set to give way over the thorny problem with Jess, or to see reason over Ernie's future now. She smiled at having performed the usual balancing trick, sizing people up and sorting out their problems. She was good at that; in a way it was like mixing minute quantities of medicine at work and weighing them on the little brass scales.

'Well done, Frances,' Jess said later. 'Ern's thrilled to bits.'

'Yes. I'm sure it'll help make him more responsible.' Frances struggled for the right word. Even so, she went to bed that night with her fingers crossed, hoping to goodness that she was right.

*

So, during April, Duke Street got used to Ernie in his long white apron making his wobbly way between the stalls, his basket loaded with fresh bread and eggs. It was a wonder to see him keep his precarious balance on his sit-up-and-beg, his long legs pedalling, his elbows stuck out wide. But the noises of the street didn't distract him; not the roar of the taxi-cabs, nor the rattle of the tram-cars. He swerved round horses and carts, and barrows piled high with fruit. With total dedication he would steer his way to number 11 Meredith Close down the side of Coopers', to the black door with the lion knocker; or to number 32 Oliver Street, past the Board School to the house with the broken basement window. He would deliver his goods and wobble back to Henshaw's with his empty basket, perhaps stopping for a word with Nora Brady at her fish stall, or more likely Annie Wiggin, whose own stall stood right outside his corner shop.

'Blimey, that was quick, Ern,' Annie would call. Spring had arrived, so she'd switched her black shiny hat for a pale straw one, decked out with red ribbon from her range of haberdashery.

Ernie grinned. 'Mr Henshaw says we got a busy day ahead of us.'

'Oh well, better not hold you up, then.' Annie could talk and serve at the same time, measuring lace along the length of her arm from shoulder to wrist, and throwing in an extra few inches for good measure. She would wrap it in a cone of white tissue paper, exchange it for money and give the right change without even pausing. 'How's that sister of yours getting on, Ern? The one with the baby. Is it born yet? Can't be, else we'd all get an earful of its yelling through the window of a night. Jess, ain't it? Tell her I was asking after her.' Annie's one-way conversation rattled on as Ernie propped his bike on its metal stand. 'And tell your pa I was asking after him an' all, miserable old bleeder!'

Mrs Henshaw was on the doorstep for a breath of air and her eyebrows shot up at Annie's bad language. 'Come along inside, Ernie. There's another order ready here.' Her primly curled head turned away.

Ernie followed her into the Aladdin's cave of soup-tin pyramids and stacks of silver-wrapped chocolate bars while Annie grumbled on. 'Bleeding slave-drivers. Call themselves Christians, they won't even give the poor blighter five minutes' peace. I know what I'd do with their bleeding orders if I was him!' She jammed pins into a pincushion, voodoo style.

Late spring and early summer also brought perfect days for Sadie. Her bike rides with Charlie Ogden had become a regular thing since Duke's first reluctant consent. Escaping from grimy Southwark on a Sunday morning, through Rotherhithe and the newer suburbs further east, they might stop off by the river at Thamesmead. Their more adventurous rides took them far afield along quiet country roads full of the scent of flowers, the woods and hedgerows. They would pile their bicycles alongside dozens of others at a country inn and step inside for ginger-beers out of stone bottles. Once, Sadie had ridden back home with a sheaf of bluebells tied across her handlebars, and their perfume had filled the living room.

Still Duke complained that women couldn't ride bicycles to save their lives. 'When a motor comes up behind, why they gives a scream and falls off,' he teased. 'I seen it.'

'Pa!' Sadie protested with a flounce out of the room. But she didn't worry; her cycling trips with Charlie were too well established for her to mind much.

Charlie came to the tiny backyard of the Duke every fine Sunday. He now had a cycle on permanent loan from the lamed brother of one of the women who worked with his mother in the hosiery department at Coopers'. Sadie's family had clubbed together to buy her a shiny new one of her own. Her heart skipped a beat as she heard his bell ring below, and she would be downstairs in a flash, not bothered about coat or hat.

Once on the road, she felt exhilarated and free, despite her cumbersome skirts, her good mood heightened by the knowledge that Charlie would glimpse her slim ankles and calves. He would show off in turn, riding ahead with a dare-devil call of, 'Look, no hands!' They'd sit to rest on the high grassy banks and Charlie would confide his dreams; how he'd leave the East End behind him for good once he'd passed his scholarship to go to college in Birmingham or Manchester.

'Is that what you want, Charlie?' Sadie lay back in the grass on one of these days out, staring into blue nothing. It all seemed so far ahead. 'What about your ma and pa?'

'What about them? I want to be an engineer. I'll make machines that change the world, like flying machines. I'll be part of something wonderful like that, Sadie, to make my life really mean something! I won't rot away in Paradise Court!'

Hesitantly she said she understood.

'I got a friend at school living out in Putney now. Posh house, a garden even. I wouldn't want to bring him down the court if I could help it, would I?'

Sadie bit back a sharp reply. Paradise Court was good enough for her; she didn't always want something better, like Charlie did. But then maybe he was right; there was a whole big world out there. 'C'mon, let's go.' She sat up and brushed the palms of her hands, unsettled by the turn of conversation.

That was the time when he caught her wrist and stared at her. They knelt face to face, and Charlie tilted his body towards her and kissed her on the lips. 'Don't take on,' he whispered. 'There's all kinds of things I want in this life!'

'Not just books, Charlie Ogden?'

He kissed her again. 'Not just books, Sadie Parsons. And not just a house with a garden.'

That night she had a scolding from Frances for being late and giddy with it. 'Out till all hours, God knows where. Honestly, Sadie, it's not as if you ain't been brought up to know better.'

Sadie went out mouthing Frances's words, mimicking her. She banged the door of the room she shared with Jess. Jess sat at the open window, a shawl thrown loosely over her night-dress. She started as Sadie came in, then went back to staring over the rooftops up into the star-filled sky.

Jess's baby was due in July. In June she finally agreed with Frances's plan for her to go out into Kent, to spare Duke the details of childbirth which held bad memories for him since Pattie's death. A letter from his sister Florrie had finally made up her mind on this.

Florrie was living with a married son in Brighton. She heard the family news on the grapevine, and saw fit to write and tell Jess what a silly girl she'd been, but there, least said about that soonest mended. Only she'd better not cause her poor pa any more trouble, what with business going downhill all the time amidst all this talk of war. Before they knew it, they'd have lost Robert to the army and all the pubs would be empty of custom, and then where would they be? 'Your pa's had enough trouble for one life,' Florrie wrote. 'It's my place as your godmother to tell you this for your own good, Jess. Be a good girl and don't cause no more. Go away somewhere nice and quiet until the worst is over, and be glad if you've still got a home to go back to. I'll close now, wishing you health and happiness, your loving Aunt Flo. PS: My rheumatics is better, thanks to the sea air, Tom says.'

The letter stormed Jess's sensitive heart. She was a burden, a disgrace. If not only Frances but others saw it that way, it must be true. She would go into Kent soon and lie low. Everything was arranged through the friend of Frances. In the meantime, Jess kept to her room, except to cook and clean.

Florrie in Brighton wasn't the only one to be troubled by prospects of war. If it wasn't bleeding Ireland, it was that demon Kaiser, the bar-stool politicians in the Duke muttered darkly. Joe O'Hagan shuffled in one evening, furnished with a sixpence from his daughter Daisy's purse. He was a depressing enough sight in himself, pale and drawn, with a listless eye. Daisy had given him the money to spare her mother the sight of him for an hour or two. 'Go drown your sorrows, Pa!' she cried.

Mary sighed after his retreating footsteps. 'Go ditch them on some other poor fool, you mean.'

Arthur Ogden saw Joe enter the bar. He was at a terrible loose end himself, having read through the *Daily Express* headlines. His glass was empty, as was his pocket, so he hailed the newcomer with a faint hope of some improvement there. 'Hello, Joe. Some bleeding bertie's got himself shot, it says here,' he said as he thrust the newspaper under the illiterate newcomer's nose. 'And it says the whole of Europe's turned upside down over it.'

'That beats me,' Joe said in his nasal drawl. He ordered two pints of half and half; one for Arthur. 'All I know for sure with this shambles you call a government is that they can't even sort out the mess in their own backyard.' He sat by Arthur to make up a gloomy pair. The cellarman Joxer was there to serve them their drinks, and he scowled from under dark brows. Joxer had nothing particular against them. He never smiled and he never spoke to the customers at the bar, preferring a shadowy existence in the cellar. No one knew where he slept or how he lived. He was a drifter who'd found an unexpected soft spot in Duke's heart, and was accepted as such.

'By "backyard" I take it you mean Dublin?' Arthur took up the conversation with a self-important air. 'You mean your home turf?'

'Certainly I do. It's in a state of chaos, I'm telling you here and now. And we've no need of any Kaiser to go complicating things.' Joe spoke bitterly and brought the short conversation to an abrupt end.

'Drink up,' Robert encouraged. 'And cheer up, for gawd's sake.' He was taking over from Joxer and found himself rattled by the dreary talk. An army career didn't appeal, not when there was a good chance of being shot at into the bargain. He'd disagreed with Duke about it recently, resenting his father's patriotic talk. He certainly wasn't as keen as his father's generation had been to fight for king and country. 'It's the twentieth century, Pa. We do things in a different way now,' he insisted.

'Tell me that when the fighting starts,' Duke replied. 'And if you do I'll say you're no son of mine!'

'Anyone'd think you'd just got your call-up papers,' Robert told Arthur and Joe. 'You two are out of it whatever happens, ain't you? So bleeding well cheer up!'

Joxer's mouth bent in a sarcastic grin as he passed by. His night's work done, he was drifting off to wherever he spent his lonely nights. But instead of heading off down Duke Street, he turned and swung open the door again. 'Trouble!' he announced. 'Up the street!'

As word went round, people crowded out of the pubs and houses into the street. It was a clear June night when curiosity could be satisfied without the dampening effect of cold, wind or rain.

'What's happening?' Annie asked, darting quick as a flash up the court to the pub corner. 'What's all that bleeding noise?'

Dolly and Amy Ogden rushed up the street after her. Whatever it was, it came from up near Coopers'. They could hear shouts organized into a kind of high chant, then the crash of splintering glass. Amy broke into a run; more than her mother could manage. Ahead of her she saw Robert Parsons with Frances at his side. Even Duke had come downstairs and strode along, leaving Jess and Sadie with Ernie to look down from the window. He strode along, right up the middle of the street past a stationary hansom, the horses champing at the bit.

'Window-smashers!' someone gasped. 'It's them suffragettists!' A mob had gathered on the corner of Duke Street and Meredith Close. Now everyone converged on that focal point.

Frances heard the word spread like wildfire. 'Window-smashers!' The sound of splintering glass grew louder. Soon it was plain that the mob was made up entirely of women.

Some of the men in the crowd of onlookers pushed their hats to the back of their heads and whistled in amazement at the sight.

Terrified by the violence, but thrilled by their daring, Frances drew level with Coopers' shop front. She held her breath. She'd never seen a sight like this in all her life. Twenty or thirty women pelted stones and rained hammer blows against the plate glass. They'd broken through in several places, so the windows were crazed in giant spider's web patterns all along the length of the department store, which was twenty yards or so fronting on to Duke Street. Now they'd run down the side into Meredith Close. As one woman succeeded with her hammer blow, another would dart forward and add her own force. Glass caved in on the expensive goods on display, glinting like dangerous jewels under the street-lights. The women cheered, their faces savage with delight as they surged down the close together. Then the police arrived, whistles blowing, truncheons at the ready.

'Police!' women's voices cried, sharp and hysterical.

The onlookers stood back to let the men in uniform through. 'You need bleeding strait-jackets, not truncheons,' Arthur Ogden warned. Amy and Dolly stood speechless at his side, joining in the crowd's lust for action. It looked like none of the women would go quietly. Trapped down the close, they fought tooth and nail.

Then there was a hush in the crowd as Jack Cooper and his son rolled up in their big black motor car. They both jumped out and pushed roughly through. Faced with a devastated shop front, the older man stopped dead in his tracks as if the life-blood had suddenly drained from him. He stared in disbelief at the expanses of shattered glass. But Teddy strode angrily over the shards and turned the corner into the close.

The women outnumbered policemen by about three to one, and although one or two had been manhandled off up the street into waiting vans, the gathered crowd hadn't lifted a finger to help. They stood passively, waiting to see the police get the better of the law-breakers, but by no means determined to see it over quickly. So the women were able to fight back by kicking and scratching, shouting all the while at the tops of their enraged voices.

Frances found herself at first roused and then moved to tears. She stood back from the main crowd, watching the struggles of the ones who were roughly taken off to prison.

But Teddy Cooper, beside himself, began lashing out at the women still at large. He lunged at one whose face was already bleeding from flying glass and caught her off balance. Down she went on to the pavement amongst the scuffling, stamping feet. Frances heard her scream. She saw Teddy Cooper poised to smash his boot down on her. Two policemen turned and moved to restrain him. Then Amy Ogden rushed forward.

The woman screamed again. For Amy, the sound brought back a terrible memory. She flung herself at Teddy, yelling his name and sobbing at him to stop. He had time to wrench himself free, there was time to recognize dawning contempt on his face as he made out his assailant, before the policemen took hold of him and dragged him clear of the two women; one knocked full length on the pavement, one desperately calling his name.

It was only a matter of time now before reinforcements arrived and the mob of women was subdued. More uniforms swept up Duke Street and into the close. The crowd saw it was all over and broke up. The last women were carried off. Still Jack Cooper stood there staring at the ruins of his shop, while the police took details from Teddy. Amy was led quietly away by a puzzled Dolly.

Duke and Robert stood their ground as the crowd melted. Regardless of his like or dislike of the local employers, Duke's sense of fair play was upset. He was against the mayhem caused by these women and had to feel sorry for a man whose livelihood stood in ruins before his eyes. So he went up to Cooper. 'You'll need a hand to clear this lot up,' he said. Robert was sent to round up a few fit and sober helpers, along with brooms to sweep up the mess.

Cooper nodded slowly, emerging from his daze. Teddy had gone inside to assess the damage. Unnoticed, Frances stood and watched as the men set to. She felt nothing now after the shock of events; just a coldness round her heart towards these men.

There was a story her mother told her when she was very young about a girl whose heart was pierced by a fragment of glass, and the glass froze her heart so she could no longer love and no longer cry. She became the Ice Queen's child.

The story settled in Frances's mind again now. Robert and her father had no right to help Frank Cooper. She saw it clearly as she turned and walked home. It was the women, driven to desperate action, who needed help. Who cared about the state of a few broken windows when women had to fight these mighty injustices? Frances's rebellious thoughts took shape from this one violent episode. She went slowly back to the Duke, but she felt the ties with her home, her family, her whole history break with each step she took.

Chapter Ten

'Them women need a good hiding,' Duke grumbled when he got back from sweeping up the glass. 'That's what they need.'

Frances couldn't bear to hear him lay down the law. Her hair came loose as she swung round to confront him. 'How can you say that? Do you know what they do when they get them to Holloway? They stick a tube down their throats to feed them! Think of that. It's downright disgusting!'

But his own code was violated. 'Women who go about smashing windows need the feel of the birch on their backs!' he shouted. 'Teach 'em their proper place.' Duke roused was a terrifying spectacle.

Frances sobbed. 'It ain't right. They're sticking up for all us women, not just themselves. And look what happens.'

'You ain't telling me that what they did was sticking up for other women?' He stared at her in disbelief.

'I am! That's just it, Pa. We need to be treated equal; that's what all this is about!'

A look of scorn slowly crept on to his face. He refused to follow her wild reasoning. 'It ain't no wonder you're on the shelf, girl,' he said quietly.

'What!' she screeched in disbelief. She was the one out of control now.

'You heard. I said it ain't no wonder you can't find yourself a decent man like all the other girls.'

He regretted the words even as he spoke them. Frances looked as if she'd been stabbed in the chest. Jess ran in from the bedroom to stop her from falling in a dead faint. He could hear Sadie sobbing. But a stubborn voice reminded him that women would always try to gain the upper hand, either by worming their way in or by outright defiance. You had to fight it for all you were worth. 'I'm off downstairs to finish up,' he told Jess gruffly. 'You sort her out and get her off to bed. She'll come to her senses tomorrow.'

Jess took Frances's full weight as she half fell against her. She called out for Sadie to stop crying. 'Lend a hand. Help me get her to our room.' She struggled, but Frances pushed her off.

'You heard him!' she gasped. 'How can I stay here now? You heard what he said about me!'

'He don't mean it, Frances. Just give him a chance to calm down. Everything will look different tomorrow.' Jess put one hand to her belly as she felt the baby twist and kick. There was a sharp stab of pain low in her abdomen. She sat down and gripped the edge of the table.

'Frances, it's Jess!' Sadie rushed forward to drag her oldest sister away from the dark window. 'She's gone white as a sheet, look!'

Frances was still gripped by a blind determination to cut loose, to live her own life and begin to fight for the cause she believed in. Her lips were set in a straight line as she stared at her own reflection.

'Frances!' Sadie let out another terrified cry. Jess had used both hands to push herself upright. She began to stumble towards the bedroom door.

'Get help,' she gasped. 'It's the baby. Go on, fetch someone, quick!'

Frances spun round and ran towards her. 'Oh, Jess, no! Not yet! For God's sake, Sadie, do as she says! No, help me get her into bed!' The sight of Jess doubled up in pain pierced her heart. Selfish, selfish! she told herself. My fault, my fault! 'Oh God, no, Jess. Just hang on. Sadie, run for Dr Fry. Knock until you get an answer. Tell him what's happened.'

Sadie ran wild-eyed down the stairs, out into the street, while Frances used all her strength to lift the fainting Jess safely on to her own bed. She loosened her clothes, then ran to the airing-cupboard for towels. 'It's all right, Jess. Everything's fine. Sadie's gone to fetch Dr Fry.' She stroked her sister's forehead, cold and wet with sweat. 'Is it bad? Is it, my dear?'

Jess turned her head. 'Make this baby live, Frances. Make her live!'

'Oh!' Frances moaned. She could hardly meet Jess's pleading gaze.

'Not your fault,' Jess whispered. Then she turned to grip the bedstead as the spasm of pain came strong and sharp.

Frances felt another hammer blow to her heart. She called out for more help. Robert came running and was sent to boil up water in the kitchen. Duke came up in alarm. He rested a forearm against the door jamb, then retreated. He'd seen it before; a woman struggling in childbirth, fear in the air, the doctor arriving brisk and businesslike because things were not as they should be. The closed door. The cries.

Long into the night Jess struggled. Weakened by loss of blood, faint with pain, she gave birth to a daughter.

Dr Fry cut the cord. Frances gave him a clean square of

linen in which he wrapped the baby tight. 'Here's your little girl, Jess,' he said as he handed her over. Frances wept. She leaned over the bed.

Jess's hands shook. She saw the face of her daughter, her own child. She held her close. Dark eyes opened towards her. She looked up at Frances and smiled.

'Now we've work to do,' Dr Fry said, his voice low and kind. 'Let your sister take the child, Jess. She'll take good care.' He took the baby away from her.

Jess's world was empty. Her head swam with pain.

'We have to stop the bleeding,' the doctor told Frances.

'She will be all right, won't she?' Frances felt the light weight in her arms.

Dr Fry grunted. 'Go through and show Duke his new granddaughter,' he advised. 'I'll do what I can here.'

Duke sat with bowed head by the fire. Robert stood, elbow against the mantelpiece, keeping Ernie calm. Sadie hovered with Hettie by the kitchen door.

Frances stepped forward. 'It's a girl,' she announced.

'Thank God!' Hettie breathed. She'd come in from work, full of news about the window-smashing, only to be greeted by this crisis. Jess's time wasn't up for another month yet. But she found Sadie at the top of the stairs, her hands covering her ears.

Duke looked up.

'A granddaughter for you, Pa.' She spoke softly, held out the child towards him; her own peace offering. The family would need her now, more than ever.

'What about Jess?' Duke's face was drained, his voice cracked. 'I've been praying for her, Frances. She's still with us, ain't she?'

'She is, Pa, and she's putting up a fight.'

'Has she seen the child?'

'She has.'

He nodded. 'Then she'll live. She's got everything to live for now, ain't she?' He stood gazing down into the infant's sleeping face. 'My Pattie never saw Sadie when she was born. Never ever saw her face.'

Sadie ran up and put both arms around him. Frances cried on Hettie's shoulder. Robert frowned to stop his own eyes from filling up. Ernie hung his head. They waited.

At three in the morning Dr Fry emerged from the bedroom. He rolled down his shirtsleeves. 'Awake,' he reported. 'And asking for her daughter.'

There was a cry of relief.

'She's weak. There's a danger of infection. You must take good care.' The doctor's gaze took in each of them in turn. 'I know she's in good hands,' he told Frances. 'Your work at the chemists has taught you about hygiene during a recovery such as this?'

Frances nodded. Tears streamed down her face.

'Good. In that case . . .' Dr Fry snapped his black leather bag shut and reached for his jacket, which Ernie handed to him. 'Congratulations, Duke.' He came and shook him by the hand.

'The child?' Duke wouldn't let go until he answered.

'Small.'

'Ailing?'

'No. Only weak with the difficult birth. We'll need to get her weight up.'

Duke considered. 'Thank you, Doctor.'

'Keep an eye on them both, and send for me again if you think I'm needed.' He buttoned up his jacket.

Hettie saw him out. Dawn streaked the sky above the grey roofs as she watched the small, dark figure down the street. Upstairs, they moved quietly, careful of each other, fearful for Jess and her newborn baby.

At seven o'clock, Frances made breakfast. She was pale but calm. The others watched her for their lead. They sat down to an edgy affair of boiled bacon, hot tea, whispers and worried looks. Sadie had filled Hettie in on the row between Duke and Frances, and they all waited nervously for some solution to this problem. Frances had never in her life before lost control like that, and no one had shown Duke such open defiance.

But that had been before the emergency over Jess. Now Duke seemed determined to let the other matter drop. He listened quietly at the breakfast table as Rob discussed with Hettie the damage done to Coopers' windows in terms of cost and loss of trade. Rob didn't think any of the workers would be laid off; quite the opposite. It seemed to him they'd have to put in extra hours in the sweatshops to replace damaged stock. 'Everything'll be back to normal in a couple of days,' he said.

Frances sat and listened without reacting. During a long, brilliant dawn, measured by silence, the baby's cries, and then the early noises of carts rattling down the cobbled street, she'd decided there was no point arguing further with Duke. She would stay on at home and try to live peacefully with him. Her loyalty was to Jess now.

Like all the other men round here, her father regarded the women's demonstration as a sideshow at the fair, performed by freaks of nature. But Frances knew different. She had the ability to think things through. There was justice in the women's cause; they should be treated equally in this day and age. She used logic to soothe away the hurt Duke had inflicted; if she'd been a man of twenty-eight and still single, people would say she was a good catch, with her respectable job and good prospects. Just because she was a woman they said she was on the shelf. And old maids like her were regarded with mixed scorn and pity. When day broke Frances was ready to meet it, for Jess's sake. But things would never be quite the same in the family. They would have to get used to a new edge to her, even more remote and determined.

'It's eating her up inside,' Annie Wiggin confided to Dolly Ogden. 'She's turned into one of them man-haters, and it ain't doing her no good.'

The two women stood gossiping in the street outside Henshaw's on a sultry August day. Their subject was the Parsons family and Frances in particular. Her long-standing row with Duke was by now common knowledge. She went openly to the suffragists' meetings and wore their purple and green sash.

'He don't like it,' Annie reported. She said 'he' in an awed tone. Duke was looked up to by many of the older women and Dolly caught Annie's meaning right away. 'He ain't got no time for it and it's causing bad feeling in the house, believe me.'

'D'you think it's brought on all this trouble young Jess had with that baby?' Dolly didn't really want Annie's opinion. With her expert knowledge of the complexities of childbirth, she'd already made up her mind. 'I mean to say, the poor girl started that very night. She didn't have no chance to get away like she planned. Poor little blighter was born there and then, right above the pub. Sadie had to run for Dr Fry. Everyone down the court heard the rumpus.'

Annie nodded. 'Weeks early. By all accounts, the poor

little mite was no bigger than a wax doll. Jess was in a pretty bad way herself and all. It can't have been easy.'

Dolly seized the opportunity to confide the secrets of her own difficult labours. 'Take Charlie. Arse about face he was. Dr Phillips has a feel and tells me he's lying the wrong way "hentirely". That's what he says. It was two whole days before Charlie finally consents to put in his appearance, all nine pounds eight ounces. He was just about the death of me, I can tell you!' The stout woman reminisced with pride. 'He always was an awkward little bugger!'

Annie nodded her way through Dolly's fascinating account, but was anxious to steer things back on course. 'They thought they was going to lose her,' she said.

'Who, the baby?'

'No, Jess. Everything went black for Duke. Course he was remembering his old lady and how he lost her over young Sadie. He heard the state Jess was in and everything went black all over again. He just put his head in his hands and sat there still as a statue, with the poor girl clinging to life by a thread in the very next room!'

Even Dolly was impressed. She stared at Annie. 'How come you know all this?'

'Hettie told me. She came down the stall the other day and we had a little chat. Poor old man, he was in a state for days till he knew Jess was on the mend. Just sat there without moving for days!'

'He never! Who looked after things downstairs then?'

'Robert, of course. He ran the whole place. I'm surprised your Arthur never told you that. No one expected the old man to take it so bad.' Annie shook her head. 'The whole family was gutted, mind you.'

'And what's she decided to call the baby, then?' Dolly needed to be on her way back to work. 'Supposing the poor little bleeder decides to make it through to her christening.'

Annie had begun serving mother-of-pearl buttons to a woman from the pawn shop. She counted them on to her palm. 'Seven, eight, nine. Grace. That's threepence to you, ta very much. Hettie says they're calling her Grace. And she's a pretty, dark-haired thing, but still sickly.' Annie pocketed the money and watched Dolly on her way.

Dolly too had much on her mind. The chat with Annie had cheered her up, as other people's troubles often did, but she had several of her own, over and above the usual. For one thing, it was getting too much to put up with, these constant rows with Amy over something and nothing, with Arthur putting in his own two penn'orth. Ever since the window-smashing episode Amy had been behaving like a little fool. She claimed to hate the boss's son, but there was more to it than that. She would be always bursting into tears, turning her nose up at the food on her plate. She was getting thin; most unlike her. What's more, she looked for arguments with Charlie all the time. It was time to put her foot down, Dolly decided.

'If there's one thing I can't stand, it's a person who goes looking for a quarrel,' she told herself, descending out of the sunlight into the depths of Hosiery. Cooper had long since had his windows repaired and they were good as new. The workers had put in overtime and business was back to normal, as Duke Parsons had predicted. 'I'm going to have to have a talk with that girl when we get home tonight!'

That morning Amy had smashed her cup into the sink and stormed off. Dolly had only mentioned in passing that the case against Teddy Cooper was coming up before the beak. One of the women in the mob had done him for assault. 'Don't mention his name to me!' Amy screamed.

Her face went all twisted and she dashed her cup down. Dolly had been able to glue it back together, but it'd never be the same. 'Don't ask me what's up with her, but I'm going to put my foot down,' she said again, sitting down at the long table behind her machine for knitting the hose.

In the early afternoon, cocooned by the network of muffled sounds that comprised her working day – the hum of the machinery, the distant yell for orders, the low chat of the women – Dolly was roused by an unexpected event. She looked up in the dim light, surprised to see Bert Buggles sneak into the workshop. He headed straight for her, a look of spiteful glee in his weasel eyes. Sticking his pointed nose right up to her face, he whispered a message.

Dolly's machine clattered to a halt. She launched herself off her bench, scattering bobbins of beige silk thread.

'Hang on, Dolly, where you off to?' one of the women called. Bert had already darted away up the back stairs.

'Hats!' Dolly replied, with a face like thunder.

'Here, you can't do that,' her supervisor warned. 'You ain't asked permission!'

'Stuff your permission!' Dolly's sturdy figure never hesitated. 'My Amy's in trouble. I got to sort her out.'

They could tell by her tone of voice that the situation was serious. The women looked at each other, shrugged and ducked their heads to carry on with their work. What one had actually overheard Bert say was that Amy Ogden had laid into Teddy Cooper with a pair of scissors. Trouble that shape and size was best avoided.

Dolly took the four flights of narrow back stairs two at a time in a rush of skirts and a creak of stays. Her breath came short and there was a sharp pain in her chest. By the time she reached Amy's workshop she was clutching at her blouse and gasping. If Teddy Cooper had laid a finger on her to provoke her into having a go at him, her mother's wrath would know no bounds. She barged into the low attic room ready for anything.

The boss's son was there all right. He must have grabbed the scissors from Amy, but not before she'd nicked him on the left cheek. Dolly saw the bright-red cut and the thin trickle of blood. Teddy had backed Amy away into a corner, where she cowered in a crumpled heap. She snivelled something that Dolly couldn't make out.

Just then Teddy made a grab for her, scissors still in one hand. Out of control himself, he jerked her to her feet. 'Shut your face, you hear!' The scissors were at her throat, and Amy's head forced back against the wall.

'Stay clear,' Dora warned. The tall woman moved to restrain Dolly. They'd seen it coming for weeks, if Dolly did but know it; the barbed comments, the filthy looks from Amy whenever Teddy Cooper showed his face. 'Let them sort it out.'

But Dolly was a lioness protecting her cub. She roared across the room. Startled, Teddy lost his hold and the girl pulled free. He felt the full force of Dolly's weight against him. His head cracked sideways on to the yellowed plaster, but he swung out wildly and managed to keep Dolly at bay as she moved in a second time. 'Get these bitches off me!' he snarled at Dora, Emmy and the rest. 'And for God's sake keep them quiet!' He stood upright, trying to regain his self-control, as several women moved in to restrain the mother and daughter.

'A nice bastard you are!' Amy's hysterical voice rose, even as Dora tried to lead her off. 'He attacks women, he does!' she cried to her mother.

Dolly looked from Amy to Teddy and back again.

'Shut your face!' he threatened. His face was smeared with blood, he took deep breaths to pull himself together.

'He does, he attacks women, Ma!'

'I know. I was there, I seen him.' Dolly moved in to take Amy away from Dora.

'No, you never saw what he did to me!' Amy's body was wracked with sobs and gasps.

Dolly's arm was halfway round her shoulder. It froze in mid-air. Everyone else drew back. Even Teddy stopped cursing and fuming. 'What you on about?' Dolly asked slowly.

'He don't deserve to live, that's what! I seen him putting the boot in on that poor girl and I thinks of what he done to me, every little thing. It all comes flashing back!'

'What you saying, Amy?' Dolly stared at Teddy. 'Are you saying what I think you're saying?' She saw his head go down, the back of one hand against his mouth as he failed to meet her outraged stare.

But Bert Buggles had acted as messenger again. His route took him from Hosiery to Jack Cooper's office, where he passed on the news of trouble in his attic workshop. 'Will you come, Mr Cooper? Only, one of the girls is a bit upset,' he said in his oily way. Then he sneaked off ahead.

Jack Cooper strode upstairs, coat-tails flying. Girls didn't get upset in his workshops, or if they did he soon sent them packing. It was bad for routine, bad for discipline. The heavy man came upstairs preparing a self-important lecture on the high standards expected of those who worked for Coopers' Drapery Stores.

He opened the door on chaos. Not a single woman was at her workplace. The Ogden woman had stormed up from the basement. He saw her sturdy back view and someone else cowering in a corner. There was a lot of noise. Materials had been swept from a work top on to the floor. A girl was sobbing and swearing by turns. Mr Cooper advanced into the room.

'What's going on here?' He stood legs apart, thumbs hooked into his waistcoat pockets.

Dolly turned. The figure in the corner stepped forward.

'Teddy!' Jack Cooper's fine speech deserted him.

'It's all right, Father, I can manage here.' Teddy attempted to defuse the situation before it got any further out of hand.

'What do you mean, it's all right?' Furious, Cooper strode over to Amy and pulled her upright, for the girl had slumped against her mother, half-fainting. 'Stand up straight, for God's sake!' He turned to his son. 'I'll take over here. Let me just deal with these Ogden women.' For the first time he saw the open cut on his son's face. He frowned. 'You'd better go home and tend to that,' he said, very formal and unsympathetic.

It gave Dolly time to gather herself. Jack Cooper meant to sack them both on the spot, it was clear. But he'd hear the full story before he chucked her out, and she wouldn't mince words. She pulled Amy to her side. 'You ought to be ashamed,' she challenged. Suddenly Cooper's flabby chin and plump, gold-ringed fingers offended her. He'd begun like all the rest down Duke Street in the battle to survive, trundling barrows. He'd done well on cheap labour and high prices, working his women like slaves in the sweat-shops he set up in flea-ridden cellars, before he moved up to owning his own shop. Now he thought himself high and mighty. 'I'll deal with these Ogden women,' he sneered. Dolly launched into him. 'You and that son! Call himself a man! And listen, you can stick your job up your arse! I wouldn't work for you, not now!'

'What are you talking about, woman?' He could see she was incoherent with rage.

Dolly took a deep breath. She saw the son take another

step forward, and out of the corner of her eye the look of amazement on Dora's long face. 'Your precious son's had his wicked way with nearly every girl in this bleeding place, as if you didn't know. And now he's tried it on with my girl!' For a second her voice broke down. She took Amy by the hand. 'Look here, Mr Cooper, you go ahead and give us the push, but you'll hear me out. Your boy's done my girl serious harm and he has to pay for it. Me and Amy's going straight out of here up to the coppers!'

They sailed out of Coopers' for the very last time to a long, stunned silence.

At home down Paradise Court Arthur fumed over the loss of two whole wages coming into the house. 'What you bleeding well have to lay into the boss's son for?' he ranted. 'Silly cows, what d'you expect me to do about it now, go back down the bleeding glass factory with my lungs in this state?' He coughed raucously.

'What's wrong with your lungs, Arthur Ogden?' Dolly said evenly. 'Look, we all know we cooked our goose with Cooper good and proper, so there's no point going on about it.' She sat heavily in a chair at the kitchen table. 'Make us a cup of tea, Charlie, there's a good lad.'

Amy hung about miserably by the door leading upstairs. 'What about me, Pa? Ain't you going to do nothing for me?'

He turned on her. 'No, I ain't. How could you be so bleeding silly to think a toff like Cooper would want to walk out with a girl like you? Did you think he just wanted to hold your hand then? 'Struth, girl, you wasn't born yesterday.' He ran his hand through his thinning hair. 'If you ask me you brought it on yourself.'

Amy wailed and turned back to her mother.

'And don't go thinking your ma's taking you up to the peelers, neither. We'd be a laughing stock.'

Amy flew at him in angry despair. 'You heard what that Teddy Cooper done to me, and you ain't going to do nothing about it! But you can't stop Ma and me, can he, Ma?'

Dolly sat and sipped her tea, deep in thought. She'd already sent Charlie packing. 'Get upstairs, it ain't nice for you to hear,' she told him. Charlie had been glad to escape. Now Dolly stared cold reality in the face. Arthur was right; the family had lost the only money coming in, and there was nothing left to pawn. She stared round at the empty shelves and the one crooked picture on the wall; a cross-stitch sampler done by Amy at school. 'Bless this house,' it said. What's more he was probably right about the police. She looked up at Amy. 'Calm down, girl. Your pa's right. We done as much as we can do.'

'But I thought you said we was going to the station?'

'I did. But think about it. We've left it too long for them to believe us. Who'd take our word against Cooper's?'

'We're not going then?' Amy was stunned into silence. She sat on the doorstep, suddenly limp.

'No. But we'll let the Coopers think we are.' Dolly arched her eyebrows. 'Leastways they'll have to sweat it out for a bit.'

Arthur nodded, glad she'd seen sense.

'And I got another plan.' Dolly stood up, ready to tackle the sinkful of dirty pots and pans. 'We'll move Charlie out of his room at the top of the house again and we'll take a lodger. That'll keep the money coming in!'

*

Back at the workshop Jack Cooper re-established order and got the women settled back to work once more. He promised them a shilling each if they made up for lost time, but they'd have to take on the Ogden girl's work until he filled her position. He bullied and bribed them back into place, his sagging, mottled face betraying the strain of the recent scene. The women resented every inch of the pompous little man, every whiff of his hair oil and every stab of his stubby finger on the table in front of them. But they needed the shilling. They bowed their heads and the waters closed without trace over the scandal of Amy Ogden.

At home in Richmond, Edith Cooper bathed the cut on her son's face. After twenty-five years of marriage to Jack, she'd trained herself never to ask questions. She'd slid into place alongside him on all his upward moves from tenement to rooms above the first shop and eventually out to the leafy suburb. Her clothes and her accent improved along with her surroundings. She was by now a tall, slight, sandy-haired woman of good taste and manners, with a fondness for cameo brooches and amber necklaces, and an outstanding lack of curiosity about the business which paid for them.

She finished dabbing at Teddy's wound as Jack's car drove up the drive, and she quietly crept out of the room with her basinful of disinfected water.

Jack lectured his son. What he did with his women was his own affair, but never again would he put up with a situation where Teddy's fooling got in the way of profits at work. There were girls on every street-corner; why did Teddy have to pick them up in the workplace? From now on he strictly forbade that. He'd noted what the Ogden woman had said; there was every chance she'd lay charges against him and it would serve him right. 'Does your mother know?' he asked. He fumbled in a silver cigar box, his hand shaking.

Teddy shook his head. 'I haven't told her. Listen, Pa, how will this affect things? Will they really lay this second charge, do you think?' He was in trouble up to his neck, what with the mad suffragette and now that little fool, Amy Ogden. His self-confidence was visibly dented and he presented a pathetic figure; pale, cut and bruised, with a wheedling tone. 'You'll back me up, won't you, Pa?'

Jack treated him to a contemptuous glare. He thought of all the years bartering on the docks and barrows, the fights he'd had for the best market pitches in the early days, his first shop with his name in gold letters above the door. He pictured what he had now; the acres of floor space, the precious plate-glass expanse on Duke Street, newly restored. He'd built Coopers' Drapery Stores from nothing, and this young fool sitting before him was the son he must hand it on to. 'You don't deserve it, Teddy,' he said with grim resignation. 'The best you can do is hope the Ogden woman keeps quiet.' He lit his cigar and felt the smoke ease down the back of his throat. 'Or if you're very clever and think about it long enough, maybe you can work out a way of making her!'

Chapter Eleven

Daisy O'Hagan called up to see Hettie in the middle of one Saturday morning in August, not long after Dolly Ogden's notorious row with her employer.

'Good for her,' Daisy said to Robert, who was sweeping out in the pub before the day's trade began. It had been the talk of the street for days. 'It's high time someone took that Teddy Cooper down a peg or two.'

Robert leaned against his broom handle, keeping it propped at an angle so that Daisy couldn't get upstairs. He wore his usual teasing smile. 'You could've fooled me. Last time I seen you, you was with Teddy Cooper and you couldn't get so much as this broomstick between the pair of you. Very friendly, you was.'

Daisy flared up. 'Where was that, I'd like to know?'

'After the show last Tuesday or Wednesday, I think it was. He dropped you off down the court in a taxi; either him or his double.' Robert shook his head. 'You got a nerve, Daisy my girl.'

Daisy tossed her own head backwards and brazened it out. 'It ain't none of your business, Robert Parsons.'

'But you're breaking my heart, Miss O'Hagan, pushing me over for the likes of him!'

'Teddy Cooper's a gent, not a scuttler like you!' Daisy attempted to barge past Robert.

'Tell that to Amy Ogden,' he said quietly. 'Or Chalky White for that matter. I'm sure he'd be interested in your high opinion of Mr Cooper.' Robert had heard rumours that Daisy was still involved with the shady docker, despite her denials.

Daisy felt Robert had gone too far this time. Her temper snapped, and she raised a hand to give his cheek a smart slap, but Robert moved quickly and caught her wrist. He grinned condescendingly. 'That Irish temper of yours ain't going to get you nowhere with me, Daisy.'

'It ain't meant to, you bleeding idiot! Now let go of me.' She struggled to prise his fingers from her wrist. 'I gotta go upstairs!'

Robert, at such close quarters with Daisy, could see why she was the most popular of all the girls at the Palace. A spirited mixture of jokiness and independence overlaid a real passion. Her eyes said everything. Wide and expressive, they flashed with anger, but they conveyed vulnerability beneath. And she was so pretty and wild. He stood, unwilling to let her go.

'Look, just let me be,' Daisy pleaded. She glanced swiftly up the stairs and back into the empty bar, then stamped hard on Robert's foot with the thin heel of her boot. He yelped and let go. Daisy hurried upstairs, hot and flustered. 'Serve you right!' she called down.

'Our Rob been having a go at you, has he?' Hettie greeted her friend with a shrewd look. She worried about her a good deal these days. 'You want me to have a word with him for you?'

Daisy sank gratefully into a fireside chair. 'No need, thanks. I can look after myself.'

'So what's up then?' Hettie had spent the morning washing her hair and looking after baby Grace while Jess went out shopping. Her hair hung free almost to the waist.

She stood by the mirror over the mantelpiece, brush in hand.

Daisy sighed. 'If it ain't one bleeding thing it's another.' The grind of poverty at home was having its effect on her for a start; the lack of privacy and her father's constant grumbling. Her mother would turn to her for both money and a sympathetic ear.

Being Irish, the O'Hagans were cut off from most of the other families down the court. They were regarded as outsiders and drifters, likely to flit whenever they fell too far short with their rent. Their children tumbled up and down the stairways and hovered in alleys, got ill, picked at the gutters for scraps, crawled under the market stalls and generally went to the bad. So Mary had no one except Daisy to share her troubles with, except for occasional lifts from good-hearted neighbours like Frances Parsons. 'Ma's worried sick about Tommy,' Daisy told Hettie. 'We ain't seen hide nor hair of him since Wednesday. The little sod's gone and vanished on us again!'

'He'll turn up, won't he?' Hettie knew that Tommy often took off for a day or two, perhaps teaming up with one of the local rag-and-bone men to go picking iron off the rubbish tips. Or else he'd be cab-ducking up at Waterloo. Tommy turned his hand to anything that would earn him a copper or two.

'He mostly leaves us word though. Last time he was cutting up hay at the carter's place down Angel Yard. He got a bed in the hayloft and never come back home for a week. But he sent Ma word where he was and we never lost no sleep.' Daisy came close to the mirror to push stray hairs into the framework of pins that held her elaborate style in place. 'Any rate, I told her I'd ask around. You ain't seen him, have you, Ett?'

'Wait here, I'll ask Sadie.' Hettie went off, while Daisy

stooped to look at Jess's baby, sleeping peacefully in its crib in the corner. The tiny, unmarked face made her sigh again.

'Sadie says she ain't seen him since midweek, but she remembers him going on about them cage birds he keeps in the cellar. Said he was feeding them up so he could go up the West End and get good money for them. She ain't seen him since.' She looked at Daisy and squeezed her arm. 'Don't take on. Tom's the same as you; he can look after himself.'

'We have to in our family,' Daisy agreed. 'But I think you're right. Just pass the word will you, Ett? If anyone catches sight of him, let me know. Then Ma can stop worrying herself.' She made as if to go. 'See you later up at the stop?'

Hettie smiled and nodded. 'Six o'clock on the dot.' The baby showed signs of waking, so she went and gingerly lifted her from the crib.

'Suits you, I'm sure!' Daisy said with one of her old, lively grins.

'Cheeky sod!' Hettie cradled Grace in the crook of her arm as Daisy went on her way to look for Tommy.

To Hettie's relief, Jess soon returned to look after the baby.

'Here, give her to me,' she offered, putting her basket down on the table. She smiled at Grace and grasped hold of her tiny fist. The baby gurgled and puckered her wet lips. 'How's she been?' Jess asked.

'Fine. Sleeping mostly.' Hettie came up to look, her hair swinging free. 'Ain't it time you started to breathe more easy over her, Jess? She's eight weeks now, and Dr Fry says she's coming on in leaps and bounds.'

'I ain't worried no more,' Jess lied. 'Leastways, not like at first.'

compliments as his very own, accepting good wishes from neighbours and friends.

'About time, too!' Annie Wiggin exclaimed. She leaned into the pram, then stood up wreathed in smiles. 'Ain't she a picture! I ain't never hardly seen such a pretty little thing!'

'Oh, Annie,' Jess demurred.

'Why thank you, Annie!' Duke beamed back, chest out, head up.

'There's a couple of yards of spare lace at the back of my stall here. I want you to have it for any little dress or smock you make up for her.' Annie handed a small packet of tissue paper and lace to a surprised Jess. She held up her hand to wave off protest. 'I been keeping it handy, hoping I'd catch you. It ain't nothing much, but I hope it comes in.'

'That's very kind of you, I'm sure.' Duke took the packet from Jess and put it in his pocket. He smiled again and strolled on, steering them through the crowded market.

Jess raised her eyebrows at him. 'Who'd have thought old Annie Wiggin would go all soft over little Grace!'

'Course she would,' Duke remonstrated. 'Anyone would. And less of the old. Annie's a spring chicken.'

'Leave off, Pa. She's fifty if she's a day.' Jess paused, and seeing Ernie pedal by on the far side of the street, raised her hand and gave him a big wave. Ernie wobbled and waved back.

'She's not. And besides, I'm nearly sixty,' he reminded her. 'Old Duke Parsons with a brand new granddaughter.' They walked on in the sunshine, proud as peacocks.

He was in a good mood back behind the bar when a new customer came in. Since most of the men had gone to watch the Crystal Palace versus Bury match, business was slack and the newcomer stood out all the more. Smartly dressed in a dark suit and bowler hat, he approached the bar and gave his order. Duke took in his clean-shaven, sallow skin, his confident air. 'Are you just passing through?' he enquired, pushing the glass towards him. 'Or visiting down the court?'

'To tell the truth, I'm looking for a room,' the young man said pleasantly. 'I thought the local pub was as good a place as any to start.' He took a long draught of the cool beer, glad to be out of the hot sun.

'That's true,' Duke said. 'We get to hear most things.'

'I don't want nothing flash to start with, just a respectable room till I get set up proper. You heard of anything?'

Maurice Leigh was moving on from the Balham Empire. He'd been offered the manager's job at a new picture palace on St Thomas Street at a starting salary of two pounds ten shillings per week. Convinced as he was that moving pictures was the entertainment form of the future, he'd seized the chance to get a new establishment underway. He was full of plans and bursting with enthusiasm. Lodgings were a minor detail which he hoped to sort out without too much bother.

Duke studied the stranger. He wouldn't recommend lodgings unless he approved of the enquirer. By his voice he was East End born and bred, but not from this neck of the woods exactly; more Bethnal Green. By his looks, his background was Jewish; second, maybe third generation of emigrants from Eastern Europe. Duke was practised in the art of pinning down newcomers. 'You found work round here?' he asked with some scepticism. Jobs were still like gold dust, though that might change again as men enlisted and went off to the war. The rumblings had turned into certainty, with the declaration on the 4th of August. Even now posters were going up on street-corners calling the young men to arms.

Maurice nodded and confirmed Duke's theory. 'I'm the new manager at the Gem Picture Palace. This area's nice and handy for my work, see, if I can find a place.' He drank up, took a watch from his waistcoat pocket and looked about.

'Well, maybe I can help.' Duke came to the conclusion that the man was a good prospect. 'It just so happens there's a room going down Paradise Court.' He leaned over and gave details of Dolly Ogden's place. 'Not grand, of course, but she keeps her place clean. I know for a fact she's looking for someone. I'd try there if I was you.'

Maurice thanked him and went quickly out. He smiled and lifted his hat to Jess in the hallway, ready to hold the door for her to slip out on her last errand of the day.

She dipped her head and thanked him before picking up her skirts and sailing off. Maurice watched her go, half absent, half appreciative. Then he went straight off down the court to knock at Dolly Ogden's door.

It was a godsend. He was a clean young man with a proper job. His manners were perfect. Dolly went into raptures over her new lodger. He'd gone up and looked the room over, and decided there and then that he'd take it. Charlie would have to move his things out double quick to make room for Mr Leigh, and never mind pulling a face about it. Needs must. She bustled about in high excitement, threatening to dust and polish Arthur unless he moved himself out of the way. 'His rent's set at seven and sixpence and he seems quite happy,' she told him. She knew how persuasive the sound of money coming in was to her husband. 'Amy's out looking for work this minute, poor girl, and Charlie boy himself should be earning before the next twelve months is up. By then I'll have got myself another job and all.' Her calculations put her into good heart. 'So just you behave yourself, Arthur. With a bit of luck we'll pull through this bad patch.'

Charlie cleared the set of drawers in his attic room, and swept his school books from the little work-table into an orange-box. He was furious. The indignity of sleeping in Amy's room, with an old curtain slung across the middle for privacy caused a burning sensation in his throat, but he bit back the words of angry protest and followed his mother's instructions. What could he do? At least until he finished school, he must live here under her terms and conditions. As he stacked his books on the window ledge in Amy's room, he stored up the confidences he would share with Sadie during their precious bike ride next day; his feelings of being born in the wrong place at the wrong time, prince by nature, pauper by birth. It didn't make him feel any better when Maurice Leigh returned with his two suitcases, dumped them in Charlie's room, took his hat off to Amy and started to flatter her shallow vanity with his polite attention.

'Ain't I seen you before?' Maurice asked, curiosity roused. He recognized her soft features and fair colouring, probably on the arm of someone he knew. He racked his brains.

Amy blushed. 'I don't think so, Mr Leigh.'

'Yes, I've got it. At the Empire, a few weeks back!' Maurice saw being polite to the landlady's daughter as a price he had to pay for cheap lodging near to his place of work.

By now Amy was brick red and beginning to chew the corner of her lip. 'No, I don't think so.'

'With Teddy Cooper, wasn't it?' His memory for faces was sharp. He rarely got it wrong.

'No!' Amy couldn't bear to be reminded of the worst mistake in her life. Neither did she want her mother to know that Teddy Cooper had since been in touch with a mixture of threats and promises. 'If you keep quiet,' he said, 'I'll help you find a new job. If you go gabbing to the police, I'll tell them you made it all up and demand your proof.' Unwisely, she'd accepted a present of ten shillings to tide her over. She regretted it at the time, but told herself that Teddy could be very persuasive when he wanted to be. And in a way she was pulling one over on him, she thought, since he'd absolutely no idea that her ma now had no intention of going to the police. Perhaps she could string him along for a few more weeks and make something out of the whole sorry business. Amy was a dangerous mixture of naïvety and manipulativeness, bound together by the glue of dishonesty. So, 'No!' she said to Maurice Leigh, recognizing him at once as the young under manager at the Balham Empire. 'We never met!'

Maurice merely nodded, and after a little more small-talk he went up to his new room. The sun had gone down over the slate roofs of Paradise Court, and deep shadows filled the alleyways. A narrow dormer window gave a bird's eye view of the place. From here you could squint down and see the kids playing at pitch and toss, hear the clang and clatter of their metal horseshoes. The women stood at their doors and gossiped as their men came home from the match. A street like any other.

Part Two

LONG
SHADOWS

LONG
SHADOWS

Chapter Twelve

Robert had given the first match of the season a miss that afternoon for the sake of a good work-out with Walter down at Milo's gym. It was September. News of the brave boys out in France filtered through, but, for Rob, life went on much as before.

Football was only the second love in his life to boxing, a sport in which his sturdy physique gave him a good advantage over many of the scrawnier, less athletic East-Enders. Whether it was taking swings at the huge leather punch-bags, lifting weights, or sparring in the ring, Robert seemed to excel. His balance was good, the co-ordination between eye, hand and feet very precise. He took pride in his reputation as one of the best young boxers in the neighbourhood. So far, none of his opponents had been able to mark or mar his handsome dark features.

He stood now at the ringside, towel slung around his neck, watching Walter train against one of the merchant seamen who came off the docks to lodgings in Southwark; a Norwegian, with limbs as strong and solid as the pine trees of his native country. Walter stood up to him though, and the thud of padded leather against muscle went on apace. Robert observed the technique of the two men, looking for pointers to pass on to Walter when the bout was over.

He felt rather than saw a presence behind him. Something warned him not to look round; this wasn't a friendly arrival. It was only when the sneering remarks began, under the breath and hostile, that he gave way to provocation and looked round.

'Bleeding cart-horses, both of them. Too slow to catch cold,' came the first comment.

In the ring, Walter hesitated mid-stride, while the Norwegian, oblivious to the insult, swung a hefty right to his head. Sweat sprayed over the canvas, the hostile onlookers guffawed.

Robert, who'd felt the sweat cool on his own skin after his training bout, now felt himself heat up again. He'd recognized Chalky White's scoffing tone. His jaw muscles jumped. Chalky was difficult to ignore, but retaliation was unwise. The pair in the ring side-stepped and swiped at one another, evenly matched.

'You put my old lady up in there and she'd knock 'em both dead in ten seconds flat,' Chalky pressed on.

Against his better judgement, Robert spun round. 'Know what,' he said to Chalky loud and clear, 'you got a mouth on you as big as a bleeding railway tunnel, you have, and I'm gonna close it for you if you don't watch out!'

The punch-bags all around the gym fell silent, weights sagged to the floor. Men stopped their training to listen. Only the ones in the ring continued their bout, Walter still having to defend himself hotly against the foreigner.

The smile never wavered on Chalky's mouth. He felt big and confident in front of his mates. Robert Parsons was a cocky lad with a pea-sized brain and a bad temper to match; just the sort he liked to wind up. 'You and whose army?' He grinned. Syd and Whitey Lewis were there to back him up if necessary.

'Me and nobody's army!' Robert turned and motioned to Walter and the big Norwegian to stop their bout. 'But we'll have this out here and now,' he challenged. 'You been wanting to have a go at me, Chalky, and now's your chance.' He hopped into the ring while Walter explained the tense situation to the sailor. They withdrew to the floor, breathing hard. 'C'mon, what you waiting for?' Robert insisted. 'Let's see you put your money where your mouth is.'

Chalky White had a code of his own, as Robert well knew, and it was a point of honour not to lose face in front of his mates. He was taller than Robert, with a longer reach. Though he'd not expected the hot-headed publican's son to jump the gun like this, and if anything had planned a dark meeting with him down a side alley late at night, he calculated he could probably step into the ring with him and settle things now. The kid was getting on his nerves, the way he bristled up and stared in undisguised loathing. Well, Chalky would teach him a public lesson. Slowly, and with great bravado, he climbed into the ring.

They began circling each other with raised fists. Daylight poured into the gym through long windows, casting dramatic strips of light and shade across the room. Dust motes whirled in upward blasts of air as each man danced and began to place his shot. All was silent, except for their hard breathing and the scuff of their shoes on the sprung boards.

Even to the hard-bitten men and boys of Milo's gym, there was tension in the air. With their short-cropped hair, bull necks and calloused hands, they gathered to watch Robert Parsons spar with Chalky White. As they saw it, there wasn't much in it for the victor; no glory or reward, but there was a lot to lose. This was a needle match and respect was at stake. Whoever ended up on the canvas was a man without his reputation. The spectators looked on with sharpened appetite, as Robert moved in under Chalky's guard and landed two or three heavy blows.

Chalky staggered as he took the punches to his ribcage, and saw the look of concentrated anger in Robert's eyes. He pushed him off and recovered his guard; upright, backing off, ready to side-step.

From Robert's angle Chalky didn't look so clever now. His reach meant nothing if the punch behind it lacked force, and Robert's own well-coordinated movement was backed by real muscle. He wouldn't jab to the face, but he would swing more upper-cuts to the body and jaw. That way he was sure he had his man. His eyes levelled on the target and he moved in, ducking, weaving to the left and right, displaying his skill.

In the end they had to pull him off. He'd backed his opponent into a corner and hammered blows on him until he slumped, a dead weight at his feet. Milo moved in swiftly with a bucket of cold water and sharp orders to Robert to back off. Walter Davidson rushed into the ring and seized him under the arms from behind, while Syd and Whitey moved in to rescue their leader. For several seconds Chalky was dead to the world, then the icy rush of water revived him. His head jerked, his eyes opened in time to see the back-slapping crowd follow Robert towards the changing room.

'What got into you?' Walter urged, as they stripped, towelled and climbed into their clothes. 'Ain't you got eyes in your head? Your man was already down, for gawd's sake! Why go that far?'

Robert nodded, only now returning fully to his senses. 'He had it coming to him,' he said, buckling his belt and reaching for his cap.

'That's all well and good, but Chalky White ain't the

right man to pick a quarrel with.' Walter had to run alongside Robert to keep up as he swung through the door out into the street.

'I didn't; he did.'

'But did you have to beat his brains out?' Walter caught his friend by the arm. 'This ain't the end of it, you know. From now on, Chalky's got you down as a marked man. Ain't no way he'll live down a thrashing like that without getting his own back, and some more!'

Robert pulled himself free. He walked on savagely into the subsiding evening traffic. 'Think I don't know that?' Without waiting at the kerb, he nipped smartly between cabs and trams, caught up in their roar. 'Anyhow, it don't make no difference to me now.'

'How's that?'

Robert glanced sideways. He'd got himself into a tight corner over Chalky, all right. The man's pride had taken a bad battering. 'I ain't planning on hanging around waiting for Chalky to get even,' he said.

They entered the railway arch at the top of Duke Street, their footsteps echoing, its damp stench filling their nostrils. They emerged into the setting sun. 'I'm thinking of joining up, Walt,' he said in casual, throwaway style.

Walter stopped short in sudden, stunned silence.

'What you looking at me like that for?'

'This is the first I ever heard of it, Rob!'

'So? I don't have to tell you every bleeding thing, do I?' He bridled at the shock which registered on his friend's face. 'There's a war on, Walt, in case you hadn't heard!' He reached into his jacket pocket for a pack of cigarettes, pulled it out and lit one in the shelter of the railway arch. Flicking the spent match into the gutter, he hunched his shoulders and strode off.

This was the first time Robert had broken the news to

anyone. The war was less than a month old, but already the post-boxes sported posters inviting men to enlist. Queues were a familiar sight around the Town Hall; hundreds of smiling faces clutched papers and crowded in on the impromptu recruiting office. Hope was high that the Schlieffen Plan would be defeated by Christmas and the enemy attack on Paris would be over. Robert himself was sick of queuing for work or hanging around the pub until something better came along. Though he'd warned his father he wouldn't be rushing to risk his neck for king and country if the war broke out, he didn't see any real danger in joining up now and being treated as a war hero when he came back. At least it would get him off Chalky White's turf for a time. That was it; if there was a deciding factor, it was the need to take the heat out of the rash row with Chalky and his gang.

In the meantime, he'd jolly them up at home by taking Ernie off on one last trip to the Palace. That should be harmless enough, as long as he kept a weather eye out. He was pretty certain Chalky's cuts and bruises wouldn't allow him to venture far that evening. With a bit of luck, Robert would have himself enlisted, assigned to a regiment and be gone within the week.

'What if Joxer don't turn up?' Duke grumbled his objection to Robert's plan to take Ernie to the Palace. Rob had put in time setting full barrels on the gantry and adjusting half-empty ones on their wooden chocks, but the old man didn't like being left without extra pairs of hands on a Saturday night. He wasn't sure he approved of Ernie's more frequent nights out to the music hall either. He twitched his moustache and scowled at Robert.

'Get one of the girls to lend a hand,' came the flippant

reply. Robert knew Duke didn't like to get them involved in the serious Saturday night drinking. 'Get Frances. She won't mind.' He winked, but the joke went down badly. His father and his strait-laced sister were still at odds, with Frances often on her high horse and Duke sulking. 'Anyhow, Joxer'll be here, you wait.'

Good-hearted Jess came down when she realized, and gave the bar top a quick polish, while Sadie sorted out a clean collar for Ernie and spruced him up for his night out. Jess was still in the bar when the Ogdens' new lodger called in on his way to work, smart and clean-cut as before. He was grateful to Duke for the recommendation, he said. Things had worked out well.

He stayed to chat for a little longer than he'd intended, drawn by Jess's quiet ease. He learned some details of his new neighbourhood from her and explained his job. She listened carefully and asked how they made the voices fit the pictures on screen in the new talkies. 'I read about them, but I ain't seen them yet.' It seemed miraculous to her.

Maurice caught her genuine interest and waxed enthusiastic about the new Chronophone method. It was early days and not much in demand yet, but he was sure it was the up-and-coming thing to have sound in the cinema. 'I want the Gem to be the first picture house round here to have it. They'd queue up by the hundred and pay to see that,' he said. 'It looks really and truly like the words are coming from their mouths, only it's a gramophone record played through loudspeakers. They synchronize it with the faces. Clever, ain't it?' He was proud of the word, 'synchronize', and told Jess she should come along to his new cinema. He'd look after her, see to it she got good seats and everything. 'Bring a girl friend with you,' he said. 'Tell them at the desk that you know the manager.'

Jess blushed. 'I don't know. I got a lot on here.' Duke

had come up from the cellar with Joxer, who'd recently arrived.

So Maurice was put off his stride and backed off. He downed his pint and left the pub. She thought he was too brash and pushy, he reflected as he swung out through the decorated doors. Pity; there was something about her that caught his eye. Something different to the flighty, flirty shop and factory girls like Amy Ogden, he thought with a grimace. The woman behind the bar was an ocean to Amy's paddling pool when it came to depth of character.

Being a determined sort, he planned his next move as he strode up Duke Street, crossed into St Thomas Street and between the mock-classical pillars of the Southwark Gem.

With Joxer installed behind the bar like some monumental carved beast, his features set in habitual glum expression, Jess went upstairs, the rhythm of her own evening fixed around her baby's pattern of sleeping and waking. She saw Robert and Ernie off and gathered with her sisters by the open window to watch them down the street. Frances had one of her meetings and left soon after. Then Sadie vanished off to Maudie's house. The room settled into its evening calm.

The hum of noise from the pub below kept Jess company in her dainty stitching as she sewed Annie Wiggin's lace into the smock she was making for Grace. At the back of her mind she planned how she might bring in some money to support herself and her baby by advertising on the board in the Henshaws' shop as a seamstress and invisible mender. She could do alterations to women's costumes, let out growing boys' jackets. Better than taking in washing, she thought, and it was a solid notion based on the fact that so many women were now out at work themselves. They had no time for complicated sewing work when they got home at night. Excited by her idea, she sat through the evening in peace and quiet.

Raucous shouts and thunderous applause echoed through the ornate balconies at the Palace. It was a full house, as if war talk, which depressed people in their workaday world, sent them scurrying all the faster to the easy glamour and excitement of the music hall, set on enjoyment and forgetfulness. Despite their confidence in victory and the wave of patriotic fervour that had greeted the declaration, it was a sobering experience to see sons and husbands trickle off from Victoria Station, hanging out of the carriage windows in their khaki uniforms, waving their caps. Laughter, song and dance was a refuge from that, so the audience roared at Archie Small's broad humour and they ogled the white limbs and bosoms of the chorus girls under the artificial glare.

Ernie thrilled to it all. He joined in the words of the songs which he could sing under his breath as he pedalled his bike for Mr Henshaw, belting them out now to the swelling sounds of the orchestra. After the show, he and Rob would swagger off to the stage door and join the swells. He was picking up the routine, learning the jargon. Best of all, he would meet up with Daisy and walk her home.

'C'mon, Ern!' Robert sprang to his feet as the final curtain fell. He was eager to beat the crowds. Hettie and Daisy didn't know they were here tonight, so it might prove more of a problem to get backstage. He'd have to signal through the window before anyone else arrived. Hurrying up the aisle, he expected Ernie to be hard on his heels.

But Ernie had difficulty with huddles and knots of people. They put him off his stride, standing there blocking his way. He hesitated, felt confused then flustered, then lost sight of his brother up ahead. Still, he knew where to go, he told himself. He knew to head for the stage door down that dark alley, where he'd find Robert ready to tell him off for getting lost. He nodded his head to a series of simple instructions which he gave himself as he headed out of the hall.

Robert slid easily past the groups of unhurried spectators gathered under the stone portico in feathered finery and Sunday jackets, unwilling to spill out on to the streets. Only one or two bunches of people had beaten him to it and were hanging about on the corner, or setting off in cheerful twos and threes on their long walks home. He glanced back, annoyed with Ernie, who'd been swallowed up back there. Bleeding idiot, he thought. Slowly he drifted to the corner, ready to light up a cigarette and hang about until the kid showed up.

But things didn't work out. A group of shadowy figures in a side doorway attracted his attention. He recognized Syd Swan's tough-looking outline lounging against the wall, chin jutting out, eyeing him up and down. He saw Whitey Lewis and a couple of other thugs, all obviously on the prowl tonight minus their injured leader. They'd spotted Robert too. It was time to make himself scarce.

Robert spun on his toes, hitched his collar and darted into the traffic. A passing omnibus made things easy for him; he nipped on to the open platform, swung round on the pole and waved a cheery goodbye to his pursuers. But his luck wasn't in after all. A snarl-up of traffic at the next junction brought the bus to a halt, and Syd and company had by no means given up. He could see them belting down

ert ran. He used the doorpost to brake and swung
into the dressing room. Hettie was stumbling
 him, hands to her face. In the far corner of the
clear of the rail and screen, she'd exposed the object
pped to her knees over it. She'd touched the blood
white face, she'd knelt in a pool of it and drenched
rts before she jerked on to her feet and staggered
reaming.

ert caught hold of her. He stared at the body. Blood
from the neck and chest, the face stared up at the
. 'Oh my gawd!' he moaned. Hettie had buried her
gainst him. He clung to her. 'It's Daisy, ain't it?'
 light from the corridor caught the corpse in its full
The mouth hung open, the blank eyes stared. One
as flung wide across the floor.
re footsteps ran down from the direction of the stage.
Mills had been on the point of locking up when the
ing started. Now he came running. He saw the body.
telephone the police, get help. This didn't happen, it
mething you read about in the newspapers, Jack the
 stuff, really nasty.
e was a lovely girl,' he told the sergeant. 'One of my
okers, a good dancer. She had a voice like a bird.'

the pavement towards him, jackets flying open, arms working like pistons. They meant business. Robert swung down from the platform with a shrug of apology at the approaching conductor. He had to beat it on foot if he was to come out of it clean. Lucky for him, he knew his way around, down to every last nook and cranny.

Ernie struggled on alone. The women's long skirts got in his way, the men would tell jokes standing bang in the middle of the aisle. No one seemed to care that he'd lost sight of Robert. When finally he broke through the foyer out into the street, his brother had disappeared. But Ernie clung to the idea of going to meet Daisy. That's what they did after a show; he didn't need anyone to remind him of that. He even knew the way.

Slowly, long after the main crowd had drifted off, he finally reached the familiar corner. Down this alley, at the far, dark end away from the lights, he would meet up with Robert, Robert would tell him off and then they would go inside and see Daisy.

Hettie was out of sorts as she made her way home after the show. She'd had to cold shoulder lecherous Archie Small, all because Daisy wasn't around to divert his attention. He was a slug in a cellar, slimy little man. Even the manager, Mr Mills, came looking for Daisy to give her her wages. And when it came time to link up with her for the walk back to Duke Street, could she be found? 'Silly cow's gone walking home with some new beau, most like,' one of the other girls offered. 'Let's hope he's a gent.'

'Fat chance,' Hettie said. Daisy might have thought to let her know. She was practically the last to leave the place, losing all this time looking for her, asking everyone where she was. Hettie banged the door and hurried off up the empty alley. Even the stage-door johnnies had given up and gone home, it was so late.

She met Robert coming towards her, going at a steady trot, head back, elbows out.

'What the bleeding hell you doing here?' she barked.

He stopped and doubled over to regain his breath. Behind him the street was empty. 'We seen the show,' he gasped. 'But then I ran into a spot of bother back there. Nothing serious.' He stood up, hands on hips.

'"We?" Who's we?'

'Me and Ern.' Robert's face, which had been relaxing into a grin, narrowed again. 'Why? Ain't you seen him?'

Hettie shook her head. 'No. He ain't waiting by the door neither, if that's what you think. I just come from there.'

Robert frowned. 'Bleeding idiot.'

'It ain't his fault,' Hettie said hotly. 'And I keep telling you, don't call him names!' Then she thought, standing out on the street. 'Listen, I bet that's where Daisy got to. Wouldn't you just know!'

'What?'

'She's met up with Ern and walked him home. I been looking everywhere for her.'

Brother and sister turned and began to walk the route home. Hettie was tired after her second performance of the day, and Robert still looked warily about. 'You sure about this?' he asked. 'What if Ern got himself well and truly lost back there. What'll Pa say?'

Hettie stopped and sighed. Come to think of it, she couldn't see Daisy playing nursemaid to Ernie if there was anything else in the offing. 'Let's go back and check,' she agreed. It would only take ten minutes and then at least they'd be sure. They began to retrace their steps.

The alley was deserted, dry and c[...] night. Never silent, it rustled with sm[...] behind drainpipes, along the gutter. [...] skirts and trod gingerly. 'I hate it d[...] gone quiet,' she said.

'C'mon,' Robert urged. He wishe[...] stupid idea of bringing Ernie along in[...]

'He ain't here.' Hettie pursed her l[...] to check in the deepest shadows down[...] and he'd come back none the wiser.

'He ain't gone inside, has he?' R[...] door, which stood off the latch.

'Here, you can't go in there!' Hetti[...] side and sailed in. 'Wait here. I'll go.'[...] familiar obstacles of ladders, ropes and [...] long corridor, and smelt the old sta[...] perfume, dust and sweat.

'He ain't here!' She sent a loud whisp[...]

'Try the dressing room!' With growi[...] stood hunched by the door. 'And ble[...] about it, will you!'

'If he ain't in here, I'm off hom[...] anything you like, it ain't nothing to [...] moaned. The girls' stage dresses looked[...] the low light which fell from the corr[...] purple, crimson and emerald all me[...] grey. 'Ain't no one here!' she called ba[...]

But something made her check a[...] quite right. A rail of dresses was swun[...] and a screen which the girls used to[...] tipped forward against it. Hettie wen[...] bling to set the screen upright. But sh[...] object stopping her. She pulled the [...] began to scream.

Chapter Thirteen

At the end of her meeting Frances said goodbye to friends on Union Street. She walked through the back closes off Blackfriars Road with Billy Wray, a newspaper vendor in the market with an ailing wife; one of the organizers of the lecture she'd attended that evening. As they came through on to Duke Street, they too parted company and went their separate ways.

It was then that she met Ernie. Astonished to see his tall, ungainly figure half-stumbling up the road, she ran to catch him up. 'Ern, what you doing out this time of night? Where's your hat? What happened?'

Ernie plodded on, as if dazed. 'I lost Rob,' he told her. He sounded dull and miserable. 'I never saw where he went.'

'The nuisance!' Frances said under her breath, determined to give Robert a piece of her mind. 'You mean to say he dumped you and never came back to find you?' she cried, seizing Ernie by the elbow and heading firmly for home. That was the sort of thing Robert would do; dump poor Ernie if he bumped into a few friends and got tempted by the promise of drink and girls.

'I lost him. I never saw where he went,' Ernie repeated. He was looking into the distance, straight ahead.

'Well, never mind now. We're here.' Frances ushered him through the door of the Duke and straight upstairs.

Midnight had chimed on the church clock as they walked the final stretch. The last drinkers had already left the pub.

Upstairs, Frances was glad to find that Jess was still up, greeting them with a smile and the offer of a cup of tea. 'Thanks!' Her hat and jacket were already off and hung on the peg. She turned and smoothed Ernie's dishevelled hair. 'Ern here could do with one, couldn't you, Ern?'

'What happened to you?' Jess stared at his pale, blank face. 'You look like you seen a ghost, Ern! For God's sake get him sat down nice and comfy, Frances. No, on second thoughts, you fetch that tea. I'll sort Ern out.' She bustled to help him out of his jacket and unbutton his waistcoat. Then she gently stroked his cheek. 'C'mon, Ern, it ain't that bad, surely.'

Frances soon came back from the kitchen. She still felt livid with their feckless brother. 'That Robert went and dumped him. Took him out for a treat up the Palace and left him. I just found him wandering back all by himself. It ain't right!'

'No.' Jess wanted to soothe away Ernie's hurt. 'But don't tell Pa,' she said to Frances. 'There'd only be a row.'

'Hm.' Once they'd straightened Ernie out with a hot cup of tea, Frances began to calm down. 'Did Ett get back home yet?'

'No. Sadie came in and went off to bed like a good girl, but that's all.' The sisters looked at one another, puzzled frowns on both their faces, but the ticking clock, the sound of Duke locking doors below lulled them into security.

'We'd best get you off to bed then, Ern.' Jess rose and pulled him to his feet. 'No point hoping he'll manage by himself tonight,' she told Frances. Sometimes he went all quiet and helpless, and you had to treat him like a little kid.

'Just wait till he comes home.' Frances gazed at the back of Ernie's stooped head as Jess took him gently off to the bedroom shared by the two brothers. 'He ain't never learned to use his head, that Robert.' She settled with her feet up, nursing her cup of tea. The lecture had contained lantern slides of the Seven Wonders of the World. Billy Wray had given a good talk, considering. Frances drifted off into her own world.

Jess sat Ernie down on the edge of his bed. 'C'mon, Ern, let's take your boots off.' He sat passively while she unlaced them. 'Give us a hand,' she urged. But he stared straight ahead, sitting in his shirt-sleeves, his collar unbuttoned and loose around his neck. So Jess struggled and finally held both boots in one hand, ready to take them away. 'Wait here while I go and put these down on a bit of clean newspaper, Ern.' She was surprised by the nasty, greasy feel of the uppers. They would need a good clean.

In the bright kitchen light Jess set the boots down on paper and went to wipe her hands at the sink. Her fingers were stained a sticky red. For a moment she spread her palms and stared in disbelief. Then she went straight back to Ernie's boots to scrape and scrub at them with the paper, anxious now to wipe them clean. She screwed the paper into a tight ball, went to the kitchen range, which they always kept lit for cooking, and thrust it far into the back of the fire, holding it there with the poker. She took the boot polish from the cupboard, blacked Ernie's boots and polished them until they shone. Finally, she washed her hands at the sink.

Ernie still sat in the very same place when she got back to him, but it was less than a minute more before she'd eased him between the sheets and drawn his eiderdown up to his chin. He stared at the ceiling, numb and silent. 'G'night, Ern,' she whispered. 'I got to go check on Grace now. You get off to sleep and we'll sort things out in the morning, eh?'

'What d'you suppose Ern was up to?' Frances asked when Jess returned. In a roundabout way her daydreams had brought her back to the subject. She remembered breaking off from her lively conversation with Billy and seeing poor, lonely Ernie up ahead. 'When you think about it, there's a whole hour missing between him losing Robert and ending up back here. It don't take an hour to walk that little stretch!'

Jess shook her head. 'Don't ask me.'

'No need to bite my head off.'

'Sorry.' Jess found it hard to get rid of the sick feeling in the pit of her stomach. The boots bothered her. She was sure it was blood on them.

Duke came up and told the girls to get off to bed. It was his habit of a lifetime never to retire until all the family were in and accounted for, so he sat in his shirt-sleeves, poring over the latest reports of the war in France. At two in the morning Robert and Hettie walked in looking as if the world had come to an end.

A solitary policeman came down the court still later into the night to give the O'Hagans news of their daughter's death. 'I drew the short straw there,' he told them back at the station. 'This scraggy woman comes to the door, which anyhow don't shut tight on account of its hinges. She opens it a crack and I says, "I'm very sorry to have to tell you this, Mrs O'Hagan, but your daughter Daisy has been murdered." There ain't no nice way to put it. The woman looks at me like she ain't heard. I can see through the door that the whole place is a tip. I tells her she can go along to the mortuary in the morning and see the body, and we'll do our best to find out who did it. I still ain't sure she's heard. But then she nods and closes the door on me, and I can hear my own footsteps going back down them stairs, knock-knock against the bare boards and out into the street.'

His sergeant nodded. 'Good lad. Needle in a bleeding haystack this is, though.' There was paperwork to do. He opened the black ledger and chose a pen.

'What is?'

'Finding the bloke what done it. It could be any one of them hooligans done her in, the way them girls carry on after a show. I know, I seen 'em often enough.' Dutifully he wrote down the details: 9 September 1914. A quarter to twelve. Summoned to the Southwark Palace Music Hall by the manager, Mr Frederick Mills. Body on the premises. Female. Nineteen years. Stab wounds to throat and chest area. Identity: Daisy O'Hagan of Paradise Court, music-hall dancer and singer. Time of death, half-past eleven approximately.

'Ain't you got no one particular in mind?' The young police constable was recovering from his experience as the bearer of bad tidings. He supposed it was something else you got used to in this job.

The sergeant sucked in air loudly and shook his head. 'Well, I never took to the manager, Mills, for a start.' He finished writing, blotted the page and closed the book. 'All that stuff about what a lovely girl she was. Who's he trying to kid?'

'I can see you don't reckon much to her, Serg?'

'They're all the same, them showgirls.'

'What about the witness?' The young man's imagination was more fired up by the murder than his more experienced boss's. 'You reckon he had anything to do with it?'

'Parsons? Ain't come across him before. He was pretty worked up all right. Dunno. The sister was in a proper state and all.'

'It couldn't be a woman what done it, could it?'

'Don't see why not. Like I said, it could be any bleeding one!'

Their work finished for the night, they buttoned their capes and left the sombre brick building with its barred windows and iron railings. At least they could get away to their Sunday roasts and walks in the park. Not like the poor O'Hagans, they said, walking in step away from it all.

Hettie sat up all night. The rising tide of hysteria she'd felt as she knelt by Daisy's body soon passed. Afterwards she was acutely aware of every detail; every word Fred Mills gabbled to the sergeant, the phosphoric flash of the police photographer's camera, the rubber gloves of the surgeon as he inspected the corpse, until she'd been bundled out into the corridor, baldly questioned and packed off home.

Now it seemed she was floating free in her mind, telling her own body to stop shaking, ordering her hand to raise the glass to her mouth. You know it's true, she told herself. You saw poor Daisy lying there in a pool of her own blood. She never went on home like you thought.

Robert whispered the full story to Duke. The shock had given even him a bad knock.

'How come you was there, you and Ett?' Duke asked. There were misgivings in the old man's mind. He didn't like Robert being mixed up in this.

Robert had to confess how they went back looking for Ernie. 'He got home all right in the end, didn't he?' he asked suddenly.

'Ssh! Yes, no thanks to you. I seen him coming up with Frances about midnight. Keep your voice down.' Duke didn't want to wake the others. He shook his head and glanced across at Hettie. 'What we going to do with her?' She was sitting across the room from them, upright and quiet, but seemingly out of touch with her surroundings.

the pavement towards him, jackets flying open, arms working like pistons. They meant business. Robert swung down from the platform with a shrug of apology at the approaching conductor. He had to beat it on foot if he was to come out of it clean. Lucky for him, he knew his way around, down to every last nook and cranny.

Ernie struggled on alone. The women's long skirts got in his way, the men would tell jokes standing bang in the middle of the aisle. No one seemed to care that he'd lost sight of Robert. When finally he broke through the foyer out into the street, his brother had disappeared. But Ernie clung to the idea of going to meet Daisy. That's what they did after a show; he didn't need anyone to remind him of that. He even knew the way.

Slowly, long after the main crowd had drifted off, he finally reached the familiar corner. Down this alley, at the far, dark end away from the lights, he would meet up with Robert, Robert would tell him off and then they would go inside and see Daisy.

Hettie was out of sorts as she made her way home after the show. She'd had to cold shoulder lecherous Archie Small, all because Daisy wasn't around to divert his attention. He was a slug in a cellar, slimy little man. Even the manager, Mr Mills, came looking for Daisy to give her her wages. And when it came time to link up with her for the walk back to Duke Street, could she be found? 'Silly cow's gone walking home with some new beau, most like,' one of the other girls offered. 'Let's hope he's a gent.'

'Fat chance,' Hettie said. Daisy might have thought to let her know. She was practically the last to leave the place, losing all this time looking for her, asking everyone where she was. Hettie banged the door and hurried off up the empty alley. Even the stage-door johnnies had given up and gone home, it was so late.

She met Robert coming towards her, going at a steady trot, head back, elbows out.

'What the bleeding hell you doing here?' she barked.

He stopped and doubled over to regain his breath. Behind him the street was empty. 'We seen the show,' he gasped. 'But then I ran into a spot of bother back there. Nothing serious.' He stood up, hands on hips.

'"We?" Who's we?'

'Me and Ern.' Robert's face, which had been relaxing into a grin, narrowed again. 'Why? Ain't you seen him?'

Hettie shook her head. 'No. He ain't waiting by the door neither, if that's what you think. I just come from there.'

Robert frowned. 'Bleeding idiot.'

'It ain't his fault,' Hettie said hotly. 'And I keep telling you, don't call him names!' Then she thought, standing out on the street. 'Listen, I bet that's where Daisy got to. Wouldn't you just know!'

'What?'

'She's met up with Ern and walked him home. I been looking everywhere for her.'

Brother and sister turned and began to walk the route home. Hettie was tired after her second performance of the day, and Robert still looked warily about. 'You sure about this?' he asked. 'What if Ern got himself well and truly lost back there. What'll Pa say?'

Hettie stopped and sighed. Come to think of it, she couldn't see Daisy playing nursemaid to Ernie if there was anything else in the offing. 'Let's go back and check,' she agreed. It would only take ten minutes and then at least they'd be sure. They began to retrace their steps.

The alley was deserted, dry and dusty in the September night. Never silent, it rustled with small, unexplained noises behind drainpipes, along the gutter. Hettie picked up her skirts and trod gingerly. 'I hate it down here when it's all gone quiet,' she said.

'C'mon,' Robert urged. He wished he'd never had the stupid idea of bringing Ernie along in the first place.

'He ain't here.' Hettie pursed her lips. Robert had gone to check in the deepest shadows down by the high window and he'd come back none the wiser.

'He ain't gone inside, has he?' Robert pushed at the door, which stood off the latch.

'Here, you can't go in there!' Hettie pulled him to one side and sailed in. 'Wait here. I'll go.' She negotiated the familiar obstacles of ladders, ropes and cables cluttering the long corridor, and smelt the old stale smells of cheap perfume, dust and sweat.

'He ain't here!' She sent a loud whisper back to Robert.

'Try the dressing room!' With growing irritation Robert stood hunched by the door. 'And bleeding well be quick about it, will you!'

'If he ain't in here, I'm off home. You can tell Pa anything you like, it ain't nothing to do with me,' Hettie moaned. The girls' stage dresses looked drab and creased in the low light which fell from the corridor into the room; purple, crimson and emerald all merging into shadowy grey. 'Ain't no one here!' she called back.

But something made her check again. Things weren't quite right. A rail of dresses was swung out from the wall, and a screen which the girls used to change behind had tipped forward against it. Hettie went to investigate, fumbling to set the screen upright. But she came across a large object stopping her. She pulled the whole thing free and began to scream.

Robert ran. He uséd the doorpost to brake and swung himself into the dressing room. Hettie was stumbling towards him, hands to her face. In the far corner of the room, clear of the rail and screen, she'd exposed the object and dropped to her knees over it. She'd touched the blood on the white face, she'd knelt in a pool of it and drenched her skirts before she jerked on to her feet and staggered back screaming.

Robert caught hold of her. He stared at the body. Blood poured from the neck and chest, the face stared up at the ceiling. 'Oh my gawd!' he moaned. Hettie had buried her head against him. He clung to her. 'It's Daisy, ain't it?'

The light from the corridor caught the corpse in its full glare. The mouth hung open, the blank eyes stared. One arm was flung wide across the floor.

More footsteps ran down from the direction of the stage. Fred Mills had been on the point of locking up when the screaming started. Now he came running. He saw the body. He'd telephone the police, get help. This didn't happen, it was something you read about in the newspapers, Jack the Ripper stuff, really nasty.

'She was a lovely girl,' he told the sergeant. 'One of my best lookers, a good dancer. She had a voice like a bird.'

Chapter Thirteen

At the end of her meeting Frances said goodbye to friends on Union Street. She walked through the back closes off Blackfriars Road with Billy Wray, a newspaper vendor in the market with an ailing wife; one of the organizers of the lecture she'd attended that evening. As they came through on to Duke Street, they too parted company and went their separate ways.

It was then that she met Ernie. Astonished to see his tall, ungainly figure half-stumbling up the road, she ran to catch him up. 'Ern, what you doing out this time of night? Where's your hat? What happened?'

Ernie plodded on, as if dazed. 'I lost Rob,' he told her. He sounded dull and miserable. 'I never saw where he went.'

'The nuisance!' Frances said under her breath, determined to give Robert a piece of her mind. 'You mean to say he dumped you and never came back to find you?' she cried, seizing Ernie by the elbow and heading firmly for home. That was the sort of thing Robert would do; dump poor Ernie if he bumped into a few friends and got tempted by the promise of drink and girls.

'I lost him. I never saw where he went,' Ernie repeated. He was looking into the distance, straight ahead.

'Well, never mind now. We're here.' Frances ushered him through the door of the Duke and straight upstairs.

Midnight had chimed on the church clock as they walked the final stretch. The last drinkers had already left the pub.

Upstairs, Frances was glad to find that Jess was still up, greeting them with a smile and the offer of a cup of tea. 'Thanks!' Her hat and jacket were already off and hung on the peg. She turned and smoothed Ernie's dishevelled hair. 'Ern here could do with one, couldn't you, Ern?'

'What happened to you?' Jess stared at his pale, blank face. 'You look like you seen a ghost, Ern! For God's sake get him sat down nice and comfy, Frances. No, on second thoughts, you fetch that tea. I'll sort Ern out.' She bustled to help him out of his jacket and unbutton his waistcoat. Then she gently stroked his cheek. 'C'mon, Ern, it ain't that bad, surely.'

Frances soon came back from the kitchen. She still felt livid with their feckless brother. 'That Robert went and dumped him. Took him out for a treat up the Palace and left him. I just found him wandering back all by himself. It ain't right!'

'No.' Jess wanted to soothe away Ernie's hurt. 'But don't tell Pa,' she said to Frances. 'There'd only be a row.'

'Hm.' Once they'd straightened Ernie out with a hot cup of tea, Frances began to calm down. 'Did Ett get back home yet?'

'No. Sadie came in and went off to bed like a good girl, but that's all.' The sisters looked at one another, puzzled frowns on both their faces, but the ticking clock, the sound of Duke locking doors below lulled them into security.

'We'd best get you off to bed then, Ern.' Jess rose and pulled him to his feet. 'No point hoping he'll manage by himself tonight,' she told Frances. Sometimes he went all quiet and helpless, and you had to treat him like a little kid.

'Just wait till he comes home.' Frances gazed at the back of Ernie's stooped head as Jess took him gently off to the bedroom shared by the two brothers. 'He ain't never learned to use his head, that Robert.' She settled with her feet up, nursing her cup of tea. The lecture had contained lantern slides of the Seven Wonders of the World. Billy Wray had given a good talk, considering. Frances drifted off into her own world.

Jess sat Ernie down on the edge of his bed. 'C'mon, Ern, let's take your boots off.' He sat passively while she unlaced them. 'Give us a hand,' she urged. But he stared straight ahead, sitting in his shirt-sleeves, his collar unbuttoned and loose around his neck. So Jess struggled and finally held both boots in one hand, ready to take them away. 'Wait here while I go and put these down on a bit of clean newspaper, Ern.' She was surprised by the nasty, greasy feel of the uppers. They would need a good clean.

In the bright kitchen light Jess set the boots down on paper and went to wipe her hands at the sink. Her fingers were stained a sticky red. For a moment she spread her palms and stared in disbelief. Then she went straight back to Ernie's boots to scrape and scrub at them with the paper, anxious now to wipe them clean. She screwed the paper into a tight ball, went to the kitchen range, which they always kept lit for cooking, and thrust it far into the back of the fire, holding it there with the poker. She took the boot polish from the cupboard, blacked Ernie's boots and polished them until they shone. Finally, she washed her hands at the sink.

Ernie still sat in the very same place when she got back to him, but it was less than a minute more before she'd eased him between the sheets and drawn his eiderdown up to his chin. He stared at the ceiling, numb and silent. 'G'night, Ern,' she whispered. 'I got to go check on Grace now. You get off to sleep and we'll sort things out in the morning, eh?'

'What d'you suppose Ern was up to?' Frances asked when Jess returned. In a roundabout way her daydreams had brought her back to the subject. She remembered breaking off from her lively conversation with Billy and seeing poor, lonely Ernie up ahead. 'When you think about it, there's a whole hour missing between him losing Robert and ending up back here. It don't take an hour to walk that little stretch!'

Jess shook her head. 'Don't ask me.'

'No need to bite my head off.'

'Sorry.' Jess found it hard to get rid of the sick feeling in the pit of her stomach. The boots bothered her. She was sure it was blood on them.

Duke came up and told the girls to get off to bed. It was his habit of a lifetime never to retire until all the family were in and accounted for, so he sat in his shirt-sleeves, poring over the latest reports of the war in France. At two in the morning Robert and Hettie walked in looking as if the world had come to an end.

A solitary policeman came down the court still later into the night to give the O'Hagans news of their daughter's death. 'I drew the short straw there,' he told them back at the station. 'This scraggy woman comes to the door, which anyhow don't shut tight on account of its hinges. She opens it a crack and I says, "I'm very sorry to have to tell you this, Mrs O'Hagan, but your daughter Daisy has been murdered." There ain't no nice way to put it. The woman looks at me like she ain't heard. I can see through the door that the whole place is a tip. I tells her she can go along to the mortuary in the morning and see the body, and we'll do our best to find out who did it. I still ain't sure she's heard. But then she nods and closes the door on me, and I can hear my own footsteps going back down them stairs, knock-knock against the bare boards and out into the street.'

His sergeant nodded. 'Good lad. Needle in a bleeding haystack this is, though.' There was paperwork to do. He opened the black ledger and chose a pen.

'What is?'

'Finding the bloke what done it. It could be any one of them hooligans done her in, the way them girls carry on after a show. I know, I seen 'em often enough.' Dutifully he wrote down the details: 9 September 1914. A quarter to twelve. Summoned to the Southwark Palace Music Hall by the manager, Mr Frederick Mills. Body on the premises. Female. Nineteen years. Stab wounds to throat and chest area. Identity: Daisy O'Hagan of Paradise Court, music-hall dancer and singer. Time of death, half-past eleven approximately.

'Ain't you got no one particular in mind?' The young police constable was recovering from his experience as the bearer of bad tidings. He supposed it was something else you got used to in this job.

The sergeant sucked in air loudly and shook his head. 'Well, I never took to the manager, Mills, for a start.' He finished writing, blotted the page and closed the book. 'All that stuff about what a lovely girl she was. Who's he trying to kid?'

'I can see you don't reckon much to her, Serg?'

'They're all the same, them showgirls.'

'What about the witness?' The young man's imagination was more fired up by the murder than his more experienced boss's. 'You reckon he had anything to do with it?'

'Parsons? Ain't come across him before. He was pretty worked up all right. Dunno. The sister was in a proper state and all.'

'It couldn't be a woman what done it, could it?'

'Don't see why not. Like I said, it could be any bleeding one!'

159

Their work finished for the night, they buttoned their capes and left the sombre brick building with its barred windows and iron railings. At least they could get away to their Sunday roasts and walks in the park. Not like the poor O'Hagans, they said, walking in step away from it all.

Hettie sat up all night. The rising tide of hysteria she'd felt as she knelt by Daisy's body soon passed. Afterwards she was acutely aware of every detail; every word Fred Mills gabbled to the sergeant, the phosphoric flash of the police photographer's camera, the rubber gloves of the surgeon as he inspected the corpse, until she'd been bundled out into the corridor, baldly questioned and packed off home.

Now it seemed she was floating free in her mind, telling her own body to stop shaking, ordering her hand to raise the glass to her mouth. You know it's true, she told herself. You saw poor Daisy lying there in a pool of her own blood. She never went on home like you thought.

Robert whispered the full story to Duke. The shock had given even him a bad knock.

'How come you was there, you and Ett?' Duke asked. There were misgivings in the old man's mind. He didn't like Robert being mixed up in this.

Robert had to confess how they went back looking for Ernie. 'He got home all right in the end, didn't he?' he asked suddenly.

'Ssh! Yes, no thanks to you. I seen him coming up with Frances about midnight. Keep your voice down.' Duke didn't want to wake the others. He shook his head and glanced across at Hettie. 'What we going to do with her?' She was sitting across the room from them, upright and quiet, but seemingly out of touch with her surroundings.

'Leave her be.' Robert knocked whisky to the back of his throat, felt it burn. 'She'll soon come round.'

Next morning, shock waves rippled up and down the court. No one could believe it. Poor Daisy O'Hagan was dead, stabbed through the heart by some unknown villain, her young life ebbing away in the dingy back rooms of the dark, deserted Palace. That bright, fresh young girl done away with in some dark corner; it was a cruel thing for everyone who knew her.

Hettie had sat through the night. 'I ain't going back to the Palace,' she told Frances. 'I decided I don't want to work there no more.' Her hands were folded in her lap. Frances, seeing her shiver, had thought to put a shawl around her shoulders. Now they'd all heard the horrible story and were letting the news sink in.

'Oh, Ett, that's a shame.' Frances had always recognized that her sister had talent, right from being a small child. The music hall was her life. 'I don't see why you should give it all up just because of this.'

Hettie never blinked.

'Ett? Listen, the life suits you, don't it? You like being up on that stage with the other girls. Wait a bit. Don't make no rash moves.'

'It ain't the same after what's happened.'

'Not now it ain't, course not. But just wait a bit.'

'I thought you never liked the place?' Hettie turned towards Frances. 'It weren't never good enough for you. You never liked Daisy much neither, did you?'

'Oh, Ett, how could you think that?' Frances's arms went around her sister and she hugged her close. 'I thought Daisy was a lovely girl, only just a bit lively sometimes. I never said nothing against her!'

'You never had to. She was scared stiff of you, Frances. She said you always made her feel like she had to sit up straight and talk proper.' Hettie recalled all the laughing remarks. Tears rolled down her cheeks.

'I know. I can't help it, Ett,' Frances said humbly. She cried too. 'I'm so sorry for what's happened!'

'And you'll go up today and tell Mr Mills for me? I ain't never going back, Fran.'

Frances nodded and blew her nose. 'No more singing and dancing,' she agreed.

'I thought you'd be over the moon.'

'Well, I ain't, Ett, believe me.'

But she went up that afternoon and gave the news to Fred Mills. He was sorry, he said, but he couldn't really blame Hettie. A lot of the girls were very scared by the murder and worried it would be their turn next. 'And they ain't even seen it, not like your sister, Miss Parsons.' He frowned. 'I had to clear up a lot of the mess myself. Very upsetting. I'm telling them to take more care who they hang round with from now on. You never know.'

Frances spoke to him in his small, dingy room behind the box-office. His face was grey as he stood and shook her hand; a little man whose confidence was demolished. She received an extra week's wages on Hettie's behalf. 'Hettie seems to think it's her fault, Mr Mills,' she confided. 'She thinks if she'd tried a bit harder to track Daisy down last night and walk home with her like normal, this would never have happened.'

'We could all think that about ourselves,' the manager confessed, his features blank and unreadable, his voice flat. 'Tell her not to think it though. It don't do no good, and it weren't her fault. Tell her that.'

Frances nodded once and went on her way. She walked out through the foyer, under glass chandeliers, between

162

rows of laughing faces. Glossy, smiling photographs of the stars beamed down; the comedians, singers and showgirls seemed to follow her with their eyes.

No one had been able to prevent Hettie from going to see the O'Hagans. Jess was busy with Ernie, who still hadn't recovered his bearings from the night before and was going around in a dream. She'd pushed the business about the boots firmly to the back of her mind and locked it away. Now she tried in vain to get him to eat toast and drink tea. The poor boy seemed lost in a mental maze and refused everything.

Sadie had cancelled her bike ride with Charlie Ogden to sit with poor Hettie, but she'd given in without protest when her sister insisted there was something she must do. Frances returned from the Palace to find Sadie sitting miserably in her own room. She scolded her for not looking after Hettie better, then immediately hugged her. 'It's not your fault, I just hope Hettie don't find it all too upsetting. It takes a lot to go and see the O'Hagans after what's just happened. Now dry them eyes, come with me and we'll make some scones,' she suggested impulsively. Sooner or later they would all have to pull themselves together and go down the court to number 48.

Father O'Rourke came down the tenement stairs as Hettie went up. He bowed silently. His rosary swung forward towards her. Then he went on his way. She found Mary sitting stranded in a sea of miserable children, half-finished laundry, broken furniture; the flotsam of her poverty-stricken life. Her eyes were sunken, her blouse unbuttoned at the top and torn at the sleeve. She sat on the one chair, shoulders slumped, staring with unseeing eyes.

Hettie bent over and took her hand. Beside the worn-out woman she looked proud and supple. Try as she might, she couldn't avert her eyes from the squalor of the room. This is how Daisy had to live, she thought.

An older child struggled to manage the needs of the little ones, but the dirty, ill-fed infants wailed on. There was no sign of Joe O'Hagan, who, unable to bear any more, had slunk off to roam the streets at daybreak. So Mary's bleak figure formed the focus of the children's movements. They crawled around her, dragged at her skirt and climbed on to her unresponsive lap.

Hettie felt her heart break. Robbed of words, she began to look around for practical ways of lifting the woman out of her misery. 'Go down the backyard and fetch clean water in this bucket,' she told the oldest child; a girl of about ten. 'Bring it back up here quick.' She wanted to wash the little ones' faces, and the water in the tap at the sink had dried up. She found a brush for their hair, sent the girl, Cathleen, on a second errand up the court to the Duke for milk and bread. 'Tell them Hettie says to send as much as they can spare,' she ordered. Quickly she began to make improvements to the state of the two rooms, working around the silent mother. Frances sent fresh scones along with the bread and milk, and the children set about them ravenously. It was the first food to pass their lips since Friday, Cathleen said.

At last Mary roused herself to ask Hettie tearful questions. How could such a thing have happened? Why didn't anyone try to save her poor girl?

'We wasn't there. We'd all packed up and gone home,' Hettie answered. 'It happened when the whole place was empty.'

'And how did she die?' Mary looked Hettie in the eyes for the first time.

Hettie drew a sharp breath. 'Didn't the policeman tell you that?'

'Most likely. I don't remember,' came the dull reply.

The words shaped themselves out of the images in Hettie's mind; a pool of blood, staring eyes, an outstretched hand. 'She was stabbed, Mary.'

'What with?'

'They don't know that yet.'

'Who done it to her, Hettie?' The look she gave the young woman still shook her to the core.

'They don't know that neither.'

'And did you see her?' The tortured inquisition continued. 'Did she suffer?' Mary's sobs came thick and fast. 'Did my poor girl suffer long?'

Hettie breathed in deeply. She was regaining control. Once the words were out, you had to accept them. 'They think it was pretty quick. I heard the police doctor say there weren't much sign of a struggle. Whoever it was must've sprung it on her out of the blue.'

Mary nodded, satisfied. 'She was a good girl.'

'She was, Mrs O'Hagan. Daisy was one of the best.'

People could raise their eyebrows at Daisy's goings-on, and Hettie herself used to scoff at her naïve belief that one day the right man would be standing at the stage door with a bunch of flowers and true romance. She warned her to be more careful. 'Just because they're giving you presents, it don't mean they want your hand in marriage,' she said right from the start. But Daisy had found it hard to rein back her high spirits.

As for the presents, she always brought them straight back home to this place of neglect and despair. She gave the chocolates to her brothers and sisters, her wages to Mary, and she brought them their only ray of light with her bright, loving smiles.

'She was a beauty though.' Pride shone through Mary's tears. She pulled a small object from her shabby skirt pocket and laid it in the palm of her hand to show Hettie. 'It's her birthday next Thursday. I was saving this for her.' The object was a shiny tortoiseshell comb for Daisy's hair. 'I ain't got much to give, but I was saving this for her.' Her fingers closed over it. 'She'll have to wear it for her funeral now.'

Chapter Fourteen

Hettie went back home and organized more supplies of food for the struggling family. Frances, Jess and Sadie joined in with a will. 'We got to help them get back on their feet,' Frances agreed. 'This is a bad blow for them and we all got to rally round.'

'I told young Cathleen to call here at six to see what we've managed to rustle up. Her ma ain't fit to do it. We'll ask around the other women in the court too; see what they can spare. Mary needs clothes for them kids as well as food. There's a lot to do.' Since recounting events to poor Mary, Hettie had broken out of her own lethargy. Now she was intent on doing good.

Sadie listened and slipped off to her room. She came back with two items of clothing, a skirt that had been lengthened to its limit but was now too small, and a pair of boots. 'Tell Cathleen she can have these when she comes,' she offered. 'The boots is too small for me, but there's plenty of wear left in them.' In fact, they were her favourite Sunday boots, fastened with buttons. She would have continued to squeeze her feet into them for months to come if not for this sudden emergency. Until now she'd known Cathleen O'Hagan only as the wild-haired child who ran barefoot up the street.

Hettie hugged her and began to make up a box of things

that Cathleen could take. 'Go down and pass the word around,' she told Jess. 'Pa's already opened up. They was all stood on the doorstep gossiping about poor Daisy.'

Jess went down into the pub's smoky atmosphere to talk to Duke about it. There was a lot of sympathy for the O'Hagans, he told her, especially since their boy Tommy had gone missing too. He hadn't been seen for weeks. All in all, things looked pretty bleak for them.

Maurice Leigh couldn't help overhearing. He leaned at the bar, intrigued by the buzz of scandal, but vague about the details. As a stranger, he'd been excluded from the gossip, though he gathered something pretty bad had occurred. 'What's going on?' He collared Jess, choosing her to set him straight. 'I come in for a quiet pint and the whole place is up in arms.'

Jess was struck by his direct, energetic manner. He didn't beat about the bush. His gaze unsettled her because she felt it sought her out without knowing her circumstances. At the same time, she felt she wanted to talk to him. The confusion brought colour to her cheeks. 'Something happened last night. A friend of ours got herself killed. Ain't Dolly told you?'

'I ain't seen Mrs Ogden this morning. She shot out early and I ain't seen her since.'

'Well, poor Daisy O'Hagan got stabbed to death, and now we got to round up some stuff to help the family. Daisy was the only one bringing in any money to speak of.' Jess raised her head to look him in the eye. 'That's what this is all about.'

He nodded, wanting to know more about the victim. 'Here's me thinking I moved into a respectable street!' he challenged.

'You have.' She missed the amused light in his eyes and

hotly defended Paradise Court. 'We never normally go round killing people. It's a terrible shock!'

Maurice smiled. His face, which was angular and a bit tense, relaxed. Still he stared at Jess. 'Any idea who done the girl in?' He pulled up a stool and sat facing her across the bar, more interested in engaging Jess in conversation than the murder itself.

'Well, first off, I just heard my brother Robert sounding off about the manager of the place where she worked, saying he wouldn't trust him as far as he could throw him. He was on the premises when it happened. Fred Mills, the manager, that is. But my sister Ett reckons there's a bloke there called Archie Small and he was always bothering Daisy.' Jess listed them on her fingers. 'But we think the police have got their work cut out. It could just be any Tom, Dick or Harry for all we know.'

Maurice nodded. Despite his comment about a respectable street, he was himself no stranger to the seamier side of life. A boyhood in Bethnal Green as the middle son of parents working in the book binding business hadn't shielded him from the ragged men and women who tramped the streets all night, unable to find a bed. He'd played in those streets with boys who died of fever, and knew the hollow feeling of a stomach that had gone forty-eight hours without food. His father had died when Maurice was just twelve, and the family, made homeless by the dead man's employers, had moved through a succession of ever seedier boarding-houses.

With a keen eye on self-improvement, however, Maurice had made himself useful to a landlord in one of these places, a pawnbroker who eventually set him behind the counter to conduct business whenever he was called away. Maurice was a lad he could trust. That was how he'd first become one of the flashiest and best-groomed boys in the area, showing off on a Saturday night in other men's pawned Sunday best. By slow and gradual stages, he'd moved into manning the box-office at an old music hall in Stepney, and from there to the Palace, and then into cinema management.

There was no doubt that the moves had been helped by his appearance. He was a dapper young man, tall and upright, and his dark colouring gave him a sophisticated air. His features were even, his jawline strong. Perhaps he was able to find work in the cinemas because he represented in the flesh an echo of the romantic actors who glamorized life on screen. Now, at twenty-seven, he was seen as well set up, ambitious and eligible. But Maurice himself acknowledged his own single-minded streak and up till now had used it as an excuse to avoid entanglements. Life was hard enough, he thought, as a single man trying to make his way. 'No complications' was his motto, and it seemed to work.

In the bar, Dolly Ogden vied with Annie Wiggin to solve the mystery of Daisy's murder.

'It ain't what you think, Annie,' she announced. 'To my way of thinking, this bloke what done her in is someone she knew!'

'No, a complete stranger, more like.' Annie felt irritated by the impression Dolly gave that she knew all the answers. 'There was hundreds of blokes in that audience. Thousands gawping at her all evening. Any one of them could've nipped back and done it easy as anything.' Annie planted her feet firmly under the table and took a long drink. Seeing Duke with his eye on her, she resisted the impulse to wipe her mouth on her sleeve.

'That's right, Annie,' Duke called across. He returned

the kindness she'd shown to baby Grace by backing her now.

Annie clutched the edge of the table in surprise. 'See!' she said, recovering enough to put Dolly in her place.

'See, nothing!' Dolly shook her head slowly, gathering herself to present her case. 'Now, look, who'd murder the girl just for the fun of it? No, this bloke must've known her, else how did he get backstage in the first place? Say, for instance, he arranged to meet up with her and she invited him in, not suspecting a thing of course. What then? Easy as pie to hang around till everyone's gone off home, and then stab her to death, see.' She appealed to her listeners, hands outspread.

Robert's ears pricked up. The murder had left him gloomy. On top of his little difficulty with Chalky White and the general feeling that life was going to the dogs, Daisy's death, lonely and brutal, had set the seal on his ambition to move away and make a complete break. He'd meant what he said to Walter about joining up. He'd thought about it long enough and planned to break the news to Duke that night. But natural curiosity diverted his thoughts and drew him into the women's orbit. 'You lot think it's a boyfriend what done this to Daisy?' he repeated.

Dolly looked up at him and nodded. She enjoyed lording it with her opinions. 'Ain't no doubt in my mind. Why, did you know her latest beau?' she quizzed.

'It were *him!*' Liz Sargent said. 'You was sweet on Daisy, wasn't you?' Unlike most of the local women, she thought Robert Parsons was too big for his boots, and enjoyed getting in this sly dig.

Robert bristled. He set a tray of full glasses down on the women's table. 'We was all sweet on Daisy, Liz. She was a real postcard queen.' He regarded her through narrowed eyes; her thin, grim mouth, her prominent nose. 'I just wish there was more like Daisy around.'

'Lay off him, Liz. He's been through a lot,' Annie said. 'Him and Ett found the corpse.'

'I'm asking you, who's her young man then?' Dolly took on the role of chief investigator. She sensed Robert had a juicy detail to give them.

'I can tell you of one that'll interest you, Dolly, at any rate.' He pulled up a chair and straddled it. 'Of course, this is between you and me and the gatepost.'

'Cut it out, Robert, just get on with it. Tell us what you know,' she grumbled. But she warmed to the flattery implied by Robert's special attention; even many of the older women found his looks and manner irresistible.

'Well,' he said in a low voice, 'the one I have in mind is the one your Amy had that bother with.'

'Teddy Cooper!' Dolly gripped his arm. 'You ain't stringing me along, Robert Parsons?'

'Cross my heart and hope to die, Dolly. Daisy told me about it herself. And anyhow I seen it with my own eyes; Teddy Cooper in a taxi with her, Wednesday of last week I think it was.'

For a second Dolly sat there stunned. The others considered it, willing to give it a hearing. Teddy Cooper's reputation was very poor, spreading beyond the sweatshops, amongst all the factory and shop-girls. He was after anyone he could lay his hands on, the younger the better.

''Struth! Where was he last night, does anyone know?' Liz Sargent asked.

'He was at the Gem,' a cool voice said. Maurice Leigh felt all the women's eyes swivel and fall on him. 'He came to see the new Karno picture. I remember seeing him there, clear as day.' His comment was greeted with hostile silence.

Jess quickly rescued him from their disappointment.

They could turn ugly if he went and ruined their nice theory. Maurice hadn't got their measure yet, otherwise he would have spoken more tactfully. 'About what time did the picture finish?' she asked, knowing that cinema shows often turned out early.

'Ten o'clock,' he confirmed. 'There was a couple of shorts on first, and then the Karno. That lasts forty-five minutes, so I can get them all out by ten. I turned off the lights at a quarter past.'

'See!' Dolly recharged her battery. 'Plenty of time for him to gallop up to the Palace. Who was he with, do you know?'

'Not with a woman, if that's what you're getting at,' Maurice said. 'I had a word with him and a bunch of his mates. Said they'd come into town to give my new place a try out. We been open a week, that's all. They seemed pleased as punch with it.'

The women nodded, warming to the well-informed newcomer. 'Thanks, Mr Leigh. So, we know for a fact he's got in with Daisy. We know he had time to go over and meet up with her.' Dolly paraded the evidence. 'And of course we all know what he's bleeding well like!' By now she was willing to swear on the Bible that Teddy Cooper was the one. Her hatred of him ran deep. 'There's nothing'll stop him and his filthy tricks!'

The others sat silent and sympathetic. In their minds too Teddy Cooper, the boss's son, leapt from womanizer to murderer in one easy bound. 'And of course Daisy was a lively girl with a bit of a temper herself. It ain't as if she'd take it from him if it didn't suit her,' Annie chipped in. 'What I mean to say is, the girl could put up a fight.'

'She could,' Robert agreed. 'Poor cow.' With his forearms folded along the hooped back of the wooden chair, he rested his chin and fell silent.

'So!' Dolly took it up again. 'She puts up a scrap and it turns nasty. Only he's not like other blokes. He's a devil when his temper goes. He snaps and comes at her with a knife. It's all over in seconds.' She led them through the scene. By the end, the jury didn't even need to go out. 'He's guilty as sin, I'm telling you!' Dolly declared.

'Don't tell us, tell the coppers!' Liz suggested. 'They ought to know about this.'

'They been round?' Dolly asked.

'Only to the O'Hagans' place,' Annie reported.

'They talk to you at the Palace last night?' Dolly asked Robert directly. 'Did you think to mention Cooper's name?'

'The state Hettie and me was in, we never even thought to mention our own bleeding names!' He got up to go. 'I wouldn't pin too many hopes on the coppers, though. Not if I was you.'

'How come?' Dolly was all for marching up to the station and laying a charge.

Robert shrugged. 'I dunno. I just got the feeling they wasn't that interested.'

'The poor girl's lying there dead!' Annie protested. 'What d'you mean, not interested?'

'But they never knew her. To them Daisy's just another chorus girl up the Palace, a girl who made a careless slip, worse luck. It ain't nothing to them. They seen it all before.' He went off to help Joxer shift some barrels.

The women looked downcast. 'She weren't just another chorus girl to me,' Annie remarked. 'She was a beauty, was Daisy.'

'And what about her poor bleeding mother?' Dolly added. 'It's broke her poor heart!'

'Ssh!' Jess warned from the bar. She'd heard Ernie's footsteps coming down, unmistakably jerky and heavy. 'Ern feels real bad about Daisy,' she explained to Maurice. 'He worshipped her, poor lamb.'

Maurice watched as Ernie came into the bar, head down, avoiding people's eyes. He realized at once that the kid was slow; you could read it in the angle of his body, with its slight forwards tilt, and the way his face looked somehow open and unguarded. He was tall and well built, not gawky like so many of the other simple-minded kids round the streets, and he kept himself clean and tidy. His thick, dark hair was well cut, his white shirt starched, his boots polished. The family evidently did a good job of keeping him in trim and looking after him.

'Ern, this is Mr Leigh,' Jess said gently as he came and waited at her side. 'Mr Leigh's just moved in with the Ogdens.'

Maurice shook the boy's hand. 'Nice to meet you.'

Ernie nodded and looked back at Jess.

'I better see what Pa's got lined up for him to do,' she said. 'He ain't feeling himself today. None of us is.'

She linked up with her brother and took him down to the far end of the bar where the old man showed him the tray of dirty glasses to wash.

Maurice sat and studied the family group; the grey-haired landlord once probably strong as an ox, now in decline, but still upright and smart, the salt of the earth. There was the boy, led by the hand, made in the same mould as the father and older brother, but raw and unfinished. And the daughter. Maurice stared for a long time at Jess; not flashy, not even aware of how nice looking she was. She was patience itself with the boy, and gentle. She wore her brown hair high on her head, but little wavy strands escaped and curled against the nape of her neck. She wore a dark-blue blouse, high-necked, with a cream flowered pattern, nipped in at the waist. Finding him watching her, she smiled self-consciously and put a hand to the stray strands of hair. Maurice looked away. If he wasn't careful, she'd get through to him in a serious way and undermine his motto. No complications, he reminded himself. New job; plenty to do, places to go.

Little Katie O'Hagan came up to the corner of the court at six as arranged. Hettie was waiting with a cardboard box full of smocks, trousers, socks and boots; all the assorted belongings that the women of the street had been able to muster. 'We ain't having them going up before the Officer at a time like this,' Hettie insisted. The Relief Board was notoriously unsympathetic towards people like the O'Hagans, who couldn't join in the panel schemes for those who paid out national insurance contributions and who weren't eligible for any of the benefits so far introduced by liberal governments. So Hettie even persuaded some of the men to dip into their pockets to help save Daisy from a pauper's grave. She appealed shamelessly to their guilt. 'C'mon, Walt,' she cajoled Robert's friend. 'Things ain't as bad as all that if you can pay good money to go down Milo's every other day and beat each other's brains out!' She collected the money, together with the clothes, and brought them down to the waiting girl.

'Tell your ma I'll be down with a bit of something extra in the morning,' she told her. She planned to go round the market stalls for damaged fruit and veg. 'And you be a good girl, Katie, and help her all you can.'

The girl nodded, wide-eyed. Daisy used to come home and tell them all about Hettie; how kind she was, and what a nice house she lived in. Cathleen walked off a few steps with the huge box in her arms, turned round and smiled.

Hettie stood on the corner, watching her down the narrow court. Women stood or sat at their doorsteps in the evening sun, following the girl with their eyes. Children stopped playing as she passed. The bright light cast long shadows until, at the bottom of the court, the two black, towering tenement buildings swallowed the sun, and Cathleen stepped into their gloom, her grubby smock ghostly. Then she vanished up the narrow stairs.

Hettie went slowly up to their own comfortable living room, where the sun shone and life followed its natural rhythm. The window was raised for Jess to stand and give Grace a few minutes' fresh air, cradled in her arms.

'I been thinking, Ett,' she said. She looked out across Duke Street at the row of small shops; Edgars' Tobacconist's advertising Navy Cut and Flaked Virginia, Powells' ironmonger's, Henshaw's eating-house and grocer's shop. 'Nice as it is, I can't go on like this.'

Hettie looked alarmed. 'You ain't thinking of leaving us again, are you, Jess?' She was closest to her in age; there was only a year between them, and though their personalities were opposites, a strong bond held them close. Ever since Jess had come home, Hettie had looked to her for company and advice. Besides, there was little Grace to fuss over and adore. 'What's wrong? Ain't you settled here?' She went across and stood by the open window.

'That's just it, I'm more than settled.' Jess sighed. 'Pa's been better with Grace than I ever dreamt. He won't hear a word against her.'

'And no wonder,' Hettie put in. 'She's an angel.'

'And the rest of you, you've been grand too. No, I ain't gonna leave again.' She smiled at Hettie's relieved face. 'But I gotta do something to get a bit of money coming in. I tried talking to Pa about it, but he don't want to know. I mean it though, Ett, and last night, before this terrible thing with Daisy came along and hit us like a steam engine, I sat here and had an idea.'

Hettie heard the excitement in Jess's voice. Everything was changing for the sisters; Frances seemed to be backing out of the heart of family life after all these years in charge. Jess had mellowed into motherhood overnight. Sadie was all talk of Charlie Ogden, and was growing up fast. And now Hettie herself had chucked her job and stood at a crossroads. 'Go on then, I can see you bursting to tell me,' she said, breathing in the warm air. 'How you gonna earn your pot of gold, Jess?'

'It ain't worth a fortune, don't get me wrong. But it's a start. I want to take in a bit of sewing work; alterations and mending. I'll advertise in Henshaw's window and get people to bring their stuff along here. That way there's no trouble getting Grace seen to. What d'you think?' Jess looked nervously at Hettie. 'It ain't a stupid idea, is it?'

'It ain't stupid,' Hettie said slowly. 'But it ain't exactly the Post Office telephonist or the typewriter Frances had in mind.'

'Frances is Frances,' Jess said firmly, 'and I'm me. It's good-hearted of her to look out all these job advertisements for me, but honest to goodness, Ett, I don't feel like going out all day and leaving Grace with someone else. No, I know what I want, and that's to be a proper mother to my baby. She ain't got no father, and that's a fact. All the more reason for me to stay home, I say. So you see, the sewing work suits me down to the ground. I can hand over what I earn to Pa, and I'll feel we can stay here long as we want, Grace and me!'

By the end of the long, heartfelt speech, Hettie found herself smiling broadly. 'Good for you, girl,' she said, turning with a swing of her skirt and striding to the middle of the room. 'Tell you what, Jess, let's be partners, you and me. Business partners. I can come in with you if you like. If two of us take in work, we can get through twice as much and make a name for ourselves twice as quick. "Them Parsons girls do a good, quick piece of work, very neat and tidy!" That's what they'll say. We'll be snowed under with work before we know where we are!'

Jess beamed back at her. 'You sure, Ett? It's a bleeding big jump from the bright lights to this.'

'Good thing too,' Hettie said. 'I'd had enough prancing about up there. What happened to Daisy was the last straw, but how much longer can a girl go on kicking her legs about every night, without landing on the scrap heap?' She stood looking at Jess, challenging her to contradict.

'Ett, you're not even twenty-six till next birthday! You're in your prime!' Jess laughed.

'Says you.' Hettie's light-hearted manner subsided again. 'But honest, what happened to Daisy made me think. It ain't a proper life, Jess. There's gotta be more to it than that, ain't there? As a matter of fact, I think I know what it is!'

'What?' Jess lay the sleeping baby in her crib and came back.

'I ain't saying. You'll think it's daft.'

'No I won't, Ett. Go on, I'm listening.'

'No, honest. I got something in mind, but I want to keep it to myself. Sorry for dragging it up.' Hettie struggled to change the subject. 'Listen here, am I in with you on this sewing lark or not? You can be the boss, since it's your idea. I'll be the skivvy. How's that?'

'Oh no, equal partners!'

'Right you are!' They shook hands and straight away set about drafting a card to put in Henshaw's window. 'Ern can take it across for us tomorrow morning,' Hettie suggested. 'You write it out neat, Jess, with all the charges made up in a proper list.'

They only stopped work when Duke rushed upstairs late in the evening. They raised their heads in surprise at the sound of his steps.

He came into the room, arms raised wide, his face delighted. 'Girls,' he said, 'I've got a bit of good news!' Propped against the mantelpiece, he could hardly contain himself. For months he'd been worried about Robert; not enough work down the docks, too many scraps and bits of bother. Now the problem was solved in the best way he could imagine. Duke's heart swelled with pride. 'I just been talking to Robert,' he told them. 'The boy's been keeping something from me, but he just give me the news and it couldn't be better. Tomorrow morning he's going for his papers. You know what that means, don't you, girls? It means he's enlisting. He's going to join in the war effort and fight for the King!'

Chapter Fifteen

Later that week, as September rolled steadily on, Charlie Ogden stood staring long and hard at the poster roughly pasted on to the red pillar-box at the top of the court. The initials 'G.R.' sat either side of the King's coat of arms, above the giant black lettering. 'Your King and Country Need You!' He read that 100,000 men were needed in the present grave emergency. 'Lord Kitchener is confident that this appeal will be at once responded to by all those who have the safety of our Empire at heart.' They wanted only men at least five foot three inches tall, with a chest measurement of at least thirty-four inches, both of which qualifications Charlie proudly met. But you had to be nineteen. He was just sixteen. Charlie's heart fell. It would be all over before he got the chance to serve. The army offered him no escape from the present misery at home. Even lying about his age wouldn't work; Charlie had one of those fair, smooth-skinned faces with small features, and his physique, though tall, was slender. The army would have to be desperate before they overlooked his birth certificate and accepted him for duty on the Western Front.

'Hello there, Charlie!' Sadie threw open the window and leaned out. Downstairs, everyone was hard at work preparing to give Rob a grand send-off. Even Frances had left work early to come and lend a hand. 'Wait there a sec.' She disappeared from view and soon joined him on the street-corner.

'You're not thinking of enlisting, are you, Charlie?' she said breezily. 'Ain't one soldier in the street enough for you, then?' She linked arms and kept him company to his front door.

'I'd go like a shot if they'd take me.' Moodily he kicked the bottom doorstep. 'Fighting in France is better than living in this dump.' Maurice Leigh might suit his mother, with his polite ways and his rent paid in advance, but sleeping in a room with Amy was a terrible indignity for Charlie.

Sadie sighed. 'And here's me thinking you was studying hard so you could leave home and go to college.' His bad moods unsettled her. For her part, just seeing him pass by or walking with him up to school was enough to lift her spirits for the day, while their Sunday bike rides made the whole of life worthwhile. She never fell into these gloomy spells, and wondered why Charlie couldn't just sail along on her cloud with her.

'I am,' he said, head down, scuffing the step.

'Well, then, ain't no point going off to France and getting yourself shot at, is there?'

Charlie looked up with a patient but stern expression. 'Answering the call to arms is a very fine thing,' he pointed out.

'I know it, Charlie.'

'It's terrible being too young to serve.' He sat on the step, hands clasped and resting on his knees. 'All our best men are going out there, Sadie. And you know what, Mr Donaldson told us at school today that they've shipped more than fifty thousand horses across the English Channel to France. It'll be all over by Christmas.'

She nodded, secretly glad that Robert wouldn't have to see much fighting by the sound of it. He'd signed up and got his uniform, but there were a few weeks' training at his barracks near the south coast before he went off to save Paris for the French. 'Would you like to come to our Robert's send-off?' she asked. 'It starts at six tonight.'

'Maybe.' He shrugged.

Feeling snubbed, Sadie backed off. 'Well, then, I gotta go.'

No answer from Charlie, who'd resorted to notions of following Tommy O'Hagan's lead and simply vanishing as an answer to domestic problems.

Then Sadie made the common woman's mistake of pressing harder for a small commitment from him when the best tactic was to withdraw. 'But you'll still come on our bike ride this Sunday, won't you, Charlie?' There was an edge of panic in her voice. What had happened to him, and all his kisses and promises?

He shook his head, staring down at his hands. 'Is that all you think of, Sadie Parsons? Cycling out into the countryside when we're at war with Germany, and to cap it all there's been a terrible murder of someone we've both known ever since we can remember? Is that all you think about?' He got up quickly and flung open the door.

'No it ain't!' Her retaliation was too slow. Charlie was already halfway down the gloomy corridor. 'Who d'you think has been taking stuff up to the O'Hagans all week? I been up and down them stairs like a jack-in-the-box, and I tell you something, Charlie Ogden, I ain't never seen you up there offering no help!'

Hot tears sprang to her eyes as she stormed off up the court. For all his reading and studying, Charlie missed the obvious things. It was true, Sadie never saw him reach out to help others. He grumbled and dreamt a lot, but he never put himself out. But neither could she bear to argue and think badly of him. It was like making cuts into her own flesh; painful and disfiguring. Sadly she went back to help her sisters.

'Cheer up, Sadie!' Jess cried. The bar shone from top to bottom. She put the finishing touches to the bread and butter and pastries that lined the bar top. 'Put a good face on it for Pa's sake. Don't let him think you're sad to see Rob go. We gotta be happy for him!'

Sadie nodded and pulled herself together. 'What d'you want me to do, Jess?'

'Go over to Henshaw's and fetch Ernie, will you. I said I wanted him home early, but it seems like he forgot. And when you find him you can help him spruce himself up a bit for the party.'

Sadie went off to look for her brother while preparations continued. The sisters brought down huge plates of cold pressed beef, veal and ham pie and fruit tarts. Duke fussed with the bungs and chocks under the barrels in the cellar, and even Joxer showed up in collar and tie instead of his usual bare neck and scarf. At six o'clock, people began to stroll in off the street to a liquid welcome and tables heaped with food.

'Just like good old Teddy's Coronation feast, ain't it?' Annie Wiggin declared. She was first over the threshold in a new hat and her old boots. As far as Annie was concerned, a party was an invitation to reminisce. She went up to Duke and settled herself at the bar. 'You remember that, don't you? We had steak and kidney pie and boiled beef, as much as we could stuff. And we had Bass beer, gallons of it, all paid for by the King himself. I went down the chapel for my dinner that day, and then across to Stepney to see Dan Leno and good old Vesta Tilley. Was you there, Duke?'

He leaned on the bar; the ice with Annie well and truly broken. 'Not me. I was up to me ears here, serving drinks to the whole of bleeding Southwark it seemed like.'

'Them was the good old days, wasn't they, Duke?'

'What was good about them? Your old man had just buggered off and left you, I seem to recall. We was all struggling in them dark days.'

Annie nodded. 'Well, fancy you remembering that.'

'What's that?'

She smiled, weighing her words well. 'The time when my better half departed this life.'

'Course I remember. He owed me half a crown,' Duke said.

'Your Pattie had just passed on and all, and that sister of yours, Florrie Searles, was living here. She came to lend a hand in your hour of need, according to her.' Annie took a long draught from her own special pint pot.

Duke smiled at Annie. 'Florrie ain't that bad, believe me. A bit loud for some people's liking, but her heart's in the right place.'

Annie grunted. 'A voice like a bleeding foghorn. And she treated them poor kids like they was in the bleeding army and all!'

'She never meant no harm.'

'Do this, do that, bleeding parade ground . . .'

The pub was filling up and Duke went off to serve his customers, leaving Annie to bad-mouth his sister to her heart's content. Another strong-minded woman in the street had been one too many for the likes of Annie and Dolly Ogden. 'Arthur, come over here!' Annie called. 'I ain't seen nothing of your Charlie lately.'

Arthur shuffled across, one fist grasping a huge slice of veal and ham pie. 'Why, what you want him for?'

'To catch some rats for me. They're all over the bleeding place again, since young Tommy O'Hagan hopped it. As if they didn't have enough on their plates. He ain't been seen for weeks, not since that poor girl was murdered. He was a dab hand at rat-catching, he was.'

Arthur considered the job in terms of family income before he dismissed it out of hand. 'He's too busy studying,' he replied.

'La-di-da!' She looked around for someone else to take up her offer, and spotted Ernie, head and shoulders above the rest of the crowd. Say what you liked about Ernie, he was twice as reliable as all the other little ikeys put together. There he was, still looking down-in-the-mouth about Daisy, sitting by Walter Davidson. Annie hopped off her stool and went to proposition him for the rat-catching job.

Soon the pub thronged with neighbours and friends, all come to give Robert a good send-off. At last he made his grand entrance, coming downstairs in full uniform, shining from head to foot. Every button sparkled, every lapel and epaulette sat pressed and straight on the khaki jacket. His shiny boots clicked on the stone floor, his flat army cap sat fair and square across his forehead. Duke grinned at him across the room, then carried on serving pints.

Surrounded by friends from the dock, attracting the attention of the girls, Robert was in his element. The uniform made him seem special in his own eyes too, as if he'd been training his body for years to fit its rugged lines like a glove. Less than a week ago joining up had seemed like the best of a bad job; an idea that caught him at a low ebb. Now it began to offer adventure and excitement, and to invest him with a clean-cut courage over and above the tough image he'd adopted on the streets and in the gym.

He glanced with contempt at Chalky, Syd and Whitey, who had drifted in for the free drink, and made a disparaging remark about them to Walter Davidson.

Whitey Lewis sat with his arm around Amy Ogden. He'd got well in with her and a couple of her old friends from Coopers'. Chalkey, on the other hand, ignored them. It was the first time he'd been seen out and about since his defeat down at the gym. He sat slumped forward over his beer, collar up, cigarette hanging from his mouth. He'd seen but ignored Robert's entrance. Memory of his disgrace in the boxing ring still seemed to weigh heavy. His stooping look was a new thing, although the bruising Robert had inflicted had almost faded.

'Bleeding cheek, showing his face round here,' Walter said to Robert. 'You want me to go over and tell him to push off?'

'Leave him be. It ain't no skin off my nose.' Robert had risen above Chalky White and his gang. He circulated, glass in hand, enjoying his last hour of freedom.

Charlie Ogden came, and Sadie was happy. Even Frances sat in a corner with some friends from her classes, though she'd been tactful enough not to invite the women from the suffragette meetings. Their table was quiet and respectable, the least rowdy of the lot, discussing the successful case brought against Teddy Cooper by Miss Amelia Jones. Frances herself had stood up in court as a witness and described the accused's actions on the night of the window-smashing. Her evidence had helped bring about a conviction. 'It ain't right though,' Frances complained. 'They find him guilty of assault and let him off with a footling little fine. They take Amelia herself to court for smashing a window and they give her six months in Holloway. Call that justice!'

The others agreed. 'Lucky little swine,' Rosie Cornwell

said. She'd just given up her good job as a typewriter in Swan and Edgar's office to train as a nurse for the war effort; a pretty, round-faced girl with light brown hair braided into a coronet around her brow.

'Hers was a crime against property,' Billy Wray pointed out. 'His was a crime against the person. It's obvious which one they think is more serious, ain't it? Besides, he's a boss.' He spoke quietly, stating the obvious with deadly effect. 'They could get away with murder without too much trouble, believe you me.'

Frances shuddered. 'Don't say that.' She'd heard the rumours, spreading like wildfire around the streets, fanned by Dolly Ogden. No one had seen much sign of Teddy Cooper since the murder, even at Coopers' Drapery Stores. People there said the police had paid him a visit and questioned him. It was only a matter of time before the arrest.

'Why not? What did I say?' Billy didn't live locally enough to have heard the rumours. His interests were political, not personal, with his long history in the hunger marches of 1908 and 1911. 'Starved to Death in a Land of Plenty' was his banner. Tittle-tattle wasn't up his street, but he noticed Frances shake her head and go pale.

'Nothing. The girl who got murdered up at the Palace lived down our street, that's all. They say Teddy Cooper's a suspect.'

'Him and five hundred others,' Rosie reminded her, and steered the talk in another direction.

Robert stood at the bar now, grasping his father's hand. 'Time I was off, Pa.'

Duke gave his son's hand one firm shake. He felt choked with pride. In his uniform, Robert looked the perfect son, the conquering hero. 'The girls will go and see you off,

Rob. Me and Ernie will say goodbye here.' He wouldn't trust his voice to say more.

Robert nodded.

Hettie came downstairs with his trenchcoat over her arm, while Jess went out to hail a cab. She too said goodbye on the doorstep. 'There's Grace to see to,' she said quietly. 'The little beggar's hungry again. Look after yourself, Rob. We're proud of you.' She looked up into his face and squeezed his arm.

So Robert set off for Victoria with Hettie, Frances and Sadie, waving farewell to the old life.

'G'bye, Ern! Look after things here while I'm gone!' he yelled. The horses clipped smartly up the street, the old cab swayed along. Crossing the main thoroughfares in the early autumn evening, they came to the sluggish grey river. They passed high over the water along London Bridge, over the slow barges. Victoria's mighty façade, with its great ribbed awning of iron and glass, greeted them as they spilled from the cab. The station platforms thronged with uniforms; soldiers with rifles slung across their shoulders, sailors with their kitbags. All the faces looked brisk and hopeful, of young men embarking for battle, making good farewells.

Robert slung his own bag down on a bench and turned to the women. 'That one's mine.' He pointed to the mighty engine, its funnel gently hissing steam.

Hettie ignored a small convoy of wounded men crossing a faraway platform, some on crutches, some carried on stretchers. She smiled bravely. 'Write and tell us how you're getting along,' she reminded him. 'And there's no need to tell you again to make sure and look after yourself, is there?'

'You too, Ett.' Robert gave her a quick hug. 'And keep an eye on the O'Hagans.'

'Try and stop me.'

'She's a one-woman Sally Army,' Frances put in. She took Robert's hand, clasping it in her own small, gloved ones.

'Well, say a prayer for old Daisy then,' Robert said to Hettie, one foot on the carriage step.

She nodded. 'I already did.' The train door slammed, Robert leaned out of the window.

'Go give him a kiss, quick!' Frances said to Sadie, who ran and reached up to his cheek. She clung on to his coat for a second, before the great iron wheels began to turn. Robert's face drew away into the distance. He raised his cap and waved, then went and sat in his carriage, with its smell of musty heat. The train left the station, shuttling between the backs of tall houses, through black tunnels, out into the open countryside, where shadows fell deep and the place names were hazy with steam and yellow flowering shrubs.

Annie Wiggin lingered until after most guests had left. The food was picked over, all the free beer drunk. Robert's departure had signalled the end of the party, of course. 'Like *Hamlet* without the bleeding prince,' she said to Dolly. 'Ain't you lucky your Charlie's too young for this lark?'

She ambled out on to the pavement in time to see a flat-topped police car drive up. She noticed its soft rubber tyres with their smart white rims, its dicky-seat at the back crammed with three coppers in full uniform, besides the sergeant and his mate sitting comfortably inside. They all climbed out and looked up and down Duke Street. Trouble, she thought, and nipped back inside the pub for a ringside view.

To her surprise, the coppers actually followed her into

the bar in single file, then fanned out across the room. Everyone stood stock-still, as if posing for a photograph. Joxer and Duke looked out from behind the bar.

'Wilf Parsons?' the sergeant asked. 'We want to talk to your boy.'

'He just left.' Duke's voice was strained, but he returned the policeman's stare. 'He enlisted for France. You won't find him here.' Whatever Robert had been up to would pale into insignificance beside that.

'Your boy, Ernest,' the man continued.

Duke breathed out, almost scornful. 'Well, there's been some mistake there. Ernie's . . .'

'No mistake,' the officer barked. He took a creased cloth cap from a pocket and held it up for inspection. Jess gasped and took a step towards it. 'This belongs to him, don't it?' He stuffed it back into his pocket without waiting for a reply. 'We already identified it through witnesses. He was seen, you understand. This is his cap, all right. We found it at the scene of the crime.'

Jess backed off, feeling herself go faint. The sticky sensation of blood on her fingers came back to her with redoubled force. She looked round wildly to see where Ernie was. The policemen watched her like hawks.

'Where? What crime?' Duke stared around the room.

'He ain't exactly hard to spot by all accounts. Several witnesses seen him hanging about the place just before the murder.'

'Murder? What you on about?' Duke lifted the bar hinge and stepped forward. 'What the bleeding hell you trying to say?'

The policemen stiffened, but didn't move in on Duke. They waited while the sergeant explained.

'We need to talk to Ernie.' He motioned two of the men to barge past Joxer down into the cellar. 'It's in connection with the murder at the Palace. Bad news, I'm afraid. We got to arrest your boy.'

Jess cried out loud and went to cling on to Annie. Annie screeched at the nearest copper; a young man with a thin moustache. Duke lunged at the sergeant, but Joxer managed to restrain him as the two policemen emerged from the cellar on either side of a bewildered Ernie.

'You can't arrest him, you bleeding idiot!' Annie yelled. 'The poor boy wouldn't harm a fly!'

'We got to take him down the station and ask him a few questions.' The sergeant turned to speak to Jess, who seemed to be the only one to have come to her senses. She was stunned but quiet. 'I've got to warn you though that we'll most likely charge him and keep him in the cells. After that, you can go and visit him in the Scrubs. Got it?'

Ernie stared at the chaos around him. Two policemen held him by the arms. In confusion, he began to struggle. One arm was wrenched up his back, the other shackled by handcuffs. He felt the cold metal click around his wrist. 'Pa?' he pleaded.

Duke pushed Joxer off and stood up straight. His head was up, though his hands trembled. 'Go with them, there's a good boy, Ern.'

Ernie nodded and let himself be led off.

Duke's head dropped to his chest. He turned away.

'Ern don't understand,' Jess told the sergeant. 'You got to explain things to him clear and simple. You get him down the station and explain the charge, right? You tell him he's supposed to have stabbed Daisy to death. Then you listen to him. He'll tell you the truth.' She held on to the policeman's braided cuff. 'You hear me? Ernie can't lie, he don't know how. You listen to him well and good, you hear?'

The man nodded, glad the boy was going quietly. 'He was up the Palace that night, weren't he?'

Slowly Jess admitted it.

'Shh, Jess,' Annie warned. 'Don't tell them nothing.'

Duke watched the doors swing to after the men. Only the sergeant remained. 'There's been a mistake,' he whispered.

Jess made one final appeal. 'Ernie wouldn't kill Daisy!' Tears poured down her face. 'He worshipped the girl!'

The sergeant sighed. 'I've seen everything in this job,' he said. 'Most of it you wouldn't believe unless you'd seen it with your own eyes.' He looked almost sorry for them as he fixed his hat on his head and pulled the strap under his chin. 'Look after your old man,' he advised. 'He looks like he could do with a stiff drink.'

Annie followed him to the door, in time to see him clamber into the car, and to catch a glimpse of Ernie's pale, bewildered face staring out from between the blue uniforms as they drove him off up the street.

Chapter Sixteen

Ernie understood that they thought he'd done something very bad. He knew they could give him the cat or put him in prison, and he was very afraid. But his father had told him to go along quietly, and it surely wouldn't be long before they came from home and fetched him. Probably Frances would come, when she got back from sending Robert off to war, and she would sort things out. This went through his head as the policemen manhandled him from the car into the station. The handcuffs locked both arms tight in front of him. They chafed his skin as he was wrenched this way and that down the bare corridor into a room with a table and two chairs. One high, barred window provided daylight, and an electric light shone under a green metal shade. The door banged shut. He was alone.

Then a man he'd never seen before came in. He wore a long, pale coat and a brown bowler hat. A dark moustache hid his mouth. His cheeks were thin, his eyes set close together. He never smiled or said hello; just threw his coat across the back of one of the chairs and slammed some papers down on the table. He looked at Ernie. 'Sit,' he said. He turned to the policeman in uniform who'd followed him in and puffed air into his thin cheeks. Then he blew it out in a loud sigh. 'Best get cracking on this one, Sergeant. What's he said so far?'

'Not a dicky bird, sir.' The sergeant stared at the blank wall above Ernie's head. 'He's all yours.'

The inspector took a mottled blue fountain pen from his top pocket, preparing to make notes for the duration of the interview. 'Does he know the charge?'

The sergeant blinked. 'No, sir. His sister says you have to take it slow. He ain't all that bright.'

'Oh my gawd.' The inspector stared narrowly at Ernie. 'He don't look that bad to me. Come quietly, did he?' The youth looked strong enough to cause trouble if so inclined. They were charging him with a nasty business; stabbing the girl at least ten or a dozen times and leaving her to bleed to death.

'Like a lamb, sir. Better tell him the charge and get it over with.'

'Easy does it. Now listen, son, you know why we brought you down here?'

Ernie stared back. He shook his head. 'I ain't done nothing wrong.'

'That's for us to say. But you know about the girl what got killed at the music hall, don't you? Daisy O'Hagan; she lived down your street.'

Slowly Ernie nodded. Pain at the memory of Daisy creased his forehead into a frown.

'And you was at the music hall yourself that night, wasn't you?' The inspector leaned across the table towards him. 'You was seen, mate, so you gotta tell us exactly what happened. Take your time, no rush.' He eased back in his seat and held his pen poised over the paper.

The man's voice sounded gentle. Ernie looked at him in surprise. 'Rob took me to see Ett and Daisy again,' he explained. 'We went to meet up with them after the show, but I lost Rob. I never saw where he went.'

The inspector glanced at the sergeant. 'Robert Parsons,

older brother, just gone and joined up,' the uniformed man informed him.

'Oh, very handy!' The inspector raised his close-knit eyebrows. 'Maybe we'd have got more sense out of him. Never mind. And what happened to you after you lost Rob, Ernie?' he asked. 'You're on your way backstage to see Ett and Daisy, remember?'

Ernie nodded. 'Ett's my sister,' he offered obligingly.

'Good, we're getting somewhere, then. But I want you to tell me what happened next. You lose your big brother. Now what?'

Ernie had begun to tremble. 'I never saw him out in the street neither. There was people all around, but I never let them put me off. I just had to go and meet Ett and Daisy like we always do. That's what Rob says, and then we walk home with them!' For a moment his face cleared.

The inspector sighed. 'Very nice, son. But it ain't like that on this particular night, is it? What happens when you finally get to the stage door? That's the bit we're interested in.'

Drawn back to that moment, Ernie's hands shook more violently against the bare table top. 'I'm too late. They all gone home. Rob ain't there. It's dark and empty.'

'What is?'

'The alley. I got held up by all those crowds, see. I was late.'

'Steady on, don't panic. What d'you do then, Ern?'

'I don't know. I can't remember.' Ernie's voice fell to a low whisper. 'Rob won't go home without me, I know that. He's gotta be somewhere.' He swallowed hard. 'Rob gets mad with me when I get lost.' He stopped, suddenly unable to go on.

'So what did you do next, Ernie?' The inspector concentrated on the boy's face. The confession had hit a brick wall.

Their suspect had gone blank on the crucial part. He glanced down to bring his notes up to date. 'Go ahead, son, tell us.'

'I don't remember.' Ernie's blank face searched the room for clues.

The inspector frowned. 'You don't expect us to buy that, do you, son?'

Ernie raised his tethered hands to his forehead. 'I know I'm in the right place to wait for Rob. But something's not right. I don't know. I'm looking everywhere, but Rob ain't there. What am I gonna do now?' He stood up, reliving the incident. 'Then I don't know what happens. Everything's gone wrong. I don't know!'

'Easy, son, easy. What happened after you'd waited for a bit? Did you go inside? Who did you see?'

'No! I don't know!'

'Did you go inside and find Rob? Or Daisy? Did you find her?'

Ernie stood up and came to appeal to the inspector. 'It ain't right. Rob shouldn't 've gone off, should he?'

'Hang on a bit.' The inspector's voice hardened and he motioned the sergeant to come forward with a brown envelope. The sergeant tipped it and emptied a kitchen knife on to the table, then stood back. 'Try thinking about this instead. Did you have this in your pocket that night, Ernie?' He looked keenly at the suspect, devoid of sympathy. They'd reached the crux of the matter.

Ernie shook his head.

'I want you to think this through carefully, Ernie.'

He nodded, anxious to play the scene through to its conclusion and get it off his chest. 'It ain't my fault, is it? Rob should never 've gone off. I was waiting for him, like he said.' He paused. When he took up again, his voice was strangled and faint. He shook his head. 'I never meant to do it!' Ernie caught hold of the policeman. 'Tell Rob I never meant to!'

'All right, all right, ease off!' The inspector pulled away as Ernie seized his jacket sleeve. 'That'll do for now. Have him taken down, Sergeant,' he said abruptly. He pulled his cuff straight and stood up as the constables came in to lead Ernie off to the cells. The heavy door shut behind them on to a long silence.

'What d'you reckon?' the sergeant asked at last.

The inspector looked up at the ceiling and scratched his neck. 'I think it's in the bag. He's got a touch of convenient amnesia around the actual stabbing, but I don't think the jury will wear that one. Maybe we'll never get it all out of him. He'll stay clammed up in court, if you want my opinion, but it won't make no difference. The rest is staring them in the face; he was there, his cap was there. This knife here is the murder weapon, and you can buy it from the ironmonger's opposite his house. Powells', ain't it?' He flicked the blade with his fingernail and made the knife spin under the glare of the electric light. 'Very neat.'

'No blood on him?' the sergeant asked.

'Too late to find out. Maybe he had someone who cleaned him up? That'd be worth checking. You can trot back to the pub and ferret around,' he suggested. Then he shrugged, picked up the knife and put it back in the envelope. 'You happy with what we got so far, Sergeant?'

The other man nodded. 'He ain't put up much of a defence, has he? Losing your memory don't convince no one that you're innocent.'

'What above a motive? That's what the jury will be asking.'

'Maybe he found her with another bloke,' the sergeant surmised. 'The sister back at the pub reckons he worshipped the girl. The way he sees things in black and white I reckon he'd go barmy if he caught her with someone else, which she was more than likely to do by all accounts.'

The inspector nodded. 'How about the older brother? That would account for him making himself scarce with a sudden attack of patriotism. Joining up is a surefire way of staying out of bother; he must know that. Anyhow, it looks to me like it'll hang together in front of a jury. Better get him properly charged. Ain't much more we can do now.' He sat to do the paperwork; suspect arrested at half-past seven on the 14th of September 1914. Ernest Parsons, aged eighteen, of the Duke of Wellington public house, Duke Street, Southwark.

Ernie's arrest shattered Duke. Men had died at his side in the army, and he'd watched his poor wife fade away under his own eyes. In the early days at the Duke, an unemployed scaffolder from one of the tenements had collapsed on his doorstep. They'd found the wife and three-year-old daughter dead of starvation at home. Horror stories of rats gnawing babies to death in Riddington's Yard, and anarchists shot dead by police in the Sydney Street siege were part and parcel of life in the East End, and now the war against Germany brought news of families who'd lost sons or fathers, or had them sent home wounded and broken. But nothing had robbed Duke of his will to battle on like this latest blow. They'd taken Ernie off in a police car, and life hollowed out to blank horizons, a slow stumble towards nothing.

'Don't take on,' Annie patted his hand. 'They got the wrong man, we know that. Soon as they ask him a few questions, they'll see they got it wrong.' She couldn't bear to see the strong man reduced to this empty shell. She looked up at Jess, tears in her eyes. 'Tell him not to take on,

Jess. We need him to be thinking straight when the others get back home.'

But Jess's own thoughts ran riot. She'd wiped blood off Ernie's boots and burnt the evidence. She'd washed her hands clean and asked no questions. Even when news of the murder ran through the streets, she'd kept quiet. What a fool she'd been, thinking that by cleaning the boots she could keep Ernie out of trouble. 'I done wrong,' she wept on Annie's shoulder. 'I never asked Ernie about his boots. I could've got the truth out of him, but I never. I left it! I done wrong over it. Poor Ern!'

'Don't you take on neither.' Annie put her arms round Jess. 'You got enough on your plate looking after little Grace. Now you go up and pull yourself together, girl. I'll look after your old man, and Joxer here will get the place straight.'

The wreckage of Robert's send-off celebrations still littered the bar, only bringing home to Duke the fact that he'd lost both his sons at one stroke. He sat in a daze as Joxer cleared off the glasses and swept the floors. Annie sat quiet and held his hand, watching the minutes tick by. She stared at his face; saw the lined cheeks, the jutting forehead and hooked nose, watching for signs of revival. But Duke sat on, scarcely blinking, trying to imagine what was happening to Ernie right that minute up at Union Street station. 'He ain't never been away from home before,' he told Annie. 'He ain't never slept in no other bed.'

Frances, Sadie and Hettie came back from Victoria by underground train and tram. Their effort to stay cheerful for Rob's send-off had worn them into a subdued silence on their return journey, and their memories of the uniformed hordes all making their farewells held an uneasy sadness. How many of those bright young men would return on stretchers like the ones carried along the side platform? How many would never come back at all?

'Chin up,' Frances said as they stood on the tram platform, ready to alight. 'Robert made his own choice. No need to ruin Pa's day by looking so down in the mouth about it now.' The tram rattled on while the sisters turned into Duke Street and walked the final stretch.

They wondered at everyone standing, arms folded and staring, as they drew near home. The pub doors were shut. Hettie grasped Sadie's hand and followed Frances along the pavement, then across the street. She noticed people withdraw inside their open doors to avoid them as they passed close by. 'Oh gawd, I hope Pa's not been took ill by it all!' she gasped. Frances pushed the ornate brass door handle, familiar to her as the back of her own hand.

Jess stood at the top of the stairs holding Grace in her arms. The bar-room door stood wedged open. Joxer was there, leaning on his broom, staring at them. Duke sat at a table, unmarked by illness or accident, and only the mystery of the staring neighbours, the closed pub doors remained. Their father was well, at any rate.

'What is it? What's wrong, Pa?' Frances hurried ahead again, picking at the fingers of her gloves, bag tucked under her arm. Sadie raised her arms to remove her hat. Hettie smiled up at Jess.

'It's Ernie,' Annie Wiggin rushed forward to intercept them. 'Your pa's had a shock, that's all. You'd best sit down.'

Hettie's smile turned to a look of alarm. She went and grabbed Annie by the arm. 'What's up with Ernie? Is that why we're all closed up here? Oh gawd, he's had an accident, ain't he? Is it bad?'

'Sit down, Ett.' Frances drew her on to a chair. 'And you

too, Sadie. Come and sit close by me.' She stared at the bowed figure of her father. 'Go ahead, Annie, you tell us what happened.' She felt sure Ernie must be dead; she just wanted someone to tell them the news.

'The coppers came.' Annie wrung her hands. She stood beside Duke. 'They think Ernie killed Daisy O'Hagan. They took him away.'

Sadie cried out loud; the long, protesting cry of a young child, her mouth hanging wide. Frances stood up and walked to the window to stare out. Hettie hung her head. 'It ain't possible,' she whispered. 'Don't they know he couldn't hurt a fly?'

'They wouldn't listen. It's hit your pa very hard, Ett. We can't get a word out of him hardly!' Annie gabbled. Now that the news was broken, she darted round the room from one to another. 'We gotta think straight, Frances. You got your head screwed on, girl. Think what we gotta do next!'

'Why on earth would they want to charge Ernie?' Frances asked. Across the street she saw the net curtains twitch. A group of women stood out on the street by the post-box, heads tilted into the middle of their circle, glancing every now and then towards the Duke. 'What evidence did they have?'

Annie shook her head. 'His cap. They say they found Ernie's cap by Daisy's body. But that don't prove nothing!'

'Where is he?'

'Union Street station.'

'Then that's where I have to go.' Frances flinched at the idea of facing the gossips again, but she had to try and see Ernie, and the sooner the better. God only knew what words the police would put into his mouth. They could get someone like Ernie to put his name to anything they wanted. 'He can't even read his statement!' she realized.

'He'll be confessing to everything up there, just to get back home. Ett, Sadie, you two stay and help look after things here. We gotta pull round. Try and rouse Pa. Tell him we'll put up a fight for Ernie. Ain't no way the police can get away with this!'

Dusk fell down Paradise Court, and not one inhabitant remained ignorant of Ernie Parsons's arrest. The murder had been bad enough. It was a terrible thing when a girl's life was snuffed out and her family left wondering why in God's name it had to happen to them. The neighbours had rallied round. This last week the little O'Hagan kids had actually looked better and been better fed than in their whole lives before, thanks mainly to Hettie Parsons. Joe O'Hagan had turned up for the girl's funeral in a halfway decent suit. There was talk of him getting work in a Tooley Street factory making cardboard boxes, to help the family back on its feet. Mary O'Hagan looked beaten by it all, but that was only to be expected.

Now they'd caught poor Daisy's killer, and it turned out to be someone else living right under their noses; none other than Ernie Parsons. He had a thing about Daisy, anyone could see that. He was always making up to her in his own, simple way. And Daisy was none too careful about leading him on. Everyone had seen problems there; at the very least, heartbreak for Ernie. You just had to think how she'd been seen carrying on with that weasel, Chalky White, to know she'd not got the sense she was born with. Now if it had been that young man who'd gone and got himself arrested, that would have been no surprise. But Chalky had been laid low by Robert Parsons that very afternoon. He'd kept to his bed to lick his wounds. No, all the best bets had been on Teddy Cooper, the boss's son. But Ernie Parsons had been thought of as harmless. It just went to show, you never could tell.

The mild evening kept folk out on their doorsteps until long after the moon rose over the dull slate roofs. By the time Annie Wiggin made her sorrowful way out of the Duke down to the end of the court, Ernie was established as a deep one, a youth with thwarted dreams who'd turned to violence when his love was spurned. It was a crime of passion, a tragedy for all concerned. Imagination came colourful in the drab East End.

Annie trudged on down the street. 'How's he taking it?' Nora Brady called from her doorstep. 'How's Duke?'

'Bad.'

'Have they sent Robert the news yet?' someone asked.

Annie shook her head, too weary to look round. But something about the situation roused her. By the time she reached the Ogden place her mettle was up. She looked Dolly straight in the eye. 'He ain't guilty, y'know!'

'I never said he was.' Dolly backed off. Annie's vehemence surprised her. Anyway, she'd been no great subscriber to the Ernie Parsons theory, preferring her own old judgement against the boss's son. 'As a matter of fact, didn't I just say the poor boy was innocent as the day?' she claimed.

In the background, Amy nodded.

'Yes, and don't no one go round saying nothing different, you hear!' Annie's voice rose like a soap-box orator's. She shook her fist at them all. 'We lived alongside that boy for nearly twenty years, some of us. We watched him grow up, we looked out for him up and down this street. Ernie ain't the brightest of lads, we all know that. But he ain't no murderer neither. Anyone who says different will have me to answer to!'

She stormed on her way, a small, slight figure, very

ferocious. Her speech had turned the whole thing round. Opinion swayed after her; 'Fancy carting poor Ernie Parsons off. They must be barmy. What the bleeding hell they up to over at that police station?' And so on, from doorstep to doorstep.

Annie closed her own door tight shut and sank into a chair. Only then did she give way to her feelings. In the privacy of her own front room, behind the aspidistra, she began to cry her eyes out for Duke and his family, and for the poor boy locked up in a cold prison cell.

Late that night Mary O'Hagan came up the court. She waited until lights were beginning to go out in upstairs rooms before she reached for her shawl and told Cathleen to mind the little ones. It was a quiet, pale figure that trod the pavement to see Hettie. 'I must speak to her,' she told the rough cellarman. 'Will you please go and fetch her?'

Joxer told her to wait in the corridor leading to the slope down into the cellar, but Hettie soon appeared on the stairs and said she must come up. Mary had never ventured inside the pub before. She trembled as Hettie came and grasped her hand and drew her upstairs. On the landing Mary resisted. 'It's you I must speak with,' she whispered. The attractive Irish brogue belied her haggard face and the clothes hanging almost in rags from her thin frame.

Hettie looked deep into her eyes. 'You heard the news?'

Mary nodded. 'That's why I came.'

'Poor Ernie!' Hettie broke down in tears. 'This is a terrible thing, Mary. I don't know what to say.'

'Then say nothing,' came the kind reply. 'Only I came to tell you not to worry. That boy never killed my Daisy, and the sooner they find that out the better.'

Hettie looked up again through tear-filled eyes. 'It's very good of you to come here,' she told her. Lost for words, the women fell into each other's arms.

'I never wanted my trouble to land in your lap, Hettie, believe me. You been good to Daisy, and you been good to us. We have to pray to God that they'll set the boy free soon. I don't like to think of him locked away for something he never did.' Mary held both of Hettie's hands and spoke rapidly, earnestly.

'Or worse,' Hettie agreed. 'They'll hang him if they find him guilty, Mary. That's the worst of it!'

'Oh never!' Mary gasped. 'It'll never come to that. What can we do to stop it? Oh, Hettie, they can't do that to the boy. Where's the justice? Where's the sense? Oh, your poor Pa!'

Jess came out, found them sobbing anew, and took them inside. The family blessed Mary for coming; it was a great comfort. Even Duke moved out of his profound hopelessness to offer her words of thanks. 'It ain't over yet,' Jess promised. 'We got a long way to go in this family before we're through!'

Chapter Seventeen

After softening the desk sergeant's heart at Union Street and gaining just five minutes with Ernie to try and reassure him that all would be well, Frances decided to set about using her contacts to get him good expert advice. He seemed to understand that he must stay in custody until they'd sorted things out for him, but he was worried about what Mr Henshaw would say if he failed to turn up for work next day. Frances promised to explain. 'Don't you worry, Ern, Mr Henshaw will understand.'

'Will he get another boy?' Ernie asked. He pictured someone else riding the shiny black bike up and down Duke Street.

'I hope not, Ern. I'll talk to him for you.' Frances and Sadie rose to go. 'You gotta stay here and be patient, and try not to worry too much. Do as they tell you and you'll be fine.' She bent and kissed his cheek. 'Cheer up, Ern, we'll do everything we can to get you out of here.'

She and Sadie sailed out of the police station, heads high. But they carried with them the memory of Ernie's stricken face as the coppers came in to lead him back to his lonely cell.

'He loves this job, Mr Henshaw,' Frances told the shopkeeper next day. 'He's afraid you'll think badly of him for letting you down.' She was on her way to work at

Boots, calling at Henshaw's, then planning to stop at Billy Wray's newspaper stand to ask about a solicitor.

Henshaw tied the strings around the waist of his long calico apron. 'Tell him from me his job will be here waiting for him when he gets out, Miss Parsons. I ain't found a boy as steady as Ernie for donkey's years.' He looked her straight in the eye. 'And tell your Pa that Mrs Henshaw and me are sorry for his trouble. You be sure and tell him that.'

Frances nodded. 'Thanks, Mr Henshaw.'

He stood at the shop door; apron tied, sleeves rolled up, dark hair parted down the middle. He could see the effort Frances had to put into making her way to work as usual, threading through the handcarts and the men loading up their stalls with the day's produce, a neat figure in her grey costume, stepping smartly over puddles, past street-sweepers and boys scavenging for fruit.

When she reached Meredith Close, the scene of the arrests during Coopers' window-smashing incident, she found Billy Wray already at his news-stand, surrounded by billboards proclaiming wonderful advances against the Germans, and the enemy's imminent collapse. Billy greeted her with a quick handshake. He'd heard the bad news about Ernie, who hadn't? Was there anything he could do? Frances discussed the sort of legal help they needed; she was afraid the duty solicitor wouldn't take much interest in a case like Ernie's. It turned out Billy had contacts at the Workers' Education Institute on St Thomas Street. He promised to nip along there today and do his best to help. Moved by his and the Henshaws' generosity, Frances felt her nerve begin to give way. She was prepared for battle, but not for kindness. Quietly she took a handkerchief from her pocket and blew her nose.

Billy too watched her on her way, oblivious to her surroundings, walking automatically amongst the heavy morning traffic, until she was swallowed by the trams and omnibuses, emerging briefly on the far side of the street, only to disappear again amidst the sea of cloth caps and boaters jostling to work.

A telephone message made its way to Florrie Searles in Brighton. A well-meaning neighbour in Paradise Court took it upon herself to go to the Post Office to ring and tell Florrie's son, Tom, that the Parsons had landed in terrible trouble. By noon that day, the indomitable Florrie had packed her bag and boarded the express train into Waterloo.

'Wilf will go to pieces about this if I'm not there to back him up,' she told Tom. 'I know him; never says nothing, but it's all going on inside his head. And there's that pub to run. It don't run itself. Wilf needs me there!'

'Now, Ma, go easy,' the thin, middle-aged man warned. He looked up from the platform at her determined expression. 'Don't go rampaging.'

Florrie's look switched to one of prim outrage. 'Me? Rampage? What you on about? I have to go when my one and only brother lands in trouble, don't I? We make these sacrifices in our family, always have. Why, I'm practically a mother to them poor girls!' She sniffed and glanced sharply up and down the platform. 'Now listen, Thomas, no need for you to fret while I'm away. It ain't as if I never taught you how to cook and do for yourself, is it?' She cast him a worried, protective look.

Tom, afraid that she was going to make a scene, gave a quick shake of his head. 'No, Ma!'

'And it ain't as if you won't have Lizzie coming in to clean for you, Monday to Friday. She'll lay the fires of a night, and leave plenty in the pantry. All you have to do is heat it up.'

'Yes, Ma.'

'Lizzie's a decent sort.'

'Yes, Ma.' Lizzie Makins was a scrawny old skinflint whose gravy didn't stand up to scrutiny. Tom curled his thin top lip over his bottom one. The guard waved his flag and blew his whistle. Steam gushed from the engine.

Florrie thrust her son back from the side of the train. 'Stand clear, Thomas, we're moving off!' Her waving handkerchief and brave farewell echoed the scenes in romantic novels where noble heroines gave their all.

Standing on the platform in a cloud of steam, Tom felt a great weight lift from his shoulders. His mother was a large woman and a great gossip, convinced of her own indispensability in every area of life. He'd carried her, slung around his neck like an albatross, for some crime he was unaware of having committed; for being born most likely. He waved the stout figure off, and she waved back under her mountainous cream-coloured hat. He heaved a huge sigh of relief.

She arrived in Duke Street in style, throwing a penny at the boy who bobbed up beside the taxi to carry her bag. She stood for a minute in the street, gazing up at the Duke's golden lettering, inspecting the windows for signs of the least neglect, glancing down the court. 'Dreadful thing to have happened, ain't it?' she confided to the taxi-driver as she paid her fare. She rolled her eyes sideways towards the pub.

The man nodded, nonplussed.

'A terrible thing for a respectable family, but I ain't ashamed to own up to him as my brother. Oh no, we Parsons gotta hold our heads up, make no mistake!' She grasped the man's hand as she slipped the two silver coins into it.

'Good for you, missus.' He tried to snatch his hand away.

'It's at times like this you know who your real friends are.' Florrie let the man go at last, stood up straight and braced herself. She pulled her brown jacket straight across her bosom, then adjusted her giant hat. The taxi-driver sped off like a greyhound from the trap. Her bag carrier stood and staggered under the weight.

'What you got in here, missus, a bleeding iron mangle?'

Florrie tapped him on the backside with her umbrella. 'Cheek. Watch it, sonny, there's a step up here. Don't knock the paintwork. Turn right through here. Watch them edges. Here, now you can put it down. Careful!' She stood in the middle of the empty bar, surrounded by gleaming mirrors, fancy plaster cornices, dark wood panelling. The old place hadn't changed a bit. 'Wilf!' She spread her arms wide and advanced like the *Titanic*. She plunged towards him. 'Ain't no need to say nothing. Your boy's innocent, we know that. Just stop worrying. Everything's gonna be all right, I'm here to help!'

Florrie's tidal-wave effect threw up survivors. She was something to stand up to, after all, and a reminder that they'd weathered bad times before. When Hettie and Jess surfaced after the shock of her arrival, they rearranged beds, emptied drawers and resigned themselves to being buffeted by her loud opinions and enormous personality. If anything, she was larger than before; stouter around the middle, her shoulders and bosom puffed out with yards of gathered white cotton. And the hats had certainly increased in size along with the rest of her. This cream one sat like an upturned shopping basket, loaded with violent red silk poppies all around the brim. She kept it on as she distributed her possessions around the house, keeping it pinioned to her jet-black hair by half a dozen vicious hatpins.

When a sergeant called in the late afternoon to follow up the arrest by interviewing members of the suspect's family, Florrie had to be restrained. 'You stay here, Auntie,' Jess protested. 'Joxer says it's me he wants to see first.'

She let this information penetrate. 'You? What's he want with you?'

'I don't know, do I?' Jess went to make sure that Grace was sound asleep before she made for the landing.

'Leave her be,' Florrie said, waving her off. 'I looked after more babies than you've had hot dinners, girl. Better go and make sure you give that copper a piece of your mind. Ask him when they gonna let that poor boy out. Tell him it'll be the death of his old man down there if they don't!'

Florrie's voice gushed downstairs after her. Jess pushed open the bar-room door, afraid of the line the police questioning might take. Was there anything unusual about Ernie when he came home on the night of the murder? the sergeant would ask. He'd be gathering evidence and writing down what she said. She looked at him in cold fear, knowing that Duke stood in the background listening.

The sergeant pressed hard. 'Did you think to ask him where he'd been?' He sat, pencil poised.

Jess tried to hold her voice steady. 'I knew where he'd been. He was up at the Palace with Robert.'

'But he came back by himself, did he?'

She nodded. 'He got lost.'

'And would you say he was in a bit of a state? Out of breath? Upset?'

'He was very quiet. He never said nothing.' Jess glanced at Duke. She was unwilling to admit the state Ernie had been in, but she felt like a lamb being led to the slaughter. Soon the policeman would be sure to pin her down.

'Just normal?'

'Yes. He don't say much.'

The sergeant began to feel irritated by her stonewalling. 'But did you notice anything different? Was his clothes messed about, for instanc? Had he been in a fight?'

'No.'

'What about his boots?' The sergeant remembered a trail of bloody footprints leading out of the murdered girl's dressing room.

She wasn't quick enough with the direct lie. 'No,' she faltered. She met his stern gaze, then cast her eyes down, unable to hold it.

'Hm, fair enough,' the sergeant said. He was no court prosecutor, but anyone with experience could break this story. He bet his life that Jess could be brought up as an accessory after the fact. Closing his notebook, he thanked her for her time with a touch of sarcasm in his voice, then he turned to Duke.

Jess rose quickly. 'How's Ern? Is he all right?'

'He's due in court tomorrow to face charges. Then they'll move him on to a remand cell in the Scrubs.' He spoke evasively, being the one to avoid her eyes now.

'But how is he in himself? He ain't gone to pieces, has he?' Jess begged.

'He's taking it quietly, I'd say. He ain't no trouble.' The policeman nodded at Duke, asked him for a few minutes of his time, and told Jess to leave them alone together.

If there was anyone he felt sorry for in all this mess, it was the old man. When they had the room to themselves, he questioned him more gently and soon decided to call it a day. His inspector had ordered him to head back to Union Street by half four. They were due to take detailed statements from some of the eyewitnesses, having hauled in some of the low life from down Duke Street. He expected to interview Syd Swan, Chalky White and Whitey Lewis,

213

among others, and they were there when the sergeant got back to base. In fact, Chalky White was already slinging his hook.

'Hey!' He put himself between the petty crook and the exit.

'It's all right, Sergeant, let him go.' The inspector looked up from his desk and sniffed. 'He's got an alibi to say he was nowhere around.'

Chalky grinned into the sergeant's face. 'And there ain't a thing you can do about it!' he sneered. 'Ask them!' He jerked his thumb towards Syd and the others.

'That's right, he weren't well, Sergeant. He had a bit of a headache,' Syd confirmed.

The sergeant sneered back. 'Too much to drink, Chalky?'

'A crack on the head, as a matter of fact,' Whitey put in.

'All right, all right!' Chalky's pasty face shadowed over. 'Let's just say I was below par, safely tucked up in my own little bed!' He pushed roughly past.

The sergeant shrugged then let him by. 'Mind how you go,' he mocked. Then he went to join the bunch of seedy-looking hooligans, headed by a cocky Syd Swan.

'Don't worry,' the inspector said. 'There's plenty more fish in the sea. And Syd here tells me he's got some valuable information to impart.' Pen poised, he got ready to write down the eyewitness account.

Duke had seen the sergeant out of the pub, more worried than ever. Jess protested that she'd done nothing wrong, but she had to confess about Ernie's boots when he pushed her to give him the truth. 'But, Pa, it don't prove nothing! All right, so we know what Ernie walked in on! He blundered into the middle of a murder, that's what, and he came home too upset to talk about it. He literally walked into it and he never even noticed the blood. Honest, if it'd been him what done it, the blood would've got everywhere. All over his hands, his clothes, everywhere. But he'd only got it on his boots, I swear to God! Just think about it; it can't be Ernie. Why can't they see that?'

Duke's head had sunk to his chest. 'They see what they want to see. As long as they can lock up some poor sod for doing Daisy in, they're happy.' He sighed. 'We ain't doing Ernie no favours, Jess, by not telling them the whole truth.'

She was stunned, but at last she saw he was right. 'All right then, we better get started.' Pulling herself together, she sprang into action. 'If Ernie ain't the one they want, who've we got left?' She counted people off on her fingers. 'There's the manager, that other bloke who works there, and Teddy bleeding Cooper. It's gotta be someone, Pa!' Distraught at the notion that she'd made things worse for her brother, she pushed herself on. 'What's the time? I'm off up to Coopers' before they close. You wait here, Pa, and ask Auntie Florrie to keep an eye on Grace for me, will you?'

Without bothering with hat or coat, Jess flew out of the door and up the street to the drapery store.

Teddy Cooper sat back in his father's office chair, his feet up on the desk. The old man had gone off on the train to the woollen mill in Bradford where they bought most of the worsted cloth for the men's suits. He'd be away for at least three days. Meanwhile, Teddy enjoyed the luxury of driving the motor car and draining his father's drinks cupboard. With experienced foremen, the place more or less ran itself, leaving him free to flirt with the shop-girls and put in a token appearance every now and then in the workshops. Thick-skinned as he was, his unpopularity didn't dent his confidence; he strutted about the place in Mr Cooper's absence, from electrical goods into menswear, and up into household linens.

But when Jess burst into the office to confront him, even his self-satisfied smile faded. He was presented with a breathless, half-demented woman demanding to know what he'd done to Daisy O'Hagan; how she'd go to the police station and tell them all about his affair with poor Daisy if he didn't go himself. 'How can you sit there and let someone else get the blame?' she shouted, beside herself. 'The whole street knows about you! Ain't it about time you owned up, you bleeding bastard!'

Teddy stood up and motioned one of the shopwomen who'd pursued Jess through the store out of the room. He advanced and kicked the door shut. 'Don't let my father hear you chucking insults like that around,' he said coolly. 'Good job he ain't here.'

'I don't care if he *is* here! If you ain't got the decency to own up when they nab the wrong person, I can call you any names I like!' She stood, gasping and dishevelled. 'Go on then, tell me where you was when it happened!'

'Ah!' Teddy rested on the edge of the big mahogany desk and fiddled with a glass paperweight. 'So you think I'm Jack the Ripper, do you?'

His flippant crudeness shocked her into silence. She was suddenly aware of onlookers crowding round for a better view outside the glass partition.

'Well, I'm sorry to disappoint you.' He put the cut-glass sphere on the palm of his hand and balanced it.

'You would say that,' she faltered. As the heat of her anger began to cool, she grew aware of the futility of the confrontation.

'I would, wouldn't I? Even if it was true, I wouldn't be on my knees confessing to you, would I? I'd be denying it even if you had *six* brothers locked up in Union Street.' He grinned at her surprise. 'How do I know who you are? That's what you're thinking. You're the Parsons sister who went wrong, the black sheep. I know all about you, see. You push your pram along here on the way to the park. The girls here gossip about it, naturally.' He paused, circling behind her as he talked.

Jess drew herself together. She stared straight ahead. 'I can still go to the coppers and tell them about you and Daisy. You'll have to tell them where you was that night, and you ain't exactly no angel as far as they're concerned neither.'

'A nice speech, I'm sure.' Teddy drew up alongside her. His top lip curled into a sneer. One lock of fair hair had fallen over his forehead. 'Again, I'm sorry to disappoint you.'

'What d'you mean?'

'The police have already paid me a visit. I had to give them an alibi, and that meant having to drop someone you know into a nasty hole.'

Jess took a deep breath. 'Why? What alibi? You mean to say you was with someone when it happened?'

'Certainly.' Teddy went back and settled on the desk. He tossed the paperweight and caught it with a small, slapping noise. 'I met someone after I left the picture house. I've done my best to protect her of course, but the police insisted on knowing my whereabouts. I was obliged to give them her name.'

'Who then?' Jess felt herself begin to shake, afraid of his answer.

Teddy enjoyed the cat-and-mouse game. He paused. Jess was one girl in the street he'd never had much to do with. She'd been away in service, but as he stood and looked at her now he saw her as an experienced, strong-minded woman, a cut above the ones he often went with. She had wonderful wavy hair and deep, dark eyes. Her skin was dark too, almost Italian-looking. 'Are you sure you want me to tell you?'

'Just say it!' Jess fended off his nasty look.

'Well, as a matter of fact, it was Amy Ogden who I met up with.' He stared right into her eyes to study the effect of his words.

'Liar!'

He laughed. 'More insults. Why not go and ask her? Poor Amy will have to admit it, but she'll be in deep trouble with her ma. Her ma don't like me, you see.'

'I will!' Jess turned and wrenched open the door. 'I'll go and get the truth out of her, just you wait!'

Teddy watched her go. The little interlude had brightened up a dull day. Now he'd best get the women packed off home and begin to shut up shop. He went about it with a smile. Amy Ogden was his precious alibi. He enjoyed all the little ironies of that situation. It was a pity about Jess Parsons though. There was a good woman going to waste.

With a sinking heart, Jess went down the court to Amy Ogden's house and knocked on the door. Possibly Teddy Cooper was lying. She could cling on to that hope and have a word with Amy. Come to think of it, surely Amy would have had to mention this before now, especially with Dolly Ogden going on and on about Teddy Cooper being the killer. She knocked again. Amy had better not try any silly games over this; Jess was determined to get at the truth.

Maurice Leigh took his time to answer the door. He had no friends in the area who would come visiting him here; the caller was bound to be for the Ogdens, but he didn't mind coming down to take a message. He opened the door to Jess Parsons.

'Is Amy here, please?' Jess was thrown off her stride and backed off.

'No, they're all out. Come in a minute.' Maurice had just finished shaving. He rolled his shirt-sleeves down his forearms. 'Would you like to leave a message with me?'

Jess stepped over the threshold, looking suddenly dejected. 'I don't know. If Amy ain't here, perhaps I'd best be off.'

'Why, what's the trouble? Can I help?' The narrow corridor made it difficult to carry on a relaxed conversation. Maurice led the way to the kitchen, turning and holding out one arm in welcome.

Jess laughed self-consciously. 'Ain't nobody can help if what I just heard is true.'

'That right?' He stopped and waited for her to catch up, feeling her skirt brush against one leg. On impulse, he took her gently by the elbow. 'Tell me about it.'

As if the effort of standing upright had suddenly overwhelmed her, Jess sank against him. She shook her head. 'Ain't nothing I can do.'

Maurice folded both arms around her shoulders and stood there holding on to her. He realized she was in deep trouble, and he wanted to shield her from it if he could. Being near to her, feeling the soft hair at the nape of her neck, smelling the soap on her skin gave him pleasure. He kissed her cheek, then her mouth.

Jess returned his kiss, then drew back. His arms were locked around her so she turned her head sideways in confusion. As a girl she'd received boys' inexperienced kisses, and as a woman she'd borne a child. But she'd never clung to a kiss and desired it as she had this one.

219

'What's wrong?' he murmured. 'Don't you like me?'

She nodded, unable to trust her voice.

'Well, then.' He stroked her hair, her smooth, slim back.

'You don't know nothing about me,' she said plaintively. 'It ain't right.'

'What's to know?' He let her pull away; he knew not to rush her. His smile broke the mood. 'Shall I tell Amy you called?'

'Yes please.'

'I will then.'

They stood facing each other in the run-down kitchen, until Jess finally turned away. 'Thanks,' she said quietly.

'My pleasure.' Maurice meant it. From the moment he set eyes on her, he knew Jess was special. Now he knew she liked him too. That was progress, he thought, as he went upstairs to get ready for work. Tomorrow, or the day after, he'd take things further; one step at a time.

Chapter Eighteen

Maurice's kiss had unsettled Jess more than she could say. In a flurry of confusion, she locked the episode away and tried to fix her mind back on her vow to help Ernie.

Later that evening, she decided to send Hettie down to the Ogdens' place to discover the truth of what Teddy Cooper had to say.

'Get down there yourself, why don't you?' Florrie urged. 'You started this thing, girl. You'd better finish it.'

Hettie hesitated by the door.

'I'm tired, Auntie.' Jess bent her head over her sewing. 'Hettie don't mind.'

'I dare say she don't.' Florrie eyed her knowingly. 'But it looks fishy to me. Who's down there that you don't want to bump into?'

'No one!' Jess coloured up. She knew Maurice would be out at work by this time, but she was still keen to steer clear of the Ogden house for a bit. Memories of Maurice's embrace came crowding in on her again. She needed time to think. Not much chance of that with Florrie around, she thought.

'Let's both go,' Hettie suggested. 'Get a breath of fresh air. I can back you if Amy plays up. Come on.'

So they stepped downstairs together and went along the court arm in arm. Little Katie O'Hagan waved at them from the far end. Three men came out of her tenement doorway and staggered up to the pub; one of them Chalky White.

The women gave the men a curt hello. 'Blimey, if he didn't have his mates to prop him up, he'd fall flat on his face, he would,' Hettie commented about Chalky.

'Why, what's up?' Jess glanced back at the trio.

'Drunk as a lord.'

'He ain't!'

'He is too. I don't like the look of him, Jess. I ain't seen him sober for weeks,' Hettie declared. 'He ain't never out of our place these days.'

Jess too turned up her nose. 'He's another one I ain't keen on. I don't know which one I hate the most; him or Teddy Cooper!' White's slouching walk got on her nerves, and she knew Robert and he had never seen eye to eye.

Hettie grinned and told her to hush before she knocked on Amy's door. 'Mind you, what we've come here to say won't go down too well as it is!'

'Are they in?'

'They are. I can hear Dolly coming now. Hold on to your hat, girl.'

Jess stood, working out exactly what she wanted to say.

Dolly opened the door with a warm welcome. 'Don't stand out there. It's drawing in cold of a night. Now, girls, sit and have a cup of tea with us.' Her sympathy for the family's plight was genuine. 'Amy, put the kettle on. Let me get rid of these things.' She began to clear a space on the table, where piles of fawn stockings lay waiting to be finished off. She'd taken in more outwork since her dismissal from Coopers' and had to work every waking hour to make ends meet.

'It's Amy we come to see,' Jess said quietly. She blushed and looked across at Hettie.

'Best make short work of this,' Hettie went on. 'Can you cope with a bit of a shock, Dolly?'

The stout woman stood uneasily in the middle of the bare room. 'You know me,' she said, trying to smile. 'I take it this ain't a social call, then?'

Amy, sensing that she would have some awkward explaining to do, bent over the hob, her face averted.

'Look here, Amy,' Jess began again. 'I been talking to Teddy Cooper this afternoon, and he told me where he was when Daisy went and got herself bumped off.' She looked up anxiously at Dolly, who'd bridled.

'So?' Amy made a feeble attempt to brazen it out. 'What's it to do with me?'

'Everything, according to him. He says we can count him out of it, Dolly. He can't have killed Daisy.' Jess hoped Amy would come clean. Things were getting very strained. But there was silence from her corner.

'Why's that, then?' Dolly had trumpeted the theory about the detested boss's son far and wide. But her skin began to crawl with a dreadful realization. 'Amy, come over here, will you. Leave that bleeding kettle alone and come and do like I tell you!'

'Hang on, just hear what Jess wants to say,' Hettie interrupted.

'Teddy Cooper told me he was with you that night, Amy. He says you're his alibi.' Jess wished herself anywhere else in the world, rather than have to look Dolly in the face right now. She saw Amy go sullen.

'Is he right?' Dolly asked.

Amy would have lied if she thought she could pull it off. But she was trapped. If she denied it, she could keep her mother off her back, but the Parsons sisters would go and land Teddy right in it, and she was back to the old bind. Who would the police believe; her or Teddy Cooper? If she confessed, on the other hand, Dolly would kill her. So she stood in silence, waiting for the storm to break.

Dolly made a lunge for her. 'I'll get this out of you if I have to shake it out!' she cried. Humiliation came with a sharp sting. She'd be a laughing stock when this got out. She seized Amy by both elbows and shook her hard. 'Was you with him, or not? Yes or no? Yes or no?'

'Yes!'

'Hold on, Dolly!' Hettie rushed forward to restrain her. The older woman took some pulling off. Amy crashed back against a chair and sat on it, sobbing.

But her mother darted forward again and slapped her cheek. 'Bloody little fool!' she cried. 'Dirty, disgusting, bloody little fool! How could you?'

Amy whimpered. 'Look what you done!' she hissed at Jess.

'Jess ain't done nothing.' Dolly pulled herself up, her fingers still tingling. But she was back in control. 'It's you, girl! I lost my bleeding job over you! We walked out of Coopers' with our heads up after what he done to you. Stuff their bleeding jobs! And what do you do? You let him get back in with you. First you yell and scream at me and your pa for not going up to the coppers with it, then you sneak off behind our backs and get back in with him again! Tell me why, girl, 'cos I don't understand you. The man's a monster, ain't he?' She breathed heavily, appealing to Jess and Hettie in her last remark.

Hettie bent over Amy's chair. The girl had slumped forward, head on her knees, arms over her head. 'Tell your ma why you went off with him, and why you never said nothing,' she whispered.

'I just went up to the shop 'cos I wanted to try and put a bit of pressure on him.' Through her tears, Amy thought she could make them understand. The fight had brought her hair down and pulled her blouse loose at the back. 'I went to tell him I could still go to the coppers if I liked!'

'What for?' Hettie was horrified. You couldn't go messing Teddy Cooper around like that.

Amy sat up straight. 'I thought I could get some cash out of him.'

'Bleeding blackmail!' Dolly's mouth hung open in disbelief.

'And did he give you any?' Hettie handed Amy a handkerchief.

'He gave me ten shillings. He weren't nasty to me neither. He said not to worry, he'd get me another job before too long, if I was nice to him and never went up to the police.'

'Oh, Amy!' Jess stood, holding on to Dolly, who still quivered from head to foot. 'You never believed him?'

Amy gave a miserable shrug. 'He was nice to me, like he was at first. I said I'd meet up with him again that night, that's all. It didn't mean nothing, and I thought he'd be different with me this time.'

'And was he?' Jess kept a firm hold of Dolly.

Amy's full tragedy came tumbling out. 'No, he weren't! I didn't even get to go to the picture house with him this time. He met up with me outside Coopers', and we went up to the office like before.' She sobbed into the handkerchief.

'*Everything* just like before?' Dolly asked.

Amy nodded. She looked up through bleary eyes. 'But I couldn't tell no one about it, could I? Especially when Daisy went and got herself killed, and, Ma, you went on and on about it being Teddy! What was I meant to say?'

'And have you seen him since?' Hettie asked. She put her arm around Amy's shoulder, thinking how young she looked for her seventeen or eighteen years.

Amy sniffed. 'He don't want to know me. He sent me packing and he was laughing at me, saying I might cry rape once but not twice, and anyway they'd soon see what sort of a slut I was. He warned me to stay away or he'd have me thrown in gaol as a common prostitute. That's what he said.' The memory sent her off into fresh wails of misery.

Dolly stood there stunned. 'I ain't dragged you up to go off and do this kind of thing,' she whispered. 'I lost my bleeding job over you!'

Amy sobbed harder. 'Oh, Ma, why didn't we go up to the police first off?'

Dolly steadied herself against Jess. 'Your Pa said why not. They'd never have believed us.'

Jess and Hettie worked hard to pull them round after the first shock had worn off. They talked about Florrie arriving out of the blue to lend a hand, and Frances getting hold of the very best advice for Ernie through a friend of hers. If they all pulled together they were sure they could get him out. 'But we gotta admit Teddy Cooper's out of the picture now,' Jess said to Dolly out on her front doorstep again. 'Try not to be too hard on the girl, if you can help it.'

The sisters walked back up the court. They felt down, in spite of their efforts to look on the bright side. The next day, the second of Ernie's imprisonment, Frances had arranged a visiting order to go and see their brother. They'd keep themselves busy by making up a food parcel and helping Duke in the bar. The old man was determined to carry on business as usual, but he moved like an automaton, drifting from dawn to dusk.

Wormwood Scrubs was a loathsome place. The warders made visitors queue up and answer to the number belonging to the inmate they had come to see. 'Janeki 743, Madigan 621, Parsons 684.'

Terrified, Frances walked in single file along the inside of the perimeter wall, which rose twenty feet high to their left. Built like a fortress, black with age and soot, the prison must deaden the spirit of whoever set foot inside its iron doors and metal landings. She was angry and astonished that men lived here like caged beasts. Looking out of a window, she saw prisoners shuffling the narrow triangular path in the exercise yard, heads bowed and shaven. She saw their faces at the door hatches, gaunt and brutal. Doors clanged, footsteps echoed, the stench of boiled food sickened.

All eyes followed the female visitors along the landings, drilling holes into their backs, resentful of their freedom. Frances felt faint, but she clutched Ernie's food parcel and marched on behind the warder. At last he stopped and turned the key of cell number 684.

'This your first visit?' he asked, holding the door ajar.

She nodded.

'It ain't that bad,' he reassured her. 'Not when you get used to it.'

Then he locked her in with Ernie, telling her they had half an hour. Ernie rose from his iron bed and came blindly towards her, reaching out his arms. She cried as she hugged him, then broke into questions: did he have enough to eat? Was he warm enough? Had they treated him well? She opened up the food parcel, happy to see him tuck into some left-over veal pie. She told him to expect to see a Mr Sewell, a good man who would help explain things to the judge in court. Ernie must tell Mr Sewell everything he could recall about that night. 'Think long and hard before you answer him, Ern. A lot will depend on exactly what you remember.'

He nodded faithfully.

'Try to think who you saw, and where and when. Or think, did you hear any noises from inside? How long did you stand waiting outside the stage door? Mr Sewell will ask you them sort of questions, Ern, so you gotta be clear in your own mind.'

But Ernie was so pleased to see her, he just sat and smiled and nodded, and he cried silently when it was time for her to go. She got up and leaned over the table to kiss him.

'We'll look after you, Ern,' she promised. 'But it's gonna take a bit of time, so you just got to hang on here.'

'Don't have much choice, do he?' the warder said as he beckoned her out of the cell. He eased the giant key in the lock.

Shocked to the core, Frances followed him down the metal staircases, under brick arches, out through the fortress-like gate. By the time she'd travelled the streets back to Southwark, she'd come to, but when Billy Wray intercepted her on Duke Street with the offer of a cup of coffee in Henshaw's, she was glad to accept. 'You look done in,' he told her. They settled in a dark corner of the eating-house, away from the window, while Bea Henshaw went for their order.

'I got to write to Robert tonight and tell him about Ernie,' she said faintly. 'I put it off yesterday, and I still ain't looking forward to doing it.'

'No, and there ain't nothing he can do about it in his position. Has he been shipped out to France yet?'

Frances shook her head. 'No. He ought to be told what's going on back here though, don't you think?'

Billy nodded. 'Even if it is a bit hard on him. But I should think the police will be in touch with him pretty soon. I'd get a move on and write that letter if I was you. It's better if he hears the news from family in my opinion.'

'Only, I think if Robert was here Ernie would have a better chance, and I'm afraid Rob might think so too. I just hope he don't go and do nothing stupid.'

'Go AWOL? No, you gotta write and explain we're doing everything we can.' He settled back in his seat, watching with concern as Frances sipped her coffee. 'How do you feel now? You didn't half give me a fright when I saw you step off that tram. You nearly went straight under the wheels of a car, not looking where you was going.'

'That prison's a terrible place, Billy.' Frances stared down at the linen tablecloth. 'I never expected it to be that bad.'

'I fixed up for Mr Sewell to visit him tomorrow morning. That'll help keep his chin up.' If Billy Wray could have moved a mountain for Frances Parsons, he would have done. He admired her determined way. His own wife, Ada, had always been a passive sort, content to stay at home. Now, with her illness, she leaned on him a lot. Billy was a devoted husband, but he felt as he sat watching Frances that marriage was his own sort of prison. Then he regretted thinking it. If Frances had been less good-looking, he'd have things more under control. The truth was, he liked her precise, neat movements, and the graceful turn of her dark head.

'What does Mr Sewell think of Ernie's chances?' Frances asked. She knew through Billy that Sewell was regarded as a supporter of good causes such as women's rights and Fabianism. But was he any good at fighting individual cases? She had to put her trust in Billy's judgement. Knowing from their meetings and lectures how well informed he was, she turned to him in this time of crisis.

'I managed to have a few words with him about it. He says the police have built their case on what he calls circumstantial evidence, but he admits there's a combination of things that will make it hard for a jury. He says to wait till he's seen Ernie before he jumps to any conclusions.'

Frances nodded. 'Thanks, Billy.'

'Try not to worry.' He put his hand over hers. 'No, I don't mean that. You're bound to worry, it's only natural. I just wish I could be more help.'

She smiled. 'You've been very good to us, Billy. I don't know what we'd do without you.'

Frances's gratitude was cold comfort when he found himself wanting more. But she was eaten up by her family problem, and he was tied to Ada. Come to that, she probably never looked at him as woman to man. She was a spinster born and bred, they said up at Union Street. And he was married.

When Maurice Leigh heard the news about Amy's feather-brained entanglement with Teddy Cooper, he decided to steer clear of the women in his household until the upset had died down. He had a serious aversion to female hysterics, and in this sense his relationship with his landlady and her daughter was bound to be problematic. He was a poor shoulder to cry on, he told himself, so keeping out of the way seemed his best tactic.

Still, he couldn't help feeling sorry for the one who seemed overlooked in all this; and that was Charlie. The poor boy wandered in from school and could hardly find a seat to park himself on. Once, while there was some bother rumbling on down in the kitchen and Maurice was just slipping out to work, he found Charlie sitting on the stairs, chin in hands. 'How do you fancy coming up to the Gem with me tonight?' he offered. 'You can sit in with the projectionist and see how things work.'

Charlie stared back, his face suddenly alive with excitement. 'You're not kidding?'

Maurice stood in the stairwell, hands in pockets. 'I take it that means yes? Right, get your jacket on and hurry up. If you like what you see, I might even find you a little job one or two evenings a week. Keep you out of trouble!'

The two were already out on the street. Charlie walked jauntily along, cap tilted to the back of his head. 'I ain't *in* trouble.'

'Well, a boy of your age ought to be,' Maurice replied. They swung diagonally across Duke Street, getting into their stride. 'If I was you going bike-riding with a pretty girl like Sadie Parsons of a Sunday, I'd make bleeding sure I was in trouble!'

Charlie grunted. 'I don't think you should be encouraging me that way.' Privately, he realized that those bike rides, so precious at first, were beginning to lose their charm, now that the novelty had worn off.

Maurice laughed. 'No? You most likely don't need no encouraging neither.'

'That'd be telling.' Charlie followed on Maurice's tail into the plush picture house. This was it; he'd arrived! This was the future, these were the machines he wanted to learn about. Magic flickered up there on the screen. He fell in love with the giant reels of celluloid, the whir of the projector, the hot dust rising in the tiny projection room. Their lodger had offered him a gateway to heaven, and Charlie was about to dash headlong through it.

Maurice offered Jess a gateway of a different kind, which she approached timidly and full of doubt. For a start, it didn't seem right to her to be having thoughts about anything except Ernie's trial. She saw Frances moving heaven and earth to get him the best solicitor in the East End, delving into her own savings and working long hours at the chemist's shop to pay for it. She watched Hettie transformed from a music-hall girl with a spring in her step to a quiet, nunlike figure, grieving for Daisy. Duke was a shell, an empty husk; even Florrie had given up trying to jolly him along and had to leave him alone.

And Jess already felt guilty for the comfort she found in nursing little Grace and in watching her baby develop her first smiles. Sewing work had come in from the advert, and this too brought satisfaction. Jess, who less than a year ago expected to be the most miserable of women, feared she was blossoming in spite of her family's troubles. She racked her brains to see what more she could do to help, and constantly asked herself how could she rein back her hopes for the future.

'Jess?' Hettie said tentatively, in the middle of one long afternoon's sewing. She was altering the sleeves in a ladies' jacket to bring it back into fashion. Jess sat at their new sewing-machine, running up girls' petticoats for Mrs Henshaw's nieces. 'You remember me mentioning I wanted to put something better into my life than working the halls?'

Jess glanced up from the yards of fine white cotton, but she kept the treadle moving. The machine whirred on. 'You said to mind my own business if I remember right.'

'I never did. Or if I did, it was because I hadn't made up my mind then. I have now.' Hettie was moving on from helping Mary O'Hagan out of her terrible hole. Now she felt that she'd like to help others too. It grew harder to walk by the huddled shapes under the railway arches, and she began to loathe the effects of the demon drink as she watched the men stagger from the pub at night. Then one day, when she'd been lending Mary a hand by asking after

Tommy O'Hagan up at Waterloo Station, she fell in with a Salvation Army woman called Freda Barnes, who described the work done for the poor at her industrial home in Lambeth. 'We provide food, shelter and honest work,' she said. She told Hettie that she was going to man a stall of goods made by the inebriates in a special home set up by the Army, then back to the industrial home for an evening meeting. 'Why not come along?' she said.

Hettie went and joined in their rousing choruses to the accompaniment of a brass band. She was singing again, but this time she was singing for Jesus.

'I signed the pledge,' she told Jess. 'I took the plunge the other day. Look!'

Jess stopped treadling in surprise. She read the richly decorated card which Hettie handed to her: 'I Promise by Divine Assistance to Abstain from all Beverages that Contain Alcohol. Also from Opium and Tobacco in Every Form; and that I will not Gamble or use Profane Language, but will Strive to be Loving, Pure, and True in Thought, Word, and Deed.' Signed Hesther Parsons, 20 September 1914. 'Blimey, Ett!' Jess sat staring at the picture of cherubs against a twinkling night sky. 'What you gonna tell Pa?'

Hettie laughed. 'I ain't gone and done nothing terrible, you know.'

'Ain't you? Talk about cat among the pigeons,' she grumbled. She needed to think more carefully about Hettie's new fad.

'No, I only signed the pledge. I think it's common sense when you watch what drink does to a man. As a matter of fact, it wouldn't surprise me if drink played a part in poor Daisy's death.'

Jess nodded. She began to see the train of Hettie's thoughts.

'Pa won't mind,' Hettie cajoled. 'He likes to have the

Army come round collecting. He always dips his hand in his pocket.'

'If you're sure, Ett.' Jess couldn't picture pretty Hettie in a drab blue uniform and homely bonnet, all buttons and old-fashioned maroon bows. 'You ain't acting a bit sudden, are you?'

'"They that be wise shall shine as the brightness of the firmament,"' Hettie read out from her pledge card. 'Well, I don't know if I can be wise, Jess, but I should like to do a little bit of good!'

'Oh, Ett!' Jess stood up and embraced her. 'You've got a heart of gold, you have. Don't tell me I gotta get used to another angel in the family! Ain't Frances enough?'

'Listen, Jess, it don't mean we can't carry on being partners in the business, you know.'

'Good!' Jess smiled and went back to her work. 'These petticoats won't make themselves.' She'd been on the point of confiding to Hettie over Maurice Leigh, but the subject sounded trivial somehow alongside Hettie's momentous decision.

On the last Sunday of September, Charlie came calling for Sadie as usual, eager to show off about his new job at the cinema. He waited in the yard for her to finish tying up her hair, or whatever it was that took a girl so long to achieve between his ring on the bell and her coming down to unlock her bike from the shed, ready to set off. Sadie sent Jess to keep him company, and she was still standing in the side alley waving them off when Maurice came running up the court. She turned to go in, almost bumping into him.

'Damn!' He watched Charlie disappear up the street. 'I meant to ask him to work a couple of extra hours for me tomorrow night.' He didn't seem unduly upset about missing him, however, and turned instead into the alley with Jess. 'Are you busy today?' he asked.

She felt the same confusion; a mixture of liking, longing, fear, doubt. It twisted around her chest like a tight band whenever Maurice came near. 'I don't know yet. Why?'

'I thought we might walk out this afternoon?'

'Oh, I don't know,' she demurred.

'Why not? Don't you want to?' He put one hand over her shoulder against the high wall, leaning in, confident that she wouldn't move away. 'We got to stop meeting in these narrow places,' he joked. 'It ain't dignified. How about meeting up with me at the park gates at half two?'

Jess looked up at him, took a deep breath and nodded. 'Half two, then.' She was committed. Quickly she went up by the metal fire escape, and Maurice swung out into the street back home to his attic room.

'Nice to clap eyes on a cheerful face,' Arthur Ogden grumbled, as they crossed paths on the doorstep. 'Like a bleeding morgue in there these days if it wasn't for you.'

Maurice nodded and whistled up the stairs. He planned to polish his shoes, find a clean collar, have a shave.

Back at the Duke, Jess had to ask Florrie a favour. To her surprise, her aunt practically whirled her out of the place. 'Mind? Why should I mind? I been saying you should get out more! Of course, the others don't notice, but I do, girl! Blinded by their troubles, they are, but I seen you was looking peaky the minute I walked in. I says to myself, "That girl needs to get out!" It ain't no fun looking after a baby all by yourself, but no one knows that better than me!'

Jess smiled gratefully at her larger-than-life aunt, gearing herself up for the usual reminiscences.

'My Tom was always a sickly child, coughing and

wheezing. And there I was stuck with him after his poor father passed on. Day in, day out without a break. Oh, there's no need to tell me what it means for a mother to have to manage by herself.' She swept up and down the living-room carpet, baby Grace settled on one broad hip, little legs dangling. 'So you go and have a break, girl. Go out and enjoy yourself.'

Jess had put on her best hat; a dark-blue velvet one, and a new soft-collared white blouse. She liked the fashion of wearing a strip of dark silk around her neck like a loose man's tie; she thought it looked jaunty and modern. Her even features smiled back at her in the mirror.

Florrie came up close for a confidential whisper, though there was no one else in the room. 'You go and find yourself a nice young man. You got my blessing, and never mind about young Grace here. It don't mean you got to lock yourself away like a nun for the rest of your life!'

Jess turned to her. 'You sure, Auntie?' Florrie's early letter about the baby had sounded stiff and stern. But since her arrival on the scene, little Grace's soft dark curls, her rosebud mouth and huge dark eyes seemed to have melted the old lady's heart. 'Do you think I'm doing right?'

Florrie answered the appeal warmly. 'I know you are. You're a lovely girl, even if Wilf ain't never seen it in you. And you're only young once. So just leave me to get on with things here and you take as long as you like.' She gave Jess a wink. 'What's he like? I bet he's a bobby dazzler.'

Jess laughed and blushed. 'He is, Auntie. Well, I think so at any rate!'

Chapter Nineteen

Maurice decided that a walk in the local park wouldn't do for the type of treat he had in mind for Jess. He was ambitious for this courtship from the beginning, seeing it as something different. So he hopped her up on to one of the new 'B' type buses when it stopped at the crossroads, and they sat on the open upper deck in the rich autumn sunlight, all along the Embankment, up to the great green space of Hyde Park.

Jess felt the bus roll smoothly past splendid shops under mellow golden trees. She saw ladies walking white lap-dogs past the hotels on Park Lane, heard the rant of orators on Speakers' Corner. During all her years in service she'd had little free time for Sunday afternoon jaunts. Her time off had been spent visiting family and helping in the pub. Now she and Maurice alighted arm in arm from the bus and joined the people strolling through the iron gates.

'Oh, look!' She pointed to a corner of the park where a collection of giant hot-air balloons hovered at rest. A crowd of women in white skirts, carrying pale parasols, and men in long jackets and trilbies had gathered round. Children stood in small knots, heads craned back to study the tethered monsters. Then a gasp escaped as one took off. It rose slowly, silently over their heads into the perfect blue sky. Jess heard the 'oh!' and clutched Maurice's hand. 'Look, there's people in them things! How are they supposed to get down?'

He laughed and looped her hand through his arm. 'They just have to let some of the hot air out and down they come.'

'What if they want to go higher?'

'They chuck a couple of passengers overboard.'

They walked on happily together. 'Ever been to the seaside?' he asked, as they passed colourful posters on Magical Margate. When she shook her head his plans grew extravagant; he'd borrow a motor car if she liked, and take her on an outing to the sea. Jess was impressed that he had friends with cars. 'Talbot Invincible, that's the best one out,' he recommended. 'Say you'll come.'

But Jess made no promises. 'Ain't you got too much on with your new job?' she asked. They'd walked away from the crowd down an avenue of beech trees. Sunlight cast a dappled pattern over his face as she glanced sideways at him. 'From what I hear, your place is bursting at the seams most nights.'

'That's why I deserve a day off every so often.' His success in drawing audiences to the Gem away from the halls, with his clever mix of comedies, romances and the latest foreign epics had set him in good stead. He stopped and turned to face her. 'I ain't larking about with you, Jess. You know that?'

She nodded and received his kiss. Her arms went up round his neck, he pulled her close. There was an intense look in his dark eyes when she tried to pull away. Instead, he offered more close kisses which made her melt against him once again.

'I'm serious,' he whispered, his mouth against her neck. 'I ain't never been this serious with any girl.'

Suddenly she drew away. This was a temptation almost

too much to resist; to swoon in his arms and let herself be kissed into unconsciousness. But she had to get straight with him. The misery of getting involved and then having him break it off later when he discovered the truth would be too much to bear. She was pretty sure Maurice wasn't the type to have got involved in any of the street gossip since he came to live at the Ogdens. Yet telling him about Grace must surely finish things off before they'd truly begun. Jess struggled with her conscience. At last, self-denial, always a strong force in her, won through.

'What?' Maurice pulled at her wrist. 'Don't walk off. I said too much, I'm sorry.' He thought he'd scared her.

She hung her head. 'It ain't that.'

'What then?' He caught her round the waist and made her walk along the path with him again. 'Look, Jess, I ain't sure what's going on here.'

She saw it wasn't fair; that he might think she was teasing and leading him on. So she forced herself to try and explain. 'It's me. I told you, you don't know nothing about me.'

'And?' He watched her struggling to confess, felt certain there was nothing she could say which would alter this build up of feeling towards her. He held her close around the waist.

'You sure you ain't heard?' She looked fearfully into his eyes. 'Ain't Dolly said nothing?'

'No. Why should she?'

The corners of her mouth went down. 'It's to do with why I had to come back home to the Duke in the first place. I ain't always lived there, you know. Before you came to live in the court, I was in service.'

'Don't cry.' He offered to wipe the tears from her cheeks with the flat of his thumbs. His voice was soft and gentle.

'You know what I'm gonna say, don't you?'

He nodded. 'I think I can guess what's coming. But you gotta say it, Jess. Don't be scared.'

'All right then. I came home because of the son in that family I worked for. Gilbert Holden. He got me into trouble.' She paused, unable to go on. Then she gathered herself together. 'Pa took pity on me and took me back, thanks to Frances. You see, Maurice, it ain't just me. I got a baby to think about.'

His forehead went down on to her shoulder and he closed his eyes. 'It's all right, I ain't shocked,' he murmured.

'Ain't you? I am. I can hear myself telling you these things and I can't hardly believe it myself. I'm sorry, Maurice. I ain't never been more sorry in my life!' She tried to draw away, struggling for some scraps of dignity.

'It don't make no difference.' She was still the woman he desired. The old 'no complications' motto was good enough when you only felt things on the surface; easy come, easy go. But it didn't seem to operate now that he'd met Jess.

In some way which he couldn't put into words, the fact that she had this baby made him want her more. It moved her further away from the child-women he came across in gaggles on park benches and on the front row at the picture house, putting her into new realms of experience for him. 'Just tell me you like me, and you want to be with me,' he said, gathering her to him.

'Do you still want me?' Relief flooded through her as she stroked the short hair at the back of his head. 'I thought no one would want me now.'

He kissed her wet cheeks, her open mouth, her long neck as she raised her head. She felt the branches of the trees shift and whirl overhead. Then a sense of being out in the open, in public, brought her back to herself. She put her fingertips over his mouth. 'No, stop. Let's walk on. We gotta think,' she insisted. 'We gotta wait a couple of days for things to settle down, see how we feel.'

They walked on together, hands firmly clasped. In the distance, a silent, white hot-air balloon coasted gently to the ground.

By late autumn of 1914, war talk had taken over from the Irish problem and threats of strikes in all the East End bar rooms. Their British lads had joined the French and the Belgians to become an army of moles, tunnelling into the muddy fields around Ypres, Vimy and Neuve Chapelle. The Germans had been halted short of Paris, but only just. Now the two sides fought across barren wastes of barbed wire, and the faces of recruits lining up outside Southwark Town Hall looked less than exuberant, more resigned to a hard slog in the trenches.

Robert Parsons sent letters home, full of concern and advice over Ernie. When he addressed his letters to the whole family, he would tell of the crossing to Calais and the huge operation to shift men, horses and machines to the front. He told them to keep their chins up over Ernie; they'd have him home by Christmas once the lawyers had done their work. To himself, he hoped the promise didn't sound as hollow as the one about the war being soon over now looked from this side of the Channel. As for the war, he said, morale was good. He wouldn't have his pa thinking any different and anyway it'd never get past the censor. So he chatted on about meeting up with an old pal from the docks; George Mann. They were in the same regiment. George was strong as an ox; single-handedly he'd dragged a water cart out of the axle-deep mud, making him the sergeant-major's blue-eyed boy. They hoped to get leave together eventually, and Robert would bring George back to meet the family.

His letters to Duke alone were less gung-ho. He told him how hard it was to get a night's rest, sharing board and lodgings with rats. A recent infestation of lice also kept them awake. They were stationed half a mile west of the front in the Somme valley. You heard the big guns go off and longed to get at the Hun. But for the time being they were stalled, waiting for action.

'I got a lot of time on my hands,' he wrote. 'And I get to brooding about poor Ern. If I never took him up to the Palace that night, he'd never be in the Scrubs now. And if I'd not been in that scrap with Chalky White earlier in the day, I wouldn't have had to make myself scarce and drop Ernie right in it. That's a fact. It preys on my mind, day in, day out.'

Duke wrote back words of consolation. What was done was done. Ernie understood Robert hadn't dropped him in it on purpose. Now they'd have to rely on British justice to get him out. Meanwhile Robert must concentrate on the army and keep himself safe. He told him Hettie had taken the pledge and joined the Sally Army, and he sent his regards to George Mann. Frances believed she knew his sister, Susan, who came in for prescriptions for their mother.

Everyone brought stories of the Western Front into the bar at the Duke; of cousins killed or sent home wounded. Convalescent homes were set up in great houses in the Kent and Essex countryside, where the injured men lived the life of Riley.

'I ain't so sure.' Annie Wiggin delivered her opinion over a glass of porter. She'd taken to coming in of a tea-time, instead of scuttling off back down the court with her jug.

Her ties with Duke had strengthened over Ernie's arrest; she felt he'd appreciated her being there to lend a hand and would pick her out to confide in when the time was right. But Florrie's arrival had put her nose out of joint. The daft ha'p'orth fancied herself as her namesake, Florence Nightingale. She treated Duke as if he was sick instead of boosting him up. Annie thought Florrie was going about it the wrong way, sighing and dabbing her eyes at every mention of the court case. So she stayed put on her bar stool, following Florrie's every move behind the bar, looking out for Duke. 'It ain't no picnic over in them trenches,' she pointed out. 'And it ain't a nice thing to be sitting in them hospitals with your legs blown off, even if there is roses climbing up the bleeding walls!'

'That ain't very nice,' Florrie sniffed. 'Them boys is heroes in my eyes. I bet they feel proud, no matter what. I'd feel proud if my Tom joined up, then came home wounded, I can tell you.'

Annie looked sceptical. She glanced round to check that Duke was at the far end of the bar out of earshot. 'Your Tom's way too old even to enlist,' she reminded her. 'So there ain't no danger to his limbs exactly. Easy to say you'd be proud when he's just about ready to go down the Post Office and draw the pension what nice Mr Asquith's handing out.'

Florrie took the bait. Her expression flashed outrage at Annie. 'My Tom's fit as a fiddle!'

'And not a day under forty.'

'That's a lie!'

'Forty if he's a day. And what does that make you, Florrie Searles? You're pushing seventy for all your fancy blouses.'

Florrie leaned over the bar towards her skinny opponent.

Her bosom settled on its mahogany surface, squat and steady behind its whalebone plating. 'Say that once more, Annie Wiggin, and I'll throttle you!'

'You and whose army? We all know you, Florrie. We remember you from the old days, poking your nose in where it's not wanted. And just look at you now, girl. Who you trying to kid with all them beads and bits and pieces? Come down my stall and I'll deck you out with something more suited to your situation!' She was scornful of Florrie's attempts to dress like a woman half her age, and snorted whenever she saw her begin to flirt with Duke's customers. When you were over the hill, you ought to have the guts to recognize it, Annie reckoned. As for herself, she still had a bit of life in her. Florrie Searles was a good fifteen years older than her.

'Look at you!' Florrie's foghorn voice floated over Arthur Ogden's head. Duke glanced around. 'Them boots you wear is a disgrace for a start. Can't you take no better care of yourself, Annie, and show a bit of self-respect?'

'Them's my old man's boots!' Annie stood up, face to face. 'As if you didn't know. They're a keepsake, so you keep your nose out!'

Florrie had hit a raw nerve, and she knew it. 'Keepsake? What the bleeding hell do you want to remember him for? Useless article, he was, going off and leaving you in the lurch!' Florrie's throat and chest were flushed red with the effort of hurling insults. She'd never liked Annie's snappy, whippet-like ways, and she liked her even less now that she'd obviously set her sights on Duke. The poor bloke needed protecting, especially since he was so down over Ernie. Annie might catch him at a low point and he'd find himself doing and saying things he'd regret.

'My old man was lost at sea,' Annie said with fierce dignity. She held her head high and her shoulders back.

'Lost at bleeding sea, nothing! Lost in the arms of another woman, more like!'

Annie saw red. But she wouldn't descend to fisticuffs. She'd stick the knife in where it hurt instead. 'Them who lives in glass houses,' she began. She rolled her eyes and stuck her tongue in her cheek.

Florrie choked. 'You go and wash your mouth out,' she threatened. 'Thomas was a good husband to me before the consumption came and took him after we moved to Brighton for the sea air and all.'

'Consumption!' It was Annie's turn to gloat. 'Thomas Searles was a weedy little bloke all right, but it weren't the consumption what took him off, believe you me.' She winked at Arthur, who enjoyed this from a ringside seat. 'Her problem is she's got all twisted up in her mind about what's true and what ain't. She thinks her old man popped his clogs from consumption, she really does. She thinks she's a widow woman of thirty, when she's sixty-five if she's a day. She even thinks she's worth turning round in the street for a second look, but just have a gander at her close up!'

'Oh!' Florrie had gone purple with helpless rage. Small, strangled noises were emitted from her throat, the scarlet silk flowers in her hair trembled uncontrollably. 'Oh, I ain't feeling well,' she whispered to Arthur, clutching at her bodice. And she retired upstairs hurt.

Annie looked down her nose after her. 'Serve her right.'

'But it ain't true, is it?' Arthur wanted to know. He'd never fancied Florrie Searles as deserted wife material.

'Every word is God's honest truth,' Annie insisted with utter sincerity.

Arthur took his half-empty glass and went off to chat with Duke. 'All over a pair of boots,' he ruminated, eyeing the shapeless offending articles on Annie's feet. 'I dunno,

245

women fall out over some bleeding stupid things once their dander's up.'

Arthur spoke from bitter experience. His house echoed with the small artillery fire between mother and daughter ever since Dolly had found out how badly Amy had let her down. She picked fault with the way the girl sat, ate and breathed. She criticized her dress, her manner, her laziness in not finding work. The more she went on, the more Amy dug in her stubborn heels. She didn't get out of bed until eleven, then spent an hour or more at her bedroom mirror. Perhaps she'd meet up with her old mates from Coopers' at dinner time, then she'd walk on alone up to other department stores to study the goods which she had no means of affording. Evenings were spent joining up with her pals again, to hang around street-corners or outside the picture houses where they hoped for someone in the money to come along and stand them a treat.

Amy's reputation had nosedived indeed when the truth emerged about her involvement with Teddy Cooper. He bragged about his clever way of compromising her for good on that second night, feeling that it showed his clear-headedness as well as his way with women. His own friends smirked and congratulated him, while the girls Amy hung around with turned up their noses. 'Oh, Amy, how could you?' Emmy protested. 'Ain't once on the big office desk enough for you, girl?'

But Amy found she could ride out this level of disapproval, and even began to turn the episode to her advantage amongst girls younger than Emmy and Dora. She gave out the story that Teddy had found her irresistible, and that she'd used her charms to screw some money out of the poor sod. This hard veneer gave her a certain status with little Lettie Harris who'd taken over Amy's job in hats, and with other girls still at school or just on the very bottom rung of the work ladder. 'He ain't such a catch, I can tell you,' she intimated. 'He thinks he's big with all the girls, but he don't know they only put up with him 'cos he's the boss's son and they have to.'

Outside work, the girls were bolder, especially in their street-corner gangs. Led by Amy, they stood outside the Southwark Gem one night in mid-October, dropping snide, giggling remarks as Teddy and two or three cronies swaggered down the pavement into the cinema. Their brash, broad smiles antagonized the girls. 'Who do they think they are?' they muttered, watching the men's backs as they paid at the box-office window. 'Bleeding Prince Charming?' Amy had already caught Teddy's eye and brazened it out. He wasn't so high and mighty that she couldn't try and get her own back, after all. 'Come here, Lettie,' she whispered. All the girls huddled round. Before long, they'd despatched pretty Lettie to worm her way into the picture house along with Teddy and the boys. 'Ten o'clock, round the back,' they reminded her. 'Make sure you bring him all on his ownio!'

At ten, they waited quietly down the alley, tight in against the blank, high wall. Amy had managed to whip up feeling against the boss's son almost to fever pitch. Every girl had recounted a story about his ugly behaviour. Most had come out of it better than Amy, but more by luck than judgement. All detested his groping, hot-breathed presence. Amy was good at stoking up their guilty disgust. 'Might as well be pieces of meat on a slab for all he cares,' she said.

So they braved the cold autumn night, prepared to stick it out and help take him down a peg or two. They weren't sure how things would work out, but they longed to turn Teddy Cooper into a figure of fun, if only for one night, down here in the dark alley.

'What if he recognizes us?' Olwyn Williams wanted to

know. She worked in a department at Cooper's which made men's shirts. She was plump and homely, but this hadn't disqualified her from attracting Teddy's unwelcome attentions. 'Will he get us the sack?'

Amy laughed, then shivered. Vanity had kept her in her figure-hugging summer jacket long after the season was past. 'He won't dare say nothing, or he'd never live it down!' She longed to get her own back for one brief moment.

The others laughed too, making an echo down the hollow passage between two high walls. Then someone said, 'Hush!' as footsteps approached.

They made out Teddy's tall, slim figure in silhouette, backed by street-lights up on St Thomas Street. He had draped himself all over Lettie, whose head scarcely came up to his shoulder. Giggling and leaning her body towards him, she led him out of the yellow pool of light into deep shadow.

Teddy was intent on the task. Lettie was so small and slight she wouldn't put up much of a fight. He'd sent on the friends he'd arrived with, intending to catch up with them in a pub after an hour or so. She was a bit skinny and underdeveloped, but she seemed willing, so he'd come for swift satisfaction. He pressed himself against her, scarcely bothered with preliminaries such as talking and kissing.

He had Lettie backed up against the blank wall and she was beginning to struggle, just as a fierce finger poked him in the back. He grunted and swung round, expecting a drunken onlooker come to share the fun. Instead, he was confronted by five or six grinning, jeering girls.

'Charming, I'm sure,' one of them said, staring down at his state of undress.

Teddy fumbled with the buttoms at the waistband of his trousers as Lettie slipped sideways to join the row. They all stood, hands on hips or arms linked, summing him up. He recognized Amy Ogden as the ringleader. 'Oh, very funny, Amy. I expect this is your idea.' He was so livid he didn't see the danger, only the ridicule. He moved forward to shove through their rank and head off up the alley.

But Amy stood her ground and thrust him back by the shoulder. With her other hand she snatched at his shirt and dragged it free of the loosened waistband. Then she shoved him again. He felt the cold wall with the flat of both hands. He lunged forward once more.

This time, Lettie and Olwyn stood in his way. The Welsh girl stared him in the face, eyes glinting, a sarcastic smile twisting her mouth. She reached her fingers inside his collar, wrenched it and tore it free. He heard the studs snap the collar and hit the ground in the shocked silence that followed. Olwyn glanced round at Amy, who nodded approval.

The group moved in closer. 'Ain't so cocky now, is he?' a voice jeered, high and excited. 'He won't go round bragging after we finished with him.'

'Not if we show him we mean business,' Amy said. She stepped to the front of the semi-circle. 'Let's see how big and strong you are now, Mister Teddy Cooper!' Standing there with her full lips parted, her eyes gleaming with hatred, she defied him to strike out at her.

When he did, with a savage, slicing blow at waist height, she was ready. She plunged sideways, twisted and caught him round the middle to drag him off balance. His legs shot from under him, grabbed by other hands which began to tear at his clothes. He felt his shirt ripped open. The women's hands clutched and pulled at him, then one dug in her nails. He kicked and punched back, face upwards on the ground under the flailing arms and flying hair. Soon they had the clothes from his back. He rolled on to his side, trying to curl and cling on to his trousers which were halfway down his buttocks. Fists pounded his ribs, nails snatched at him as each girl fought to aim her blow. They shrieked with savage energy, fuelled by the unique satisfaction of having him at their mercy. 'Get them off me!' he cried at Amy. 'Do you want them to kill me?'

She stood back to look at the writhing heap of bodies; arms pummelling at Teddy's naked white flesh. His face and chest were scored red. He'd had enough, she decided. Coolly she went and hammered on the fire-exit door, and as help came she cleared her friends off. They ran wildly up the alley, screaming with victory. Olwyn clutched Teddy's collar like a trophy. They ran laughing and gasping on to the tram that rattled its way towards them down the street.

In response to the violent hammering on the door at the back of the cinema, Maurice Leigh wrenched open the iron bolts which he'd just locked. He darted into the alley in time to see silhouetted figures of laughing girls, and on the ground the groaning, nearly naked figure of a man.

He picked him up, recognized him at once, offered his own coat and took him inside. Teddy Cooper was a mess; severely bruised and scratched. Maurice suggested calling the police, but Cooper refused. 'It's nothing. Just telephone this number and get my father to send the car for me.' He wrote down a number for Maurice on a piece of office paper. The pain of the scratches was nothing compared with the blow to his pride, and he wouldn't forget the hyena faces of those women as they laid into him. He shivered inside another man's coat, clutching his torn clothes, covered in claw marks.

Maurice quietly made the necessary arrangements. He was alarmed by what had happened. Skirmishes like this could give the Gem a bad reputation, so he didn't push to involve the police. He knew enough about Cooper to guess that he probably deserved what had happened. Still, Maurice didn't like it when women turned nasty. His sympathy for Cooper's ex-girlfriends didn't extend to condoning what they'd done; as a man he had to back male vanity by giving it a stiff drink and hustling it half-naked into the car sent over from Richmond.

He stood on the pavement watching Teddy being driven off with his jacket round his shoulders. I expect that's the last I'll see of that, he reflected. Back to the pawn shop for a decent replacement. The man had had his come-uppance and no doubt his family would patch him up. It was time they sorted him out and put a stop to his antics with women, though. Maurice went and locked up the cinema, arriving back at his lodgings at the same time as Amy Ogden returned home after an innocent evening out with the girls.

Chapter Twenty

Next day, Edith Cooper was closeted with her husband, Jack, in the office of their department store. She sat opposite him at the great desk, determined to stay put until he gave her an answer. It wasn't her habit to make confrontations, but she'd considered things long and hard, and knew something must be done about Teddy.

'Why can't you leave him to me?' Jack asked. He drummed the desk with his fingers. 'You'll only get out of your depth, Edith, I'm warning you. This business is better dealt with by me.'

She sighed. 'I've left it to you for twenty-three years, Jack, ever since Teddy was born. But now I feel I have to put my foot down.'

Jack Cooper glared at his wife. Their relationship, stormy in the beginning, had levelled out over the years to one of mutual non-interference. As prosperity increased, so did the veneer of politeness, in direct inverse proportion to the passion they'd once felt. Jack might bully his work-force, fleece his suppliers and browbeat his rivals, but he would go home each night and listen attentively to Edith's tribulations over the upstairs maid. He dressed for dinner, complimented her housekeeping and learned not to swear in front of her ladies' sewing circle.

For her part, Edith willingly paid the price for going up

in the world. She didn't expect to play a part in the core of her husband's life, his drapery store, as long as she was left to her own devices of spending money on clothes and house. She had quiet, refined tastes and a placid temperament which had let certain things slide, she now realized. But when Teddy had come home last night with most of his clothes gone and his face scratched red raw by a gang of vengeful shop-girls, her tolerance reached its limit. 'It's a terrible thing to be ashamed of your own son,' she told Jack. 'I asked myself what Teddy could possibly have done to deserve what they did to him, but I can't bear to think about it.' Her eyes began to water and she reached in her bag for a handkerchief.

'See, you should leave it to me and not bother your head over it. Don't worry, I'll have a heart to heart with him when I get the chance.' Jack chewed the end of an unlit cigar. His own view was that Teddy just wasn't careful enough, even after the warning he'd received over the Ogden girl. What he got up to was his own business, but he was a fool for being indiscreet.

'What good will it do this time or any other time?' Edith had taken the plunge by coming into the store especially to discuss this. At home, surrounded by fire-screens and occasional tables and all the gadgetry which was the fruit of Jack's labours, she could never pluck up the courage. The more impersonal atmosphere of the office gave her the necessary determination. 'No, Jack, I want you to do something about his behaviour. I want to be able to hold my head up when I come through the store, knowing that he's behaving himself like a gentleman.'

'How's that?' Jack snorted. He might aspire to the status himself, at least in outward show, but he also scorned many of the gentlemanly attributes, such as fair play and openness.

'You know very well what I'm talking about.' Edith wouldn't let herself be thrown off course. 'I want you to *do* something, Jack!'

The stout shop-owner's patience, fragile at best, began to give way. He stood and leaned forward, resting his knuckles on the desk. 'For God's sake, woman, what do you mean, "do something"? He's a grown man, in case you'd forgotten. He goes his own way. Do you think I want him bringing down the family name and trampling it in the mud down all these filthy back courts and yards? Course not. I brought him up better, and God knows it cost me plenty. But I don't see what I'm supposed to "do" about it, as you put it. It's his choice, ain't it?'

'But listen to me, Jack.' She got up and walked agitatedly back and forth between the desk and the door. 'I'm not just speaking out of turn here. I've an idea that there is something we can do to rescue Teddy from himself.'

Her husband snorted again. 'You've been reading too many novels,' he declared. '"Rescue Teddy from himself"!'

Edith was stung. 'If they're not the right words, it's only because what your son gets up to is too filthy to describe! If you want me to be plain, I'll ask you a question. Do you want him to go on dragging girls down the back of cinemas or using his key to bring them up here for his pleasure? One night he'll go too far and the police will arrest him and put him in prison. Is that what you want?'

'Using his key?' Cooper had begun to parrot his wife's words, this time in disbelief.

'Yes. Don't you bother to keep your ears open at all? It's what the girls say when they whisper in corners; that he uses your whisky from that cupboard there to get them drunk, and then he uses this very desk to . . .!' She broke down. 'I can't say it. I didn't believe it when I first heard the rumour, so I asked directly; three or four of the women who work here for you. Then I had to believe it.' She hid her face in her hands and gave a shudder.

Jack Cooper slammed his cigar into the ashtray, making the glass paperweight bounce and rock. 'I'll horsewhip him! I will, I'll flog him!' He went and looked wildly along the shelves of the cupboard where he kept his drink, then turned with a look of violent disgust. 'Where is he? Still licking his wounds at home, I expect.' He wrenched the telephone off the hook, ready to yell his home number through to the telephonist.

'No, Jack, I want to explain my idea.' Edith's self-control was restored. She thought she could use his outrage to force a decision, so she made him replace the telephone and listen. 'I want Teddy to join the war effort. It's a good, decent thing for him to do. The army will give him some discipline for a start, and that will be something he'll never lose. Besides, Lord Kitchener tells us all young men should serve. That's true, isn't it? It's their duty. Teddy's fit and able-bodied.' She spoke quietly and firmly, ignoring Jack's sarcastic grunt. 'I've thought it all through. You could get him a commission, then he won't have to go into the ranks. I wouldn't want that. Conditions would be better for him, he'd earn the men's respect, it would change his whole life. Listen, Jack, I don't think we'd ever need worry about him again!'

Rattled more by the fact that Teddy continued to risk the firm's reputation than by the red-blooded activities themselves, Jack Cooper listened and brooded. 'How are we going to get him into uniform if he don't want to?' He was beginning to see the good side of the plan, and if he was honest with himself, he knew he could easily do without his son's so-called help around here. But he didn't see how you could force someone to join a war, commission or not.

Edith had thought of that too. 'You hold the purse strings, don't you? If you cut off his allowance, he'll go to France soon enough.' She spoke steadily, coolly.

Jack thrust his head back and stared at the wood panelling on the ceiling. His eyes darted from side to side. Edith had sewn this up nicely; he wouldn't have believed she had it in her. At last he nodded. 'Right then, I'll put it to him.'

'When?'

'When I get the chance.' He began to shuffle papers into order on the desk.

'If I know you, the war will be over and done with before you get the chance, Jack Cooper. I want you to talk to Teddy tonight.' She stuck fast until he agreed. Then she gathered her bag and gloves.

'It's a hard mother who sends her only son off to war, you know that?' Jack got in a sour dig in retaliation for the way he'd been so successfully manoeuvred.

Edith looked him in the eye. 'And it's a soft father who turns a blind eye to all his shenanigans.'

They stared at each other, then called a truce. Edith went down through the store dignified as usual, pausing for a word with the supervisors in various departments, stopping again on the pavement outside the main entrance to drop coppers from her purse into Hettie's Salvation Army collection box.

Hettie recognized the store-owner's wife and immediately drew her into conversation. There was a family down Paradise Court, she said, who'd suffered a lot of bad luck. 'You heard the business about Daisy's murder, I expect?' She approached the subject frankly, not meaning to disconcert Mrs Cooper.

The fair woman's complexion flushed bright red. 'The music-hall girl?' Uneasily she put her purse back in her bag, fearful that Teddy could be dragged into yet another scandal over a girl.

'Yes, Daisy O'Hagan. Well, her family ain't taking it too well. They live down my street and they're pretty much cut up about it.'

Edith Cooper overcame her discomfiture and nodded. 'How do you want me to help?'

'There's a lot of mouths to feed, and Mary ain't up to it all by herself. Joe, her husband, would take work if he could get it, but they already turned him down at Tooley Street. I wondered if there was anything he could turn his hand to here?' Hettie glanced back at the shiny, fatly stocked windows. 'Just a little job would do for a start.'

Edith promised to try, though she didn't normally interfere with her husband's workforce. Hettie's sincerity had affected her. Hepton drove off through the dingy, cold street while she sat on the leather upholstery, looking to right and left at the stall-holders, flower and newspaper sellers, crossing sweepers and children picking at gutters. Helping one family wasn't much, she reflected. Still, she would try, if only to resist Jack's accusation that her heart had frazzled up and died during these years of plenty.

She went home to prepare the way with Teddy. He was in a weak position, and even his confidence was knocked by the livid scars and humiliation at the hands of Amy Ogden. Edith thought she could manage to carry the day. Teddy would look good in uniform and she would be able to speak of him with pride.

All through October, Hettie was the one in the Parsons family who most often braved the bleak walls and metal gangways of the prison. She went two or three times a week to the remand wing, sometimes taking Duke to see

Ernie, sometimes going with Jess. But Jess had taken on the task of visiting people round about to see what she could dig up about the murder. Though she'd drawn a blank with Teddy Cooper, she still had names on her list, and planned to see Fred Mills, the manager at the Palace. 'The coppers don't care,' she told Hettie in a bitter voice. 'They interviewed a few witnesses and they think it's cut and dried. As far as they're concerned, Ernie did it and that's that.'

As Hettie sat across the table from Ernie in her navy-blue Army uniform, she held his hand tight. 'We're gonna pray to Jesus, Ern,' she said fervently. 'He's the one what watches over us, even in the bad times. You gotta believe that. We're gonna march under the banner of Jesus, you and me, and He ain't gonna let us down!'

Ernie nodded. He'd remembered to pray, like Hettie taught him on her last visit. It was someone to talk to in his lonely cell late at night, and Hettie promised that He heard and would answer his prayers. The warders would look in on him through the grille and shake their hard heads. The lad mouthed his prayers audibly. 'Lord, keep me safe and send me home to my pa.'

In the earnestness of her new-found religion, Hettie taught him the psalm which brought her most comfort in her hour of need. 'The Lord is my shepherd,' she began. Ernie repeated after her, phrase by phrase. 'I shall not want.'

'I shall not want.'

'He maketh me to lie down in green pastures.'

'He maketh me . . .'

'To lie down.'

'To lie down.'

'In green pastures.'

Ernie nodded again and completed the line. He liked to

258

think of green fields and still waters. He wanted to dwell in the house of the Lord for ever.

Their dream was interrupted on one occasion in early November by the arrival of the solicitor, Mr Sewell. He was a short, balding man, decisive in his movements, with a confident, cheerful voice. He introduced himself to Hettie, then told Ernie some news. 'We have a date set for the trial at last.' He drew up another chair and sat at the table. 'It's going to be the tenth of December, so that gives us more than another month to prepare.'

Hettie heard the date and felt it etch itself painfully in her mind. She smiled to reassure Ernie. 'See, it'll soon be over. Don't you worry.'

Mr Sewell was brisk. 'I've received a letter this morning from your brother Robert in France. He tells me that the prosecution counsel doesn't plan to drag him away from the front line to stand as a witness for them. So I'm going to ask for his written testimony to use in your defence, Ernie. I'm sure it will corroborate – back up – your own account of your movements that night. I'll also ask him to provide a character reference, which should help us a great deal.' He gave the sister a quick glance. 'Does he understand what I say?'

Hettie shook her head. 'I doubt it. Still, you go ahead, I'll explain it to Ern later. What about Rob's letter. *Will* it help?'

'The jury will have to take it into account. It looks very good, coming from a member of our armed forces, patriotism being what it is now there's a war on. Our job is to build up a picture of a respectable family background, you see, to impress members of the jury.'

Hettie nodded. Sewell's talk made the trial all too real. Though she was cheerful for Ernie's sake, she went home full of fear. Ernie's life lay in the hands of twelve strangers. What would they see when they came into court? Who would they believe?

The setting of a date for the trial for the 10th sent Jess straight away up to Hettie's old haunt, the Southwark Palace. She left Duke to keep an eye on Grace, since Florrie was out at the market. Joxer could easily manage the trickle of early afternoon custom. It was Saturday; a match day. Jess could be over there and home again before the football crowd filtered back through the streets into the pubs. Grace sat, plump and content, on her grandfather's knee. 'If she cries, you can give her a spoonful of that mashed veg.' Jess buttoned her emerald-blue coat and put on her velvet hat. 'Auntie Florrie won't be long down the market. Do you think you can manage here?'

Duke rallied to something like his old self. 'I ain't completely useless yet, you know.' He jiggled Grace up and down, making her smile and gurgle. 'Her and me get on like a house on fire, don't we, girl?'

'She can go down for a nap if she looks sleepy,' Jess advised, hovering by the door.

Duke growled at her to get going. Baby Grace reminded him of Sadie as a child, dark and definite. She'd soon let him know if she was unhappy. 'I'll manage here. You run along on your errand, girl; quick before I change my mind.'

Jess's arrival at the music hall coincided with the end of a matinée performance. The cheerful crowd spilled on to the street; mainly family groups all dressed up for the occasion. They bantered and inexpertly repeated jokes they'd heard onstage. Jess shuddered to think this must have been the scene on the night of the murder, with Ernie lost in just such a crowd.

She waited until it dispersed. She'd picked this time to talk to Fred Mills because she knew from Hettie that the manager never went home between the afternoon and evening shows. He took tea in his office, brought in from a pie stall, and ate it tucked away behind the main foyer, counting the afternoon takings and dividing up the wages. Jess was bound to find him there.

As she walked in under the giant circular chandelier, she crossed paths with a fat, dapper man in spats, who raised his trilby hat and asked if she needed any help. She asked the way to the manager's office. 'Certainly, this way please.' The man grinned and turned on his shiny heel. She followed him across the crimson carpet. 'Who shall I say wants him?'

Jess held her little leather bag neatly in front of her. 'Jess Parsons, Hettie Parsons's sister.'

Archie Small stopped dead in his tracks. He raised his eyebrows and studied the visitor. 'You're not looking for employment, I take it?' She lacked the sister's style. Though she was good-looking in a striking, sultry sort of way, he couldn't imagine her treading the boards for a living like Hettie.

'No, I came on a personal matter.' Jess coloured up with suppressed irritation. 'If you'd just let Mr Mills know I'm here.'

But Archie thrust both hands deep in his pockets and began to circle round her. 'Personal matter? Connected with Daisy O'Hagan, by any chance?' He knew they'd arrested Hettie's simpleton of a brother for the murder. A visit from another sister could only upset the applecart and bring the police poking their noses back in.

Things had died down nicely, as far as Archie was concerned. He didn't want questions asked about his relationships with the ladies of the chorus line. They were murky to say the least. Archie exchanged promises of work for favours from the girls; they all lived in the knowledge that he was well in with the manager and could get them kicked out at a moment's notice. Everyone knew how the system worked, except for Archie's wife, Clemmie. He didn't much want to have to face her if the truth came out. Clemmie had a bruising side to her nature. Besides, if the police realized he'd been pestering Daisy, they might drag him in as a fresh suspect. 'I should let sleeping dogs lie if I was you,' he advised Jess. 'Instead of barging in here demanding to see Mr Mills.'

'I ain't barging in.' Jess stood her ground. She looked around to see if she could spot a sign on the manager's door. She set off towards it. 'I just want to speak to him.'

Archie stepped smartly in front of her. 'I don't really think you do.' He was wondering what to say to get rid of her when Mr Mills's door opened and the manager himself came out. Jess tried to side-step. 'I'm telling you you can't go in there without an appointment,' he blustered, catching at her arm.

'Losing your touch, Archie?' Fred Mills asked with a cool smile. His unbuttoned jacket showed an expanse of starched white shirt and braces. He wore his dark wavy hair slicked back and he ducked his head forward in an insinuating way. Nothing he had to say seemed sincere. 'How can I help?' He gestured Jess out of the way into the office, allowing Archie to slip in and close the door after her.

Inside Mills's cluttered, poky office, Jess explained her mission. There was a heavy iron safe in one corner, and a stack of light bulbs in cardboard boxes against the wall. A metal shade on the desk lamp cast a small pool of light, leaving much of the room in semi-darkness, since there was no window. More of a cupboard than an office, it was Mills's domain, reflecting much about his slapdash, penny-pinching way. 'You know they arrested our brother, Ernie, for Daisy's murder, Mr Mills. The trial comes up next month, and we all have to do what we can to help get him off.'

Mills let her speak, but he was already discounting her. No need for Archie to get hot under the collar; he could deal with the girl easily enough. She lacked guile, she just came out with things straight. But if she wanted someone at the Palace to give her another little fact, a tiny piece of evidence to get her brother off, she must look elsewhere. Like Archie, he preferred things the way they were. 'What can I do, Miss Parsons?' He expressed concern, but he was half turned away, riffling through papers on his desk.

Jess heard the other man light up a cigar, and felt its pungent smoke prick her nostrils. The room was tiny and claustrophobic. 'I want to know more about that night, Mr Mills; what you found when you checked things through with the police, anything unusual that you couldn't quite place, either before or after Daisy got killed.'

Mills glanced up. 'A proper little Sherlock Holmes, ain't you? You ain't thinking of interfering with a prosecution witness, are you, Miss Parsons?'

Hastily Jess shook her head. 'Course not. Only I thought, since you was the one here inside the place when Ett discovered poor Daisy lying there, that you'd want to help. I ain't asking you to do nothing wrong, am I?' She was shocked at the idea. 'If you was me, you'd want to do your best for Ern, wouldn't you?'

Archie came up from behind. 'Listen, girl, you can't go asking Mr Mills to tell you more than he already told the coppers. What he told them's gonna come out at the trial, clear as daylight. If I was you, I'd go on home and talk things through with Ett.' He paused, drew deep on his cigar and exhaled. 'Lovely girl, that. What's she doing with herself these days?'

Jess's heart sank. She ignored the lecherous comedian as best she could. 'For Ernie's sake, Mr Mills, ain't there nothing at all that'd help? Who was Daisy hanging round with that week? Who'd want to meet up with her after the show?'

Mills looked Archie in the eye and grinned. 'A whole football team, I shouldn't wonder, Miss Parsons. She was a popular girl. Like I said, I think you should ask your sister. She knew Daisy better than most.'

'I already done that! What do you think, that I'd come over here without talking to Ett?' Jess's indignation rose to the surface. In her innocence she'd believed that people at the Palace would want to help them. Now she saw they had reasons for wanting to hide things. She turned on Archie Small. 'You was one of them!' she accused. 'According to Ett, you was one what fancied having a fling with Daisy!'

The man backed off, then he wheedled. 'Other way round as a matter of fact. Daisy O'Hagan went after anything wearing trousers, if you want to know. I had to tell her to keep her hands off me; I'm a married man.' Beads of sweat glistened on his forehead. His cigar glowed, then he was masked again by a cloud of blue-grey smoke.

Jess struggled to choke back her anger. She swung round to face Mills, finding herself sandwiched between them in this muggy, confined space.

'I'd be more careful what I said if I was you,' Mills said smoothly. 'It might just backfire in front of a jury, and the family of the dear departed might have to listen to some awkward facts about their darling girl.' He buttoned his jacket. 'Now then, if you'll excuse me, I've got a show to put on.' He pressed by her with an empty smile, then hung on a moment longer by the door. 'We know how you feel, believe me. I don't even blame you for having a go. I wish you luck on the day. But if your brother did go all haywire and do the poor girl in, like the coppers say, you ain't doing no good going round putting people's backs up, are you?'

'Leave it to the lawyers,' Archie cut in. 'They can talk the hind leg off a bleeding donkey and bore everyone to death. With a bit of luck they'll get a not-guilty verdict for him just so we can all go home!'

His false cheerfulness disgusted her. 'We need more than luck!' She stalked out into the foyer. 'What we need is the truth!' Her cheeks burned as she glared at them both. 'And it seems to me that it's in short supply around here!'

Her anger only died away in the cold evening air. When she finally got rid of their grinning, furtive faces from her mind's eye, she shook with fresh doubt. She feared that she'd done more harm than good again as she went home to confess to Frances that her search for new evidence had led to a dead end, or worse.

Ever since Ernie's arrest, Frances had kept herself in touch with the outside world through her meetings and her work. Her nerves were strung out, but she kept up the front of continuing to cope because giving in was not an idea that ever crossed her mind. She wasn't a crier or a shouter, except over her big split with Duke, when they'd leapt to opposite sides of a giant chasm over the window-smashing at Coopers'. She was a doer. If anything, she worked harder now in the pharmacy, kept herself abreast of preparations for the trial, and attended more meetings.

Her friend, Rosie, kept a watchful eye on her. 'Don't wear yourself out,' she advised. It was the evening of Jess's failed mission to the Palace. 'You have to take care of yourself, Frances, whatever happens.'

'Oh, I'm never ill, I'm not the type.' Frances sat in the coffee room at the lecture hall after a talk by the brilliant

Elizabeth Garrett Anderson on the need for better health care for women. Rosie had encouraged her to attend. 'I got the constitution of an ox.'

Rosie looked doubtful. She was a cheerful, practical woman, perversely enjoying the war effort because her training as a nurse was proving immediately useful. She felt herself moving for ever out of the trap of factory work and marriage. 'I ain't never seen an ox look this pale and thin,' she said. 'In fact, I got patients with shell-shock at the hospital looking healthier than you.'

'Thanks!' Frances stirred her coffee.

'Don't mention it.' Rosie laughed and got up from the table. 'Speaking of which, I gotta go to work on the night shift. Are you walking that way?'

Frances looked up at the wall clock. 'No, I'll hang on here. I want to speak to Billy about defence witnesses for Ernie. He's seeing Mr Sewell after a class upstairs.'

Her companion nodded. 'Don't wait too long. It's late already. And get him to walk you home. It ain't safe if you leave it too late.'

'Says who?' Frances appreciated her concern. She smiled warmly.

'Says me. Here's Billy now. I'll leave you in his tender care. Look after her, Billy. She's worn herself out as usual.' Rosie sailed out, the picture of health.

Billy took her place at the bare table with a look of concern. 'You sure you're all right?' His heart went out to her. 'She's right, you look done in.'

'The next person to tell me that had better watch out,' she warned. 'Now, what did Mr Sewell say?'

Billy discussed the latest tactics; Hettie must be prepared to be called as chief witness for the defence, since they only had Robert's written statement.

'Will Ern be called to give evidence?' Frances tried to consider how he would cope.

'It ain't been decided yet. Mr Sewell ain't sure about the prosecution line. They could chew Ernie up good and proper. On the other hand, he's working hard at getting him to remember more about what went on at the stage door. If he can do that, it could help the defence case to hear Ernie give his version. Sewell says we'll wait and see. He says he'll discuss it with you if you call into his office.' Billy delivered all the information without once taking his eyes off her face.

Frances put on her gloves and got up to go. The wall behind her was lined with red and blue books, a gaslight on the side wall shone its soft light on her face and made a halo of her hair. People passed downstairs and through the entrance hall, hidden from view. Suddenly Billy seized her hand and came to stand close by her. She didn't react.

'I ain't got no right,' he began. One arm was around her shoulder. 'Tell me I ain't!'

'That's right, Billy, you ain't.' Gently she tried to extricate herself. She felt a fool. How had she missed the signs of his interest, to be taken so much by surprise now? Was it that she'd given up thinking of herself as a desirable woman? She had one hand against his chest, the other clasped in his at waist level, forming a barrier between them. 'We mustn't mix things up. It'll ruin us!'

But he felt he'd stepped off the edge of a cliff. He'd trodden this path for a long time; studying Frances, watching her, helping her. He could have gone on for a lifetime; only, as she slid her slim white hand into her glove, his heart had missed its footing and gone tumbling down. He kissed her long and hard.

Their simplicity went smash. She found she liked his

kiss, and he knew she liked it. She couldn't say it was a mistake and go back to how they were. New knowledge got in the way. Slowly she drew away, searching in his face for what they should do next.

Billy put his hand to her face and held his palm against it. Not for the first time he told himself that he was forty-three years old; a newspaper vendor with a sick wife, a mother-in-law and a discontented outlook. No catch for someone like Frances. He wanted to turn back the clock ticking overhead, not five minutes, but twenty years. He wanted his time over again.

Frances reached up and held the hand that stroked her face.

'Would you have me?' he whispered.

She nodded. 'If things were different, yes.' Her voice was full of longing.

'Will you have me as it is?'

Her heart jumped at the directness of the question. How many women said 'yes' on the spur of despair? 'No, Billy, how can I?'

He let his hand drop to his side. 'Like I said, I ain't got no right.'

The caretaker trawled the building for people left gossiping in classrooms. His footsteps approached the coffee room.

'But we'll be friends,' Frances said hurriedly, with no experience of the torment involved.

He nodded. 'We'll try.' He had a better idea of the misery in store behind that harmless phrase.

She gathered herself and went out into the hallway before him. The caretaker shuffled towards them, ushered them out and locked the door against them.

Billy walked Frances to the corner of Duke Street as usual. When they parted, exhaustion overtook her. She arrived home at last and met Duke toiling his way up from the cellar, preparing to close down the empty bar. Her father looked at her strained, tragic face and held his arms wide. She sobbed silently against his chest, before they went upstairs to join the others. They sat together until long after midnight, missing Ernie and Robert, dreading the start of the trial.

Part Three

SHOULDER
TO
SHOULDER

Chapter Twenty-One

As the winds blew through the trees in Hyde Park and tore off their golden leaves, the Parsons family hoped and prayed for a new lead that would clear Ernie. October turned into November.

'A miracle's what we need,' Florrie confided to Dolly Ogden.

'Or for Ernie to remember what did happen that night,' Annie put in.

'Exactly, a bleeding miracle,' Florrie insisted. She shook her head and went on wiping glasses at the bar. 'He always clams up when he gets into a state about something. Always has. You can't get a word out of him. Duke reckons he just blocks things out, as if they ain't never happened.' She was 'worrying herself to a shadow over him', as she told Tom on the telephone.

But Paradise Court as a whole had other events to consider. Tommy turned up one night out of the blue. It was the 5th of November. He strolled down the court, his new jacket collar turned up against the cold wind, whistling and poking his way into the alley at the back of the Duke, where he caught Charlie Ogden in a clinch with Sadie Parsons. He rattled a dustbin lid and watched them spring apart. 'Ooh, someone's clicked!' he crowed, ready to move swiftly on.

273

Charlie had been busily impressing his girlfriend with his mastery of the screen kiss. He'd studied it in detail from the projection room at the Gem; you had to draw the girl towards you by the waist, so she leaned her face back, then you craned towards her with heavy-lidded eyes and put your mouth firmly against hers, gently forcing her lips apart. It worked like a dream until Tommy O'Hagan came and interrupted them. 'Bleeding hell, Tommy!' he called out, dragging Sadie with him out into the court.

Tommy turned with a cheeky grin, relaxed and unconcerned, as if he'd just taken a stroll down the park before tea. He had more flesh on his bones and shoes on his feet, besides the new jacket. This one didn't skim his backside and fail to fasten across the chest like the other. An optimistic streak must have told him that he'd grow into this one eventually, since he was filling out nicely and losing the peaky look of the Barnardo's posters. 'Now then, Charlie, is that what they teach you at school nowadays? "Bleeding this and bleeding that"!'

Charlie approached him warily. 'Where you been, Tommy?'

'Here and there. Why, did you miss me, then?' Tommy glanced ahead towards the grim tenements. 'Blimey, the old place still looks horrible as ever, don't it?'

Sadie clutched Charlie's hand. 'Ain't you heard, Tommy?'

'Where I been I ain't heard nothing, believe me.' Tommy had taken it into his head to go downriver and look for a ship. It was a spur-of-the-moment decision; things couldn't be worse at sea than they were at home, he reckoned. He met up with a Norwegian captain and persuaded him to take him on as dogsbody on his fishing boat. They set sail straight away. After five days of throwing up and staggering about the place like a lunatic, he'd found his sea legs. In no time, the oily smell of fish had crept into every pore. All day he cleaned each cog and wheel of the old boat's engine with filthy rags, and all night they would chug and grind in his dreams. But the food made up for the grimy work, even though everything tasted of engine oil. There was plenty of it at any rate. One short voyage was enough, however, so Tommy inherited the first mate's jacket during a drunken brawl on their first night ashore, then he hightailed it back upriver.

With money in his pocket and a determination to make a success of himself before he headed home to Paradise Court, he turned his hand to wheeling and dealing on dry land. He set his sights on a barrow and a pitch outside Waterloo, his old hunting ground. So he befriended a feeble old-timer who had a fruit stall and persuaded him he'd be better off with his feet up by the fire as winter drew on. He offered him cash, of course. The old codger snatched his hand off.

Now Tommy was part of the early morning scene at Covent Garden, and all day you could hear his raucous shout between the great main archway of Waterloo Station. This evening he'd come home to show off.

He turned to Charlie. 'Why's she got a face on her? Ain't she pleased to see me?'

'Pleased as punch, Tommy,' Charlie faltered. He and Sadie fell into step beside him. 'You going straight on home?'

'Looks like it.'

Sadie tugged at Charlie's sleeve. 'Leave him be, Charlie!'

They halted, and Tommy headed on without breaking his stride. They heard him whistle a romantic tune and saw the derision of the unattached and fancy free in his swaggering walk. 'Blimey!' Charlie shook his head. 'He ain't half in for a shock.'

It made Sadie cry all over again, to imagine Mary's

haggard face as she told Tommy the news about Daisy. Charlie's hug contained nothing of the screen hero this time; he was finding it hard to hold back tears himself.

Maurice Leigh had also done some hard thinking since his golden walk in Hyde Park with Jess. In the cool light of day, the problems of being involved with a woman who had a kid in tow shone clear and sharp. He summed them up in the dreaded word, 'ties'.

For Maurice this wasn't the callow reaction of irresponsible youth. At eighteen or nineteen, perhaps, being tied down went against a natural spirit of fun and denied the opportunity all young men needed to play the field. But he was now in his late twenties, smart and successful, and outwardly in a position where a man might want to settle down with wife and family. However, life had made him wary of such a move. His Jewish background, strict and claustrophobic when his father was alive, had invited bad name-calling at school and turned him into a poor attender. There was a particular hatred of Eastern European immigrant Jews, to which group Maurice's family belonged. They survived in small, isolated pockets in areas like Bethnal Green, and he recalled all too well the heavy sentimentality of family ties and the strict moralizing which held him almost in chains and apart from other boys.

Since the work in the book-binding shop kept the family hovering only just above the desperate poverty of the homeless and jobless who roamed the East End streets at the turn of the century, Maurice quickly learned to suspect the value of his closed community. His father worked for an uncle who ran the small business; his mother's brother. He paid the men a pittance to make them stoop all week over glue and leather, doling out gold leaf for the page

edging with miserly caution. His meanness eventually cast
the fatherless family on to the street; he needed the garret
to provide lodgings for his new employee, he said. Maurice's mother begged for Marcus, Maurice's oldest brother,
to be taken on in his dead father's place, but the uncle
refused to consider it. So much for family loyalty. The
brothers lived on their wits to support themselves and their
mother in a series of run-down rooms until she too died of
tuberculosis when Maurice was just fourteen. Then he was
alone and free.

Working to survive, he primed street-lamps, got birched
so regularly at his industrial school for hopping the wag
that he soon gave up going altogether, and eventually fell
in with Monty Phillips, the pawnbroker who also ran a stall
selling secondhand clothes on the railings down the rag
fair. From here life took off. Decently dressed in other boys'
clothes, he used his spare time to gamble over cigarette
cards or to pinch a bicycle for a day to ride out into the
countryside, when he showed off his athleticism by storming ahead up the hills and freewheeling down the other
side, hands in pockets. Ditching the bike back with its
owner, he would buy a fish supper and retire to bed under
the counter at Monty's. No complications. No ties.

From this start, he'd moved on through a mixture of
opportunism and hard work into his present respectable
job. He was still convinced that his motto held good. What
did he want with a woman and a child? The difficulty was,
this wasn't just any woman. This was Jess.

He was annoyed with himself for prolonging the unfamiliar state of indecision, which had now lasted more than a
month. He and Jess danced around each other whenever
they met, half longing, half afraid. He took her out once or
twice a week, and at times the passion was intense. But the
relationship seemed to have stalled. She felt she didn't want

Maurice to see Grace; the commitment would be too great. And she worried about Ernie. For his part, Maurice worked hard at the picture palace and bided his time.

On the day after Tommy O'Hagan turned up in the court, he decided to shelve these things and go to join a session at Milo's gym. It was the nearest place to Paradise Court for a good, strenuous training bout. He was as quick with his fists as with his brain, and straight away impressed regulars, including Walter Davidson, with his clean punching and neat footwork. Maurice had finished his work-out and stood chatting with Walter and Milo himself, when Chalky White approached to introduce himself.

They shook hands. 'Nice piece of work,' Chalky said. He stood, arms akimbo, clutching the ends of a towel which was slung like a scarf around his neck. His own singlet was damp from a work-out on the weights.

Maurice immediately resented the condescending tone. In the code he had been attuned to all his life, 'Nice piece of work' signalled, 'This is my turf'. It was an unasked for seal of approval from the gangland boss. Maurice felt he didn't need it, so he nodded once and kept quiet.

Chalky pumped him for information on where he lived, where he'd come from, what he did. It didn't take him long to work out the Jewish connection, and this put an extra edge of superiority into his conversation. 'Maybe I'll bring my girl down your place this Saturday,' he told him, as if bestowing a favour. He'd found a replacement for Daisy in yet another girl from the chorus line at the Palace, but he didn't usually meet up with her until late at night. So he also went out to pick up a casual girl earlier in the evening, in a pub or at a dance, and he and his mates would parade the streets, girls in tow. Meeting up with Maurice gave him the chance to angle for free tickets to the Gem; one of the up-and-coming places to be seen.

She knew he nattered and worried about Robert too. It was a couple of weeks since they'd had a letter from him. Two sons in the firing line, if you looked on the black side. Poor old man, he needed all the help he could get.

'It'd be nice to see you there,' was Maurice's non-committal reply. He kept his eyes on the pair who'd just stepped into the ring and begun to spar.

'Reckon I might put a bit of business your way,' Chalky boasted. He'd already taken against Maurice as a tight-arse.

'Fine.'

'Me and my mates, Syd and Whitey up there.' He pointed to the two boxers.

Not so tough, Maurice thought, casting a critical eye. Neither would last two minutes in the ring with him. If Chalky was only as good as these two at handling himself, there was not much to worry about. 'Best come early and miss the queues,' he advised. 'The place gets packed out and I have to turn people away these days.'

Chalky rubbed the towel across his face. Jumped up tight-arse, he repeated to himself. Leigh had just made a bad move, treating him like a nobody. Chalky would show him different as soon as he got the chance. He spat a ball of phlegm on to the floor and strode off.

Milo, still standing nearby, pulled a face at Maurice and went about his business. 'Bad move,' Walter said later when Maurice went to the changing room to put on his outdoor clothes.

'I ain't bothered.' Maurice combed his hair in the speckled, steamy mirror. 'I can deal with his type no trouble.'

In this reckless mood he went straight up to the Duke to invite Jess to a dance that Friday night at the Town Hall. 'I'll get time off,' he told her. She looked doubtful, glass and tea-towel in hand. Duke kept an eye on her from the cellar steps.

'Oh, I don't know. I ain't been to a dance in ages. I've forgotten how.'

'All the better. That means I can teach you; the Tango, the Turkey Trot!' He looked animated. 'Go on, Jess, say you'll come!'

In the end she nodded. 'I'll see if I can.'

'This Friday, eight on the dot. Make a date!' He drank up, chatted amiably with Arthur and Dolly at a table by the door, then went on his way in high spirits. 'Babe! Come along! O, kid! O, kid!' He hummed the latest American dance. 'Hug 'em. Hug 'em. Put your arms around me, Babe!'

In the bar, Florrie warned Duke not to be a misery. 'The girl needs some fun, just like everyone else.'

Duke concentrated on tapping the new barrel. 'I ain't said nothing.'

'You don't have to, your face says it all. You'll put her off going if you go round looking like that.'

He sighed. 'I ain't exactly feeling on top of the world, Flo.'

'Same as the rest of us, Wilf. It ain't no better for Jess. And she's doing her best for Ern. In fact, she's more than pulling her weight if you ask me, getting the sewing off the ground with Ett. She's a good girl if you did but know it.'

Duke grunted. 'But do you think he knows about . . . you know?' He tilted his head sideways, glancing up through the cellar ceiling. 'He ain't in for a shock when he finds out, is he?'

Florrie tutted and shoved him to one side while she turned on the tap and let beer froth into her jug. 'No, she told him about Grace weeks since. He took it well, she says.'

'It makes me mad!' He went behind the gantry and put his shoulder to a second barrel, wedging the chock up a notch with angry force.

Florrie stepped back in surprise. 'Steady on. What got into you?'

'I'm just thinking of him what done this to her. I tell you, if I could get my hands on him, I'd throttle him!'

'Yes, and you won't even let on to your one and only sister who it was, and that's a fact!' Florrie stood, arms crossed.

He shook his head. 'No. Frances said not to. They don' want no one poking their noses in.'

'Including me.' Florrie sniffed and folded her arms, do her best to assume a wounded look. 'It ain't for wa asking, Duke Parsons!' In fact, she'd nagged them to to get at the truth.

'Jess says it ain't important no more.' He cle teeth and hammered at the chock with the e massive fist.

Florrie regained her momentum and beg him once more. 'Well, he ain't gonna be a fa is he? So in a way she's right. And the soor and about and finds herself someone else better. Tell her she can go to this dance your blessing.'

'First time for years,' he grumbled. up and shrugged. 'He seems a decent

'Go tell her!'

Florrie stood and watched her stooping a little as he eased his sti steps. He carried his troubles we recently warned Frances not to for the trial, just in case. She'd and passed the message on to he said to Florrie. 'There's no more.'

Chapter Twenty-Two

Annie Wiggin did brisk business on her haberdashery stall during the week leading up to the dance at the Town Hall. She sold silk flowers for head-dresses and corsages, all shades of ribbon to thread through lace collars and cuffs, tiny buttons of pearl and glass, filigree buckles and the inevitable yards of delicate lace.

Late on the Friday, Jess sent Hettie down the market. The mission was to, 'buy something to brighten up this bodice when I've finished running it up on the machine'. Her feet treadled hard and her hands steered the silky jade-coloured fabric through the swiftly stabbing needle. She held a clutch of pins in the corner of her mouth, and mumbled that it would never be finished in time. She would have to go to the dance in her ordinary day wear of white blouse and blue skirt.

'Calm down, Jess.' Hettie had finished her day's task of altering waistbands on three pairs of trousers. She clattered her scissors down on the table and stood up. 'There's heaps of time. And it's gonna look lovely on you.'

Jess came to the end of a seam. She took the pins from her mouth and put them in a shallow tin. 'It ain't had no proper tacking. I just slung it together in a big rush.' She held up the nearly complete garment for inspection.

'It looks fine to me.'

'It ain't too low-cut?' Jess asked. 'You don't think it needs a bit more lace round the neckline to raise it?' The bodice was shaped and cut to show off both bust and arms.

Hettie laughed. 'I told you, it looks fine to me. I'll nip down to Annie's for matching ribbon, so we can ruche it up here around the shoulders. With my black skirt and belt to finish things off, you'll be the best-dressed girl there!'

Hettie rushed off to consult with Annie, who showed her which ribbon would best do the job. Jess's dark hair, with its fashionable wave, needed a pale cream flower or two to set it off. 'What about you, Ett? Ain't you going dancing with your sister?'

Hettie blushed. 'No. Sadie's going along early with young Charlie Ogden, but I'm staying home to help with the baby. Dancing ain't for me these days, Annie.' She paid for the ribbon and flowers.

'Why not? It was not so long since.' Annie gave her a reproachful look. 'Life and soul of the party, you was, Hettie Parsons.' She launched into a well-meaning speech. 'No need to chuck out your dancing shoes for good, is there, girl? We all know it was a terrible thing what happened to Daisy, and you had a nasty shock yourself, finding her like that. But it don't mean you have to go overboard on the tambourine bashing and hymn singing, do it? Why not have a bit of fun as well?'

Taken aback, Hettie defended herself hotly. 'I signed the pledge, Annie. I'm not going near if there's alcohol on sale, I promised.' She regarded the oath seriously, taking it to earnest extremes.

'That's rich, with you living right over the Duke!' Annie scoffed. 'What's your pa say about you saving poor sinners and helping to empty his till while you're about it?'

'He ain't said much,' Hettie replied quietly.

'I bet he ain't. I expect he's waiting for you to grow out

of it, girl. Honest to God, Ett, it breaks my heart to see you decked out in that bleeding horrible uniform, when I think of how you used to be.'

'It's vanity that lands us in trouble in the first place,' Hettie insisted. 'Anyhow, I made up my mind.'

'Pity. It used to brighten my day, seeing your hats all trimmed up with the bits and pieces I sold you off this stall. Pretty as a picture!'

'Well, I am sorry about that, Annie.' Hettie smiled self-consciously and squeezed Annie's hand.

'Not half so sorry as the scuttlers round here. They miss you and Daisy something rotten.' She looked wistfully at Hettie's pale, serious face. 'No hard feelings?' she checked.

'No hard feelings. I'm happy the way I am now. I feel I can be a bit of use.' She set off home with Jess's carefully wrapped trimmings, glad she'd stood her ground. They'd have to get used to her and her new mission; her Quakerish uniform and tambourine bashing, as Annie called it.

Frances came in from work just as Jess was trying on her finished outfit. She took off her hat and coat and hung them in significant silence, avoiding looking directly at Jess.

Already in a bad state of nerves over the whole business of accepting Maurice's invitation, Jess's confidence collapsed. 'Oh, Frances, you don't think I should go, do you?' She came up close to her unresponsive sister, while Hettie and Sadie hung back frowning.

'I never said that,' Frances replied, sinking into a chair. 'I'm all in. Sadie, make me a cup of tea, there's a good girl.'

'You don't have to say nothing,' Jess went on. 'I can tell by your face you think it ain't right.'

Sadie had already jumped a few steps ahead. 'Does that mean I can't go neither?' she wailed at Hettie. She knew

Duke would only let her go to the early part of the dance if Jess was there to supervise things. She stood in her best blouse, hair swept up for the very first time, close to tears.

Frances intervened with a weary shake of her head. 'Don't take on, Sadie. Just make me that cuppa, will you?'

Miserably hanging her head, Sadie went off into the kitchen.

There was an uneasy silence as Jess considered sending back word to Maurice. Frances's disapproval would hurt her badly and bring a poor atmosphere into the house when they least needed it. 'It ain't right, is that what you think?' she persisted.

The phrase struck a chord in Frances's memory. It was Billy's phrase before he kissed her. Suddenly her rigid distinction between right and wrong began to crumble. It was true, she'd thought Jess's affair with Maurice, coming close on the heels of the baby and in the very midst of their worries over Ernie, was ill advised. Better to wait at least until after the trial, she thought. As she stood all day and weighed, rolled and cut paste for pills, she divided moral issues into neat and tidy boxes, and thought life could follow prescribed patterns. Jess shouldn't enjoy herself with a new boyfriend. Ernie should be at home, not in prison. Everyone should do what was right.

But her memory played this sudden trick. She pictured herself in Billy's arms responding to his kiss, not fending him off as she should have done. Love, longing, loneliness were enormous forces pushing people into one another's arms. Who was she to judge? Humbly, Frances took hold of Jess's hand. 'Don't mind me,' she sighed. 'I'm just tired out. Why don't you go off and have a good time? You and Sadie with your Cake Walk and your Dandy Dance!'

Sadie came in with the tea to hear the last part of this speech. Her face lit up, then she teased her oldest sister.

'It'd be nice to see you there,' was Maurice's non-committal reply. He kept his eyes on the pair who'd just stepped into the ring and begun to spar.

'Reckon I might put a bit of business your way,' Chalky boasted. He'd already taken against Maurice as a tight-arse.

'Fine.'

'Me and my mates, Syd and Whitey up there.' He pointed to the two boxers.

Not so tough, Maurice thought, casting a critical eye. Neither would last two minutes in the ring with him. If Chalky was only as good as these two at handling himself, there was not much to worry about. 'Best come early and miss the queues,' he advised. 'The place gets packed out and I have to turn people away these days.'

Chalky rubbed the towel across his face. Jumped up tight-arse, he repeated to himself. Leigh had just made a bad move, treating him like a nobody. Chalky would show him different as soon as he got the chance. He spat a ball of phlegm on to the floor and strode off.

Milo, still standing nearby, pulled a face at Maurice and went about his business. 'Bad move,' Walter said later when Maurice went to the changing room to put on his outdoor clothes.

'I ain't bothered.' Maurice combed his hair in the speckled, steamy mirror. 'I can deal with his type no trouble.'

In this reckless mood he went straight up to the Duke to invite Jess to a dance that Friday night at the Town Hall. 'I'll get time off,' he told her. She looked doubtful, glass and tea-towel in hand. Duke kept an eye on her from the cellar steps.

'Oh, I don't know. I ain't been to a dance in ages. I've forgotten how.'

'All the better. That means I can teach you; the Tango, the Turkey Trot!' He looked animated. 'Go on, Jess, say you'll come!'

In the end she nodded. 'I'll see if I can.'

'This Friday, eight on the dot. Make a date!' He drank up, chatted amiably with Arthur and Dolly at a table by the door, then went on his way in high spirits. 'Babe! Come along! O, kid! O, kid!' He hummed the latest American dance. 'Hug 'em. Hug 'em. Put your arms around me, Babe!'

In the bar, Florrie warned Duke not to be a misery. 'The girl needs some fun, just like everyone else.'

Duke concentrated on tapping the new barrel. 'I ain't said nothing.'

'You don't have to, your face says it all. You'll put her off going if you go round looking like that.'

He sighed. 'I ain't exactly feeling on top of the world, Flo.'

'Same as the rest of us, Wilf. It ain't no better for Jess. And she's doing her best for Ern. In fact, she's more than pulling her weight if you ask me, getting the sewing off the ground with Ett. She's a good girl if you did but know it.'

Duke grunted. 'But do you think he knows about . . . you know?' He tilted his head sideways, glancing up through the cellar ceiling. 'He ain't in for a shock when he finds out, is he?'

Florrie tutted and shoved him to one side while she turned on the tap and let beer froth into her jug. 'No, she told him about Grace weeks since. He took it well, she says.'

'It makes me mad!' He went behind the gantry and put his shoulder to a second barrel, wedging the chock up a notch with angry force.

Florrie stepped back in surprise. 'Steady on. What got into you?'

'I'm just thinking of him what done this to her. I tell you, if I could get my hands on him, I'd throttle him!'

'Yes, and you won't even let on to your one and only sister who it was, and that's a fact!' Florrie stood, arms crossed.

He shook his head. 'No. Frances said not to. They don't want no one poking their noses in.'

'Including me.' Florrie sniffed and folded her arms, doing her best to assume a wounded look. 'It ain't for want of asking, Duke Parsons!' In fact, she'd nagged them to death to get at the truth.

'Jess says it ain't important no more.' He clenched his teeth and hammered at the chock with the edge of his massive fist.

Florrie regained her momentum and began to badger him once more. 'Well, he ain't gonna be a father to the kid, is he? So in a way she's right. And the sooner Jess gets out and about and finds herself someone else who will be, the better. Tell her she can go to this dance, Wilf. She needs your blessing.'

'First time for years,' he grumbled. Then he straightened up and shrugged. 'He seems a decent sort at any rate.'

'Go tell her!'

Florrie stood and watched her brother's broad back, stooping a little as he eased his stiff legs up the steep cellar steps. He carried his troubles well, considering. Sewell had recently warned Frances not to hold out too many hopes for the trial, just in case. She'd come home white as a sheet and passed the message on to Duke. 'Don't tell the others,' he said to Florrie. 'There's no point dragging them down no more.'

She knew he nattered and worried about Robert too. It was a couple of weeks since they'd had a letter from him. Two sons in the firing line, if you looked on the black side. Poor old man, he needed all the help he could get.

'Frances, it ain't the Cake Walk no more. That's old hat. No, these days it's the Turkey Trot. I been practising with Charlie!' She went and dragged Hettie across the floor with her arms slung around her shoulders, walking with wriggling sideways steps.

'Oh my Lord!' Jess looked at Frances in wild-eyed alarm.

'Go on, get out of here quick before I change my mind,' Frances moaned. She put one hand over her eyes and squinted through her fingers as Sadie rushed for her jacket. 'And mind you're back by ten!' she called.

Sadie and Jess grinned, and sailed downstairs together.

Maurice and Charlie met up with Jess and Sadie in the fuzzy halo of the street-lamp outside the pub. They walked four abreast up the greasy pavement, hopped on to a tram and joined the steady stream of young people heading for the Town Hall.

The dance was held in a huge central room bedecked with strings of coloured electric lights. It buzzed with expectation as the band arrived on the raised platform to strike up the first tune. One novelty of the occasion was the array of uniforms on show. Recent recruits to the army and navy, or veterans sent home on leave strutted through the hall. Khaki mingled with navy-blue under giant coloured posters which displayed men at arms, women in nurses' uniform or busy in munitions factories. 'Are YOU in this?' read the challenge below. It was the first time the war had seemed real to many of the young civilians gathered there, but the uniforms seemed to inspire rather than depress them. Many minds were made up as they talked, wide-eyed and eager, to the battle-scarrred heroes of the day.

Teddy Cooper turned up in the grey-blue uniform of a pilot in the Royal Flying Corps; the most glamorous outfit of all with its belted jacket and breeches. After nearly a month of haggling at home, he'd conceded defeat and agreed to serve the war effort, but on his own terms. Not for him the mud and sweat of a Flanders field. He preferred the soaring blue reaches and a mission to bring back information on enemy positions. His mother complained of the danger involved in piloting the flimsy bi-planes, but Teddy declared they were safe as houses. He'd fight a clean war of darting raids across the Channel. A rumour that the Flying Corps was preparing to drop bombs on the enemy sounded to him an exciting but unlikely development.

So he stepped into the dashing uniform and role in adventurous spirits. The Town Hall dance would be a good send-off; a chance to be admired and envied.

Ugly duckling civilians like Walter Davidson and the Chalky White gang hung back in the shadows while the boys in uniform glided on to the dance floor with the best-looking girls. Chalky, adrift again from his latest girlfriend, eventually picked up Olwyn Williams, who'd recently ditched her job in the shirt sweatshop at Coopers' and taken work as a bus conductress. The war had opened many jobs to women, and Olwyn was one of the first to seize the new opportunity. She liked the uniform: a military-style jacket, a shorter than usual plaid skirt and jaunty brimmed hat with its company badge. And she liked the independence. As she swung by on Chalky's arm, she winked at Amy Ogden. Amy had picked up Syd Swan, regarded as a slimy customer by most of the girls. 'That's the ticket, clippie!' Syd grinned inanely at Olwyn. Amy pulled him back on course to instruct him in elementary tango. He enjoyed the sweaty, grappling aspect, but the nifty footwork was beyond him.

Soon the music and heat generated by hundreds of dancing couples set the evening in swing. Charlie danced energetically with Sadie, having picked up more handy tips from the American bioscopes, where women with crimped hair and pouting dark lipstick swooned in the arms of broad-shouldered, square-jawed heroes. Jess stood at the side with her arm linked through Maurice's. She smiled at the new style of dancing. 'I hope you don't expect me to try nothing like that,' she said, looking prim.

Maurice was flattered by the effort Jess had put into her appearance this evening. There were complicated swirls in her thick hair, and tiny pearl-drop earrings in perpetual motion as she turned her head this way and that. Her sloping shoulders and full breasts showed to advantage in her new, tight-fitting bodice. Her arms were long and slender. 'What, ain't you never done the tango?' he asked, taking her by the waist and leading her on to the dance floor. 'It's easy. You just slide around a bit. Let yourself go, trust me!'

Jess laughed. 'If you let go of me, Maurice Leigh, I'll crown you!' She felt herself tipped backwards in a dangerous, plunging motion, then pulled upright by the strength of his arm around her waist.

He held her, his cheek against hers, feeling her soft, smooth skin against him. He felt her mouth smile. 'Oh, I won't let go of you, Jess, don't worry,' he whispered. He pulled her close, to breathe in the clean, perfumed smell of her hair.

The strutting music of the tango merged seamlessly into a more sedate waltz, leaving only the romantically inclined couples on the floor. Sadie and Charlie went off hand in hand to the refreshment bar. Amy Ogden struggled into a more upright position with Syd Swan, whose arm still snaked around her, too close for comfort. Chalky threaded through the couples in the opposite direction to his ex-partner, Olwyn. He paused to wink at Syd and then

considered Jess as she danced with Maurice. He knew
enough street gossip to register surprise that she was out
on the town. Slowly he lit up a cigarette, flicked the match
to the floor and circled in their direction, preparing a
cutting remark. He fancied somehow hitting the newcomer,
Maurice Leigh, with the bombshell about Jess's baby. With
narrowed eyes he halted again and exhaled smoke by jutting
out his bottom lip and directing it straight up in front of
him.

Maurice spotted Chalky's intention to come over and
upset things. He could see the sneering face draw near. Jess
was oblivious, her head against his shoulder. This was
awkward timing; Maurice could hardly snap Jess out of the
slow, smooth movement of the waltz without alerting her
to Chalky's sly approach.

Jess felt Maurice stiffen, and glanced up to see the cause.
Chalky White stood close by, in the middle of the revolving
pairs, his snake eyes fixed on them.

'What's he think he's staring at?' Maurice muttered, now
that Jess had seen.

'Take no notice,' she pleaded. She wanted the music to
stop so they could walk swiftly away.

But then luckily Chalky's attention was diverted. Amy
had spotted Teddy Cooper in his smart uniform and
whispered something to her new boyfriend, Syd Swan,
which made him swear loudly, then round up a couple of
mates. They soon started to square up to Teddy and his
officer-type pals, facing each other in a corner of the hall. A
space had cleared and a ripple of excitement spread through
the room. The band wavered, then played on, now almost
ignored. Chalky responded quickly, dropping his vendetta
against Maurice and roughly pushing through the middle
of the dance floor to side with Syd. Jess breathed a sigh of

relief. 'Time I went and rounded up young Sadie,' she told Maurice. 'I promised Pa I'd send her home safe and sound.'

Maurice kept one eye on the trouble brewing in the corner; shirt-sleeves were already rolled up, each side taunted and mocked the other. He went with Jess to the refreshment table. 'Let's walk with them,' he suggested. 'There's a bit of a scrap on the cards over there. They can sort it out while we take Sadie home, then we can come back and pick up where we left off.'

Jess smiled and nodded. Charlie, who thought it was a bad idea, was soon overruled. Sadie left with a long face, pleading for half an hour more, but soon they were out in the cold, windy street, huddling together and half running for warmth, until they came under the railway arch on to Duke Street, when Maurice and Jess chose to walk diplomatically ahead, leaving the young couple to their midnight kiss.

'Don't she look lovely tonight?' Jess glanced back, then slid her arm close inside Maurice's. 'Ain't no wonder he's smitten, poor boy.'

Maurice glanced back. 'Hm. He's more smitten with himself than anyone else, if you ask me.' He smiled at her. 'Do you think we're past standing in an alley like them?' He turned her towards him in the full glow of the street-lamp and took a bold kiss.

'Just like a couple of kids,' Jess protested. She steered him on down the street past Henshaw's frosty window, past the unlit courts. 'Come on, Sadie. It's too cold to hang about,' she called.

Sadie grumbled and called them spoil-sports, but they got home just fifteen minutes late and delivered her into the anxious care of a tired-looking Frances, who stood wrapped in a shawl at the head of the stairs.

Charlie watched her go with a lingering look, then trudged into the bar to meet up with his ma and pa.

'Do you reckon it's safe to go back to the Town Hall now?' Jess asked. Her feet felt like blocks of ice and her cheeks tingled, but she wanted to avoid any chance of Maurice getting involved in a brawl. If Chalky had it in for him in some way, they'd best steer clear.

'Storm in a bleeding teacup,' he told her. 'But come down to my place to keep warm, if you like. Ain't no rush, is there?'

Jess let herself be guided down Paradise Court, and over Dolly Ogden's whitened step. Caution went flying on the wind and she let her feelings surface. Soon she was clinging to Maurice in the safety of his room.

He felt her willingness, and every fibre in his body wanted to take advantage of it. Her body seemed part of him already, open and defenceless. He held her close and ran the flat of his hand up and down her back. For a second his mind raced ahead; what if she regretted this later? She might be angry at being rushed into the situation and blame him for it. It might raise a terrible memory. So he pulled back a fraction and stared into her face. 'Are you sure?' he murmured.

Jess stroked his forehead. 'Don't frown.' Then she kissed his face. The voices of her upbringing had fled; the elderly chorus of Sunday schoolteachers and maiden aunts who stood in line down the years, shaking their heads and speaking of respect, decency, reputation. All she saw was Maurice's face, his deep brown eyes and the desire there. 'Kiss me again,' she whispered, drowning in the warm moment.

He unhooked the small fastening of the blue-green silk bodice. There was a layer of thin white silk beneath, held in place by a tie on each shoulder, which easily slid away.

Then he ran his fingertips over her breasts, felt her shiver as he bent to kiss them, felt himself driven on beyond thought by a desperate need to have her.

Jess felt him lift her and gently lay her on the bed. Her eyes were closed. She heard the small snap of his collar studs, the rustle of his shirt lifted over his head. She opened her eyes as she felt the side of the bed dip, and reached out to touch the smoothness of his shoulder and chest. She rested her forefinger in the shallow dish beneath the Adam's apple, then she raised her finger and brushed it across his mouth. He bent with an urgent groan to smother her neck and breasts with kisses, before he pressed her back with the full weight of his long, strong body and kissed her mouth until her lips ached.

Now he roused her with his hands, caressing her in open celebration of her beauty as she consented to more and more intimate moments. He stroked the sleek line from hip to thigh, resting his head against her belly. For the first time in her life she felt delight pass from a man's touch into her own body, and she responded with unselfconscious pleasure. They taught that you gave away something precious to the man you loved, but they had it the wrong way round. She felt Maurice offered her the gift of himself, unguarded, utterly whole. That men could be like this stunned her mind and roused her body. She thrilled and held him to her.

Their love-making over at last, they lay intertwined, falling from breathlessness into gentle contentment and then the strange, redundant moments of shyness, when she gathered the sheets around her and wondered what was the next move. Her clothes lay scattered on the floor. She gazed at him, not knowing what to do or say.

Raised on one elbow, he smudged away signs of her tears, as he had done once before. 'Don't go and cry on me,' he whispered. 'I ain't no good with a handkerchief!' He seemed to read her mind, for, without rushing, he went and gathered her things and put them on the end of the bed within reach. 'You've got lovely hair,' he murmured, running one hand back from her brow across the shining dark mass on the pillow. 'Listen, you get your things on while I go down and make us a cup of tea.'

She laughed. 'You'll give Dolly the fright of her life if they've just got back and you go down like that!'

'The thrill of her life, you mean.' He grabbed some clothes. 'Anyhow, Dolly's up at the Duke, well away by now, I shouldn't wonder.' He went off down the dark stairs.

Jess lay flat on her back for a few moments, staring at the shapes made on the sloping ceiling by cracks in the plaster; a human profile, a starfish. Then she roused herself and got dressed, glad when she went down of the low fire in Dolly's kitchen grate. Maurice kissed her and they hugged close together while they sipped the tea. It was midnight when he took her back up the court. The last drinkers spilled out of the pub. Charlie, Dolly, and Arthur met them fair and square on the doorstep.

Dolly, her free and easy tongue loosened by an evening's sociable drinking, hollered blessings at them. 'That's a girl, you enjoy yourself. You only live once and that's a fact!' She winked at her lodger. 'Mind you treat Jess right, Mr Leigh. She needs someone to look out for her. Don't we all?' She gave Arthur, as inert as his wife was lively, a hefty nudge which unbalanced him on top of Maurice. Maurice set him straight with a good-natured smile.

By this time, Jess could feel herself blushing from head to toe, so she gave Maurice a hasty kiss on the cheek and fled upstairs.

*

Hettie had spent part of the evening with Mary O'Hagan, and become a willing helper in the crowded bed-time routine of the three older children, who washed in cold water at the restored kitchen tap, scraped a comb through their hair and climbed into one big bed, at the end opposite to the three younger ones, already sound asleep.

She noticed signs of improvement. Besides the running water, there was a white cloth on the kitchen table and a piece of net curtain draped across rough twine to block out the worst of the grimy outlook down on to the back court. Mary herself had tidied her hair and made sure her blouse was clean and decent. The washing she'd taken in that day was already laundered. It awaited the iron in neat piles. She welcomed Hettie with a calm smile and offered tea, making only half-hearted attempts to keep the children from clinging to the visitor's skirt.

During the evening, Mary pieced together the family's latest news; Tommy was still on the scene, putting his mind to earning good money in place of poor Daisy. 'Poor boy, he never believed she'd been done in first off. I had to hang on to him to stop him racing straight over the Palace to bring her home. It was all right for us, we had time to get used to it, but poor Tom, it hit him like a hammer. I never seen him look so bad.' Mary's thin, serious face went distant. Hettie took her hand. 'He never got a chance to come to the funeral, see. He never seen her laid in the ground.'

Hettie sat with Mary, marooned in grief, waiting for the sad tale to continue. She said silent prayers.

'At any rate, the poor boy had to believe it in the end. Now he's up with the lark every day, off to Covent Garden, working his barrow to bring back the pennies.' Mary sighed. 'I'm proud of that boy, Hettie. And you'll not believe this, but his poor pa's found work as well. He heard of a job going down at Coopers', and he went across right that minute and they took him on. He came home grinning fit to bust, all swelled up with pride. Now he's bringing in a few shillings again.'

Hettie smiled. Her talk with Edith Cooper had eventually paid off.

Mary patted her friend's hand. 'Joe's not a bad man, only he's been down on his luck. What's a man to do without work, I ask you, except sit on his backside and get down?'

'And worry about rent day coming round,' Hettie agreed. She tried to imagine doleful Joe O'Hagan grinning fit to bust.

Mary nodded. 'We done many a moonlight flit, me, Joe and the kids, and I ain't ashamed to admit it to you. But please God, things will be different now. We turned a corner, thanks to you!' She returned Hettie's hand to her own lap. Through the doorway, six tousled, sleeping heads lay without pillows. The women sat on in companionable, peaceful silence.

A week later, on the 11th of November 1914; a day engraved on their minds for ever, Edith and Jack Cooper stood among the proud parents at Victoria Station, waving their son off to war.

Young men swung up into the carriages, feeling their importance, knowing their destiny. Individual differences faded, marked only by a tartan band on this soldier's cap, a line of gold braid around that sailor's cuff. To a man, they looked down from the open windows with a mixture of defiance and fierce bravado. Instructions from mothers centred on food and frequent letters. Fathers stood by silent, hands behind their backs, feet apart, heads raised to look at the gathering clouds of steam under the giant glass canopy.

'Write soon, Teddy!' Edith Cooper cried, strangled with guilt now that the moment had arrived. Perhaps it was too great a test, merely to restore their good name. He looked young and vulnerable, too fair and soft to face the harsh realities of war. But it was too late.

'Don't fuss, Mother.' Teddy frowned. His Flying Corps uniform encased him in a tough, worldly shell. He leaned out and shook his father by the hand. The train whistle shrieked, the wheels began to shunt. His mother cried along with all the rest.

Teddy leaned out until he lost their heads in a sea of waving hands. Then he ducked inside the carriage and sat down heavily on the buttoned cloth. Soon he was in conversation with an army captain, exchanging regiments, training camps, news of the front and so on. Edith and Jack sat in silence as they drove along suburban streets beneath skeletal trees all swirling in November fogs, between faint pools of gaslight.

Next day before dawn, a heavy knock on the doors of the Duke announced the arrival of a telegram.

Duke came down and slid back the bolts with dread certainty. It was Robert. He held the door open a fraction and took the envelope without speaking, then he closed the door and stood in the empty hallway. The paper shook in his hand.

'I'll open it, Pa.' Frances had come quietly down in her shawl. She put one hand on his shaking arm. The other girls had gathered at the top of the stairs, clutching the necks of their night-dresses. Florrie soon joined them.

He handed the telegram to her.

Frances tore it open. She read the official message and sighed. 'Robert's wounded. He's in the field hospital.'

'Alive?' Duke breathed.

'Wounded. It don't say how bad.' She had to lean on him for support now. She looked up at her sisters.

'But alive.' He took the message and reread it. 'They don't tell you nothing. What we supposed to think?'

Florrie, Hettie, Jess and Sadie came down to stand in the cold hallway. They crowded together for comfort. 'We gotta be patient,' Florrie said. 'They'll look after him and send him back for proper nursing when he's strong enough.'

Frances nodded. Her friend, Rosie Cornwell, took care of cases like that. 'Soon as he gets back, we'll be able to tell. We can go and see him for ourselves . . .' But she remembered the terrible injuries Rosie described; men without limbs, shell-shocked, scarred, with terrible stammers, or blind from exploding bombs. Sadie began to cry.

'Stop that, girl, we ain't lost him,' Duke told her. His hand still shook as he took hold of the banister rail. 'He's one of the lucky ones. We gotta remember that.'

Chapter Twenty-Three

A dark gloom settled on Duke and his family as they waited for news of Robert. A day went by. Hope flickered that his wound would be slight, that his recovery would be swift and complete. After all, he was a strong, fit young man with a good fighting spirit. If enemy shells had failed to finish him off, there was no reason why the doctors and nurses couldn't patch the wound and put him back together as good as new.

This was the opinion of people up and down Paradise Court. They read the bullish reports of battle and transferred the illusion of national invincibility to individual cases like Robert Parsons. He knew how to take care of himself, none better. He'd lived on his wits all his life, and no one had ever got the upper hand. They held in their minds a picture of the tall, strapping lad manhandling great barrels down into the cellar, and the girls remembered him in particular as brazen, handsome Robert Parsons, the ladies' man.

'Any news?' Annie Wiggin asked Florrie when she came into the bar for her evening drink. Though she still looked askance at Florrie's bossy ways, she preferred a quiet word with her rather than bothering Duke directly. Annie felt his unspoken hurt keenly, but she had developed the tact to keep her distance. She knew all too well the torment of waiting to hear news of a loved one. Her old man had put her through two whole years of it before she finally gave up hope.

'Who is it you want to know about this time, Robert or Ernie?' Florrie was up to her elbows in soap suds, washing glasses. 'If it's Ern, there's nothing new. We're moving heaven and earth to get him off. His trial comes up in less than a month.'

'It's bleeding criminal!' Annie said, fired up all of a sudden. 'That's what it is. Makes my blood boil to think of the poor sod banged up in some prison cell. What d'they think they're up to, accusing an innocent man?' She took a savage gulp from her full glass, then calmed down. 'You been to visit?'

Florrie nodded. 'Ett took me along with her last week. White as a sheet, he is, and pining for home. He don't know what's hit him, not really.'

'Any rate, he's in good hands.' Annie had kept in touch with Frances about the work being done by Mr Sewell on Ernie's behalf. 'We gotta hope for the best.'

'Ett says we gotta trust in Jesus,' Florrie said. She turned to lean across the bar and lowered her loud voice. 'Tell me if I'm speaking out of turn here, Annie, but Jesus by himself ain't enough, not to my way of thinking.'

'It's a start, though. With Him on your side, things is bound to get smoother.' Annie didn't consider herself religious, but she paid lip service to God's existence as a kind of insurance premium. 'I go along with Ett. I think we should trust Him.'

Florrie's eyes narrowed further. 'Don't get me wrong, I ain't against a well-meaning prayer or two, don't think that. All I'm saying is it's a good job we got Jess and Frances both doing their bit and all. And it's a good job we got

British justice. Twelve good men and true. I'd rather put my trust in them, if you want to know.'

Annie's mouth went down at the corners. She glanced sideways to make sure that Duke was well out of hearing. 'No, Florrie, I'd put my money on Jesus if I was you. Them other scales is weighted against the likes of Ernie, believe me!'

'No thanks,' Florrie snapped back.

Annie saw she'd put her man-sized boot in it. 'Don't mind me. Of course, we gotta hope for the best, I know that.' She took another swig from her glass. 'Anyhow, what's the news from France? Are they sending Robert home for a drop of Blighty?'

Florrie slung a damp tea-towel across one shoulder and picked up a wooden tray full of clean glasses. 'They are. We got word this morning. They put him on a train last night; he gets back within the hour.'

'Well, that's good, ain't it?' Annie's face lit up with genuine pleasure. 'That's what you all been waiting for.' She nodded at Duke. 'I hear you're getting your boy back tonight!'

He came across. 'We got a telegram. Hettie's going up to Guy's to see him.'

Annie faltered. 'He ain't coming home then?'

'Not straight off. He has to stay in the hospital.' Duke tried to keep a steady gaze and a level voice. 'They want to keep an eye on him for a bit, that's all.' He changed the subject. 'Now then, Annie, what's this I been hearing about you giving young Amy Ogden her old job back? I never knew business was that brisk these days.'

Annie shuffled on her seat. 'It ain't brilliant, I gotta admit. But she's been out of work a fair while now, and I promised her ma I'd keep her out of harm's way. It's coming up to Christmas; you gotta do your bit.'

'There's a lot wouldn't.'

'Well, she ain't a bad little worker. She keeps going on about the bleeding weather though, and I have to tell her to shut it or it gets me down. Otherwise I ain't got no complaints.' She finished off her beer.

Duke picked up the glass. 'Have another one, Annie? It's on the house.'

Annie beamed at sour-looking Florrie. 'Don't mind if I do, Duke. And you tell Jess and Hettie they can come down my stall and get special rates any time they like. Anything they need. I hear their own little business is taking off nicely these days. Cotton thread, darning wool, shoulder pads, bias-binding; I got everything they need nice and cheap. You just tell them that from me, you hear.' She settled in for a good evening. Trouble brought out the best in folk, she thought. If you couldn't trust Jesus or justice, at least you could be sure of your friends and neighbours.

When she heard the news about Robert's home-coming, Sadie went straight down to Charlie's house. Everything had been so gloomy lately that this ray of light made her jump up to visit, even though she knew Charlie didn't like her to call. 'Tell Pa I'm at Charlie's,' she shouted up the street to Frances, just coming home from work. 'Ain't it brilliant? Robert's been sent back home!'

Frances nodded quietly and went up to see Jess and baby Grace. 'I wish to goodness Sadie would calm down a bit,' she complained. 'She's a harum-scarum, and it ain't as if she's a little kid no more.' Frances's own mood had been thrown off balance by a chance word of Billy Wray. Rosie had called in to tell her that his wife, Ada, had been admitted to the women's hospital and was very ill.

Jess glanced up from the bed, where she sat cleaning and

changing the baby. 'Leave off, Frances,' she said. 'It's been tough on Sadie lately. She's only thrilled at Rob being sent home, that's all.'

Frances sighed. 'We ain't heard what's wrong with him yet, though, have we?' She sat heavily at the other side of the bed.

'Ett's just gone off to find out. We'll know before too long, at any rate.' Jess kept busy. She hoped it was bad enough to get him sent home for a good long time, not too bad to have done permanent damage. With luck, they'd have him at home for the trial. He'd be able to come and give evidence in person. Every cloud had a silver lining, she thought.

'Give me a cuddle of my favourite niece!' Frances declared with sudden warmth. She bent to pick up the child, gathering her close and breathing in the smell of clean skin and talcum powder. Grace, fully awake and curious, began to poke her chubby fingers against Frances's lips and nose.

Dolly came slowly to the door to answer Sadie's knock. 'Why, it ain't your birthday, is it?' She stood on the doorstep, arms folded. 'What's up? I ain't missed nothing important, have I?' She too knew that Charlie was funny about Sadie coming to the house.

'No!' Sadie laughed out loud. 'Not yet. But Rob's been sent back. He'll be arriving any minute. I came to tell Charlie!'

Dolly nodded and eased herself back down the corridor. 'In that case, you'd better sit in the front room while I go up and get him.' She smiled pleasantly in response to Sadie's infectious excitement, glad there was something to smile about at last. Maybe the girl would cheer up her moody, touchy son. 'He ain't at work with Mr Leigh tonight, so he'll have a long face on him if I know anything about it. You got your work cut out with him, girl.'

Sadie was shown in, and sat down on a rickety *chaise-longue* in the Ogdens' empty front room. The sofa was covered in torn black calico, with its horsehair stuffing sprouting through in places. It wobbled noisily on the bare, uneven floorboards. The grate lay empty in spite of the cold weather, and the walls, once decorated in fawn-flowered wallpaper, were patchy with damp, dark stains. Soon she heard Dolly's footsteps return downstairs and go through into the kitchen. Several nervous minutes later, she recognized the sound of Charlie's own scuffing feet.

As the door opened, she sprang up to greet him. 'Guess what, Charlie, good news!' she began, darting forward.

Charlie frowned and backed off against the closed door. He felt the bare, bleak meanness of his family circumstances more than he could put into words, but he turned it against Sadie herself. 'I thought I told you not to come bothering me here.'

She paused. The smile faded. 'I didn't think I was bothering you,' she murmured.

'You didn't think, full stop.'

'I thought you'd be glad, Charlie.'

He moved uneasily towards the window, avoiding her gaze. He didn't want to be deflected from saying what he knew he must say. Her big, dark, liquid eyes would put him off. 'Robert gets back tonight, Ma told me,' he said, his voice flat. He stared out at the row of identical houses opposite; no gardens, no railings, no net curtains, nothing. 'That's good.'

Sadie stood there unnerved. She looked a fool, she realized. Dolly could never keep her mouth shut, not even for a second. Sadie's insides started to churn. She clutched the buckle of her belt and began to back off towards the door. 'I just wanted to tell you myself, that's all.'

Charlie nodded. He had to say what he'd decided one night last week when he sat in the projection room at the Gem. Pictures of America flickered on the screen; a great train journey across the Wild West, depicting the exploits of cowboys and gun-slingers. The world was a vast, unexplored territory. The dusty little room was dark. It smelt of hot metal, it whirred as the film rolled past the bright lens. He was stuck in prison and the camera showed him freedom. 'I want us to stop walking out together,' he said in an empty way. 'It ain't no use going on, now the winter's here. It ain't as if we can ride out on Sundays, is it?' He glanced round to judge the effect of his words. The room fell quiet.

'But we can go again in spring,' Sadie said at last. She stared at the back of his head. 'Can't we, Charlie?'

'No, we can't.' He hated her docility. Didn't she realize he was chucking her? Why wasn't she angry?

'Why not? Do you have to give your bike back? We'll get you another one, then it'll be fine.' She came close up behind him, reaching out her hand.

'It ain't fine!' He turned on her. 'Ain't you heard what I said? I want us to stop walking out together, that's what. I'm sick of it!'

Sadie stepped to one side, averting her face as if he'd struck her on the cheek, half-turning away so that her long plait swung round in front of her shoulder. She clutched both hands together.

'What did you have to come here for?' he raged. 'Why can't you stay out of my way? You're always hanging round, showing me up. Can't I do nothing on my own? Can't I?'

His head was thrust towards her, then he rushed past her, pushing her off balance. 'I ain't ready to be tied down,' he said finally. 'Can't you see that?'

Sadie gathered herself. He still stood by the door, one hand on the handle. It seemed he wanted her agreement to break off on his terms. Well, he could think again. 'I ain't tied you down, Charlie Ogden. I enjoyed being with you, and either you lied to me or else you enjoyed being with me too. That ain't tying you down. I listened to all your big ideas and I never said nothing. But you never listened to nothing I said, I know that now. I listened while you rabbited on about being hard done by because you ain't got a garden or a room of your own. Well, poor thing! I ain't got a room of my own neither. I got one brother wounded in the war, no one knows how bad, and one other brother in gaol accused of murder. I got a sister struggling to bring up a baby on her own. And I think they're the bleeding best there is!' She paused, but only to draw breath. 'I love my family, Charlie Ogden, and I loved you too. Not any more. You don't know the meaning of the word, and I'm sorry I wasted my time waiting for you to find out!' She swept past him at the open door. 'Fine words and big ideas, Charlie. That's you from top to bottom. Well, you'd better just go off and do them fine deeds so you can live with yourself, and I wish you lots of bleeding luck!'

Charlie watched her go. The front door slammed.

'Blimey, where did that come from?' Dolly asked from down in the kitchen. She'd overheard every word. 'I got her down for a little mouse, but she put you in your place, son.' She sat sewing stockings. 'Not half!'

Sadie's feet hardly touched the pavement as she flew back up Paradise Court. For the first time in her life she'd been deeply hurt and angry, with Charlie and with herself. But she quietened herself as she pushed through the decorated doors and went upstairs. No one would want to hear her troubles, what with Robert due back tonight. She looked flushed and her heart beat fast as a cat's. 'Ain't Ett back yet?' she asked. Baby Grace was up with a touch of colic, being walked back and forth by Jess, who'd administered gripe water. Frances had the ironing board out by the fire. Freshly ironed clothes lay all around in warm piles.

Charlie waited to confide in Maurice Leigh when he arrived home from work. He came out of the bedroom on to the landing and waited for the older man as he heard his key turn in the lock. 'I had a word with Sadie and I put a stop to things,' he told him, his face grave. 'I told her I didn't want to be tied down.'

Maurice stood, hands in pockets, his hat tipped back. 'No complications?' He remembered his own old, confident motto.

Charlie nodded. 'It's one thing walking out every now and then, but I don't want her hanging around my neck, do I?'

Maurice agreed. 'Course not. But you thrown a good-looking one away there. You sure you know what you've done?' He kept his expression serious, though Charlie's tragic face was a bit over the top in the circumstances. He was young and intense.

Charlie frowned. 'Looks ain't everything.' But he had a sharp flash of memory; Sadie's perfect features stared out from a mass of rich, dark hair as his arms encircled her in the Turkey Trot. 'Brains is important too. She gotta be able to keep up. I ain't gonna be round here much longer, see.'

And then Maurice did smile at the forced bravado. 'Good for you. Beauty and brains. Sounds perfect.' He nodded. 'What would your ma say if I took you up the Duke for a quick drink before closing?' Maurice put a chummy arm around Charlie's shoulder. 'Let's go down and find out, shall we?'

Charlie hesitated. 'Mind you, I wouldn't want to bump into her, would I? Sadie, that is.'

Maurice tutted. 'Hair of the dog,' he declared. 'The sooner the better. Face up to things, come on.' He had his own reasons for wanting a last drink at the pub before closing time. Besides, Charlie had some growing up to do, in his opinion, and he didn't mind lending a hand.

That tea-time, Hettie had insisted on making the short journey to Guy's Hospital alone. 'They won't want crowds of people hanging around the first night,' she warned. 'There'll be a whole bunch of our boys coming home wounded on that train, and you know what Rob's like; he won't want a fuss.'

Reluctantly the others agreed. 'Be sure you ask him everything; how long he's got before they send him back. Every last thing!' Jess was most particular. 'Don't forget nothing.'

'No need to jump the gun,' Duke grumbled. 'Give the boy a chance.' He squeezed Hettie's hand as she set off. 'You look nice and smart,' he said. She was dressed in her greeny-blue outfit and feathered hat.

Hettie grinned. 'Yes, well, I didn't want him dying of shock on me,' she conceded. 'He ain't had time to get used to me being in the Army yet.'

'Me neither. But you go and cheer him up, girl.' The old man watched her step out along the dark street. It didn't seem five minutes since the big send-off. This was modern war, modern life. It moved along too fast. He shook his head clear of hopeless thoughts and went back to work.

Hettie entered the huge doors of the hospital and stepped into an alien world. Outside was the monstrous roar of traffic, the clerks coming home from work, builders clattering up and down scaffolding, factory hands streaming out to the shrill sound of hooters. Inside, all was calm, clean and quiet. Nurses glided down corridors, shrouded in white aprons and nun-like head-dresses. A doctor stuffed a stethoscope into his jacket pocket and went from one ward to another. There was a glimpse of dormitory-style beds and men in pyjamas sitting playing cards at a table by a radiator.

Hettie turned on the spot, wondering where to go next.

'Name?' An overweight man behind a desk inside a glass-partitioned room stuck his head through an open window. Visitors were an untidy intrusion, apparently.

'I want to see Robert Parsons.' She stayed calm, unbuttoning her jacket in the overheated atmosphere.

The cross man checked a list. 'He's in E Ward. Third on the right,' he barked. 'You a relative?'

'His sister,' she confirmed.

He nodded her down the wide corridor straight ahead.

Hettie trod quietly, chin up, refusing to look to left or right at the men in their beds until she reached the sign which told her that this was Robert's ward. By now the smell of disinfectant had seeped through her clothes and into her pores. Sickness, disease, pain were all around. She hesitated, then pushed the door.

She saw a man in a wheelchair, one leg stretched out and resting on a metal platform, his hands shaking, his dark head sunk forward on to his chest. Another lay immobile on his side, bedclothes up to his chin. Another was flat on his back, staring at the ceiling. Hettie looked quickly away from a fourth patient wandering slowly towards her, one side of his face a mass of burned flesh, scarcely healed. Then a nurse came quietly down the central aisle. She smiled at Hettie.

'Robert Parsons,' Hettie whispered, low and nervous.

The girl nodded and led the way down to the far end of the ward. 'Don't expect too much,' she warned. 'And try not to tire him.'

Hettie flashed her a look of panic, but met no response. Instead, the nurse gestured to Robert's bed and went on her way. Hettie approached the bed, afraid and at a loss.

Robert lay propped against pillows, his eyes closed. His face ain't been touched, thank God, was her first reaction. She would have nightmares about that other poor man's burned face. But second thoughts snatched away this reassurance. Robert opened his eyes and she saw that his face had changed beyond measure.

He was Robert, but not Robert, the same in form only. His moustache was shaved, his dark hair very short. His eyes opened in a blank stare which took in her presence but showed no recognition. His hands lay trembling on the folded-down sheet, a wire frame made a tent of the bedclothes.

'Robert!' Hettie rushed forward with a mixture of relief and apprehension. She wanted him to be the same, or at least have a sign that he would be the old Robert eventually. 'It's me, Ett!' She grasped one hand and kissed his cheek.

He submitted to the embrace. She felt his whole frame tremble. There was nothing in his expression to show he knew where he was or why.

'Pa sends his love, and everyone at home.' Hettie struggled for normality. She smoothed his pillow. 'Don't worry, no need for you to talk to me if you're not up to it.' He seemed to be looking at her in bewilderment. 'I'll have a word with the nurse on my way out. She'll put me in the picture.' She drew up a wooden chair and sat close by the bed.

Robert's head rested back on the pillow and he gave up the struggle to make sense of his surroundings. He gazed emptily at her face, unresisting as she stroked his hand, unresponsive to her news.

'We're all keeping well, and baby Grace is thriving. You should see her now. Pa keeps plodding on. Well, he would, wouldn't he? Auntie Flo's settled herself in good and proper, and Ern's just about bearing up.'

Robert sighed and turned his head to the wall.

After a few minutes, the same young, fair-haired nurse returned. 'That's all for today,' she suggested. 'Come back and see him tomorrow.'

Hettie jerked to her feet. She bent to kiss her brother and blindly followed the nurse up the aisle between the beds. 'He ain't always gonna stay like that, is he?' she pleaded. They'd reached the radiator where a group of men sat and played gin rummy.

'Shh!' The nurse glanced at her other patients. 'Your brother's suffering from shock, that's all.'

'It'll wear off, won't it?'

The nurse nodded. 'In time. He needs to rest.'

'He'll know us if we come back tomorrow?'

'Maybe. It might take longer, considering his injuries.' She studied Hettie's face. 'Weren't you told?'

Slowly Hettie shook her head. 'We ain't been told nothing, only that he's wounded.'

'Well, it was bad, I'm afraid. He lay in no man's land for quite a time, apparently. He lost a lot of blood.' The young nurse saw she'd better get the news over with. 'Someone went over the top to get him and bring him back. He owes his life to that friend.'

Hettie nodded. 'It's his legs, ain't it?' She remembered the wire cage that lifted the bedclothes high in a ridge shape.

'One leg in particular. The right one. They had to amputate it there and then. There was no hope of saving it.'

Hettie hid her face in her hands.

'There are deep shrapnel wounds to that side of the body as well. He was in a lot of pain, but he's well sedated now.'

'Is that why he don't know me? It's the stuff you give him for the pain?' Hettie clutched at straws.

'Partly.' The nurse was reluctant to commit herself. She touched Hettie's elbow. 'Listen, why don't you go on home now and come back tomorrow. Wait and see.'

Hettie nodded and walked mechanically through the doors up the corridor to the main entrance.

The porter at the desk spotted her. 'Bad news?' he asked.

Tears came to her eyes as she nodded. 'Worse luck.'

'Never mind, I seen it day in, day out,' the man said. 'Poor bleeders, won't none of them ever be the same again. It's a bad business, if you ask me.' He wandered from his office and saw her through the door. 'You get a cab, girl,' he advised. 'Blow the expense. You don't want to be walking home in this.' He stuck his hand out into the rain which pelted into the dark puddles. 'Here, I'll go and get hold of one for you.'

He signalled to a taxi idling at the gate, went up to the driver and thrust his head close to the window. 'Take the girl home. She's had a bit of a shock.'

The cabman nodded. Hettie saw the back door swing open and remembered it was Robert's ambition to own a taxi. She got in. 'Paradise Court on Duke Street,' she said. The taxi jolted forward through the rain. What am I gonna

tell Pa? Hettie wondered. This'll break his heart once and
for all. The thought of it choked her with more unshed
tears. All too soon the taxi rolled past Coopers' and drew
to a halt outside the Duke.

Chapter Twenty-Four

Annie saw Hettie walk, head bowed, from the taxi to the pub door. She'd positioned herself by the window as lookout, and she could see from Hettie's bearing that the news wasn't good. She went out quickly to meet her in the corridor. 'How bad?' She grasped Hettie's wrist and stared anxiously into her eyes.

Hettie reported the bare facts.

Annie gasped and nodded. 'Poor bleeder. Now, chin up, girl. I'm right beside you. You think you can manage to tell your pa?' She had an arm around Hettie's waist for support. 'You go on up while I fetch him.'

Glad to be relieved of at least part of the burden, Hettie did as she was told. Her limbs felt heavy, her head light as she climbed the stairs looking pale and shocked. Frances, Sadie and Jess welcomed her in silence.

'I'll go get Pa!' Sadie stammered. She looked wildly at Frances.

'No, Annie's fetching him.' Hettie shook her head and stood as if in a dream. 'I can hear him now.'

They waited for what seemed like an age as Duke's heavy tread came upstairs.

'He ain't gonna die, is he?' Sadie cried, terrified.

Jess held her tight. 'Hush!' she said.

Duke appeared in the doorway, Annie hovering behind. He knew from Annie's manner that he should expect the worst, so he came up grim-faced but prepared. 'Sit down, girl,' he said to Hettie. Frances brought a chair from the table and sat her down. 'Now take your time, just tell us what he got.' He was determined to stay calm, whatever the news.

Hettie looked up at him and took courage. He was strong enough to take the blow, after all. She saw the set of his jaw, the broad shoulders. 'It ain't just a Blighty one, Pa. He never even knew who I was. He looked straight through me!'

Duke nodded. 'But what's he got?'

'Shrapnel down his right side.'

He nodded again.

'And his leg.' She pointed to her own right thigh with a shaking finger. 'They had to take it off.'

A shudder gripped them, but Duke was the first to recover. 'Anything else?'

Hettie shook her head. 'He's full of stuff for the pain. He don't even know where he is or nothing.'

Duke remembered his own fighting days; the wild, rolling eyes of men too close to bullet and blade, the death-haunted look of those who crawled back to consciousness as their shattered bodies were lifted on to stretchers off the battlefield. He knew enough to realize that the horror would fade. But he drew a choking breath and looked blankly at Annie.

Her eyes widened in a defiant challenge. 'Now don't you give way, none of you. It ain't like you, Duke Parsons!'

Her words were a key to action. Frances went straight down to Florrie to hand on the news. Jess took Hettie's hat and coat, Sadie went to make tea. Duke talked of Rob getting well enough to come home and told Hettie not to worry, the shock would wear off; Rob would soon be his old self again. Annie nodded in satisfaction.

'I'll be off then,' she said, as soon as Sadie brought in the tea.

Duke followed her on to the landing. 'Thanks, Annie,' he said. He bowed his head in embarrassment.

'Ain't nothing to thank me for,' she said, a touch too quick and sharp. There was a catch in her voice.

'Well, thanks anyway.' Duke rested his arm on the banister and stared down at the patterned carpet. 'Robert!' he said with a sigh and a shake of the head.

'Yes,' Annie agreed. 'Robert.'

Duke looked up. 'You know he was the best boxer around here, Annie. The best by a mile.'

'He was.' Her eyes filled with tears. Quickly she grasped his hand, then turned and went downstairs.

The round of visiting Robert in hospital began next day. They went in shifts, with a determined cheerfulness, bustling down the ward with fruit, flowers and messages from half of Paradise Court.

Robert gave a sign of recognition as Duke bent over him. Next time, he reached out his hand to Sadie. Then he asked to be propped up and he spoke to Jess. Each visit saw such an improvement that the good cheer grew less forced and began to spread to other casualties in nearby beds.

'Bleeding hell, mate, how many sisters you got?' The man with the burned face, a sergeant from a cavalry regiment, asked enviously.

'Four.' Robert looked up the length of the ward, waiting for the influx of visitors. It was his fifth day in the hospital. His head was clear now, but each day opened up fresh memories of the moment when the shell landed with a soft whistle and a thud before the whole world exploded in a cascade of mud and stones. He preferred to keep talking about other things; anything to keep his mind off that moment. So he looked for the day's visitors with visible impatience.

'Blimey. Ain't none of them married?'

'No. Why?' He was prickly with the other men. Their scars and injuries reminded him of his own.

'Nothing. You can lend me one if you like.'

Robert glanced at the man's disfigured face. We're all in the same boat, he thought. 'You'd better ask them, pal,' he grinned. 'Here they come now.'

Sadie and Frances hurried down between the rows of beds with bright hellos to right and left. Frances brought him a book on the motor car from the library. Sadie sat on the edge of his bed. She stared critically at him. 'I been thinking, Rob,' she began.

'Oh, don't do that,' he reproached.

'No, I been thinking. You should grow back your moustache.'

He laughed. 'You think so?'

'Yes. You look ever so much more handsome with it, don't he, Frances?'

The older woman entered into the spirit. 'You do, Rob. Irresistible.'

He felt the stubble on his chin. 'How about a beard to match?'

'Oh no!' Sadie gave a little shriek. 'That's old hat, that is!'

'Old hat, is it?' He winked at his neighbour. 'A great big bushy beard?'

'You'd look like some old grandpa, wouldn't he, Frances. Don't let him grow a beard.'

The teasing went on from visit to visit, though sometimes there was a more serious interlude. Hettie explained
her decision to join the Salvation Army after Daisy's
murder, and she gave news of the O'Hagans. Eventually,
Robert asked Jess about Ernie.

'His trial comes up on the tenth,' Jess told him. She
described her fruitless visits to Teddy Cooper and Freddie
Mills. 'I ain't got nowhere, and the coppers are playing
things close to their chests.' Now that Robert was prepared
to talk about things, she leaned in close to the bed. 'Rob,
there ain't nothing else that you can think of that might
help, is there? I know you told it all once already in the
written statement for Mr Sewell, but if you can bear to
think again and go through it, not missing a single thing!'
She spoke urgently. 'Ernie goes blank when he gets to the
part about waiting for you outside the stage door. He keeps
on saying he's sorry. That don't look good, you see. But we
can't get him to remember what he did next. No one can.
And then they're gonna ask him why he just ran off and left
the place, instead of waiting till you showed up.'

'He can't remember that neither?'

She shook her head. 'And there's one other thing, Rob.'
Jess checked up and down the ward. 'If they get me up on
the stand, they gonna ask me how Ernie was when he got
back home.'

'And?'

'I'm gonna have to say how I cleaned him up.' She
explained about the blood on Ernie's boots. 'If I swear on
the Bible, I won't be able to tell a lie, will I? Then they're
gonna ask me why I ain't said nothing sooner.'

Robert threw back his head and pinched the skin on his
exposed throat. 'Bleeding hell!' he said. Then he looked
directly at her. 'How many weeks have we got? Two?
Three?'

'Three.'

'Get me out of this bleeding bed!' he cursed. 'Tell Mr Sewell I'll get myself to that bleeding court if it kills me. Tell Ern not to worry, I'll be there!'

Jess soothed him and promised to give Ernie the message. 'It'll make a difference to him, Rob, honest to God. He'll want you there to help him.'

'I'll be there,' Robert promised. 'I'll be in a bleeding wheelchair, but I'll be there.'

Ernie's trial began at ten o'clock on Tuesday, the 10th of December; a peculiar cross between entertainment and reality. The newspapers had got hold of it as an example of what can go wrong in a family if rules of conduct are too lax and discipline not maintained. The *Express* in particular painted a picture of a motherless boy dragged up in rooms over an East End pub, daily witness to drunkenness and all kinds of brutish, hooligan behaviour. Duke was picked out for special blame. 'Modern parents should not allow the art of flogging to pass into the limbo of forgotten achievements,' the paper intoned. Flogging would have set the accused on the right track and prevented the tragedy at the Southwark Palace. Such families, knee deep in vendettas and street fights, were a hotbed for violent crime.

They printed a picture of Ernie above a caption which read, 'It's a fair cop!' It set the courtroom buzzing with expectation as people crowded into the public gallery, awaiting the arrival of the accused.

Quickly the court filled up. Men came in with bundles of official-looking papers, which they laid out along tables in precise order. A woman came to sit on a high stool behind a typewriter. The jury-box was soon occupied by two rows of serious men, more at ease behind shop counters or desks in banks and offices than in this heightened atmosphere where life and death was at their disposal.

There was a stir in the gallery as Duke Parsons entered below into the main body of the court. He pushed his son in a wheelchair, with all four of his daughters following behind. A ripple of identification ran through the ranks of spectators, then one of puzzlement. This didn't look like the ruffian family depicted in newspaper accounts.

Duke was dressed in a dark suit, a heavy watch chain slung across his broad chest. His starched collar, the shine of his boots could attract no whiff of disapproval. There was even something dignified about him as he manoeuvred the wheelchair down the central aisle, then stood to one side to let the women pass into a row of seats kept vacant for them.

Frances didn't allow her gaze to flicker. She looked straight ahead, as if in church. The story in the paper had sliced into her soul, then brought out her proud resistance. By her presence she would prove every word a filthy slur and a lie. Hettie followed, holding Sadie's hand, each taking their tone from Frances. They'd taken care to dress up, not flamboyantly, but decent and smart, to give Ernie a boost and to prove the reporters wrong. Even Hettie had shed her Army uniform, to appear in court in her best green outfit. She felt it would attract less attention, and she didn't want to risk offending some members of the jury with her teetotal stance. Jess bent to speak a word with Robert, nodded, then proceeded to her seat. Duke set the brake on the wheelchair and sat down at last, shoulders back, head up.

'Wounded in France,' ran the whisper around the gallery. 'Oldest son . . . volunteered for action . . . saved by a pal.'

Robert took the force of their concentrated gaze. He

wanted to meet expectations. How would a proud, wounded hero react? He felt unsure, aware of the gap between their perception and his sense of the truth as it happened, there amongst the roaring guns and stuttering rifles. So he resorted to a stiff glare at the empty judge's seat. It seemed to satisfy. You could almost hear and touch public opinion as it shifted and swung behind the whole Parsons family.

Up in the gallery, Annie Wiggin and Florrie Searles, strange bedfellows during this crisis, helped things along. They conferred over the quality of the jurors; one looked pinched and mean, another too full of himself, but one, two, three on the right looked solid, decent sorts. Dolly Ogden, standing behind, poked Annie to draw her attention as the lawyers came in. Then a door rattled out of sight and two police officers preceded Ernie out of the cells. They walked impassively ahead.

Ernie emerged from his lonely, dark wait and ducked his head away from the massive room full of strangers. He stopped dead, until a third officer moved him on from behind. Then he shifted on again into the dock. There was a sea of faces, a babble of voices as he climbed three steps and sat alone and terrified in the seat of the accused.

A warder jerked him to his feet as a gavel rattled down on a desk and the procession of crimson and fur robes and curled wigs approached the platform from the side.

The judge sat in the central carved seat, flanked by lesser court officials. As he settled, pulling his robes close around his legs, he glanced at Ernie. Removed by ritual and by long years of administering justice, his cold eyes simply registered the usual; a raw young man spruced up for the occasion, but with a downtrodden look. He flickered a second glance into the body of the court to where the relatives sat, tight-jawed and upright. He was impassive to the point of boredom, hoping for no nonsense and a swift conclusion.

The family hardly spared a moment to assess their chances with Judge Berry. Ernie claimed every scrap of their attention as he struggled to hold up his head. Once he'd spotted them, he kept his eyes glued to their bench, and as proceedings began, his every move was dictated by his pa's silent, patient signs. He stood when Duke stood for the judge to enter. He sat at Duke's firm nod. He swivelled his body towards the men in wigs when they began to talk, but his gaze never stole away from the reassuring sight of his family all lined up to help.

Robert meanwhile suffered badly from the stares of all his old friends up in the gallery, facing them for the first time since his injury. He knew they were judging the changes in him; the stigma of his wheelchair, his white, drawn look and trembling hands. But all protest was beyond him. Just as in the hospital, you had to submit. Here it was different rules and regulations, but they kept you tied down just the same. They prevented you from speaking out when your family was under attack, and people drove their knives of accusation into the heart of your existence. The very language shanghaied him; the 'm'luds', 'm'learned friends', 'aforesaids' and 'incriminating evidence'. Their posture spoke of privilege as they hooked their thumbs inside the front bands of their silk gowns and strutted down the centre of the court, wigs perched, pivoting on metal-tipped, polished shoes. He sat there angry and helpless as the prosecution presented their case.

Hettie took the witness stand first and swore her oath. She stood up high, recalling the night in question; the time, the place, the position in which she'd discovered her friend's body. In the corner of the gallery, almost hidden, stood Mary and Tommy O'Hagan. Hettie answered with honest simplicity and a touching faith in the truth. Earnest prayers had shown her the way; the blame would shift and rest on the right person if only she told the truth.

'Tell me, Miss Parsons, were you expecting to meet the victim, Daisy O'Hagan, on that particular night?' Charles Forster, prosecuting counsel, paused by the witness stand. He was a tall man with white hair and shadowy grey features. His voice was deceptively smooth and polite. 'It was your custom, was it not?'

Hettie nodded. 'Daisy never said nothing about going off by herself. That's why I went back to look for her.'

'Had you already looked?'

'Yes, and I asked around the whole place. One of the girls said she'd seen her go off to meet someone at the stage door, but that was earlier on.'

'She went off to the stage door, you say?' Forster sounded merely curious.

'That's what they said. I ain't seen her.'

'Did they say whom she'd gone to meet at the stage door?'

'I don't know. Some gentleman, I expect.' Hettie returned his stare.

'Did they say *which* gentleman?'

'No, sir. It could've been anyone.'

'Hm.' Forster's expression was disapproving. 'So it seems the victim had an assignation at the stage door.' He raised an eyebrow at the jury-box. 'Let's proceed. What did you do next, Miss Parsons, when you failed to find your friend?'

'I seen Mr Mills looking for her, and . . .'

'Mr Mills?'

'The manager. He had her wages. He wanted to get hold of Daisy to hand over her money.'

Forster nodded. Sewell, sitting beside another bewigged figure, wrote a short note and slid it along the table. 'But eventually you left the building, Miss Parsons?'

'Yes, sir.'

'Assuming that the victim had met her gentleman friend and gone off. Now tell the court why you returned and made the unfortunate discovery.'

Hettie gave a small frown. 'I met up with Robert out on the street.' She looked down at the barrister and answered his brief prompt. 'My brother, Robert. He asked me, had I seen Ernie 'cos he'd lost him. Ernie's my other brother.' She glanced towards the dock. 'I said we'd best go back. Ern was bound to be waiting at the stage door. He never went nowhere without us. So we went back.'

There was more urgent scribbling at both defence and prosecution benches.

'And was he at the stage door?'

'No, sir.'

'That was most unusual, you say? So where was he, do you know?'

'No, sir. It was after that I went in and found Daisy, like I told you.' Hettie's head went down for the first time. Her eyelids pricked with tears.

'And when in fact did you next see your brother, Ernie?'

'Back home, sir.'

'Not where, but when, Miss Parsons. That same night?'

'No, sir. He was already in bed when me and Rob got back. I never saw him till breakfast.'

'I see.' Forster backed off with raised eyebrows. He sniffed, checked the brief on his desk and finished with his witness with an air of quiet satisfaction. The case had begun nicely.

The sergeant and the inspector from Union Street cemented it firmly in place, identifying for the jury the time of events, the unusual amount of violence used against the victim, the position of the murder weapon after it had skidded across the floor away from the body.

'Thrown down in haste, would you say?' Forster suggested.

The sergeant nodded. 'I'd say so, yes, sir. Not very clever. Done in a panic before the murderer ran off.'

'What kind of knife, Sergeant Matthews?'

'Kitchen knife, sir. Ordinary type with a bone handle, a six-inch blade.' The sergeant performed his duty with minimum fuss. 'Available from any ironmonger's.'

'Including Powells' of Duke Street, Sergeant?' Forster loaded his voice with quiet significance.

Mayhew, the defence counsel, objected. If the type of knife was commonly available, he argued, the fact that it was on sale at Powells' could not be considered relevant. The judge agreed. Jess looked along the row at Frances and nodded.

Forster inclined his head towards the bench. Unfortunately, the police had not been able to pin down the shopkeeper, Powell, over the purchase of that particular knife. He had to let it go, but he turned energetically back to his witness. 'Did you subject the weapon to forensic scrutiny, Sergeant Matthews?'

'We did, sir, and we found fingerprints on the handle.' The sergeant rocked on to his heels as a ripple of renewed attention ran through the room.

'Could you identify those fingerprints for the court?'

'Yes, sir. They appear as item number three in evidence for the prosecution. They belong to the accused, Ernest Parsons.'

There was a gasp. Prosecuting counsel executed a turn and clipped his heels together. Then he dipped his head to the judge and returned to his seat.

Duke sat looking steadily at Ernie, while the others dropped their gaze under the dual weight of confusion and shock. Ernie had touched the knife. Fingerprints couldn't lie. Defence cross-questioning continued in a haze, and they were well into the inspector's testimony before the family could gather their concentration.

'Now, during your interview with the accused at Union Street police station, Inspector, did he give an indication as to why he had waited at the stage door in the first place?' Forster was in full swing.

'Yes, sir. He expected his brother, Robert, to join him there, to wait for the girls, Hettie Parsons and Daisy O'Hagan.'

'And did he? Did his brother eventually join him?'

'We don't know, sir. According to him, the last thing he can recall is arriving at the appointed spot.' The inspector turned a page on his notepad set down on the ledge in the witness-box. He looked up sharply to field the next question.

'But you found fingerprints belonging to the accused on the murder weapon, did you not? Do you have any other evidence to corroborate Ernie Parsons's presence at the scene?' Forster led him on, sure of his ground.

'Yes, sir. We found his cap, item number two in evidence for the prosecution, down in one corner of the girls' dressing room, as if it had fallen off and been kicked about a bit.'

'In a struggle? Is that what you suggest?'

'That's how it looked to my men, yes, sir.'

'And in his written statement, is it true that the accused admits to having done something he was sorry for on that occasion?'

This was another question guaranteed to raise the tension in the court. There was an intake of breath. Robert gripped the arms of his wheelchair until his knuckles turned white. Hettie, unnerved by her own time on the stand, stared down at her lap.

The inspector cleared his throat and picked up the notepad. He read in a loud, clear voice. 'Yes, sir. He said, "I never meant to do it. Tell Rob I never meant to!" He said it twice, sir. There was no doubt.'

Forster nodded and pursed his lips. '"I never meant to do it."' He repeated the phrase deliberately and looked accusingly at Ernie. '"I never meant to do it." We all do many things we never mean to do, on the spur of the moment, and often they give cause for regret. Our temper snaps, we lose control, isn't that so, Inspector?'

'In crimes of this type, that's true in my experience, yes, sir.'

'And would you say that the accused has a temper like anyone else? That he might be prey to jealousy if the girl he wants is seen taking up with another man, for instance? That he might very well lose control and snap, as we say? What would be your opinion on that, Inspector?'

'Like you say, sir, he ain't no different. Same as the next man, if provoked. Only not too bright and not open to reason, in my judgement. I can see a case of him choosing the wrong girl and having to stand by and watch her chuck him over for someone else. Well, it's obvious what might happen then.' The inspector gave a worldly shrug.

If his family could stand up and shout, right then and there, 'You don't know Ernie. He ain't the same. He's gentle as a lamb, there ain't no harm in him!' they would bring the trial to a shambling halt. But you had to live with him to know him; poor, gentle Ernie, just bright enough to realize his own shortcomings, ever anxious to make himself acceptable in spite of them. He never 'wanted' anything in his life and just took it; least of all Daisy, least

327

of all a life. Yet he sat with a puzzled frown, shaking his head at his pa, seeing through a daze that things were not going well now.

Fred Mills came next, suave and sneering about Daisy. Yes, it was possible she was seeing more than one man at once. Yes, he'd seen her walk home with Ernie Parsons on more than one occasion, but that wouldn't stop her from going with other men. She liked the ones who gave her presents and she knew how to lead them on. Mills painted the picture of a cheap flirt who might provoke a man to violence. He seemed not to care that her mother stood in the gallery, and he cast a cold look at Hettie, sitting subdued and strained alongside her sisters.

Mayhew cross-examined him. Had he managed to find Daisy and give her the wages owed?

'No, sir. The other girls told me she must have gone off early, so I left it.'

'Was that normal, Mr Mills?'

'Not really, no.' The manager's mouth twitched sideways. He looked disgruntled.

'And weren't you suspicious? That a girl should go off home without her wages?'

'I'm not her keeper,' came the flippant answer.

'Yes or no will do, Mr Mills,' Judge Berry interposed wearily. 'And we keep a civil tongue here.'

Mills breathed loudly through his nose. 'No, I wasn't suspicious. I didn't think it was my business.'

'Weren't you worried?' Mayhew pressed the point. He was dogged; a dark-haired, olive-skinned man, much younger than his opponent, Forster. 'Forget suspicion. Weren't you perhaps alarmed that a girl in your employ, not yet twenty years of age, seemed to have simply disappeared into the maze of London streets, late at night, in the dark?'

'No,' Mills insisted through gritted teeth.

'So you stayed inside the building and forgot all about her?'

'Yes, I went back to my office.'

'To count the takings, no doubt. Did anyone see you during that time?'

The witness stared him out as he answered with a note of triumph. 'In my office, you mean? As a matter of fact, yes. I was with Archie Small.'

The gallery gave a deflated sigh. 'Just when he was getting his claws into the oily bleeder, he comes up with an alibi!' Florrie scowled her disbelief.

Annie grunted. 'Them two's thick as thieves,' she grumbled. 'Mills and Small. I wonder what they've got to bleeding hide!'

Mayhew, dashed but not defeated, came at his witness once more. 'Would you please describe your relationship with the victim, Mr Mills,' he said coolly.

'What are you getting at?' Mills was visibly rattled. His suave exterior gave way.

'Answer the question,' the judge commanded.

'I gave her the work. I paid her wages.'

'So you never took what might be called a romantic interest in Daisy O'Hagan, Mr Mills?'

The manager's laugh struck a dry, hollow note. 'Not me, mister. Strictly professional, that's me.'

Mayhew continued with his sceptical tone. 'And what about your friend and alibi, Mr Small? To your knowledge, was he in any way other than professionally involved with Miss O'Hagan?'

Mills turned to the judge. 'He's a married man, Your Honour!'

This time, some spectators responded with a laugh. Moral outrage sat absurdly on the cynical manager's shoulders. Berry's hooded eyes closed for a moment in exasperation. Mayhew, seeing that the judge's tolerance had reached its limit, backed off. But Mills was exposed as a nasty character. Set alongside Hettie, with defence evidence yet to come, Mills had come off badly. Archie Small would back up his alibi, no doubt, but first the court must deal with a witness whom no one in the gallery had expected.

Syd Swan came on to the stand to open disapproval. No one liked the blunt-featured, crude individual who took a sly interest in all the girls and had fingers in many of Chalky White's shady deals.

In the gallery, Dolly frowned at Amy for having taken up with such an unpopular figure. 'You can certainly pick them, girl,' she growled. Swan had never completely emerged from the pimply stage; there was something grubby and unappealing about him. His head hung slightly forward off hunched shoulders. He looked furtive even when trying to impress, as now.

'Hush, Ma!' Amy squirmed.

Down in the middle aisle, Robert's grip on his wheel-chair tightened. His skin felt lousy, as in the trenches. Just looking at Swan made his flesh creep. But yes, he had been there that night, hanging around under a dark archway, giving chase when he spotted Robert. Now no doubt he'd have more 'incriminating evidence' for the jury to consider. Robert's throat constricted with rage and helplessness.

New spectators entered the public gallery as Swan swore the oath. Maurice Leigh and Walter Davidson had met up by chance outside the courtroom and made their way in together, discussing Ernie's case as they went. Maurice had come as early as he could, to lend Jess moral support. 'I only hope it goes the right way,' he said to Walter. 'It'll break Jess's heart if they go and hang him.'

The phrase stunned good-hearted Walter. It seemed out

of the question until you heard it spoken. 'They wouldn't,' he said quietly.

'They hung a flower seller in Shoreditch that time. Margaret Murphy, the one what done her kid in.' Maurice peered through the door to seize their time to enter. The court usher was handing the Bible to the witness. 'And they hung that farm boy last year. Eighteen years old. Then they found out he hadn't done the murder, too bleeding late.'

'Not this time, they won't.' Walter strode past Maurice into the mass of spectators. He spotted Chalky White coming in through an entrance opposite, then lost him in the crowd.

Forster's questions for Swan were brief and simple. He established his witness's rivalry with the older Parsons brother, Robert, which had come to a head after the performance at the Palace. He pictured for the court the chase that took place between them just at the crucial time when the accused had come out of the theatre in search of that brother. Robert listened, a bitter taste in his mouth, unable to look at either Ernie or Duke.

'Now then, Mr Swan, what did you do after Mr Parsons had given you the slip?' Forster could feel the initiative returning to him.

'We walked back to the Palace.' Syd stood gripping the ledge of the witness stand. He leaned forward, eager to lay the blame.

'How many of you?'

'Three or four.'

'For what purpose?'

Syd shrugged. 'I dunno. We was having a lark, that's all.'

'Looking for girls, Mr Swan?'

He leered. 'Could be.'

'But you didn't find any?' Forster pretended to condone the rough code of picking up fair game in the street.

'We left it too late, see.'

The judge sat back in his seat. Forster rolled his eyes at his witness's informality. 'Whom did you see outside the Palace after your return?'

This was Syd's star part. He leaned even further out of the box. 'We seen Ernie Parsons.'

'Where, exactly?'

'He was running up out of the side alley from the stage door, going hell for leather. Never seen nothing like it. He was moaning and yelling something, I couldn't make out what. First we heard him, then he comes pelting out on to the street, a proper bleeding mess.'

'In a panic, would you say?'

'Not half.'

'You say you couldn't make out what he said, Mr Swan?'

Syd paused. He caught Chalky's eye up in the gallery, certain that his standing had shot sky high with his leader and all the rest of the gang. 'Just one word,' he told the court. 'I just made out the one word.'

'What was that?' Forster stopped pacing and rested one knuckle on top of his pile of papers. He looked directly at Ernie as Swan gave his final answer.

'"Daisy,"' came the reply. 'Lots of times, over and over, before he runs off like a mad thing. "Daisy. Daisy. Daisy."'

Chapter Twenty-Five

An unofficial jury gathered that evening in the public bar at the Duke. Some felt that the first day of the trial had gone as well as could be expected. They liked Mayhew's style; he came across straight, unlike the puffed-up, insincere Forster.

'I reckon him and Sewell make a good team,' Dolly told Florrie, who stood staunchly behind the bar while the rest of the family pulled themselves together upstairs. Joxer too had come in as regular as clockwork through all this, steadily minding his own business and never missing a day. 'Frances did well to find them two.'

Florrie nodded. 'They got Ernie's best interests at heart. They're thinking of leaving well alone and not dragging him on to the stand as a witness.'

'Why not?' Amy couldn't see the point. Surely they'd want to get Ernie to stand up and say he wasn't guilty for all to hear.

'They think he might panic.' Florrie couldn't make up her own mind about this. On the one hand, she thought Ern could win the jury over, on the other hand he might well go to pieces.

'If that bleeding Forster gets at him,' Annie explained, 'he can twist things round and make them look bad. Poor Ernie ain't no match for him.'

Everyone nodded uneasily.

'But we'll have other witnesses speaking up for us.' Florrie tried to rescue the mood.

Arthur Ogden, well dug in by the pianola, agreed. 'We got Robert home for a start.'

'They'll take to him all right,' Dolly said. 'They're gonna have to see they ain't dealing with a pack of ruffians when he gets on the stand. He'll wear his uniform, I hope?' She glanced at Florrie for confirmation. 'Well, he still looks big and handsome, poor bloke, and very decent. He'll stand up for Ernie.'

Several bystanders picked up on the awkwardness of her choice of phrase, and stuck their faces deep into their beer glasses. Amy wondered privately how they would manage to get the wheelchair up the steps into the stand. Walter Davidson frowned and shook his head in Maurice's direction.

'Ain't Hettie done well?' Annie put in to change the subject. 'There ain't a drop of cunning in that girl. Nice and clean and honest, she came across. And not going on about Jesus neither, thank God.'

Dolly turned up her nose. 'It's all right, Annie Wiggin, everyone here knows you ain't been to church in a month of Sundays. If you ask me, Ett should've worn her Army uniform and all.'

Annie disagreed. 'It'd put them off. They're all fond of a drink or two, I bet.'

'Who is?' Arthur was slow to follow.

'Them geezers on the jury. They like Ett the way she was, an honest, good-looking girl.'

No one mentioned the police evidence and the weight it must carry. 'That Syd Swan's a bleeding smarmy bastard,' Walter said with unusual force.

Amy felt her face glow red. Walter realized he must have

missed something. When no one put in a word in Syd's defence, Amy stuck her head in the air and waltzed out.

'You put your bleeding foot in it there, mate,' Annie told Walter. She nudged him and looked over her shoulder at the swinging door.

'Serve her right,' Dolly said. Her relationship with her daughter hadn't improved of late. There were fewer rows, but each pretended she couldn't care less what the other thought. Dolly said Amy could go out with whoever she bleeding well chose and get herself done in, like poor Daisy O'Hagan. Amy said she could look after herself and do as she liked. 'Walter's right. Syd Swan's a nasty, creeping sort. Look how he tried to put the blame on Ernie today,' Dolly said. She looked at her beer as if it had suddenly turned sour.

Just then, the door opened again. Jess held it wide from outside to let Robert wheel himself through. The awkward silence broke as Walter moved forward to greet his old friend. He admired the man's nerve; shot to bits, just out of hospital, but wheeling himself in to see the old crowd. Walter caught Robert's eye and shook hands with genuine warmth. 'What'll you have to drink, Rob? The usual?'

Jess managed a smile as she joined Maurice at the bar. The deep affection between them grew day by day, despite the poor circumstances. An important step had been taken when they first allowed people to notice them as a couple at the Town Hall dance. Now, whenever Maurice called into the Duke for a drink, the shout went up to go and tell Jess that her young man was here. 'You on your way to work?' she asked him as he looped an arm around her waist.

'Yes, I got ten minutes though.'

'How do you think it went today?' She looked up into his face.

'We was saying, well as can be expected.' Maurice's own feeling was gloomier and perhaps more realistic than the general opinion. He'd picked up the police evidence from a fellow spectator, and seen the reaction to Syd Swan's dramatic testimony. But he didn't want to dash Jess's hopes.

'Hm.' Jess looked worried none the less.

They switched to safe small-talk, and as Maurice got ready to go, he crossed paths at the door with a crowd of new drinkers, including Syd Swan and Chalky White. They came in off the street with careless bravado. Instinctively Maurice ducked back into the room to keep an eye on things and to make sure Jess could cope with the unwelcome intrusion.

Chalky and Syd were all dressed up. They strode in as if they owned the place, knowing smiles passing between them. Whitey Lewis went up to Florrie to order drinks. Someone went over and fingered the keys of the pianola, setting up a tuneless sprinkling of notes.

Florrie's glance darted towards Robert. He'd picked up on their entrance right away, though his back was turned. His jaw was clenched tight. Walter put one hand on his shoulder. Behind them all, Duke came through the double doors.

'Give the men a drink, Florrie.' He sounded matter of fact, striding across the bar and lifting the counter flap. He reached up to a high shelf for clean glasses, lining them up for Florrie to fill. All the while he kept his eyes fixed on Syd Swan.

Some of the regular drinkers began to mutter. Dolly led an exodus of women away from the bar to the furthest corner of the room. But the gang enjoyed this demonstration in a thick-skinned, insulting way. It proved they were having an effect.

Duke switched his gaze to Robert. The boy's suffering

was too much to bear. 'Pa!' Jess cut in. 'You gotta get rid of them!'

He took a deep breath. A fight was the last thing he wanted. But he was landlord here, and he could sense everyone was behind him in slinging them out. He would keep it calm, but he'd get them out. He counted five of them, then nodded firmly in the direction of each one of his own supporters; Walter, Maurice, and if it came to it, Arthur Ogden and some of the older men. Joxer lined up alongside his boss. One look at his grim face and iron-hard frame would send most men running for the door.

Syd looked uneasily at Chalky for direction. He'd agreed to this for a lark, and because Chalky had been set on carrying it out. 'It's my local,' he'd bragged. 'Ain't no reason why we can't go in for a quiet drink, is there?'

'You want to set the bleeding cat among the pigeons, you do.' Whitey had woken up to the possibilities. He was keener on a good scrap than Syd.

'You're right there, Whitey. What's wrong with reminding them Parsons that they got themselves in a spot of bother when their boy done that poor girl in?'

Out on the cold street the gang had laughed at Chalky's false concern for Daisy. Majority opinion went with their leader's plan, so they dived into the Duke, grinning like monkeys, scattering the kids hanging round the doorstep for crumbs of news about the trial.

Now there was a serious possibility of a fight.

'You just drink that down, gents, and then you can leave the premises,' Duke said loud and clear.

'Or else?' Chalky checked around the room and guessed that numbers were evenly matched. 'You don't want to throw us out, old son. It won't look good when it gets out. More rough stuff. As if you ain't got enough bother already.'

Duke didn't hesitate. Chalky's cheap taunt roused him to anger at last. He slammed open the bar flap and moved out to face Chalky. 'I'm the one who decides that, mister, and I'm chucking you out, no matter what!' With Joxer, Walter, Maurice and Arthur lining up behind him, he stood his ground.

Chalky snorted. He took a long, slow pull at his drink, draining it to the dregs. All eyes were on him. Jess had crossed over to Robert, who wrenched at his chair, trying to drag it into the centre of action, restrained by Dolly and Annie. Chalky withered him with a pitying look, then he turned back to Duke. 'Listen, we don't want no trouble.'

Duke's fist ached to smack Chalky's jaw. He held it ready clenched, but he could see they would slither out of a confrontation now that they'd thrown the place into turmoil. He felt Walter drop his guard and Joxer shift to one side.

'We're on our way!' Chalky derided them with his insolent cheeriness. All five men put down their empty glasses and turned away. Arthur made a grab at Whitey's coat sleeve, but Maurice pulled him back. Someone spat on the floor as the gang left.

Duke went straight over to Robert for a soothing word. 'Easy there,' he told him, 'you gotta do your bit in court tomorrow.'

But the humiliation had been too strong. 'What bleeding good will it do?' Robert demanded. He pulled his chair out of their grasp. Walter and Maurice came over, while other customers resumed their drinking. 'They already made up their minds Ernie done it. And for all we know, he did!'

Duke turned sharply away. He looked lost for words.

'He don't mean it, Pa!' Jess leapt forward.

But Robert was hurting too much. 'We don't know, do we? Me and Ett was on the scene that night and even we can't say for sure that Ern never did it!' He was beside himself.

'He *never* did it!' Jess clutched both arms across her stomach and fended off all doubt. Her face went wild with shock.

'No, he never.' It was Walter's calm voice backing her up. 'It stands to reason, Rob. Ernie never done nothing like that.'

Jess grasped his hand with relief. 'See!' she said. 'We gotta keep hold. Ern's innocent!'

'Well, who did it, then?' Robert had subsided into sullenness.

Duke sighed, bent to unhitch the brake on his son's wheelchair and began to wheel him out. 'If we knew that, son, we'd be home and dry,' he said.

Frances's sense of duty had taken her along to the hospital to enquire after Ada Wray. It was the first evening of the trial; reason enough to get away from the Duke and to try to keep calm. She was averse as ever to bar-room gossip and found herself uneasy with her neighbours' sympathy, however well meant. So she hurried along the rainy streets, intent on seeking out her friend, Rosie Cornwell, for news of Billy's wife's condition.

But it was Billy himself she met first in the hospital grounds. She recognized him, thinking it odd that he should be sitting outside on a bench in the cold, dark evening, staring ahead. They'd not met alone together since that evening in the coffee room at the Institute, and at first she almost redirected her track so as to miss passing close by. But then she changed her mind.

'Billy?' She went and stood by the bench, waiting for him to stir. 'How's Ada?'

Billy sat forward, resting his arms on his thighs, his cap slung between his hands, head down. Without giving any sign of recognition, he told Frances that Ada had died that afternoon.

Frances sat beside him. 'Oh, Billy, I'm sorry.' To her Ada had been a shadowy figure whom she'd met only once at a social evening; a faded but evidently pretty woman with a plump, pale face and carefully arranged light brown hair. She was quite pleasant but uninterested in Billy's 'causes', as she called them. Her mother lived in the house with them, and the two women were friends and allies.

Billy nodded. 'You came a long way out of your way to ask after her.' He kept his head down. Any effort seemed too much.

'I wanted a breath of air and a talk with Rosie,' Frances explained.

He glanced up at last. 'How's the trial?'

'I don't know, Billy. We just had one day of it.'

'I been thinking about you.'

'Don't, Billy,' she interrupted. 'Thanks, but don't say nothing.' She stretched out her hand in the dark and put it over one of his. Then she quickly withdrew it. After a few moments more she stood and said goodbye. They parted in the glimmer of dripping lamplight, with no witness to their sad, lonely scene.

Next morning in court, Mr Sewell came and drew Duke to one side to inform him that they'd decided against calling Ernie to give evidence. 'We don't think he's up to it, Mr Parsons. I've had one last talk with him, and I'm afraid he still insists that he can't remember anything that took place beyond that stage door.'

Duke didn't look surprised. 'He blocked it out, I should think. When he's upset he goes into a world of his own; that's just Ernie.' He was aware of the crowd outside shoving down the corridor for the second day of the trial; idle spectators, newspapermen, supporters.

Sewell agreed. 'Yes, I understand that from my talks with him in prison. It's like getting blood out of a stone.' He sighed. 'No, we can't take the risk of letting the prosecution have a go at him. He's easily led, you see, into saying what he thinks you want to hear.'

'No need to tell me that,' Duke argued. 'He'd put his own head into the noose, is that what you mean?'

Frances slipped her arm through her father's. Sewell looked uncomfortable. 'I wouldn't put it quite like that, Mr Parsons. But tactically it's best if we rely on the evidence of others, don't you agree?' He disliked any whiff of defeatism until the case was finally over. 'It really is going as well as we expected.' His own confidence was vital once the family started to go downhill like this. He turned to Jess to check final details in her account. 'Don't let Forster frighten you,' he warned. 'Stand up to him. Don't let him think you've got anything to hide.'

His unwitting words followed her on to the witness stand, the first to be called that day. Everyone sat or stood in place exactly as before; all the court officials with their own special piece of ritual to enact, the all-important Judge Berry presiding in his crimson robes and white kid gloves.

Forster got to work right away. Jess was the final witness for the prosecution, with information relevant to the state of mind of the accused when he returned home. She felt her fingers tingle to the touch of the calfskin cover of the huge Bible with its big gold cross. Her voice emerged faint and unfamiliar to swear the oath.

'Now, Miss Parsons, we want to hear how your brother, Ernest, behaved when he got back home from the music hall. He was alone, was he not?'

'No, sir. He came in with Frances.'

This was a bad start. Forster looked irritated by the contradiction.

'Frances is my sister, sir.' Jess offered to help.

'Quite. You have a large family, Miss Parsons?'

'Yes, sir.'

'But it was you who dealt with your brother and got him to bed?'

'Yes, sir.'

'How did he behave?'

'He was upset.'

'How, "upset"? Was he raving and moaning?' Forster reminded the court of Syd Swan's last account of seeing Ernie outside the Palace.

'Oh no, sir. More dazed. Upset in a quiet sort of way, sir. Frances found him outside on the street looking lost, and she brought him on up. Then I took over.'

'Quite, again. You say he was dazed. Did he say anything to you?'

'Yes, sir. He said he'd lost Robert outside the theatre. He looked for him everywhere, but he never found him.'

'Is that all?'

'Yes, sir.'

'Now, Miss Parsons, what time did your sister, Frances, bring the accused upstairs with her?'

Jess faltered. 'About midnight, sir.'

'Speak up. About midnight, you say?'

'Yes, sir.'

'And we know that the audience came out of the music hall at five minutes to eleven.' Forster included the jury in his calculations by walking close to their box. 'Does it take more than an hour to walk from the Palace home to Duke Street, Miss Parsons?'

'If you're lost, it could do, sir.' She wanted to point it out as a fact, but the barrister turned it into a facetious remark with a frown and a sigh.

'Let's say he was *pretending* he'd got lost, Miss Parsons. Let's just suppose. If you came straight from A to B, from the Palace to the Duke of Wellington public house, how long would it take you? Walking briskly, as the crow flies?'

'About twenty minutes, sir.'

Forster placed his fingertips together and looked directly at the foreman of the jury. 'More than forty minutes unaccounted for, by my reckoning, sir.' He raised his eyebrows, then turned with a swish of his silk gown. 'Now, Miss Parsons, we're almost there. We'll return to your brother's distress when he did finally make his way home. Didn't you think it might amount to something more than his simply getting lost?'

'No, sir.' She could feel Ernie's full gaze fixed on her. 'I never.'

'So you thought the best thing to do was to pack him off straight to bed? Did he object?'

'No, sir. Like I said, he was a bit dazed.'

'I imagine he was, Miss Parsons. Now think carefully, and remember your oath. We've learnt from fingerprint evidence, and the presence of the cap of the accused that he had indeed been in the room where the murder had taken place. He doesn't deny that outright, at least. He only goes so far as to tell us that he can't remember having been there! Now, did he mention this vital fact to you?'

'No, sir.' Jess fell into the same dull, monosyllabic replies. Her mouth felt dry. She looked up to the gallery for Maurice, but a sea of faces looked back.

'Hm. It would account for his distress, would it not? If

he had been in that room, I mean? No, don't answer that, Miss Parsons. That was merely for us to ponder. Now, he mentioned nothing about the murder. That suggests he was trying to conceal it from you?'

'Maybe, but maybe not.' This was where Jess knew more about Ernie than they did in this court. 'If he's upset, he goes quiet, sometimes for days on end. It's a kind of shock, I think.' She spoke eagerly, turning to the jury. 'He don't remember nothing till he comes out of it, then he's right as rain again.'

'Very convenient, Miss Parsons.' Forster stood and demolished her with a single look and phrase. 'Selective amnesia, I think they call it, gentlemen.' He shared a joke with the jury, then reached the pinnacle of his questioning of this particular witness. 'Let's say he was concealing it. We must ask ourselves, was there anything about him to suggest that he'd been in a struggle?'

'No, sir.' Jess looked down at her own trembling hands.

'He'd lost his cap. Did you not notice that?'

'Yes, sir.'

'Perhaps in a struggle?'

'It didn't strike me at the time, no, sir.'

'Was his clothing torn?'

'No, sir.'

'Were his boots dirty, Miss Parsons?' The tension in Forster's naturally high, thin voice rose a further pitch.

Jess hesitated.

'Yes or no, Missie!' Judge Berry barked.

'Yes, sir.'

'Was there blood on them?' Forster realized he had her. Honesty was such a flimsy commodity in these circumstances; it could be turned both ways.

'Yes.'

Forster's head went back. 'What did you do? Did you clean it off?'

'Yes.'

'Louder, Miss Parsons.'

'Yes.' She looked up for help. There was none to be found.

'You cleaned blood off his boots, yet you say there was no sign of a struggle on him?' He sounded shocked, disbelieving.

Jess's lip trembled. She hung her head.

'That's all, Miss Parsons.'

Forster sat as Mayhew stood, quickly rethinking his tactics. This was more damning than Sewell had led him to believe, and the witness was in no state to act as character reference for the accused. But there was one point he must make clear in the minds of the jury. He would get it over with quickly. 'Miss Parsons, I'm sorry to distress you further, but let's be clear about this matter of the blood.'

Jess fought to look him in the eye.

'It was on your brother's boots, you say?'

'Yes, sir.'

'Was it on his trousers?'

She frowned. 'No, sir.'

'Speak up!' Judge Berry snapped. 'So we can all hear your answers, Missie!'

'No, sir!'

'Was it on his jacket?' Mayhew picked up the thread.

'No, sir.'

'Was it on his hands or his face? Was it anywhere at all, except on Ernie's boots?'

'No, sir,' she said, loud and clear now.

'That's odd,' Mayhew remarked. He looked quizzically at the jury. 'This is an exceptionally neat murderer, whose hands and clothes carry not one stain of his victim's blood, don't you think?' He waived any further questions and watched Jess half-stumble from the witness-box, then he bent to confer with the solicitor. Numb and weak, Jess returned to her seat.

'Good for you,' Hettie whispered as she sat down. 'You stood up to them, and Mr Mayhew nailed them good and proper.'

They brought Frank Henshaw to the stand next, to provide a good character for Ernie. The defence case would rest on the clean record to date of the accused. They would dismantle press reports of bad living and poor family support, and ask how a young man of unblemished reputation and admittedly limited capabilities to think for himself could suddenly transform himself into a vicious, frenzied attacker of a defenceless woman. His employer was the first port of call in the journey to re-establish Ernie's good name.

Henshaw took the oath and acknowledged judge and jury. He stood full square, hands behind his back, a solid tradesman like them. Mayhew established him as a chapel-goer and a thriving businessman, with the pick of a dozen errand boys to deliver his groceries. 'So why choose Ernie Parsons, Mr Henshaw?' Mayhew sounded relaxed. The shopkeeper wouldn't let them down.

'I knew him as a reliable lad,' Henshaw explained. 'I've known the family more than twenty years, ever since they came to live on Duke Street.'

'But as a chapel man, a Methodist, we might imagine you to have objections towards the family who lived at the pub, surely?'

Happy to be drawn out, Henshaw contradicted this view. 'I ain't one to ram my religion down another man's throat, sir. Like I say, I get on well with the Parsons family.

I offered work to Ernie and he turned out like I expected, a steady, honest, reliable lad.'

'He presented no problems at all, Mr Henshaw?'

'None, sir. And my wife, Mrs Henshaw, she found him just the same. You tell him what to do and it's good as done. The best lad we had in years.'

Mayhew nodded. The words penetrated even Ernie's bleak misery, and those who watched him saw his head go up and a faint look of pride appear on his face. A lump rose to the sisters' throats. Sadie allowed her hopes to rise.

'No questions,' Forster said abruptly, hardly bothering to stand, dismissing the witness as a tiresome waste of time and unworthy of cross-examination.

A new figure took Henshaw's place. The reporters in the gallery licked their pencils and began to scribble anew as the woman's faint voice repeated the oath. 'I, Mary Kathleen O'Hagan do swear by Almighty God . . .'

Annie Wiggin shouldered people aside for a better view. 'Good for you, Missus!' she said under her breath. Who better to give evidence for Ernie than the mother of the corpse? She glared in triumph at the surprised prosecution bench, and hoped that the shrivelled scarecrow of a judge would sit up and take notice. Morale rose. Dolly came and settled close to Annie, shoulder to shoulder.

Mary found the ordeal truly terrible. Naturally reticent, and worn down by long years of struggle, her instinct at the best of times was to shy away from the limelight. And this was the worst of times. But she did it for Hettie. She put on her one worn and dowdy brown coat and she came to court. She knew she looked what she was; a poor washerwoman from an immigrant family, whom life had treated badly.

'Thank you for taking the stand, Mrs O'Hagan,' Mayhew

began gently. Sewell had done well to get her here. She was a strong weapon in the emotional argument. He said he really only had two questions for her. 'Firstly, did your daughter, Daisy, ever talk to you about the accused, Ernie Parsons?'

'She did, sir. She mentioned him to me every so often.' Mary swayed and grasped the brass rail which ran along the top of the witness-box.

'Did she like him? Would you say she got on well with him?'

'She did, sir. She told me there was no harm in the boy and she liked to have him come to see the show. She was a good-hearted girl, sir, and she knew she could make Ernie's day, just by being friendly and nice with him.'

'Did she like him better than some of the other men who came to visit her backstage?'

'She did.' Mary's voice grew stronger. 'Some she didn't care for at all, sir, but they could be difficult to shake off. She knew her own mind in these things, sir.'

'But Ernie?'

'She liked him a lot, in a friendly way.'

'Not a romantic way, Mrs O'Hagan?'

'No, sir. They was just friends.'

Mayhew nodded. 'She trusted him?'

'Yes, sir. We all do.'

'Good. Thank you, Mrs O'Hagan. Which leads me to my second question, and this is really very important. In your opinion, would the accused be capable of committing this brutal act against your daughter?'

They held their breath as Mary paused. Her face looked long and weary. There were dark shadows under her eyes, and a hopelessness at the centre of her being. But she pulled herself upright.

'Do you understand the question?' Mayhew asked softly.

'I do, sir.' She looked straight at Ernie and her whole heart went out to him. 'I don't believe he done it, sir. Whatever they say against him, I don't believe he killed my girl!'

Chapter Twenty-Six

Ernie's defence counsel hoped he'd judged the public mood right as he watched Robert Parsons swear the oath. A special provision had been made for him to give his evidence from the floor of the court, still seated in his wheelchair, and it was true that he cut a sympathetic figure. Poetic phrases gathered around the injured man's head; 'Cut down in the flower of his youth', or more gloomily still, 'Think not for whom the bell tolls'. And that was the problem. Robert stood for the frailty of the human condition as well as for glorious sacrifice. Worse still, his uniform was evidently useless on him now, except as an emblem of the supreme indifference of war. But this pessimistic knowledge lay deep under layers of brash patriotism. Although the generals battling it out in Belgium and France were now prepared to admit that the war might well continue beyond Christmas, the demon Kaiser remained a figure of intense public hatred against whom the British Tommy would willingly fight to the death.

Mayhew banked on this image of the common-or-garden East End boy giving his all for king and country as he began his even-paced questioning of the wounded soldier.

Robert listened, and explained why he liked to take his young brother to watch the shows at the Palace. 'To give him a bit of a break. He was always on at me to go and watch Hettie and Daisy with him.'

'Why was that? Couldn't he go by himself?'

'No, sir. He needs someone with him. He ain't too good by himself.'

'No confidence?'

'No, sir.'

'What would happen to Ernie out on the streets alone?'

Robert didn't hesitate. 'He'd get lost. Pa never let him go off, especially at night. And we wouldn't want him to neither.'

'He'd get lost, you say? So it was entirely consistent for him to do so when he was separated from you on the night of the murder? I mean, you weren't surprised to hear he'd got lost while trying to find his way home alone?'

'No, sir.'

'And what was the reason for your separation?' Mayhew let the jury get used to the sound and look of this, his last witness. Robert's deep, sure voice with its military overtones came across well.

'I came out ahead of him. I told him we had to get a move on if we wanted to nab the girls. They didn't know we was there. So I shot off. But Ern's a bit slow in a crowd. I never thought of that, so I lost him somewhere. Then I ran into a bit of bother of my own.' Robert was reluctant to tell this part of the story, knowing that it was his own hot temper that had caused him to make an enemy of the powerful Chalky White, and this had led directly to his altercation with Syd Swan that night. Still, Sewell had convinced him to tell the whole truth, after Jess's experience on the stand. 'I planned to give Swan and his mates the slip as quick as I could, then double back for Ern.'

'How long were you gone?'

'About a quarter of an hour.'

'So you arrived back at the Palace at eleven fifteen?'

'Yes, then I met up with Hettie and heard there was no sign of Ern, so we set off home together, then we thought better of it, so we cut back again and went inside to check.'

'Inside the Palace, using the stage door?'

'Yes, sir.'

'At what time?'

'I'm not sure exactly. Before half eleven.'

Mayhew nodded. 'Now we won't trouble the court with another description of events surrounding the discovery of the body. Suffice it to say that the disaster coincided with your enlistment into His Majesty's regular army, and that your brother's arrest for this murder occurred on the eve of the fourteenth of September, the very day that you left Duke Street to join your regiment?'

'Yes, sir.'

'It must have been a terrible blow, Private Parsons?'

'We was all staggered. Frances wrote me the news and I jumped right up and said, "Oh no, that ain't right!" They had to sit on me to stop me jumping on a train back home to put them right about Ernie.'

'What was so incredible?' Mayhew had taken off his gold-rimmed glasses and swung them from his forefinger. He nodded encouragement at Robert.

'I knew in my bones they got it wrong. That's the first thing. Now, if they told me Ernie killed a bloke to stop him laying a finger on Daisy; maybe, just maybe I could see that. He'd die for that girl.

'Second thing, like you said yourself, sir, why wasn't he covered in blood then? All right, so suppose he goes into the room and suppose he finds her lying there. The poor bloke goes to see what they done to her, don't he? He goes over and he tries to get her up. Only she don't get up, and he gets blood all over his boots, like we heard. But if he'd been the one, it'd be all over his hands and clothes and all. And there ain't no sign of that.' Robert followed the logic without flinching at the details. 'He ain't never seen a dead body before. I bet he's scared stiff. He finds the knife on the floor beside her, and he grabs it and throws it away 'cos that's what done the damage. Now he's upset. He knows she ain't gonna wake up and he goes wild. He gets up and he runs out of the place quick as he can. That's when he bumps into Swan. By the time Frances runs into him, he's practically back home, and he's trying to block out what he just seen.'

'Explain to us why he would do that, if you please, Private Parsons.'

Robert sighed. ''Cos if he talks about it and tells anyone he's seen Daisy lying in a pool of blood, then it's true, ain't it? If he locks it up inside his own head, it can still be a bad dream. He can wake up. Daisy'll waltz into the room like normal, and everything's fine!'

Mayhew let this version sink in before he finished off. 'Private Parsons, why did you enlist with the army?'

Robert registered slight surprise. 'They need blokes like me,' he said, more subdued.

'Blokes like you?'

'Yes. Fit and strong. We can do out bit.'

Mayhew left it at that. 'And did your family approve?'

Robert looked straight ahead. 'Pa was with the army in India. He says it's the making of a man.'

'So you did it in part for him? Your family has a strong loyalty to king and country?'

'Yes, sir.'

'And finally, Private, could you tell us briefly the extent of your present injuries and how they occurred? No need to go into distressing detail, of course.' Mayhew's voice was respectfully lowered. He wanted to finish with this strong emotional impact.

Robert recalled for them the place, the time, the circumstances of the order to go over the top. He didn't tell them of the bitter cold, the muddle of command and counter-command, the sprawled bodies of comrades face down in the mud, the soft whine and thud of enemy shells. He said he was knocked unconscious by the explosion, and woke to find himself snagged on barbed wire, being hauled back to the Allied trench on the back of George Mann, a private in his regiment. 'He went on his belly with me slung round his shoulders, lying on top of him. He could've left me, but he never. They got me on a stretcher and they took me off in an ambulance. I never got a chance to thank Mann. Everything went black again. Next thing I know I'm in the field hospital. I've lost my right leg from the knee down, and they've had to patch up my hip and side.'

Silence reigned. Mayhew thanked him sincerely for gathering the strength to appear in court. He folded his glasses into his waistcoat pocket and sat down.

Forster stood and manoeuvred himself into position alongside the jury-box. This mood of reverence required quick deflation. 'Private Parsons, what was your relationship with the deceased?'

Robert pulled himself round to answer the snappy question. 'We was friends, sir.'

'No more than friends?'

'No, sir. We had a lark. We grew up in the same street together.'

'But she was an attractive girl, would you say?'

'You could say that, yes.'

'Private Parsons, the question is not whether or not *I* would say she was attractive, but what *you* have to say about the matter.' Forster's urbane voice picked up Robert's speech mannerisms and played with them. 'Did you find her good-looking?'

'Yes, sir.'

'Have you had lots of girlfriends?'

Robert's resentment began to show through. 'A few.'

'You're a good-looking man.'

There was a muttering in the gallery at the overt insensitivity of this remark, but Forster wasn't out to win any popularity stakes.

'You were a favourite with the ladies?'

'It ain't for me to say.'

'Oh, come, no need to be modest. You had the girls practically falling at your feet, didn't you? Weren't you what we call a ladies' man, Private Parsons?'

'I went about with women, if that's what you mean.'

'But not with Daisy O'Hagan?'

'No, sir.'

'You never flirted with her?'

The momentary pause cast doubt on Robert's answer. 'No, sir, not really.'

'Be precise, if you please,' Forster drilled into his man, his voice dry and sharp.

'Only for a lark, sir.'

'Did your brother, Ernie, see you flirt with Daisy, "for a lark", as you say?'

'How would I know?' Robert felt himself being led helplessly into muddy insinuations. He reacted sullenly.

'Let's say he did. He saw you with your arm around her, let's say. Yet according to your own words, the accused would "die for that girl". Isn't that what you said? Wouldn't he then feel jealousy when he came across you two spooning together?'

'We never spooned!' Robert interrupted.

'Well, call it what you will. We reach the point where

Ernie, dimly perhaps, begins to realize that you're the sort of brother who will steal a girl from a fellow the moment his back is turned.' Forster allowed Robert to glare at him for a few seconds before going on. 'So he must seize his opportunity in double-quick time. The bees are buzzing round the honey-pot, you might say.'

Judge Berry, who until this point had sat resting his chin on his hand, forefinger to his lips, suddenly leaned forward. 'Where is this colourful metaphor leading us, Mr Forster? Bees and honey-pots; what's the point, if I may ask?'

'The motive, m'lud. That's where we're leading. "By indirections . . ."'

'"Find directions out." Yes, quite, Mr Forster.' Judge Berry sighed but allowed him to proceed.

'Now, Mr Parsons, we've reached the night of the murder. The accused loses sight of you in the theatre. But he heads for the girls' dressing-room in any case. You admit that he could view this as an unlooked-for opportunity?'

'What are you getting at?' Robert frowned and twisted a finger inside his uncomfortably tight collar. He felt hot and flustered.

'I mean, he has Daisy all to himself, doesn't he? We all know how much he adored her. But what would Daisy make of Ernie's advances, there in the dressing-room, all alone?'

Robert let out a short laugh. But before he could frame an answer, Forster forged ahead.

'Exactly! Let's just say, she wouldn't respond well. And who can blame her? She's a popular girl. She has the pick of all the East End scuttlers. Surely she would prefer you to your brother, Mr Parsons; a good-looking ladies' man like yourself? After all, wasn't it you she liked to flirt with? Wouldn't she make these feelings quite plain to Ernie? And then what?'

'Then, nothing!' Robert found his voice. 'I'm telling you, you're going about this the wrong way!'

Forster glanced sharply at the jury, as if to say, *Pay attention. The witness is rattled*. Then he concentrated his sharp gaze on Robert once more.

'Do you believe that Daisy O'Hagan would reject Ernie's clumsy advances, Mr Parsons?'

'Course she would!'

Forster cut back in. 'Would she laugh at him? Would she put up a fight?'

Robert looked helplessly towards Duke. The old man's gaze was fixed on Ernie.

'Does Ernie panic in a fight?' Forster insisted.

'How should I know?' Robert couldn't find the right answer to put his finger on and clear Ernie of these ridiculous suggestions. Everything he said just dropped him deeper into Forster's trap.

'Well. *We* know the murder is the action of a man who suddenly loses control. We can tell that by the number of wounds inflicted on the corpse. This is no professional, premeditated act.' Forster took time to glance around the court. 'Would you agree, Mr Parsons, that this murder was committed by someone who did not accurately judge his own power to inflict harm? Would you say that it was a frenzied attack, from what you yourself saw of the body?'

Robert took a deep breath and nodded. 'But Ernie never fights! He ain't never hurt no one!'

'Quite.' Forster's jaws snapped shut. He paused. 'He never fights. But he is a strong young man. Therefore he has no idea of how much damage his violent actions can inflict, when his temper is provoked beyond restraint. His thin thread of self control snaps when Daisy rejects him. A sudden idea takes hold; if he can't have her, then no one else will. Maybe she is laughing at him even now. He takes a knife he carries in his pocket; a common or garden kitchen knife available at the local ironmongers'. He advances. He's surprised by how easily the sharp blade plunges into the soft flesh. And by the blood. He steps quickly to one side. But there's no turning back. Again and again he plunges the knife into Daisy. Then the struggle is done. He releases her. She slumps dead to the floor.'

Hettie hid her head in her hands and wept at the description. Frances felt pure hatred for the prosecutor. Sadie and Jess sat holding hands, stunned as Robert began to shout; incoherent words of rage that offended the jurors' ears and challenged the authority of the court.

'He can't bleeding well say that! He's a bastard, he is, putting pictures in their heads. This ain't what I call justice!' Robert ranted, raising his fist in an impotent, destructive gesture as Duke rose from his seat, intent on being the first to reach his son's wheelchair. He spun the chair on the spot and rushed him down the aisle.

'Easy, take it easy.' Duke slammed the chair through the double doors at the back of the courtroom, to the sound of the gavel rattling down on to the desk and to the rising consternation of spectators in the gallery. Duke leaned his head back against the closed door. It had been too much to expect. 'I'm sorry I put you through that, mate,' he said.

Robert sagged forward in his chair, hot tears stinging his eyes.

'A pity,' Mayhew said to Sewell, shuffling papers into order on his desk. 'If he could just have kept his temper . . .' The gamble hadn't quite paid off. He cast a cool eye over the jury to assess the effect of Robert's outburst, getting ready to repitch his summing-up speech. Meanwhile, Forster was making his own last push.

The jury heard again the mountain of evidence pointing to the guilt of the accused; the time, the opportunity, the motive, the forensic reports. They would recall the words from the accused's own lips: 'I never meant to do it', and his intense secrecy after the event, so clumsily covered up by the sister, Jess. It was a poor defence, was it not, to simply 'forget' one's exact movements in the room where the murder occurred, but it was the typical defence of a guilty man, not too bright, who saw all the fingers of accusation lining up ready to point in his direction.

Forster polished off his final speech with a common-sense touch, a sad but true tone which spoke regret that these things happened when men of this type were pushed beyond their limit. Nevertheless, a conviction was imperative. 'Despite your inevitable softer feelings of sympathy, gentlemen, which are perfectly natural when you see the distress of the accused as he sits in the dock listening to horrific accounts of his own actions, do not lose sight of the decision you must reach.

'Do not believe, as defence counsel would have you believe, that Ernest Parsons is incapable of committing this crime. They say he is a simple man, unable to negotiate the streets of London alone. Certainly, he is simple, but not incapable, as we have seen from the testimony of Mr Henshaw. No, Ernest Parsons can hold down the very sort of job which requires detailed knowledge of these streets, as Henshaw's errand boy. Moreover, we are sure that he harbours the ordinary feelings of men towards the gentler sex; this much is clear. Those feelings include possessiveness and jealousy, do they not, gentlemen? No, you may discount the view proposed by Mr Mayhew that this is a saintly simpleton, a kind of divine idiot. This is a man; a man who snapped, who killed in a frenzy the woman whom he loved "not wisely but too well". Can there be any reasonable doubt left in your minds that this is so? And likewise any hesitation that this man must pay the ultimate penalty which the law demands? Your duty is not a pleasant one, gentlemen. No man here says that it is. But it is plain, and it is a duty which we must carry out without flinching, in the name of justice. We must find the defendant guilty as charged.'

There was a terrible hush in the courtroom. Forster's speech was delivered watertight. It sent hopes spiralling down in the public gallery. It numbed the Parsons women, so that Mayhew's own summing-up speech had to beat its way with heavy wings through the gloomy atmosphere of the court.

He must rely on the unblemished family history, he must recall for the jury the whole-hearted support showered on the accused by his own family and community, not least from the mother of the supposed victim. 'An unprecedented thing, in my experience,' Mayhew said. 'A brave and selfless act by a woman who has suffered much, yet driven here by her belief in the innocence of the man whom the prosecution would hang.

'He sits before you, as he has sat through all these long weeks in prison, more boy than man, in utter sorrow and confusion. He denies nothing that is true, yet he does deny this brutal murder. His statement takes you as far as his own memory can possibly take you, and what this amounts to is that he was simply in the wrong place at the wrong time. As a result, his entire world collapsed, wiping out any observation of detail which might have helped him escape this charge; a shadow in a corner of the alleyway, a struggle overheard, a name called out in terror.' Mayhew's gaze raked the courtroom and the gallery, seeking out the guilty name to no avail.

He lowered his eyes to the jury once more. 'No one can deny the hideousness of the crime you have to consider; the brutal murder of a beautiful and defenceless young woman by a man without a conscience, a man sufficiently cool and cruel to let another stand accused here, who would let *his* blame hang the man who stands before you now. Two victims of one crime, gentlemen; consider that. The shadow of doubt looms large under the hangman's noose, and so it should, for this is an irrevocable act. This is a decision which may colour the rest of your lives.

'Look around this court, gentlemen, and let your gaze rest on Ernie Parsons. Study him.' Mayhew led them with a gallant gesture to where Ernie sat looking at his sisters with a fixed stare, waiting for them to tell him what to do next. 'This man is no liar, this man is no murderer. He is simply trapped by circumstance.' His final appeal was low, almost inaudible to all except the jurors. 'For God's sake, gentlemen, release him from that trap, and find him not guilty!'

Forster turned to his own assistant, as Mayhew returned, head bowed, to his seat and the jury received the judge's directions. 'Heart versus head,' he said drily. 'Let's see which way they swing now.'

When word came back that the jury had reached a verdict, Sewell took Duke aside one last time. 'There is a procedure,' he warned. 'In all these cases it is the same.'

'The black cap? Is that what you're getting at?'

'Yes. Innocent or guilty, the cap will be there in readiness. You mustn't jump to conclusions.'

Duke nodded. 'I'll tell the girls,' he promised as they took their places in court. The unreality of the occasion was only heightened by speaking of these things, when in truth he thought his heart must stop dead at the awful irresistibility of it all.

The jury returned to complete silence, each man in

procession, his gaze set straight ahead, tight-lipped, narrow-eyed. They sat as three loud knocks announced the re-entry of the judge. The Sheriff and Mayor followed in robes of crimson and ermine. An official carried the square of black cloth ceremoniously outstretched, and last of all came the chaplain, all in black.

Then Ernie was brought up from the cells into the dock. He looked anxiously for Duke, found him in his usual place, and fixed his eyes upon him.

The thing was played out in a daze. They knew in their hearts by the grim, fixed look of the foreman what the verdict was to be.

At last the clerk to the court cleared his throat. 'How do you find the defendant?'

'Guilty, m'lud.'

A scramble began in the gallery. Reporters left to be first on the telephone to their editors with the news. Uninvolved spectators nodded and drifted off into the next courtroom. Friends stood stock-still. The morbid hung on for the last details.

Judge Berry placed the cap on his head. It was over. He was satisfied, reciting the words which sealed the man's fate.

'Taken from this place . . . Eight o'clock on the fifth day of January 1915 . . . hung by the neck until you are dead . . . and may God have mercy on your soul.'

Chapter Twenty-Seven

Ernie was taken stumbling from view, and life lurched on around the vortex, the black certainty that he was to die.

Mayhew came to shake hands with Duke. He felt it had come about partly through lack of other suspects. 'There's a strong urge to convict when public opinion is roused. They need to blame someone, and of course we were unable to implicate anyone else.' He shook his head. 'I am truly sorry, Mr Parsons.'

Duke couldn't trust himself to speak. The girls wept and clung to one another. Robert covered his face with his hand.

'Can I see the boy?' Duke said at last, turning to Sewell, who went off to arrange it.

Maurice came down to help Jess and the women. Walter came for Robert. Annie sat in the rapidly emptying gallery next to Florrie and Dolly. She'd sent Tommy off home with the news, and now she turned to comfort Duke's sister. 'You go ahead, have a good cry, girl.' The old woman's stricken face streamed with tears. Annie put an arm around her shoulder.

Florrie choked back the tears, for the family's sake. She didn't want to make a fuss. 'Only, when I think what they're gonna do to Ern, it breaks my heart!' she wailed, overcome once more.

Annie drew a sharp breath. 'Don't say that, girl. I can't bear it.'

And it was Dolly's turn to put her strong arms around skinny Annie and let her weep.

Duke was taken along dark, bare corridors to the cells below the courtroom. Two warders guarded the door to Ernie's cell, and they avoided the father's eyes as he was silently marched inside the room. One officer remained there with them.

The boy seemed bewildered. He sat hunched over the table, hands clasped. He looked up at Duke in mute appeal, then turned away. At last he realized that even Duke couldn't help him now. For the first time in his life, Ernie recognized the limits of his father's power; up till now he'd thought he was invincible.

The turning away was too much for Duke. He stood by the door immobile, as cold as stone. In that windowless room, where condemned men accepted their fate, the electric light glared.

Ernie looked back and saw his father's weariness; the shadows on his face, his weakness and age. He got up and approached him. 'Don't worry about me, Pa. Tell Ett I remembered my prayers. Tell them all to come and see me.'

Duke nodded. 'We'll be there, mate.' He held his son close to him. 'We won't let you down.'

The weeks in prison had taught Ernie new rules. You did as you were told and never spoke your fears. He glanced at the warder. 'I gotta go now, Pa.' He began to ease himself free.

Duke released him. 'We never let you down, did we, son?' He wanted to be able to walk out with Ernie's trust restored.

'You never, Pa. I let myself down. I never remembered what happened to Daisy. I think I should've.' Ernie had walked across to the warder, but he turned again for a moment. 'That's right, ain't it, Pa? I should've remembered?'

Duke nodded. 'I know you tried, Ern. But it ain't easy for you, and it don't do to think of it now.'

Ernie shook his head. 'Would it've helped her? Would my remembering wake her up?'

'No, son, but we could've helped you.'

Ernie sighed. 'I'm sorry, Pa.'

'Don't be, Ern. What's done is done.'

The boy bowed his head and submitted to being led away. Another warder came in for the old man, gave him one brief, sympathetic glance, turned and took him off up the corridor, up the stone steps back into the courtroom. Duke heard heavy doors slam and lock. They battered his heart with grief and loss.

There was no cheer in the court as Christmas week drew near. People drifted in and out of the Duke, but they lost their natural rhythm when talking of Ernie and the terrible outcome in court. Some, like Arthur Ogden and even Syd Swan, refused to mention it at all, though it must have preyed on their minds.

When Syd took Amy out to the Gem in the week after the verdict, her heightened sense of drama made her want to chatter to Syd about the awful prospects facing Ernie now; the hangman's noose and the condemned man's last request before he went to meet his Maker. Syd refused to listen, as he ushered her through the shiny doors, relieved when their turn came up at the ticket office and they could sidle in for the latest Keystone adventures. Amy was all very well, but she never knew when to stop. Maurice Leigh watched them take their seats without his usual courteousness, and at home, later, he openly warned Amy off her association with Swan.

Dolly Ogden treated the subject of Ernie with an outpouring of powerful sympathy. She went the opposite way to Arthur and Syd, but her interest wasn't prurient, like Amy's. 'You come and tell that girl how sorry you are,' she chivvied Charlie. 'You gotta act like a man. They need all the help they can get these days.'

So Charlie went up to the Duke and asked to see Sadie. He was shown up to the living room, where the women sat. He said his awkward sentence, cap in hand, aware of the inadequacy of the words. He wondered for a moment if Sadie would turn on him.

But Frances thanked him for her, and said they appreciated his coming. It was a kind thought. Sadie sat in a chair by the fire, looking young and lost.

'Is there anything I can help with?' he faltered.

Sadie looked up at him through her grief.

'I don't think so, Charlie,' Frances said softly. 'But we're very grateful for the offer.' She showed him downstairs and closed him out of their misery.

If Dolly talked too much, running through the trial time after time with Flo at the bar, pouring out venom against Forster and the prosecution witnesses, it was accepted in good spirit and taken as a sign that Dolly really did care. In one way, Flo was glad to talk about things. She trod on eggshells around the place herself, now that the verdict had sunk in, not knowing how anyone was going to react in the long run. 'I went up the Post Office and telephoned to my Tom,' she told Dolly. 'He couldn't hardly believe it, said for me to save the newspaper account for him to read, but

I told him I couldn't bear to have it near me. Not with the things they write!'

The *Express* had followed up its early reports on the case with an expression of righteous indignation on the subject of lawlessness and the evil of wrongdoers such as Ernest Parsons, who made it unsafe for respectable women to walk the streets at night. They looked forward to his punishment with ghoulish pleasure.

'Don't take no notice,' Dolly consoled her. Florrie's flamboyant style had taken a knock this last week. Her rouge was put on crooked, her black hair showed grey at the roots. 'They can write what they like, no one round here thinks he done it!'

Florrie raised her pencilled eyebrows. 'Thanks, Dolly.' In private, she thought the touching faith might make things worse. She heard Sadie sobbing her heart out night after night, and Hettie's prayers, and Jess questioning everything, urging Frances to work on Sewell for an appeal. Florrie sighed. 'We're worn out with worry, I don't mind telling you.'

To make things worse, she had noticed a severe falling off in trade at the pub, since the government had decided to restrict opening hours for the duration of the war. It was to encourage sobriety and to concentrate people's attention on the war effort, but Florrie's point of view was that folk needed to drown or share their sorrows up at the Duke. She worried about the empty bar stools and full barrels in the cellar, the dwindling takings in the till. But she wouldn't trouble Duke with it, as Christmas approached, and the dreaded New Year.

Annie was one of the customers who stayed loyal, and she dealt with Duke in a clear, matter-of-fact manner which encouraged him to talk things through. 'Ain't no need to put on a show for me, Duke,' she advised. 'I don't expect it.' A couple of draymen had just finished rolling fresh barrels along the corridor to the cellar, and Duke had helped heave them on to the gantry. Now he stood at the window watching the men jump on to the cart, taking up the reins and positioning the splendid shire horses, ready to set off and merge into the busy traffic on Duke Street. He didn't shift position as he felt Annie come up alongside.

'Will they get rid of them in the end and all? What do you think, Annie?'

'What you on about?'

'The horses. Will they put them out to grass and go for the motor car?' He watched them take the strain and lift their huge hooves. They were great dappled grey beasts, with creaking leather straps, silver bits, golden brasses.

'Not before you and me are six feet under, if you want to know. I say they can keep their electric tramcars and their motor omnibuses for all I care. No, them drays is a sight for sore eyes, and they'll see us out, Duke.'

'I hope you're right.' He seemed happy to reminisce, briefly caught up in the shallows of memory, ignoring the approaching tidal wave. 'My old man brought us up over a carter's yard up in Hackney. Did I ever tell you that, Annie? There was one old grey in the yard, a bit like them two out there, and we called him Major, and my pa would hitch him up to a cart of a Sunday and take us kids out in the country for a day, riding back high on a load of hay, just smelling the sweet smell of the countryside all the way between the factory walls, down the cobbled streets back home. I could lie on that hay at the journey's end and stare up at the stars. Then Ma would come out with a face as long as a poker and shout where the bleeding hell did we think we'd been. I remember once Pa told her we'd stopped for a dog that he ran over on the road. He tried to save it, but it was too far gone. He had to bury it. Ma said never mind burying no stray dog, our bleeding supper was burnt to cinders. She made us pay for that day out, make no mistake.'

Annie smiled. 'We never got no days out in the country when we was kids. My old man was a bootmaker, and poor as a bleeding church mouse, with eight mouths to feed.' She stared down at her old standbys. 'That's why I knows a good pair of boots when I sees one.'

'Ain't it time you gave those up to the rag-and-bone cart, Annie?' Duke turned and frowned down at Wiggins's ugly legacy.

'Waste not, want not, I say,' came the gruff reply. Then she drew a small, slim wallet out of her pocket and showed it to her friend. 'Now look here, Duke, I had an idea what Ernie might like.' She opened the small brass clasp on the blue velvet wallet. It opened to reveal a concertina of small, framed photographs. 'I went up and down the court and I asked your girls and all, and they dug out a photograph for me, and I stuck them in here so we could get Ernie to remember that all the folks round here are thinking of him and praying for him. What do you think?' She handed the album across. 'I know he ain't one for books or letters, or nothing like that. But I thought he might like photographs. He can sit and look at his friends in a picture, can't he?'

Duke studied the brownish photographs. There was Tommy O'Hagan standing behind his fruit barrow, a grin splitting his face. There was Charlie Ogden on the back row in a Board School picture, with Sadie, neat in her white smock and black buttoned boots, sitting cross-legged at the front. There was a hand-tinted, glamorous head and shoulders one of Amy. Frances had provided a photo of the whole family, taken four or five years earlier, of them standing on the front doorstep of the pub. Ernie stood in the centre of the group, between Duke and Robert. And Mary O'Hagan had given up her favourite picture of Daisy, onstage, with white flowers in her hair and a sparkling laugh lighting up her face.

Annie grew uneasy at the long silence. 'If you think it'll only upset the poor boy, I'll take it back,' she suggested.

But Duke shook his head. 'It's just the thing, Annie.' His voice was hoarse. 'I'll take it in to him tomorrow.'

Now Hettie prayed fervently each morning and night, and went over to Lambeth to see her Army friend, Freda Barnes, as often as she could. Freda still helped to run the industrial home, dishing out soup and blankets to the poor creatures who came in off the streets at night. She was a plain-featured, grey-eyed woman in her mid-thirties, broad-faced beneath her navy bonnet, very down to earth and not at all smug. She encouraged Hettie to throw in her lot with them. '"Yea, though I walk through the valley of the shadow of death, I will fear no evil; for thou art with me, thy rod and thy staff they comfort me."' Hettie clung to her belief, seeing that it bolstered Ernie in his hour of need. She even invited Robert to attend an Army meeting with her.

Robert went once, but he preferred his old haunts. He allowed Walter to wheel him down to the gym, where Milo devised some weights which Robert could lift from a sitting position in his wheelchair, and a special punch-bag to exercise with. The hospital hoped he would soon progress from chair to crutches, and they promised an eventual artificial limb which would restore him in many ways to his old lifestyle. He worked at his recovery with fierce fanaticism. Nothing, nothing in life could be as bad for him as being treated like a cripple. They looked down at him in a wheelchair, and saw him as something less than human, so his pilgrimage took him through terrible pain on to crutches, too soon, and with several relapses before he could stand face to face with the next man once more. Now they admired him at the same time as they shied away from him. His experience was too raw, too recent, and he raged against each day as it brought him closer to the one set for Ernie's execution.

Maurice came in whenever he could, and took over some of the heavy tasks in the pub which Robert had once helped Joxer with. It gave him time with Jess, when the doors were closed and she came down into the bar, sometimes with Grace, sometimes alone.

She'd relented in this run-up to Christmas over her intention to keep her life with her baby daughter separate from her life with her lover. Maurice was especially tender after the verdict. She decided to trust him with getting to know the child.

She brought Grace down one day when she knew Maurice was at work in the cellar. She called him into the bar. 'Shh!' she said. 'Try not to wake her.'

His footsteps were heavy on the stone steps. He stared at the child, who was indeed stirring in her sleep. She opened her dark eyes and turned her head towards him.

'She can see your watch chain shining in the light.' Jess smiled as Grace freed one tiny hand from her fine white shawl and stretched it out towards him.

Maurice, mesmerized by Grace's dark stare, dare not move. At last he reached in his pocket and released the chain from the watch. He swung it gently towards her and let her catch its cold, shiny links. He glanced shyly at Jess. 'She looks like you,' he said.

There had been a sudden and drastic change from his freewheeling, quick-thinking pattern of old, which still had to operate while he was at work, or out and about. With Jess, however, things took on an intensity; not because she made much of Ernie's tragedy, rather because she was determined not to be defeated by it. She battled on for him, and seemed to Maurice to be living and breathing in a different sphere from mere mortals, where all trivialities fell away, leaving only her true self, pure and unadulterated. He was in danger of worshipping her, he realized, and there was nothing he could do to stop himself.

One sunny weekday morning before Christmas, he took her and Grace off to the park. Then he invited her along to a new Gaumont talkie, and got Hettie to back him up in making her go. He told her he was worried she would make herself ill over Ernie. 'You done everything you could. You done your very best,' he said.

'And it weren't good enough.'

They walked together after the picture had finished, back up Duke Street in a world of their own.

'Jess, you gotta stop hurting yourself over it. Sewell's working on an appeal, ain't he?'

'We need new evidence.' She thought of Ernie in the condemned cell. He was gentle with visitors, asking for news, never talking of his own situation. He'd told Frances that, when it came to it, he'd want her to write down a letter from him to Duke.

Maurice held her close. They stood outside the lively yellow warmth of the Duke. Strains of music filtered through the closed windows and doors. 'Come home with me,' he said softly.

In the empty house they made love again, with great passion between them. The ache of grief made her cry in his arms, and her tears healed the loneliness of his youth. He loved her clean smoothness, the slant of her shoulders, the curve of her back. She took his strong body to her, a little afraid of its power. They entwined. She was all softness until she pressed back against him and returned her female desire for his longing. Then she vied with him for pleasure, stroking and kissing him, and sighing as he held her. He looked down at her; her eyes looked deep into him with full consciousness of what she desired. What he could give, he gave, overjoyed by their union, their clinging limbs, their warm touch.

This time, the way back to cold reality was slow and gentle. They lay in each other's arms, murmuring to one another. He told her she was the best thing to happen in his life, kissing her eyelids, her forehead. She said she'd been wary of him at first.

'Too pushy?' he asked.

Jess nodded. 'I ain't used to all that attention. I lived a life below stairs, remember.'

'And wasted you were too, girl!'

She laughed.

'What about your pa? Ain't he made a fuss of you when you was little?'

'Not much.' She remembered winning the school races for him and bringing home the prize. 'It was all Rob, Rob, Rob with him, 'cos he was the first boy. Who wants three girls on the trot?' She said it without bitterness. 'I ain't complaining.'

'Well, you got plenty of attention from me from now on, if you want it?'

'Is that a question?' She turned on her side and propped herself on one elbow.

'If you like.' He was teasing, stroking the corners of her mouth and reaching across to kiss it.

'Funny sort of question. What was it again?' Her laugh, so rare of late, lit her up.

'Let's get married, Jess.'

She fell suddenly serious. 'You mean it? You don't want no more time to think?'

'I been thinking about it since I first clapped eyes on you.' He wanted to sweep her along. 'Say yes, Jess. Just say yes!'

She sat up in bed, hair tumbling about her shoulders, spreading her arms wide. 'I ain't gonna say no, Maurice, am I?'

'What are you on about?'

'Ain't I sitting here in your bed thinking we're bound to get married some day?' Strangely, it hadn't been a large question in her own mind. Then she realized that it was because she trusted him. 'Just as soon as you got round to asking me!'

'Say yes!' he demanded.

'Yes'.

He lay back flat on the pillow, speechless. It was Jess who kissed him and got up, got ready to go home to Grace. 'It ain't all plain sailing,' she warned.

Maurice's arm circled her waist as she sat again on the edge of the bed. 'No need to remind me.'

'But I love you, Maurice. Just remember that.'

'Then I'm happy,' he said simply. In his direct, optimistic way, he didn't see what could possibly go wrong.

Frances had arranged to meet up with Sewell in the prison. It was the Friday before Christmas. She greeted him in a subdued mood, and, it seemed to him, defeated.

'Never say die, Miss Parsons,' he reminded her as the warder showed them to Ernie's cell. They'd come for one last try to break down the barrier in Ernie's mind about events on the night of the murder. 'The doctors tell me that sooner or later it will all click into place,' he said. 'Like a camera shutter; click, as sudden as can be. And it will all be in place in perfect detail.'

'I hope so, Mr Sewell.' Frances went and sat by Ernie's side of the table. His face lit up to see her. Then he fixed his attention on Mr Sewell, screwing his gaze on the solicitor's face.

Frances noticed that Ernie held the little photograph album sent in by Annie. It was open at the picture of Daisy with white flowers in her dark hair.

'Now, Ernie,' Mr Sewell began. 'You understand why we're here?'

He nodded. 'To remember what happened to Daisy.'

'That's right. Let's just think about that. We're standing outside the stage door. What colour is it, Ernie?'

'Green. Dirty green.'

'Good. Is it closed?'

'Yes.' Ernie's eyes crinkled with concentration.

'Good. Is there anyone there in the alley with you, Ernie? I know we've asked you before, but you're doing very well this time. Just take things slowly. Now, is there anyone in the alley?'

Frances put one hand over Ernie's and stroked it softly.

'No, I'm by myself. I'm waiting for Rob. I know he'll be mad at me.'

'He's not mad,' Sewell reassured him. 'He's worried about you, but he's busy. He'll be back soon. He won't be mad.'

Ernie nodded. 'I never meant to do it,' he whispered; the old refrain.

'Do what, Ernie?' Sewell too lowered his voice.

'I never meant to get lost. Tell Rob.'

'He ain't cross,' Frances said. She grasped his hand tight. 'You never meant to get lost. We know that.' She glanced up at the solicitor, a light in her eyes. 'Now, Ernie, what happened while you was waiting for Rob? Did something scare you?'

Ernie's own eyes fogged over. He sighed heavily.

'What do you see?' Sewell leant forward across the table. They'd met up with the same invisible wall, the boy was giving in.

'What can you hear?' Frances urged.

'A noise. Someone's screaming.' He gripped the photograph. 'Daisy. Daisy's screaming. I can tell it's her. She's shouting. There's something wrong!'

'Daisy's inside and she's screaming. The door's closed, Ernie. What do you do?' Sewell pushed hard.

'I open it. I have to go in there, even if Rob comes along and I'm not there waiting for him. That's right, ain't it? I have to go in. Daisy needs me.'

'That's right, Ern.' Frances could hardly breathe. There was a moment when she thought, No, we can't go on. We can't make him live through it all again. It's a cruel torment. Once was enough. But Sewell was firm. He pressed on.

'She does. She needs help. Do you run inside, Ern?'

Ernie nodded. 'The screams are loud now. I have to run. They're coming from her dressing room, where they get changed. No, now they've stopped!' Ernie jolted to a halt. He was trembling. His eyes filled with tears.

'The screams have stopped, Ernie. Where are you now?'

'In the corridor,' he said, dazed and slow.

'Good. Do you see anyone?'

'No. I can hear someone running off. I turn the corner. But I don't see no one.'

Sewell let out a sharp breath. 'What do you do now? Now that Daisy's stopped screaming and you've heard someone run off?'

'I go in.'

'Go in where?'

'Into the dressing room – ' He paused.

'Who's there, Ernie?'

'No one.'

Sewell nodded. 'How do you feel now, Ernie? Daisy's not there. How do you feel?'

'Scared.'

'What of? Is someone in there hiding?'

'No. He ran off. I heard him.'

'But you're still scared?'

'Something's wrong. Something's happened to Daisy. I have to find her.'

'Where? Where do you look?'

'All over. I can't see her. But I know she's still here.'

'Do you find her? Where is she?' Sewell glanced at Frances, willing her to keep her own nerve.

'No, I can't find her!' Ernie looked wildly round, his eyes streaming with tears.

'Not at first, no. But you keep looking?'

'Yes. And the rail with the dresses hanging, I see it move.'

'How? Did it move much, Ernie?'

'A bit. Not much. One of the dresses falls down. I have to pick it up.'

'You go over.'

'I pick it up. It's caught. It's soft and silky, but it's caught.' Ernie gasped. 'I'm pulling it hard. There's a noise.'

'What noise?'

'Someone hurting. A hurting noise. Behind the dresses. I have to kneel down to see. It's dark behind the dresses.'

Ernie paused again, but both Frances and Sewell stayed silent. They let him lead them on at his own pace now, through the terrible remembering.

'I can feel something move, like a little animal moving. Something grabs my neck and pulls me down. My hat falls off. I lose my hat, Frances!'

'It don't matter, Ern. We'll get you a new one.' She thought her heart would break.

Ernie went on. 'It's Daisy lying down there moaning. Daisy's holding my neck and moaning. Her face is all white. She says something. Twice. I have to bend right down to listen. I see all the blood. I'm kneeling on the dress, getting it dirty. I lost my hat. There's a knife. I have to get it out. I have to be careful. It hurts. I take it out, quick as I can. She's not moving no more. She won't get up. Oh, she won't get up no more. I know it now.'

Racked by sobs, Ernie's head went down.

'What next?' Sewell held steady. He put a hand on the boy's arm.

'I have to go to meet Rob,' Ernie said blankly. 'I have to go, don't I?'

'You do. But before that, tell me one more thing, Ernie.' The solicitor held on to his arm. 'This is very important. What did Daisy say to you when you found her lying there?' He was after a final incriminating detail; Daisy's revelation of the murderer as she lay dying.

Ernie stared down at the photograph. 'She said it twice. She said "Ernie" twice.' It broke him, the memory of Daisy whispering his own name as she died.

They stayed a long time to comfort him, and the warder didn't interfere. Frances told Ernie he was brave. Brave as Robert in the army. She said there was hope now. What he'd done had given them new hope. At last he sat quietly, his eyes full of trust.

They left the prison at last, and went straight away to Sewell's office. Frances allowed her own spirits to rise.

'This is very good, ain't it, Mr Sewell? Ernie would never

make it up.' She grew animated, standing up in his office and beginning to pace beneath the shelves of heavy, leather-bound law books. 'They'll grant us an appeal now, don't you think?'

The solicitor smiled and nodded. He too stood up. 'I think we have a very good chance. You can go home and pass on the news. I'll be in touch as soon as we have a date for the new hearing.' He was more than pleased with the outcome.

'Before Christmas?'

He considered her eager expression. 'I should say between Christmas and the New Year, Miss Parsons.'

Her face fell.

'Yes, I know. It must be a torture for you all.' He came and shook her by the hand. 'Never say die, Miss Parsons. We're doing all we can, believe me. This time everything will depend on the medical men, and on Ernie. So keep up his spirits as best you can.'

Frances promised and left the office. There was new energy in her stride as she walked past the clerk at his desk and the telephonist busy speaking into her mouthpiece. She took the first tram home and alighted outside Coopers'. Billy Wray stood selling the evening papers. He noticed her as she made a bee-line straight towards him.

'Mr Sewell's managed to get up an appeal, Billy!' She was breathless. 'He was marvellous with Ernie today. He got him to remember every single thing about the murder. We're so glad you went and picked him out for us.'

People threaded between them, around his stall, down the close, or waiting at the kerb to cross the street. He felt jolted out of his own dull misery, back into life. 'Listen,' he said. 'I'll finish up here and you slip home. Give them the good news. Then meet me at Henshaw's and tell me all about it.'

She nodded her agreement. The family must know as soon as possible. Then she'd come and share it with Billy.

'We owe it all to him if Ernie gets off,' she told Robert. 'We got hold of Mr Sewell on his recommendation, and he's the best there is.'

Robert let his own hopes revive. 'We ain't beat yet,' he agreed. He wanted to go along to the Scrubs with Duke to help give Ernie a boost. When the news had been entirely bleak, he could hardly face the ordeal of a visit. Before long, the whole pub was looking on the bright side, and Frances left them to it, to make her own way back to the coffee shop.

Bea Henshaw had the news from Billy. She rushed to the doorway to greet Frances in a state of real pleasure, flustered but determined to have her say. She was a brisk, prim woman as a rule, but hopes for Ernie had given her a high colour and a breathless manner. 'Oh, Frances, we heard! Such good news. Your pa must be thrilled. Oh, my dear, we pray for him every single day. We want Ernie back with us, believe me!'

She led Frances, by now exhausted, to the table where Billy sat. Frances joined him, aware that circumstances had removed formalities and plunged them in the deep end again. Still, she stopped to ask about Ada's funeral, and the arrangements he'd had to make. 'You don't think me selfish for not asking sooner, do you, Billy? I've got a lot on my mind.'

Likewise, he told her. His mother-in-law had decamped and gone to live in Bermondsey with another daughter, to his secret relief. 'But I must say it leaves the house feeling big and empty, so I've got a plan in mind to sell up and move into a room above the Institute. I want to give up the newspaper stand, all in good time, of course.' He said the market life no longer suited him, and there was a chance to help the printer on some of the Workers' Education Centre publications.

'Lots of changes,' Frances commented. 'And now a new chance for Ernie.' She tried in vain not to let her hopes fly too high. Billy understood more about the process of appeal in such cases, and pointed out the complications. 'Still, we're banking on Mr Sewell and the doctors,' she told him. 'And we're grateful to you, Billy. We really are.'

He nodded. Frances kept on upsetting his balance like this by giving him sympathy or gratitude when he wanted something else. He wished things weren't so complicated by protocol, or by guilt and grief. Still, he offered her his arm and walked up the street with her. He was glad above all to have been of use.

Chapter Twenty-Eight

The Christmas truce came in the trenches, when British Tommies listened in wonderment to the familiar strains of 'Silent Night' sung in a strange tongue across the battlefield, and emerged to shake hands with the enemy, so like themselves. It meant little to the Parsons family or to the inhabitants of Duke Street and Paradise Court.

Local drama pushed national interests to one side as the day of Ernie's execution drew near. They sat round their firesides late at night, connected by a taut wire of dread, talking endlessly about the progress of Sewell's appeal. A hearing had been granted for New Year's Eve.

But on the morning of Christmas Eve, another, unexpected disaster struck. Edith Cooper travelled into town on the train and made her way to her husband's department store. This was unusual in itself, and her pale face, her dazed manner alerted the shop-girls to expect bad news. She walked between the counters bright with Christmas gifts, decked out with red ribbon and glass baubles. She gave no response to polite greetings, so that word went up ahead to the office that Mrs Cooper was here and all was not well.

Jack Cooper came to the top of the wide stairs to meet her, then led her into the privacy of the office. There could only be one reason for her being there.

'I had to tell you face to face,' she began.

'It's Teddy.'

She nodded. 'Oh, Jack, he's been shot down and killed.'

The words sank in like a stain. In those seconds of disbelief, Cooper went and picked up an invoice from his desk to file it in a drawer. He saw the paper shake in his hand. He looked up at his wife. 'They sure it was Teddy?'

Edith took the telegram from her bag and handed it to him. 'I read it over and over, Jack. There ain't no mistake.'

Jack Cooper sat at his desk and sank his big head into his hands. They'd snatched his boy, his only boy. He knew on the instant that he would have given his own life for Teddy's, but no one had offered him the chance. He was old, Teddy had been young, with his whole life ahead of him. The world was turned upside down. 'How? How could it happen? I thought he said them planes were safe.'

Edith went and bent over her husband. 'He wanted to fly them. It was his decision. We didn't have any way of knowing the dangers; this is a terrible war, Jack.'

He looked up. Shock had stunned him, but a strong idea already broke through that Edith was to blame. She'd forced the issue and made Teddy sign up. Then he was struck by her own misery, as she no doubt took this blame on herself; a double burden of grief and guilt. So he reached out for her hand. They thought of bullets ripping through the fabric of moth-flimsy wings, the rattle of rifle fire against propeller blades, the man in his cockpit gripping the joystick, the sudden end.

From the hosiery sweatshop in the basement to the hat workers in the attic, news of Teddy's death swept through the building. There was no false sympathy for the man himself, but a sober awareness of the new family situation, bereft of son and heir. Most of the women felt quiet fellow feeling for the grieving mother. She'd always behaved well and done her best with her wayward son. Teddy himself might have turned out all right in the end. Hindsight already softened perception of his womanizing ways. A pity he'd had no real chance to prove himself in civilian life, they said. They craned at windows to watch Jack Cooper take his wife out to the car.

'Stop whining, Lettie,' Dora Kennedy snapped, as the women in the hatters' workshop got back to work. 'And don't snivel over that bolt of best silk neither.' She rolled back her sleeves and seized the hot iron. 'We all know them's crocodile tears.' Tall, bony Dora would in fact miss Teddy's bravado and quick wit more than most. She liked to watch him in action with the Amy Ogdens and the Lettie Harrises. But she wouldn't let on that her world was a greyer place without him. There was no room for sentiment in her grim armoury.

Lettie wiped the tears with the heels of her hands and sniffed loudly.

'Here.' Emmy handed her a grubby cotton rag. She knew that Lettie had got news yesterday that her older brother, Arnie, was missing in action. As it happened, most families had at least one worry of this kind; brothers injured or missing, sons killed. 'Lay off, Dora,' she warned, against the hiss of steam and the thump of the iron.

All day they picked on Bert Buggles for being too mean to buy the girls a Christmas box of chocolates, for lounging in the corner with his racing tips, and for sloping off early when there were still orders to finish and pack. They clung to normality, while the war relentlessly robbed them of their menfolk.

Down the court, Christmas came and went under leaden skies, amongst aching hearts. A few regular customers braved the swing doors of the Duke's public bar, but they soon drifted out again. No holly decked the fine mirrors, no tunes played on the pianola. The place was like a morgue, they said.

Two days before Ernie's appeal, Robert sat quietly over a midday drink at the Duke with his friend and saviour, George Mann. George had himself received a shoulder wound bad enough to get sent home to recover. By now he was on the mend, almost ready to return to the war. But he looked in on Robert and was introduced to his family, bashful in the face of their immense gratitude.

In his talk with Robert he took a different view of things. Losing a leg was bad, but not the end of the world. He'd seen poor bleeders with their faces shot away, unlucky enough to survive. These days you got the order to go over the top and you saw men running in the opposite direction. They were rounded up and shot like dogs. The end couldn't come soon enough for George, yet he'd always reckoned on being strong-willed enough to withstand anything they threw at him. 'It ain't like it says in the papers, you and me both know that, Rob. Some mornings you wake up and you think you've landed in hell.'

Robert agreed. He appreciated the visit. Duke had taken to George, with his brawny, strapping figure and modest, level-headed way. He spoke out plain and simple; saving Rob from the battlefield was what any man would do for another.

Duke offered open house to George as soon as the war was ended, when he hoped to return to his old job on the docks across the water. 'Drop in any time, mate. You'll always find a welcome here.'

As George shook hands again and got up to go, a

message came with Joe O'Hagan. Would Robert be kind enough to call in on Mrs Cooper at the shop? Or would it be more convenient if she came and visited him here?

Robert sent back the message that he would find his own way there, and went up the street with George. There was a pea-souper of a fog, so acid and thick that it caught in their throats and enveloped the passing traffic, which roared and rattled past almost invisible. Swinging himself forward on his crutches, Robert welcomed the fog, for it hid his awkward, maimed figure. He parted with his comrade at Meredith Close. 'Look after yourself.' He freed one hand from the crutch by leaning heavily on the other.

George shook him warmly by the hand. 'Don't worry, mate. They ain't made the bullet yet that's got my name written on it!' He winked, nodded and walked off, smart and upright in his immaculate khaki uniform. The fog soon swallowed him, and Robert turned to go into the store.

Edith felt she simply wanted to talk to someone who'd been in the war like Teddy, someone who knew the suddenness and randomness of death. She wanted to hear that her son's end had been quick and sure.

Robert explained the job of the Flying Corps pilots. It wasn't quite as simple as flying overhead to determine enemy positions, for of course the enemy wanted to stop them and sent up his own planes to scare off the allies. They had gunners in the cockpits, sitting tight up behind the pilots, with machine-guns mounted on swivelling rests, and these gunners were highly trained and deadly. It depended on the skill of the pilots to dip and weave out of the line of enemy fire, but there was bombardment from below too. Robert had watched the dog fights in the air and counted himself lucky to be ankle deep in mud and filth, protected by sandbags and barbed wire.

'I hear the Hun's got hold of something new; a forward-mounted gun that fires between the propeller blades, specially timed to the split second. It means they can come straight at you, instead of sideways on.'

Edith sighed and nodded. 'Teddy never wrote and told us that.' They were in her husband's empty office. Robert looked uncomfortable, but he spoke calmly. She was grateful to him for putting himself out. How opposite to Teddy he was; dark and solid, very earnest.

'He ain't allowed to. It's all very hush-hush. But we knew them boys took a terrible risk every time they set off. You'd see them go up in flames and drop like a stone, straight down. They got plenty of guts going up there on a wing and a prayer to get shot down.'

Edith nodded again as tears welled up. 'Thank you.'

'No, I mean it. You wouldn't get me up there in one of them things, I can tell you.' He leaned forward. 'Will you tell Mr Cooper we're very sorry the way it happened. It ain't easy.'

She registered the pain the other family must be going through. She said she was glad there was an appeal for Ernie; it must surely succeed. They sat and looked at each other, caught between despair and hope, bitterness and nobility; the handsome, maimed young man and the gracious, grieving mother.

Ernie appeared at the appeal looking thin and unwell. The flesh had fallen away from his face, giving the brown eyes a wide, startled look. Prison pallor had settled on him and his movements were more stumbling than ever. Still, he put on a brave face for his family as he finally came on to the witness stand.

His account of the discovery of Daisy's body was consistent with the version he'd given to Sewell and Frances in prison. The memories were still painful; they were often broken by long pauses, to the obvious irritation of the judge. Many times the family longed to step in to save him his agony.

Though fewer onlookers had gathered in the gallery, stalwarts like Annie, Florrie and Dolly remained. They'd nodded their heads wisely during the evidence offered by the eminent medical men, remarking that it had been obvious from the start. The poor bloke had been shocked out of his wits, anyone with an ounce of common sense could see that.

Then came the vital summing up. Mayhew approached the jury as humane, decent men. They would recognize truth as it had been presented to them here. They would see that Ernie Parsons was sincere. 'You cannot hold it against a man for caring too much, for holding Daisy O'Hagan so dear in his simple heart that the discovery of her murder led to a state of complete shock and amnesia lasting several weeks, until the impact of her death gradually settled in his confused mind. You will surely believe him now.'

He walked along the row, appealing to each juryman in turn. His voice carried conviction and understanding. 'Remember, gentlemen, the law tells us that to convict a man of murder you have to know! You have to *know* that a man is lying when he protests his innocence. More important still, you have to *know* that there is no other possible explanation, no other possible culprit.

'New evidence has been brought to light here in this court today which shows us that there was indeed someone else present at the scene: a cry, a struggle, a frantic attempt to escape without being seen, and then a cold-blooded willingness to let another man hang for a crime he did not commit. All changes in an instant, does it not, gentlemen?

And the horror of the guilty verdict rears up to confront us as our worst nightmare.'

Characteristically, Mayhew lowered his voice as he came towards the end of his plea. He rested both hands on the lapels of his gown and stood full square before the jury. 'Consider the condemned man for a final moment.' The heads of the jurymen all swivelled at his bidding. They kept Ernie in their sights as they listened. 'No pressure in the world could make this man confess to the murder of Daisy O'Hagan. No police interview, no energetic cross-examination by my learned friend here today has brought about the slightest deviation in his account. And this is not because you see before you an accomplished liar and a fraud. No, this is because your man is innocent.' He paused. 'I was going to say as innocent as the day he was born, because in this case it would not be inappropriate. In this country we do not hang a man as a scapegoat for the heinous crime of another. That is not justice, gentlemen. Consider him once more, and I beg of you, go off and grant his appeal against conviction.'

Ernie sat mute in the dock. Duke and his family prayed with all their hearts. Forster could say what he liked; surely he could not sway the jury now.

But prosecuting counsel adopted a condescending tone. He could understand the softer feelings called out by the defence. How easy it was to feel sorry for someone under the shadow of the noose. 'We would be hard-hearted men indeed if we did not balk momentarily at such a punishment. But, more surely still, we would be weak-willed cowards to back off from our original conviction.' Forster twisted them to his point of view; the patrician whose sophisticated ideas they must accept.

'After all, what does this "new evidence" amount to? No more than a simple change of story; an invented scream, an invented attacker and an invented loss of memory. As for medical opinion, gentlemen, take that as you will.

'Our eminent doctors would freely admit that amnesia can be faked. They tell us that memory loss is possible in such a case as this, they do not tell us it *is* so. And as my learned friend so wisely pointed out, "You have to *know*." We do not know that the accused is sincere. We have only his word. Yet we have his fingerprints on the murder weapon. We have his bloody footprints leaving the scene of the crime. This is what we *know*, gentlemen!' He paused before he finished his man off. 'So let's have no more nonsense about changing our minds and such like. Let us have the courage to stick by our decision and to see justice done.' He bowed, then went to sit, lips pursed, eyes busily scanning the papers on his desk.

'The devil!' Annie muttered.

Florrie and Dolly looked down anxiously at Duke and the rest. They felt the spider snares of abstract justice entangle them.

Once again the judge and jury retired. Once again the endless wait, the fluctuating hopes and fears. The family scarcely talked, their minds fixed on Ernie's own feelings as he sat in his cell and awaited the verdict.

The announcements were made. The appeal was lost.

Ernie was taken from them a second time and they were plunged into the pit. Hopeless, speechless, defeated, they filed from the court.

That evening, Duke sat at the living-room table and addressed a letter to the most eminent man in charge of law and order throughout England: the Home Secretary. Sewell said it was the only avenue left open; a plea for mercy and a stay of execution. They had four days.

Duke's letter flowed on to the white page. It spoke of the difficulty the family had in understanding the ins and outs of the law. He did see how bad it looked for Ernie, and how his simplicity could be turned against him. It described his son's character as loving, obedient and gentle.

'Ernie has lived an honest life and I hope we taught him the same, since the death of his poor mother when he was little. Ernie ain't like other boys. He needs more help with things, and it breaks my heart when I think of him trying to cope with this latest piece of bad news.

'He ain't never committed no criminal acts in the whole of his life, and you have to believe me when I say he ain't no murderer. I swear on the Holy Bible in front of me.

'But the law is the law, and they seen fit to convict my poor boy and turn him down on appeal earlier today. His sisters, his brother and me know they mean to hang him before the week is out, so I write to you now, sir, for you to step in and stop this terrible thing before it is too late. If you don't help us, it don't bear thinking about.

'The boy accepts it all, and I left him calm when we came away from court. But his sisters and his aunt ain't coping, and we're all broken-hearted.

'Like I said before, sir, we want you to stop the hanging. We know you can do this for us, and save our boy from the noose.'

Duke signed himself as 'obedient servant'. He pushed the letter adrift into the middle of the table. Sadie, Hettie and Robert read it through with dull eyes. Jess came out of the bedroom carrying Grace. She nodded; yes they should send it straight off. Florrie and Frances agreed. The light was turned down low, the embers settled in the grate as Duke sealed the white envelope, set it down, then bowed his head over clasped hands and prayed.

Chapter Twenty-Nine

Sewell took charge of the delivery of the vital letter. For the family at the Duke, time passing became a nightmare, like having hideous foreknowledge of an assassin lying in wait around a corner, but being powerless to stop him. The minutes ticked by on the living-room clock.

In the cold first week of the New Year, business was almost at a standstill in the pub and out on the market stalls in Duke Street. Liz Sargent stamped her feet and blew on to her hands behind her boxes of fish. 'Might as well pack up here and sod off home,' she complained to Nora Brady.

Nora looked up at the heavy grey sky. 'It's gonna bleeding well snow if we're not careful.' She tried to cheer herself up by changing the subject. 'You thinking of going up the Duke tonight for a singsong?'

Liz shrugged. 'Ain't gonna have the time of our lives up there, are we? Like a bleeding morgue, according to Dolly Ogden, and I ain't a bit surprised.'

Nora jutted out her bottom lip. 'Who'd want the job of hangman in this day and age? It ain't natural. Do you think he has kippers for his breakfast the day he does it?'

'Don't.' Liz shuddered. 'I heard he has to have a chat with the poor bleeder and shakes him by the hand. Just think. You know you're for the chop, and you have to act matey with the geezer what does it.' She shook her head. 'How they taking it?'

'Who?'

'The family.'

'Bad. They sent a letter off to the Home Secretary, asking him to lift the noose from round the poor boy's neck. But they ain't hopeful.' Nora had spoken with Annie. 'They ain't letting on to Ernie though. They tell him he's bound to get off, trying to keep his spirits up.'

Liz looked doubtful. 'I think I'd tell him the score if it was me. How long they gonna go on fooling him?'

'Long as they can. They only got two days to go.'

This and similar conversations were held in hushed voices up and down the street. Snow threatened, trade was bad. The war lumbered on and Kitchener wanted more men. People said times were so bad that all the able-bodied young men flocked to enlist. 'And they come back home in a box, or not at all, like poor Teddy Cooper. Or useless, like Robert Parsons.'

Amy Ogden, standing freezing behind Annie's haberdashery stall, overheard such remarks. It brought back memories of when Teddy was alive and she had a steady job at Coopers', before all this trouble. She lapsed into self-pity; she'd only done what any girl would, making the best of her looks and setting her cap at the boss's son. She knew there were those who still blamed her, but they didn't see how she herself had been badly treated by a so-called toff, and her own family had ditched her over it. A girl had to make her own way now, and she didn't expect to have to freeze to death over a load of glass buttons and stay-hooks. Amy snivelled. Life looked bleak on this early January day.

'Bleeding misery,' Annie grumbled. 'If you don't cheer up, girl, I'm gonna have to lay you off work again. You're scaring my bleeding customers.'

Amy glanced up and down the half-deserted street. 'Ain't no bleeding customers.'

'No, that's because you scared them all off, like I said. What's got into you, anyway?' Annie, like Nora Brady, was deciding to call it a day. She began to reach under the stall for the lids to the cardboard boxes full of needles, thread, ribbons and lace.

'Nothing.'

'Here, catch hold of these.' Annie handed her the lids. 'If this is "nothing", I don't want to see "something".' She considered that Amy might make a bit more effort and think of someone other than herself for a change. 'What's the problem, girl? You gonna let on?'

'I got something on my mind, Annie. Just leave it, will you?' Amy found the right-sized boxes for the lids. The cold had pinched her nose and cheeks and chilled her to the bone. She felt truly miserable.

'Ain't we all?' Annie sighed. She thought of Ernie.

Amy hesitated, then took the plunge. She had to get it off her chest. 'Syd let something drop last night. It keeps bothering me, I don't know why.'

Annie stood with an armful of boxes, ready to load them on her small handcart. 'Come on, spit it out, girl.' She'd no liking for Syd Swan since his gloating performance at the trial.

'Oh, it's nothing. Forget I said anything.' It was a small niggle; something not quite right in Syd's recollection of the night of the murder. He was always going on about it, boasting how he'd helped to finger the killer. Last night, on the tram home from the Gem, he'd let slip a fact he'd never mentioned before.

'What did he say exactly?' Annie insisted. The slightest thing was worth knowing.

'Nothing much, Annie, really. He just dropped Chalky's

name into the conversation, like he was there at the Palace that night.'

'Chalky White?' Annie looked puzzled. He'd never entered the picture during the trial. She understood that Robert had flattened him earlier that day, and he'd had to hide away in his room. The police had never even had him in the picture, as far as she knew. 'Weren't he busy licking his wounds?' she asked.

'That's the way I saw it. So I says to Syd, "I thought Chalky stayed home that night?" And he says, yes, he did. He says I must have made a mistake; he never mentioned Chalky's name. I said he did. We had a blazing row on the tram. Syd just blew up at me.'

'But you still say he did mention it?' Annie seized the suspicion like a terrier. She dropped her boxes on to the cart and turned to grab Amy's hand. 'Syd did say Chalky was up the Palace the night of the murder?'

'Let go, Annie, you're hurting!' Amy withdrew her hand. 'Yes, he did. Then he turns round and tells me I must have gone round the twist; Chalky's name never passed his lips. Give me a bad fright, he did.' Feeling sorry for herself, she sniffed and turned on the tears. 'He said for me to keep my mouth shut, or else. Now he's gonna have a go at me again.'

'Never mind, you done the right thing, girl.' Annie quickly put her thoughts in order. 'You pack up here and take the cart on down the court. There's something I gotta do.' She nodded and set off up the street.

'Annie!' Amy's terrified voice called after her.

Annie turned.

'Don't say it was me. I'll get a beating off Syd if he finds out.' She stood in dismay at the chain of events she seemed to have unleashed.

Annie agreed, then hurried up to the Duke.

Duke stood behind the bar as usual. He'd just opened

up for the evening, determined to go through the motions. There'd been no word from the Home Secretary. Two days had gone by, and no word back. Each hour on the hour he went to the door and looked for the cream letter with the House of Commons seal. It never arrived.

'Duke!' Annie clattered through the doors and across the nearly empty bar. 'I got something to tell you!' She gasped and clutched the edge of the counter for support. Her hair had come loose from under her hat, her dark eyes were fired up. 'I knew things weren't right, and now I put my finger on it, thanks to a certain person!'

'Calm down, Annie.' Jess had come straight downstairs to see what the fuss was about when she saw and heard Annie make her frantic entrance. She wanted to spare Duke any extra trouble, so she took the older woman by the arm and looked to Florrie for help. Her aunt came over from the window, where she'd been busy wiping down tables. They got ready to walk Annie out smartly through the still swinging doors. 'We know how you feel. None of us is taking it that well. But it don't do no good making a fuss. You gotta let Pa be. So come on, Annie, girl. Let's get you home.'

Annie shook herself free and pushed them to one side.

'Act your age, woman,' Florrie said severely. She pulled her blouse straight. 'You can't barge in here like this.'

'Shut your mouth, Florrie Searles! And you, Jess, you listen to this!' Annie reached across the bar and laid hold of both of Duke's hands. 'It's the night of the murder, right? Your Rob's come out of the Palace and he has to hang around for Ernie. He sets eyes on that nasty piece of work, Swan, and two or three of his mates, and he gives them a run for their money.'

Duke nodded and sighed. 'What is this, Annie? This ain't nothing new.'

'Not yet, it ain't. But you just hold on. Rob seen Syd and that bloke, Whitey, and one or two other hooligans. But he ain't never mentioned Chalky White, has he?' Annie delivered her news at a gabble. 'And Syd Swan ain't mentioned him neither. So we think he ain't there that night, and no one gives him a second thought.'

Jess came forward. 'What you saying, Annie?'

'I'm saying he *was* there. There at the Palace. But he weren't hanging round with the gang, or Rob would've spotted him, see!'

Jess nodded. She looked quickly at Duke.

'So where was he?' Annie demanded.

'Backstage.' Jess's two simple syllables, delivered flat and deadly quiet, set up a flock of suspicions.

'Chalky White,' Duke said. He looked Annie in the eyes. 'You sure?'

She nodded. 'Think about it. They never go nowhere without him, and he ain't one to stop home for a couple of cuts and bruises. He was there all right!'

'And he'd fallen out with Daisy, Pa.' Jess had been carried along by Annie's reasoning. 'I can just see him getting his own back.'

'She threw him over. Ask Ett. You seen her in here with him, ain't you? And he didn't like it one little bit when she said she didn't want nothing to do with him. Ask Rob. I think she had a bellyful of trouble with him.' Annie refused to calm down. She released hold of Duke and shook Jess by the arm. 'What we gonna do?'

'I don't know. I'll go and get Maurice for a start. You stay here and see who else we can round up. Tell the others. Ett's upstairs working. Tell her to find Rob.' Jess flew towards the door. 'That's right, Pa, ain't it?'

Duke hesitated. 'It ain't much to go on.' He narrowed his eyes and thought it through. 'But it's better than nothing. You spotted something there all right, Annie. And when we lay hands on Syd Swan, he'll squeal, don't you worry. I know his sort.' He nodded at Jess, then went down into the cellar to fetch Joxer. They would gather all their help, then decide what to do.

Maurice was setting off for the Gem when Jess tracked him down. He handed over the cinema keys to Charlie and told him he was trusting him to open up the box-office. He'd get to work as soon as he could. Charlie walked on, but he stopped on Duke Street to let Tommy O'Hagan know what was going on. 'They're after Syd Swan. Anyone know where he is?'

Tommy had finished work for the day, and eagerly took up the cry. He ran up the street and passed the word. Soon all the kids on street-corners and doorsteps swarmed off down the alleys. Word was out; Syd Swan was wanted. Don't let him know, but go back and tell them at the Duke. There was trouble brewing; big trouble.

Tommy knew the gang's usual haunts and he was quick on his feet. He used all the short cuts, looking in all the likely places. It was he who landed back at the pub with the first news. 'Syd's down at Milo's,' he reported. 'With Chalky.' His breathless message provided the key.

The men left the pub straight away. Florrie was glad that Duke had decided to stay put and let the others deal with it. It was a young man's game, he realized. Walter Davidson said they didn't know what to expect exactly, but that he would keep an eye on Rob. Duke sent Joxer and Maurice to back them up. 'Don't do nothing stupid,' he warned. 'We want the truth, not a bloodbath.'

'We want Ernie out of that place,' Rob reminded him. 'Whatever it takes.'

Sadie, Hettie, Jess and Frances came out into the dark

street to watch them go. They stood in silence. It was a last chance for Ernie; no one else could help him now.

Milo came up the long, shabby room to greet Rob and his friends. 'Good to see you out of that chair, mate.' His smile wavered. 'What's up? You ain't had no more bad news, I hope?'

Men exercised and trained in all corners of the room. Iron weights rattled against the wooden floor, there was the thud of punch-bags, the scrape and squeak of shoes on canvas. The raised platform of the ring was occupied. Inside its ropes, Chalky White and an opponent were sparring.

'There's Swan, over there!' Walter pointed him out. He was standing fully dressed, with his elbows hooked over the low rope bordering the ring, shouting encouragement to Chalky and measuring his form.

Maurice took Milo to one side and quietly explained their mission. The small Irishman nodded. 'I wish you luck, mate.' He stood by and watched as the newcomers closed in on Swan.

Chalky spotted them first, as he moved his sparring partner round the ring and came into a position which gave him full view of the intruders. He went flat on his feet and dropped his guard, eyeing them warily. They looked an ill-assorted group: Joxer in his waistcoat and shirt-sleeves, Robert on his crutches, Maurice dressed up smartly for work and Walter buttoned up inside a greatcoat. But he could see it was trouble. Syd turned to investigate.

Robert stood forward of the group. They were framed by the long, black windows of the gym which reflected the yellow glare of electric bulbs. Curiosity had brought other men up close, their attention on Syd and Chalky to see what they would make of the interruption. Many breathed heavily. They stood about idly, their hands still strapped with tape, their singlets damp with sweat.

At a signal from Robert, Maurice and Walter moved in on Syd. 'We hear you've got a new story,' he began, 'about who was where when Daisy got done in.' He kept his eyes on Chalky, as the other two moved Syd up against the nearest wall. 'You might be interested to hear this and all,' he told Swan, without deflecting his gaze from Chalky.

'I ain't said nothing, Chalky!' Syd protested. They'd caught him off guard. Maurice and Walter had backed him right into the corner.

'Shut it!' Chalky warned. He stooped under the ropes and vaulted down to floor level. 'What the bleeding hell do you think you're up to?' He was face to face with Robert, aware of Joxer's bulky figure in the background. A taut nerve flicked in his cheek and pulled down one corner of his almost lipless mouth. He saw Robert give another signal to the two who'd cornered Syd.

Walter laid into Syd's body with well-rehearsed skill and timing. Syd aimed a return blow but missed, as Walter ducked. They heard the air expelled from his lungs by Walter's second, thudding punch. He collapsed forward as Chalky began to move in to join the fight. But then Joxer loomed up from behind and hooked a massive arm around Chalky's neck. He locked his elbow in position, forcing the man's head back, half-strangling him.

Maurice caught hold of Walter. 'Wait! See if he's ready to talk!'

Syd gasped and clutched his stomach, then he swung out, dribbling saliva, coughing, catching Maurice on the side of the jaw, so that Maurice had to lunge back at him to prevent him from running off. Joxer held tight to Chalky, keeping him pinioned against his own chest. Soon he ran him straight at his accomplice, like a battering ram, and bundled them back into the corner. He was so powerful that both men went sprawling.

Chalky looked up from his humiliating position. His hand slipped sideways into Syd's jacket pocket and he pulled out a knife, gleaming silver, long and sharp. He crouched, and a sneer came on to his face. Syd came up beside him. They edged forward, mocking and jeering as Maurice and Joxer were forced to back off.

'Go on, Syd, tell us why you never said Chalky was there.' Robert held his nerve. 'Couldn't be that he was busy backstage, could it?'

'Prove it,' Chalky snarled. He sprang at Robert with his knife, slashing through mid-air in wild, stabbing movements. Robert raised one crutch to protect himself.

The onlookers backed away. Milo ran to his office to use the telephone to ring Union Street station.

Joxer saw Chalky come at Robert with his knife. He put one shoulder down and charged, so heavy and strong that he knocked the attacker off course. He reached down for the knife as Chalky's arm flailed backwards, then grabbed his wrist and shook the weapon free. It clattered to the floor. Robert swung at it with his crutch and knocked it out of reach. Now Joxer was enraged, and he punched at his man's body and face, letting go a battery of blows.

Syd crouched back down and watched in dismay. Walter wrenched him to his feet and throttled him against the wall. 'Spit it out!' he ordered. 'I'm not stopping Joxer until we get what we want from you!' They heard Chalky groan under the weight of the cellarman's punches.

'All right, all right, he was there!' Syd broke down. 'So what? Call him off. He'll bleeding well kill him!'

Chalky groaned again. He'd fallen on the floor and tried to curl up, but Joxer rolled him over with one foot and bent to drag him upright again.

'Right, he was at the Palace,' Maurice challenged. 'We got that. Now what?'

'Now nothing.' Syd winced as Joxer landed another blow to Chalky's body.

Walter flattened him against the wall again. 'He went to see Daisy, didn't he? You was hanging around waiting for him. He went backstage and done her in!'

'No!'

They heard Chalky slump to the ground as Joxer let him go. The big man moved across towards Syd.

'Come on!' Robert urged. There'd be another murder committed before long. He saw Syd cower in Joxer's shadow, and realized he couldn't take punishment like Chalky. 'It was Chalky, wasn't it?'

Syd's nerve broke down. 'Yes!' he gasped.

Robert heard the confession. His head went down and he took a deep, shuddering breath. Maurice held him up. Joxer towered over Syd, while Walter kept an eye on their murderer, still lying half senseless on the floor.

'Call him off,' Syd pleaded. 'I said it was Chalky, ain't I? He went looking for trouble, said she had it coming. I thought he was gonna smack her about a bit, that's all. I didn't know he was gonna do her in!'

Chalky groaned and lifted a hand in protest. They pulled him to his feet. Vivid bruises already stood out on his cheekbone, a trickle of blood ran from one corner of his mouth. He knew it was all over.

'Get the police,' Maurice said.

Milo hovered in the background. 'They're on their way.' There was a stunned silence throughout the gym.

402

'Ask him why he did it,' Robert said, his voice shaky. 'Tell him I want to know.'

Daisy had laughed at him, it was as simple as that. He'd called her out from her dressing room into the dark alley, and she'd put her hand to her mouth and laughed at his black eye. She said she was glad Robert had given him it; it was no more than he deserved. She didn't want to go round with his sort, how many times did she need to tell him? He'd better make himself scarce. She laughed in his face and went to call Fred Mills for help.

That was when he followed her inside, after all the others had left. Fred Mills spotted him and left him to sort the girl out. It was none of his business, the manager said. Daisy wouldn't stop laughing. She'd gone hysterical when he started to push her about. Then he drew the knife. It was over in seconds.

'You done the girl in because she laughed?' Robert repeated. He shook his head in disbelief. 'And I bet that Fred Mills seen you at it. I bet he knows.'

Chalky stared sullenly back.

'Bastards, they were all in on it. They let Ernie get it in the neck without lifting a finger!' Robert stammered.

'Not any more.' Walter put an arm around his shoulder. 'We nailed them this time, mate. We nailed them good and proper.'

Chapter Thirty

Tommy O'Hagan was proud of the part he'd played in the arrest of Daisy's true murderer. He'd come a long way since he used to hang about Waterloo Station on the off-chance of earning a penny or two cab-ducking, or pestering the carters' yards to cut up hay. He'd seen life in the raw and been to sea. He'd set up his own barrow. He'd officially left school. 'No more Miss Sweetlips for me,' he told Sadie, remembering all too well Mr Donaldson's less-than-affectionate use of the cane, the books thrown as missiles, the hog-tying of boys to radiators. 'School's a mug's game for the likes of Charlie Ogden, not for me.'

Sadie appreciated how much Tommy had come on. He worked for himself and was doing very well. He was even thinking of hiring a lad and taking on Billy Wray's stall as well. He'd been practising the newspaper vendor's raucous, incomprehensible cry. And he'd filled out to fit his new jacket; no longer the skinny, ragged-arsed kid. He combed his hair, used a razor at least once a week, and prided himself on his valuable contribution to the family budget.

'You know something, if I'd been around when our Daisy got herself done in, they'd never have nicked Ernie in the first place,' he bragged.

'Oh, bleeding Sherlock Holmes now, are we?' At the

moment, Sadie would forgive Tommy anything. He'd slung his arm around her shoulder, leaning back against the bar with his other elbow. The room was crowded out with all their friends and family. Ernie sat at a table, the smiling centre of it all.

Tommy polished his nails against his chest. 'You just gotta keep your eyes peeled, that's all. You gotta be one step ahead.'

Sadie shoved him sideways and broke free. She stood, hands on hips, studying his white neck scarf, his bold brass buckle. 'Talk about big-headed!' She flashed him a challenging look. 'You're still nothing but a peaky blinder, Tommy O'Hagan, with that stupid cap and everything. Who you trying to kid?'

Tommy exaggerated his disappointment. 'Oh, Sadie, don't say that. Here's me thinking we'd clicked.'

'The day I click with you, Tommy, is the day they cart me off and throw away the key.'

'I'll go and chuck myself off London Bridge, you heartless girl.'

'And spoil your nice new jacket? Don't do that, Tom.' Sadie was aware of Charlie sitting with his family at a nearby table. She flirted with Tommy for all she was worth.

Maurice's words about throwing over a good-looking girl came back to haunt Charlie now. Sadie, restored to high spirits by Ernie's last-minute reprieve, sparkled. There was a time last year when he'd sat on a grassy bank with his arms round that girl, taking for granted the nearness of her creamy, smooth cheek, the soft intensity of her dark-fringed eyes. He'd showered her with bluebells and run laughing with her across a sweet-smelling carpet of flowers under branches newly green. He'd given her up, and now he must watch her flirt with Tommy. He frowned.

'Serves you right,' Dolly said. She followed his gaze and read his thoughts. 'You made your own bed there, son. Now you gotta lie on it.'

'Leave the boy alone.' Arthur cottoned on to his son's regret. 'No need to rub it in.' He pulled at his pint, ready to play the man of the world. 'Love them and leave them. That's my advice, Charlie. Ain't none of them worth losing no sleep over.' He winked and drank again.

Dolly laughed uproariously. 'Look who's talking; love them and leave them! A proper little Romeo, ain't you, Arthur Ogden? If you want to know the truth, I think you chucked over a real gem there, Charlie.' She waved at Sadie and called her over to join them. 'Just sit tight and be nice to the girl. I'll try and bring her round for you. You never know your luck.'

But Charlie blushed red to the roots of his hair. 'No, Ma. I told Mr Leigh I'd go ahead and open up.' He pulled a big bunch of keys from his jacket pocket. 'I gotta dash.' He leapt for the door as Sadie approached.

Amy grinned. 'Mister Leigh this, Mister Leigh that,' she mimicked. 'You'd think the sun shone out of that man's backside.'

'Hush, Amy.' Dolly stood up to embrace the youngest Parsons girl. 'Sadie, we're over the moon for you, girl. We can't hardly believe it. This is the best bit of news we had in ages.' She held her close and patted her on the back. 'When they took Ernie away it was as bad as losing one of our own, I can tell you. The whole street was cut up. But now he's back!' Even Dolly ran out of words at last. She held Sadie at arm's length, eyes glistening. 'How about organizing a singsong to celebrate?' she asked. 'Go on, you got a voice like a canary when you get going. And Amy here. You girls get over there and sort it out for us, put us in the mood.'

Sadie smiled down at Amy. 'Come on,' she said. She linked arms and they threaded their way through the crowd gathered to join in Ernie's home-coming. When they reached the pianola, she turned to the older girl, who still looked downcast after the strain of recent events. She had put on an unconvincing show of dolling herself up for the occasion with flowers and feathers in her hair, but her conscience was uneasy. 'What's up, Amy?' Sadie wanted to know. 'You don't look yourself tonight. It ain't Syd, is it?'

Syd Swan was in deep trouble for concealing material evidence from the Crown. Chalky was firmly behind bars and without its leader the gang had disintegrated. In fact, Whitey and a couple of others had moved across the water until the fuss died down, and Syd was rumoured to be holed up in his ma's place in Walthamstow. Amy knew she was safe from him at present, but she didn't underestimate his long-term resentment. She felt no regret about his absence from Duke Street. 'No, it ain't Syd,' she confessed.

Sadie softened towards her and took her by the hand. 'Has any of us said thanks to you yet, Amy?'

'No, what for?'

'For fingering Chalky for us. That took plenty of guts, that did.'

Amy inhaled deeply. It took her a while to realize that Sadie meant it, then she shrugged.

'It did. And you was on the ball to pick it up in the first place, from what I hear. We got a lot to thank you for.'

'Oh, I ain't been too clever on the whole,' Amy protested. 'Not really.'

But Sadie wouldn't hear of it. Her gratitude bubbled over, and soon everyone within earshot was saying, yes, Amy Ogden was the one to thank. Without her, Chalky and Syd would have got away with it. They wouldn't all be sitting here now celebrating if not for her.

'You know,' Dolly said to Arthur, surprise registering in her voice, 'that girl of ours done us proud.' She sat nodding. 'All right, so she put a foot wrong here and there. Don't we all? But her heart's in the right place, ain't it?'

Amy's head had gone up, pleased as punch. She was getting ready to sing alongside Sadie Parsons.

Arthur breathed a sigh of relief. 'Blimey, you mean you two ain't gonna be at each other's throats no more?'

Dolly smiled blithely back. 'If they can climb out of the trenches for a Christmas truce, I reckon Amy and me can call it a day. That's what I say. Anyhow, I been thinking.'

'Oh, bleeding Nora!' Arthur hated it when Dolly schemed. It usually cost money.

'No, seriously. I been thinking. I want to send the girl to learn how to be one of them typewriters. I been talking to Frances, and she says it's the up-and-coming thing; girls working in offices.'

'Clackety-clack, bleeding machines,' Arthur grumbled. But he could see the writing on the wall. Dolly had ambitions for Amy. Well, it was better than open warfare in the house. 'Where's the money coming from?' he argued.

Dolly eyed him severely. 'You gotta get a job, Arthur. That's where the money's coming from.'

Arthur definitely drew the line at that. Moving with the times was one thing, and having ambitions above your station. But sending a sick man out to work to pay for it was quite another. He wheezed into his beer. He and Dolly would bicker about it for weeks, then Dolly would work miracles to find the money and send Amy off to college. There was no stopping her.

Before Amy and Sadie could get the singing into full swing, Hettie and her friends came round with the collecting tin for the Salvation Army.

'Cashing in, eh?' Robert winked. He hadn't got used to

this transformation in his fun-loving sister, but he respected her decision. He tipped a few coins into her tin.

'Why not?' Hettie retorted. 'Don't you think God deserves a bit of the praise and some thanks round here?' She held out the tin and rattled it under the noses of some of Rob's friends. Walter Davidson dug deep in his pocket. 'It's God kept us going through the darkest hours, ain't it, Ern?'

Ernie heard her shout and nodded back. He wanted to wallow in the moment, to agree with everyone, see the smiles on people's faces. He still couldn't believe the moment when the key had turned in the lock and Duke had come into the cell specially set aside for the condemned man. He was with Mr Sewell, who delivered the news. They'd caught the real murderer. Ernie was free to go.

Duke had confirmed it; it was true. Rob and the girls were waiting outside at the prison gate, all of them. The warder held the door wide open. Ernie was reprieved. He had remembered to thank God, and the warder who'd looked after him without harshness or contempt.

'Good luck, mate.' The warder clapped him on the shoulder and sent him on his way. At the gate, he fell into everyone's arms and they took him home in a taxi. He slept in his own clean bed.

'All right, all right, less of the Onward Christian Soldiers, thank you very much,' Robert murmured. 'It used to be Frances what was bad for business, but she turned out normal lately, and you stepped in for her.'

Walter kicked him under the table. 'Give it a rest, Rob.' He was fascinated by the change in Hettie, knowing there was a good-looking, vivacious woman lurking under that poky bonnet. He could understand her turning to the Army, though, and thought Robert was being too hard.

'She don't mind, do you, Ett?'

'Not if you cough up all the coppers you got in your pockets, Robert Parsons; I don't care what you say.' She asked after Walter's bruised hands and said thank you to him for the hundredth time. Her combination of natural warmth and zeal for the cause was irresistible. She and Freda took record amounts, before they set up the singsong with Sadie and Amy, turning their faces to the ornate ceiling and bursting with praise for the Lord.

Walter grinned at Rob. 'I wouldn't argue with her if I was you, pal.' He was happy to sit and talk things over with his friend. For the first time since his return from the Front, it seemed Robert wanted to look ahead and make plans. They brought up the old dream of owning a taxi.

'Whoever heard of a one-legged taxi-driver?' Robert complained. 'Or a one-legged docker when it comes to it.'

'How about a one-legged motor-car mechanic?' Walter didn't see that his injury would stop him in the long run from learning how to take care of car engines. 'We could still be partners; Davidson and Parsons, Hackney Motor Carriages.'

For a few minutes, their conversation took off; men who knew about the combustion engine would be in high demand after the war. Modern transport was going along those lines. Robert recalled his brave friend, George Mann, having to heave the horse-and-cart munitions wagon out of the mud. 'It's had its day, that kind of thing. From now on it's going to be motorized everything.' He agreed it would be a good line of work to get into. 'Only one problem,' he pointed out.

'What's that?' Walter was reluctant to fall back to earth just yet. He fancied a whole fleet of taxis, shiny and black, with running-boards and big chrome bumpers. He wanted an office with a telephone, and people ringing up to be taken into the West End.

'It's the little matter of pounds, shillings and pence, mate.'

'Ah.' Walter sighed. 'Ain't no harm in dreaming.' Then there was one other problem he thought it only fair to point out. 'It ain't on the cards right away in any case. I been thinking, Rob. I ought to join up.'

Robert's mood switched in an instant. 'Enlisting?' He tried not to give away his own doubts and fears.

'I think I ought.' Lord Kitchener's face with its black moustache and piercing eyes had begun to appear on posters. The finger of accusation pointed at those who still thought to let others lay down life and limb for their country, but not themselves. Walter had too much pride to resist the call for long. 'I ain't keen on aiming at the Hun down the barrel of a gun, don't get me wrong. I ain't one for all that. But I'm fit and strong, Rob, and it don't seem right to hold back no more. This jamboree's going on longer than they thought, ain't it? If I join up straight off, do my bit and come home a hero, there'll be a job waiting for me at the end of the line, won't there?' He attempted a confident grin. 'Then we can start saving for that taxi.'

Robert found it hard to look him in the face. 'Good for you, mate.' He shut out the mental pictures of mangled bodies, blank terror, the insanity of slaughter for ten yards of mud.

'I'm off up the Town Hall on Monday morning,' Walter promised. 'Then you won't have one up on me no more.'

'Well, drink up,' Rob said. 'It's on the house.' Awkwardly he took the two glasses by hooking his thumb through both handles and dangling them from one crutch.

Duke served the beer and looked straight at his son. 'You sit down, mate. I'll get Joxer to fetch them across.' The cellarman had reported for duty as usual the minute Chalky had been taken into police custody. He said nothing as he buttoned his waistcoat and left the gym, and he didn't intend to discuss things thereafter. He knew he had a job for life with Duke, and they'd each mind their own business. His face was expressionless as he brought Robert the two pints of beer.

Duke stood happily behind the bar, back in charge, his old, unflappable self. With Ernie at home and enjoying the limelight for once in his life, he felt that nothing could dent his sense of all being right with the world; not earthquake nor calamity nor war. Thanks to family and friends, he added to himself.

He sent extra drinks over to Frances and her friends, Billy and Rosie. Even Frances had let her hair down and sat there having a good time like the rest of them. She was human, after all, in spite of all that nonsense about the suffragettes.

Billy was in the middle of telling them how the Workers' Education Movement was putting its shoulder behind the war effort, especially as far as women were concerned. 'Just like Mrs Pankhurst and the suffragettes,' he said. 'We gotta unite against the common enemy.' The women's movement had ceased hostilities against the government; no more window-smashing or burning of post-boxes. And since women were beginning to form the nation's workforce – on the buses, in the factories, out in the fields – the Workers' Education people were putting together leaflets and holding classes especially for their benefit.

'Talking of workforces,' Rosie said, standing up and preparing to go. She gathered her cloak around her nurse's uniform and put on her gloves. 'My night shift starts in half an hour.' She bent to kiss Frances on the cheek and told her to give her love to Ernie.

So Frances was left sitting face to face with Billy Wray.

She told him how the chief pharmacist, a married man, had just joined up. 'That leaves me in charge.'

'About time too.' He said he had great faith in her abilities. 'You got the right frame of mind,' he told her. 'Very particular in everything.'

'A fusspot, you mean?' She blushed, feeling a strong urge to throw off her finicky spinster image.

'Very precise. Very neat.'

'Oh Lord, Billy, don't I wish I weren't sometimes!' She confessed she wouldn't mind a bit of Dolly's free-and-easiness, a touch of young Sadie's rebellious high spirits. 'It ain't that much fun being the responsible one, day in, day out.'

Billy smiled at her. 'It don't mean to say that's all there is to you.' He paid her the compliment of implying a hidden depth and intensity to her character, calling to mind their one stolen kiss under the watchful bound volumes of Ruskin and Sidney Webb.

It was too soon for him to make any move. He wanted to do the decent thing by Ada's memory for a start. And he was no moonstruck youth. He had just enough confidence in himself to realize that Frances was playing the same waiting game; observing convention and biding her time. She for her part was no mere flighty girl.

Frances sighed. 'Sometimes it does take a catastrophe to pull out the best in us, like they say. I mean, it's the war that'll give me the chance I want in the pharmacy. And it was the trouble over Ernie that pulled me and Pa back on to the same side, acting as a family again. And take Jess over there; having the baby really proved her mettle. There's times we'd all have given up over Ernie if it hadn't been for her, I don't mind telling you. It's funny, she's my sister, but I don't think I ever really knew her till now.'

413

Billy liked to hear these things. An only child himself, he envied her her large family. 'Jess should count herself lucky and all,' he reminded her. 'She ain't never gonna be on her own.'

A sudden gust of cold air and an influx of women from the market and from Coopers' turned the tide of conversation. The pianola thumped out another tune, second nature to Hettie from her days at the Palace. Liz Sargent encouraged her to sing up. Little Lettie Harris jumped in to do the Huggie Bear with Sam the leather worker.

'Nothing like a good knees up.' Nora Brady sidled up to Robert. 'Just what the doctor orders.' She picked up her skirts and made him do away with his crutch. Then they swayed along to the music, arms around each other's waists.

'What's your old man gonna say, Nora?' Rob asked, his good humour restored. He pulled Ernie to his feet and made him link up with Nora's free arm. 'Now you've got two new beaux?'

'He ain't gonna say nothing,' came the bold answer. 'Not when he's banged up in Parkhurst for six months, now, is he?' She laughed like a drain. 'While the cat's away, you know the rest!' And she took Ernie by both shoulders to give him lessons in the latest American dance craze.

The noise rose as the evening got into full swing. The dreary tenements at the bottom of Paradise Court spilled out their occupants, and the poor but respectable terraced houses emptied in turn. Older children were left to care for infants and little ones. Keys turned in locks. Even the penniless unemployed turned out tonight to call in at the Duke and help Ernie celebrate.

'Annie, you don't half look a treat!' Nora shrieked at the late arrival. The music played on, the bar was alive with bright lights, curling smoke, reflections in mirrors, the clink of glasses. There was the uproar of competing conversations.

Annie had lingered in front of her own glass, making a special effort. She'd been in and out of first this blouse, then that. Finally she'd chosen a smart one of shiny green and white striped poplin. She arranged her hair in softer, more flattering folds, put rouge on her cheeks, then scrubbed it off again. At last she set off for the pub.

Robert Parsons gave a cheeky whistle, Liz passed by with a nod of approval. Annie crept nervously towards the bar.

'Blow me!' Florrie said in a voice laden with sarcasm. 'Look what the wind blew in!'

'I see you're done up like a dog's dinner as usual, Florence.' Annie didn't wait for the full force of Florrie's scorn to land on her before she returned the insult. 'I keep on telling you, girl, but you ain't got the sense you was born with. Them magenta ribbons ain't you at all. And I should tone down the black dye a bit and all, if I was you. In fact, I'd say it was high time you gave in gracefully.'

'Who asked you, Annie Wiggin? Any rate, this ain't magenta, it's scarlet!' Florrie took the bait as usual. She rushed across to serve Annie so that Duke didn't need to stir himself. As she pushed the porter towards her, she leaned over the counter and her eyes popped. 'Blimey, Annie!' She clutched the bar for support. 'I think I must be seeing things!'

'Very funny, ha, ha!' Annie began to beat a retreat, but Nora too broke off dancing and came and seized her by the arm.

'Do you mean what I think you mean?' Nora said to Florrie. She gazed down at Annie's feet. 'Or is our eyes deceiving us?' She fluttered back into someone's arms, as if in a faint.

'Very funny, very funny!' Annie grumbled. She wished now she hadn't taken the plunge in such public fashion. It was true; she'd bought herself a pair of brand new boots.

'My, but they're a pair of bobby dazzlers.' A group led by Nora gathered round, to Florrie's satisfaction. The boots were black and pointed, with neat raised heels and dainty scalloped edges where the laces threaded through. They were immaculate.

But if they thought they could get one over on her, they'd another think coming, Annie told herself. 'So what? Ain't you never seen a new pair of boots before?'

'Not on you, Annie, no.' Florrie's tone kept up the derisory note. 'You mean to say you finally thrown over the memory of old man Wiggin after all these years?' She arched her eyebrows in the direction of Duke, but her brother stolidly refused to join in the taunting of Annie.

Annie gathered herself. She felt ladylike in her new boots, and well above Florrie's low aim. They gave her movements new snap and vigour. 'As a matter of fact, yes, Florrie. I thought it was time I laid his old boots to rest along with him, God rest his soul. Me and Duke's been in mourning long enough, ain't we, Duke? We think it's time to liven things up.'

Florrie gasped at Annie's audacity, and was even more surprised when Duke seemed to happily concur in the use of the first person plural. Annie evidently wasn't using 'we' in the royal sense.

Duke smiled awkwardly and came out from behind the bar. He felt himself moved by a sense of destiny. 'I see you took my advice about them old boots, Annie!' He took her by the arm and led her to a seat in a corner.

Annie retaliated as of old. 'Ain't nothing to do with your advice, Duke. I spotted these down the market. They was too good a bargain to miss.'

The hum of celebration continued all around them; the soaring girls' voices, the lively conversation, an outbreak of laughter. 'Too good to miss, eh?' Duke said meditatively.

'Yes, some things are too good to pass by.' Suddenly Annie's voice dropped. She realized that neither of them were talking about boots any more.

'That's it, we'd be fools to pass by certain things in this life.' He sighed. 'I'd go a long way before I found a friend like you, Annie.' He took her hands in his own large, work-worn ones.

She struggled to reply. 'Now, don't you go all soft on me, Duke Parsons. Just 'cos I bought myself a new pair of boots.'

He cleared his throat. 'Annie Wiggin, I think you and me should get spliced!' It was hasty, he knew.

'Blow me down!' was Annie's reply.

'Come on, Annie, you can't kid me you never knew what I was leading up to!' he protested. She'd gone coy on him.

'I never! You could knock me down with a feather!' Her heart fluttered. Her hands still rested in Duke's.

'Well?'

'I thought you'd never ask!' she answered at last, her face radiant. 'Blimey, Duke, you certainly took your time!'

Duke and Annie stood up and linked arms, then went across to the table where Jess and Maurice sat in self-conscious conversation. He held up his hands for quiet.

'Now as you know, I ain't one for public speaking,' he began. His voice rumbled into the newly created silence. He gestured for Ernie to draw near. 'You're all friends here, not just customers. We grown up and we grown old together, some of us.' He had a tone of deep tenderness, his arms around Ernie's shoulder. 'So I don't have to tell no one here what it means to have Ernie back home.'

417

A cheer went up for Ernie, and an outburst of applause. Once more, Duke put up his hand.

'Without you we'd never have come through this like we have, still in one piece, and we ain't never gonna forget what we owe you, as long as we live.'

Sadie, standing at the pianola with Tommy and Amy, sighed happily. Hettie stood proud and smiling by the door. Frances squeezed Billy's hand. Robert stood shoulder to shoulder with Walter, while Jess hung on to Maurice's arm.

Duke took up the thread, his voice thickened with emotion. 'Now, I aim to do this whole thing right and make it a home-coming to remember.' He cleared his throat. 'Ernie, I got one more bit of news for you. Frank Henshaw sent word he wants you back at work on Monday, eight o'clock sharp.'

Ernie nodded. The last shred of doubt about his future fell away.

'And more than that. Jess here, and Maurice have asked me to announce their news.' Duke raised her up to stand alongside him. 'They asked me to tell you they plan on tying the knot just as soon as they can.'

A buzz passed round the room, then another cheer.

Duke continued. 'We ain't known Maurice long, but we say welcome to the Parsons family.' He turned to shake his prospective son-in-law vigorously by the hand. 'As long as you think you can put up with us, that is.'

Maurice grinned sheepishly and put an arm round Jess's shoulder. 'You mean I'm stuck with the lot of you?' He had no qualms now. Once he'd decided, he went ahead. He was already talking of finding bigger lodgings down the court, or nearby on Duke Street, so Jess and Grace would still be on the doorstep. He'd approached his employer for a rise in wages, describing his plans to marry and settle down.

He'd been offered more money in return for helping to set up another new cinema down the road in Dulwich.

Jess basked in the contentment spreading through the room. She was the luckiest woman alive, with Maurice and Grace, the one to pour her hidden passion upon, the other on whom she could dote so tenderly. She felt like a passenger rescued from the wreck of the great *Titanic*; she'd kept her head in the icy waters and climbed into a lifeboat with those she loved. She reached out and kissed her father, then Ernie, then Maurice.

But Duke hadn't reached the end of his own long, unaccustomed journey into speechifying. 'Now, girls,' he said to no one in particular, 'I expect you're all thinking of buying a new hat for Jess's wedding, and I ain't one to force you into no unnecessary expense.' He paused to look round and clutch hold of Annie's hand. 'So Annie and me, we thought we'd better make it worth your while and follow up with a wedding of our own. No need to buy another hat, see, Dolly. You can wear the same one to both!'

Annie stood beside him, looking small and spry, like a preening bird. She dipped her head and looked sideways up at him, then stared straight at Florrie with a new sense of territory. Her head went back, her chest out. Until this moment she hadn't really believed in Duke's proposal. His announcement of it had stunned everyone in the room. Well, that was one in the eye for his sister, Annie thought with undisguised triumph.

Florrie shook her head as if a bee had landed on her nose. Of all the foolish things. After all these years. Annie Wiggin, of all people. She couldn't pull one sensible thought together. Then it came with startling clarity; Annie had wormed her way under Duke's guard and into his affections when he was at his lowest point over Ernie. Of course, that was how she'd managed it. Otherwise, how could it be explained?

There was not a single thing about Annie that cut her out from the common crowd of middle-aged women whose husbands ran off and left them in the lurch. She was no beauty, that was certain; thin as a whippet, all skin and bone, and her mouth needed a permanent muzzle. No, it wasn't romance that had drawn Duke in her direction. She'd just wormed her way in, out of spite against Florrie.

But if she thought Florrie would pack her bags and toddle meekly back to Brighton, she was making a big mistake. She, Florrie, was made of sterner stuff, and there was many a slip between this moment and, 'Do you take this man to be your lawful wedded husband?' Florrie chuntered on to herself. She had of course turned down umpteen decent offers in her own time. It was the only dignified course for women in their situation.

Still, congratulations for both couples poured in. 'I ain't gotta call you Ma, have I?' Robert winked at Annie.

'You do and I'll knock your block off,' she said.

'I see marriage ain't gonna soften you up none,' Arthur Ogden observed. 'Not that it does in most cases, if you ask me.' He looked ruefully at Dolly.

'It ain't gonna change nothing,' Annie insisted. 'I'll run my stall of bits and bobs, and Duke will run this place like before. We ain't gonna live in each other's pockets, don't you worry.'

The men slapped Duke on the back, bought him drinks and admired his nerve.

'Well, we're living in dangerous times,' he told them. 'It makes a man feel reckless, don't it?'

Hettie, Frances and Sadie came across to complete the family group. The Parsons were back together and the heart had been restored to Duke Street and Paradise Court. They might have been posing for a picture as the music struck up. They stood, arms intertwined, a fading photograph in an album, seen through a haze of smoke, features already beginning to blur. They held position for a moment in time, in harmony, completely happy.

AFTER HOURS

For the Holmes family of Beckwithshaw

PART ONE

For better, for worse

CHAPTER ONE

November 1923

The great Wurlitzer rose into the auditorium as Sadie
Parsons settled into her plush velvet seat. Richie Palmer had
brought her along to the Picturedrome as a special treat.
The organ came into view with a cascade of rich notes
which rang out through the vast cinema. Overhead, the
projection light flickered, cigarette smoke mingled with
dancing motes of dust. Onscreen, the titles came up for the
cartoon shorts.

'Hurrah, it's Felix!' someone in front stood up and yelled
in a raw voice of recognition. An animated drawing of a
cheeky cat strutted across the screen, while the organist
played his 'Keep on Walking' signature tune. The front row
went wild.

'Sit down!' another voice called from further back. 'And
take off yer hat!'

The enthusiastic boy in the wide flat cap subsided into his
seat, then subtitles appeared with a moving ball of light which
bounced from word to word in time with the music. A
thousand people sang as Felix the Cat danced the Braziliane.

Wreathed in smiles, Sadie joined in. It was Saturday night
in a miserable November. The year of 1923 was grinding to
a close amid more food shortages and strikes in London's
East End. Victory in the Great War seemed hollow to the

maimed men bearing placards who still trudged the streets of Southwark looking in vain for work. But here, in the fabulous new Picturedrome, singing along with Felix, they could forget their woes.

Richie shifted closer to Sadie and slid his arm along the back of her seat. She shot him a quick, shy glance, but his square, handsome face gave nothing away. He sat silent, chin up, smoking his cigarette, while the Wurlitzer sank into the floor amid a sea of coloured lights.

The audience clapped and stamped, impatiently calling out for the main picture to begin.

'Get a move on, why don't you?'

'Ta-ra-ra-boom-de-ay!'

'The bleeding thing's broke down!'

The boys in the front row stood on their seats and jeered. The magic square of light from the projection room stayed obstinately blank.

'Give us our money back, or else!'

'Fat chance!'

Seats clattered on their hinges, the boys shook their fists at the screen. Calls of 'Sit down, for Gawd's sake,' came from further back. 'And take off your bleeding hats!'

'What's the betting them little pests talk all the way through the picture?' Sadie whispered to Richie. She'd made all the running so far this evening, though it had been his suggestion to come and see the new Valentino film. He was hard to weigh up; scowling through his cigarette smoke, but with his strong arm quietly resting along her shoulders. She pursed her lips and concentrated on the screen instead.

More titles appeared at last. A woman sat down at the piano to one side of the screen and played rousing introductory music. Valentino's flashing eyes peered down from beneath an exotic turban. Sadie sat transfixed.

But the antics onscreen which so fascinated her scarcely held Richie's attention. He'd got what he wanted, just sitting here alongside his boss's sister; he'd got her to say yes after months of being put off. Close to, her dark hair escaping in wavy strands from under her close-fitting crimson hat, her heavily lashed eyes and full mouth were all that mattered. Light, reflected from the screen, flickered on her pale, triangular face; real, living and warm, sitting close to him in the darkened cinema.

Tension onscreen mounted. The pianist thumped out her set-piece struggle music. Sadie held her breath. Valentino vanished amid swirls of tent canvas and clouds of sand. The pianist played heartrending music, tears brimmed, Sadie dabbed them away before the houselights came on.

Richie sat forward and ground his cigarette into the floor. He stood up and hitched his jacket square on his shoulders, hardly glancing behind to check that Sadie could keep up as he made his way through the crowd towards the Exit. She fixed her eye on him, hatless, and head and shoulders taller than most. 'Nuisance!' she said to herself. She wrapped her warm coat around her, tucked her bag under her arm and wove her way up the aisle. Walter wouldn't have treated her this way, she knew. She began to regret accepting Richie's invitation. He couldn't even be bothered to escort her out of the cinema like a gentleman.

All ravishing, romantic thoughts flickered out with the last whirrings from the projector. Real life was a chain of trouble and daily problems; like her brother-in-law, Maurice Leigh, who was the manager of the picture house and who now stood talking to Richie in the foyer.

Sadie pulled up short, looking for an escape. But Maurice spotted her and beckoned her over. 'How's my favourite little sister?' he greeted her. 'Beautiful as ever, I see.'

Maurice stooped to give Sadie a peck on the cheek. Dark and dapper in his fashionable suit, Maurice was all smiles. He was genuinely fond of Sadie. 'You know Richie Palmer, don't you? He works at the taxi depot for—'

'Leave off, pal. She's with me.' Richie stepped forward and spoke abruptly. He took Sadie's arm.

Maurice cleared his throat and kept control of his expression. What would Jess say about her kid sister flirting with the mechanic when he went home and told her, he wondered. Though the smile stayed steady, his voice caught him out. 'Did you enjoy the picture?' he asked.

Sadie nodded, hot with embarrassment. 'Smashing, except for them little hooligans in the front row.'

Maurice's smile tightened. His eyes flicked from Sadie to Richie and back again. 'Don't worry, sis. By this time next year them front-row pests will be back-row Romeos, and you won't get a peep out of them.'

'But there'll be hundreds more of the little blighters to take their place.' She laughed. She held her head up; she had a right to a night out when she felt like it. Walter Davidson, her official beau, was always busy down at the depot. She stared defiantly at her brother-in-law.

Maurice laughed back. 'They pay to get in, don't they?'

'And the rest of us! We don't chuck away hard earned cash to hear their kissing noises in all the best bits, or them yelling "Oo-er!" and sucking their lips at every end and turn.' She and Richie followed Maurice towards the grand exit.

The manager turned, hands in pockets. 'You're getting past it, Sadie.' Still his eyes narrowed when he glanced at her companion, but he held out a cigarette and a light to him.

'Cheek.' She pulled her hat over her forehead and tucked back the stray curls, ready for the cold night air. She waited while the two men discussed this and that: a good result for the Palace, a new refinement in car engine design. Though he seemed to have hopped the wag for much of his school life, Richie was car-mad. He knew all there was to know, even about the most up-to-date models. So Walter and Rob had been glad to offer him steady work taking care of their two Morris Oxford taxicabs. They'd seen him strip down an engine, spread pistons, gaskets, casings, nuts and bolts all over the floor, and have it put back together in working order before the day was out. But he was a bad timekeeper. They talked often about having to lay him off. The threat hung over him, ready to enforce the next time he put a foot wrong.

At last Richie nodded goodnight to Maurice and led Sadie out into the street.

'Say hello to Walter from me,' Maurice called after her. He stood, hands in pockets, still watching the two of them like a hawk. 'If you run into him before I do, that is.'

She gave him a curt nod. At twenty-five years old, she reckoned she didn't need to ask Maurice's or anyone else's permission over whom she chose to go out with. Before the war, maybe, when she was younger and things were different. Frances, her eldest sister, lived at home with them at the Duke in those days, and she'd kept Sadie well in line. But not now. She stepped out confidently, arm-in-arm with Richie Palmer, high heels tapping along the dark pavement, a shapely leg showing beneath the tube skirt of her dark red coat.

Behind the bar at the Duke, Annie Parsons called last orders. She made a show of sweeping the empties off the bar and carrying them down to Ernie at the sink. 'Don't none of them take a blind bit of notice,' she grumbled.

'Look at them all sitting there without moving a muscle. They got bleeding cloth ears, all of them!'

Ernie nodded and grinned. He enjoyed this nightly ritual; his stepmother yelling out last orders, only to be ignored, his pa, Duke Parsons, happily serving pints of best bitter, Annie grumbling behind his back.

'Now, don't go on, Annie.' Duke leaned his elbows on the bar, gold watch-chain swinging forward from his broad chest. 'It's a Saturday night, ain't it?'

'And it'll be the same on Sunday, Monday and blooming Tuesday night!' Annie breathed hard on a glass and polished it to perfection. 'According to you, Wilf Parsons, there's no such thing as licensing laws. Oh, no, it's all "Drink up, Jim, and have one on the house!" with you.' She reached on tiptoe to put the glass on its shelf above the bar.

'We just gotta be thankful we can plod along,' Duke growled back. It was the same reply as always. 'No one's flush with money down the court these days.'

'Play me a different tune, Duke.' Annie shook her head and wiped on. They'd been married almost ten years now, and the patter was always the same.

'Well, who am I to deny them a drink when they've cash in their pockets to buy one?'

Ernie nodded at this too, and plunged more glasses into the sudsy water. Year in, year out, the routine reassured him and bound him safe in the arms of his large family. Gradually the terror of being accused of Daisy O'Hagan's murder had receded into the darkest recesses of his simple mind. He knew what he knew; he was innocent, he washed glasses, Duke and Annie would look after him.

'How about a sing-song, our Amy?' Arthur Ogden, a permanent fixture at the bar, called out to his daughter.

Amy had rolled up at the Duke for the evening with

some of her pals from the living-in quarters at Dickins and Jones, where she worked as a shop assistant. They'd signed themselves out, all five of them, writing down the Duke as their destination; East End girls glad of a good night out. They jumped at the chance to sing along to a tune on the old pianola.

'Let's have that Scottish one, "I love a lassie"!' Ruby Thornton sprang to her feet and made a beeline for the stack of pianola rolls. '"A bonnie, bonnie lassie!"' she trilled above the hubbub of glasses, striking a bold figure with her dyed blonde hair cut daringly short.

Amy's mother, Dolly, got there first and ferreted around in the cardboard box containing the rolls of perforated paper. 'It's here somewhere. I don't mind singing along to that one myself.'

'More like "One of the ruins that Oliver Cromwell knocked about a bit",' Arthur muttered to Bertie Hill. He didn't expect a reply. Hill was a miserable blighter, unpopular due to the fact that he'd recently bought up Eden House, the old tenement block at the bottom of the court where the O'Hagan family still lived. A new landlord was always treated with suspicion: he could start thinking about turning out tenants and razing the whole lot to the ground, like they did down Meredith Court last year. 'Did you hear they found two baby skellingtons buried in one of them cellars?' Arthur said out of the blue. 'Never put a name to them neither. Said they could have lain there mouldering for twenty years and nobody knew a thing!'

Charlie Ogden, standing at his father's side after an evening on duty at the Gem, gave the old man's drinking arm a nudge. 'Lay off, Pa, for God's sake.' Life was gloomy enough. 'He's had one over the eight,' he explained to the landlord.

Bertie Hill smiled his tight, humourless smile and drank up. He rapped his empty glass down on the bartop, picked up his trilby hat and prepared to go home. 'Time for my beauty sleep.' He smirked. He'd taken a back room in his own tenement to tide him over. The story went that he'd been a copper, up on the other side of the water, who was thrown out of the force for being crooked; a rumour seized on by Dolly and some of the market women. 'He looks like a copper,' they agreed. 'And he smells like one. Carbolic soap, and the stuff they use to scrub the station up Union Street.'

Few people said goodnight to Hill's burly, sandy-haired figure as he made his way through the etched and bevelled glass doors of the Duke of Wellington public house.

They carried on with their sing-song, which was in full swing by the time Richie Palmer came along Duke Street arm-in-arm with Sadie. Bertie Hill tipped his hat to them both as he turned and disappeared down the court.

'My poor feet!' Sadie hesitated fifty yards down the street and sighed. They'd walked all the way from the Picture-drome and it was almost midnight. The strains of 'Stop yer tickling, Jock!' and the shrieks of the women easily reached them as she stooped to examine the splashes on her pale cream stockings.

The walk home had been mostly silent, with Sadie still half-cross, half-guilty that she'd agreed to come out with Richie in the first place. She thought of faithful Walter stuck behind a telephone in the taxi office. At last, as they'd come down by the side of the giant Town Hall, she'd been driven to sarcasm. 'My, ain't you the chatterbox!' She'd tugged at Richie's arm to signal that they should cross the road. It was cold, the damp had seeped through the thin leather soles of her shoes, and she was downright miserable.

At first he hadn't responded, only shoving his hands deeper into his pockets and trapping her arm against his side. 'Well, if it's small-talk you want,' he said, hurrying her up the kerb, ducking down an alley towards Union Street.

'Small-talk, any talk.' She frowned. 'Anything would do. Like, why you asked me to walk out in the first place.'

He stopped suddenly. 'Like, why you said yes,' he countered. He stood looking down at her, the mist settling in his straight, dark hair.

'Because I wanted to see the picture,' she said awkwardly. When he spoke, she noticed that he slurred his words together slightly.

'You could do that any time.' He looked down at the pavement as they turned from each other and began to walk on.

'Then it was because you asked me, I expect.' She went a step or two ahead.

'You could've said no, like you always did before.' He followed Sadie's slight, small figure, warmly wrapped in soft red cloth. The hat made a bell shape on her head.

'And don't I wish I did say no!' She turned exasperated. 'You ain't been very friendly to me, Richie, and I don't know why!'

'What's friendly?' He came up close, took her by the elbow.

'Talking. Telling me about yourself.'

He shrugged. 'What's to tell?' The shadowy alley where they stood was full of scuttling, whispering sounds. Footsteps echoed along the main street. 'Talk,' he said, shrugging again. 'Hot air.'

Sadie found herself staring up into his face. His eyes gleamed, then he turned away, though he still held her arm in its tight grip. In profile, his forehead jutted over a long, straight nose. His top lip had a slight upward tilt, his jaw was set strong and firm. She raised one gloved fingertip to his lips.

He bent and kissed her. Her hat fell backwards from her head and the glossy halo of wavy hair came free. Her lips, soft and warm, opened slightly.

She felt the dampness of his hair, the hard smoothness of his collar. She was in his arms and she was kissing him.

Then he eased back and stooped to pick up her hat, brushing puddle-water from its velvety surface with his coatsleeve. 'Don't put it back on,' he said as he handed it to her, 'I like to see your hair.'

The compliment took her by surprise as much as her own sudden desire to kiss Richie Palmer on the lips. 'That's more than Pa did when I first came home with it all chopped off.' She stuffed her hat into her bag, trying to lighten the mood. 'Pa's got old-fashioned ideas, especially about women's hairstyles. He said he'd divorce Annie if she ever came home with her hair looking like mine! And I don't know what else.'

Richie put his arm around her shoulder. He felt the light sweep of the offending haircut against his wrist. 'I like it.' He almost smiled as they walked on up the alley. Their silence was easier, though a question still hovered as they saw Bertie Hill raise his hat to them and heard the raucous music drift towards them from the pub.

'And will you go with me again?' Richie stopped and drew her into the shelter of Henshaws' doorway, out of the cold rain that had begun to fall.

Sadie shook her head. 'I don't know, Richie. Maybe I ought not?' She looked away, catching her own reflection in the eating-house window.

'Why?' the low, slow voice insisted.

12

'What will Walter think? Or Rob, for that matter. You could lose your job over something like this.'

His mouth twitched down into a grimace. 'It ain't my job you're fretting over.'

She frowned and tried to sidestep him back on to the street. 'Maybe. Maybe not. But I am bothered by us walking out together again, Richie, and that's a fact. I wish you wouldn't ask me right now.'

He leaned against the door, rattling it with his shoulder, letting her step by. 'Well, then, I expect you'll let me know when I can ask again. Send me a telegram. Call me on the telephone.'

'Don't be like that.'

'Then don't you.'

They walked the last few yards down Duke Street in another kind of silence. At the brightly lit double door she paused to look up at him, but Richie turned and walked across the street without looking back. She didn't even know where he lived; not one thing about him. Yet she'd kissed him on the lips. She darted inside the pub, a hot flush of guilt on her cheeks.

CHAPTER TWO

'This allotment will set me up good and proper,' Arthur Ogden declared as Sadie came in. Annie stood behind the bar patiently paying attention. 'You just see if it don't!'

'Good for you, Arthur.' Annie went on wiping glasses. She waved at Sadie. 'Hello there. Bleeding long pictures they show up at that Picturedome place!'

'Picture*drome*.' Sadie rolled the second 'r'.

'And come again tomorrow. We was worried about you, girl.'

'Well, there's no need.' She drifted into the emptying room, perched on a stool and placed her bag and gloves on the bar. 'Here I am, safe and sound.'

Arthur, listening in, returned Charlie's earlier nudge with a vengeance. 'Look lively, son, and buy the girl a drink. Can't you see she looks done in?'

Charlie dug into his pocket and ordered Sadie a glass of port wine.

Duke obliged. 'You never walked back, did you?' he asked his youngest girl as he pushed the glass along towards her. 'Who was you with? Them typewriter pals from work?'

'That's right.' Sadie nodded. She sipped her drink to avoid meeting Duke's eye.

'And what's the matter, couldn't you get Walter to send

14

out a taxicab to pick you all up?' Charlie interrupted. 'That's a bit tight of him, ain't it?'

Sadie gave her old boyfriend a scornful look and turned to Arthur. 'What was that you was saying about an allotment?' she prompted.

Charlie's brows went up as he pulled at his own pint glass. 'Them typewriters ain't wearing trousers and trilby hats by any chance?' he muttered.

Again Sadie ignored him. 'Go on, Arthur, tell us about your cabbage patch.'

'Hallotment,' Arthur announced, very grand. 'Down the side of the railway embankment on Meredith Court.' The words rolled inside his mouth and slipped over his tongue. He drew descriptive pictures in the air with his free hand, while the other stayed clamped around his empty glass. 'It's going to make me a man of substance, I can tell you. That little patch of land is going to bring pride *h*and prosperity to the Hogden family!'

'Pride and what?' Amy breezed up to say goodnight. 'Leave off, Pa, and say goodnight. Time I was off.'

'Shame!' Dolly squeezed Amy's arm as her daughter made a sour face. Though Amy fretted about having to live in at the Regent Street shop, Dolly knew she liked her life in the West End better than the office life Dolly had once planned for her. She didn't waste much sympathy on Amy's grumbles as she watched her, Ruby and the rest out of the door. Then she turned back to Sadie. 'Arthur ain't boring you with tales of his giant Brussel sprouts, I hope?'

Sadie laughed, feeling her balance return, her heartbeat slow back to normal after the confusing episode with Richie Palmer.

Little Arthur bridled and drew himself up. 'No I ain't! You just wait, Dolly Ogden, till them rows of carrots come up perfect, and all them beautiful onions and cabbages. When I've sold them on the market at a tidy profit, you'll be laughing on the other side of your face!'

Dolly's smile was as good-humoured as ever. 'You ain't never held the right end of a spade in your life, old man. And you don't know a dandelion from a dockleaf. No, it's another of them flash-in-the-pans, if you ask me.' She eased her husband's grip from the empty glass and stood him upright, then pointed him in the direction of the door. 'And we all know who'll be down there digging and weeding, don't we?' she said to Sadie with a wink. 'And that man's name ain't Arthur Ogden.'

'Nor Charlie neither,' her son warned. 'You won't catch me dirtying my hands for a few frostbitten turnips.' He drank to the dregs, then put down his glass.

'I never thought it was,' Dolly called cheerfully. She shepherded Arthur through the front hallway on to the dismal street.

There was the round of goodnights, scraping chairs, swinging doors before the bar eventually emptied, leaving Duke to lock up behind his regulars. Annie laid clean towels over the row of shiny new pump handles, then she dimmed the gaslights. It was already the early hours of Sunday morning.

'Bye bye, Sadie,' Charlie said. He stayed to the very last, still curious about her flushed face and evasive manner when she first came in. He looked a slight, sensitive type in his Prince of Wales tweed jacket, with his light brown hair brushed across his forehead from a side parting. His face was still fresh, smooth, even slightly womanish. He regarded his long-lost sweetheart from under furrowed brows. 'I hope you ain't doing nothing I wouldn't do?'

Sadie flicked her hair behind one ear, pouting back at him. 'I'd go help Dolly get your pa home safe if I was you, Charlie.'

She outstared him easily, and he went off down the court with the usual Saturday night feeling that his own life stood still as the rest of the world hurried on by. Twenty-six, still unattached, still working for Maurice Leigh in the chain of cinemas he managed, but going nowhere fast. His work hours were unsocial, his teenaged dreams of bursting upon the world of cinema with wondrous improvements had so far come to nothing. He'd talked to Maurice about the chances of improving synchronization between sound and vision on the new talkies by incorporating the soundtrack on to the edge of the cellulose film by a series of patterned dots, like on a pianola roll. Maurice had listened approvingly, nodded his head, considered it carefully. Then he'd told him that as far as he could judge, there wasn't the demand for it as yet. 'They flock to *see* Negri and Pickford, not to *hear* them talk,' he'd advised. 'Hold your horses. Work at it, Charlie; it's a bright idea. But bide your time.'

That was in the very early days, in his first flush of enthusiasm. Now, however, Charlie was in a rut, and he knew it. He'd chucked his chances over his scholarship for grammar school by throwing in his lot with the moving pictures game. At the same time, nearly ten years ago, he'd chucked his chances with Sadie Parsons. Sadie was considered the smartest, most admired girl around, and didn't Charlie know it.

'What's eating you?' Dolly asked as he crossed the threshold of his terraced home down Paradise Court. He'd slammed the door behind him. She sighed. 'No, don't tell me, I don't want to know. Just lend a hand up these stairs with your pa, for God's sake, and don't stand there looking like a wet weekend.'

It was Rob Parsons' last job of the evening to pick up his sister, Hettie, from the Mission on Bear Lane; a favour he did every Saturday night, when Southwark's streets were full of helpless, hopeless drunks who'd turned up too late to get a bed with the Army. They curled up instead in the tunnelled walkways that ran under the railway line, or lurched out of alleyways in blind, aimless pairs.

He pulled up outside the new redbrick Mission with its arched windows; worn out, easing his artificial leg into a less painful position, wanting his own bed. He watched a woman with a small child stagger unsteadily in the direction of his idling cab. He saw his sister emerge and come down the steps, leaned over and opened the passenger door. 'Hop in, Ett, I'm freezing to death out here.'

She stepped on to the running-board, then collapsed exhausted into the leather seat. 'Sorry!' She loosened the stiff ties to her dark blue bonnet and sighed.

Rob eased the Bullnose into gear and edged away from the pavement, too late to avoid the woman with her outstretched hand. He dipped into his pocket, found two coins and flung them to her through the window. Hettie had closed her eyes and sunk her head against the seat. The woman, hair loose, scrawny-armed, backed into the mist with her child. The car rolled off down the road, heading for home,

'Had a hard night?' Rob glanced at his sister. This work for the Army, on top of the dress business she'd set up with Jess, was wearing Hettie out. She sat pale and still beside him.

'The usual. How about you?' She opened one eye and rolled it towards him. 'You ain't exactly a bundle of laughs yourself.' She studied his slight frown, the jaw set tight. 'Ain't nothing wrong, is there?' It didn't take much to see that Rob had something on his mind.

'Nothing I can't put right.' Rob steered through the empty streets, long since rid of their tram and bus traffic. In the fog, the old acetylene lamps on his car scarcely penetrated the gloom. 'Electric headlamps,' he muttered, changing the subject. 'That's the up-and-coming thing, Ett. Electric. Powered by a battery that starts up the engine and works a windscreen-wiper too.' He turned at long last into the home stretch of Duke Street.

'Never! Did you go over Ealing way tonight?' Hettie enquired. She knew that her brother often picked up their brother-in-law and took him home to his posh new neighbourhood after work. She pulled herself out of her own exhaustion and tried to make pleasant conversation.

'I picked Maurice up from the Picturedrome and drove him over.'

'And did you see Jess?'

He shook his head. 'I never stopped off. There was another job waiting.'

'You've been busy, then?'

'Pretty much. Could be better.' They drew up outside the Duke. Hettie prepared to get out.

But she turned back and touched his elbow. 'Rob,' she began.

'What? Get a move on, Ett. Let me drive this old girl down the depot. I need some kip.'

'I know. But Rob, something happened tonight. I can't get it off my mind.' She looked out of the cab window at the lights dimming inside the pub.

'Down the Mission?' Rob knew she never made a fuss unless it was something serious. He studied her for a moment, finding himself wishing that she would ease up, get out of that drab Salvation Army uniform that looked like it came out of the Ark, and be more like the old, carefree Hettie, pre-Daisy O'Hagan, pre-Ernie's trial. She used to dance and sing her way through life then.

'Yes.' She shook her head. 'Don't mind me, it's probably nothing.' She pushed down on the door-handle. 'It's just we gave a bed to a newcomer tonight. In pretty bad shape. I ain't never set eyes on him before.'

'And?' Robert prompted.

'He was rambling on a bit, drunk, of course. It felt like trouble, that's all.' She began to regret giving voice to her worry.

'Trouble? Who for?'

'For Annie and Duke.' But she opened the door and scrambled out. 'Look, forget it, Rob. Pretend I ain't never mentioned it, OK?'

He blew out his cheeks and shrugged. He guessed it was something about the old man's habit of serving after hours. Rob sometimes got a bit hot under the collar about that himself, thinking that one of these days it could get them into trouble. They were tightening up the licensing laws again. He'd even heard they planned to put a full stop to alcohol altogether in America. But he nodded at Hettie. 'As you were, Ett. My lips are sealed.'

She leaned in and nodded. 'Thanks, Rob. I expect it'll all blow over. The poor old geezer'll have sobered up by morning. He'll be on the move again. Sorry I brought it up.'

Rob watched her slip quietly down the court, by the side of the pub to the back entrance. She'd brushed it off, whatever it was, but he made a mental note to warn Duke to be careful about who he served after hours.

Now he had his own bone to pick with Sadie; something he hadn't wanted to mention to Hettie until he'd had it out with their wayward kid sister. He turned the car back on to Duke Street, recalling his little chat with Maurice earlier that night. The railway arches at the top of the street loomed into view. He'd park the Bullnose and lock her up for the night. Then he'd hurry back on foot.

Maybe Sadie would still be up, having a cup of cocoa with Hettie before they both went off to bed. He pocketed a list of scribbled messages left on the table by Walter, then went out and bolted and padlocked the big wooden doors. 'Davidson and Parsons', it said on a newly painted sign, 'Taximeter Cabs for Hire'.

He went off down the street, shoulders hunched, cap pulled well down, a familiar late-night sight limping home to the Duke.

CHAPTER THREE

Jess heard the click of the front-door lock. Maurice was home from work. She looked up from the paper pattern she had carefully laid on to the silky silver-grey fabric on the front-room table, under the glow of the standard lamp. First he would steal upstairs to look in on sleeping Grace and little Maurice, then he'd come back down to tell her about his day. Taking three pins from her mouth, she tucked them neatly into the pattern to secure the cloth beneath. Then she glanced into the mirror over the mantelpiece. Strands of hair had worked free of the loose bun at the nape of her neck. She tucked them back into position and straightened her blouse into the waistband of her skirt.

Maurice took the stairs two at a time. Along the landing, he spotted Grace's bedroom door standing open. When he peeped inside, it was as he'd suspected; that little monkey, Mo, had decamped from his own room further down the corridor and come to snuggle up beside his big sister. Their two dark heads lay together against the white pillow, round-cheeked and peaceful, their breathing light, almost silent. He tiptoed across the carpet, turned down the blanket on Mo's side, and, careful not to wake him or Grace, he took the boy in his arms and carried him to his own bed. He smoothed the pillow, stroked his farehead, then bent to kiss his son's soft cheek.

At the sound of his return downstairs, Jess came to the hallway. She greeted him with a smile and an embrace, noticing the usual smoky, damp smell of his overcoat and the shadows around his eyes. He was working too hard. She took his coat and hung it on the hallstand.

'Mo's been on his travels again,' he mentioned as he took off his jacket and unbuttoned his waistcoat. 'Sometimes I think he gets there in his sleep.' Maurice hitched up his shirtsleeves and followed Jess into the dining-room.

'Did you take him back?' Through in the kitchen, Jess put the kettle to boil on the gas stove. It was a point of difference between them; she liked to leave the two children snuggled together, but Maurice insisted that Mo should get used to waking in his own bed, now that he was six and going to school.

'Yes. But don't worry, he's still fast asleep.' He wandered into the kitchen for a cosier chat. The sight of Jess, reaching for cups from the pantry cupboard, her slim waist shown off by the tight-fitting skirt, pleased him. His arms encircled her from behind and he kissed her neck.

She returned his embrace with a light kiss on the cheek, then went to stir milk and sugar into the cocoa, waiting for the kettle to boil.

Maurice leaned against the cupboard watching her. 'What've you been up to while the cat's been away?'

'Not playing, if that's what you think. Sewing.' She glanced up. 'I've an order to finish for Monday.'

'And can't Hettie do it?' He didn't like to think of Jess always working, making clothes for the well-to-do women of their new neighbourhood. He felt it could damage their name here in Ealing; people always found a way of looking down on others. As an East End Jew he knew this all too well.

'Hettie's at the Mission on a Saturday night, you know that.'

And because he was feeling edgy about the dressmaking business which Jess and Hettie ran from a small shop on the High Street, he grumbled on. 'Sadie came up to the Picturedrome tonight,' he said.

'Yes?' Jess handed him the cocoa, still smiling. 'To see the great screen lover with her pals, I expect?'

Maurice didn't answer directly. 'She was wearing that red outfit you made for her. You can't hardly miss her.'

Jess laughed. 'Don't she look a picture?' She enjoyed the way Sadie chose to look these days. As a young and single woman, she could get away with the new short skirts, the dark eye make-up and lip rouge.

Maurice grunted. 'I expect Richie Palmer thinks so too.' He wandered off into the sitting-room, moved a newspaper from a low table and sat with his feet propped up, head back, trying to wind down.

'Richie Palmer?' Jess had to call through from the kitchen. 'What's he got to do with it?'

'That's what I thought. But that's who she was with tonight. Richie Palmer from Rob and Walt's place.' He predicted to himself the effect this piece of news would have.

Jess came through, hands on hips. 'Maurice, you ain't kidding me?'

He shook his head. 'You could've knocked me down with a feather. What's she see in him, for God's sake?' They knew Richie only as the surly mechanic at the taxi depot; hardly a likely candidate for Sadie's attention, even if she wasn't already walking out with one of the bosses from there.

Jess frowned and shrugged. 'It's her business. And I expect they was just friendly, that's all. You know how much Walter has to work these days. You can't blame Sadie for going out and enjoying herself.'

Maurice applied this to his own situation. The idea of Jess going out and enjoying herself, as she called it, touched a raw nerve. 'Some would.' He bent forward to pick up the newspaper. 'Like your pa, for instance.'

Jess went and crouched by his chair, one hand on his shoulder. 'Oh, Maurice, don't go telling tales on Sadie! Pa's got enough to cope with.'

He glanced at her over the newspaper and curbed his next remark. Instead he said, 'Why don't *you* have a quiet word with Sadie, then? Explain how it looks to other people when she goes two-timing Walter for some shady character like Richie Palmer.'

Jess breathed out sharply and stood up. 'Maybe Sadie don't care how it looks to other people.'

'Then she should, tell her.' Maurice closed the subject. 'It says here the Welsh miners are on strike again for more pay.' He pointed to a headline. 'It's back to the old hunger marches, it seems like.'

Jess looked at the photograph of coal-blackened faces beneath worn-out caps; a ragged procession of half-starved men. 'Quite right too. They deserve a decent living,' she said hotly.

'But not strike for it. Look what happens to the whole blooming country if they go on strike, what with winter coming up.'

Jess turned away. 'There's no talking to you, Maurice.'

She went out into the polished hallway, automatically pausing to listen to any sound from the bedrooms. All was quiet, so she slipped into the front room to take up her sewing. Half an hour later, she heard her husband close the sitting-room door and go quietly upstairs. Then she switched on the radio, turning the loudspeaker volume low, listening as she cut and tacked the silvery cloth to news of hardship in the Welsh valleys; children working in the pits while her own two slept soundly in their beds.

'Come to bed, Duke,' Annie said. She stretched across the hearth and tapped his hand. 'You look done in.' The fire flickered low in the grate, Hettie and Sadie were both safely back home.

'You go,' he told her. 'I'll hang on here. I want a word with Rob. I don't expect he'll be long.'

'Hm.' She was unconvinced but, nag as she might, she knew the old man would never get himself off to bed before all the others were in. Old habits died hard. 'Rob can look after himself, you know.' She rose stiffly from her seat, ready to go through.

'Better than most, I reckon.' In spite of the loss of one leg during wartime action, Rob managed to keep himself fit and active. It hadn't stopped him from learning to drive either; a goal he'd set his heart on as soon as the war was finished. If people said, 'No, you can't do it,' to Robert, you could bet your life he'd prove them wrong. So he'd worked, saved and borrowed the money to set up this taxicab business with Walter Davidson, down at the old carter's yard. They were making a go of it too, though both their cars were past their best and cost them plenty in repairs. Duke was proud of Rob. He'd settled down and got over the bitterness of what had happened to him in the trenches. 'That's him now,' he told Annie. He heard the bolt being shot across the back door.

She stooped to kiss his cheek. 'Chin up.' She thought he looked a bit down tonight. 'It'll all seem different in the morning.' His old face seemed sunken. After all, he was going on seventy and still putting in a long day's work.

Duke sighed.

'Look here, business ain't that bad. We get by.'

He nodded. 'Don't mind me, Annie. You go off, get some sleep, and I'll ask Rob to take us out in that contraption of his to see Jess and the littl'uns.'

Annie's face lit up. 'When?'

'Tomorrow.'

'Oh, Duke, that sounds nice!' She loved visiting the posh house that Maurice had set Jess up in, with its lawned front garden and fancy leaded windows. Grace and little Mo would tumble over themselves to answer the doorbell. Jess would give the warmest of welcomes.

'Consider it done,' he said, as she disappeared happily off to bed. He rose to greet his son and offer him a nightcap before he dimmed the last lamp.

But Rob, flinging his cap on to a chair, looked round, disappointed to find Duke alone, sitting up in the small hours. 'Where's Sadie?' he demanded.

'Gone to bed. Why?' The old man went to fetch the whisky bottle from the cupboard. He recognized the tone of voice, registered trouble brewing. 'Sit down, have a drink, son. You look as if you could do with one.'

Rob swilled the whisky round his glass, then knocked it back. The stump of his leg hurt where it was strapped tightly to the artificial limb, and the daylong effort of changing gear with it had taken it out of him. 'You'll never guess what Sadie's been up to now!'

'Hush. Ain't no need to yell, Rob. Whatever it is, can't it wait till morning?'

'No, it bleeding well can't.' Robert's anger boiled over. 'She's only two-timing Walter, that's all. She's a rotten little flirt, Pa, and she don't deserve a decent bloke like him.'

Duke sighed over the inevitable row between his hot-headed son and his youngest daughter. 'Two-timing, you say? Mind you, they ain't exactly engaged,' he reminded Rob. His own whisky hit the back of his throat and trickled down.

'As good as. Look, Pa, you don't mess about when you got someone steady. You gotta tell her.'

'In the morning,' Duke agreed. 'We'll get the full picture off her, then we'll see.' He blamed himself if Sadie was turning flighty. He'd spoiled her in the past, let her have too much of her own way. He didn't hear the bedroom door click, or see the white figure advance down the landing. 'If she is pulling the wool over Walter's eyes, we'll have to sit down and talk to her then.'

Rob, with his own back to the door, wasn't satisfied. 'Walter's my best pal, Pa. I've known him all these years and he ain't never said or done a rotten thing to no one. She can't just come along and make a fool of him!'

'Keep your voice down,' Duke warned. But then he turned to see Sadie herself standing there, almost as pale as her long cotton nightdress. He retreated to the fireplace, seeing that it had gone past remedy. Sadie and Rob would go at it hammer and tongs; they'd wake the whole street before they'd finished.

'Who's making a fool of who?' Sadie trembled as Rob

28

whipped round to face her. She held herself steady by holding on to the door-handle. 'And who's been telling you fibs, Robert Parsons?'

Rob snorted. 'Oh, so Maurice is a liar now, is he?'

'Maurice?' Her heart sank and her voice went faint. Events slotted together: her brother-in-law had opened his big mouth as soon as ever Rob had picked him up to take him home to Ealing. Soon everyone would know about her and Richie Palmer.

'Yes, Maurice! That shut you up, didn't it? He saw you in the back row with that hooligan. As if you didn't know!'

'We wasn't in the back row,' she protested, a red flush creeping up her neck.

'No, but you was *with* him, you admit that much?' He went and faced her, daring her to deny it.

'So what?' Up went her chin. 'What's it to you?'

'Oh, nothing,' Rob sneered. 'You're only my sister. Walter's only my best pal and business partner.'

'And what do you think?' she asked hotly. 'You don't think I'm cheating him, do you?'

'What am I supposed to think?'

'Now, hold your horses, you two.' Duke stepped in between the flashing looks and raised, accusatory voices. 'I don't know what's going on here, but this ain't the time or the place for it, I do know that.' He could see Annie advancing down the landing, a shawl covering her nightdress, her hair in a long braid over one shoulder.

Robert laughed and backed off to pour himself another drink. His own face was patchy and flushed. 'Oh, I get it,' he said sarcastically. 'You arranged everything with Walter beforehand. He gave permission for you to go spooning with Richie Palmer?'

Duke's brow wrinkled. He switched his gaze to Sadie.

'We wasn't spooning! And I was going to tell him just as soon as I got the chance!' she insisted.

'Oh, you was going to tell him,' he mimicked. 'Well, that makes everything swell, 'cos if *you* don't, I will!'

Sadie felt Annie appear at her shoulder and turned to grab her in heartfelt appeal. 'Oh, Annie, ask Rob not to! If he tells Walter, it'll hurt him. I gotta talk to him myself in my own way. I *will* tell him, I promise!'

'Steady on.' Annie led a shaking Sadie by the wrist and sat her down by the fire in Duke's own chair. 'And you steady on too, Rob. Give the girl a chance to tell her side. We gotta hear the whole thing and give ourselves time to calm down.' She put an arm around Sadie's shoulder. 'Don't take on, girl. You only went to the pictures with Richie Palmer, I take it? So far as I know, it ain't a hanging offence.'

In the face of Annie's kindness, Sadie dissolved into tears. 'But I never meant it to get out, Annie. I knew it'd hurt Walter if he found out. Only I wanted to see the picture, and Walter's so busy, and it's a Saturday night, and—'

'Strike a light!' Rob said roughly. He paced across the patterned carpet.

'I didn't mean no harm!' Sadie crumpled into Annie's arms once more.

Annie glanced up at Duke. 'You ain't fifteen no more, girl. You're a growed woman. You can walk out with more than one young man if you like, you're welcome. And there ain't no law against it.' She held up a hand to stem Rob's noisy protests. 'Only, I do think you oughta clear it with Walter first.'

Sadie sniffed and pulled herself together. Her dark hair fell as a curtain to shade her face. 'I ain't never going to see

Richie no more,' she vowed. 'It ain't even as if he's nice to talk to.'

In the background, Rob snorted.

'But you'll still tell Walter what you done?' Annie checked.

Overwhelmed by family pressure, and her own swelling sense of guilt, Sadie gave her promise. Rob heaped more insults on to Richie's head, calling him a no-good drifter who'd end up on the scrap-cart before too long. She watched as Annie calmed Rob down, and saw her efforts to cheer Duke up, before she dried her own eyes on a handkerchief and slid off to bed.

In her own room, Sadie found Hettie sitting in the wicker chair, her long hair flowing over her shoulders.

'It was only a little fling,' Sadie insisted quietly, defiance stiffening her stance once more. 'I weren't never going to see him no more!'

'I know. I heard.' Hettie looked her full in the face. 'Walter's the best there is, surely you know that?'

'I do, I do! No need to rub it in, Ett!' Sadie rolled back her sheets and stumbled into bed. She pulled the covers tight under her chin. 'I could kill that Maurice,' she muttered. 'Landing me in this fine mess!'

Hettie shook her head. 'I don't know about him landing you in it, but did you notice Pa?' she asked anxiously across the darkened room. 'I been worried about him lately, Sadie. I don't suppose you saw how he took it all?'

But Sadie, exhausted, was already falling asleep.

Jess worked quickly and expertly, running up seams on the machine, watching with satisfaction as the dress took shape. The trimming would be a wide band of glass beads handsewn around the hem and plunging neckline. A sash would tie tight around the hips to show off the straight shape that all the customers preferred these days.

She thought back to the time when she and Hettie had rustled up an outfit ready for her to go with Maurice to the Town Hall Christmas dance. That had been the beginning of it all for her; the escape from drudgery and the stigma of Grace's illegitimate birth. That tight bodice and clinched waist seemed to belong to a different world. How long was it, for instance, since she and Maurice had been out dancing? Before they came to the new Ealing house that faced on to the Common? Before Mo was born? Well, staid, well-to-do women didn't dance along to the new whispering baritones, or cavort to the Charleston. What would people think?

She used one of Maurice's phrases to laugh at her own silliness, then snipped a thread and held the dress up for inspection. Not going straight up to bed with him had been her small act of defiance after their scratchy conversation about Sadie. Now that was lost in a sea of reminiscence, as she delved deep into their marriage.

There was no doubt about his success as the forward-looking manager of the biggest cinema chain in the city, and it had given them a lot of what other people could never dream of having. They'd moved away from their East End roots, and up in the world. With careful planning, they were able to instal a telephone, and gradually buy the new, streamlined furniture that was replacing the carved mahogany style of her childhood. Soon Maurice would start looking for a Morris Cowley motor car; not brand-new, but still dearer and more stylish than the Model T, as far as small cars went. Jess tilted her head from side to side as she re-ran word for word the endless conversations about whether they could afford to buy and run a car, and if so, what type? And how much? And petrol at one and six a gallon.

The biggest problem for Jess in all this, setting aside the wrench of having to move away from family and friends, was a growing feeling that Maurice's ambitions were all well and good, but that he gave no room for Jess's own dreams to take root and grow. They basked in the sunshine of his success, his good business sense and eye for fads in the fast-moving picture trade, which kept his cinema chain well ahead of all East End rivals. But her own poor little business, dressmaking with Hettie, was overshadowed and neglected. She even felt that Maurice would uproot it if he could, and throw it away like a useless weed. He never said so in so many words. But then he never praised her efforts either, and sometimes suggested that Grace and Mo might prefer it if she gave up the work. 'It's not as if we need the money,' he told her, in a spirit of husbandly generosity. 'I earn enough, and I don't like the idea of you working your fingers to the bone. It's like the old sweated labour.'

'That's all you know,' she challenged. 'Our little shop is in a good spot on the High Street. We're getting to be very fashionable with a certain class of lady round here.' They'd graduated long ago from the repairs and alterations of their humble beginnings above the Duke.

'The trouble is, wives round here don't go out to work much.' Maurice's dark brows had furrowed. 'It ain't Paradise Court!'

'I know it ain't!' She'd looked at him long and hard. 'What about Hettie?' she said finally. 'Don't I owe it to her to keep on?'

So he'd let the matter drop, and she often stayed up late at night, after the children had gone to bed, making up orders for chiffon party dresses and crêpe-de-Chine visiting outfits. During the day, she would enjoy her time with Hettie in their chic little shop. She took pleasure in the cut and quality of their tailormade clothes.

'You know it's two o'clock in the morning?' Maurice's voice interrupted her train of thought. He peered round the door, sounding subdued, seeing her still sitting there in the pool of light.

Immediately she felt contrite. 'Can't you sleep?' she asked as she stood up and came halfway to meet him.

'No.' He'd come down dressed in pyjamas. 'Was it my fault?'

'What?' She glanced at his ruffled hair, his tired face. 'No, it's mine. I should've realized.' She could never sleep when Maurice stayed up late either. She went and put her arms around his neck. 'You should've let me know before now.'

He kissed her. 'I knew you were busy.'

Stroking his cheeks she whispered, 'Not too busy,' and felt his arms tighten around her.

'You'll come now?' he murmured. Their passion, undimmed by the years, rekindled easily. His arms pressed her to him. She leaned back to unpin her hair and let it fall loose to her waist. Tilting sideways, he kissed her neck, then led her from the room.

The light burned all night long. In the morning, Maurice came downstairs and turned it off before he opened the curtains and went through into the kitchen to make tea for Jess and take glasses of fresh milk up to Grace and Mo.

CHAPTER FOUR

November faded into a raw, dripping December, accompanied by rain and fog. They were short, cold days, harbouring a continuing fear of hunger in the docklands. Still, the East Enders found things to be cheerful about, whistling the old wartime songs in the streets, standing in long, damp queues to watch Crystal Palace rout the northern opposition, then emulating their heroes during Sunday matches in their local park.

On the second Saturday of the month, Palace were to meet up with arch-rivals Derby County. Walter Davidson and Rob gave themselves a rare afternoon off from taxi work, leaving Richie in charge of the depot. Tension between the three of them had slackened off during the weeks since Sadie's heart-to-heart with Walter, when she confessed the mistake she'd made in going to the picture-house with Richie. She told him she hadn't realized how it might look; she hadn't meant any harm and she was truly sorry. She didn't mention the kiss.

Walter had kept both her small hands in his during the confession. He said he understood how much she liked to go to the pictures, and he didn't blame her for taking a night out. He was sorry he couldn't leave work to take her more often himself, only they were still building up the

35

business, getting known beyond Duke Street, down Union Street and Bear Lane. It was wrong of him to neglect her, he knew. There was really nothing for him to forgive.

After this, Sadie felt worse. For a start, she might have welcomed a small show of jealousy on Walter's part; there was her female pride at stake. Second, her confession had only been partial, to save Walter's feelings, she told herself. But she'd deliberately missed out the tumult in her heart when she kissed the silent, infuriating Richie Palmer. From now on she must keep out of his way, as a safeguard to her own peace of mind. Her stolen night out with him would be the one and only.

Duke and Annie approved when they saw her and Walter back together. Walter was part of the scenery; steady as they came, loyal and true, a big support to Rob when he first came home wounded.

Walter's own war had been spent as a motor-bike dispatch rider around Ypres. It had kept him out of the thick of things on the front line, but he stored many terrible memories which he would forever keep to himself. His belief in the justice of the Allied cause had kept him going through thick and thin. Later, he'd trained as one of the first drivers of the new military tanks, and was in the last push of the autumn of 1918. He came home a hero to a country exhausted by war, unable to offer him a means of keeping body and soul together. So he and Rob resorted to their boyhood dream of setting up by themselves. They took casual employment on the docks and markets, working like navvies to scrape money together. Over the years, their meagre savings of one pound a week rose to thirty shillings, or on a good week, thirty-five. Still, their target seemed miles off.

Help came along for the pair of them at last in the

unlikely shape of Mrs Edith Cooper. She heard of their struggle to start up from one of the girl assistants in her husband's drapery store. Mrs Cooper held a soft spot for Robert; he'd come to talk kindly to her on the death in action of her only son, Teddy. She'd seen in Robert all the maimed and wounded victims of the war, the wasted youth, the terrible price of victory. This dainty, fastidious woman, an East Ender herself in the days before her husband's success, had once more requested Rob to visit her at home. She offered him a loan of £200 to be paid back according to a set plan at a low rate of interest. She wished him well, shook his hand and stood at her window, shielded by a long net curtain, watching him to the gate. Rob went with his head high, eagerly in spite of the impediment of his leg. Tears stood in her eyes. Her husband, Jack, sneered and told her she'd be lucky if she ever got back a penny of her investment. 'Throwing good money down the drain,' he complained. 'And times are this bad.'

Cock-a-hoop, Rob and Walter sat up late debating whether to spend their cash total of £350, £150 of which they'd saved for themselves over a three-year period, on one brand-new Morris Cowley with its revolutionary American engine, or on two older, used Bullnose Morrises. They'd gone for the latter; two cars meant twice as much business when there were two of them able to do the driving. They found premises to rent at the old carter's yard under the railway bridge, installed a telephone and put up their nameplate. For two years now they'd struggled to repay their loan and to make ends meet. Each month, with a gleam in her eye, Edith Cooper unsealed the brown envelope and held up the five-pound note to show her disbelieving husband.

It was a rare Saturday when they decided to take time

off, but the Derby County game was a needle match and the whole of Southwark would be making a mass exodus to the Palace ground in Sydenham. When they spotted Tommy O'Hagan trudging along Duke Street through the pouring rain, water rolling from the brim of his trilby hat, they pulled up to offer a lift. The car, notorious for its poor road-holding, skidded to a halt.

Tommy quickly gestured to his companion to hop in too, and the pair of them slid gratefully into the back seat. Glancing in his mirror, Rob saw that the uninvited guest was Bertie Hill, the unpopular new landlord of the O'Hagan tenement block. Tommy, keeping an eye open for the main chance as usual, had obviously thought it wise to keep well in with the man. He sniffed and shook his hat on to the floor. 'Blimey, Rob, ain't we glad to see you.'

But Hill was the sort to put a dampener on the conversation with his snide remarks. He would assume familiarity where there was none, and managed to put Rob's back up the moment he stepped on the running-board. 'Whoa, Dobbin!' he cried as the cab slewed sideways into the pavement. 'Ain't you got no control over the old girl?'

'About as much as you've got over your mouth, I'd say,' Rob replied. He slapped on a grin from the outside without meaning it, before he pushed the car into gear and set off at breakneck speed. 'Mind you, I have to admit the brakes ain't so hot,' he remarked, deliberately swerving wide of the giant tramcar which bore down upon them.

Bertie Hill took a damp Woodbine out of his breast pocket, lit it and inhaled deeply. 'Now, a Daimler,' he said slow and easy, 'there's a beauty of a car, if you ask me.'

'I was in a Daimler once,' Tommy told them. 'She went like a bird, all the way down to Southend and back. Next thing I knew, the geezer what drove it was cooling his heels up the station at Union Street. Turns out this Lefty Harris had nicked the Daimler from Earl Somebody-or-other. Tries to lay it on me. I says I can't even drive the bleeding thing, so how the hell can I nick it? In the end, they had to let me go.'

Walter and Rob enjoyed the story. Tommy had a way of dissolving tension. He was always in a scrape from wheeling and dealing on the market, always one step ahead, but at the same time a strong family man who took home much of what he earned to his ma and pa. He kept just enough to socialize and get by. He had been the mainstay of the O'Hagans after Daisy's tragic death, reckoning he'd no time for the birds or for settling down.

'Hey, Tommy, there's just one thing wrong with that,' Rob protested. 'You can drive almost as good as me!'

'But the coppers don't know that, do they? They take me out and put me behind the wheel of one of their Model Ts. I looks it all about like this, and takes hold of the handbrake. "Is this to turn the engine, or what?" I ask. And I let it go and we freewheel down the hill until the copper grabs hold of the wheel and slams the handbrake back on. "Just wait till I get my hands on that Lefty Harris!" he squeaks. He's gone as white as a sheet. They give Lefty six months in the Scrubs, no messing.'

'And *did* you nick the Daimler?' Walter leaned back to listen to Tommy's reply. Rob had begun to edge the car into a side street not far from the ground.

Tommy looked at him, all wide-eyed innocence. 'You know me, Walt!'

'That's why I'm asking, Tommy, believe me!' Walter winked, and the subject was closed.

Rob parked the car. The four of them pulled their hats down and joined the trudge up the street towards the turnstiles.

Sadie stared down at the rain-sodden street. 'Look at them poor blighters,' she said to Hettie. Two women, shawls over their heads, pulled a sack half-full of coal along the pavement. 'I bet they've been picking by the railway.'

From the comfort of their living-room above the pub, Hettie and Sadie watched the women drag the sack. 'A land fit for heroes,' Hettie remarked, sinking into the shadow of Giant Despair. With an effort she shook herself free. 'I dunno, Sadie, there's a lot of work to do before we can afford to rest.' Picking up her bonnet and fixing it on her head, Hettie got ready for her long, busy shift at the Mission.

'Anyone'd think you can do it all single-handed, the way you work yourself to the bone, Ett.' Sadie thought her sister looked worn out. 'Them women struggling down there ain't your fault, you know. You shouldn't take on.'

Hettie tied the bow smartly under her chin. 'They ain't my fault, but they are my sisters, Sadie, as sure as you are, and I can't let my sisters suffer in silence. We all gotta work and pray, and ask God to forgive our sins, until we reach the Heavenly gate.'

'And I suppose I gotta watch *you* suffer in silence?' Sadie refused to let the point drop. She knew that Hettie worked herself to the point of collapse on behalf of the poor down-and-outs.

'I ain't suffering,' Hettie protested. 'I'm doing God's work.'

She looked so pained and surprised that Sadie regretted

her sharp tone and went up to her. 'I know you are,' she said gently. 'And I'm just a horrible sinner, getting at you when I know you're a hundred times better than me!'

Hettie smiled. 'Who's counting?'

'I am. I'm a wicked woman, and don't I know it!'

'How? How are you wicked?' Hettie linked arms and fondly stroked Sadie's wavy hair.

'Pa thinks I am. The other day he asked Frances not to bring me no more lip-rouge from her chemist's shop because it ain't ladylike.' Poor Sadie had been kept under strict control since her escapade with Richie.

'And what did Frances say?'

'She told Pa not to be so old-hat. All the girls wear lip rouge these days.'

'See.' Hettie smiled. 'Frances has her head screwed on.' Of the four sisters, Frances was the one they looked up to. Even Duke stood in awe of her since she'd married Billy Wray, the widowed ex-newspaper vendor, and gone to live with him above the Workers' Education place in Commercial Street. 'You ain't wicked just because you wear a touch of make-up. Same as the women who come into our shop; they ain't terrible vain things just because they want a dress to look nice in.'

'But you don't know the half of it,' Sadie told her. Her one serious transgression, the luxurious, forbidden kiss was beginning to worm its way out of her conscience.

'I know one thing.' Hettie glanced at the clock on the mantelpiece. 'I'm gonna miss my tram if I don't get a move on.' She gave Sadie a quick smile. 'Why not come to church with me and Ernie tomorrow?' Her hand was already on the doorknob.

Sadie half-nodded and smiled. 'I'll think about it.'

But as soon as Hettie vanished downstairs, Sadie's

41

brooding mood returned. Feeling the urge to shake herself free of it and make herself useful, in a pale shadow of Hettie's own missionary zeal, she decided to heat some soup and nip down to the depot with it. Rob and Walter would be glad of a warm lining to their stomachs on an afternoon like this. Quickly she set the pan to boil on the range. She put on her broad-brimmed grey hat to keep off the rain, and slipped into a matching wrap-around coat. Then she set the pan inside a linen teatowel at the base of her shopping-basket, tied the towel in a knot to secure the top of the pan, and set off on her errand.

Puddles barred her way when she reached the cinder-strewn yard where Rob and Walter garaged their two cars. One of the Bullnoses stood safe inside, under the brick arch of the massive railway bridge. The other was missing; presumably out on a job. Carefully she picked her way across the yard, trying to shield her basket from the worst of the rain. 'Rob?' she called as she peered inside towards the corner office. There was no sign of life. 'Walter?' Cautiously she stepped inside.

Richie Palmer eased himself from under the stationary car and stood up. He'd recognized the voice and the ankles, and thought for a moment that if he stayed put, Sadie might well conclude there was no one there and turn right around. But he'd look a fool if she spotted him hiding, spanner in hand. So he got up to face her, watched her spin round at the clink of metal as he rapped the spanner on to the ground. This was a meeting he could well do without.

'Where's Rob?' Sadie felt her throat go dry.

'At the match. They both are.'

'Oh.' This possibility had never occurred to her. She was

42

irritated; even her good deeds turned against her. Richie was the last person she'd planned to bump into. 'Are you sure? They never take a Saturday off.'

'It's Derby County.'

She tilted her head back. 'I brought them some soup.'

Her remark hung in the air. Richie looked steadily at Sadie, aware of how she'd avoided him since their night out together. It was clear that she wished the ground would swallow her. 'I'll tell them you dropped by,' he said.

'Oh no!' Even being here, alone with Richie, would upset Rob if he found out. He'd think she'd planned it. 'No, never mind. I'd best be off.'

He didn't respond, wiping his hands on a rag slung from a hook on the wall. Then she felt ashamed of treating him so badly, and angry that this was how others arranged her life for her. Why shouldn't she talk to him? Talk was only talk. 'Shall I leave you this soup?' she offered.

He wished she'd make up her mind; either he was below notice, or he wasn't. When he'd taken her out to the picture palace, she'd proved in one unguarded moment that she found him attractive. Then she'd gone and cut him dead. Now she was being friendly all over again. Cat and mouse. He stared silently at her.

His gaze succeeded in unnerving her. 'It was Rob, really,' she explained. 'He went mad at me for walking out with you.'

'Were we walking out? I thought we went to see a picture.'

She nodded and turned away, resenting being teased.

'I ain't good enough, I don't suppose?' Richie stood in her way.

'It ain't that. Rob don't care about that. But it's Walter he's thinking of. Walter's his pal!'

43

'And does Walter own you? What about you? What do you think?' He kept his distance, but didn't offer to shift.

''Course not. Only, I owe it to him. Oh, I don't know!' She backed off. 'It's best left alone.'

'Is that what you think?'

His look, his slow voice hooked her like a fish on a line. 'Yes, it's what I think!' She felt the rain slanting against her back as she stepped outside.

'And is it what you feel?'

'It's the same thing, ain't it?' With a sudden change of mind, she rushed forward and thrust the basket into his arms. 'Don't ask me!' she cried.

'You said that before.' He caught her by the elbow. 'Remember?'

The shock of his touch ran through her. She felt herself tremble, then she struggled to get free.

He let her pull away and stand upright, but he'd brushed his face close to hers, smelt the rose of her soap or perfume. 'I'll move on, then,' he said abruptly. He decided in an instant. 'It ain't no good hanging round here waiting for this whole thing to blow up in my face. Your Rob's got a temper. I'll go; you won't have to worry no more.'

'No!' Once more she let herself down, gave herself away. 'I mean to say, there's no need. You're wanted here to work on the cars.'

Richie looked away. 'You'd best get out of here. They'll be back soon.' The match would be over. He had several messages from customers to hand over to his bosses when they returned. 'You can have a lift if you want.'

'No.' She darted out into the heavy downpour, careless of the huge, dirty puddles. 'I can walk, thanks.' And she ran off, her thoughts as ragged and confused as ever.

Richie deposited her basket on the desk, squatted down,

took hold of the front bumper of the old Bullnose and swung himself from view once more.

Palace had lost two-nothing. The home crowd had sung 'Abide with Me' right through to the dying seconds, to no avail. Bertie Hill blamed the muddy conditions, Walter said that County were the best side on the day. Rob coughed the engine back into life as the other three flung open the doors and piled into the car. He swung his disappointment into the violent turning of the starter-handle, but he'd forgotten to retard the engine. The motor caught fire and turned at full speed, kicking back the handle, nearly taking his thumb with it. Rob cursed and climbed into the driver's seat. They drove in subdued silence; only after they'd drowned their sorrows in a pint or two of best bitter would they be able to take their defeat philosophically. The inside of the car smelt of wet worsted and stale cigarette smoke. The windows steamed up, the old car refused to grip the wet road.

'Thanks for the lift, pal,' Tommy said. Rob had stopped to drop Bertie and him off at the Duke. 'Another day, another dollar, as they say.' He shrugged and slammed the door shut.

'You been watching too many American pictures,' Walter warned. But he knew Rob was anxious to get back to the depot. The rain would mean plenty of taxi business tonight; people didn't like standing in a queue for the tram, getting soaked on their night out.

But halfway down Meredith Court, the Morris started churning out steam from under the bonnet. The plugs had overheated and the car was losing water fast. 'Bleeding thing!' Rob cried, mouthing curses as Walter scrambled in the boot for the emergency canvas bucket. He filled it at a nearby standpipe while Rob lifted the bonnet and eased the cap off the radiator. Minutes ticked by. Richie would already have booked them in for jobs, expecting them back by now.

Walter shook his head. 'This old girl's on her last legs, you know that?' His face was serious as he refilled the radiator. 'She ain't reliable no more.'

Rob sighed. He leaned against the door biting his thumbnail. 'Got a spare three hundred and forty-one quid on you, pal?'

Walter gave a hollow laugh. He felt in his pockets. 'Well, it just so happens . . . no!' He slammed down the bonnet and chucked the canvas bucket into the boot. 'Things are a bit tight right now.' He turned the starter-handle while Rob advanced the engine. They'd lost a good fifteen minutes waiting for it to cool.

'*We beat 'em on the Marne,*' Rob growled, swinging the car back into the slow crawl of traffic. He chanted the old war song with savage irony.

> '*We beat 'em on the Aisne.*
> *We gave them hell at Neuve Chapelle . . .*'

He blew his horn furiously at a cyclist who had wobbled out from behind a crowded omnibus.

> '*And here we are again!*'

'Steady on, Rob!' Walter warned. He made a grab for a hand-hold as the car swerved to one side. 'Ain't a thing we can do about it.' He resigned himself to getting Richie to strip down the engine of the old car one more time.

'Maybe. Maybe not.' Rob's brain was a riot of ideas,

some feasible, some not. They could sell both Morrises and buy one new Cowley. They could team up with another outfit, cut down on overheads, start saving all over again. They could borrow more money. 'Maybe not!' he repeated, careering through puddles with a hot hiss of steam. He pulled to a halt outside the depot, leaped out and slammed the door as he went inside.

Walter jumped into the serviced car still parked inside the garage. Richie handed him an address, saying the woman had already rung up twice to ask where he was. Rob started up the engine, Walter put his foot down and was on his way. Rob went into the office to check the next job on the list.

'What the bleeding hell's this?' he asked, shoving a basket to one side. He glowered at the scrawled messages.

Richie frowned. He stood in his shirt-sleeves, a wide leather belt buckled carelessly round his waist, his collarless shirt open at the neck. 'Sadie brought it in,' he answered. His choice had been to get rid of the basket and avoid awkward questions, or to leave it on view. Some stubbornness in him had chosen the second option. Now he stood looking steadily at Rob as the information sank in.

Rob, never one to ask questions, pounced on the one unacceptable fact. 'She never came down here?'

'She did.' Richie took his jacket from a peg behind the door.

'By herself?'

He nodded.

Rob kicked a chair to one side and slammed the office door shut. Its glass panels rattled. His eyes widened, his fists clenched as he pinned Richie into one corner. 'Now listen, Palmer, you leave that girl alone, you hear me? You lay one finger on her and I'll break your neck!' He faced his strong, able-bodied opponent head on, without a scrap of fear. Even when Richie unfastened his belt and swung its brass buckle out in front, wrapping the leather strap around his wrist for a firmer grasp, Rob refused to back off. 'Come on, then! Come on! What you waiting for?' He crouched low and made a beckoning motion.

'You don't want a fight,' Richie warned him, low and menacing. 'Ain't nothing worth fighting over.'

Further enraged, Rob swung at him. Richie dodged sideways, escaping from the corner. He was three or four inches taller than Rob, younger, fitter.

'I'm telling you, lay off my sister. She ain't interested, get it? She don't want nothing to do with a hooligan like you!' Rob spat with ineffectual rage. He swung again, once more missing his target.

'You'd better ask her that.' Richie put the desk between himself and his boss. He never even raised his voice.

To Richie, things had suddenly changed. Five minutes ago he'd been prepared to vanish, without wages, without explanation! He'd take his cap and jacket off the hook and never show up again. This thing with Sadie was too complicated. Since he never knew which way she'd jump, he felt the whole affair was out of his control, and he was uneasy. Besides, whenever he saw her, his urge to hold her and the memory of kissing her that once resurfaced and threw him further off balance. He didn't like that feeling one bit.

Now it was different; Robert had come charging in with orders, with the idea that he could lord it over Richie and rule his life. Richie had never been able to bear being told what to do. Brought up by Barnardo's, he'd learnt to follow his own instincts to survive. He took the children's home for what it gave him – food and shelter – but he hated the rules and Christian browbeating that went with them. He left there when he was ten years old. His teenaged years on the streets had toughened him up and taught him never to trust. Then two years of army service had fuelled his obsession with car engines. He gleaned information and experience from working on supply lorries that travelled between the Belgian coast and the front line. Like many uneducated men, the war had at least given him a trade. Otherwise, it only served to reinforce his rebellious spirit.

He had one sergeant-major who treated him like dirt; Richie got the worst billets, the most dangerous tasks in a battle of wills to see if he would crack. But it came to a bad end. The sergeant-major had sent Richie over the top on reconnaissance once too often. He and the other men had stayed put in the trench until they heard a hail of enemy fire. But the sergeant left his own strategic retreat a second too late. A shell had landed in the trench over Richie's head, leaving the sergeant-major hanging on the old barbed wire. Later, Richie would sing that wartime favourite with vicious enjoyment.

Rob wore a dark moustache, just like that sergeant-major. His upright bearing gave him a military air. He was the type who never showed a soft side. His temper was always ready to flare and he didn't like to be crossed.

'Look, I ain't gonna take none of your cheek, you bleeding idiot.' Rob jumped down Richie's throat. 'Sadie's spoken for. Why can't you get that into your thick head?' He got ready for his third lunge, this time raising the heavy brass phone, holding it like a club. The wire wrenched from its socket and dangled uselessly.

Over his head, beyond the glass partition, Richie spotted the rapid approach of Rob's eldest sister, Frances. He lowered the belt and unwound it from his fist. Instinctively

Rob dropped his own guard. 'You heard me,' he warned. 'You leave her alone.'

Richie turned away and took his jacket without a reply. But the set of his shoulders spoke defiance. 'Try and make me,' he suggested. It was in the angle of his cap, in his curt nod at Frances as she came in. He loped off across the cinder yard.

Frances Wray, as she now was, had spoken earlier on the phone to Hettie. She'd set off for the Duke as soon as she could, hoping to catch her sister before she left for the Mission. Hettie's tone had been uncharacteristically down-beat. Though she'd been quick to deny that anything was amiss, Frances had decided to leave work and pay her a visit.

Since Rob's depot was on her way and it was raining hard, Frances thought she might ask Rob for a rare favour and catch a lift to the Duke. Now she shook out her black umbrella and closed it, glad to find someone in. 'Cheer up, it might never happen,' she told Rob. His face was like thunder.

'It already did.'

Frances glanced after the retreating figure of Richie Palmer. 'Well, anyhow, run me up home to the Duke, there's a good chap. I need to see Hettie and I'm afraid I've left it late.' Frances sighed. 'Why do customers always have to come in at the last minute? You'd think they'd show more consideration. Don't they know we have our own lives to lead?' She'd been mixing pastes and making up pills until well after five o'clock.

'No, didn't you know?' Rob tilted his chin up and fixed his tie straight. He was beginning to recover from his argument with Richie. 'You ain't a human being. You're a machine for peddling pills and potions, that's all.'

'Ta very much, Rob.' By now they'd climbed into his cab and backed out of the yard on to the dark street. Frances sat quietly in the passenger seat, listening to the swish of the tyres through the puddles. In her feather-trimmed hat and fawn, tailored outfit, she looked quietly respectable as always. 'Ett didn't sound her usual self,' she commented, separated from the familiar sights of Duke Street by the steamy windscreen. 'She ain't mentioned nothing to you, has she, Rob?'

He came to a halt outside the pub. 'There was something, but she didn't say what. I think she's got a lot on her mind. She won't even say nothing to George, though, so there's no use asking me.'

George Mann, also a pal of Rob's, stayed quietly in the background of Hettie's life, and he had become part of the Parsons family. He'd taken Joxer's place as cellarman at the Duke, after Joxer had uprooted and drifted off on his silent, lonely way. George had been glad of a job during the lean period after the war. Duke said he owed him a steady place after he'd snatched Rob from certain death on the battle-field; it was George who'd lifted the wounded soldier on to his back and staggered with him to safety. 'He'll stick like glue,' Annie warned. She knew the type; strong and silent, pretty much alone in the world, fond of his home comforts, and quickly falling for Hettie.

Her heart and soul were with the Army, however, and at first she gave him little encouragement. Then, almost passively, she began to accept his persistent attention. Duke had acknowledged Annie's point of view. But, 'He'll do for me,' he said, 'now that Joxer's slung his hook.' For more than three years George had grafted and quietly impressed.

'And she won't say nothing to Sadie?' Frances enquired, still wondering about Hettie's troubles. She prepared to brave the wet street.

Rob tossed his head.

'I take it that's a "no"?'

He followed her into the rain. They shifted as quick as they could into the front porch. 'Sadie ain't listening to no one at present,' he said in disgust.

Frances braced herself and pushed open the door. Annie, busy at the bar, waved noisily. Duke looked up, pleased by the rare visit from his eldest daughter. She was thirty-nine, with a sensible marriage under her belt and a good job at Boots, and he felt proud of her if a little distant. He still didn't hold with her opinions, which were too modern for his taste, though since women had got the vote, he'd noticed she'd quietened down a good deal. Still, there was something aloof about her; she meant well, put her husband and family at the top of her list of priorities, but she lacked the common touch. 'One look from her would freeze a man's beer in its pint pot,' was Arthur Ogden's way of putting it.

Frances went upstairs ahead of Rob, only pausing to shake the rain from her jacket and hang it up. From the landing she heard the telephone ring, and Sadie's voice as she answered it. Something made her hesitate.

'Ett, is that you?' she heard Sadie ask. 'Calm down, Ett. Don't get worked up. It ain't like you . . . Yes, I can hear. But are you sure? . . . Yes, I think I heard Frances come upstairs just now. Hang on a tick, Ett. Don't go away. I'll go get Frances for you.'

Slowly Frances turned the handle and went in. She looked at Sadie's pale, shocked face, saw her standing holding the telephone mouthpiece out towards her. She went and took it from her.

'Oh, Frances!' Sadie cried. 'Ett's here, and she's in a fix. She's at the Mission and she says Willie Wiggin has just turned up!'

'Annie's old husband?' Frances held the phone to her ear in disbelief. Everyone in the court knew the story of how Annie had been deserted by Wiggin, who'd gone off to sea and eventually been declared missing, presumed dead. Ett's voice sobbed along the wire, while Sadie made a grab for her arm, pleading over Ett's incoherent tears. 'Tell her there's some mistake, Frances! Tell her it's just some mad old drunk. It can't be Wiggin. It can't be!'

CHAPTER FIVE

By the time Frances and Sadie arrived at the Bear Lane Mission, Hettie had managed to calm down. She was standing at a long trestle-table doling out soup and bread, quakerish in her navy-blue uniform. She looked tense, but under control. Her two sisters signalled they would wait by the refectory door until the soup queue was served. Hettie nodded and wielded the big metal ladle, though the smell of potato and mutton from the steaming pot was as much as she could stomach. Doggedly she worked on, dealing kindly with the row of shuffling, dejected tramps.

'Oh my God!' Sadie breathed. It was her first view inside the Mission, and it struck her as a picture of hell. The refectory was a long, bare room with arching roof beams and high, narrow windows. Tables were set out in rows along the length of the room, and hunched shapes huddled over their meagre rations.

These men, segregated from the women and children, were clothed in rags. They sat to eat, wrapped in old trenchcoats tied around with sacking, padded out with newspapers. Bundles of rags perched on the benches beside them; they were reluctant to be parted from one scrap of their belongings. Their feet, under the bare wooden table, were shod in old, misshapen boots, stuffed with paper that was worn to a waterlogged pulp. Many were caked in mud. They scoured their empty enamelled bowls with crusts or dirty fingers, chewing with toothless gums. Their faces were caved in by poverty; unshaven, shadowy, suspicious.

'They're the lucky ones,' Frances reminded her sister. 'At least they got a bed for the night.'

Sadie looked on in horror, her gaze flicking from one face to the next, praying that this wasn't the man claiming to be Wiggin; or the next, or the next.

At last Hettie finished her work, wiped her hands on a linen towel and came across the hall. She was composed, pausing when an inmate stuck out his hand to accost her and accuse her loudly of some uncommitted crime. 'It's a crying shame!' the old man shouted. 'So it is. It's a shame, and I want something done about it!'

Hettie bent to soothe him, promised that everything would be all right if he took his empty bowl to the hatch and picked up his bed ticket for a good night's sleep. She patted his hand until he released her and she could go on her way. She woke another man, fast asleep at the table, and helped him to his feet, not flinching at the sight of a livid, distorting burn that scarred one side of his face.

Sadie came forward almost in tears. To her, Hettie was an angel. She could solve everything, find a way through for these hopeless cases. She would be able to dissolve away this small problem over Wiggin. 'Hello, Ett.' Sadie gave her a brave smile, aware that Frances had come up quietly beside her.

'We came as quick as we could,' Frances said. 'Where is he? Do you want us to try and get some sense out of him?'

Hettie nodded. She led the way out of the refectory,

down a long cream and brown corridor towards the men's sleeping quarters. The dormitories, well aired, with rows of bunks to either side, were a step up from the old work-houses, but offered few luxuries. A warm blanket, a promise of breakfast in return for a chore successfully carried out, was what persuaded the homeless to stay on after their spartan suppers. Included in the bargain was a dose of hymn-singing and allelujahs, which most considered a price worth paying in return for refuge from the elements.

Hettie turned right, up a narrow flight of stone stairs. 'The thing is, he keeps coming back regular as clockwork, every Saturday night.' She spoke quietly over her shoulder to her two sisters. 'First off, I hoped it'd be just the once. They drift off and we never slap eyes on them again, some of them. But he came back the next week, I think it was the last Saturday in November, and I hoped to goodness he'd change the tune and stop going on about this woman called Annie. It was a load of rubbish mostly, but it put the wind up me.'

Frances listened carefully. The upper storey of the Mission contained more men's dormitories. Glancing to either side, she could see barrack-like rooms, each of which gave beds to thirty or forty men. 'Just "Annie"? Is that all?' She grasped at a straw. After all, there were hundreds of Annies round here, lots of room for Hettie to have jumped to the wrong conclusion.

'At first, yes. I had to help him to bed, he was so drunk. He moaned the name "Annie" over and over, then it was "Paradise Court". He held on to my arm. He told me he'd left his Annie down the court and gone away to sea. But now he'd come back to find her.' Hettie stopped and turned helplessly. 'I prayed hard, Fran. And God forgive me, I prayed for him to go away and never come back! I was glad when he went the next morning, poor old sinner. And I can't tell you how much I dreaded seeing him come through them doors again!'

'But he's here now?' A deadening feeling had seeped into Frances that the old tramp's story might indeed be true, and that here was someone who could turn up out of the blue after twenty-odd years and set their lives in turmoil. Her voice flattened out into a monotone, jerking between her narrowed lips.

Hettie breathed in sharply. 'I was in Reception earlier on, helping the major with admissions. The major calls out names and issues blankets, I write down the name and give each man a number for his bed ticket. "Wiggin," the major says. It comes over loud and clear, the first time I've heard it. My hand can hardly write it down for shaking. I look up and see he's back right enough. And now I've got his last name and a face to put it to.'

'So you telephoned us? It's all right, Ett, you did the right thing. We'll help you sort this out if we can.' Frances managed to control her fears and take charge. 'Show us where he is and let's see what we can do.'

'It's Annie and Pa I'm worried about,' Hettie whispered, leading the way into a dormitory. 'Whatever'll we do, Fran?'

Frances gave her a brief shake of the head. The three women went in at last, and two of them being in civvies attracted a certain amount of attention. Eyes swivelled in their direction from the bunks and from groups of men huddled by radiators. 'Oo-er!' came the old-fashioned call from shrivelled, cracked lips. A cackle went up, fuelled by Sadie's obvious blushes. Then a lone baritone voice struck up into the sudden silence.

'You are the honey, honeysuckle, I am the bee,
I'd like to sip the honey from those red lips, you see . . .'

Sadie shuddered and forced herself to walk on.

'This ain't the place for the ladies to kip,' another, rougher voice called out. 'You missed your way, I think!' His laugh turned into a hoarse cough.

'Ain't we the lucky ones?' someone else cried. 'Good tommy in our bellies and fine lady visitors!' His wild eyes stayed riveted on Sadie's fashionable short skirt.

'Nah!' His companion from the bunk above cut in. 'They ain't no fine ladies. They're soul-snatchers, just like the rest!' He sneered and spat on to the floor, before rolling over and pulling the blanket over his head.

Hettie, used to the name-calling, went right down the central aisle, reading off the number on the end of each bed. But when she came to the one supposedly occupied by the man who called himself Wiggin – number 407 – she came to a sudden halt.

'Is this it?' Frances had followed close on her heels. She stared at the empty bed, the blanket thrown to one side.

'Where is he?' Sadie panicked more at the idea that the man was lost than at the previously dreaded idea of having to confront him. He might drift back on to the streets, find his way down to Paradise Court before they could check his story.

'You looking for the old Jack Tar?' The man with the decent baritone voice jumped up from his bottom bunk and approached them. He was among the most sober and alert of the men, ready for a good mystery. 'He jumped ship.' He smiled, eyeing the three women in a lively way. 'You should've seen him. He was punching the air and shadow-boxing like the devil. Then he stands up on the edge of the

58

bedstead. Blimey, I thought he was a goner. He topples forward and crashes down, then he rolls over and makes for that door on his hands and knees. Gone. Man overboard.' He winked at Sadie. 'I don't like these soul-snatchers and their jingle-jangle music no more than the next man. But I reckon I have to put up with it unless I want another wet night under the arches. That's the way it is. But not that old bag of bones. I reckon he came to just enough to see where he'd landed up, and the idea of all that song and prayer at five in the morning was too much for him. So he hopped the wag. And who can blame him?' He glanced from Sadie to Frances, then to Hettie, trying to make her rise to his bait.

Sadie had to back off from the reek of the man's breath, while Frances went to look through the far door leading into another dimly lit corridor. 'You mean he went this way?' she asked.

The sober man, standing upright, with his hands casually in his trouser pockets, nodded.

'How long since?' Hettie spoke sternly.

'Five minutes.' The man's cocky smile faded.

'Where does this lead?' Frances asked Hettie. The three of them had made their way from the bleak dormitory on to the darkened landing.

'Down some back stairs to the refectory,' Hettie reported. The cackle of catcalls and insults had begun again as the men's insolent cheerleader recovered his nerve and set up his tune of 'Honeysuckle' once more.

Sadie shut the door behind her. 'Let's be quick,' she said. 'Maybe we can catch him up.' She darted down the stairs; it was vital to get hold of this old tramp before he could spread his wild story.

But down in the refectory, an adjutant stood on a raised

platform, praying for the batch of souls who'd just partaken of the skilly and hard rolls. Fifty or sixty men bowed their heads, more likely in sleep than prayer, as the Army preacher began his speech of salvation: 'Poor as you are, hungry and ragged as you are, be sure that you will feast in Paradise. No matter how you starve and suffer here, you will rest one day at God's heavenly feet. Pray with us, dear brothers, that the path may not be long and weary, that we may feast on His Host and pray for His forgiveness . . .'

Anxiously, Sadie, Frances and Hettie scanned the rows of bowed heads. At last Hettie had to admit that she recognized none of the captive audience. 'No,' she signalled, retreating from the hall.

'Where's he got to?' Sadie frowned. She looked all about.

'What'll we do now?' Frances was the one to think ahead. They must talk face to face with the man before they could frame a real plan of action.

'My bet is he won't get far,' Hettie told them. 'He ain't strong. I don't see how his legs could carry him all the way up to the court, even if he could find his way at this time of night.' They stood in the churchlike entrance, looking out at the pale faces pressed against the window; the men who'd arrived too late for shelter. 'Leastways, he ain't managed it up till now.'

Sadie nodded in relief, but Frances shook her head impatiently. 'We're jumping way ahead of ourselves,' she told them. 'We're supposing things before we know they're true. How do we know for sure this *is* Annie's old husband? He's given Hettie a load of gibberish, he's got a couple of names right. But who's to say he is who he claims he is? No, we gotta take this one step at a time.'

Hettie frowned. 'You ain't heard him, Frances.'

'Exactly. I could kick myself. We missed him by five minutes. But you say he shows up here every Saturday?'

'Now the weather's turned bad, yes.'

Frances took a deep breath. 'Right, here's what we'll do. We'll wait a week. Then we'll come back early in the evening and talk to him.' She quietened Sadie's protest. 'A week ain't long to wait after all these years. We don't say nothing before then. Not a word.'

'But maybe we should warn Annie?' Hettie had had more time to consider this option. 'If it was me, I think I'd want to be the first to know, not the last.'

Frances knitted her brows. 'I don't know, Ett. What difference does a week make, like I say?'

'And what about poor Annie? She'd be like a cat on hot bricks.' Sadie imagined how their stepmother would feel. 'Not knowing if it really is Wiggin or not. That don't seem right.'

So Hettie gave in. She saw that it was two to one, and she trusted Frances's judgement most of all. 'Next Saturday, then,' she agreed.

Frances and Sadie pulled on their gloves and tucked their collars up around their chins. They kissed Hettie on the cheek and she waved them goodbye, watching them brave the army of lost souls who had been locked out. Then she went back to her calling.

61

CHAPTER SIX

Now every tramp in the streets of Southwark seemed to pose a threat to the happiness and security of the Parsons family. Hettie's description of 'Wiggin' as just over five feet tall, thin, bent by age, undermined by drink, a tiny, shambling figure of a man, could be taken to include many of the more hopeless cases taking shelter under the railway arches, staggering out to beg for a few small coins.

More than once that week, gazing through the window of her chemist's shop, beyond the bright purple, blue and red carboys on display there, Frances had cause to start and wonder. An old tramp would thrust his nose up to the window, tattered grey coat hanging wide, his body wrapped in woollen rags, his trousers shiny with grease and many sizes too big. Or she would be behind her counter, sorting loofahs and sponges to size before pricing them, when she would glance up at another of these fearful sights; rheumy-eyed, skin lined and engrained with dirt, holding out a skinny hand for a dose of black draught to help ease his permanent hangover. Once, a man so scared her on her evening route home, as he lurched out of a derelict shop doorway and crumpled into a heap at her feet, that she rushed on and fled upstairs to the comfortable flat she shared with Billy. There she poured out the whole story of 'Willie Wiggin'.

Billy Wray was startled by the state his wife was in. He promised whatever help he could. They'd been married for six years, following a decent period of mourning for his first wife, Ada, and he was still devoted to Frances. Like most of the rest of the world, he put her on a pedestal, admiring her cleverness, her interest in good causes, always respecting her opinion. For her part, Frances trusted Billy with her life, often went to him for advice, and gave wholehearted support to the workers' publications which Billy edited and composited from a back room of the Institute. He was a self-taught printer, having given over his newspaper stall on Duke Street to young Tommy O'Hagan, and he put his painstakingly acquired skill to work in support of the many new unions for shop and factory workers which were springing up in the East End. Now in his late forties, he had mellowed into a sinewy, spare-framed man; his fair hair had turned grey and thinned at the temples, but he was still very upright and smart.

He greeted Frances's distressing tale with concern, then shook his head. 'Ain't no getting away from it, it sounds like bad news,' he told her as he brought a cup of tea from the kitchen and got her to put her feet up by the fire. 'It's turned you into a bag of nerves for a start.' Personally he thought it unlikely that fate would push this very same tramp into a ragged heap at Frances's feet. He heard from her that a police car had pulled up at the kerbside when they spotted her in trouble, and hauled in the vagrant for a breach of the peace. This had upset his sensitive wife all the more.

Frances sipped the tea. 'That ain't the point though, Billy. The point is Annie and Pa. What'll this do to them if it turns out to be true? If this really is Wiggin come back after all these years?'

He sat opposite her, leaning both elbows on his knees. 'Don't you think you owe it to Annie to let her know as soon as possible?' he asked softly.

She stared back, bit her lip and sighed. 'Not yet, Billy. Not when it's coming up to Christmas and all. Let's wait until Saturday and we can see what's what.'

Saturday the 20th was when things would come to a head. Frances kept in close touch with Hettie by phone. On the Friday she took another call from the pub. It was eight-thirty on a cold, clear night. Hettie asked if she and George Mann could pay them a visit.

They arrived at the Institute within the half-hour. Billy shook George's hand and showed them both up to the tasteful modern room which Frances had made into a home suitable for the respectable, childless couple they were. A valve radio stood on a sleek, veneered sideboard, with a pair of headphones hung neatly to one side. The pictures on the walls were light, modern watercolours in ash frames which Billy had made himself. The rows of books on the alcove shelves were to do with social issues such as education and family planning, or else slightly controversial modern novels, many by women.

Frances made their visitors feel at home. Billy offered to send down to the local pub for beer, but George shook his head. It seemed matters were too serious.

'What is it, Ett?' Frances stood up and took off her steel-rimmed glasses which she'd lately taken to for reading. Her own hair was greying at the temples, but it was cut into a good, shoulder-length bob which gave her an up-to-date air. 'It's Wiggin again, ain't it?' She dreaded the next day and their planned return to the Mission.

Hettie nodded. She nudged George's arm. 'It's bad this time, ain't it?'

The cellarman hung his head and studied the backs of his own broad hands, placed squarely on his widespread knees. All eyes were on him and he wished it otherwise. Reaching up to ease his necktie, he coughed. 'I'm afraid it is.'

'Well?' Frances's anxiety broke through in a schoolmistressy prompt.

'I bumped into him,' George said apologetically. 'Without intending to, you understand.'

Frances felt the stuffing go out of her. She leaned forward in her own chair. 'Oh, George, no! What happened? Tell us, quick!'

'It was earlier today,' George began. He felt his colour rise. Frances scared the living daylights out of him, if the truth be known. 'I heard the dray roll up for a delivery, and I went out to meet it.' He stared at the fawn, flowered wallpaper for inspiration. Hettie nudged him again. 'Well, there I was lifting the barrels off the cart, and I'd just stopped for a chat with Harry Monk, the carter. We call him Harry the Priest on account of his name ... and anyhow, we're chatting ten to the dozen, then I turn to roll the first barrel down the slope. But instead I bump into this old heap of rag and bones. He was standing in the road, waving and going on something shocking.'

'What was he saying?' Frances gasped. It seemed as if the old runaway had found his way to the court after all.

George breathed out through his long, straight nose. 'Not a lot. Just a name. Annie's name. He kept shouting it over and over.'

'And did she hear?'

'No. I reckon she was out down the market.'

'Let's be thankful for small mercies,' Frances breathed, composing herself by folding her hands in her lap. 'What do you think, Ett? Does it seem like Willie Wiggin to you?'

Hettie nodded. 'George told me the second I got back home from the shop. Then I rang you. 'Course, George here didn't have a clue who the old man was, and when he tells me, he's all of a puzzle about it.'

George came back in. 'I was thinking, what's the old sod want, shouting for Annie like that? I'm hoping Duke don't come out and hear. It wouldn't look too good, you know. So Harry and me, we hoiked him up on to the old dray cart and laid him out comfy under one of the horse blankets. He was asleep as soon as his head touched the boards.'

'Drunken stupor, more like.' Frances failed to muster any charitable feelings towards the old tramp, but then her gaze dropped under Hettie's reproachful stare. 'So what happened next, George?'

'Harry said he'd take him right on up the Mission for me. He has to pass that way anyhow.' He turned to Hettie. 'I knew you and your pals could fix him up, and I knew Harry had only to drop off another four barrels before he makes his way back to the brewery. So I says yes, that's the best thing for him, and that's the last I saw of the old chap. As far as I know, the Mission's where he ended up.'

Billy broke the silence that followed. 'Like I said, it's a bad business. It was a narrow squeak, only saved by George's quick thinking. What if Annie *had* been in this afternoon? Or what if Duke had heard the row and come out to investigate? What if Duke had been the one to spot him?'

Both Frances and Hettie froze at the very idea. So far,

their plan had been to keep the tramp away from Annie until the case was proved either way. But the effect on Duke had also preyed on everyone's minds.

Billy continued. He stood, arms behind his back, back to the fire, offering his best advice. 'Look, you plan to visit the old man tomorrow, don't you? Well, my idea is that you should talk to Annie *before* you go, give her the chance to come along with you. It's *her* old man, when all's said and done.'

'*May be* her *ex*-old man!' Frances protested.

'No, if it is him, then there's no ex about it. That's a knot you can't untie for love nor money. If I was a betting man, I'd lay money on it,' Billy said quietly. 'How come he found his way back to the Duke otherwise?'

'Coincidence,' Frances suggested. 'And where's he been all these years?' She still felt it was impossible; like a man rising from the grave. She sprang to her feet and began to pace the floor. 'And if so, even if it is him, what right's he got to come back now and upset everything?'

'What's "right" got to do with it?' Billy shook his head. But his wife looked stricken, so he went and put an arm around her shoulder. 'Don't take on. Let's wait and see.'

George waited a decent interval for Frances to recover. 'I think the same as Billy,' he told Hettie. 'Annie's gotta be in on this. I can't look her in the eye no more, knowing what's brewing behind her back!'

Hettie's eyes filled with tears. 'You're a good man, George, and you're right. We gotta tell Annie!'

'Tomorrow,' Frances insisted. 'Let them have one more night's peace together. We'll tell her tomorrow!'

*

Sadie had planned a full day before the dreaded visit. She spent Friday evening at Jess's house, stopped over, got up at six when the household was still fast asleep, then made herself breakfast of boiled egg and toast. She changed into her work blouse and dark blue skirt, brightened up her outfit with the red hat and coat, then hurried out to the Underground.

She sat all morning at her desk in Swan and Edgar's office, checking through bills and typing out invoices. For once, as long as time flew by, she didn't mind working on a Saturday morning. That afternoon, she would stop off at Duke Street market to buy small Christmas gifts for the family; a new striped tie for Ernie, a box of Ashes of Roses face powder for Jess. That was if the family managed to celebrate Christmas this year. Fear of what lay ahead if this really did turn out to be Annie's husband made her shudder and pull her coat close. She clocked out of the building at twelve sharp, and set off down the cold street.

'Hey, missie, what do you call this?' her supervisor, Eric Turnbull, called after her. He came rushing out in his pinstripe waistcoat and shirt-sleeves, his glasses perched on his forehead, hissing at her with his affected lisp. 'You don't call this a letter to a valued customer, I hope?' He came and thrust a piece of paper under her nose.

Sadie wrinkled it and stepped smartly back. 'Is something wrong, Mr Turnbull?' She was afraid she'd been genuinely caught out; her concentration had been poor all morning and the shiny typewriter keys had swum before her eyes.

'Wrong? That's putting it mildly, I'm afraid, Miss Parsons.' He stabbed at the paper with his forefinger. 'Look, here's a capital F! Who ever heard of a capital F for "faithfully"? And this here, this is a comma where there should be a full stop. And here, a full stop where we all know we need a comma!' He looked aghast. 'Where did you go to school, may I ask?'

Sadie sighed. 'I'm sorry, Mr Turnbull. I've got a lot on my mind.'

Turnbull, who saw his job as a balanced combination of bullying and humiliation, was about to continue his tirade, when Sadie's ears picked up the familiar hooter call of one of Rob's taxis. Her spirits lifted at once. She hadn't expected a lift and supposed that it was either Rob or Walter turning up to do her a favour. 'I'm sorry, Mr Turnbull, I gotta go. That's my taxi!' She fled across the pavement. 'I'll put it right first thing on Monday morning. I already clocked out, you see!'

'Taxi?' The supervisor choked on the word. He watched Sadie step on to the running-board. Even he, in his elevated position, had to catch a bus home. How could Sadie afford to take a cab?

Sadie had collapsed with a loud sigh of relief into the front seat before she realized that the driver was neither Rob nor Walter, as she expected, but Richie Palmer. Immediately she stiffened and sat up straight. But it was too late. Richie rejoined the flow of traffic, his hands firm on the wheel, his chin jutting forward.

'Surprise,' he said quietly. 'Walter sent me out on a test run. I just put a new patch on the radiator.' He tapped the dashboard. 'She runs like a dream, touch wood.'

'How did you know I was at work?' Sadie challenged. She still felt glad about getting one up on Turnbull, and she looked at her rescuer with a bright smile. She perched crosslegged on the leather seat, her hand on the armrest.

'A little bird told me,' he said. In fact, he'd overheard Walter discussing it with Rob. When they'd sent him out in the car, he'd seized the golden opportunity to meet her out of work with both hands, knowing that she would finish at midday.

She laughed. 'Thanks anyway. You got me out of a tight spot back there.' She wouldn't have put it past the small-minded Turnbull to have dragged her back to retype the dratted letter then and there.

'Pay me back if you like.' Richie took up the joking tone. He was showing off with his driving, nipping in and out between omnibuses and lorries.

'How's that?' She noticed him take a detour down towards the Embankment, but she didn't object. Their speed on the wide road thrilled her. Walter always drove well within the twenty miles per hour speed limit.

'Come along and see the new Chaplin picture.'

She shot him a look. 'You got a cheek!'

He shrugged. 'You can say no. It's a free country.' He shot on to Blackfriars Bridge and over the river.

Sadie looked down at the immense stretch of steel-grey water. Coal barges chugged upriver to feed the power-stations, a small cargo ship crossed their wake and headed out to sea. 'So it is,' she agreed. 'I can say yes. I can say no.'

'Which is it to be?' Richie overtook a trail of slow cars behind an old horsedrawn dray. ''Cos I'm sick of hanging around.'

Sadie remembered their last conversation at the depot and her tone altered. 'I thought you said you was moving on?' she reminded him.

'Something came up.' He glanced at her, held her gaze. 'Is it yes or no?'

'The new Chaplin, you say?' She knew that details of the invitation were a diversion. Yet she couldn't muster the courage for a direct reply.

'Tonight,' he put in quickly.

'Oh, no, I can't. Not tonight.' The visit to Hettie's Mission was firmly fixed. She noticed the flicker of a small muscle on the side of his jaw.

'Rightio.' He swung left, thin-lipped, avoiding her eyes.

'But maybe I could sometime next week!' She rushed into it after all. This was the last offer she'd get from Richie Palmer. He wouldn't stand being put off once again.

His eyelids flickered. 'Monday?' he suggested.

She nodded. 'But not the Picturedrome this time. Let's go somewhere new.'

'You choose,' he agreed. His voice, laconic as ever, betrayed none of the triumph he felt.

'Meet me out of work at six.' It was all fixed, for better or worse. Minutes later, he pulled up at the end of Duke Street and dropped her off to do her shopping in the market.

When Sadie finally arrived home with her basketful of Christmas novelties, she found the pub already crowded with men celebrating a home win, or else trying to escape the pre-Christmas frenzy of shopping for turkey and tree. Ernie and Duke, all hands to the pump, worked to slake their customers' thirst. George had been called on to lend a hand. He was serving beer to a couple of men she'd never seen before; apparently friends of Bertie Hill, who stood in close conversation with them. At present, there was no sign of Annie.

With her basket over her arm, and her feet touching the ground for perhaps the first time since her decisive taxi ride, Sadie ran upstairs. She had about an hour to get ready before she, Hettie and Frances went off to the Mission. She burst into the living-room, totally unprepared for what greeted her.

Annie sat in her own chair by the fire, staring into its glowing depths. Frances stood uneasily to one side, twisting her wedding ring around her finger. Hettie was over by the window, as if trying to melt away to nothing.

'You ain't gone and told her?' Sadie cried. She rushed forward to hug an unresponsive Annie. 'You ain't never gone and told her! Look what you done!' She hugged the slight, stiff frame. Annie was the only mother Sadie had ever known, and she could see how much they'd hurt her by dropping this terrible bombshell. Annie bowed her head on to Sadie's shoulder.

'We had to, Sadie. It was for the best,' Hettie told her. 'Don't think it was easy, for God's sake.'

'But we ain't sure. We don't know nothing for sure!'

Frances lifted one hand to her mouth. 'He was here, Sadie. He was outside the Duke yesterday afternoon, only thank God Annie was out.'

Sadie drew a deep breath. She rested a cheek against Annie's fine grey hair. 'Look, we ain't sure, Annie. Chin up. You never know.'

Annie spoke for the first time. 'It's him all right. I can feel it in my bones.' She managed to straighten up and sit with her shoulders back. 'I should've known it was too good to last.' She looked round the room, from the sewing box on the table to the clock on the mantelpiece, to Duke's empty chair.

'Don't say that!' Sadie wanted to cling to her shred of hope. 'We'll go and find out all we can for you, Annie. You just gotta stay here and hope and pray.'

But Annie, who'd never shirked anything in her life, would meet trouble full on. That's the way she would have it; not to be caught unawares by a misplaced concern for her welfare. 'Frances and Ett done right telling me, girl. And there ain't no way I can let you three take my trouble on your young shoulders.' She stood up. 'If anyone's staying here, it's Frances and you, Sadie. I'll go along with Ett and put everyone's minds at rest.'

Hettie came obediently forward.

'You sure, Annie? You sure you're up to this?' Frances saw the determination on her stepmother's face. 'It ain't nice down at the Mission. Why not stick to our first plan? Let us go and talk to him.'

But Annie shook her head. 'You can do one thing for me, though.' She looked from Frances to Sadie. 'You two can go down and fetch Duke for me. And one of you can stay and cover for him in the bar.'

This time it was Hettie who objected. 'Annie, can't it wait? It'll only upset him something dreadful.' The thought of Duke in distress pushed her to the brink. 'Wait till we know for sure.'

But Annie stood firm. 'Just go down and fetch him, there's a good girl,' she told Sadie. 'If old Wiggin is back in the picture, I gotta tell him now. Whatever happens, we ain't got no secrets between us, Duke and me.'

CHAPTER SEVEN

Duke steadied himself by holding on to the banister rail. He took an age to climb the stairs. It was the first time in their nine years together that Annie had called him away from serving behind the bar on a Saturday night.

'She ain't ill?' He looked up at Frances, feeling his heart pound, grasping the rail.

Frances shook her head. 'She wants you to go see her in your room, Pa. She's got something to tell you.'

The muscles in his chest contracted, he took two or three short breaths and carried on his way. 'Ain't no need to drag me up at this hour, is there?' he grumbled. 'Don't she know it's our busiest time?' He tried to trick himself into believing that this was a trivial problem, not worth abandoning routine over.

Frances saw his hand shake as he turned the handle to their bedroom door. She retreated into the living-room to wait with Hettie.

Annie sat on the double bed. She raised her head as she heard Duke come in. It was painful to her to see the misery of apprehension in his eyes. 'Come and sit down over here, Duke.' She patted the white counterpane and smoothed a place where he should sit.

'You ain't ill?' he said again.

Annie took his hand. 'Fit as a fiddle.' He was shaking. She must get this over with. 'No, but I got bad news. Are you ready for this, old son?'

Rob? Jess? The little ones, Grace and Mo? Their names sprang to mind. He imagined harm or danger to each one in turn. 'It ain't little Grace?' he said. His darling, his first grandchild.

Quickly Annie shook her head. 'No, it ain't nothing like that. It's us. Now, you gotta hear me out, Duke, then we can see what to do.' She cupped his hand in both hers and drew it close to her, shutting her eyes and rocking gently as she told him the news. 'Something, or I should say someone, has turned up. Now it might be something or nothing, we don't know yet; I gotta go with Hettie to find out. What it is, Duke, we think Willie's showed up again down at the Mission. Leastways, he says he's my old man, and I reckon I ought to go and find out.'

Duke sat quiet. No one was dying. No one was hurt. He was grateful for that. The actual news caught him stone-cold. 'That's a winder, that is.' He sighed.

'I had to tell you.' Annie stroked his lined cheek. 'Poor Ett, and the others, they was in agony, but you and me gotta deal with it. What do you say?'

He nodded. 'What do you think, Annie, is it him?' His voice stuck in his throat. He had to recollect where he was by concentrating on Annie's silver brush and comb set on the dressing-table. He caught sight of his and Annie's reflection in the mirror.

She sighed. 'Something tells me it is, yes.'

Duke's head sank to his chest. Beside him, Annie seemed small as a child, her eyes bright with tears, her chin up.

'If it is him, we'll have to think what to do,' she urged.

The room seemed clouded, nothing would stay still even

for a second. 'Give me time.' He nodded, he made a supreme effort to raise his head and got to his feet. 'Off you go with Ett, Annie.' He raised her up too. 'She'll look after you and make sure you come to no harm. I'll still be here when you get back.'

She didn't want to let go of his hand. ''Course you will, silly old sod!' Annie brushed away her tears. 'Where else would you be? Now, just you get down them stairs in the bar where you belong!' She dabbed her eyes with the corner of her apron and went to the wardrobe to fetch her boots.

To Hettie, the streets had rarely seemed so mean and cold. Rob had volunteered to run her and Annie to the Mission. Just as well; a freezing mist shrouded the shopfronts and dwelling places, the streetlamps failed to pierce the gloom.

'Turn left here.' Hettie leaned forward to tap Rob's shoulder. 'You just missed Bear Lane. What you playing at?'

He swore and took the next left, then left again. 'Can't see a bleeding thing,' he complained. He checked in his overhead mirror, caught sight of Annie sitting ramrod-straight on the back seat, her black coat buttoned up, a wide-brimmed grey hat shading her face. 'Everything all right back there?' he asked.

Annie nodded. 'Blooming lovely. Keep your eyes on the road, young Robert. Ain't no use us having an accident right this minute, is there?'

Rob grinned. 'That's the spirit, Annie.'

'Hm.' She took a deep breath as the taxi drew up outside the Salvation Army hostel. 'Ready?' she asked Hettie.

'Ready as I'll ever be.' Remarking on how well her stepmother was managing, Hettie got out of the car and held out her arm.

Annie climbed out, then paused to thank Rob.

'Ain't nothing. Good luck!' He gave her a worried smile.

'We'll need it. Ain't no point you hanging round here, though. Gawd knows how long it'll take, and you need to get off and earn some pennies.' She turned and stared up the forbidding stone steps. Then she took Hettie's arm again and marched straight up them. 'Don't mess about now, Ett,' she warned. 'Or I might just turn tail and run!'

Hettie took her swiftly past the huddled queues, straight through the entrance hall to the major's office. There Annie was greeted by the firm handshake of a tall, upright woman with long grey hair tied back in a plain bun, her blue uniform crisp and smart with its maroon epaulettes and brass buttons.

'Major Hall, this is my stepmother, Annie . . . Parsons.' Hettie hesitated over the second name. 'She's come to see Wiggin, one of our admissions. He's in the sick bay.'

The woman checked down a list pinned on a notice-board. 'Ah yes, we admitted him yesterday afternoon. We had to bring the doctor in. Yes, yes, of course.' She came out from behind her wide desk. 'Thank you for coming, Mrs Parsons.'

'I'm only doing my duty,' came Annie's stolid reply. She wondered whether the major knew about the strange circumstance behind her visit.

Major Hall nodded. Behind her spectacles her grey eyes shone frank and clear. 'Not without a struggle, I imagine,' she said kindly.

Annie grunted. 'How is he?'

The major glanced at Hettie. 'Don't expect too much,' she warned them. 'The doctor recommended rest, but he said recovery would be slow, if at all.' She waited for them to take this in. 'The drink has undermined him, I'm afraid. He's an old man, and he's not strong.'

'Will he know me?' Frown marks creased Annie's forehead. She clutched her black umbrella close to her chest.

'Why not go up now and see?' Major Hall suggested. There was a businesslike quality in little Annie that she'd taken to at once. 'Remember, God is with you.' She smiled. 'A rod and staff, a comfort still.'

'Hm,' Annie said again. 'I need something along those lines, and that's a fact!'

Hettie glanced at the major's raised eyebrows as Annie turned and marched out of the office. 'Good luck!' Major Hall nodded, thinking that Annie was the type of soldier they could do with in their ranks.

The Mission's sick-bay was less crowded than the main part of the building, and staffed by nurses in starched white uniforms. The inmates, stripped of their filthy rags, lay in clean white beds, many awake and staring at the high, arched ceiling. Some were moaning and calling out for help. Annie's determination met another test. She hated illness and decay; they made her afraid, then angry. She hated hospitals and doctors and the idea of not being able to look after yourself. It was a fate she herself intended to avoid at all costs.

'You still feeling all right?' Hettie sensed her hesitation at the door.

Annie sniffed. The strong, sharp smell of disinfectant was overwhelming. The soft shoes of the nurses squeaked over the polished tiled floor. 'Just tell me where he is,' she managed to gasp. 'There's a good girl.'

'Third bed on the right.' Hettie pointed. 'I'll come with

you if you like.' She had to overcome her own growing fear to make the offer. This could be a turning point for the whole family. She thought of Duke busy behind the bar.

But Annie patted her elbow. 'You wait here. Third on the right, you say?' She saw that the man in the bed was awake as she advanced slowly down the aisle towards him.

It was the wreck of a human being; a shrunken, demented old man who writhed to escape from his sheets, who fought the air with his fists and cried out at invisible enemies. He was foul-mouthed and frightening.

Annie took a final step forward. She drew a chair from under the bedside table and sat close to the bed. 'Willie?' she said quietly.

The man continued to beat the air, sitting upright at the sound of her voice. She saw his face. There was no flesh, just skin and bone. The mouth opened in an awful curse; it was toothless, a gaping, slavering black hole. The skin was covered in sores, the head shaved. The red-rimmed, swollen eyes could scarcely open. He tore at his sheets with twisted hands.

Annie looked at him in terror. 'Willie?'

The mouth issued another thick, incoherent curse. The face turned again in her direction, but the eyes stared straight through her. It was Wiggin.

She put out a hand to touch the cold claw that tried to beat her off. 'Willie, it's me, Annie.'

He pulled away. The name seemed to mean something to him at least. 'Annie! Annie!' he roared, like a man just home from the pub and demanding his supper. 'I'm back, Annie! Annie! Annie!'

She shuddered. 'It's me, Willie. I'm here.' She tried to restrain the fighting hands.

More terrible curses, a violent coughing fit, a struggle to be free. 'Wiggin, sir! 02753!' He lay back at last and gasped the number, hands held to attention at his sides. His head jerked upwards and back.

'Willie, it's Annie.' She withdrew her hand, spoke as if to a feverish child.

He stared back without recognition. 'You ain't Annie!' he accused vehemently. He wrenched his head from the pillow and tried to sit up. 'I ain't never seen you before! Annie! Annie!' The screams rose in pitch, then his body convulsed and he fell back. A nurse came and put her arm around Annie's shoulder.

Annie looked up broken-hearted as Hettie rushed to help. 'He don't know me, but it's him all right.'

Annie and Duke decided on a family gathering. Sunday would be a good day to bring over Jess, Maurice and the kids from Ealing. Frances would come along to the Duke with Billy; they would meet up in the afternoon, once everyone had had time to come to terms with the shocking news of Wiggin's reappearance.

On his wife's return from the Mission, Duke had gone straight upstairs to hear the worst. He was prepared for it and took it without flinching. 'No, don't tell me.' He sat down heavily in the wicker chair. 'I can see it in your face, Annie. It *is* Wiggin, ain't it?'

Annie sat on the bed, white and drawn, her hat lying across her lap. 'He's in a bad way, Duke. They reckon he might not pull through.'

'And if he does,' Duke said slowly, 'we're in a fix, ain't we?'

'Two husbands is one too many for me, you mean to

say?' Annie looked up, grasping at the shreds of her old fierce and lively self, shaking a fist at fate.

'For any woman living, I should think. Well, Annie?'

She stood up to embrace him. 'Two like you, Duke, would do me any day.'

'Try telling that to the vicar.' Gently Duke let her go. 'It looks like we ain't married no more, don't it?'

Annie's dark eyes blazed. 'We're married, Duke. They can say what they like, ain't nothing can alter how I feel about that!'

The last nine years had been the best of her life. Marriage to Duke Parsons had brought double helpings of happiness that she'd never dreamed of before. He was a stubborn, proud, old-fashioned type of husband; breadwinner, decision-maker, grumbler, worrier. A generous-hearted, stalwart friend. It wasn't as if they never had a cross word, and Annie gave as good as she got. But they believed in each other, that was the thing. Neither had had a moment's doubt since they'd reached that altar and promised, 'For better, for worse.'

'The law says different,' Duke pointed out. 'You know how I feel, Annie, and I know what you're going through, believe me. But we got to try and keep a clear head here. For a start, what's going to happen to Wiggin now?'

'He's staying put. He ain't going nowhere, not for a week or two.'

'But he can't stay at Ett's Mission for ever.'

'No. I already thought of that. That side of it ain't so much of a problem. I still got a bit put by from the old market-stall days, and I can dip into that and find a place for the poor old sod to stay. I'll pay his rent for a bit.'

Duke's frown deepened. 'You're sure you can manage that?'

She nodded. 'Call it my rainy day money. And if this ain't a rainy day, I don't know what is.'

He saw her mind was made up and began to follow her line of reasoning. 'It'd be somewhere nice and handy, I take it?'

'I thought of the tenement down the court. Joe O'Hagan was just saying this new landlord has kicked a lot out for being late with the rent. There's plenty of rooms free. Willie could take one on the ground floor with no steps.'

'That's the ticket,' Duke agreed, though his heart was sinking. 'You think he can get by?'

Annie recalled the wrecked piece of humanity she'd just encountered. 'No, Duke. I'll have to look after him.' She looked him straight in the eye.

He lifted his hand to stroke her hair. 'I know, Annie,' he said sorrowfully. He cleared his throat, rising to the challenge of her selflessness. 'I been thinking about it. We gotta do the right thing, and I'm saying to you now, love you like I do, and will do to my dying day, I gotta tell you you're free. You ain't under no obligation to stay on at the Duke, see.'

'Free?' Annie repeated the word like a death sentence. 'You ain't sending me on my way, Duke?'

His voice broke down. 'Never in this world, Annie darling. Only, we gotta do what's right.'

Annie went and clung to him. 'I'm trying. But this is hard. I'd cut off my right hand for this never to have happened!'

'But it has.'

They talked long into the night, growing calmer, trying to look ahead into the future. The first thing they wanted to do next morning was to include everyone else in what had taken place. They asked Hettie to break the news to

Jess, while Sadie explained to Ernie that Duke and Annie had hit a problem they wanted to share with the family. Everyone was coming to Sunday tea.

Ernie nodded and went and got his best collar from the top drawer. He polished his boots and paid special attention to his teeth and hair. It was Ernie's wide, simple smile that greeted Mo and Grace that afternoon as they leaped upstairs.

'Now you all know this ain't the sort of Christmas get-together we had in mind,' Duke began. They'd arrived in Sunday best, as smart a bunch as he could wish to greet; the two men in their tight-fitting suits with wide lapels, the girls beautifully kitted out, thanks to Jess and Hettie's skill with the needle. His grandchildren were shiny clean in white collars and socks. 'No need to say why not, worse luck,' he went on. He looked down at Annie, who sat in her own fireside chair, turning her head this way and that with birdlike precision, her face glad as little Mo scrambled on to her knee.

Duke stood next to her, back to the fire, with the others gathered round, sitting or standing, and Rob leaning against the mantelpiece in his usual self-assured pose. 'Annie's asked me to start doing the talking,' he said. 'She wants you to know she ain't thrilled by Wiggin turning up out of the blue. But he's a sick man, and Annie wants to look after him.'

Frances leaned across and murmured to Billy. Jess warned Maurice to hear Duke out.

'Now, we all know her too well to try and change her mind. So she's been down the court this morning to have a word with Bertie Hill about renting a room.'

'How sick?' Maurice asked, in spite of his wife's warning. It was where everyone's thoughts were tending.

'Pretty bad,' Duke confirmed. 'But if he does pull through, Annie wants to have the room ready and waiting.'

'Even after what he's done to you?' Again Maurice was the one to give vent to a common feeling. 'This is the one what left you in the cart, remember? Not so much as a by-your-leave, according to Jess here.' He recalled the details of Annie's story; how Wiggin had taken off during one of his regular trips to sea. He'd told Annie he'd be away for two or three weeks. Weeks turned into months and months into years, and not a penny, not a word did he send. She wore out his old boots, tramping up and down the court, scrimping and saving to get by, building up a life for herself by running her haberdashery stall on Duke Street market. She'd been abandoned, but she refused to let it beat her. Only after years of silent struggle did she give Wiggin up for dead and set her sights on the widowed landlord at the Duke. When Duke had eventually proposed marriage, Annie had her runaway husband officially declared missing at sea, presumed dead; only to having him turn up again now, doing his Ancient Mariner act.

Now Annie felt it was her turn to speak. She touched Duke's hand. 'It ain't that simple, Maurice. Yes, he left me in the lurch, I don't say he didn't. But it depends how you look at things. According to the law, and Duke and I have talked this one through, Willie and me is still married.'

Sadie looked at Frances in alarm. Rob stood up and moved restlessly round to the back of the group, out of his father's gaze. The others stared wide-eyed or frowned at their own feet.

'But according to Ett, he don't even know who you are!'

Frances intervened. 'How can you still consider yourself married to him?'

Annie ploughed on. 'It's not me. It's the law, Frances. Ask Billy, he'll tell you the same thing as me. Anyhow, I ain't that hard-hearted. I gotta find the poor bloke a roof over his head, whatever he done. You all see that, don't you?' She pleaded for their understanding. 'Duke seen it straight off!'

Jess came up and took Mo gently from her, stooping to kiss her cheek. 'Poor Annie,' she said. She carried the boy back to her own chair.

'Thanks, Jess.' Annie sniffed into her handkerchief. 'And your pa has told me he won't hold me to vows that ain't legal no more. He says I can go.' Her voice trembled, her hands shook, a solitary figure in her big fireside chair.

'Not to Wiggin!' Sadie's outrage broke through.

Ernie heard Annie's last words with dawning dread. Slowly the picture of how things might change formed inside his head. He wandered out on to the landing and sat at the head of the stairs, frowning at the wall.

Annie shook her head. 'No, I ain't never going back with him. There's no law says I have to be his wife again, as far as I know; only the one saying I can't be your pa's no more.'

'More's the pity.' Frances looked up at Billy. She knew what Annie and Duke must have gone through to reach this decision.

'Pity is right,' Annie said. 'Anyhow, the plan is, I'll move my bits and pieces out of here this evening, back down the court to my old house.' She moved swiftly on. 'I'll need a hand from you, Rob, to carry my trunk in your cab. And I'll need plenty of elbow grease to get the old place shipshape again. Where's Ernie? Grace, sweetheart, you run and find him and ask if he'll sort out the rats in the cellar like he used to.'

Her enforced cheerfulness drove Hettie to tears. She'd prayed all morning in church for this not to happen; Annie having to move out, down to her dusty, deserted house in the corner of Paradise Court.

'Don't take on, Ett. Ain't nobody died yet, is there?' Annie couldn't bear it if good, strong Hettie broke down. She spotted Ernie drift back into the room, gazing uncertainly from her to his pa. 'Listen here, Ern!' Annie went and seized him by the hand. 'I ain't going far. Ask your pa; he says it's for the best. And I can carry on working behind the bar. So cheer up, things ain't as bad as they look!'

She repeated her own advice to herself later that evening when she sat down at her own lonely fireside, amid the smells of carbolic soap and lavender polish, with only the silver-framed portrait photograph of Duke smiling down at her from the mantelpiece.

CHAPTER EIGHT

The women of Paradise Court approached the Christmas of 1923 with a mixture of dread and determination. This was the time when finding presents for the children and a bit of extra meat for the table became a pressing burden to people already working through the night to exist, taking in washing or going out to clean in hotels and restaurants. Those who could bring home leftover bread and a knuckle of boiled bacon considered themselves lucky. The others took in still more outwork. Katie O'Hagan, for instance, sat the little ones around the kitchen table with cardboard and paste, where she supervised the making of matchboxes. She was set on buying their mother, Mary, something special for Christmas out of the one penny per hour which made up each child's average earnings.

Some of the men tried hard too to make this a time of seasonable enjoyment. But many were demoralized by chronic unemployment in the docks, and they took refuge in the pubs, often staying till well after midnight. Joe O'Hagan, his health failing, struggled to keep on his porter's job at Jack Cooper's drapery store, but nevertheless was one of the Duke's regulars, along with the unemployed Arthur Ogden. On the Monday of Christmas week, he came in with twelve shillings worth of hard-earned tips, laid it on the counter and demanded a supply of drink to keep him going through the festive season.

Annie looked at him tartly from behind the bar. 'What'll it be, Joe?' To her mind, a man wasn't a proper man unless he could regulate his drinking and put his family before his own need to block out harsh reality.

'The usual.' Joe sighed and rolled his cap to fit in the pocket of his worn jacket. 'Times are bad, make no mistake,' he told Arthur in his flat, sad voice. 'A man in work is a lucky man, believe me.' Over the years, Joe's hangdog look had increased; he stooped under the weight of his responsibilities, his pale, thin face was lined as tissue-paper, and his wide mouth had turned down in a permanent scowl.

Annie noticed his hand shake as he raised his glass to his lips.

'Go easy,' Duke warned Annie under his breath. 'Make sure he can get home in one piece.'

'I'll see him on his way,' she promised. Under the brand-new arrangement of Annie living at the bottom of the court, she could easily walk Joe home to Eden House.

Dolly Ogden's sharp ears picked this up. Tingling with curiosity, she leaned over the bar for a confidential chat. 'You made a nice job of them front windows of yours, Annie. I seen you out there yesterday afternoon with your leather and bucket. Shining like a new pin, they are now.' She nodded her approval.

Annie sniffed. She intended to give nothing away.

'Took me aback a bit, I can tell you.' Dolly creaked still closer, her old-fashioned stays straining against the bar-top, Like many of the older women, she stuck to the clinched and corseted look of her own youth. She derided the new, flat-chested style, showed off her cleavage and hid her girth behind strong laces and whalebone. 'I never thought in a month of Sundays that I'd be seeing you move back in down the court!'

'I seen you on your doorstep, Dolly.' Annie went on steadily serving. 'I never seen you offering to lend a hand though.'

'I never liked to butt in, Annie.'

'Since when?' Annie put money in the till. 'Pull the other one!'

'Anyhow, I seen Rob and Ernie helping to carry your stuff down. Charlie was working, otherwise he'd've lent a hand.'

'But not me with my bad back,' Arthur put in. 'Can't lift nothing heavy these days. It goes without a by-your-leave, and there I am, laid flat out. I have to go steady on the allotment, else I'll put it out good and proper.'

'But it don't stop you lifting a pint glass,' Dolly observed. She felt cheerful; the pub's shiny mirrors and fancy windows took her out of herself, the company and a fine old gossip did her good. 'Annie, you and Duke must have had a ding-dong battle for you to pack up your stuff and move out!'

'No.' Annie clamped her mouth tight shut. She swept empty glasses from the bar and took them to the sink.

'You can't fool me, Annie Parsons! It don't make no sense otherwise.'

'It don't to you, Dolly. But it do to Duke and me.'

'It ain't natural, Annie. A man and wife can't live in separate houses. I mean to say, Arthur here snores something shocking, but I ain't kicked him out of bed yet and we been married twenty-eight years.' She sighed; Arthur's snoring was one of the crosses she had to bear.

Annie knew it would only be a matter of time before the news broke. She spotted the sturdy figure of Bertie Hill come through the doors; she must tackle him about renting a room for Willie. Then the whole world and his wife would know. She shook her head at Dolly. 'Wait and see,' she advised. 'And don't go bothering Duke about it. You'll find out soon enough, and when you do, I don't want you poking your nose into what ain't none of your business, you hear me, Dolly?' She fixed her to the spot with the ferocity of her stare.

'Me?' Dolly attempted outrage, but she knew Annie meant business; no tittle-tattle. 'Don't take on, I'll mind my Ps and Qs,' she promised. Then she shook her head. 'It don't seem right to me.' She thought Duke looked worried and worn out, and she could tell Annie was only putting a brave face on things. 'It don't seem right at all.'

On the same Monday before Christmas, Sadie had to perform her own version of 'doing the right thing'. She went to work, and after Turnbull's public dressing-down over the badly typed letter, she'd put her head down and got through more than her fair share of work.

She sat at a long desk with three other typewriters, all women. They were all under thirty, nicely dressed, their nimble fingers flashing across the black and silver keyboards, sitting upright at their tapping machines. The work may have been repetitive, and Turnbull's standards ridiculously high, but it was clean work, and they had the sense of belonging to the modern age, free of the slave labour of factory and domestic work.

Turnbull's bark was nasty, but it was worse than his bite. In fact, the chief clerk held uneasily on to his own job; the women had proved themselves to be fast and efficient office workers, and he knew that his era of pen and paper and handwritten ledger books had passed for ever. He was a tall, thin man with grey hair that grew low on his brow but was combed straight back in a thick, greased pelt. He wore a grey moustache and thick glasses. At home he had a wife ill with tuberculosis, and three grown-up, unmarried daughters.

When lunch-break finally came, Sadie made her excuses to the other girls and slipped out to the depot to see Walter. She hoped to find him alone; Rob had mentioned a business appointment and Richie had been given a day off. But she knew she had only half an hour to break her news. Her stomach felt tight ard fluttery as she half ran down Meredith Court, across the cinder yard into the gloomy garage.

Walter looked up from the desk with a smile. The sight of Sadie was enough to raise his spirits as he pored over the lists of figures which Rob had left for him to study. She came towards the office, stepping neatly between lathes and hoists, looking anxiously towards him. His smile faded as he came to meet her. He altered his expression and prepared himself for a serious talk.

Sadie had known Walter for most of her life. He'd been a pal of Rob's at school, then he'd worked at Coopers' and stood by the family all through Ernie's trial, before following Rob off to war. Unlike her brother, Walter had survived unscathed and come home to take up the old dream of running a taxicab business. The Army had helped build up his physique. His tall frame had filled out and he wore his wavy brown hair short and neat. He spoke little about life in the trenches and he even hid his disappointment with King and Country when they failed to offer him a decent means of making his living. He saw other young East Enders, more prepared to skirt wide of the law than he was, rising in the world through dubious trading on the docks or on the markets. Others got themselves a training in trades he didn't understand or care for; hotel work in the West End, or making new-fangled electrical equipment in the great new factories that sprang up wherever they demolished the old blocks of flats.

Walter lacked the ambition of a Maurice Leigh, but he was steady and determined. Over Sadie he was downright dogged. This was the woman he set his heart on, once she'd outgrown her schoolgirl crush on Charlie Ogden. She had spirit and good looks, and the war had brought Walter enough self-esteem to suppose he could win her if he set his mind to it. He knew he was braver and more steadfast than other men, thought that even if it was a deficiency within him that had let him go over the top into enemy fire without hesitation, then this was the same quality that made him reliable and loyal. He had patience. He would save towards the taxicab dream, and he would be there for Sadie, to take her dancing or to her favourite pastime, the picture-house.

In time this had won her over. She knew other men who were flashier, funnier, more charming, but not one paid her the same level of attention as Walter. He admired her looks, her decision to better herself by taking typing classes at night-school, the ease with which she held down her job at Swan and Edgar. As far as Walter was concerned, she could do no wrong. To be quietly adored was not the fate of every girl she knew, so for two or three years Sadie had counted her blessings and basked in Walter's affection.

Now she knew that what she had come to say must hurt him. 'Walter, I got something to say.' She took off her hat and sat down at the desk.

'I heard about Annie and Duke. Rob told me.' He hoped this was it; that Sadie had slipped out of work to tell him

92

her troubles at home. But it didn't seem to be that. She could hardly bear to look him in the eye.

'It ain't that, Walter.' Sadie sat twisting the fingers of her gloves together. 'Though it's bad enough, believe me. No, this is about you and me.' She paused. How could she say that she meant to break off?

But this intimation was enough. Walter got up and turned his back for a second. Then he faced her. 'You don't want us to go on no more?'

Hearing him speak it out loud was a shock. She felt her safe world go crash. But that was just it; it was too safe going out with Walter. She was twenty-five years old and she'd seen so little of the world, done so little for herself. People were bound to think that going out with Richie Palmer was no substitute for Walter Davidson, who ran his own set-up and adored her through and through, as anyone could see. Richie was footloose; a moody type who might take off one day, never to be seen again. But he'd kindled her desire, an uncomfortable flame that let her know she was alive and desirable herself. She'd never felt that with Walter. She knew he respected and admired her, but he'd never treated her with true passion. She shook her head. 'I don't think I do, Walter.'

He longed for her to deny it. He wanted her to vanish from the room. He'd raise his head again, and there she would be, dashing across the yard towards him during her lunch-break, a smile on her face. They'd talk of this and that. He'd kiss her soft mouth. 'What happened?'

'Nothing happened, Walter.' She hoped to get away without telling the whole truth.

'Yes it did. You found someone else?'

She nodded once, then changed her mind. 'No, not

exactly. Only, I find I . . . *want* someone else. I ain't got him yet. I ain't cheated on you, Walt!'

'But it's Richie Palmer,' he said quietly. Her silence confirmed it. He thought it through. 'He ain't good enough for you, Sadie.'

'You *would* say that.' She felt a spurt of defiance burst through her guilt.

'But he ain't. He's a drifter. And have you thought what Rob will say now?'

She was angry. 'What's it matter what Rob says? Or anyone else? What matters is what you say, Walt! I ain't heard about that, have I?' She stood up to face him.

'What difference would it make?' He felt defeat settle on him. He wouldn't make a fool of himself by fighting. Pride held him up. 'I ain't going to beg you not to do it, Sadie. I ain't that kind. You know how I feel about you.' Against his judgement, he reached out to put his arms around her. For a second, her head rested against his shoulder. When she raised it, her eyes were full of tears.

'I'm sorry, Walter. I truly am.' She seemed to recognize and feel his distress. When a strong man was hurt, her tenderness overflowed. Yet she was the one to hurt him. In confusion, she pulled herself free.

He breathed a deep sigh. 'I ain't gonna say nothing to Rob,' he told her. In his own mind this wasn't completely altruistic; the affair would grow out of proportion if Rob found out, and there'd be less chance of things blowing over and of his getting back to normal with Sadie.

'Thanks.' She grasped his hands. 'I'll tell them at home in my own time. And you won't take it out on Richie neither? It ain't his fault.'

This was harder to promise, but Walter quickly saw wisdom here too. 'His job's here as long as he wants it,' he said. 'As long as he keeps to time. And I'm here too, Sadie, waiting for you. You'll think of that sometimes?'

The tears flooded over as she nodded once and headed for the door. She was convinced now that she'd done the wrong thing. 'I must be mad,' she said through her tears. 'Letting go of you, Walt.' He took a step towards her, she met him eye to eye, then turned away. 'I gotta go now!' she whispered.

She sat red-eyed at her desk all afternoon, convincing herself that she would call it off with Richie. She would creep back to Walter and eat humble-pie, say what a terrible mistake she'd almost made, ask him to go on as if nothing had happened. Yet she knew again, as the black hand of the clock ticked towards six o'clock, that Richie would be out there waiting after work, and that something strong in her would welcome the sight of him, that her good resolution would dissolve away, and that she would fling herself into their evening out together regardless.

Monday, Tuesday and Wednesday crawled by for Annie and Duke. Bertie Hill had cast the pub landlord an odd glance when the request came from Annie for a room in the tenement, but his rule was never to ask questions where money was concerned. 'Tired of serving after hours?' he quipped. He took the first month's rent in advance and counted it out on to the bar. 'Can't say I blame you neither.'

'It ain't for me.' Annie faced him without blinking.

He looked up. 'Oh, well, ain't none of my business.' His face had an insolent half-smile.

She resented his attitude. 'That's right, it ain't,' she snapped.

'It's room number five, down the back,' he told her.

She knew those odd numbers on the ground floor; they faced on to ash-pits and rubbish heaps stacked up against the factory wall. Their windows overlooked sooty bricks, the filthy yard bred disease and harboured rats. Her stomach turned. 'Ain't you got nothing facing out front?' she demanded.

His small, mean eyes blinked, he shook his head. 'A view costs extra. Besides, ain't none of them for rent right now.'

Annie knew quite well that Bertie Hill was lying. He shoved up the rents and stuck tenants wherever he pleased. It was useless to argue.

'Take it or leave it.' He shrugged.

She nodded. 'I'll send Ernie down for the key later on.'

That was Tuesday. On the morning of Christmas Eve, Wiggin walked half-naked out of the Mission sick-bay, down the main corridor, demanding his clothes. Major Hall telephoned Annie to warn her he was on the move. 'He's not really fit to go,' she told her. 'But he insists. I thought you would want to know.'

'I'll come and fetch him,' Annie promised. 'What kind of Christmas present do they call this?' she grumbled to George Mann, who was shifting new barrels into position in the cellar. 'Tell Duke for me, will you? He's out buying last-minute things. Tell him I have to go fetch Willie.'

She flew out into Duke Street, her coat still unbuttoned, running to catch the tram that would take her down Bear Lane and noticing with sharp irony that for once the day was fine and clear. She reached the Mission just in time to see the huddled shape of her old husband come stumbling down the broad front steps, elbows up, fending off all offers of help from two Salvation Army officers. She rushed up and seized his arm.

'Hush, Willie! . . . There's gratitude for you!' She tried

to quieten him, apologizing to the people who'd saved his life. 'I'll take you back now. I found a room down Paradise Court, I made it nice and clean for you. Come on, now.' She struggled against his shoves and curses.

'He won't take in much of what you tell him,' the Army man advised. He didn't envy Annie the task of getting Wiggin home.

Annie grunted. 'He still don't know me, do he?' She stood trying to attract his attention. 'Willie, behave! It's me, Annie!'

Again the name clicked deep inside his memory. He investigated her features for a few seconds, then he pulled away.

'Now, it ain't that bad,' she joked grimly. 'I ain't changed that much, have I?'

'Wiggin, 02753, sir!' he told her. 'See that big one in the uniform there?' He hissed and pointed to the Army man on the steps. 'He ain't what he seems!' With a mysterious gesture, he beckoned Annie down the street.

'What's he mean by this number lark?' Annie wanted to know.

The woman Army officer came down quickly to speak with her. 'We think it's a prison number,' she said quietly. 'He don't hardly know where he is most of the time.'

Annie shook herself straight. 'Prison?' She looked at Wiggin through narrowed eyes. 'No wonder you never came home, you old scoundrel!'

'Try to keep him off the drink,' the young woman advised.

'That's like saying, try to keep the rain from falling,' Annie retorted. 'You hear that, Willie? You've to stay on the wagon!' She set off, remonstrating with him all the way down the street, deciding not to risk taking a tram back to

Duke Street. Though the Army had cleaned up his clothes and the stench was certainly less, they couldn't clean up Wiggin's language for him. He shuffled along, foul-mouthed as before, shouting at invisible devils that tormented him and hovered just out of reach.

Duke and Annie decided to make the best of Christmas that year, for the sake of their customers, and for little Grace and Mo. With Wiggin holed up in Eden House, Duke gave strict orders that he must not be served in the pub, telling Annie that her old husband was in such a poor state that he would never have the strength to stagger further than the end of the court in search of the liquor that was killing him.

But Wiggin on the trail of drink was a cunning animal. He collared a lad on the street and sent him up the pawn shop with the ex-army greatcoat which the Mission had donated as their last act of charity towards him. With sixpence from the coat, Wiggin gave one penny to the lad and ordered him to spend the other five on gin and to bring the bottle back down the court. After that was gone, he would have to beg and steal his way towards the next drink. He had no pride, felt no gratitude, possessed no intention in life, save that of oblivion.

Annie found him on Christmas morning, dead drunk on the stone floor.

In the afternoon, Jess and Maurice came with the children, and there were presents, music and games. Ernie had his new tie from Sadie. He gave Grace a parcel of chocolate wrapped in silver and purple, and Mo a painted wooden soldier. No one spoke of family troubles. Maurice and Rob talked business, while Billy asked Ernie about his longtime job with Henshaw's. 'Mr Henshaw ain't there no more,' Ernie told him sadly. 'He passed away. But Mrs Henshaw says she needs me more than ever. She wouldn't know how to get by without me!'

Duke overheard and winked at Frances. 'Cheer up, girl. Have a drop of sherry,' he insisted. 'Come on, Frances, it's time you let your hair down for once.'

She tried for his sake. But she didn't relax until Annie came in, and she saw her father and her stepmother smile at one another and go on as before. If they could cope, then surely to goodness she could too.

Jess and Hettie gossiped with Sadie, the three of them heads together at the table loaded with cold ham pie and sandwiches. They sat under swathes of holly and mistletoe, talking shop and fashion, discussing the merits of various face powders and the desirability of the recent trend among women to take up smoking.

'It's only what the men do,' Sadie protested. 'You see it in all the films these days.'

'Yes, and I don't like it,' Jess put in, playing the respectable lady and mother. 'It makes them look . . . fast.' She drew the line at her own shorter skirts.

'I don't know. I like the look of them silver holders.' Hettie sprang her opinion on them. 'Not that I'd take up smoking cigarettes myself, but I don't object to them that do.'

For a time, it seemed a normal Christmas afternoon. It was only when Annie stepped out to check on Wiggin that the heart went out of their quiet celebrations and they were reminded of the problems which the new year held in store.

Rob was the first in the family to tackle trouble head on. He didn't like the way Christmas slowed London down, taking people off the streets and business out of his pockets. He would grumble about it to his occasional girlfriend, Amy Ogden, who was home for a few days, staying at her mother's place.

Amy had many boyfriends, none of them steady. She called it moving with the times. Quite the career woman, with ambitions to become supervisor of the hat department at Dickins and Jones, she was one who didn't hesitate to hitch up her skirts when fashion dictated, or to lounge elegantly against a doorpost, cigarette-holder in hand, playing the vamp. She wore long strings of false pearls and shiny rayon stockings. She curled her fair hair with the new Marcel wave, and though she worked hard at reducing her weight to suit the new, boyish styles, she never succeeded in slimming down her curves. Rob advised her not to bother. 'It ain't natural,' he told her. 'Anyhow, I like you just the way you are.'

Amy enjoyed flirting with Rob. It came naturally. She could make him laugh with her sly imitations of the narrow-voiced, la-di-da customers she dealt with in the shop. She did the accent well and made herself cross-eyed with the effort of looking down her nose. They both enjoyed sending up the middle classes; the flappers, the bright young things.

'You're only jealous,' he taunted. ''Cos you ain't got what they got.'

'What's that?' Amy blew smoke from between her red lips. She'd teased Rob for being all dressed up when she'd dropped in at the pub to arrange an evening out with him. It was tea-time one Monday early in January.

'Cash,' came the swift reply. 'The pound in your pocket to buy one of them nice new hats.'

'Says who?' Amy countered airily. 'Anyhow, Rob, how about a night at the pictures with your best girl?' She changed the subject, wondering why he was already dressed up in his suit.

'Maybe. I got something to do first.'

'Something more important than taking me to see this new Greta Garbo picture they're all on about?'

'Much more. I gotta see a man about a dog.'

'Come again?' Amy showed she was put out. She went into a sulk over her cigarette.

'A woman about a loan, if you must know.' Rob picked up his trilby hat and his walking stick. He'd arranged to visit Mrs Cooper personally to pay the last instalment of his loan. He thought it would be wise to wish her Happy New Year in person.

Amy frowned. A woman? 'Best of bleeding luck,' she said to his back as he swung through the doors.

Rob's appointment was for five o'clock. He used the lift up to the office and arrived on the dot, catching the eye of the shopgirls, who knew him of old. But today he wanted to impress with his businesslike attitude, so he resisted the temptation to stop and chat. Injury hadn't diminished his darkly handsome appearance. His square face was clean-shaven except for the moustache, and his shoulders were still broad and straight. He brushed his short dark hair to one side, took pride in himself, but avoided close involvement with women. He didn't want pity, neither did he want to be anyone's second-best. For who would put up with an injured husband if they could find an able-bodied one?

As the lift door clicked and slid open, Rob stepped out on to the carpeted landing. He saw that Cooper's office door was open and Mrs Cooper herself stood there uncertainly, waiting for him to arrive. She was a slight figure in a purple-grey outfit, with lace and a gold brooch at her throat.

Rob followed her into the office and drew out a long brown envelope from his inside breast-pocket. He handed it across the desk. As she opened it, fifteen pounds in single pound notes fluttered out. 'But this is too much!' she declared. 'Are you sure you can afford all this at once?'

He nodded and they fell to pleasantries for a while; the cold, clear snap of weather, the cost of living. Then Rob cleared his throat. As for business, he said, he had great plans for the future. 'My partner Walter and me, we want to go in for a more modern type of car, a Morris Cowley.'

Edith Cooper listened politely. Since the war and the loss of her only son, Teddy, she'd faded and pined. She was thinner, much older-looking, greyer, more subdued. Not a day went by without her thinking what might have been if she hadn't insisted on Teddy joining up. He might not have been killed in that plane crash; there might have been grandchildren, a future, a family to cushion her old age. She found herself drifting off as Rob carried on explaining the benefits of replacing the old cars with brand-new ones.

'As you know, I'm a good risk. I pay my debts on time. Never been late with an instalment,' he reminded her.

'No, never,' she agreed. She rested her thin arms along the padded armrests of the swivel chair. In the background, the whir and ping of change machines racing along their taut wire tracks punctuated their conversation.

'So I would like to set out another proposition.' Rob came to the crux of the matter. 'If you could see your way to advancing us another two hundred pounds, we would pay it back at a more favourable rate of interest than before, and use the money to invest in a new motor car. I've worked out the figures and set them down here, if you'd like to take a look.' Rob knew how to behave with Mrs Cooper; impeccably polite, direct. That way she would go on trusting him.

Edith frowned. She gazed down at the gold watch hanging as a pendant around her neck. She realized that her husband was due back from the cotton suppliers at any time now; it had been her idea to fix Rob's appointment so that she would have the satisfaction of seeing her husband's face when he realized that her 'bad risk' had paid off. But there was no way he would permit her to make another loan.

'We must expand to survive, you see,' Rob said. 'Each year the competition gets stiffer. I can see which way the wind blows; before too long all the old carters' yards will be shut down and the heavy stuff will go on motor lorries. That's something for the future, of course.'

She nodded once. 'You want to borrow another two hundred pounds?'

'Yes.' Rob sat forward in his chair. 'I won't let you down, Mrs Cooper.'

But she had faded back into her chair. 'I'm afraid it's impossible,' she said. Her hand tapped the chair arm, she glanced out of the window, heard the lift bell jangle below.

'How's that?' Rob had convinced himself of success. He'd worked out the figures to make absolute sense.

'Oh, it's not that it wouldn't be a good investment.' She shook her head and raised a pale, thin hand to reassure him. 'No, I'm quite sure that what you say is very fair, and I wish I could help, I really do!' She looked at him in mute appeal.

Rob quickly caught on. He saw how much his proposal had embarrassed her. He glanced at the oldish fixtures and fittings around the place; out of date now and slightly down-at-heel. It dawned on him; Coopers' was struggling, just like everywhere else. It had hit hard times since the coming of the massive new West End stores, it had grown shabby and unfashionable. And he'd never even noticed.

He stood up at once. 'I'm sorry, Mrs Cooper. I'm sorry the investment don't seem a sound one to you.' He was gentlemanly enough to spare her further embarrassment. Amid his own crashing disappointment, he wanted to ease Edith Cooper's position.

She nodded and stood up to shake his hand once more. 'Thank you, Robert,' she said quietly. 'And I wish you luck.'

He went out, walking tall, knowing in his heart that it was more than luck they needed to keep the taxi business afloat. He pretended not to catch sight of Jack Cooper's florid, overweight figure coming into the store as he left.

'What did Parsons want?' Cooper snapped suspiciously at his wife as soon as he reached the office.

'He came to pay the last instalment of his loan,' she told him calmly.

Cooper grunted. His features were sunken into folds of flesh, his eyelids drooped. 'Well, you needn't think it'll make any difference,' he told her. 'We'll get no more cotton or rayon yarn from Hazlitts'. No supplies without payment first; that's the form these days.'

Edith rose from her chair in alarm. 'What'll we do without the yarn, Jack?'

He sneered at her. 'What'll we do without the yarn? Close down Hosiery, of course!' He would have to lay off ten women, and that would only be the start.

CHAPTER NINE

'And what will all them women do for work now?' Jess frowned as she paused to rethread the needle of her sewing-machine. Hettie had come into the shop one morning in mid-May and told her the bad news. Coopers' were laying off still more of their workforce. This time it was the hatmakers and some of the sales assistants in the shoe department, following on the heels of the hosiery workers laid off at the start of the year.

According to Hettie, they'd held off till spring to see if trade picked up, but the displays in the big plate-glass windows had failed to attract enough customers into the drapery store. Among those with money to spend, the talk was all of Selfridges in the West End, and Woolworths, whose proud boast of 'Nothing Over Sixpence' brought in the crowds.

Hettie sat in the sunny window seat, putting finishing touches to a peacock-blue dress. Their workroom was at the back of the shop, overlooking a long garden which at this time of year was white with blossom; a world away from Coopers' attic sweatshops. 'A job's a job,' Hettie agreed. She thought of poor Dora Kennedy, who'd been in that hatters for donkey's years, suddenly out of work. At fifty or so, she was likely to be on the scrapheap for good.

'It don't seem right.' Jess resumed her sewing. The steady whir of the machine had a calming effect. 'If you ask me, Ett, Coopers' is on its last legs. I don't think they can stagger on much longer.' If the store closed down, it would leave a big gap in Duke Street; an employer of that size, even one as tight-fisted and autocratic as Jack Cooper, would be sorely missed.

'Rob told me that was the way it looked just after Christmas. He wanted to set up some business with Edith Cooper, but she had to turn him down flat. She weren't able to help.' Hettie's needle flew in and out of the soft rayon silk.

'No, now him and Walter have to get by with them two old cabs instead of buying new motorcars. Rob says they ain't reliable no more. They're on their last legs and all.' Jess sighed.

Not for the first time, the sisters counted their blessings in landing this little shop in Ealing High Street. They'd established a niche in the market as a high-class ladies' dressmaker's specializing in finely tailored, hand-finished articles made to a customer's own specifications. This way they could follow the latest fashion whims. Since the opening of King Tut's tomb earlier that year, it had been all things Egyptian. Now their ladies wanted tight-fitting, square-necked shifts with bold designs in turquoise and gold. They dressed their window accordingly with a fan of peacock feathers, lapis-lazuli necklaces and gold cloth to capture the mood of the Pharaoh's tomb. Jess was the one with the eye for design, Hettie the skilled seamstress who checked every detail.

Generally their customers called by appointment, and the shop space presented a quiet, exclusive air. The long glass counter displayed one or two expensive hats, a pair of kidskin shoes, good-quality accessories. The shelves were stacked with bolts of shiny cloth, the walls hung with Jess's design sketches and photographs from fashion magazines. They had a developing reputation for good work combined with flair, and were reckoned ladylike in their dealings with customers, and very fair in the prices charged.

'What do you think of the set of this sleeve?' Hettie held up the blue dress for examination. It was part of a large, rushed order for a lady planning a spring wardrobe to take with her on a cruise ship holiday. She'd heard of the Parsons sisters by word of mouth and descended on them with a flurry of ideas and requirements.

Jess cast a critical eye over the garment. 'I think we need to take a bit more fullness out of here.' She pointed to tiny gathers around the shoulder arch. 'That line over the top should be smooth as we can make it, and all the interest comes in the trim down the front of the bodice, here.'

They were so busy discussing details that they overlooked Maurice, who'd come in the back way. It was half past two, and he'd called in on his way to work.

Their absorption in their task irritated him. He had a strong and childish notion that sewing up a piece of cloth was more important to Jess than him or anything else these days. What on earth could she find so fascinating about the set of a sleeve? He threw his hat on to the window seat and turned to look up the garden, hands in pockets.

'I hope you remembered, you gotta take Mo to the doctor after school,' he said without preliminaries. They thought he might have a slight ear infection, and Frances had suggested they go and get it looked at.

Jess checked herself, hearing the impatience in his voice. Hettie withdrew into the shop to busy herself there. 'Hello, Maurice! Fancy seeing you! Ain't this a nice surprise!' Jess went up to him and teased him, brushing some white petals off his dark suit. She offered her husband a kiss on the cheek. ''Course I remembered. What do you think I am?'

He smiled self-consciously. 'Sorry, Jess, I never meant to snap. Will you ring me and tell me what the doctor says?'

'The minute we get home,' she promised.

'And can you fetch that book from the library for me? The one on aeroplanes I want to read.' Maurice had his usual subconscious reaction; the more Jess's involvement in the shop seemed to take her away from her role of house-wife, the more small errands he found for her to do.

Again Jess had to bite her lip. 'If I get the time,' she told him, then regretted saying even this.

Maurice went tight-lipped. She'd proved the point he was trying to make; running the shop got in the way of smooth family life. But he wouldn't argue about it now. 'I'd best be off. I'll be back just after midnight.' He picked up his trilby and brushed the pile all one way with the back of his sleeve. Returning her kiss, he strode out into the garden, up the side alley to his beloved Morris, bought that February, brand-new after all, gleaming by the kerbside. He jumped into it and glided off down the High Street.

'Don't say nothing!' Jess warned Hettie, as her sister looked to see if the coast was clear.

'Would I?' Hettie said sweetly. 'You know me, Jess. I never interfere!'

Jess laughed, then sighed. 'Maurice sees things one way, and I see them another, that's all.' They worked in silence. 'He's got his dreams, see, and there ain't much room inside his head for other people's.'

Hettie considered this and nodded.

'And he does love them kids. He thinks the world of them.' The sewing-machine whirred, stopped, restarted.

'And just think, Ett, he picked me up when I was down. He took me on when Grace was tiny, and there's many wouldn't, not with a baby hanging round my neck.'

'I ain't arguing,' Hettie repeated. 'Only, you was down but not out, remember! You was coping. You was more than coping!' She thought how Jess had come home to the Duke, pregnant and abandoned, how she'd held up her head and helped the family through the awful time of Daisy O'Hagan's murder and Ernie's trial. She'd been the backbone, the strength of the family, fighting every inch of the way. 'No need to feel so grateful to him, Jess. I should think Maurice was over the moon when he found you.'

Jess blushed and laughed. 'He was,' she admitted. 'And so was I.'

'Well then.'

They continued working quietly. Only, all that seemed so long ago; a different lifetime, two other people. Jess sat there, afraid of the gap opening up between her and her husband, unsure of how to deal with it. 'If only he didn't work so late,' she put in. 'There ain't no time to talk.'

Hettie nodded. 'But he does, and that's that. A job's a job, remember, and Maurice is working his way right to the top.'

She should be proud. She had a dozen reasons to be grateful. Jess snipped and tied and oversewed, willing herself to accept things as they were, thinking of the life that lay ahead for her two children; a nice house, proper schooling, summer holidays and lovely things to wear.

For Rob, the improvement in the weather as summer approached was sometimes enough to lift his spirits. They hadn't managed to scrape together the money to buy new cabs; so what? Richie Palmer worked to keep the two old Bullnoses on the road, and they could get by for a bit longer. He was thinking this as he pulled in one afternoon in late May at the new petrol pump outside Powells' ironmongers on Duke Street. He got out and lounged against the car in the spring sunshine, watching the young lad, Jimmie, work the petrol up the gauge by turning the pump-handle in big, energetic circles. Eight turns of the handle for one full gallon. Rob checked carefully. 'Don't you go short-changing me,' he warned. 'I ain't one of your toffs who can afford to take under the gallon, you know. Top it right up.' He knew the boy's trick of flipping the pointer over the gallon mark with a quick flick of his finger.

The lad shrugged. 'Who, me, mister?' He was all fair-haired, blue-eyed innocence. He finished turning the pump, then drew a wash-leather from the back pocket of his overalls. He set to work on the windscreen, whistling as he wiped.

'All right, all right, no need to make a meal of it!' Rob cuffed the back of Jimmie's head and tossed a penny for him to catch.

The boy grinned. He'd secretly flicked the gauge, *and* earned a penny tip. He was well on his way to another night out at the picture-house.

Rob climbed back into the car, easing his leg sideways. Up and down Duke Street, taxicabs were on the lookout for passengers. Suddenly his mood swung the other way. 'This game ain't worth the candle,' he told himself as he joined the flow. 'Leastways, it's getting that bleeding way, unless Walter and me come up with something new.' The truth was, money problems kept him working from dawn until well after midnight, then kept him awake at night. For months he'd set his nose to the grindstone and not noticed

110

much of what went on around him. Any time he took off work, he drove up the West End and took Amy out. This was getting by by the skin of his teeth, he realized. Still, it was no worse than for anyone else, except perhaps lucky sods like Maurice.

Think of Annie. She had to come up the court each day, call in on Wiggin to sort out his food, his coal, his cooking. Then she would carry on up to the Duke to work behind the bar. Just who was married to who was the cause of much comment in the pub, after Dolly Ogden had first put two and two together and identified Annie's old husband, Wiggin.

'No wonder Annie's moved out!' she declared to an astonished Arthur. 'When you think about it, her and Duke, they've been living in sin!' She laughed uproariously.

Arthur sniffed. 'No they ain't, you silly cow. They tied the knot in good faith, didn't they? Just because Wiggin turns up out of the blue shouldn't mean she gets turfed out of here, does it?' He spoke in a loud voice, above the hum of voices in the pub. Duke overheard and moved away.

'Hush!' Dolly hissed. 'You'll get us chucked out if you're not careful!'

Rob was looking daggers at them. 'It ain't funny,' he warned.

'No, it ain't,' Dolly agreed, overtaken by decency. She coloured up. 'No offence, Rob. Only you gotta admit, it *is* a turn-up for the book!'

After a time Rob had got used to the gossip and learned to ignore it. Opinion was strongly on the side of Annie and Duke continuing to live together as a married couple. Only Mary O'Hagan told her daughter, Katie, that she could understand their dilemma. They would hear Wiggin crashing into things and fighting his invisible devils in the room below, and they would admit that as long as he was alive and kicking, there was not much that Duke and Annie could do. Tommy overheard and put in his two ha'porth. 'I don't know about *alive* and kicking,' he said with a sour look. 'But the sooner he kicks the bucket, the better.'

Mary said a quick Hail Mary an her son's behalf. But Tommy said it was a common opinion. 'The old scoundrel ain't worth wasting your breath on,' he insisted.

Because of work and worry, Rob didn't spend too much time trying to work out his family's problems. If the present arrangement between Annie and Duke held up, that was enough. Who could expect a trouble-free life these days? He had noticed that things had cooled off between Walter and Sadie, but it drew no comment. Again, that was their business, so long as Sadie behaved herself, and he had no evidence that she wasn't.

Deep in thought, Rob swung the car down Meredith Court, its tank newly full. There, at the fringe of his vision, standing on the pavement outside the Lamb and Flag, were two figures, a man and a woman. They'd just come out of the pub and paused to kiss goodbye before heading their separate ways. Rob had passed well down the street before it clicked; that was Sadie in her new cream-coloured jacket and skirt, and she was with Richie Palmer. He flashed a look in his mirror. They were gone.

Thumping the steering-wheel with the heel of his hand, Rob pressed on. He slammed on the brakes in the depot yard and hauled himself out of the car. Tact wasn't part of his make-up; he'd go in and let Walter know the score, and they could have it out with Richie when he next showed up.

Walter saw that something was eating Rob as soon as he put the telephone on its hook and looked up.

'I just seen Sadie with Palmer!' Rob came in and slammed the office door. 'And they was more than just good friends, I can tell you!'

Walter steadied himself by placing his palms flat on the desk. 'I know, Rob. No need to shout.'

It stopped him dead in his tracks. 'You know? What the bleeding hell's going on round here?'

'Me and Sadie's broken off, in case you hadn't noticed.'

Rob grunted. If two people broke off, it was up to them. 'It ain't because of Palmer, is it?'

'Maybe.' Walter had watched Sadie fling herself into the affair. He'd read the signs; secretive telephone calls to the garage during her lunch-break, Richie sprucing himself up to go out on a night. You didn't have to be a genius to see that Sadie and Richie had hit it off.

Wrong-footed, Rob let loose his rage against the mechanic. 'Slimy customer, he is. Stealing another man's girl from under his nose. Well, he's got it coming to him now!' His fist came down on the desk. The telephone jumped on its hook.

'Steady on, pal.' Walter wasn't sure how much of this he could take.

'I bet he's cock-a-hoop, he is!' Rob imagined the tales Richie would spread among his friends of how he'd broken up a beautiful friendship and shown his bosses up for what they were: one man who couldn't keep his girl, and another whose sister was a cheap little flirt. 'Well, not for long. 'Cos the minute he steps foot in here, he'll find himself out of a job and in that bleeding dole queue. Then let's see how fascinating he is to the women!'

Walter stood up and shook his head. 'No, Rob, you ain't gonna sack him. I promised.'

Again Rob needed a second to get the measure of this.

'Promised? Promised who?' He leaned forward on the desk, elbows locked, arms braced.

'Sadie,' Walter explained. 'I said I wouldn't take things out on Richie.'

'And you never said nothing to me?' Rob felt a fool. All this had gone on behind his back. 'Don't I have a say in it? Palmer's ruining a girl's good name, and that girl happens to be my kid sister!'

'I ain't standing up for what he's done, Rob.' Walter felt he was in a hopeless position. 'And maybe I would like to clock him one, to tell you the truth. But I can't.' He reached for his hat and opened the door. 'Anyhow, I got a fare to pick up over the water,' he said. 'Now don't do nothing stupid, Rob. Take it easy.' He paused a moment longer. 'What you gonna do now?'

Rob turned away in disgust. 'Knock his bleeding head off,' he muttered. 'If he shows his face in here.'

'No, you ain't,' Walter insisted.

'All right, I ain't.' Rob limped to a shelf behind the desk to pull out a black ledger. 'I'm gonna do some paperwork, that's what I'm gonna do.' He thumped the book down on the desk.

Walter breathed a sigh of relief. 'I thought you mentioned Amy might drop by?'

'Maybe.'

'Well, why don't you two head off to the picture-house soon as I get back? I'll hold the fort here.'

'Maybe,' Rob said again. He stuck his head into the lists of figures, refusing to look up as Walter choked the engine into life and headed off to collect his fare.

*

Amy Ogden signed out of her crib at Dickins and Jones with the information that she was heading down to home turf on her night off.

'Cheerio!' Sammy Hutchinson called from his top-floor dormitory where all the male assistants stayed. He saw her step smartly into the narrow alleyway as he hung his work shirt out to dry.

Amy stopped to wave. 'I know, Sammy, "Don't do nothing I wouldn't do!"' It was their refrain whenever they spotted one another going out on the town. 'Would I?' She blew a kiss then ran on to the street, heading for the Oxford Circus tube and all points south.

In the railway carriage, she took her little mirror from her clutch-bag and checked her lashes and lips, happy with an arrangement of beads and feathers forming a circlet around her newly blonde hair. She would knock Rob dead tonight, if he did but know it. She'd get him to take her out in the car, maybe downriver into the countryside. 'It's a nice night,' she said to herself as she mounted the stairs into the warm evening light, under hoardings advertising Pears' Soap and Nestlé's Milk. Nothing could dent her mood; not even the usual sights of ragged children clustered in doorways and grim-faced women shuffling down from the railway embankment with an armful of potatoes or some half-rotten cabbage leaves.

'Nice night,' she repeated to Rob as she waltzed into his narrow office in a strong swirl of lily-of-the-valley perfume and face powder.

'Is it?' He glanced up, his face a picture of peevish displeasure.

Amy laughed out loud. 'It was till I came in here!' She seized the black ledger he was poring over and slammed it shut. 'Robert Parsons, get your hat. You're gonna take me for a drive!' she announced.

'Am I?' He smoothed his moustache and frowned up at her. 'And who'll run this show while we're off hobnobbing?'

'Walter will. Won't you, Walter?' Amy's voice wheedled as she heard Walter Davidson come into the office.

'I already told Rob I would.' He hung his hat back an its peg.

'Oh, come on, Rob, it ain't as if it's a weekend or nothing!' Amy was unashamed as she perched on his knee and slung her arms around his neck.

He swung her back on to her feet. 'All right, hold your horses while I hand on these messages to Walter. Go and wait in the car.'

She grinned. 'That's the ticket'' She was pleased with her persuasive powers as she went out to sit and wait. Rob always came round, no matter how grumpy he was at the start. She slid into the passenger seat and anticipated their evening out: a drive out of the city, a drink in a country pub before they found a nice quiet lovers' lane, some woodland spot where Rob would spread a blanket on the ground in the moonlight, among the primroses. It would be almost romantic, almost like it was in the pictures.

'You ain't going out tonight, then?' Hettie asked Sadie. It was unusual enough for her to comment on.

Sadie shook her head. She'd just met up with Richie for a quick drink after work, but this was her evening in for washing her hair and curling up with a good book. There'd been precious few lately, since she'd got caught up in the storm of emotions connected with Richie Palmer.

'Put the flags out,' Hettie said, caustic for once. 'It's

about time you stopped to let your feet touch the ground.'
Although the whole family knew that things had cooled
between her and Walter, Sadie had not confided her new
state of affairs to anyone. She grew tense when the subject
was mentioned, and more secretive as the weeks went by.

'Don't go on, Ett,' she said, affecting concentration. But
the words on the page blurred. Although Hettie let it go
and drifted downstairs to help in the pub, Sadie's own
thoughts were enough to make the print swim before her
eyes.

The simple fact was, she couldn't get Richie Palmer out
of her mind. He was locked in there, a secret she dare not
share because she didn't want to admit the strength of her
feelings for him.

Richie took her out three or four times a week, usually
well away from Duke Street. Still poor in the word department, he never said he loved her, but actions spoke louder
than words. He wanted to be with her, touching, kissing,
walking close by her side. She'd grown used to his face: the
heavily lidded eyes, the straight nose, the full mouth. It was
like a contour map she could trace inside her own head and
conjure up to catch herself out while she sat typing, or
reading, as now. The sound of his voice ordering a drink
would echo in her mind, and she would look up, surprised
to find herself at home or at work. His image filled her
dreams, not pleasantly as a romantic hero, but as an
obsession she couldn't move away from, sentenced to go
wherever he went, though he might not even acknowledge
she was there.

'Fool!' she told herself. She would have to get up to look
in the mirror and talk straight at her reflection. 'What's
happening to you? What has happened to your life?' But
any resolution to distance herself from Richie melted away

as soon as they met. He would clasp her hand, walk her along, claim her.

The trouble was, she read things into his silences, even if she suspected they were the wrong things; her romantic heart leading her to false conclusions, she lacked a guide to put her straight. Her sisters would never understand. Theirs would be a paler version of Rob's antipathy to Richie, and they would side with Walter, her old flame.

She told herself versions of Richie's life story, half making it up, snatching at fragments that he himself let slip. He'd always been alone; she knew that much. He'd built a shell around himself, fooling people with a hard, tough exterior. But really he was easily hurt. He was proud, despite his poor beginnings, with the pride of an animal strong enough to protect his own territory; in this case, his heart.

Sadie would gaze into his face before she kissed it. It seemed to her that even his words had to fight to escape through clenched teeth in case they betrayed him. She got used to his low, indistinct voice. It was one of the things she loved best.

Her evening at home had turned as always into the fascinating study of the workings of Richie Palmer's mind, when she heard footsteps on the stairs. She recognized Rob's tread and a lighter step, probably a woman's. Before she had time to close her book and slip away, Amy Ogden had opened the door and entered the room laughing.

'Oh no you don't!' Amy swept in. 'No sneaking off, Sadie Parsons. Put that kettle on and make us a cup of cocoa while we put our feet up. We been out driving, and we need a nightcap before Rob drives me back to the barracks!' She pretended to give a smart salute. 'I ain't signed out for the whole night, so I gotta get back.'

Something about the way Sadie put down her book, a

small, superior smile perhaps, irritated Rob. Sadie needn't get on her high horse about Amy; she was no better than anyone else round here when it came to it.

While Sadie put the kettle to boil and Amy chatted on, Rob decided to knock his sister off her perch, as he called it. 'Ain't the Duke good enough for you no more, then?' he dropped in, stretching his chin over her shoulder, pretending to sniff the cocoa.

'What you on about now?' She shrugged him off, hoping that he wasn't planning to annoy her, totally unsuspecting.

'It's the Lamb and Flag now, I take it?'

The spoon froze in mid-air. Sadie couldn't frame a reply, remembering that she'd been in the Lamb with Richie earlier that evening. What had Rob seen? Was her secret out? Eventually she stammered something about popping in with a friend.

'O-ho!' Amy spotted gossip. 'She's got a guilty conscience, I'd say, Rob. Just look at her, she's red as a beetroot!'

'Shut up, Amy!' Sadie threw the spoon on to the table. She turned to confront her brother. 'Come out with it, say what you want to say!'

Amy pretended to retreat behind a magazine, her mouth puckered, eyebrows raised. She kept her ears wide open: it promised to build up into something she wouldn't miss for the world.

'I'll say what I gotta say tomorrow morning down the depot, when Richie Palmer comes in.' Rob met her gaze. His voice had fallen to a low, deliberate pitch.

The sound of Richie's name opened the floodgates of Sadie's panic. 'No, Rob! That ain't fair, you leave him out of this!'

'I'd leave him out if he'd leave you out.' Rob intended

119

to see this argument through. He forgot all about Amy sitting there, ears flapping, as he launched into Sadie for letting down the family's name. 'He ain't nothing but a grease monkey, and you know it!'

'Keep this between you and me, Rob. You ain't got no right to talk about Richie that way!'

'No, but I got the right to tell him to move on all right, and that's what I plan to do first thing tomorrow morning.'

Amy's eyes shone. She turned back to Sadie, awaiting her next move.

Sadie took a deep breath. 'You do that, Rob Parsons, you give Richie the sack for no good reason, and that's the last you'll see of me round here!' She began to shout and flounce towards the landing.

'Tell the whole bleeding street, why don't you?' He sneered as he took out a cigarette and lit it.

'I mean it. You get rid of Richie and I go too. 'Cos you make me sick, that's why, with your bullying and throwing your weight around. Who do you think you are, telling me what to do, lording it over everyone like you do, when you're really just as bad. No, you're worse! We all know what you get up to in the back of that taxi, and it ain't nice!' Sadie shot a glance at Amy, who turned to her magazine to hide her own blushes. 'So don't think you can go on about other people and get away with it yourself, you bleeding hypocrite!' The rush of words left Sadie shaking. Her throat felt constricted, there were hot tears in her eyes.

Slowly Amy clapped into the silence. 'Hurrah!' she drawled. 'You tell him, girl.' To her credit, she recognized a good show when she saw one and didn't take Sadie's insulting implications personally.

Rob shrugged. He blew a funnel of smoke towards the

ceiling. 'It don't make no difference,' he pointed out. 'Go ahead, bawl away all you like, Sadie. But tomorrow morning, first thing, I go down that garage and I give Richie Palmer his marching orders.'

CHAPTER TEN

It was a desperate Sadie who tried to intervene between her brother and her lover the following morning. She waited at the entrance to the taxi depot, a grey woollen jacket slung around her shoulders, gazing up the length of Meredith Court, not caring who saw her watching out for Richie in the morning light.

Walter Davidson came into work at six-thirty from his lodgings further up Duke Street. He guessed at once what the matter was.

Sadie ran up to him. 'Oh, Walter, thank God you're here! You gotta stop Rob. He's got it in for Richie now, unless you can do something to stop him!' Her pretty face was screwed up in an agony of fury and despair. She hadn't had a wink of sleep, anxious to beat Rob down to the yard, slipping out of the house before anyone else was up, to stand waiting in the cold dawn.

Walter swung open the gates and walked ahead towards the office. He flung his newspaper on to the desk and hung up his hat, considering his next move. 'I ain't told Rob nothing about you two,' he assured her. Being near Sadie still had the power to disturb his even temperament. He had to turn to one side to busy himself with opening bills and letters.

'I know you ain't. The problem is, he seen us!' Time was running out. Any moment, either Rob or Richie would be coming into work. 'And now he says he'll show Richie the door, but it ain't his fault, and we ain't even doing nothing wrong. I came clean with you, Walter. You gotta tell Rob that.'

Walter sighed. 'It won't make no difference.' He'd spotted Richie sloping in across the yard. Rob himself wouldn't be far behind. 'You know Rob.'

Sadie choked and slumped down at the desk. 'It ain't fair,' she sobbed, head in hands.

'Listen, the best thing is for me to break it to Richie and give him his wages before Rob gets here,' Walter decided. 'Then it's up to him if he wants to have it out with Rob. If he's got any sense, though, he'll take the money and hop it.'

Sadie knew he wouldn't. She couldn't imagine Richie running away from a fight.

Richie had come into work as usual, collar up, shoulders hunched down Meredith Court. But when he spotted Sadie in the office talking to Walter, looking upset, it only took him a second to work things out. He stared warily at them both, then glanced over his shoulder to see if Rob was following him in.

The moment Sadie looked up and saw him, she reached a further level of panic. Common sense fled as she dashed out to meet him, desperate to warn him so he would be ready to face Rob. Rob mustn't get it all his own way.

But there was no time to explain. Rob's uneven footsteps crunched across the cinder track, he turned the corner into the yard. Richie pushed Sadie to one side, telling Walter to take care of her. He stood, feet wide apart, facing Rob.

'Right, Palmer, you know what this is about! Take your

nasty face out of here, and don't never show it no more!'
Rob was fired up by the scene that confronted him, Sadie
crying, begging Walter, of all people for help. He acted
without hesitation, his dark eyes narrowed in an angry
frown.

Richie gestured again to Sadie to stay out of it as she
tried to break free of Walter. He faced Rob with a cool
stare. 'Don't worry, I'm on my way,' he drawled. 'You can
stick your job, Parsons. I'm sick of it anyhow.'

Rob, who had been building up for a straight fight, was
caught off guard. 'Go on, get out!' He punched out the
words, still expecting resistance from Richie, who, after all,
was big and strong enough to give him trouble.

The mechanic turned down the corners of his mouth,
shot Rob a pitying look from head to crippled toe, and
turned his back. Rob lunged clumsily. Sadie wrenched free
of Walter and caught hold of her brother, pulling him back
by the sleeve. She saw Richie hesitate as Rob swung round
to push her off, but he walked on, head high, away from
the depot.

'Right, Rob Parsons, that's it!' Sadie was screaming at
the top of her voice. 'You just wait!' Her helpless threats
echoed under the dark roof arch. 'You just wait and see!'
She ran out across the yard, up Meredith Court, too late to
spot where Richie had headed off to. Weeping tears of
angry frustration, she made her way home.

'What are you up to at this time, girl?' Duke came along
the corridor to investigate the noises in Sadie's room. It was
still early, not half past seven. He was only just up and
dressed.

'I'm packing my bag, Pa, what's it look like?' Sadie could hardly see through her tears. She flung underthings from a drawer into a canvas bag, hands shaking, her stomach in knots.

'It's Rob, ain't it?' Duke knew there'd been a row the night before. Annie said so, and warned him it looked serious. Rob and Sadie were at each other's throats again, she said, and with their tempers, things could turn nasty. So Duke was expecting more trouble.

Now Sadie blurted out Rob's crime of sacking Richie. She was still beside herself, crying and trembling.

'And what's it to you?' Duke asked slowly. These days Sadie never confided in him. He prepared for a shock.

'Richie and me's walking out, Pa! That's why Rob done it.'

'Because of Walter?' It began to make sense. Rob's loyalty to his friend would override everything else.

'But Walter knew,' she insisted. 'I ain't done nothing behind his back, not since the first time.'

He looked at her shaking and crying. She was a slender, pale, dark-haired young woman, still a girl to him. Hettie wouldn't go and make a fuss like this, he thought; nor Jess, nor Frances, not over a lover's tiff. 'Pull yourself together, girl,' he said sternly. 'No need to go on.'

But she turned on him. 'Go on, Pa, take his side! You and Rob won't never understand.' She flung more clothes into the bag, tears dripping off the end of her nose. 'Ain't no use talking to you!'

'I never said I was on Rob's side.'

'You don't have to say it. Well, you won't have to watch me "going on" no more, as you call it, 'cos I'm leaving! And good riddance, says you!'

'I never said that neither.' Duke tried to steady his voice. It looked like Sadie was serious. 'Just hold on, Sadie. Where you off to, for God's sake?'

Her eyes flashed as she weighed the impact of her reply. 'To Richie's!' she said, swinging the bag off the bed, reaching for her coat and hat.

'Never.' Duke sat down heavily on the edge of the bed. He blew out through his cheeks.

But Sadie swept on down the stairs. Hettie came out of her room, still in her night things, just in time to catch a glimpse of the bag Sadie carried, before the door slammed in the hallway below. 'Pa?' Hettie peered into her sister's room, saw Duke sitting bewildered.

'Sadie's gone,' he reported.

'Where to?' Hettie came and put an arm around him.

'To Richie Palmer, she says.' He shook his head. 'Now why, Ett? Why would she do that?'

Hettie scrambled the facts together; *this* was the secret Sadie had been keeping to herself all through the spring!

'Why's she leaving us for Richie Palmer?' Duke repeated.

Hettie comforted him. 'I expect she loves him,' she murmured. 'That must be it, mustn't it?'

Sadie's morning was spent tramping the streets of Mile End looking for Richie's lodging-house. She had only a rough idea of where he lived, and had to stop to ask many times. At last, just before midday, she arrived at an old tenement block in Hope Street. This was it. She went in under the arched brick entrance and up some dirty stone stairs until she came to number twenty-five, knocked on the door and waited amid sounds of children name-calling down in the alley, heavy drays carting sacks of flour to the biscuit factory down the street, and the smells of stale cooking and fumes from cars below. When she realized she would get no reply, she sat down heavily on her canvas bag to wait.

A woman passing by on the balcony stopped to peer in at her. 'Have you tried his work?' she asked, not unfriendly. 'You'll find him down Southwark way, I think.'

Wearily Sadie nodded. 'I know where he works, thanks. He ain't there, though.'

The woman, who wore a square of coarse brown cloth tied around her head and a shapeless dress, whose muddy coloured skirt had come apart from the bodice in places, stood and summed up Sadie's plight. 'You his girl?' She seemed taken aback by the younger woman's smart cream outfit and stylish appearance.

Again Sadie nodded. 'You ain't seen him this morning, then?'

'I ain't seen him all week,' the woman replied. 'You never know with him. I sometimes think what's the use of having him as a neighbour, as a matter of fact. I never hardly see him.'

The words sank heavily on to Sadie's shoulders as the woman went on her way. She'd never asked Richie about his life in the tenement, and he'd never volunteered any information. According to the woman, it seemed a rootless, detached sort of life. With time to kill, exhausted after the morning's crisis, Sadie sat wondering what she'd let herself in for. After all, she'd left home and landed on Richie's doorstep without even letting him know. At last, round about four in the afternoon, she heard footsteps come up the stairs.

Richie turned on to the landing and saw Sadie waiting there. He held his key in one hand, stone-cold sober despite a day-long binge at the pub to help him block out the morning's events. He stared at the bag lying at her feet, then without saying a word he unlocked the door to his rooms and stepped inside.

Sadie lingered on the doorstep. Should she follow him in after all? This was a big move an her part and she waited to see how he would react. But Richie lifted her bag in silence, as if everything was understood and settled in that moment when he'd turned the corner and seen her there, smoothing down her jacket, putting one hand up to her dark hair. He led her in and closed the door behind her.

There was one room for living in, with a window facing out on to the landing, overlooking the busy street. It had a sink, a table and one wooden chair. The other, darker room to the side of the block was for sleeping. Richie had a piece of faded red cloth pinned permanently across the narrow window, a mattress on the floor, and one coat hook on the back of the door. He watched Sadie's face as she took a quick look around.

'Not much, is it?' he said.

'It ain't.' She marvelled how he could live like this, wandering back into the living-room and peering out of the window into the street.

'You can change your mind.' His hunched shoulders and lowered head suggested he didn't care if she did. Inside, he wanted to lock the door, throw away the key, keep her here for ever.

'I can.' Her own head went up. She flicked her hair out of her face and stood squarely facing him.

'So will you stay?' He gestured to her bag on the bare floorboards. 'That's what you got planned, ain't it?'

'Are you asking me?' she challenged. 'Do you want me to?'

He leaned back against the crumbling wall and turned his head away. 'Don't play games with me, Sadie. I ain't in the mood.'

Suddenly serious, she went up to him and put her arms around his neck. 'I'm here, ain't I? It took me all morning to find the place, for God's sake!' She kissed him on the lips.

He responded, held her close. 'Stay, then.'

There was only the present as they embraced once more; no thought of the future or the consequences of what they were doing. They had a place to themselves, however poor. Sadie had made the break from home.

She and Richie made love for the first time, shy and tender. There were tears, which he kissed away. Then he kissed her neck and shoulders. If they thought they could beat him, they were mistaken. He had her now, in spite of them. He would love and care for her for ever.

May days lengthened into early June. Sadie left the tenement rooms in Mile End each morning, and travelled by tube to her job at Swan and Edgar. Richie took casual work wherever he could get it. Since neither wanted to accept help from Sadie's family, they cleaned and painted the two rooms themselves. Sadie's first purchases were another chair, some bedlinen and a tablecloth. Eventually she wrote to Hettie, telling her where she was, but saying she would prefer not to come over to the Duke to visit until Rob saw fit to apologize to Richie.

'Never in a month of Sundays,' Duke said sadly.

Hettie put the letter on the table with a shake of her head. 'Let's wait and see, Pa. Leastways, we know she's safe and well.' Sadie sounded happy. There was no disguising her enthusiasm as she wrote about her new set-up with Richie.

Duke didn't like it, but Sadie was twenty-five years old and he had to get on with his own life as best he could. Summer nights brought more people out on to the streets to gossip and watch the children play. Some of them drifted into the pub for a drink before they went to bed. Trade improved slightly, though much of it went on late at night, well after hours, to Annie's disgust. 'What can I do?' Duke shrugged. 'We gotta earn a crust.' When the doors of the pub finally closed, he fretted after Sadie. And the truth was, he'd rather have the place alive and full of people, than close early and sit at his hearth without Annie.

One rule he did intend to stick to was his ban on Willie Wiggin. 'Ain't no one here will give him a single drop to drink!' he told Annie, and she would nod in satisfaction when she saw him keeping his promise. She was trying to dry the old drunk out, and largely succeeding. Though his liver was ruined, the doctor said he might not get rapidly worse as long as they kept him away from the drink. She kept her eagle eye on him, and gave orders to the tenement children to run no more errands for the lodger in number five.

But Wiggin sober was as much of a problem as Wiggin drunk. He turned to argument, accusing the O'Hagans of deliberately driving rats into his room, claiming that Annie came in to steal his money when he lay asleep, trudging up to the post office and claiming dole that he wasn't owed. He was impossible to handle, mean and vicious, and still cunning in pursuit of drink.

On the first Saturday afternoon in June, Wiggin was seen making his way along Duke Street towards the public park.

Katie O'Hagan, who ran Annie's old haberdashery stall with all her predecessor's verve for business, spotted him wandering back an hour or so later, obviously the worse for wear. She passed the word along, 'Tell Annie, Wiggin is off the wagon!' She saw it'd be a miracle if he didn't get run over by a bus, the silly old sod. Katie wound five yards of white ric-rac braid on to a scrap of card, took threepence in payment and craned across the stall to watch Wiggin's progress. When she saw his shambling figure stagger to a halt at the corner of the court, then drift crabwise towards the door of the Duke, she thought direct action was called for. 'Watch my pitch!' she yelled at Nora Brady on her nearby fish stall. Then she skipped down the busy street, eager to warn Annie personally.

She found her wending through the crowd from the other direction, her basket full of fruit and veg, taking her time and chatting in the evening sun. Annie turned to Katie's call, but her smile vanished when she saw the girl's pointed little face looking serious and she heard the latest news. Quickly she went towards the pub, just too late to stop a confrontation between Duke and Wiggin.

'I said, a pint of best bitter!' Wiggin had to cling to the bar to make his demand. His head lolled from side to side, he had trouble shaping the words. He stood there unshaven, shouting his order.

Duke raised the wooden flap and came out from behind the bar. He took Wiggin by the elbow, feeling many eyes on them as he steered Annie's old husband towards the door.

Arthur Ogden watched, then grunted into his glass. Joe O'Hagan wiped his mouth with his sleeve. They couldn't help but make a comparison between the two men; Duke still sturdily built, wearing a crisp striped shirt under his dark waistcoat, vigour in his grasp. Wiggin, on the other hand, had never been much of a figure, even in his youth, and was now shrunken, bent and unkempt, his mind permanently fuddled by drink.

'Come on now, Willie, let's get you safely back home.' Duke never raised his voice an these occasions. In fact, he managed to suggest he was doing a man a favour by refusing to serve him. Even with Wiggin he was considerate, steering him out on to the street.

'You take your hands off me, filthy swine!' Wiggin roared. He exploded into a writhing mass of fists and elbows. He kicked, he staggered, he spat and thumped. 'I know you, Wilf Parsons! A man just has to come in for a little drink and you throw him out! Yes, I know you!'

Taken by surprise, Duke hesitated. Maybe Wiggin wasn't as far gone as they imagined. Annie still said he didn't know her, ranting and raving at her each time she went in to cook and clean. 'You know me, do you, Willie?' Duke turned him round to face him and stood him up straight.

Wiggin came out with a barrage of obscenities that made some of the nearby women shriek in mock horror. Rob left off talking to Tommy O'Hagan at his news stall to come to Duke's assistance. If necessary, they'd lift Wiggin clean off his feet and cart him down the court between them.

'That's the way, Willie. Easy does it.' Duke managed to swivel him in the right direction again. 'Just get one thing clear, will you? You won't get served a single drop in my pub, understand? Shouting and carrying on don't make no difference. Just don't come back and try it on no more.' He was only sorry he'd not got rid of the old nuisance a minute or two sooner, as Annie came towards them, a worried frown on her face.

Wiggin put his fists up again. 'Oh, you serve those you

like, no bother! I seen you. Same old Duke Parsons, serving right through the night. I seen your light. It always shines, long after closing time. Ha!' He raised a gnarled finger and pointed an inch away from Duke's face.

'Shut up!' Annie stepped in to take over from Duke. She grabbed Willie's elbow and shoved him on down the pavement. 'You just shut your noise, you hear!' God knew who was listening as he ranted on. 'I told you lots of times,' she muttered to Duke, 'if someone like Willie blabs, we're done for!'

Wiggin roared on down Paradise Court. 'We all know you ain't no angel, Wilf Parsons!' Children laughed, women backed away, seeing in Wiggin the terrible shape of things to come, unless their old men cut down drastically on the drinking. 'We know about you, Parsons! Refuse a man a drink at tea-time, and serve your pals right through the night!'

Annie bundled him down the street and into the tenement. She slammed the door behind them, worried to death about the after-hours serving. It just took one man, one enemy, to ruin Duke for good.

Back in the bar, the crowd of weekend drinkers closed over Wiggin's interruption as if it had never happened. Only one or two paused to comment. Tommy O'Hagan turned to Bertie Hill and expressed his usual opinion that Wiggin was a man who'd outlived his usefulness. He was sick of hearing him clattering about in the room below theirs, and thought it a shame that the old wreck should come between Annie and Duke, who'd never done anyone any harm. Now he was even issuing drunken threats. 'He belongs in the knacker's yard if you ask me,' Tommy said.

Hill raised his glass but said nothing.

Rob came in and leaned on the bar, winking at Ernie to

bring him a pint. 'I'll knock his block off before too long,' he promised. 'He ain't fit for nothing, and that's a fact.'

'People ain't animals. You can't cart them off to the knacker's yard, however much you feel like it.' Hill's tone was infuriatingly reasonable. 'It ain't right.'

'Oh, ain't it?' Rob replied. And, 'Oh, can't I? Well, we'll just have to see about that.' He admitted that he'd cheerfully strangle Wiggin if he thought it would solve anything. He swallowed down his beer in a couple of gulps and went on his way.

'Joke!' Tommy reminded Hill, recalling the landlord's old police background and noticing his dark look. 'Don't take no notice of Rob.'

Hill shrugged and drank on in silence. The waters closed over the event.

'Funny thing, that,' Arthur remarked to Dolly when she called in later that evening. 'Did you know, Duke had to chuck Wiggin out?'

Dolly gave a short laugh. 'That's life.' She pondered the situation with an ironic smile.

'Funny, though, when you think about it.' Arthur saw that Annie had popped back to help behind the bar as usual. No one could have told from looking at her and old Duke what the pair of them must be going through. They handled it well, considering.

Two weeks later, Tommy and Rob had cause to tackle the subject over again.

If there'd been any warning, any suggestion that Wiggin could do real damage, Rob said, they'd have done things differently. 'Only no one except Annie took him serious, see?' He was just coming to terms with events. The letter from the magistrates' court had arrived that morning, 20 June. 'It hit Pa like a bombshell,' Rob went on. 'And I still feel a bit shaky myself.'

'Are you sure Wiggin's your man?' Tommy could just make out from the official wording on the letter Rob had handed him that the coppers planned to drop down hard on poor old Duke. He made out the words 'summons', 'investigation', 'evidence'. There was no doubt, they were on to him with a vengeance.

'You heard him. He might be a useless old drunk, but he knows enough to give us a real headache round here. God knows what Pa can do about it now.'

Tommy shoved the letter back to Rob and leaned both elbows on the bar. George Mann had taken over the serving, with Ernie there as usual to help with the clearing away. There was no sign of either Duke or Annie. Regulars dropped in every now and then for a quick word of commiseration, but they drifted off again when they found Duke was missing. 'It's hit him pretty hard,' Dolly said to Charlie, who came in on his way to the Gem. 'I ain't never known him to leave the bar to George on a Friday night.'

'*Someone* gave the game away,' Rob was still insisting. 'And who's the first one that comes to mind?'

'Wiggin,' Charlie admitted. He didn't like to see the Parsonses in more trouble over this. 'What'll happen now, Rob? What does the summons mean exactly?'

But Rob was taken up by his own train of thought. 'You show me a pub in the whole of the East End that don't serve after hours!' He clenched his fist and smacked it down on the bar. 'We're forever getting warnings from the coppers and sticking them on the fire. Pa couldn't make ends meet if he stuck to licensing hours, for God's sake!'

Tommy, standing nearby, saw the light at last. He gave a faint whistle. 'Bleeding hell, Rob. You mean to say your old man could lose his licence over this?'

It took Duke himself several hours for this realization to sink in. While Rob and his friends fretted in the bar, he sat upstairs with Annie, motionless in his chair by the empty fireside. Hettie would soon be back from the dress shop. He'd have to explain all over again.

'Try looking on the bright side,' Annie begged. 'What if they can't prove nothing? Who'd take Wiggin's word in a court of law?'

'We can't be sure it was him.' Unlike Rob, Duke didn't want to jump to conclusions.

'No, but let's say Wiggin's word don't prove reliable, according to the magistrate . . .'

Duke shook his head. 'The police don't get up a summons without checking their facts,' he insisted. 'I reckon they already sent their men in for evidence. Someone we don't know. You seen anyone, Annie?'

She searched her memory. 'I can't think of no one, Duke.' She tried to build up his hopes because she knew the pub meant everything to him now. He'd already given up his marriage, Sadie had gone off with Richie Palmer, and now it was his home on the line! She couldn't go down the court, leaving him to despair.

'How long have I been here, Annie?'

'Thirty-five years. I remember it, Duke. Jess was just a little baby.'

'Well, I'm too old to change my ways now,' he sighed. 'What is it they reckon? Three score and ten years? I had my fair share, when you look at it that way.'

'Ain't nothing wrong with you!' she snapped. 'You'll go on for years yet!' She raised herself and walked to the window, looking out at the market traders packing up for the day. 'How long before we have to go to court exactly?'

'Two weeks.'

'Fourteen days to get something done,' she promised.

But Duke got up to join her. 'Ain't you forgetting something, Annie?'

She turned to look up at him.

'They caught me redhanded, remember?'

She threw her arms around his neck and held him tight. She willed him to fight back. She cursed Wiggin and their own carelessness.

Annie and Duke looked down together on the barrow boys trundling carts over the cobbles. They saw two of the youngest O'Hagan girls ducking in the gutter for bruised apples. A pianola tune drifted through the open window below, churning out a Viennese waltz above the hum of street life. She glanced up at his lined features, saw that his eyes were moist. She couldn't bear it if he lost everything because of Wiggin; wife, home, occupation all gone.

PART TWO

Suspicion

CHAPTER ELEVEN

June 1924

The whole of Paradise Court was up in arms when they heard what Wiggin had done.

'You know what this means, don't you?' Arthur Ogden sat on an upturned orange-box among the rows of young cabbages and leeks on his allotment.

Dolly, bent double over the tender plants, gave a short reply. 'Yes, it means no more drinking after hours. And a bleeding good thing too!' She stood up to roll back her sleeves and fix her hair.

'You don't mean that. Think about it, if Duke does get chucked out over this and a new man comes in, and that new man happens to be a stickler for the rules, what then?' Arthur groaned at the prospect of many early nights ahead.

'It'll do you no end of good,' his wife insisted. She eased her back after her labours. It was a fine summer's evening. Swallows darted overhead, an old black tomcat sat blinking on the fence, while in the background a train shuttled by. Dolly wiped her face with her apron. 'No, it ain't you I'm bothered about, Arthur. It's old Duke. What the bleeding hell's he gonna do if they take away his licence?'

There was no answer to this. Arthur sat silently brooding.

'I mean to say, it's the same as uprooting one of them cabbages and chucking it on the compost.' Dolly jabbed

141

with her trowel. 'If he goes, what's left for him except the scrapheap?' The idea of the old man minus his pub was unimaginable. 'It's his life, Arthur, you gotta admit.' She sighed and bent slowly to begin weeding once more.

'Maybe Annie will take him back?' Arthur sat, arms folded, contemplating the ripple of pink clouds in the eggshell sky.

Dolly shook her head. 'Never in a month of Sundays. There's Wiggin standing in the way. Don't ask me why, but Annie still sees herself as married to the old sod. She has old-fashioned views on the subject.'

Arthur changed tack. 'Well, then, he could go to live with one of his stuck-up, bleeding daughters.' He gathered phlegm, coughed and spat. 'That Frances, or that Jess.'

'Jess ain't stuck-up.' Dolly pointedly ignored his reference to Frances. 'Anyhow, that ain't the point. The thing is, what's an old man like him to do when they take away both his home and his job? Come to that, what's Rob and Ernie and Hettie gonna do?' She dug savagely at a dandelion root, heaving it free in a shower of earth. She flung it into a nearby barrow.

'Like I said, it ain't good news.' Arthur stood up. Talk of problems at the pub had helped him to work up a thirst.

'You can say that again. It's like an axe over their heads, and there ain't nothing they can do.' Dolly hacked away at another root.

'I think I'll just pop along there and see how he is,' Arthur said. 'I expect he'll need cheering up.' He took his cap from his pocket, unrolled it and put it on.

'Have one for me!' Dolly watched him go, meandering up Meredith Court past the blank windows of Coopers' Drapery Stores. That was the other big news of the week: Jack Cooper had closed down and thrown eighty-five workers on the dole. On Monday the bailiffs had moved in and cleared the place. Not that she wasted an ounce of pity on the shop owner. He'd been a pig in his time, and Dolly herself had rowed with him on Amy's behalf. The son, Teddy, had behaved badly towards Amy, and Jack Cooper, quite wrongly in her opinion, had stood by him. That was all water under the bridge: Teddy Cooper was just one more dead hero, and Amy had got on in life in spite of the setback. Still, Dolly wasn't sad to see the shop go under. Something better would come in its place. Meanwhile, though, half of Duke Street was out of work.

When Arthur arrived at the Duke, he found Tommy O'Hagan standing his pa a drink, and soon muscled in on the act. Tommy was good for a pint these days. He earned a pretty penny on his stalls, selling daily newspapers on one, and a range of brushes, paints and varnishes, pastes and wallpapers on a new stall on the corner of Duke Street and Union Street. Soon he planned to open a little shop and call it The Home Decorator. Arthur admired his get-up-and-go.

Joe O'Hagan stood at the bar, his baleful eye fixed on Duke. Even as he picked up his glass and sipped the froth, he kept the landlord in his sights. 'It happens to the best of us!' he announced, apropos of nothing.

'What does, Pa?' Tommy pushed back his hat and drank a long draught of cool beer.

'Getting the push. I've had it all my life, and it ain't pleasant, believe me.' Joe's Irish accent seemed to give his bleak words a musical edge. 'I've had the push so many times I lost count. The railways, the canals, they given me the push when I was a young man. I was a fine figure in them days.' He tugged at the dark brown liquid, pulling it down his scrawny throat in gulps. 'The bottle factory, and the cardboard box factory and the cabinet makers, they given me the push in my time. And now Jack Cooper.' He followed Duke's activities behind the bar, inviting him to come over and share the misery of being put out of work. With the closure of Coopers', Joe had lost his part-time portering job. 'Who'll take me on now?' he complained.

Duke came across at last. 'What's that, Joe? You ain't moaning, are you?' He winked at Tommy.

'He is, and he's giving us a earache.' Tommy had had a lifetime of his father's grumbling while his mother, Mary, struggled on.

'What, you ain't sixty yet, are you, Joe? There's plenty of life in the old dog yet!' Duke stacked glasses ready for the evening trade.

The worn-out little Irishman gave a hollow laugh. 'Tell that to them as pays the wages.' And he began another long, self-pitying lament.

But Tommy cut him off. 'Stow it, Pa. Duke don't want to hear it. Things ain't exactly rosy for him neither.'

Duke sniffed. 'You can say that again.'

Arthur remembered the reason he'd called in. 'How's things, Duke?' he asked in a tone of deep commiseration.

'They been better, thanks, Arthur.' It was four days since the police summons had landed on his mat. Duke managed business as usual, but only just, as he felt the clock ticking towards his court appearance on the fourth of July.

'Any news of who dropped you in it?' Arthur's nose for gossip was almost as sharp as Dolly's.

'Nothing definite.'

'It was Wiggin,' Joe said with finality. 'Everyone knows it was him. We hear him, day in, day out, cursing and swearing and calling you all the names under the sun, Duke. He's the one, you can bet your life.'

'Ain't none of us will have nothing to do with him,' Arthur assured Duke. 'We sent him to Coventry the day it happened. Ain't no one said a word to him since.'

'Much good may that do.' Tommy polished off his pint and pulled his hat down on to his forehead. 'No, what we need is for someone to finish him off good and proper. Bang goes your witness, bang goes your case!'

'Now, now, less of that!' Duke shook his head.

'I was only trying to look on the bright side.' Tommy's wide grey eyes opened still further. He gave a wink and sauntered out through the swing-door.

'Take no notice,' Joe advised. 'With a bit of luck, Wiggin will drink himself to death before you get to court, Duke.'

'He'd best get a move on,' Arthur pointed out. 'He's only got just over a week.'

Duke went and pulled a pint for a new customer. He told George to tap a fresh barrel, then gave Ernie the first of his evening chores. 'Put fresh sawdust in them spittoons, and sweep around a bit, there's a good lad. Let's have the place spick and span.' He himself checked the gas mantles. With a grunt of satisfaction he rang up fourpence on the till. They were good and ready. He pulled out his watch; it was half past seven on Tuesday, 24 June.

While Duke stuck to business as usual, the rest of the family racked their brains over what to do. Though the taxi work kept Rob busy as ever, he made a special journey over to Maurice's house one night, soon after the bad news had come. It was late. There were few lights on along the tree-lined streets as Rob pulled up and rang the bell.

Jess came to the door to let him in. The strain of worrying over Duke told in her pale face and serious expression. She kissed her brother's cheek, took his hat and led him into the kitchen, where Maurice sat at the table in his shirt-sleeves, looking dog-tired after a long day at work.

'What do you reckon?' Rob pulled out a chair and joined him, sighing deeply. 'It don't look good, do it?'

Maurice tilted his head sideways, his sharp features half in shadow. 'Licensing laws are pretty straightforward, to tell you the truth. If you're caught breaking them, you land in the cart good and proper.' Jess had spilled out the facts to him as soon as Hettie had rung her on the previous Friday night. As far as he could see, Duke had dropped himself right in it.

'Don't say that,' Jess put in, quiet but tense. She handed Rob a small glass of whisky. 'Rob ain't come all this way just to hear that. We know Pa's in the cart. What we have to do is work out a way of getting him out.'

Maurice nodded. He, too, realized how much his father-in-law *was* the pub, and the pub was Duke. 'Right, let's think. First off, who owns the licence?' he asked Rob.

'The brewery. Pa's a tenant and he's a bleeding good one. The best there is. They know him. There's never been a scrap of trouble in more than thirty years!' Rob grew hot in Duke's defence.

'Till now.' Maurice went briskly on. 'The chances are, the brewery won't want no trouble over it themselves. They'll let Duke take the blame, never mind the profits he's put their way, and they'll just sit by till it's all blown over.'

'Oh!' Jess frowned. 'Typical, ain't it? Not a bit of trouble for thirty-five years! Then, soon as Pa steps out of line, they drop him!' She was close to tears. Why couldn't Maurice be a bit more positive?

'There *is* one thing.' Maurice worked things through. 'The brewery will want to stay out of it, right? They'll let

Duke go to court next week and lose his licence. Then they'll issue a new licence to someone else, a new landlord, and get him into the Duke as quick as ever they can.'

Jess put both hands to her ears. 'Oh, Maurice, don't!'

'No, hang on a minute. They won't like it one little bit. It gives them a problem, see, if they have to get a new man. But if we could find a way of helping them out of their difficulty; if we can find a new landlord for them before it comes to court, I think they'd jump at the chance!'

'Find the brewery a new landlord?' Rob echoed. 'Either I'm dim, Maurice, or you're round the bend, pal.' He stood up in disgust.

'No, listen. 'Course, we don't want just any old landlord.' Maurice spread his hands flat on the table. 'Look, say Duke is bound to lose his licence on the fourth? It's what they call a foregone conclusion. Well, we have to get to the brewery before then and say there's no need to go as far as court. Duke agrees to give up the tenancy.'

Jess jumped up and turned away.

'No.' Rob stopped her from leaving. 'I think I'm with you, Maurice. If the brewery can keep their noses clean, they might listen to what we have to say. But it depends on the name we come up with for the new landlord, don't it? Someone who'll let Duke stay on, someone who wants to take on the licence in name only, but let Pa run things same as always?'

Maurice nodded, his face broke into a smile. 'What do you think?'

'Good one!' Rob saw it straight away. 'You ain't thinking of volunteering for the job, are you, Maurice?'

Jess sat down again, listening hard. She turned her head from her brother to her husband and back.

Maurice shook his head. 'I got enough on my plate.

Anyhow, I wouldn't go down too well with the brewery. My face don't fit,' he said wryly. In the East End, immigrant Jews weren't considered good landlord material. 'And the name ain't right. No, I was thinking more of you, Rob old son. You're on the spot, see. You know the ropes. If you ask me, you're a good bet to put up to the brewery. What do you say?'

Rob smacked his palm on to the table. 'Bleeding brilliant!' He beamed at Jess. 'Sis, you're married to a flipping genius!'

Maurice, too, was pleased with himself. 'I'll set up a time to go and see them. You and me, Rob, we'll go along together. Let's see what they got to say.'

'What will you tell Pa?' Jess asked.

'What do you think?' Rob looked back at her for advice.

'Don't tell him nothing yet,' she decided. 'It'd be cruel to raise his hopes before we pull it off.'

Maurice nodded. 'Wear your best suit,' he said as he showed Rob to the door. 'I'll telephone you tomorrow.' They shook hands. 'Let's try to keep it in the family and keep everyone happy.' But he lowered his voice for a word of caution. 'Don't bank on nothing yet, Rob. We're doing our best, but we got an uphill struggle to keep Duke where he belongs.'

He went inside to help Jess clear away for the night. She was warm towards him as they got into bed, and she lay close, resting inside the crook of his arm, one hand on his chest.

'Better now?' he asked gently.

She nodded. 'It don't seem right. How can life be so cruel to Pa? He ain't done nothing to deserve it.'

'No, he ain't.' Maurice kissed her hair.

'And how can *I* be happy with Pa in trouble?'

He held her tight. He would ring up and try to pull a few strings with the brewery, he would do what he could. He liked it better when Jess relied on him and turned to him for help. He kissed her warm face and lips, remembering how it was in the early days; the trust between them, the unbroken passion and tenderness.

'And how are *you* bearing up?' Dolly leaned across the bar to grasp Annie's hand. It was Saturday evening and the usual singalong hadn't picked up, so Dolly gave up her vocal efforts to come and have a chat with her beleaguered old friend.

'Better since you stopped making that horrible din.' Annie wasn't about to succumb to Dolly's sentimental overture. 'Dame Nellie Melba you definitely ain't!'

A couple of young lads standing nearby in their cheap suits and trilby hats caught on. They laughed, then squawked in imitation of Dolly's operatic rendering of 'Sister Susie'. 'More like Vesta Tilley,' one scoffed, referring to Dolly's deep voice. 'Only she ain't wearing no trousers!'

'Very funny.' Dolly did her best to ignore them and turned back to Annie. 'I was saying to Charlie earlier on, ain't it a shame Wiggin had to show up when he did? He set the cat among the pigeons all right.' Dolly was dressed up for her night out in a white lace collar and a bottle-green dress of crushed velvet, whose ample skirt took up much room at the bar. She leaned closer to Annie. 'I think you're a saint to put up with it like you do. I'm a churchgoer myself, but I admit, I wouldn't give him house-room if he showed up on my doorstep and I was you.'

'Well, he didn't, and you ain't.' Still Annie was reluctant to be drawn into Dolly's gossip trap. She had too much on her mind as it was.

Undeterred, Dolly went full steam ahead. 'Especially after what he done to you, Annie!' She tutted in all directions, hoping to enlist sympathy for Annie's cause. But all she succeeded in doing was catching Frances Wray's cool gaze. Frances had been tea-time visiting and was just on her way out. She'd popped into the bar to say goodbye to Annie.

Dolly Ogden wasn't fond of Frances. 'I say she ain't natural!' she would hold forth to Arthur on many occasions. Between them the couple had set up a small campaign against the best educated of the Parsons girls, ever since her support for the window smashers way back before the war. 'It ain't nice for a woman to join marches and behave the way she does.' And when she left the pub to go off and marry Billy Wray, it was their opinion that the street was better off without her snooty face poking its nose in everywhere. Dolly felt Frances's disapproving gaze fall on her now, and it provoked her. 'I was just telling Annie, Frances, I wouldn't give Wiggin house-room. Not after what he went and did!'

Frances didn't respond at first, but when Dolly bustled across, all green velvet and lavender-water, to accost her face to face, she turned and sighed. 'What's that, Dolly?'

'I'm only saying what every single soul in this court says!' She rose up and defended herself. 'Wiggin ruined everything for Annie, we all know that. I'm just expressing my sympathy, that's all!' Two or three drinks had made Dolly indiscreet and raised the volume of her voice.

'And I'm sure she's grateful.' Frances noticed that Annie had made herself scarce. She tried to make her own excuses and leave.

But Dolly seized her wrist. 'Look here, Frances, the people round here, we care about Annie and your pa, so don't think we don't!'

Aware of several girls from the market sitting nearby, all ears, Frances tried to pull away. 'I know it,' she said quietly, trying to unwrap Dolly's fingers.

'Well, we want to know how you can stand by and let it happen.' Dolly's temper suddenly lit up. Frances Wray was a cold fish all right.

'We're not just standing by, Dolly. But what can we do?' At last Frances freed herself. She felt knocked back by Dolly's burst of anger, but separate from it. It was nothing to do with anything that she, Frances, had said or done.

'You can try getting them two back together for a start!' the older woman's voice fell into a stage-whisper. 'Don't you see how miserable it is for them?'

Frances blushed self-consciously, feeling all eyes on them. 'Hush, Dolly. Anyhow, this ain't none of your business,' she said abruptly.

This was lighting the blue touchpaper as far as Dolly was concerned. 'Ain't none of my business?' Her voice shot up several decibels once more. She turned to address their audience. 'Ain't I known Duke since he first came here?' she demanded. 'Ain't I known Annie even longer than that? And Lady High-and-Mighty here has the cheek to say it ain't none of my business!'

'I never meant it like that.' Frances felt herself go red. 'I'm sorry, Dolly.'

Dolly ignored her. 'I've known Annie, girl and woman, and it breaks my heart to see what Wiggin's done to her.' Real tears came to her eyes.

'I said I was sorry.' It was Frances's turn to take Dolly by the wrist and lead her to a quiet chair. 'Calm down. Just sit quiet a bit and tell me what you think we should do.' She looked nervously over her shoulder in case Annie or her pa showed up in the bar.

It took a few seconds for Dolly's sobs to subside. 'I ain't made of stone,' she protested.

'No more am I,' Frances said quietly.

Dolly looked up at last.

'We're all going through it, believe me. Ernie, for a start. He's beginning to panic.' Frances herself stayed awake at night, failing to find a solution to any of their problems.

'You want to get Annie and Duke back together?'

'I'd give an arm and a leg to help. But Annie won't listen. She says the law's the law, and the law says she ain't married to Pa no more!'

'And you've given her a talking to?' Dolly was sniffing and coming round from her outburst.

''Course I have. We all have. She won't shift. And Pa agrees with her, bless him.' Frances sat upright, her pale colouring highlighting her delicate features, her bobbed hair swept straight back from her high forehead.

'But have you got her to think straight?' Dolly became more secretive and urgent as she leaned across. 'You know, about how her and Wiggin got together in the first place?'

Frances was puzzled. 'How do you mean?'

Dolly stared back. 'You mean, you don't know? She ain't told you?' It had never occurred to her that the family didn't know the full story, that Annie had kept it quiet.

'Ain't told me what, for God's sake? What are you on about, Dolly?' Frances was exasperated by the big eyes and exaggerated whispers. 'Tell me straight, was there something fishy?'

'Why not ask her?' For once Dolly's lips were sealed.

'How can I if I don't know what you're on about?' Frances battled to stay calm. The pub had filled up. Duke was behind the bar now, but as yet there was no sign of Annie.

'We was sworn to secrecy,' Dolly declared. 'All them years ago. I ain't saying another word.' She gathered her dignity and stood up. 'Like you said, Frances, it ain't none of my business.'

'Dolly!' Frances sprang up to restrain her.

'All right then.' Swiftly Dolly changed her mind and whispered in Frances's ear. 'Annie was just a girl, mind. She weren't a Southwark girl born and bred. Her family was over in Hoxton, I think. Anyhow, when she came to live in the court she was already hitched up with Wiggin. We never took to them, not at first. Things was said behind their backs and Wiggin treated her bad from the start.'

Frances sat Dolly down and forced herself to be patient. She was totally in the dark about this.

'We took to Annie all right when he was away at sea. She kept things nice and clean and she never went on about her other half. She never told us nothing about herself neither; she was close on that score. Only, the story went around that Wiggin weren't her first husband, that she'd been married before.'

Frances shook her head in disbelief. 'How could she? She ain't never said nothing to us.'

'She wouldn't.' Dolly's stare held secret significance.

'Why not?'

''Cos the story was she'd been married to a man called Kearney. He married her when she was sixteen and he was no better than Wiggin turned out to be second time around. They lived like rats in a cellar in Hoxton, and he used to knock her about, and one day when he was short of money for a drink, he took Annie along to the market, met up with his old pal, Wiggin, and he sold her! They said Wiggin bought her for twenty-seven shillings, which was a tidy sum in them days.'

Frances gasped. 'Oh my God, it ain't true!'

'Calm down, I ain't said there's been a murder or nothing.' To Dolly, it was one of the things that went on in the old poverty-stricken days. A bargain would be struck, the second marriage would even be given the respectability of a forged certificate.

'But why didn't she tell us?'

'It ain't something to blow your horn over, is it?'

'But don't she see what it'd mean?' Frances began to get over her shock.

Dolly shook her head. 'No, she don't. I ain't that clear myself. All I know is, it went on, and a lot of women got trapped that way. It ain't very nice, but there it is.'

'And what happened to Kearney?' Things could be even worse in one sense, if Dolly's version of events was true.

'I haven't a clue. You'd better ask her that. Choose your time, Frances, and get her to tell it all. You're the one can do it if anyone can. And you're the one who can sort out this mess for her.'

Frances took a deep breath. 'This needs thinking through.'

Dolly smoothed her skirt and bodice. 'I'd do more than think about it if I was you. And don't take too long about it.' She gazed across at Duke's sturdy figure; as much a fixture round here as the bar itself or the bevelled, fancy mirrors. 'Let's get Duke and Annie back together,' she insisted. 'It'd be a start at any rate.'

*

While Frances hesitated over how best to approach Annie on the delicate topic of her marriage to Wiggin, Sadie put in a brief appearance at the Duke.

She chose a time when she knew Rob would be absent, preferring to avoid him, but anxious to call in to see how Duke, Hettie and Ernie were bearing up. First she spoke to Hettie on the phone. 'Will Pa want to see me?' she asked. "Cos I can stay away if he'd rather. I don't want to cause no more trouble.'

'Pa ain't mad at you, Sadie,' Hettie assured her. 'He just wishes you and Rob could make things up.'

'Well, we can't, Ett. Not after what he did to Richie.' This was a firm new principle in Sadie's life, that she wouldn't talk to Rob again so long as he refused to apologize for what he'd done.

'Come over anyway. Rob's out seeing someone. Pa's resting.' It was the Monday of the week of the court case, and stalemate. They waited and worried in a kind of limbo. 'Come and help cheer him up,' Hettie said.

Sadie arrived looking as neat and pretty as ever. There was colour in her cheeks and a liveliness about her as she embraced Hettie and Ernie at the top of the stairs, then went into the living-room to see Duke.

'Surprise, Pa!' She stepped forward, holding out her arms, still half afraid of a lukewarm reception.

Duke held her for a second or two before he let go, then he looked her up and down. 'My, but you're like your ma,' he said quietly. 'Didn't I always say you was like Pattie? Now, Ett, put the kettle on while Sadie makes herself at home. Sit down here and put your feet up and tell me all your news.'

Sadie felt swamped by a rush of emotions. Where she thought she'd feel defensive over Richie and angry with

Rob, keeping a distance from her old life because of it, she found now that she was overwhelmed with homesickness. She'd settled in with Richie in his Mile End tenement, and she was deeply in love with him, but she saw now what it was to have her heart pulled in more than one direction. Duke was old, she realized. He put on a brave front, but he was old and hurting badly. He was tired and sad, and she wanted to help. 'How are you coping, Pa?' She took a cup of tea from Hettie and set it down in the hearth.

'Bearing up.' He eased himself back into his chair.

'And have you got any plans?'

'Not yet. Let's see what happens on Friday first.'

Hettie explained that if the magistrates ruled against them, they would be given a short time to make other arrangements.

'But does it mean you'll have to move away from Duke Street?' Sadie glanced at the familiar objects; the clock on the mantelpiece, a pair of matching Chinese vases with a blue design.

'Let's wait and see,' Duke insisted. 'Listen, girl, I ain't gonna think about it till Friday, and that's that. Just tell us how you're getting along. How's work? How's your young man?'

'I'm fine, Pa. Work's the same.' She blushed. 'Richie's fine too. He looks after me, so no need to worry on that score.' The young lovers were still in the honeymoon period of fulfilling one another's wishes, being there when needed, bringing home little presents of cufflinks and brooches. Their two rooms now looked bright and cheerful. Sadie had imprinted her presence in the shape of new white curtains, proper plates and cups, a pole across the bedroom alcove to hang her clothes. Richie looked on with bemusement at this advancing domestication, but he let her proceed, knowing it pleased her.

Duke listened and nodded. 'He's good to you, then?'

'He is, Pa.' Sadie's face broke into a radiant smile. You have to know him to see how good. He ain't one for talking, and he don't have much yet in the way of belongings, but he loves me, I know he does.'

'Well then, we'll see.'

'Thanks, Pa.' Sadie sprang from her chair and hugged him once more.

'What for, girl?' He smiled as he patted her shoulder.

'For not staying mad at me. For letting me come home to visit.'

Duke sighed. 'Ah, Sadie, don't you know I miss my little girl? It's lovely to see you looking happy, ain't it, Ett? It's one less thing for us to worry about.'

They settled down to talk in the old, easy way, almost forgetting their pressing troubles as Ernie finished his chores and joined them, and Annie came up the court with fresh scones and strawberry jam.

Sadie was long gone, back to her new home in Mile End, when Rob returned home. The summer evening had turned to soft drizzle as he trod his well-worn path from the depot up Duke Street, but he was oblivious to it. There was something lifeless in his walk, a bleakness in his gaze, an overall impression of defeat in the way he reached the pub and climbed the stairs.

He'd set off that afternoon with Maurice to see the brewers, their hopes high. Maurice had arranged everything; they arrived at four on the dot and were shown into a room whose oak-panelled walls were lined with hunting prints, its leather chairs and polished tables lending an atmosphere of a gentlemen's club. Rob was dressed up smart, according to his brother-in-law's advice, hoping to impress the brewery boss as a likely candidate to take on the problematic tenancy at the Duke. They had to wait ten minutes for the manager called Wakeley to arrive.

He was a tall, thickset man, built in the mould of one of the grey drayhorses that pulled the beer along the cobbled streets. He wore a good tweed suit with a high-buttoning waistcoat. His handshake was firm, his eyes wary.

Maurice opened up the conversation. He spoke well, reminding Mr Wakeley of the good service Duke had done for the brewery over many years. He told him that Duke was well liked and respected in the community, predicting a fall-off in trade if he were to be ousted.

Wakeley listened and nodded. 'But,' he said frankly, 'Mr Parsons seems to have overstepped the mark on this occasion. With the police involved, there isn't much we can do, I'm afraid.'

Maurice leaned across the table. 'We know that, Mr Wakely. And we can see the hole you're in.'

Wakeley nodded. 'It brings us into disrepute, you see. The case will come up in the local paper. It don't look good for the brewery to have its landlords seen to be flouting the law.'

'Right!' Maurice seized his chance. 'So we've come with a proposal that'll help to avoid all that.'

The manager inclined his head. 'Is that so?'

'Yes. Say Duke were to give up the pub without the fuss of going to court? That gets you out of any bad publicity, see. But say then, Duke goes. What happens to trade? It plummets. You lose in the long run.'

Wakeley frowned. 'I don't see where this is leading, Mr Leigh.'

'You see, the Duke of Wellington public house without

Duke ain't the answer.' Maurice felt Rob shift uneasily beside him and pushed on. 'So we came up with an alternative.'

Wakeley leaned on the table and pressed his fingertips together. 'Which is?'

'Which is that you hand on the tenancy to someone who keeps the trade rolling in. Someone connected to Duke.' Maurice turned to Rob. 'That's why Robert here came along with me. We talked it over, and Rob would like to take on the tenancy. That way, Duke don't get turfed out, you keep your trade, and everyone's happy!'

The manager seemed to consider the proposal. 'Keep it in the family, eh?' He turned to scrutinize Rob. 'You're fit enough to take on the job?' he inquired.

Rob nodded. 'If you mean the leg, it ain't stopped me so far.'

'And what is your present business, Mr Parsons?'

Rob couldn't tell from the manager's unsmiling face how things were going. He described the taxi firm he'd set up with Walter Davidson. He pointed out how much time he'd put into the pub over the years, organizing the cellar with George Mann, serving behind the bar.

Wakeley listened. 'It might work,' he admitted. He offered them both cigars from a fancy silver box. They refused, but he took one for himself and rolled it between his fingers. 'It's a pity you didn't bring it forward sooner.'

Robert's heart sank. 'How's that?'

'Well, the fact is, Mr Leigh, Mr Parsons, I wanted a chance to meet you in any case. The brewery has its own ideas on Friday's court business, naturally, and we had intended to approach Wilf Parsons to ask him to step down on a voluntary basis.' He was brisk, matter-of-fact.

Maurice leaped in. 'Let us talk to him, then. Rob and me

can get him to listen. I think we can get him to step down as long as Rob can take over.'

'Ah!' Wakeley sat back. 'There's the rub.'

'What? Ain't I good enough?' Rob showed his exasperation.

'Of course. It's not that. Only, our proposal that Mr Parsons should step down of his own accord is based on a different outcome.'

'What's he on about, Maurice?' Rob got to his feet and walked the length of the room. 'Come clean, Mr Wakeley. What is it you're saying?'

Wakeley looked him straight in the eye. 'The fact is, Mr Parsons, we have someone else in mind.'

Maurice tapped the edge of the table with his fingertips. 'A different landlord?'

'Who? Who the bleeding hell can you put in Pa's place?' Rob's control snapped. So much for dressing up and playing the part. 'They got another plan in mind all along,' he said to Maurice in disgust.

'Now, I can't tell you that, Mr Parsons. You wouldn't expect me to. But we want a fresh start; move with the times, that sort of thing.' Wakeley stood up. He clipped the end of his cigar then turned to Maurice. 'No, the best thing you can do, Mr Leigh, is to go back to your father-in-law, explain the brewery's point of view, and advise him to go without a fuss. *Before* Friday, if possible.' He stood firm behind clouds of blue cigar smoke.

Rob took a sharp intake of breath. 'Let's get out of here,' he said to Maurice. He felt stifled. 'Ain't no point hanging round.'

Maurice conceded defeat. They went out of the office, pointedly refusing to shake Wakeley's hand or make any promises on their part.

'We was set up!' Rob said angrily as they found their way

out of the nearest exit, through the stables lined with heavy tack. 'If they want us to do their dirty work, they can think again.'

Two great shire horses stirred restlessly inside their bays. Maurice shook his head. They crossed a wide yard towards the iron gates overlooking a railway siding. 'I gotta go back and tell Jess,' he said, not relishing the task. 'What you gonna do?'

Rob sagged forwards, hands in pockets, shoulders stooped. 'I'll go and tell Pa to expect the worst. There ain't no way he can win now.'

'We done our best.' Maurice turned his starter-handle. The car fired. 'We can say that.'

'And it ain't good enough.' Rob climbed into his taxi.

The two cars slid into the crowd of bicycles and pedestrians filing out of the brewery gates to the sound of the hooter that signalled the end of the working day.

CHAPTER TWELVE

The bad news filtered down Paradise Court that the brewery didn't intend to stick up for Duke when he went to court.

Charlie Ogden met Katie O'Hagan on the market and told her that it was all up; Duke had seen the writing on the wall. He'd admitted defeat. Charlie had got the news from Walter Davidson, who'd got it straight from Rob Parsons.

'He ain't gonna fight?' Katie was devastated. She was a fiery slip of a girl, with a green tinge to her eyes and her father's wide, Irish mouth. Undersized, but making up for her lack of height with non-stop activity and determination, she regarded the Parsons set-up as the ideal home she'd never had. Duke was a rock in the neighbourhood. He ran the pub like clockwork, never took sides in petty quarrels and looked on his family with affectionate pride. And in Katie's eyes, Hettie was an angel of mercy, a saint. 'Does that mean he'll have to pack up and go?'

'Duke's finished,' Charlie told her. 'Ain't nothing he can do.'

She passed on the news to her ma and pa. Joe cursed Wiggin. 'Who they gonna get to fill Duke's shoes? That's what I'd like to know.'

'. . . a new broom?' Dolly Ogden listened to Mary's account with rising scorn. 'Who they trying to kid? Listen,

162

they got the best landlord there is in Duke Parsons.' It was almost unheard of for her not to be first on the scene when a new development occurred. 'And you say Duke ain't gonna fight no more?' she shouted at Mary, as if it were her fault.

'That's according to Katie.' Mary was on her way to deliver a calico sack of clean table linen to Henshaws' when she bumped into Dolly. 'She says they tried talking to the brewery, but they didn't want to know. They got someone else in mind.'

Dolly mouthed Mary's last words to herself, then exploded aloud once more. 'Who the bleeding hell can they get in Duke's place?' she demanded. Then she stormed up to the market to have her say among her women friends. 'The brewery's dropped Duke in it,' she reported. 'They're kicking him out after all these years. It's a bleeding disgrace!' Dolly overlooked the little matter of serving after hours. Who could blame Duke for giving people what they wanted?

Next day, the Thursday, Frances came across to Duke Street to talk things over with Hettie. She still hadn't felt able to broach the important subject with Annie, finding the problem over the licence enough to deal with at any given time. The sisters sat in the living-room together while the business of the pub went on below.

'Is he thinking straight?' Frances asked. They talked in hushed tones, their eyes dark with worry. 'Has he thought what he's gonna do after tomorrow?'

Hettie was dressed in uniform, ready to go out. Her bonnet lay on the table, her Quaker-plain jacket was buttoned to the chin. 'I don't know, Fran, it's like he can't bring himself to think about it. I asked him yesterday after Rob came back from the brewery, should I look round for another place for us? And he just looked up at me with dying eyes. Yes, like he wants to pack up and die.' Hettie's eyes filled with tears. 'I been praying and asking God's help, but I ain't getting no answers.' She sobbed on Frances's shoulder.

'Hush, we'll sort something out, Ett. Just hush, my dear. Don't you cry.' Frances's self-restraint cracked under the strain of comforting Hettie. They sobbed quietly for a few minutes, to the sound of doors swinging, glasses clinking, people drinking in the bar below.

Then Frances blew her nose and went down the court in search of Annie. She needed to tell her that Duke had agreed that she and Hettie should compose a letter to send to the magistrates, admitting his offence of serving after hours and agreeing to give up his licence. Everyone understood, after listening to Rob, that all was lost. Now Frances wanted to spare her father the unnecessary distress of appearing in court.

She didn't find Annie in her own little terraced house, but she was still anxious to explain the latest development to her face to face, before it had time to reach her in a buzz of rumour. So she went on from Annie's house to the tenement, expecting to find her busy tidying up at Wiggin's place.

Frances had never before ventured into number five Eden House, the misnamed tenement where Wiggin had holed up with Annie's support. She disliked the feel of the whole building in fact, objecting to the lack of privacy whenever she came to visit the O'Hagans on the upstairs floor; the dark, bare corridors, the peeling plaster. For the inhabitants it was a poor sort of life, overlooked by the tall walls of a furniture factory at the back, with one toilet shared between all the tenants on each floor. As Frances went under the crumbling stone entrance and down some steps to the semi-basement rooms at the back, she instinctively pulled her cardigan around her and knocked briskly at the shabby door marked number five.

She stood and waited. There was someone in there, she was sure. 'Hello. Annie, is that you?' Frances shivered in the damp, cold corridor. She knocked again.

Inside she heard a shuffling sound of something heavy being dragged across a bare floor.

'Mr Wiggin?' Frances's suspicions were aroused. It seemed he didn't intend to answer the door. 'Is Annie there, please? It's Frances Wray. I need to speak to Annie.'

'I don't know you!' Wiggin's muffled voice came back at last.

Frances heard more grunts and gasps as he shifted the heavy object towards the door. 'I tried Annie's place. She ain't there. I was hoping to catch her. It's very important.'

There was a stream of abuse as Wiggin clattered around inside the room. The message came through loud and clear; he didn't want to be disturbed.

Frances backed off in distaste, then she set her head at a determined angle. 'Ain't no use calling me them names, Mr Wiggin,' she retorted. 'I heard them all before. They don't bother me.'

Wiggin responded by throwing open the door. He clutched on to it to peer out at Frances, a respectable figure in the fawn cardigan and skirt looking him straight in the eye. He swayed unsteadily, growled and spat out phlegm at her neatly shod feet.

Frances stepped quickly back, out of reach. 'I want to know, have you seen Annie?' she persisted. 'Ain't she dropped by with your breakfast today?'

Wiggin's eyes were red, his breath stank of strong drink. He tottered in the doorway, cursing Frances for coming there. 'Annie-this! Annie-that!' he minced, with his top lip curled. 'I ain't seen Annie. Annie don't live here. See for yourself!' He flung open the door, overbalanced and fell against Frances.

She caught him by the shoulders, filled with disgust, but shocked at how little he weighed. He was skin and bone, easy to drag inside the room and pull on to a poor bed in one corner. There were signs of Annie's efforts; clean curtains at the window, a tidy grate. But Wiggin seemed to have been on the rampage, scattering bread and milk across the floor, dragging an old chest out of the alcove by the hearth. As Frances eased the old man on to his bed, the smell coming off him made her feel sick. He collapsed on his back, wheezing and cursing.

'Does Annie know the state you're in?' she said coldly. 'Has she gone for the doctor?'

Wiggin's chest heaved and erupted. Frances realized with horror that he was laughing. His thin lips stretched back, showing ulcerated gums that were red-raw. He clutched his chest, convulsed with unseemly laughter.

'It ain't funny.' Frances made a snap decision to leave him where he was, noticing an empty bottle by the bed and another half-empty one on .the mantelpiece. Satisfied that he had left off laughing and subsided into a lethargic stupor, she quickly closed his door and fled.

Now alarm bells rang, not just for Wiggin. Frances had to find out where Annie had got to. Coming up the court, she bumped into Patrick O'Hagan, a boy of about thirteen who played truant and loitered his life away in the alleys and courts. He nodded when Frances rushed by and asked him if he'd seen Annie lately.

'When?' Frances grabbed his arm. 'Which way did she go?'

'Ten minutes since,' Patrick guessed. 'She went home.'

'But I tried her door. Are you sure?'

The boy nodded. 'Sure I'm sure.'

Frances turned on the spot and headed down the street towards Annie's house again. Why hadn't Annie answered her door? Why had Wiggin laughed? She mentioned Annie going to fetch the doctor and he croaked his delight. She knocked hard at Annie's door for a second time. She tried the knob. It turned in her grasp.

'Annie?' Frances hesitated on the doorstep. She called gently, 'It's me, Frances. Are you in?'

'I can't come and see you now, Frances.' Annie's voice drifted down the narrow stairs. 'I'm upstairs having a lie-down.'

This was unheard of. 'I'm coming up.' She mounted the bottom step.

'Leave me alone, there's a good girl. I'm just resting.'

'Ain't you heard me knock before, Annie? I need to talk.' Frances carried on until she came to the landing.

Annie's bedroom door opened. She came out fully dressed, her face averted. She trembled and reached out to the banister for support. 'I didn't want no one to see me,' she whispered.

There was a gash across her left eyebrow, an inch long, just missing the eye. A trickle of blood still ran down her cheek. The eye itself had swollen and begun to bruise. Frances stopped in her tracks. 'Oh, Annie!' she whispered.

'You found me out, Fran.' Annie tried to smile.

'Did Wiggin do this?'

'I slipped. I slipped and fell awkward against the mantelpiece.'

Frances felt herself turn cold with anger against Wiggin. She went up to her stepmother and led her gently back to bed. 'Don't stick up for him,' she pleaded. 'Not right now.'

Annie sighed. 'He had a bottle by the bed. I wanted to take it away from him. I asked him how he came by it.' Her account began, slow and flat. She was in a state of shock. 'He got his hand on it first, he held it by the neck and brought it down on my head, just here.' She pointed with a trembling finger. 'I must have blacked out for a bit. When I came to, he was panicking, trying to pull the old chest across to the door. I got up and out in the nick of time.'

'Just rest, Annie. Don't say no more.' Frances stroked her forehead. 'I'm so sorry!' She crooned until the trembling stopped and Annie was able to rest her head on the pillow. 'Shall I go for the doctor, dear?'

'No need for that,' Annie protested. 'But Wiggin might need him. He's set on drinking himself to death, I think.'

'Leave that for now.' Frances helped Annie to loosen the neck of her blouse and slip between the sheets. 'Put yourself first for a change.' She took off her shoes and put them under the bed. 'I gotta talk to you about Wiggin, Annie.'

'Later,' came the faint plea.

'No, now. You gotta rest and listen to me. I heard a story about him the other day.'

'Who from?' Annie turned to look at Frances, pain evident in her tight lips.

'From Dolly.'

'Oh, her.' Annie sighed. 'You don't want to take no notice of what she says.'

'Maybe not. But I gotta tell you. She went on about how you two met in the first place.' Frances felt she must go carefully, but go on she must. She blamed herself for not trying to get Annie away from Wiggin soon enough. 'It was over in Hoxton, I think?'

Annie closed her eyes. 'I'm tired out, Frances.'

'I know you are. You had a bad shock.'

'He ain't never turned on me before today. Not since he came back. And I don't think he knew me. I could've been anyone getting between him and his next drink.'

'Don't make excuses for him, Annie. I can't bear to hear it.' Frances smoothed down the sheets and patted them. 'About this business in Hoxton. Dolly says Wiggin weren't your first husband after all.'

Tears rolled from the corners of Annie's closed eyes. Frances dabbed them with her handkerchief. 'Don't tell no one, Fran. Don't tell Duke.' She turned her face to the wall, sobbing quietly.

'I won't say nothing if you don't want me to.' Frances took Annie's hand in hers and prepared to listen.

'I was just sixteen, not very old. It's true, I was married then, before I met Wiggin.' She opened her eyes and gave Frances a sharp look. 'Ain't there nothing Dolly Ogden don't know?'

Frances smiled. 'That's more like it. No, there ain't, so you'd best own up.'

'My pa was a cobbler by trade. He mended shoes all his life, and pots and pans when they needed a patch. There was a lot of mouths to feed, and when Michael Kearney came along and offered to take me off their hands, they thought it was a godsend.' Annie paused. 'It weren't, as it turned out, but I couldn't go back and tell my pa that, could I?'

Frances shook her head. 'Did he treat you very bad?'

'He liked a drink, and drink didn't improve his temper. I stuck it out for a year before I left him.'

169

'*You* left him?' Frances asked. 'That ain't what I heard.'

'I was married to Kearney for a year,' Annie insisted. 'Then I was married to Willie Wiggin.'

'But how? That's the real question.' Frances tried to battle a way through Annie's evasiveness. Unless they came to the crux, all these painful reminiscences would be for nothing.

'I think you know the answer to that,' Annie said slowly. 'Let's leave it, Frances. It's hard enough to hold my head up as it is.'

All Frances's notions about women's rights rose to the surface as she considered Annie's injured face and her struggle to come to terms with the past. She felt another surge of anger. 'You ain't done nothing to be ashamed of. Not a single thing. The man who done this to you, that's the one ought to be hanging his head in shame. And Kearney. Two men who put their heads together and make a bargain over a wife! It's disgusting.' Frances couldn't help but show her feelings, though she was trying to keep a level head for Annie's sake. 'Ain't that what they did? You was Kearney's wife, and he went and sold you to Wiggin?'

'They was drunk,' Annie whispered.

'And you was seventeen!' Frances ran out of words to express her disgust.

'It happened in them days. It was the old way of going on.'

'But it weren't the proper way, not even in them days. Ain't you ever thought it weren't right, Annie? Ain't you considered that?'

Annie shook her head. 'Right or wrong, Wiggin struck a bargain and showed me the piece of paper that made everything open and above board. He said he'd got it from the Register Office and there was no going back on it. Kearney wanted rid of me. Willie took me in. I wore a ring. What could I do?'

'And what happened to Kearney? Didn't he sober up and want you back?'

'Happy ever after? No, he never did get back on his feet. I heard he went on a binge, then he went from bad to worse. He had to go round the builders begging for work, when everyone knew he weren't fit for nothing. One took him on though, and he was still drunk when he went up a ladder one day. They say he just keeled over and that was it. He fell twenty feet to the ground.'

'He died?'

Annie nodded. 'A month after I went with Wiggin. Well, I was in the cart then. Wiggin was no better than Michael Kearney, but I had to stick it out. We got moved on out of Hoxton and we came over to Paradise Court. You know the rest.'

Frances patted her hand. 'I wish you'd told us.'

'And be made a laughing stock?' Annie shook her head. 'Would you own up to being sold on the market like a bolt of cloth? Be honest, what would you have done?'

'The same as you, probably. But let's get one thing straight; you ain't ever been married to Wiggin, no more than I have. Not in the eyes of the law. That marriage certificate Wiggin said he got from the Register Office, it ain't worth the paper it's written on, not without a proper divorce from Kearney.'

Annie considered this, her expression growing agitated. 'And in the eyes of the Lord?' she asked.

Frances paused. 'I ain't no expert, Annie, but I can't see that God would object if you said a prayer or two and told him you done your best for Wiggin, but you can't do no more, and you've decided to follow your heart for once and go back where you know you belong.'

'With Duke?' Annie trembled.

'With Pa. You and him should be together, Annie.'

'He needs me, don't he?'

'He does. He's lost the Duke. That's what I came to tell you. The brewery want him out. He ain't gonna fight it, and he ain't got nowhere to go.'

Annie had her chat with the Almighty, bathed her bruised face in warm water, covered her cut with antiseptic and lint, got dressed and marched with Frances up to the Duke. She spent half an hour with Duke telling him how things stood. First he swore he'd knock Wiggin clean off his feet and got up to do it then and there. Annie restrained him. 'He's already flat on his back. Out cold with drink,' she promised. 'No, you and me gotta talk.'

Duke was ready to believe every word. 'You threw yourself away on Wiggin,' he said. 'We all knew that.'

'And for nothing.' Annie sat in her old fireside chair. 'We was never properly married after all, according to Frances, the law and God Almighty.'

Duke smiled. There was a light in all this. 'Well, if them three agree, it must be right.' He leaned forward to take her hand.

'I never left you for Wiggin, Duke. I left you 'cos I thought we couldn't be married no more.'

'But now we can?'

'I've come round to that way of thinking, Duke. Yes. Thanks to Frances.'

'Thanks to Dolly,' he reminded her. 'It was Dolly tipped Frances off and got things moving.'

Annie sniffed. 'No need to go overboard. We'd never hear the end of it. No, let's move your things down the court here and now. No grand announcements. They can just get used to me and you being back together, and let them say what they want.'

It was agreed. The furniture, Duke and Ernie would move in with Annie. Hettie arranged to live with Jess and her family in Ealing, which would help in running the shop. Rob made a temporary arrangement to share Walter's lodgings. Practically, it all made sense.

'I gotta keep an eye on Willie,' Annie warned them.

They had to let her follow her own charitable course. But Duke insisted on sending Ernie along with her to Eden House, in case Wiggin turned nasty again. Annie gave in to this pressure. She felt safer in Ernie's presence; he was good and strong, and slow to anger. He knew his job was to protect her.

By Friday, 4 July, when Duke should have come before the magistrate, he was ready to leave the pub he'd run for thirty-five years. They crowded out Annie's tiny terraced house with his and Ernie's belongings; the old clock with its quarterly chimes, the two fireside chairs, the old kettle.

The Duke stood empty, cloths covering the pumps, the gauze mantels unlit. No sound came from the pianola, no laughter from the drinkers at the bar. Upstairs in the kitchen, a tap dripped, floorboards eased and creaked in the cool night air. Life that had gone on, year in, year out, voices that had filled the rooms had vanished.

Someone would come and cover the walls with new paper, set different slippers in the hearth. The tap dripped into the stone sink, measuring each empty second. Regulars approached the etched and intricate doors, saw no lights, moved on down Duke Street, grumbling about the changes, blaming the brewery for spoiling their weekend pleasure.

CHAPTER THIRTEEN

If anything brought home to Hettie the fact that she, Rob, Duke and Ernie had left the pub for good, it was a chance encounter with George Mann on the Monday after the move.

Hettie had a night off from Army work, and was hurrying down Duke Street from the tram stop. She was dressed for the summer evening in a light, wrapover dress in pale blue art silk, with a matching cloche hat pulled well down over her forehead. But every few yards, someone would call out to her; Katie O'Hagan from her haberdashery stall, or Bea Henshaw from the eating-house doorway. Then, when she spotted Ernie on his delivery bike, it was she who waved a loud hello. Her brother jammed on his brakes and stuck out his legs to come to a halt, a broad smile breaking out at the sight of Hettie. She hurried across the busy street towards him.

'Hello, Ett. You look nice.' He beamed at her.

Hettie grinned. 'Thanks, Ern. You don't look too bad yourself.' He was dressed up in a smart white collar and tie, in spite of the heat. 'How's things?'

Ernie's smile stayed put. At twenty-eight, he still had the gauche air of a teenaged lad. Sturdily built, with the family's dark brown eyes, his hair brushed carefully to one side, he still took pride in his job as Henshaw's errand boy, never putting a foot wrong in his daily deliveries of fresh bread, butter and eggs. 'Things is fine,' he told her.

'How do you like your new room, Ernie?' Hettie knew that Annie had sorted out a back bedroom for him, arranging his bits and pieces; his photographs of the family and poor Daisy O'Hagan, his collar studs and cufflinks, on an old mahogany dressing-table.

He nodded. 'It's fine, thanks.'

'Good. Well, I'm off to visit Pa,' she told him. 'Will I see you down there?'

'What time is it?'

'Half past five.' She'd left the dress shop early and come over by tube, specially to see how Duke and Ernie were settling in. 'I got some teacakes from the baker's near us. Your favourite.'

He nodded and mounted the saddle once more. 'I'll ask Mrs Henshaw if I can knock off early,' he promised eagerly.

'Watch out!' Hettie warned. Loud trams rattled by, buses lurched from the pavement. 'See you in a tick.'

He nodded and launched his heavy bike into the traffic, weaving skilfully in and out.

Hettie sighed as she lost sight of him amongst the clutter of market stalls, then went on her way. Ernie seemed all right, bless him. Like a child, he was happy if *they* were happy; his pa, Annie, and his brother and sisters. She knew all too well, though, that Duke would hide things from him to spare his feelings.

Intending to ignore the empty pub windows, Hettie ducked her head as she approached the court. She took the corner at a trot, only to come straight up against a ladder, propped over the doorway, jutting out onto the pavement.

Looking up, she spotted George at the top of it, taking down the small sign over the door.

'Wilfred Albert Parsons. Licensed to sell intoxicating liquor from the premises known as the Duke of Wellington public house, Duke Street, Southwark'. She knew that sign; its small, neat, gold lettering on a black background, her father's little-used first names. She stopped, stunned to see George take out the last screw and ease it from the wall.

'Hello, Ett.' George looked down, still holding the sign aloft. Then he swung it sideways, intending to slot it under one arm before he descended the ladder.

'Here, George, I'll take it,' Hettie offered. She held her arms out.

He handed it to her. 'Got it?'

She nodded. Close to, the gold letters had begun to fade and flake. Hettie waited for George to come down. 'The brewery ain't chucked you out then, George?'

'Not yet.' Back on *terra firma*, he took hold of the base of the ladder and swung it level with the pavement. Then he laid it flat, close to the wall.

To her shame, Hettie realized she hadn't given a thought to George's future once the battle to keep the Duke had been lost. Neither had she considered their own future together. Their quiet affair, going along gently through the years, had relied on them both simply being there at the Duke, day in, day out, coming and going. They never made arrangements to see one another; George would simply take it into his head to walk her along to the Mission, or she would come into the bar and chat with him while he worked. Now all that, too, would change. 'They'll have to keep you on as cellarman, don't you worry,' she told him. 'They can't afford to do without you.'

He shrugged. 'Let's wait and see who they put in as landlord. Maybe we won't see eye to eye.' He felt embarrassed at Hettie standing there in her light outfit, holding the old licence board in her gloved hands. 'Here, let me take that.'

But she shook her head. 'Can I have it as a keepsake?'

He nodded, wiping his own hands on his trousers. He edged her on to the doorstep, as a man wearing a sandwich-board over his shoulders sought room to pass. The board was written over in big, neat letters. It read, 'I know 3 trades, I fought for 3 years, I have 3 children, and no work for 3 months. But I only want ONE job.' The man looked respectable in a trilby hat and tweed jacket, but his shoes were worn and he walked with his head hung low.

Hettie followed George's gaze to read the message, then she turned back to him. 'Hang on here as long as you can,' she advised. 'Jobs ain't ten a penny, remember.'

'You won't think badly of me?'

Hettie glanced at the upper storey of the old pub; the rooms where she lived for most of her life. 'Never, George.' She turned to him with a sad smile.

He said he would keep the licence board safe for her while she visited her pa, and Hettie promised to walk out to the park with him later that evening. 'Thanks, that'd be nice,' she agreed, blushing. It was like starting afresh; she felt young and silly over the formal invitation.

Relieved, George took the board from her. 'How long will you be?'

'A couple of hours. I promised Ernie I'd do him toasted teacakes. You could join us,' she suggested suddenly.

It was George's turn to colour up. 'No, I have to finish here. Will you call in on your way back?' A knot of tension dissolved inside his chest: he'd been afraid that Hettie wouldn't care for him if he held on to his job as cellarman under a new boss. And he thought perhaps her affections had faded to the level of friendship only. Undemonstrative himself, with a long sense of being beholden to the Parsons family as a whole, he never pushed himself on Hettie, though he loved her steadily. His strong physique, quiet manner and untalkative nature gave no sign of vulnerability. He was good-tempered, reliable George Mann, steady as a rock.

Hettie nodded. 'About half-seven then?' She put a hand on his arm and reached to kiss his cheek. Then she went on her way past the Ogdens', past the tenement, down to Annie's corner of Paradise Court.

From her own new home in Mile End, Sadie could only keep in touch with her family through phone calls and brief letters. In those early days of living with Richie work took up much of her time, and when she got back at night, traipsing up the stone stairway to the rooms they shared, there was often a feeling in her heart that made her want to hide away and cry.

At first she couldn't tell what this was; after all, she'd got what she wanted by taking a risk over Richie, and the home she was making for him gave her pleasure. Most days on her way home from the office, she would call in at the ironmonger's to buy a new pot or pan, or at a china shop for eggcups decorated with cornflowers or a little glass powder dish for her new dressing-table.

Yet she was sad. She would fuss in the living-room, putting up a picture or introducing lace curtains to stave off this uninvited feeling. She typed all day, cooked, cleaned and sewed in the evenings. One sunny Sunday afternoon, she even made the acquaintance of her neighbour; the woman who'd greeted her decently when she first arrived.

Sarah Morris belonged to the band of now elderly East End women who had dragged up a large brood in the old Board School days, dealing on a daily basis with lice, eye infections, outbreaks of diphtheria and constant hunger. Her husband, Harry Morris, had died in a drunken street fight, leaving her and the four small children only hardship and his ukelele, which Sarah kept hanging to this day on the wall of her miserable front room. She told Sadie she never took it down to play, but she would hum 'Ukelele Lady', remembering how happy she was when Harry was alive. 'Bacon, bread and butter for tea every weekday,' she boasted. 'Harry was a glassmaker. He held down a good job. Only, drink was his downfall, you see.'

Sadie took this to heart. It depressed her to think of families broken up and suffering. And she began to ask Richie not to stay out so late. She'd only come to live with him a few weeks since, yet often he seemed to prefer the company at the pub to being with her. 'Why do you have to stay there till they close?' she asked.

'That's rich,' he said. 'Coming from a landlord's daughter.'

She had the grace to smile, sitting up in bed waiting for him to get undressed. She'd put a glass shade over the gas mantel on the far wall; its light was soft and warm on his strong back. Soon she'd forgotten her lonely, anxious evening.

Richie always undressed as if there was no one else in the room, casting his clothes carelessly on to the floor, whereas she would turn away out of modesty, or if possible slip into bed before he came in. She was still startled by the beginnings of intimacy, willing to let him take the lead, unsure of herself. But when he got into bed and held her close, when he began to kiss her, she would cling to him, arms clasped around his neck, loving his weight and strength.

Richie slid into bed now, resting back on the pillow, staring up at the ceiling. It had been a bad day; they'd laid off the casuals at the docks in large numbers, Richie among them. Tomorrow he would have to scout around for different work. Previously, when he'd lived alone, it wouldn't have worried him. But now there was Sadie. He decided to keep quiet about the job situation until he found himself something else. Not for the first time, he silently cursed Rob Parsons for kicking him out of his steady job at the taxi depot.

'Frances telephoned me at work today,' Sadie said. She curved her body against his side, slipping her slim legs under his. 'She says Pa and Ernie have settled in at Annie's place. Wiggin ain't popular down the court, though.'

Richie turned to look at her through half-closed eyes. 'Ain't the drink finished him off yet, then?'

'No, worse luck. Annie still goes in to look after him, even after what he's done. I wish she wouldn't.' She knew how hard that must be for Duke. Ernie went along to keep an eye on Wiggin these days, in case he turned violent. All this Sadie learned second-hand from Frances or Hettie.

'Someone has to.' Richie slid one hand along the pillow, under Sadie's dark head. Her hair fanned across his arm, he leaned to kiss her mouth.

She put her arms around his neck, gazing at him. 'Richie, what harm is there in you and me going to visit one Sunday?' she said softly. 'Pa would like to see us, I know.' She paused. 'And Rob ain't living with them no more.'

He frowned and pulled away, lying back once more. 'It ain't me they want to see.'

Sadie leaned up on one elbow, letting the sheet fall from her shoulder. Her hair swung across her face. 'Oh, but it is. Pa wants to see us both. And I want you to come!'

'Why?' He turned his head away.

'So they get to know you.'

'They don't want to know me.' He was stubborn. Anyway, there was no other member of the Parsons family he was interested in except Sadie.

'You're wrong there.' Sadie felt the rejection badly, but her tone came out wheedling and high. 'And I don't like to visit without you. Think of me once in a while, why don't you?'

Richie felt they were on the brink of their first quarrel. 'I think of you all the time, Sadie.' He turned to her and gathered her in his arms.

'Do you, Richie?' She stroked his cheek, ran her fingertip across his brow. 'Ain't I being very nice to you?'

He kissed her again. 'It ain't you, Sadie, it's Rob. You know what I think of him.'

'But I don't mean us to visit Rob.' She made one last protest.

'Don't talk about it,' he whispered. 'I ain't going to change.'

Their way out of a quarrel was to make love, swept up in the touch of skin against skin, melted by kisses, so that in the end nothing could matter more.

Only, next morning, as Sadie got ready for the daily grind, she returned to the subject of his staying out late. 'Why don't we go to see a picture tonight?' she suggested. She put on a broad-brimmed straw hat with a deep crown and a green chiffon band. She turned from the mirror, her face eager and fresh. 'I can see if I can get out early and meet you if you like.'

Richie's mind was back on the search for work. He shrugged by way of reply, then took his place in front of the mirror, razor in hand, ready to continue shaving.

Sadie went and picked up her bag from the table. 'Shall we?'

He shook his head. 'I ain't sure what I've got on tonight.'

'Another session down the pub, I shouldn't wonder!' she retorted, suddenly angry. 'Don't mind me. I can always go to the pictures by myself.' She flounced from the room and down the steps.

Richie went on shaving. He wasn't worried by this. As long as Sadie went on wanting to go out with him or take him visiting, that was the main thing. Whether he said yes or no was beside the point. Carefully he wiped the specks of lather from his throat. If she ever stopped wanting that, then he would start to worry. It didn't occur to him that this might be leaving things late. And he didn't recognize the importance of family to Sadie, never having had one himself.

But Sadie sat on the top deck of the bus, eyes smarting. She took deep breaths, hid her face from the gaze of other passengers with the broad brim of her hat. Now she knew what that nagging, aching feeling was, that she staved off with housework and physical arousal. It was loneliness.

Feeling sorry for herself and helpless, she swayed with the motion of the bus, under green trees, past the park. How could she be lonely when she had Richie? she wondered.

*

Pills, ointments, suppositories, powders and plaster. Gripe-water at one and six a bottle, Clarke's Blood Mixture for four shillings. Frances's days were laid end to end, measured out like the medicines she dispensed, the patent remedies she sold over the counter. The only task she disliked was fishing out the leeches from their wide-mouth jar, the black, sluglike creatures that shrivelled into long worms when prodded, which doctors still recommended for sucking out poisons.

Otherwise, skilled and patient as she was, Frances was content with her work, choosing a small bottle of 4711 cologne to take home to Annie, and remembering that Sadie's favourite face powder was Ashes of Roses. She took care of everyone's needs, treating her small nephew and niece to milk chocolate bars whenever she went over to Ealing to visit, taking Duke leaflets and books from the Workers' Educational Institute which she thought might interest him.

'You'll wear yourself to a shadow,' Billy warned. Early August had turned sultry, energy drained from the streets as people stayed indoors or continued to take their annual trips to Kent to combine hop picking with a break from grimy, noisy London. A change was as good as a rest, they said.

'Nonsense.' Frances buttoned her fawn jacket across the hip. 'You're sure you won't come?'

Billy glanced up from his print machine. 'Where is it tonight, Ealing?' He felt uncomfortable visiting Jess's place these days, the house was stuffed with too many gadgets and ornaments for his liking. He stuck to his old nonconformist ways. And though Maurice Leigh still professed to support the ideas of Ramsay MacDonald and the Labour Party, Billy remained doubtful whether a man could live in what he considered to be the lap of luxury and still be a socialist. Frances and he disagreed over it. 'Jess and Maurice deserve to be comfortable,' she would say. 'They work hard for it.'

Frances told him that she was going to Paradise Court to see Annie and Duke. 'There's a book here I want to lend them.' In her considerate way, Frances had realized how heavily time lay on their hands.

'In that case . . .' Billy wiped his hands and switched off the electric light over the machine. He smiled at his wife. 'Give me a minute to go and fetch my jacket. We'll walk over together.'

They took their time, enjoying their quiet walk, noticing a new flower shop open on Union Street, wondering what would eventually happen to Coopers' old drapery store. 'I hear he's left with nothing,' Billy said.

Frances paused to gaze in at the empty shop. Dust and cobwebs; that was all that was left. 'Poor Edith Cooper, I don't know how she'll get on,' she said quietly. Though she didn't say so, she had no sympathy for Jack Cooper, who had brought things on himself. She knew him as a pig-headed, overbearing man who neglected his East End roots after he became a wealthy store owner, treating his women workers abominably. But his wife was altogether a gentler, more charitable sort who'd suffered greatly after Teddy Cooper was killed in the war.

'They say they'll have to sell their big house now.' Billy offered Frances his arm and they set off steadily up the street once more. 'Just to pay off his creditors.'

She shook her head. 'There ain't no one safe these days.'

But as they approached the corner of Paradise Court, their quiet conversation came to an abrupt halt.

Billy stopped short and pointed to the pub. 'Blimey, look at that!'

Frances felt a jolt of anger. Workmen were busy on the building. Scaffolding ran up the front and down the side. Gone was the old green paint, the woodwork stripped bare by blowlamps. All the old green and gold signs were down from the now bare stone frontage. 'What's going on?' Frances gripped Billy's arm.

'Steady on, they're giving the old place a fresh lick of paint, that's all.' But Billy, too, was astonished at the transformation. He took an empty pipe from his pocket and began to suck at it.

Frances couldn't have felt worse if she'd been publicly stripped bare herself. She was scandalized. 'What for? Weren't it good enough?' She recalled how Annie would come out each day, regular as clockwork, carrying her stepladder and a bucket of hot soapy water to wash down the paint around the doorway and windows.

'I expect they want to make a new start,' Billy said quietly. 'When the new landlord comes in.'

'But look at this!' Frances stepped towards smart new signboards propped face down against the door. She caught sight of George Mann working inside the bar and called him out. 'What's going on, George? What are these here?'

George nodded a silent greeting at Billy, wrinkling his eyes against the low sun. 'New signs,' he said, reluctant to have anything to do with them.

'Why do they need them?' She poked at them with her shoe. 'Think of the expense. It's a crying shame!'

'Come on, Frances,' Billy urged. 'Let George carry on here.' He led her to one side, as two men in paint-splashed overalls, carrying a plank between them, made their way into the pub. Inside, they caught a glimpse of walls stripped to the plaster, gas-fittings ripped from the wall, dust-sheets covering all the fixtures.

She dug in her heels. 'Just a second, Billy. I want to take a proper look.' In growing dismay she peeped inside, then as she stepped back, one of the new signs tipped sideways to reveal the words underneath. The blackboard was decorated in modern, straight letters in a style just coming in. Frances read the words out loud. Instead of The Duke of Wellington, it read The Prince of Wales.

'They ain't thinking of renaming the old place?' Billy turned to George. 'That can't be right, surely?'

But George nodded. 'You should hear what they say about it around here.'

'Ain't it going down too well?'

'You could say that.' George turned to Frances. 'I'm sorry,' he said, shaking his head, 'the brewery says it's more up-to-the-minute.'

Frances was stunned. The Duke was to be the Prince of Wales after Prince Edward, the dilettante young heir apparent. She stared at the new signs.

George thought it best to give the full picture. 'They're talking about new windows for downstairs. They ain't sure yet.'

'And does Pa know?'

'He can't hardly help it. Not after Dolly went down earlier and told them the worst. About the name, that is.'

Frances took a deep breath. 'Let's go and see how he's taking it,' she said to Billy, marching in high dudgeon down the court.

George looked at Billy. 'They don't like it, but there ain't a thing they can do about it,' he said sadly.

*

In one way, Duke felt there was nothing more they could do to harm him. If you lost everything, he said, why lose any more sleep over a couple of new signs?

When Frances and Billy showed up, full of fresh indignation, he was sitting in Annie's back kitchen surrounded by family and friends. Rob stood smoking like a chimney by the back door, his face glowering. Dolly made cups of tea. Tommy swore he would never set foot inside the pub again.

'Bleeding stupid.' Dolly frowned. 'What do you think, Frances?' She thrust a full cup and saucer into her hands.

'I know what I think,' France said scornfully. 'How are you, Pa?' She took off her cotton gloves and put them in her bag. She sat down in Annie's empty chair, opposite Duke.

'Bearing up,' he said as always.

'But did you take a look on the inside?' Dolly went over and made a lot of noise at the sink. 'Stripped bare. And God knows what they plan putting up instead. Pictures of young girls half naked with their hair all over the place, I shouldn't wonder.' She grumbled about modern taste.

'Pa?' Frances touched his hand, urging a smile. 'Have you been up to take a look?'

He shook his head. 'It ain't worth making a special trip for.'

'But ain't you been out at all?' Frances frowned. She sipped her tea.

'It's too hot.'

'It ain't that hot, Pa!'

'Leave it, Frances,' Rob said from the doorway. 'If he don't feel like going up on to Duke Street, he don't have to.'

'But a breath of fresh air, Pa. It'd do you good.'

'Annie goes on at me just like you do,' he told her. 'Maybe tomorrow. I'll see how I feel.'

'Where is Annie?'

'She's up the court seeing to Wiggin. She ain't roused him so far today.'

Frances only had time to grumble quietly about Annie doing too much, when heavy steps came running down the passage. Ernie burst in, white in the face. 'Annie says come quick!' he gasped. He seemed to stagger sideways and Tommy had to leap forward to catch him. By now he'd clamped his mouth tight shut, unwilling to say another word. Saying something out loud meant it had happened. If you kept quiet, it would go away. He shut his eyes to block out the misery of what he'd just seen.

'Sit him down here!' Frances sprang up to help Ernie to her seat.

Duke stood up too. 'Look after him, Frances.' He beckoned to his son. 'Rob, you and me will go and take a look.'

'But what is it? What happened?' Dolly insisted. 'What's the matter with him? He ain't going to faint, is he?'

'Help me loosen his tie,' Frances said. 'And Billy, will you make sure Pa and Rob can manage?' She sat Ernie forward in the chair, head between his knees.

Both Billy and Tommy made off after Duke and Rob. The four of them arrived at Eden House together. 'This way!' Tommy yelled. 'Wiggin's in the room under us, down the back.'

They ran down the dark hallway, footsteps ringing in the hollow, tall building. Annie waited for them at the door to Wiggin's room.

Duke pushed his way to the front, relieved that she seemed to be unharmed. 'Is it Wiggin?'

She showed him in. The room was empty and in a dreadful state, the stench of stale alcohol, urine and decay almost unbearable. Wiggin had ripped down Annie's curtains and tried to block the light with old newspapers. His trunk was slewed across the room, the blankets on the bed slashed and torn. Broken bottles had been smashed across the bare floor, and as Duke advanced inside, he saw a dark stain seeping into the boards by the hearth.

'Where is he?' Rob snatched the blanket from the bed and looked wildly round. 'He ain't hit you again?'

Annie shook her head. 'I ain't got a clue where he is,' she admitted. 'I sent Ernie down for help. I think we'll have to set off looking for him.'

Rob relaxed. 'What's Ernie getting so het up over?' As far as he was concerned, if Wiggin had gone missing it was good riddance to bad rubbish.

Duke went over to the hearth. He stared down at the dark patch on the floorboards, still damp. He bent slowly and brushed a fingertip across it. 'This.' His finger was stained rusty red. 'Blood. Ernie can't stand the sight of it.'

'Whose blood?' Rob went to join Duke. 'Wiggin's?'

'Who else do you think?' Tommy kicked around amongst the broken glass. 'There's drops of the stuff over here and all.'

'So where is he?' Billy asked again. He turned to Annie. 'Ain't you seen him at all today?'

She shook her head. 'I ain't got no answer when I came up this morning. So this time I knocked and knocked, and when I got no answer I went to Bertie Hill for the key and let myself in. I thought he was still in here, asleep or dead drunk. I could smell it through the door. But I come in and he ain't nowhere to be seen. I think maybe he's made off up Duke Street on another binge.'

'Maybe he has,' Rob agreed. 'He'll be flat out on the park bench with the other old dossers.'

'Except there's this.' Annie pointed to the bloodstain. 'Ernie spotted it and it gave him a nasty turn. I had to send him down to you, Duke.'

'And it's time to get you back home and all,' he told her, taking her by the arm.

'But we gotta look for Wiggin, remember?'

'Tommy and Billy will take a look, won't you?' Duke agreed to send them off to reassure Annie more than anything else. 'He'll most likely come staggering back of his own accord if we hang on long enough.' He put an arm around her shoulder as they made they way out. 'Rob will see to the mess here. Bring a brush and a bucket of hot water with a scrubbing-brush,' he told him.

Rob went ahead with bad grace. 'Anyone would think I ain't got better things to do,' he grumbled. But he agreed to clean the room, for Annie's sake.

Back home, they calmed her with tea and sympathy. Ernie was upstairs resting, Frances said. 'Billy and Tommy will find Wiggin,' she promised Annie. 'He ain't gone far.'

'It's the blood.' Annie looked up, pale and strained. 'Look, Frances, I know he's a bleeding old nuisance, I don't say he ain't. But he could be out there down some alley, down a siding, he could be dying!'

It was the River Thames that gave up the secret of Wiggin's final journey.

He'd been in the water overnight, the police said. The current had taken him downstream and washed him up against a Norwegian fishing boat unloading for Billingsgate. A fisherman had heard the body knocking against the hull and spotted what he thought was a piece of flotsam. Only when he went for a pole to push it off, it bobbed and turned face up in the water, and he saw what it was. He called in the police. It took several days to track down Annie, Wiggin's only living relative.

Since his disappearance, Annie had been forced to relive the nightmare of his first vanishing act all those years earlier. She went in on herself, refusing to admit that it would be better if he never came back, a constant caller for news at Union Street station. The discovery of the body came as a relief in the end. She and Duke went straight to the morgue and she calmly identified Wiggin, not flinching at the bruised and battered face.

'Was it a drowning?' she asked the attendant, imagining the old man, drunk and weak from loss of blood, toppling over a bridge to his death.

But the man covered the body and shook his head. 'Bled to death. Looks like he was stabbed. Don't ask me. I ain't no expert.'

'Stabbed?' Annie echoed.

Duke and Annie went to the police station to check. 'They're saying Wiggin didn't drown after all?' Duke asked.

The bulky desk sergeant wheezed over to check the file and nodded. 'Vicious attack with sharp implement,' he confirmed. 'Dead before he hit the water.'

Annie's relief turned to distress.

'Weren't hardly nothing to identify him by,' the sergeant continued. He went to a cupboard. 'Just a few old rags. You might as well take them while you're here.' He heaped Wiggin's clothes on to the counter, including the old greatcoat that Annie had rescued from the pawnshop. 'Or you can let us burn them if you like.'

Annie sniffed and nodded, unable to speak.

'Go steady,' Duke warned. 'This ain't easy.'

Ignoring him, the sergeant pushed the heap of clothes to the floor. 'It was the old coat. It had Sally Army tickets in the pocket. We dried them out and went down and checked the numbers with the local spike. They took a look in their registers and came up with his name. They told us about his connection with you. Seems like you was his good Samaritan. Anyhow, that's how we found you.' He sounded proud of the policework behind it. 'At least you can give the poor old blighter a proper funeral.'

Duke took Annie away once more. They stood in a queue for a bus back to Duke Street. Neither felt up to the walk.

'He was stabbed, they say?' Annie puzzled over this all the way home. 'He'd been in the water overnight, but he ain't drowned, he was stabbed?'

'Let the coppers work it out,' Duke advised gently. 'You gotta try and forget it.'

But as they walked down Paradise Court together under a stormy sky, Annie insisted otherwise. 'It ain't right to forget about poor Wiggin,' she said. 'For a start, we gotta give him a send-off, Duke. We gotta put him away splendid, whatever happens.'

CHAPTER FOURTEEN

There was hardly a soul to mourn the violent death of Willie Wiggin. The sailor who'd dragged his battered corpse from the river spent one sleepless night, tossing and turning to rid himself of the old tramp's staring, sightless eyes and the hollow knocking against the boat's empty hull. The police wrote him down as one more dosser destined for a pauper's grave until they turned up an ex-wife to claim his remains and take him off their hands. The unsentimental Tommy O'Hagan told his sister, Katie, that at least they'd get a good night's sleep in future, without the old drunk clattering about below. Dolly Ogden even came out with it straight to Annie's face: she was better off with Wiggin dead and buried, the whole street agreed on that.

Nevertheless, on the morning of 8 August Paradise Court did turn out to 'put him away splendid'. They felt they owed it to Annie and Duke, who laid on a good spread in Annie's front room. Not many bothered with the graveside ceremony, just Annie, Duke and a few family and friends. Mary O'Hagan stood silent in the background as the priest threw soil on the coffin. She said a prayer and remembered the day when the police came knocking on her door with similar news. Daisy too had been stabbed. Mary crossed herself and stood head bowed for Wiggin.

Hettie and Jess had discussed who should stay in charge of the shop, and it was Hettie who came over to the funeral for an hour. She met George on the corner of the court, under the pub's new black and gold sign. He had on a smart jacket and cap, coming along at Hettie's suggestion.

'We're meeting up with the others at the cemetery,' she told him, taking his arm and walking briskly down the noisy street. 'Then Annie's asked us back to her place.' She looked nice in a grey silky dress and a straw hat with a curling brim. George was proud to walk her along to the funeral.

By the graveside, Hettie sang 'The Lord's My Shepherd' in a full, rich voice which soared into the still, blue sky. She sang of quiet waters with such purity that she brought tears to Annie's eyes.

'God rest his soul,' Annie said to Duke as she turned away. Upright and steady in his dark suit, he walked by her side to the cemetery gate. ''Cos he ain't had a happy time this side of the grave.' She dabbed at her eyes with her handkerchief.

Later, back at the house, she told Hettie that today would have been Wiggin's sixty-seventh birthday.

Dolly and Arthur Ogden were among the first to turn out in neighbourly fashion, to go down the bottom of the court and give Annie a boost. It would be a shame if she'd gone to all that trouble over sandwiches and cold pies if no one showed up. Since it was a Friday morning affair, they dragged Charlie out of bed to get dressed and show his face. 'Come and pay your respects,' Dolly said.

'Wiggin ain't worth it,' Charlie complained. He valued his lie-in after working late.

'But Annie and Duke is!' Dolly brooked no argument, as usual. The Ogdens would show up in force.

Rob dropped in, and Katie dragged Tommy off his paint and wallpaper stall to put in an appearance down the court. The hot, sunny day lent an odd festival air to the occasion; Annie's door stood wide open, and mourners brought their food and drink outside on to the pavement to chat.

Billy Wray had come in Frances's place. He talked politics with Joe O'Hagan, predicting more miners' strikes during the coming winter. 'Coal's losing a million pounds a month,' he said. 'Pits are closing all up and down the Welsh valleys, and the owners want to make another cut in wages.' He supported the Federation slogan, 'Not a penny off the pay, not a second on the day'.

Joe wondered where it would all lead. He himself cared less about the miners than the present newspaper outcry against one Patrick Mahon, murderous resident of Crumbles, near Pevensey in Sussex. 'They say he chopped up the body,' he told Billy, having steered the conversation towards the sensational case. Joe's morbid interest in such things no doubt sprang from his own daughter's death, for which Chalky White had eventually got the drop. He followed every detail of the current scandal. 'Her name was Emily Kaye, and she was his mistress.'

'I hope they string him up,' Arthur put in. 'Like they did that Edith Thompson a couple of years back.'

Billy retreated to the safety of Annie's front room for more pork pie and tea from Hettie. 'How's Jess and family?' he asked conversationally.

'They're fine, thanks. Mo and Grace ain't at school for the summer holidays, so Jess is pretty busy.' Hettie told him they were considering taking on help, both in the shop and at home.

He nodded, took his tea out into the court and, spying Joe and Arthur still hard at it, sought out the less lurid company of George Mann. The two men talked of more layoffs on the docks and a threatened strike on public transport. The TUC were heading towards a general strike, Billy felt sure.

'Ramsay MacDonald's against it,' George pointed out.

'But he's sitting on his backside in Westminster, he ain't the one being squeezed by the owners.' Billy felt strongly on the point.

Tommy, pie in hand, had overheard. 'That's why I work from my own stalls,' he put in. 'Ain't no one breathing down my neck.'

'Not till you get yourself hitched, Tommy, no!' George nudged him. 'Ain't it about time you were looking round for a missus?'

But Tommy had no intention, he said. 'Women is a thing I leave alone. It don't pay to get hitched. Look at Annie!'

They spotted her small, slight figure dressed in a long black skirt and high white blouse, bustling around with replenishments.

Tommy struck a serious pose, thumb in waistcoat pocket, chewing as he spoke. 'No, what I mean to say is, women is trouble. I've had my fling, I can tell you, but they always go screeching and carrying on before too long. Then, when they got you well and truly hooked, what do you get? A missus rowing, kids squalling, no coal in the grate and no food on the table. A missus only makes a man miserable. And kids? I won't have them. Look at my ma when we was young, washing and scrubbing till all hours just to keep us fed, and the little ones always crying for bread. No, I'm happy as I am, with my stalls and my mates, and having a beer when I like, and no blessed missus to come home to, ta very much!'

Billy and George applauded Tommy's long and eloquent

speech. 'Blimey!' George winked at Joe. 'I see you brought him up not to fall for the first pair of flashing eyes.'

But Dolly stood prepared to take Tommy on. 'What makes you think any girl would fall for you?' she demanded. 'You ain't exactly no prize catch, Tommy O'Hagan.' She said women liked tall and muscular men like George, not skinny ones like Tommy, or Arthur for that matter. She squared up to him. 'You may be a fast mover and a fast talker, Tommy, but you *h*ain't no *H*adonis. You need beefing up with a bit of muscle, you do. And you won't get far with just them big blue eyes neither!'

'Oh, Dolly, ain't I the one for you?' Tommy cried, as if stricken. 'And here's me thinking I was God's gift.'

'Well, you ain't, Tommy, believe me.' It was her turn to wink at the older men then stroll off.

'Blimey!' Tommy recovered an upright stance, his confidence intact.

The occasion had begun to go with a swing and, by the end of the morning, Dolly was congratulating Annie on a good show. 'Just like the old Coronation days,' she said. 'And we need a good get-together since they closed you down, Duke.' She nudged his arm. 'We miss our Saturday night sing-songs, don't we, Arthur? The Lamb and Flag, it ain't a patch on the Duke.'

'The Prince of Wales,' Annie corrected her with a pinched look. 'You could always try there when they open up them brand-new doors.'

'Ha!' Dolly countered. 'Over my dead body, Annie. Over my dead body.'

At Annie's insistence, the police had begun a desultory investigation into the circumstances behind Wiggin's death.

A few days before the funeral, they'd come down the court, a fresh young constable and the cynical desk sergeant from Union Street. They intended to poke around in Wiggin's old room and to speak to the other inhabitants of Eden House.

'Who cleaned up the mess?' the sergeant asked Bertie Hill, who let them into the room with his key. It was bare except for the bed, the trunk and a hessian sack full of what seemed like rubbish; paper, broken bottles, stale food.

Hill shrugged. He didn't like having police on the property, or having his time wasted. But he knew, as an ex-copper himself, that they had a job to do. 'Maybe it was Annie, the old girl what kept an eye on him.' He thought a bit longer. No, come to think, it was Rob Parsons from the Duke-that-was. The pub on the corner.' He explained to the two policemen the tangled connection between Wiggin, Annie and Rob, taking trouble to point out the things the family would have against the old tramp.

'And Rob Parsons cleared up the evidence?' the sergeant repeated. He paced the room in his shiny boots and came to a standstill by the hearth. 'Looks like he did a proper job.' He looked at the faint stain under his feet and bent to take a closer look.

The enthusiastic constable, whose short blond haircut and smooth face under a too-big helmet gave him the air of a scrubbed schoolboy, surmised that the stain was blood and that a fight must have taken place in the room. 'Broken glass. Blood stains. It could've been the end of a broken bottle what finished him off. Looks like the job was done right here, then they lugged the guts up the Embankment and dropped it off the bridge.'

The sergeant ignored him and turned to Bertie Hill. 'You say you didn't hear nothing?' He knew of the man's reputation. Everyone in the force had heard how, a couple of years before, the whiff of scandal had pushed him back into Civvy Street before a proper investigation could get started. Two or three coppers in Hackney had been taking money from the protection gangs to steer clear of their patches. They'd been dropped in it by a notorious gang member called Gyp the Blood, whom police had hauled in on other, more serious charges. Hill, like his two colleagues, had made a sharp exit from the force.

'Not a dicky bird.' Hill knew the ropes. He didn't want to get involved.

'And when did you last set eyes on him alive?' The sergeant sniffed and stared up at the ceiling.

'I never saw him.'

'Never? How did he pay his rent?'

'He never. The old lady did. She did all his shopping and cooking. He never went out.'

The sergeant sniffed again, as if the smell was bad and it was emanating from Hill. 'You never got on with him, then?'

'I never had the chance. His rent was paid, that's all.' Hill stared steadily back.

'Ain't never had no visitors and such like, I don't suppose?'

'No.'

'Just his old lady?'

'His ex-old lady, like I was saying.'

'And what about this Rob Parsons?'

Hill laughed scornfully. 'No, he ain't no angel of mercy coming to help a poor sinner. That's more his sister, Hettie.'

'So he weren't fond of Wiggin neither?' The sergeant got round to the only line of investigation on offer. After all, Parsons seemed to be the one who'd interfered with the room. If the old woman wanted an investigation, they'd give her one. He liked to inject a touch of irony into life.

Hill frowned, seeing an opportunity to lay it on thick. 'He only said he'd like to do the old bloke in.'

The young constable looked downright eager. 'How's that?' The sergeant turned down the corners of his mouth and poked at the bag of rubbish with his toe.

'In the Duke. I heard Rob Parsons swear he'd cheerfully strangle Wiggin. Him and Tommy O'Hagan from upstairs, they was always on about it. They all think it was Wiggin turned in Rob's old man, see. For serving after hours. The old man lost his licence over it.'

The two policemen considered this. They thanked Hill and set off up the court, noticing the renovations underway at the pub. That part of Hill's account was true, at least. 'No chance of a quick one in there,' the sergeant commented about its locked doors and empty windows. 'How about the Lamb and Flag?'

'Ain't we going to question this Robert Parsons?' The keen young officer was disappointed.

The sergeant looked at him with a sigh. 'Where's the rush? I reckon Annie Whatsername will soon stop bleating about a proper investigation once she hears her stepson's in the frame.' He saw no point in putting much energy into the case; when it came to it, who could care less what had happened to the old tramp? He would go through the motions of an investigation, but that was all.

Sadie Parsons guessed rightly that Rob would take time off to go to Wiggin's funeral. Hearing long-distance of all that was going on, usually through Hettie, she knew they'd all be gathered at Annie's house for the morning of the eighth.

So she applied for a half-day's holiday through her supervisor, Turnbull, and though he frowned and prevaricated, she pleaded compassionate grounds over the funeral, and he was forced to agree. This lie was the first and least obstacle the day held for her, for she had no intention of attending the service to bury Wiggin.

'Ain't you going into work today?' Richie asked from under the sheets. It was eight o'clock on the morning of the funeral.

Sadie was dressing in a V-neck dress without sleeves, part of the cream outfit which Jess and Hettie had made up for her that spring. 'It's Wiggin's funeral, remember.' She offered no further explanation.

'You ain't going to a funeral dressed like that.' He sat up to light a cigarette.

'Says who?' She put on a small cloche hat and pulled it firmly down. 'It ain't nothing formal. Annie don't want it that way.' She smiled briefly. 'How about you?'

He shrugged. 'Ain't no use going down the Labour Exchange and joining the queue again.'

'Well, it's too late for the docks.'

'I know that.' He inhaled deeply. 'Ain't no use going down there neither, not with these lay-offs building up.'

Sadie forced down a bubble of anxiety. 'Never mind.' She went to kiss him before she left. 'Something will turn up.' This morning she was keen not to upset him, so she hid what she wanted to ask; how were they to go on paying the rent, which had just gone up by five shillings a week, or make the place decent and buy food and clothes on her wage only? She knew Richie was trying hard to find work, but wishing and hoping didn't pay the bills.

'When will you be back?' He made much of the kiss, reluctant to let her go.

'Usual time. I'm going on to work after.' She pulled away at last.

He released her and watched her head for the door. She was edgily bright, as if she was hiding something from him. He had an uneasy feeling that the funeral was not where she was headed.

Sadie walked herself into a calmer frame of mind. She timed it to arrive at Meredith Court as the mourners gathered in the next street. She expected to find Walter all alone in the taxi depot.

Her daring deviousness made her heart beat rapidly as she entered the yard. Both cars were parked, and she spotted Walter in his shirt-sleeves, resting against one of the taxis. He was reading a newspaper. She hurried up to him with an awkward admission to make, and a request that would hurt her pride.

Walter looked up as he heard her quick footsteps. She caught him completely off guard. 'Sadie!'

She laughed nervously. 'I ain't a ghost, Walter.' She stood beside him, hands clasped, looking up from under her hat.

'Rob's at the funeral.' He folded his paper, trying to collect his thoughts. In her cream dress she looked slim and girlish.

She nodded. 'I came to see you. I got something to ask, but I've been trying it all ways, and I can't get it right. The words, I mean.'

'What is it?' Her confusion shot down all his defences and made him take her by the arm to lead her into the office. He sat her down and took the phone off its hook. 'Fire away,' he invited, looking intently at her.

'First off, is Rob still mad at me?' she began awkwardly.

'He don't say.' Walter knew better than to upset the applecart by prying into Rob's private affairs.

'Are *you* mad at me?'

He shook his head.

'And are you still upset with Richie?'

'Ah!' He looked down at his desk and spoke softly. 'Ain't Richie got himself fixed up yet?'

Sadie sat opposite him, swallowing her pride, battling to keep both hands and voice steady. 'He ain't, Walter. Things ain't easy.'

'You want us to give Richie his old job back?'

She took a deep breath, pushed on to the offensive by a crowd of uncomfortable feelings. 'He's good at what he does, ain't he? And it weren't fair, what Rob did. I wish you'd talk him round for me.'

'It ain't that easy.' Walter took a few seconds to dampen his own reactions and put them to one side. He tried to look at the problem with clear vision. 'You know what Rob's like as well as I do, Sadie.'

'That's what I'm doing here with you now. Ain't no way I can talk Rob round. But *you* might. You go over it again with him; tell him Richie didn't do nothing wrong, asking me out. Tell him you ain't bothered about me no more.'

'That ain't true,' he said simply.

'Only in the friendly way, then!' Sadie grew desperate. 'You see, Walter, Richie's tried for work, and it's a strain on him. I can't bear to see him low. He needs this job!'

Walter put his head to one side, looking warily at her now. 'Does he know you came here?'

She jumped. 'No. It was my idea. He's not to find out.'

Walter weighed this up. 'That's something, at any rate. Now, the way you see it is, I talk Rob round. I say, "Let's get Richie Palmer back to work on the cars. We need him here." Rob says yes. We go straight to Richie without mentioning your name in all this?'

Sadie nodded. 'It's asking a lot, I know. But you and me are good friends, ain't we? We'll always be that.'

Walter knew Sadie inside out: impetuous, kind, the petted youngest child. She sat there full of torn loyalties, battling with things she couldn't control. 'I'll have a go,' he promised.

Sadie grasped the edge of the desk. 'Thanks, Walter. I knew you'd help.' She stood up, relief flooding her dark eyes. 'You'll telephone me at work?'

'If I get anywhere with Rob, yes. But not today. You gotta give me a couple of days. It ain't likely I'll get the chance to talk to him over the weekend. It's our busy time.'

Sadie nodded and impulsively kissed him on the cheek. Then he watched her rush out across the cinder yard, a sense of loss rekindled in his heart. He put the phone back on its hook, smoothed his newspaper flat on the desk and walked slowly into the yard, where he leaned a forearm against the side of his cab and gave the tyre one hefty, heartfelt kick.

'Temper!' a voice said. It was the cropped constable, hot on Rob's trail. He'd seen a young woman looking hot and bothered dash out of the gates. 'A case of *cherchez la femme*,' he smirked.

Walter stood up straight. 'What's that?'

The policeman strolled across. 'Robert Parsons, is it?' Confidence oozed from him. He stood, feet wide apart, hands behind his back.

'He's out,' Walter said, wary now. 'What's it about?'

The policeman ignored his question. 'You're Walter Davidson, then? The partner.' After the visit to the tenement earlier in the week, the sergeant had more or less dumped the Wiggin murder case in his young colleague's lap. Diligently he set about gathering information on their one and only suspect. Parsons was part-owner of a small taxicab business down Meredith Court. There was a mixture of interesting things in his background. He was sent home wounded from the war with a chip on his shoulder. His brother was had up for murder, but got off. There was a strange coincidence, for a start. He'd been something of a boxer in his day, before the war, and was known for his hot temper.

Slowly Walter nodded. 'Shall I tell Rob you came looking for him?' He glanced over the constable's shoulder. 'No need. Here he comes now.'

Rob had left the funeral and cut along the back way, down a narrow alley running the length of the factory wall from Paradise to Meredith Court. So he came across the yard from an oblique angle and stopped suddenly in mid-stride. The sight of a copper talking to Walter gave him a start. But he soon came forward with a clear conscience. 'There ain't been an accident, I hope?' he asked. He was feeling relaxed. The funeral had gone off better than expected.

'No. I'm looking into the death of William Wiggins. I have to ask you a few questions, sir, if you don't mind.' The policeman drew himself up to full height.

'Cor blimey!' Rob threw down his cigarette butt, amused by the young copper's punctiliousness.

'This is a serious matter.' The policeman recognized the attack on his fragile authority. He'd only been in uniform for six months. 'I have to ask you to think back to where you was on the night of Wiggin's death on the third of August.' He sounded stiff and mechanical, even to himself.

'How the bleeding hell should I know?' Rob hadn't been expecting this. As far as he was concerned, the policeman was taking a liberty.

Walter shot him a look.

There was a short pause, then the policeman cleared his throat. 'That don't sound too good, for a start.'

Rob took a step towards him. 'What the hell's it got to do with you where I was that night?'

'I'd think about it if I was you, never mind why.'

But Rob saw only the absurdity of it all. 'You ain't saying I . . . I ain't one of your suspects?' He laughed at the idea.

'Just answer the question. Where was you on the night of the murder?'

'Not at home, for a start. Ask him.' Rob nodded towards Walter. 'I'm staying at his place. Go on, Walt, tell him I was out. All night! But it ain't against the law, so far as I know.'

The policeman turned to the more respectable-looking partner. Reluctantly Walter had to agree.

'Where then, exactly?'

'I ain't checked my diary, I can't say.' Rob's face set into a sarcastic scowl. This was beginning not to be funny. He dug in his heels. In any case, the coppers twisted everything you told them.

'But you must have some sort of alibi,' the policeman objected.

'Well, I ain't. Sling me in the nick for it if you like.'

Walter walked across the yard to remonstrate with him. 'Give the man an answer, Rob. Just tell him what he wants to hear and then we can get rid of him.'

'Let him find it out,' Rob scoffed. 'Ain't that what he's paid for?' He gave the stiff-looking officer a look loaded with scorn. 'I ain't saying a dicky bird!' He went into the office and slammed the door.

Walter shook his head. The young constable gave in and went off up the court, tight-lipped. He'd been well and truly got at, but that wasn't the end of the matter, as Rob Parsons would soon see.

CHAPTER FIFTEEN

Richie's Friday was spent fruitlessly wandering the streets of Mile End in search of work. 'No Vacancies' was the word everywhere he went.

He trudged on in the August heat, hearing children wail from high in the tenement blocks, and the strains of blues music issuing through coffee-house doorways in the insalubrious back streets. The slow, decadent notes captured his mood and drew him towards the windows. Inside, there would be women sitting round tables under a haze of cigarette smoke, their eyebrows arched, their lips painted blood-red.

Richie looked, but never entered. Everything cost money. Charlie Chaplin's white face, with its bowler hat and black wedge of moustache, stared down from a billboard over the entrance to a picture-house. These days he couldn't afford to take Sadie to see a film, even if he wanted to. He went home with empty pockets, and was already there, curtains drawn, stretching his legs out across a chair, when she came in from work.

'Here I am, I'm back!' She flung down her bag and whisked back the curtains to let in the sunlight. 'Ain't it hot? I couldn't half do with a cup of tea.' She waltzed round the room, picking up his jacket from the floor, lifting his legs and putting the chair back under the table. 'But first off, what wouldn't I give for a kiss!' She perched on his knee, pecking at his cheeks with friendly little kisses.

'Steady on.' He almost overbalanced backwards in his chair, letting her tip off his knee, then pulling her upright. 'What's got into you all of a sudden?'

She laughed. 'Nothing. The sunshine, that's what. Ain't it a beautiful day?'

'That depends.'

'On what? Oh, I'm sorry, Richie. Ain't you had a good day?' Excitement at what she'd dared to do on his behalf had made her ignore his slog to find work. She kissed him more softly, this time on the mouth.

He let her cuddle up. 'How come?' he asked.

'How come what?'

'How come you ain't miserable? Ain't funerals meant to make you cry?' He stroked his broad thumb against her smooth cheek, his hand cupped around the nape of her neck.

'That was this morning,' she replied, a shade too quick.

'And?'

'And some of us have been to work since then.' His probing made her irritable, but she was straightaway contrite. 'Sorry, I never said that.' She nuzzled up to him, arms slung around his neck.

He sighed and looked directly into her eyes. 'You ain't having me on by any chance?' She was, he was certain. She was too breezy, too determined to cheer him up.

'In what way?' She opened her eyes wide, but couldn't hold his gaze.

'About going to the funeral.' For Richie, there was nothing worse than being made to look a fool.

'I ain't!' she protested faintly.

'I think you are.' He looped his arms around her waist, taking her own hands and pinning them to the small of her back.

She looked up with a half-smile. 'You got a suspicious mind, Richie Palmer.' She was caught between denial and the excitement of her secret.

'Don't. Don't play games.'

His deep, muffled voice swayed things. 'Promise you won't be mad at me,' she said. 'I'll tell you all about it, so long as you see it's all for the best.'

He leaned away. 'How can I, before you tell me what it is?'

She was committed anyway. 'Oh, all right, I ain't been to Wiggin's funeral, you're right about that.' She held a hand to his mouth before he could interrupt. 'I did something for us instead!' She wanted to rush ahead, get into the calm waters without experiencing the storm. 'Just listen. I went to see Walter. He never expected me. I just showed up at the yard. I talked to him, and he promised he'd try to talk Rob round into giving you your job back. What do you think?' She ended up breathless, trying to read his reaction.

Richie broke away from her.

'I said, what do you think, Richie?'

He headed for the bedroom, kicking the door open.

She followed him. 'I asked you nicely, don't be mad,' she pleaded. His silence was like a blow. It knocked her self-control from under her. 'Richie, please don't do this. It ain't fair.'

He turned to yell at her. 'What did you have to go and do that for? You can't push me around! Do this, do that. Work here, work there!'

His savage voice frightened her. 'That ain't fair,' she whispered.

'And it ain't fair of you to go behind my back. You could've asked me first.'

'You'd have said no.'

'Too bleeding right! No, I won't let you go crawling back to that pair! No, I don't want their bleeding job; understand?' He despaired of her naivety and selfishness.

'And where would your "no" leave us?' Sadie found the courage to fight back. '"No" leaves us bleeding well on the breadline, Richie! That's what. If you ain't gonna let Walter give you your old job back, we'll starve to death and you won't lift a finger to stop it!'

They shouted at each other, face to face. His eyes were hooded and averted, hers angry and desperate. Sadie only came to his shoulder, but, slight as she was, she would stand up to him.

'We ain't on the breadline!' he retorted.

'Not yet, we ain't.'

'That's bleeding stupid.'

'It ain't, it ain't! I went to get you work, Richie, that's what. Any work is better than nothing. If you don't start bringing something in soon, we're in the cart!' She began to sob and beat a rhythm on his chest with her fists.

He caught her wrists. 'What are you going on about? They given you the sack? It's that swine, Turnbull, ain't it?'

She shook her head. Her hair fell forward. Wet strands stuck to her cheek. 'No, they ain't given me the sack. Not yet. But they will, soon as they find out.'

'Find out what?' He held her roughly, tempted to shake some sense out of her.

'Will you listen to me, Richie? Swan and Edgar don't keep on women like me!'

'What you on about?' He let her hands drop, stood back. She was trembling and crying.

211

'Girls who ain't married and go and get themselves pregnant!' She turned to flee from the room.

Richie beat her to the door. He put out his arm to bar her way. 'Say that again!' he whispered.

'I'm pregnant, Richie. I'm gonna have a baby.' She staggered into his arms and buried her head against his shoulder.

Overwhelmed, he stroked her hair. 'You ain't?' He shook his head.

'You can ask the doctor if you don't believe me,' she sobbed. 'What are we gonna do, Richie? What are we gonna do?'

That weekend, as the weather changed from clear blue to grey and thundery, Walter Davidson made sure to drop a word in Duke's ear about the police poking round the yard after Rob. He judged it best to give the old man a chance to look after his headstrong son's interest, since Rob seemed set on a suicide mission all of his own. 'He won't give them what they want,' Walter warned Duke. He'd gone calling to Annie's house on the Sunday morning specially.

'And what's that?' Duke listened, head down, taking it all in. 'What do the police want with him?'

'Where he was the night Wiggin was done in, that's all.' Walter stood in the front room, eyes on the aspidistra, fiddling with his hat. He felt bad about tipping more trouble in the old couple's lap.

Annie drew a sharp breath.

'Why not? Why won't he say?' Duke persisted.

Walter shrugged. 'You know how he is. He don't like coppers.'

Duke stood up and walked to the bay window. 'Ain't he got the sense he was born with?'

'You know he ain't,' Annie put in. She cut a quaint figure; fifteen years out of date with her high bun, her leg-of-mutton sleeves and long skirt. Now what? she wondered. Surely the coppers weren't serious about Rob. She went to the empty grate and rattled away with the poker to no good effect, except to ease her own frustration.

'I thought maybe you'd talk to him.' Walter began to back out of the room. 'Put him straight.'

Duke nodded. 'It's good of you, Walter.'

Walter acknowledged their thanks and left quietly. Annie showed him out. When she closed the front door, she hurried straight back to Duke. 'You ain't to think the worst!' she warned him. 'They ain't about to arrest Rob just 'cos he won't tell them where he was.'

'They will if they want to.' Duke still stared out through the net curtains at the row of narrow, terraced houses opposite. He thought back to Ernie's arrest; how they could snatch someone away and lock them up in the shadow of the hangman's noose for months on end, just for being in the wrong place at the wrong time. If they could do it to poor Ernie, they could certainly do it to Rob.

'Now, I said, get it out of your head that Rob's in for it. We gotta work out a way to make him come clean, that's what we gotta do.'

Duke turned towards her, heavy and slow. The sunlight showed every wrinkle, the unkindness of the years. 'Annie, you don't think Rob done Wiggin in, do you?' There was panic in his eyes.

''Course he ain't. Rob ain't never picked on no one Wiggin's size in his whole life, you know that.' She was full of defiance, standing hands on hips.

Duke nodded. 'That's true. Only there's his temper.'

'Never,' Annie repeated. 'So forget it, Duke.'

Duke sighed. 'Right then, I'm off down Meredith Court,' he told her, 'to see if I can catch the blighter in and talk some sense into him.' He went out into the passage and took his cap from the hook.

'You want me to come along?'

'No. Man to man is best,' he told her. 'I ain't gonna pull no punches. The truth ain't that savoury, you can bet. He might not want you to hear.'

Annie tutted. 'He needs a good thrashing, that Rob. At his age and all!'

Duke went over to the taxi depot, but missed his son by a few minutes. Walter had arrived back and let Rob go off for the morning to collect Amy Ogden and take her out for a spin. He told Duke he'd tell Rob to come straight over to Annie's place when he got back.

Meanwhile, Rob and Amy drove out of town in high spirits.

'And I as good as told him he could sling his hook, bleeding nuisance!' Rob was boasting to Amy about the police visit. The car windows were open, the road ahead was clear, and though the day was heavy and grey, threatening rain, they'd both jumped at the chance to drive out into the Kent countryside and breathe some fresh air.

'Bleeding cheek!' Amy agreed jauntily. She flung her hat on the back seat and leaned sideways out of the window. 'What did Annie have to say?'

'I ain't mentioned it to her.' Rob sat in his shirt-sleeves, enjoying the speed on the open downhill stretches.

'The coppers ain't serious, then?' The wind whipped at Amy's hair, tugging it back from her round face. Rob had to veer into the side as a car approached from the opposite direction. 'Watch out!' she cried. A hedge scratched at the side of the car.

Rob swerved into the middle of the road again. 'I don't know if they're serious. I ain't a mind-reader.'

'And did you tell them where you really was that night?' Amy's smile was suggestive. She faced into the wind once more.

'Let them find out for themselves.' There was a patch of woodland ahead. Rob planned a short stop somewhere off the road. He noticed Amy's interest in her surroundings increase as he slowed the car to a steady ten miles per hour.

'Ain't this grand?' She sat up straight and adjusted her tight blue skirt, wriggling to straighten out the creases. 'Nice and shady, nice and quiet.'

'Are you thinking what I'm thinking?' Rob leaned over as he steered the car on to a level verge; an area of grass backed by wild hops, blackberry bushes and hawthorn.

'Oh, so now *I'm* the mind-reader, am I?' Amy liked to catch Rob out. He'd grow touchy and she would cuddle up to him and get the better of him. They would end up kissing and laughing at nothing. He had a handsome smile, and when he laughed, he would throw back his head and she would tickle his neck to make him laugh even more.

'Rightio, then, we won't stop!' He began to edge the car back towards the road.

She flung out her arm and grabbed the steering-wheel, pouting at him. 'Now, don't be like that, Rob. 'Course I want to stop.'

He wrenched at the brake, leaving the car pointing nose

down towards the road. Amy jumped out and stretched her arms above her head. 'We can pick blackberries.' She began to make for them through the long grass.

'They ain't ripe.' Rob strolled behind, hands in pockets. 'Come on, Amy.' He put an arm round her waist to lead her further into the wood. She pretended to resist and he felt he would like to kiss her then and there: she was warm and soft, her skin smelt of sweet, flowery perfume. He put his lips to hers.

After a while Amy pushed him back. 'Not here, Rob. Let's go away from the road a bit.' She knew what the intense look, the close contact would lead to, and she invited it. Rob was a good lover, not too rough, not too gentle. He went directly for what he wanted, but he didn't leave her out of it. He knew she liked soft words, and was neither too shy nor too selfish to deliver them. Lots of men never spoke at all when they made love; it left Amy cold. But not Rob. He was tender, and he made sure she had a nice time. Often, when they made their opportunities and she lay in his arms feeling that nothing in the world was nicer than this, she imagined she might actually be in love with Robert Parsons. But then she would gather her clothes and her thoughts about her and tell herself not to be silly; she'd known him as a pal all her life. Theirs was a pleasant arrangement, that was all.

This particular day ended badly, however. Their open-air love-making had been good, as usual, but heavy raindrops began to splash on to the leaves overhead, and they had to hurry to dress and get back to the car. Amy was still buttoning her white blouse as she ran. She jumped into the car while Rob went to the front to turn the starter-handle. Feeling the rain come down heavier, he wound and swore. The engine stayed dead. He turned again, the rain began to pour. Amy sat safe and dry inside, watching it run down the windscreen. She checked her lip rouge in her hand-mirror. Rob was a blurred shape through the downpour. The engine still refused to start.

For five minutes, Rob struggled on. Cold rain drenched his shirt and trickled down his face. He swore himself blue in the face. In the end, he gave in. He came and stuck his head through the window. 'I have to get to a telephone.'

Amy sighed. 'How long will that take?'

'I don't bleeding know, do I?' He stood in the rain, dripping wet. She looked out and laughed. His dark hair was plastered to his skull. He glared at her, then strode off down the road in the direction they had come. It would take hours to sort this out; Walter would have to come out with a tow-rope. Amy would bleat on about being late back to Dickins and Jones. Before he knew it, the whole of Sunday would be wasted.

Eventually, after tracking down a telephone box and spending a wet afternoon cooped up in the car, alternately bickering and canoodling with the infuriating Amy, Rob spotted Walter's Morris come bowling down the hill towards them. The rain had eased, and it wasn't long before the tow-rope was fixed and Walter had them facing in the direction of home.

'Bleeding car,' Rob muttered. Walter had come up to his driver's window to check that everything was ready for the tow back to town.

Walter looked him in the eye. 'We need a good mechanic, that's what.'

'You can stow that for a start.' Rob picked him up in a flash. 'If you mean Richie bleeding Palmer, I'd rather take a running jump first.'

'Ain't no good *us* trying to tinker with these old engines, though.' Walter sounded as if he was only trying to be realistic. 'Let's face it, Richie knew his way around them.' He seized his opportunity on Sadie's behalf as best he could.

Rob stared back. 'Over my dead body.'

Walter sighed and went ahead to his cab. 'By the way,' he called back, 'your old man wants a word with you. He says it can't wait.'

Rob agreed to be towed through town, straight to Paradise Court. As he'd guessed earlier, the whole day had gone to rack and ruin. 'Might as well get it over with, whatever it is,' he told Amy. They left behind the hedgerows and the woods for the lamp-posts and fire-hydrants of the urban sprawl. 'We'll pop in there first off, then I'll nip you over to Regent Street in Walter's car.'

'But I'll be late,' she complained. 'I only signed out till five. You know how hard they came down on me last time.' She arched her eyebrows.

'That was different,' he pointed out. 'Now, don't go on about it, there's a good girl.' He concentrated on the task of easing the old jalopy on the end of a tow-rope down the narrow streets and byways of Southwark to Paradise Court.

Annie invited Amy to sit in the front room with her as Rob followed Duke down into the back kitchen. 'Duke wants to have a chat,' she explained. She would sit with Amy, asking after her work prospects, reliving the old days on the market stall, while Duke sorted out the problem of the alibi with Rob.

Duke sat his son down at the scrubbed kitchen table, a stern look in his eye. He laid his cards on the table, explaining how Walter had seen fit to tell him the way police thoughts were tending over Wiggin's death. 'And a good thing he did too,' Duke warned him. 'Before you say anything against Walter, I wish to goodness you had a grain of his sense, Rob, I really do.'

Rob frowned and mumbled, 'I don't see it's his business.'

'Where's your common sense, Rob?' Duke pulled him up short. 'Sometimes I think I ain't come down hard enough on you when you was young. Especially when you was sent home wounded, and we all had to pray for you to pull through. After that, I *know* I ain't come down good and proper, 'cos of what you went through.' He paused. 'We was all soft on you then. I was about to say that I let you get away with murder.'

Rob frowned and shifted in his seat. 'Oh, come on, Pa, you ain't saying I had anything to do with Wiggin?'

'What am I supposed to bleeding well think? The coppers come sniffing round and you ain't got the nous to tell them where you was that night. No, you put their backs up good and proper. I call that well done, son. Bleeding well done.' Duke had worked himself into a state. His voice, usually quiet, low and steady, had risen. He slammed the table.

'Pa!'

'Don't "Pa" me! I ain't had my full say. Think about it, the copper goes back to Union Street. He gets the old files down. "Parsons . . . Parsons?" He looks you up. He sees the trouble we had over poor Ernie.'

'That was donkey's years back. Anyhow, he got a not guilty.' Rob found his voice.

'But mud sticks, don't it?' Duke wouldn't be shut up. 'What do you want to do to this family, Rob? Drag us through all that lot again? Ernie can't stand no more, you know that. He had a shock, and he ain't never got over it, not altogether. Annie and me, we got to put him first if the coppers get on our backs. I'm telling you, son, I ain't gonna listen to no excuses, I'm just telling you to get up that station first thing tomorrow morning, and tell them, word for word, what you got up to the night Wiggin copped it!'

Rob stood awkwardly, catching his leg on the table. 'And if I don't?' he challenged.

Duke rose to his feet, looked at him fair and square. 'Then you can say goodbye and we can say good riddance, Rob. 'Cos I ain't never gonna open this door to you no more.' His voice choked, his head dipped and shook sadly.

Stunned, Rob backed off. He mounted the step into the hallway, calling roughly for Amy to come. He was halfway to the door before Annie ran out, followed by a puzzled Amy.

'Just tell him "yes"!' Annie pleaded. She caught Rob's arm from behind. 'It ain't that hard, is it?' She'd guessed from the outcome of Duke's chat, Rob storming off like this, that he'd been stubborn and hot-headed as usual. 'Think before you dash off and do something you might regret.'

Rob shook himself free. 'It ain't me, Annie. I ain't got a word in edgeways.'

'You don't have to. Just tell him the truth. Get yourself off the hook, for God's sake!' Annie felt acutely the pain of the family splintering and breaking up.

'Tell him what?' Amy came slowly down the dark, narrow hall. She glanced back at Duke, standing head bowed in the kitchen.

Annie turned to her. 'Try and talk some sense into him, Amy. Spell it out.'

Amy frowned and patted her hair. 'I would if I could, Annie. You know me, always ready to help. But blow me if I got a clue what's going on round here!' She stood, left out, like an actor who's walked into the middle of the wrong play.

'It's Rob. They're after him. They think he had something to do with Wiggin . . . you know!' Annie couldn't bring herself to say it out loud.

Amy's mouth fell open. She stared at Rob. 'They think you done the old sod in?'

He made a move to grab her arm. She pulled back. 'Amy!' he warned.

'Yes they do!' Annie insisted. 'Look at Duke. Look what it's doing to him. He can't stand it all over again, not after Ernie. It'll break his poor old heart.'

Amy drew herself up and walked slowly down to the kitchen. She saw Duke, the picture of misery. She knew she could sort it all out in a tick. 'Don't take on, Duke.' She put a hand on his arm. 'Ain't no need to worry.'

'Easy to say,' he sighed. He cast a reproachful look at his son.

'No, honest. Rob ain't had nothing to do with Wiggin being done in. It ain't possible.'

'Why not?' Duke glanced up at Amy, his hopes revived.

''Cos he was with me,' she said, keeping her head up, spelling it out loud and clear. 'He was with me all the time it happened. We spent the night together, Rob and me!'

CHAPTER SIXTEEN

'What happens when Dickins and Jones gets to find out?' Annie turned to quiz Amy on their way up to Union Street station that Sunday tea-time. She knew the big West End stores liked to keep a strict eye on their living-in assistants. 'What happens if they catch you hopping the wag?'

'It ain't like school,' Amy retorted. She walked arm-in-arm with Rob up the damp street, following Annie and Duke's steady pace.

'More like a bleeding prison,' Rob grumbled.

'They gonna give you the sack?'

'Yes, and if they do, where does that leave her?' Rob seized on this as the reason why he'd kept quiet about his whereabouts on 3 August. 'On the dole, that's where.' It was partly true; he'd seen himself as doing the decent thing by Amy in refusing to drag her name into the mud. If he upset things for her at work, another new crib would be hard to come by.

'Oh, hush, Rob.' Amy calmed him down. 'I expect they'll land me with a fine, that's all.' She'd got a friend, Ruby Thornton, to forge her signature and sign her back in. Ruby and she would probably both be carpeted and lose half a week's wages. 'Let's get this over with. Ready?' She drew a deep breath as their little group gathered under the blue station lamp. Then they went up the steps together.

Duke pushed open the door and marched up to the desk. He announced their business to a red-haired, freckled youngster in uniform. The constable studied them, head to one side. 'I'll go get the sergeant,' he said.

Soon the old warhorse himself came wheezing out of a back office and ushered them through. He sat them down in a dark green and cream room at a deal table surrounded by six wooden chairs. A dark green metal lampshade hung low over the table. The sergeant slammed down his file and began turning pages until he found his place. 'I hear you want to give a statement?' He looked wearily at Rob. 'You don't half choose your time, pal. I was just about to clock off for the night.' He sat, pen poised.

'Go ahead, Rob.' Annie sat opposite her stepson, upright and stern.

Slowly Rob began. 'I'd like this set on the record. On the night of August the third I took Amy Ogden to the pictures at the Elephant and Castle. And after that, I drove her to my taxi depot in Meredith Court, where we spent the night together.'

Annie frowned and stared at the table. Duke looked up at the ceiling.

'Steady on.' The sergeant's pen scratched slowly over the page. '. . . "Taxi depot in Meredith Court, where we spent the night together,"' he repeated. Finally, he looked up at Rob. 'Anything else?'

'Ain't that enough?' Rob felt he'd been through the mill, with his pa and Annie sitting there and criticizing his every move. 'What do you want, a blow-by-blow account?'

The sergeant didn't blink. 'Times of day might help. When did you end up at the depot, for a start?'

While Rob hesitated, Amy jumped in. 'Half-eleven. We stopped for a drink at the Lamb.'

The sergeant nodded as he wrote it down. 'Decent little pub, that.' Then he glanced at Duke. 'Not a patch on the old Duke, of course. Now, what time was it when you took Miss – er – Ogden here back home?' He turned to Rob and Amy. The girl seemed to be brazening it out nicely. She sat, with her puckered red mouth, her pencilled eyebrows and blonde hair, a free-and-easy sort.

'Half-seven next morning, Sunday that was.' Again Amy supplied the details.

The sergeant wrote it down.

Rob stared at his broad, flat face, the seamed forehead, the thinning grey hair, oiled back and parted down the middle. 'Is that it?' He stood up, ready to go.

'Hold your horses. I ain't up with all the details on the Wiggin case,' he confessed to them all. 'I handed over to Constable Grigg. But he'll want to have this signed by you, Mr Parsons. And Miss Ogden, if you give a statement here and now, it'll save Constable Grigg the bother of coming up Regent Street for it.'

Amy's eyes widened. She hadn't expected they would go to such bother, and to avoid this disastrous possibility, she eagerly gave her own account, corroborating exactly what Rob had said. 'Rob dropped me off at half-seven all right, only you don't need to tell them that at the shop, do you?' She still hoped to salvage her reputation and escape the fine, offering the sergeant, who seemed a man of the world, a sly wink.

The sergeant jumped on this. 'Ain't you told them when you got back?'

Amy's colour rose over her tactical blunder. She sensed Rob's impatience, spotted Duke and Annie's worried glances. 'I had to get someone to sign in for me on the Saturday night,' she confessed. Now Ruby would be in trouble with the bosses for forging her signature.

'So we just got your word to go on that you was down the taxi depot, doing whatever it was you two was doing down there. But according to the book, you was tucked up nice and comfy in your own little bed?' The sergeant shoved the statement book towards her and watched her sign in her childlike hand.

'But they sworn to tell the truth,' Duke put in anxiously. 'Rob's giving it to you straight, I know he is.'

'And Amy,' Annie assured him. 'Else why would she go and ruin her good name, if it weren't the truth?'

The sergeant seemed to agree. 'I'll mention that little fact to Constable Grigg.'

'But this is the end of it, ain't it?' Duke stood up, troubled by the way the interview had turned out.

The sergeant had a soft spot for the ex-publican, who'd had his bellyful of troubles lately, a salt-of-the-earth type, as anyone could tell. 'Well, he ain't off the hook yet,' he explained. 'Sometimes young Grigg's like a rat down a drain; he finds it hard to let go when he thinks he's on to something.'

'But he ain't, is he? Rob ain't mixed up in nothing like this.'

The sergeant nodded. 'From what I hear, he's a bit of a hot-head. And he rubbed my constable up the wrong way all right. That's the thing, you see.' He offered to shake Duke's hand as they all stood up to leave. 'Pity he never came in with his alibi first off, but I'll have a quiet word,' he promised.

As the family left, he closed the file and looked out after them. He decided to keep Grigg off their backs for a bit;

give him the nice little job of going up the Embankment to talk to any of the dossers who might have seen what went on that night. At least it would take the heat off Duke Parsons for a bit. The poor old blighter looked like he couldn't take much more.

August 1924 came to an end, and there was a lull in the police activity over Wiggin's death, as far as Rob, Amy and the residents of Paradise Court were concerned. Street attention focused instead on the shiny new frontage of the Prince of Wales. Workmen came to fix electric lights both inside and out. The smell of fresh paint and varnish, provided by Tommy O'Hagan at special cheap rates, hung heavy in the still, hot air.

'So when do you lot pack in?' Tommy quizzed one of the decorators as he took the money for a tin of brown varnish and a metal comb to pattern the surface. The redecorations seemed to be taking an age.

The young lad, whose own pasty, pliable features seemed to have been pressed on to his face like putty, gave a shrug. 'We've to clear out by the end of September. That's when the new licence comes through.'

'Any word on the new landlord?'

'No, it's all very hush-hush,' the boy replied.

'I expect they're worried in case they have a lynching on their hands if news gets out too soon.' Tommy pushed his cap to the back of his head and settled in for a gossip. The decorator's lad had to stand, varnish pot in hand, and listen to the ins and outs of street politics; everyone was against the brewery and for the old landlord, Duke Parsons. 'What did he do wrong, for God's sake? Put more money in their tills, that's what.' Tommy was gathering an audience in his loud defence of Duke. 'Gave the people round here more of what they wanted, that's what. A nice place to meet your mates and have a quiet drink, that's all.'

'A bit of a sing-song on a Saturday night,' Nora Brady joined in. 'Where's the harm in that?'

'A place to pass the time of day without no one breathing down your bleeding neck,' another, henpecked voice cried.

'A pub that was a cut above some!' The consensus was instantaneous. Feeling came through loud and clear that since the brewery had turfed out Duke Parsons, the heart had gone out of Paradise Court.

Residents moved in and out, as usual. Seamen came and went from Eden House. Willie Wiggin's old room was re-let to a young American fireman from a transatlantic cattle steamer, recognizable by his shiny peaked cap and his disconsolate air. He told Bertie Hill he planned to stay only a few weeks before finding an empty boat to sail back home.

'If he can save his money and stay off the booze,' Joe O'Hagan told Arthur. 'The way I look at it is, he's already been on one binge and drunk away all his wages. Even if he finds work round here, and it don't fall off trees, my bet is that's where his money will end up again, down the bleeding drain.'

But Katie stood up for him. 'He ain't like the men round here, Pa. He don't drink.'

Her father swore she was a fool. Every man worth his salt enjoyed a good pint. 'Hey, you ain't gone and fallen for him, have you?'

She denied it hotly. Which meant she had, her mother realized. The young American's name was Jack. He had wide, grey eyes, a frank expression and a good physique.

Mary noticed he spent much time hanging around the market, looking for the chance to home in on Katie's stall. Her daughter would respond by laughing and looking coy by turns. Mary's heart was squeezed. She remained tight-lipped when Katie came home chattering ten to the dozen about Jack Allenby. 'See!' she reported to her father. 'They ain't allowed a drop to drink in America. Soon as his ship docked and he got paid off, he sent every penny back home to San Francisco, to his mother and his little brothers and sisters!'

'Good for him,' Joe retorted, on his way out to the Lamb and Flag.

But the most significant move into the court was Jack and Edith Cooper's return to one of the terraced houses opposite Annie and Duke.

The house had been rented out for years to immigrant families and transient workers, and was sadly neglected now. It had belonged to Edith Cooper's mother until her death from cancer in 1910. It stood empty for three years, then Jack saw a way to capitalize on Edith's small inheritance by renting it out. Now it was the only thing they could rescue from the bankruptcy courts, since the old East End house was in Edith's name and therefore untouchable. Swallowing their pride, they came back to their roots with worse than nothing. Jack carried a chip on his shoulder so huge that it turned everyone against him. Edith's life of genteel luxury lay in ruins. So they sat in cold and hostile silence in the kitchen of her mother's grimy house, before Frances and Hettie Parsons came calling one Sunday in mid-September, with a polite invitation for tea at Annie's house, which Edith shed a tear over accepting, and at which Jack snorted with bitter contempt.

Annie welcomed Edith to her house, hiding the shock

she felt over her altered appearance. The store-owner's wife's hair had been left to fade from rich autumn brown to its natural grey. She wore it in a plain bun low on her head. Her eyes were red-rimmed and lifeless, her cheeks drawn. Of course, the light cream and fawn coloured clothes were still good, but she wore them without conviction, as if they'd been made for someone else and suited her ill. They'd been tailored in better times for the graceful, confident figure she once possessed. Annie was careful to draw the line between compassion and patronage, offering tea and thin sandwiches, taking care to outline how bad things were in general for the people round here. Still, her sharp eyes picked up the large amber and gold brooch which Edith wore pinned to the high neck of her cream blouse. It seemed that the bailiffs hadn't taken quite all, she remarked to Frances afterwards.

Hettie wished Edith Cooper well and shook her hand before she got up to go and catch her bus to Ealing. 'It's early days for you, I know,' she said, 'and I expect you and Jack will want time to get your feet under the table before you start looking around for the next thing. But it just so happens that me and Jess are looking for help in the shop. Nothing too hard. Just someone to help keep the order book straight and help with appointments and so on. I thought you might like to think about it for yourself.'

Edith considered the sweetly delivered offer.

'Shall I mention your name to Jess?' Hettie urged.

After a long hesitation, Edith agreed. She took Hettie's hand between her own. 'If you think I'd suit. I'll have to ask Jack, of course.'

Hettie nodded. 'No rush. Think about it while I talk to Jess. We've a little place on the High Street, not too grand.'

Edith smiled for the first time since her move. 'Thanks so much, I can't tell you . . .' She struggled for words.

After Hettie and Frances had both gone, Annie let Edith weep on her shoulder. 'Hettie's got a heart of gold,' she told her. 'But she won't offer a person work if she don't think she's up to it.'

At that, Edith cried some more.

'And you tell that old man of yours, you plan to take up Hettie's offer,' Annie insisted. 'Whether he likes it or not.'

'There you go again.' Jess laughed. Hettie had gone into work next day and described the Coopers' plight. She asked her sister to think of having Edith to work in the shop. Jess sat scalloping the hem of a white chiffon dress which hung to a sporty knee length, and was designed to be worn with a jaunty embroidered skull cap set off with a swirling white feather. 'Thinking of others as usual!'

'But Edith could be just what we want.' Hettie pleaded her cause. 'You know how nicely she speaks, a real lady. And she ain't pushy. She knows stock-keeping. It'd leave us free to design and make here in the back room, instead of the "Yes, madam, no, madam" lark out front.'

Jess laughed again. 'I ain't arguing.'

'Does that mean yes?' Sitting at her machine by the window, Hettie paused. She kept her fingers crossed.

'Yes, 'course. I think it's a marvellous idea.'

Hettie's eyes lit up. 'Then I'll go across next weekend and fix it up,' she promised.

For a while the two women worked on in silence, sitting heads bowed, amid yards of clean-smelling new fabrics, surrounded by scissors, pins, measuring-tapes and dressmakers' dummies.

'I been thinking,' Hettie said at last.

'Don't do that. It can lead where you don't want to follow,' Jess joked. 'And then you're in a fine mess.'

'No, honest, Jess. I been thinking about George and me.' For weeks they'd been dancing around one another, unsure of their next move.

'See!' Jess snapped a thread and shook out the skirt of the dress. 'What did I say?' She made it a rule these days to push all worries about herself and Maurice to the back of her mind.

'I mean to say, George and me, we've known each other for years now, but we ain't getting nowhere fast. Not to my mind, we ain't.' Hettie allowed a sigh to escape.

'Don't he make you happy?' Jess took up the subject in earnest; it was rare enough for Hettie to give time to her own concerns.

Hettie thought hard, letting the whir of her machine carry the talk forward. 'Not happy exactly. Contented is more like.'

'And ain't that enough?'

'For me it is.' Hettie's own horizons weren't grand. She'd seen a terrible thing happen to Daisy O'Hagan, and she experienced the effects of raw poverty each time she walked into the Bear Lane Mission. So expectations in this life had to be limited, she knew. It was a subdued life at best, rising to glory at last in Christ's presence. Only, she wasn't so blinded by the light that she didn't notice the hopes and dreams of other, more secular beings. 'I think George wants more,' she admitted.

'Does he want to marry you?'

'He ain't asked me.'

'But does he want to?'

Hettie nodded. 'I think he does.'

'And do you want him?'

'I ain't sure, Jess. That's what I been trying to explain. I like George. There ain't no harm in him, and he's good and honest.' She shook her head, annoyed with herself. 'I'm not saying it's him; it's me!'

'Your heart don't race when you see him?' Jess remembered the quick, passionate longing she'd felt for Maurice in their first years together.

'No,' Hettie said quietly. 'I feel warm towards George, but I ain't head over heels and that's a fact.'

For a while silence overtook them again.

'Do you want to break off?' Jess stood up to hang the nearly finished garment around one of the dummies. She stepped back to assess the hang of the skirt from the hip.

'No,' came the quick answer. 'Only I don't know if it's fair on George, the ways things are. Should I tell him I ain't head over heels, Jess?'

Jess considered this. 'He knows you ain't, I expect. And he still sticks with you.' She nodded, satisfied with her work. 'You can stop worrying about George. What about you, Ett? Do you need a bit of mad passion in your life?'

They both laughed, then grew serious again. 'What do *you* think?' Hettie said at last.

Jess smiled. 'I say, passion ain't everything.'

'Meaning?'

'Meaning, I'd take care of what you got, Ett. George is a lovely man and he loves you to bits. Another woman could come up and offer him the whole world, and he'd say no thanks and stick with you. You'd go a long way to find that again in a man,' Jess said sadly. She went across and hugged Hettie's shoulders. 'There, that's what thinking does for you.' She put her cheek against her sister's. 'I'd best be off to collect Mo from school. I'll be back in a few ticks,' she said.

When Maurice got home late that evening, Jess had cause to refer back to her conversation with Hettie. 'Passion ain't everything,' she'd said. It could get you into a marriage, but it didn't make you stick.

Maurice went upstairs for his ritual of looking in on Grace and moving Mo back to his own bed, breathing in the calm of their sleeping bodies. But it wasn't enough to take the edge off a frustrating day. When he went downstairs to greet Jess, he began to relay his trials and tribulations without pausing to ask her how she was.

'We had a projectionist off sick at the Gem, and a reel of film broke down at the Palace. Ten people asked for their money back at the end, and I don't blame them. On top of that, Charlie nearly bit their heads off for asking. I had to step in and keep the peace.' He sighed as he unlaced his shoes and kicked them off under the table. Then he loosened his tie and took out his collar studs. 'I been thinking; Charlie ain't up to it lately.'

Jess picked him up. 'Ain't he allowed one mistake?' She thought Maurice was sometimes hard on his employees, expecting 110 per cent from them all the time.

'I ain't talking about *one* mistake,' he said irritably. 'I'm talking about him going round like it's the end of the bleeding world. People don't go for a night out to look at his miserable face. I have to keep on telling him to cheer up.'

Jess stood in her blue, satiny dressing-gown. 'Is that all he's done wrong?'

'It's enough.' Maurice himself found Charlie's glum face depressing.

'But he ain't never late. He ain't never down on the takings, you said so often enough yourself. He's got a good head for figures, and he ain't never let you down.' She tried to rescue Charlie Ogden's image before Maurice consigned him to the reject pile. He made so few allowances for the differences between people.

'Look, Jess, I ain't asking for your point of view.' He was tired, he had too much on his mind. You had to run just to stand in one place in the cinema business, and Jess didn't appreciate that he needed a bit of care and affection when he came home late at night. Instead, she was forever standing up to him, wanting an argument.

'Shh!' She put a finger to her lips and glanced upwards to the children. 'If you ain't asking for my opinion, why bother telling me all your problems?' she demanded in a whisper.

He flung his loosened collar on to the table and turned away. 'Where's the bleeding milk?'

'Shh! It's in the pantry, the same as always.'

'Don't I even get a decent cup of cocoa made for me when I get in?'

'If you ask nicely, yes.'

They stood face to face, she looking at him in cool disdain, he sulky and spoiling for a fight.

'Anyhow, you helped me make up my mind. I thought about it, and I decided Charlie ain't up to it no more. I used to think he was on the ball, full of ideas and so on. But now he's standing still while things go racing ahead of him. The fact is, I'm gonna have to let him go, ain't no two ways about it.'

Jess stared at him. 'You ain't giving Charlie Ogden the sack? Not after all this time?'

'And what if I am?'

'But what's he done, when all's said and done? You can't sack a bloke just because he don't go round smiling all the bleeding time!' Jess never swore, but she was beside herself. 'What's got into you, Maurice Leigh? I can't believe I've heard this.'

'Well, you wouldn't understand,' he said. To make things worse, he changed tack and tried to belittle her reaction. 'Hold your hat on, I can see you've had a hard day yourself.' He adopted measured tones and waited for her to calm down as he stood over the pan of boiling milk. 'You get yourself off to bed. I'll finish off down here.'

Jess was almost speechless. 'I ain't had a bad day,' she countered, drawn into an irrelevant distraction. 'In fact, I had a very good day. We took orders for over ninety pounds' worth of stuff, and we took on a new assistant to help run the shop.' She gathered her dignity as best she could.

Her success was just the thing to grate on his nerves again. 'Yes, and Mo never sees his own mother.' He flung the worst thing at her; the one he always used when his back was against the wall. She never found a reply to that one.

Jess retired hurt. But tonight she didn't go and cry into her own pillow. She went upstairs and along the landing to the spare back bedroom, took blankets from the chest and curled under them on the bed, praying that Maurice wouldn't soften and come to seek her out. She wanted to be left alone; every nerve ending cried out, every grain of her being detested what was happening between her and Maurice.

*

On the morning of 1 October, the smart black doors of the Prince of Wales were opened for business. George Mann shot the bolts and swung them open, letting the sun shine into the bar with its dainty white window drapes and pale, plain walls. The pub stood ready for business.

George stood on the step, looking up and down the street. A light drizzle dampened enthusiasm, and the crowds weren't exactly flocking.

Arthur Ogden strolled casually down Duke Street, first on the scene. He stood, hands in pockets, his cap pulled well down. 'Lor' lumme!' He glanced inside and whistled in exaggerated surprise. But it wasn't the new decor that had brought him nosing around. He was after the vital piece of information; the one everyone had been seeking. 'You got the new man in there, I take it?' he said, nodding and winking at George. The name of the new landlord had been held back by the brewery like a state secret. Not a soul down the court had been able to winkle it out.

George nodded.

'Come on then, who've we got?' Arthur shoved past and stuck his nose inside the inner door. He caught sight of a stocky, fair-haired figure in waistcoat and shirt-sleeves standing behind the bar. 'Blimey!' Arthur couldn't believe his eyes. He scrambled back on to the street. He blinked in broad daylight. Had his eyes deceived him? He darted back inside for a second look. Then he was out on to Duke Street, bad back forgotten, dancing through the market like a bantamweight, darting into Henshaws', in and out of the market stalls to deliver the news. 'Would you bleeding believe it?' he crowed. 'The blooming brewery, guess who they gone and got for landlord?'

'Who?' came the cry.

Tommy ran out into the middle of the street, Nora Brady

left her fish stall, Bea Henshaw poked her head out at Ernie and told him to go and find out what the fuss was about. Dolly Ogden came trundling up the court.

'Who?' Tommy demanded. 'Spit it out, Arthur!'

'They only gone and got in Bertie Bleeding Hill!' he gasped.

The news dropped into a stunned silence. The doors of the Prince of Wales stood ready to receive customers, and behind the bar stood the ex-copper, owner of Eden House, and now new licensee of the old Duke of Wellington public house: Bertrand Gladstone Hill.

CHAPTER SEVENTEEN

The only person on Duke Street who was pleased with the new situation was Alf Henderson, the landlord at the Lamb and Flag. Trade was booming, with an influx of new regulars since the mass boycott of the Prince of Wales.

Henderson, a whippet-like man in his mid-forties, with wayward grey-brown hair that had the texture of scrubbing-brush bristles, a narrow face and a long nose, couldn't believe his luck. He doubled his orders of beer from the brewery almost overnight, barrels emptied almost as soon as they were tapped. Less meticulous in his methods than Duke Parsons, his cellars were often awash with slops, his spittoons full to overflowing with sawdust and cigarette butts, his glasses ringed with tidemarks from the day before. None of this mattered, however, as the Ogdens, O'Hagans, Walter Davidson, Nora Brady and her market pal, Liz Sargent, Rob Parsons and many others from the Duke crowded through his door, eager to slake their thirst.

'I ain't never gonna set foot inside that horrible new place,' Liz Sargent declared, her hatchet-face stuck glumly over her pint of porter. 'Makes me bleeding sea-sick just to look at it.' She was referring to the new cone-shaped wall lights and streamlined look that gave the Prince of Wales the air of an ocean-going liner.

Nora Brady nodded her agreement. 'Like I says to Annie just the other day, you can see it all now.' The gossip grapevine had turned it all around; Wiggin had been wrongly accused, Bertie Hill had planned every move.

'Yes, you don't have to look far to see who turned old Duke over to the coppers after all.' Liz enjoyed the gloomy talk; it suited the nights that were drawing in and turning cold. Already there was a nip of frost in the air.

'No, and it weren't Willie Wiggin,' Nora said darkly. 'So I hope whoever done him in ain't done it just because of that.' A miscarriage of justice would be a terrible thing; supposing Wiggin had been murdered due to the impression that *he* was the one who'd lost Duke his licence.

Liz reached up to readjust the hatpins in her brown straw hat. She jabbed them into her bun to hold the hat tight in place. 'They ain't still after Rob, are they?'

'They are!' Dolly muscled in, her instinct for gossip undimmed by the change of venue from the Duke to the Flag. 'Ain't you heard? That young copper was down Meredith Court again last week. It seems he ain't happy.'

'Why, what happened?' Nora finished off her drink. She wiped her mouth with her kippery apron and stood up ready to return to her stall.

'Let's just say, Rob weren't too happy neither.'

'Did he clock him one?'

'He would have if Walter hadn't stepped in.' Dolly shook her head. 'They still can't get enough on Rob to arrest him, but they're having a bleeding good try.'

'So, if Wiggin didn't do the business with the licence, who did?' Alf Henderson came round collecting empties, a stained red and white teatowel tucked into the waistband of his trousers. He dropped ash on the table from the cigarette hanging out of the corner of his mouth, and left it there untouched. His motive in finding out the identity of the police informer was clear; he had to be sure he didn't get caught out by the same bloke.

Dolly regarded him with open pity. 'Ain't you put two and two together yet, Alf?'

'And made five, like you, Dolly?' came the quick reply. 'And rob you of the thrill of telling me?' He was a quick-talking, edgy man with a snappy temperament.

'I've a good mind not to let you in on it,' Dolly huffed. 'See how *you* like losing your licence.'

'Come off it, Dolly.' Liz didn't want to run the risk of sacrificing another Duke Street watering-hole. She beckoned Alf across. 'It's obvious, ain't it? Since they opened the old Duke under a new name with Bertie Hill in charge, the whole street's been buzzing with it. Don't you see, it was Hill what dropped Duke in it!'

Alf wasn't slow to see the logic. 'But you can't be sure,' he objected.

Once more, Dolly swept aside doubt. ''Course we're bleeding sure. Think about it, we been pottering along at the Duke nice and quiet, year in, year out, with no one to bother us. Duke opens and closes the doors when it suits his customers. We take no notice of all that after hours lark. Then along comes that snake, Hill. He buys up the old tenement and shoves up the rents, a real old Scrooge. He comes drinking at the Duke, but he ain't welcome. It's never his shout, and he never sticks his hand in his pocket to pay his round. He trots home to bed at half-ten like a good little boy.'

Alf nodded at each emphatic point.

Dolly sailed on. 'And when we come to mention it, we seen him skulking round the place with strangers. They was narks, plain as the nose on your face. He gets Duke in a whole heap of bother with the coppers, then he goes straight down the brewery and sticks his name at the top of the list to be the next landlord, before anyone else gets a look in. The brewery keeps the lid on it; Hill's promised them lots of fancy changes and more money in their tills. He had it all worked out, see.' Dolly had been the very first to spot the conspiracy, forgetting all charges against Wiggin, the moment Arthur had darted on to the street shouting Bertie Hill's name.

'I ain't never taken to him.' Joe O'Hagan, wise after the event, had found his own cramped corner at the over-crowded bar. He rebuffed an approach from a Salvation Army collector, a girl of about eighteen with a mass of wavy, light brown hair tucked under her blue bonnet.

'Just tell your Tommy to give him the cold shoulder, then,' Dolly reminded Joe. 'We don't want no one round here breaking the boycott. We're gonna starve him out, see. If no one buys nothing from the bleeding traitor and the pub stands empty, week in, week out, the brewery will soon get sick of that, and Bertrand Gladstone Hill will be out on his arse!' She grinned in anticipation, ordered Arthur to buy her another drink, and then she settled down at Liz's table for a game of cribbage.

Among the rampant changes and the campaign to freeze Hill out of his new tenancy, George Mann found himself at a loss. He was no more pleased than the next man at discovering the identity of the new landlord, but he decided to hang on as cellarman for a few days, until he'd had a chance to talk things through with Hettie. He went about the business of rolling the empty barrels up the ramp and through the bar, out front on to the pavement, ready for collection. When the drays rolled up to deliver the new ones, he shouldered them from the cart and rolled them on the return journey down into the cellar. There he set them up on the long gantry, tapped the vent holes to allow the keg to breathe and inserted a new tap in one end. No need to worry about giving them a chance to settle before use, however; the barrels stayed full, just as the bar above stayed almost empty of customers.

George quickly learned how to handle his new boss's unsmiling demeanour and lack of experience in the job. He ignored them both, relieved of the necessity of maintaining a false cheerfulness by the former, and simply covering up the latter with his own expertise. George could have run the pub single-handed, with trade the way it now was.

It had one advantage: Bertie Hill's intention of keeping a clean nose with the brewery meant that he stuck to the letter of the licensing laws, so George got off early on the first Saturday night after an evening of desultory passing trade, despite the elegance of the new surroundings.

'Word will soon get round,' Hill assured his trickle of customers, including Jack Cooper. 'Then things will really take off.'

Cooper nodded and knocked back his whisky. He didn't care where he drank, so long as people minded their own business and left him to his. His skin was mottled by years of over-indulgence, and sagged badly around the chin and eyes, which had all but disappeared behind folds of flesh. His appearance was going downhill fast: the good suits to the pawnshop to support his growing drinking habit, the bowler-hat fingermarked and scuffed. These days he neglected to shave and wash. Grime had collected beneath his fingernails, and his shoe leather was grey and cracked. He didn't even care that Edith left him daily to his own devices, setting off at dawn on the bus to Ealing, getting into her stride as the new assistant at Hettie and Jess's dress shop. She took care not to mention it to him, lest his temper flare, when he would snarl abuse about her descent to shop-girl status at the grand old age of fifty-five.

That Saturday, George left the pub at half-ten on the dot. He took his cap from the hook in the hall and collected his old sit-up-and-beg bicycle from the alleyway at the back. Then he shot off in the direction of Bear Lane, to meet Hettie out of the Mission. On his way, he met Rob Parsons, the two men stopped to chat, and George promised Rob that he would see his sister safely home to Ealing.

'Blimey, you ain't gone and got yourself an old jalopy, have you, George?' Rob knew it was too late for the trams and buses.

George grinned. 'No such luck. But a pal of mine's just got hold of an old Matchless motor-bike and side-car. I was planning to ride over and borrow it, then take Hettie home in that.'

'Ett in a side-car, eh?' Rob gave a low whistle. 'Best of luck, mate.' He flicked his cigarette butt into the gutter. 'How's things?' he asked obliquely.

'You mean at the Duke?' George stuck by the old name. 'Slack, Rob. Ain't nothing doing.'

Rob grunted with satisfaction.

'I been thinking of handing in my notice,' George went on. 'I don't sleep easy in my bed no more.'

Rob shook his head. 'Think twice before you jump ship,' he advised. 'No one holds it against you for hanging on to the job.'

George nodded. 'Thanks, Rob. I'd best be off.' He set off again, pedalling hard uphill towards Commercial Street, where his friend, Herbert Burrows, lived. After a rapid bargaining session over the loan of the motor-bike, a gleaming black and silver roadster with a four-cylinder engine, George took the machine out of the back yard on to the road. He kicked the pedal starter and roared the motor into action with a twist of the handlebar throttle. He set off and within minutes was approaching Bear Lane in a cloud of blue smoke and petrol fumes.

Taken aback, Hettie caught sight of him as she came out of the Mission. She accepted the lift and stepped gingerly into the three-wheeled, sporty little side-car. 'Good job I tied my bonnet on,' she joked nervously. It was her first time in such a contraption, which seemed dangerously fast, unstable and close to the ground. She found going round bends too terrifying for words, and the roar of the exhaust as George came down the gears to stop at junctions jarred her nerves.

At last, Ealing Common hove into view, edged by gas-lamps, covered by a fine autumn mist. George slowed to a halt outside Jess's house, jumped off the saddle and ran gallantly to open Hettie's low door. She felt her knees wobble and her hand shake as she stepped out.

'You wasn't scared, was you?' George grinned.

'Not a bit. Just chilly,' she said airily. Then she laughed. 'Scared to death, if you must know.' She invited him in for cocoa, glad to have him there to help break the atmosphere that was bound to develop between Jess and Maurice when he got home from the cinema.

When Maurice did walk in, George was already sitting with his large hand wrapped around a blue and white striped mug. He was there when Maurice told Jess that he'd carried out his threat to sack Charlie Ogden for not pulling his weight. Jess could only sit there in silent, helpless anger. Then George changed the subject by dropping his own bombshell. 'I decided, I'm gonna finish at the Duke tomorrow,' he announced. 'I ain't happy under Bertie Hill. I'm gonna look around for a new place.'

When they got over their surprise, Hettie, Jess and Maurice nodded, understood, showed their appreciation. At just gone midnight, Hettie showed him to the door, waiting for him to fix his cap on his head, back to front, to keep the peak out of the wind. Then she kissed him gently and gratefully.

'I did the right thing, then?' he asked. 'I don't want no one thinking bad of me.'

'No one could,' she whispered. 'Least of all me, George. I think you're a lovely man, and I'm a lucky woman, that's what I think.'

Their embrace, close and warm, sealed his decision. Next day, his day off, he went specially to the Duke and told Hill he could stick his bleeding job on someone else, if he could find anyone in Duke Street low enough to take it on.

In the middle of October, Sadie went back to the doctor to have her pregnancy confirmed. The baby was due in May.

After her row with Richie over going behind his back to see if she could get his old job back, she hadn't dared follow up the possibility, and Richie was still without work. True to his word, Walter had in fact telephoned to say that Rob was fixed as ever against the idea of reinstating Richie. Rob was in a spot of bother himself, and Walter advised her to leave the problem alone for the time being. He was sorry, but try as he might, he hadn't been able to help.

As her troubles mounted, instead of going under as might have been suspected, Sadie's backbone seemed to stiffen. As soon as the baby became definite, the tears and pleas vanished and she became determined to manage. She put it down to an experience she had on coming out of the doctor's surgery with the news that she was indeed pregnant.

She thanked the doctor, a bookish-looking young woman with horn-rimmed glasses, who'd chosen to come and work in London's East End after a medical training in Edinburgh. She was observant enough to notice that Sadie's left hand lacked a wedding ring. 'And you think you'll be able to manage?' Dr McLeod asked, remarking Sadie's slight figure and pale young face.

Sadie nodded. 'Yes, thanks. We'll be fine.'

'We?'

'Me and Richie, the baby's pa.'

Reassured, the doctor smiled. 'And you have family to help?'

'Ain't no need. We'll manage.' Sadie's head went up as she walked from the surgery and headed, only partly consciously, by bus along the leafstrewn and windswept roads to Green Park, where she alighted and gave herself one precious half-hour to absorb the news.

It was five o'clock, the sky already lead-grey and fast losing its light. The leaves of the sycamore trees hung from their branches like so many limp yellow flags. Brown ones, already fallen, crunched underfoot. A cold breeze made her pull her red coat around her, shoulders hunched, cutting across the grass to avoid the paths where tramps slept upright on the benches and stray dogs searched for scraps. No lamps were lit, and it was easy for Sadie to feel herself swallowed by the dusk, to sense a calm beginning to envelop her, here under the trees, among the green and gold and autumnal browns. She stopped to look up through the branches of a great horse-chestnut tree, watching leaves loosen and spiral to the ground. 'Well,' she thought, as clearly, as certainly as she'd ever thought anything, 'I'm gonna have this baby.' Immediately she talked to the child in her womb as if it had life of its own and was capable of hearing. 'Don't you worry, everything's fine now. I'm gonna take care of you and see to you, and you ain't never gonna be left on your own.'

She strode on across the grass. 'We'll have each other, and Richie will grow to love you as much as me. There'll be the three of us, and we don't need no one else. There's gonna be just me and you and Richie. Life's a wonderful thing, I promise. The world's a beautiful place. Look at the trees, them leaves, that sky.'

She walked herself into a trance, only breaking out of it when she reached some far railings, and the sound of trams, buses and other traffic broke into her daydream. Then she caught sight of the clock in the square tower of a church opposite, saw that Richie would be expecting her. She turned to go home to Mile End, and to talk over realities; the fact that she would lose her job as soon as her condition began to show, that they must meanwhile scrape and save every penny, that he must find work at all costs.

For days after Maurice announced that he'd gone ahead and sacked Charlie Ogden, Jess could hardly bring herself to speak to him. His apparent heartlessness frightened her; how could he throw on to the scrapheap someone who'd trusted and relied on him for so long? Charlie had even cut short his school career to go into the cinema business, dreaming the boys' dream of bright lights and success, albeit from the wrong side of the flickering screen. True, his enthusiasm had waned along with those early dreams, but he was reliable, he knew all there was to know about front-of-house, and besides, the Ogdens were close neighbours of the Parsonses, and Jess felt personally responsible for letting them down.

What would Charlie do now? His slight stature and sensitive air made him ill-equipped to vie for work on the docks, or even on the markets, and Jess couldn't see him chained to a factory bench for the rest of his days. These thoughts churned in her head, like a whirring engine that drove her further out of sympathy with her husband's action. Maurice himself, his mouth set firm, his eyes avoiding hers, refused to discuss it.

When she heard of it, Amy sparked like a firework. The idea that Charlie had been badly used lit her anger and sent her running in all directions: to the Gem where she demanded but failed to get a confrontation with Maurice Leigh, down Paradise Court to her own house, where Dolly sat grim-faced, Arthur fumed helplessly, and Charlie himself was nowhere to be seen. Then Amy went down to Annie's house, muffled in her fur collar and black wrapover coat, hammering at their door to see if Duke could be persuaded to reason with Maurice on the phone.

Annie came to the door. 'Duke ain't well,' she reported. 'I sent him to bed with a hot-water bottle and a dose of cough mixture.'

Amy was near the end of her tether. 'I'm sorry he ain't well, Annie. But have you heard what they done to Charlie?' She got rid of some of her frustration by taking Annie through events step by step. 'It ain't right, you gotta admit. Maurice is getting as bad as them bosses in the mines and in the mills up north. He's playing God; ain't nobody gonna stop him?'

Annie shook her head in embarrassment. She'd asked

Amy into the front room. 'I ain't got the full story,' she reminded her. 'I'd have to talk to Maurice.'

Amy seized on this. 'You're a pal, Annie. You do that, and I'll nip across to the depot and see if I can get Rob on our side. I tell you what, by the time we're finished, Maurice will be sorry he started any of this.'

Annie saw her out and watched her go, running up the court between pools of gaslight, disappearing round the strangely quiet corner where the new electric lights glared from the walls of the pub. Quickly she shut her door and went to think over this latest event.

'Rob?' Amy dashed into the taxi depot. He was sitting by the telephone, feet up on the desk, catching forty winks. He awoke with a start.

'Where's the bleeding fire?'

'Ain't no fire, Rob, but I'll light one under Maurice Leigh's backside if he ain't careful!' Once more she recounted the full story. 'You have to tell Maurice to give Charlie his job back, right this minute. Get on the phone to him, why don't you?' She thrust the telephone towards him.

'He'll be at work.' Rob sniffed. 'Anyhow, I can't go barging in. It's his affair, ain't it?'

Amy snorted. 'You bosses, you're all the bleeding same!' She recalled how quick Rob and Walter had been to get rid of Richie Palmer the minute the mechanic crossed them over Sadie.

Rob was stung. 'No, we ain't. Ours was different.' He stared back at her. 'From what you say, Charlie ain't done nothing wrong.'

'Not a blind thing. It's that Maurice. He's too big for his boots these days. Well, if there was a union Charlie could join to look after his rights, he'd sign up like a flash.'

'Steady on, Amy.' Rob stood up. He found himself torn

249

two ways. His instinctive sympathy in any situation was still for the underdog, even though he respected Maurice's business sense and strong ambition. 'Listen, I'll have a word with Maurice as soon as I can. That'll have to do for the time being.'

Amy subsided into Rob's vacant chair. 'That's something, at any rate.' At last she'd run out of anger over Charlie.

'You're your mother's daughter all right.' Rob perched on the desk and smiled down at her. 'I like it when you get mad,' he said suavely.

'Yes, and you've been watching too many Douglas Fairbanks pictures,' she grumbled, already melting under his flattery.

'Ain't I told you, you're the splitting image of Gloria Swanson?'

'Only when you want something out of me, Robert Parsons.'

Rob's expression was one of pained innocence. 'Me? How could you?' He leaned forward to kiss her on the mouth. 'See, all I wanted was to give you a kiss.'

Amy tilted back her head, closed her eyes and sighed. 'And here I have to go and spoil a good thing.'

'Why, you don't have to get straight off, do you? Can't you stay a bit longer?'

She nodded, opening her eyelids. 'It ain't that. But now I'm here, there's something I gotta tell you.'

Rob leaned back, took out a cigarette and lit it. 'Fire away.' He expected another of the little melodramas that Amy went in for.

She decided not to beat about the bush. 'I ain't sure yet, Rob, but I think I'm having a kid.' She said it straight out.

She'd known for weeks, but only just got around to having it confirmed.

Rob looked as if he'd been shot. He sat rigid, ready to keel over at the news. 'How?' When he did find his voice, out came this childish question.

'How do you think, Rob?' She arched her eyebrows. There: she'd gone and spoiled anything they might have had going for them. She had sense enough to realize that by dropping this hot potato in his lap, Rob would want to run a mile. That was the end of their little jaunts and nights together. 'I thought you ought to know, that's all.' She stood up and gathered her coat about her.

But Rob threw down his cigarette and caught hold of her arm. 'Amy, have I got this right? Are you saying this kid's mine?' He knew he wasn't her only boyfriend, far from it.

Amy, apparently so blasé, seemed wounded by this. 'I wouldn't be telling you if it wasn't yours, now would I? I'd be dropping the bad news on some other poor bleeder.' Her voice was dry, edging towards a break. She tried to pull free and walk away. 'It's all right, Rob. I ain't gonna hold you to nothing. I know we been playing a dangerous game and breaking a few rules here and there if we wanted to stay out of serious trouble. In the end, I only got myself to blame.'

But he stood in her way, still trying to take in the news. 'What you gonna do now?' he whispered.

'Leave it to me,' she sighed. 'A friend of a friend . . . You know the rest.'

'You gonna get rid of it? Is that what you want?' Rob was confused. But he stood in her way, barring her exit.

'Look here, Rob, forget it. Forget I ever said it. I'll deal with it by myself. I won't be the first girl who's had to, and I'm bleeding sure I won't be the last.'

'And you say he's mine?'

'*It*,' she insisted. 'Yes, yes! Got it? Come on, Rob, let go of me. I gotta go.'

Her determination seemed to set him on his own course. Never in his wildest dreams did he think this would happen. At the same time he knew his precautions weren't thorough, but so far they had been without any consequences. Now it had happened, and something told him this wasn't a life you could just throw away. Perhaps he'd seen too much of that in the trenches – human life trampled in the mud and barbed wire – ever to contemplate wasting it himself. But there was a more positive idea too; a flickering notion that he might be a father, a good one at that. No one had planned it this way. He didn't think Amy had trapped him; she was too smart to risk it. No, it was one of those things. Looking at her now, he saw her struggling for control, wanting to walk clean away. 'Don't,' he said, pulling her close. 'I want you to stay.'

'I can't, Rob. I ain't in the mood.' Tears had begun. She was ashamed of her weakness.

'No, I mean I want you to stay with me.' He held her. 'I want us to keep this kid, Amy. And if you like we'll get married beforehand, just to make it all legal and above board for him when he's born.'

CHAPTER EIGHTEEN

Duke was ailing, Annie realized. Bronchitis had settled on to his chest, worsened by thick smog; that combination of wet mist, factory and traffic fumes that they called the London particular. It sank on the lungs like an acrid, cold blanket; filthy, bitter-tasting and thick.

It held up the traffic and clogged up both mind and body. No one felt like venturing out, and if they had to, they muffled up behind thick woollen scarves wrapped two or three times around the face. Other figures would emerge out of the yellow mist, insubstantial as ghosts. Sensible folk stayed in and waited all through late October for the fog to lift.

Duke sat indoors, struggling for breath. Annie tried him with poultices and inhalations to ease the congestion. Frances brought flowers of sulphur, friars' balsam, various pick-me-ups, all to no avail.

'It ain't the same down this end of the court,' he confided to Frances. 'Don't say nothing to Annie, but up at the Duke I could catch my breath, even in the worst of these pea-soupers.' He drew breath through a crackle of congested phlegm and fluid, shaking his head in helpless frustration.

Frances knew it was a state of mind as much as anything. Duke was pining for the beer barrels and pumps, the routine, the company of the old way of life. Down here he felt useless, his life's work valued as nothing by the brewers. It was a bitterness that found no expression, and dragged him into a decline, like the murky fog all around. She patted his hand, shook her head sadly at Annie and trailed off home.

But Annie refused to let Duke sink into apathy. She walked him about the house, wrapped in thick layers of vests, cardigans and scarves folded tight across his chest. She got people to visit and keep him cheerful; he was fond of Walter popping in for a chat, and Arthur Ogden needed no encouragement to come on an evening and put his feet up by their hearth for a game of dominoes and a steady supply of malt whisky. 'Purely medicinal,' he assured Annie, who kept a critical eye on the bottle. 'It helps clear the chest.'

But there was one visit, far from welcome, that occurred as the month drew to a close. There was a knock on the door, and Annie opened it to the uniformed figure of Constable Grigg.

Her smile turned to a frown. 'You come to tell us the name of the one what done Wiggin in?' she barked; a terrier on her home ground.

Grigg stepped over the threshold, shaking out his cape and spying the row of hooks in the hall to hang it from. Reluctantly Annie led him through to the kitchen, where Duke sat, pale and drawn, wheezing heavily. The policeman took in the tidy scene; Annie's copper kettle singing on the old-fashioned hob, the polished steel knobs, the blacked grate. A tub of coloured wooden spills sat on the mantelpiece, next to a fat biscuit barrel and a framed photograph of the whole Parsons clan. Grigg spotted Rob in the back row, recognizable by the black moustache and the jaunty set of his hat. Duke and Annie sat on the front row, bang in the middle, staring proudly out. 'I'm sorry you ain't feeling too good,' he said, thrown off his investigative stride. 'This won't take long, I hope.' He sat on the wooden chair offered by Annie, then cleared his throat.

'It ain't the time it takes I'm worried about.' Duke regarded him with suspicion. 'So long as you get the right man in the end.' It was the first they'd seen of the police since Annie and he had gone up to Union Street with Rob and Amy, and they'd begun to hope that the trail had gone elsewhere. The reappearance of the keen young bobby was by no means good news. 'You seen Rob's statement, I take it?'

The policeman nodded. 'And I went to see him too. There's some things that don't add up, though.' He was feeling increasingly uncomfortable as he pulled out his notebook and pencil. It was his idea alone to pursue the case. His sergeant had put him on to other cases, but at the end of the day he kept coming back to this one, and it was Rob's fault, he told himself. Rob should never have tried to make a fool of him during that first interview at the garage; that's when Grigg had dug in his heels, and never really let go since.

'Like what?' Annie tried to deflect attention from Duke. 'Rob's made it plain where he was, ain't he? What more do you want? It cost Amy Ogden plenty to come clean over that, so I hope you ain't bothered the girl by going up Regent Street and pestering her.'

'No. I've been following other leads. Wiggin knew some of the old dossers and I been asking around, but they ain't giving me nothing new so far. That's why I'm here, see. We're back to square one in some ways.'

Annie sighed and looked at Duke. 'Trust Wiggin.' Even though he was dead, he was still heaping trouble on their heads. 'Look,' she said, 'we already told you all we know. Wiggin went missing more than twenty years since. When he showed up again, I put a roof over his head and I paid his rent. No one knows what he got up to while he was away, except to say he was in prison some of the time, and for the rest he had a bleeding good go at drinking himself to death. By the time he holed up in Bertie Hill's tenement, his mind was unhinged. He weren't easy to look after, I can tell you. All he knew was how to get hold of the next drink.' She told the story quietly, with painful resignation.

Constable Grigg nodded. 'I got all that.' He finished scribbling a few notes. 'Now, what I want to know is exactly what happened when you went and found him missing on the fourth of August.' He sat, pencil poised.

Duke coughed and shifted in his armchair. 'Ain't nothing to tell. She goes in the room with Ernie, finds it turned upside-down, sends for help.'

'Hang on. When did you last see him alive?' Grigg concentrated on Annie.

'Saturday tea-time. I took his tray.'

'How did he seem?'

'Quiet. No trouble.'

'Any drink in the room?'

'Not that I saw. But he'd hide it, see. He was cunning in that direction.' Annie told it without emotion.

'But there *was* drink in the room on Sunday, when you finally got in?'

Annie nodded. 'Broken bottles, spilt liquor; you could smell it from outside the door. No sign of Wiggin, though.'

'So who brought him the drink?' Grigg sucked the end of his pencil. He imagined a session of hard drinking in the fetid cell they called a room, a drunken fight, a lunge with a broken bottle, then the messy business of clearing away the corpse. But how had the murderer got the body up to the river? It was too far to drag it, and too obvious. You'd need a car to hide it in. This brought him back full circle to Rob Parsons. 'Look,' he said, turning to Duke, 'I ain't clear what your son, Rob, was up to. First off, he refuses to give an alibi. Then, when he comes up with one, it's all cobbled together over a girl he's supposed to have spent the night with, only she ain't with him, she's tucked up in her own bed, according to another version. Then there's the business of getting rid of the evidence.'

'How's that?' Duke picked him up sharply.

'Cleaning out the room, removing traces of the victim's blood.' The policeman reverted to official jargon as he saw Duke's colour rise.

'That ain't got nothing to do with removing the evidence,' he protested. 'I told him to do that.' His knuckles gripped the arms of the chair. 'That was me, see. I sent him down here for a scrubbing-brush and bucket to tidy the place up a bit. Rob only did it 'cos I told him to.' A man's every deed could backfire, he realized.

Grigg tapped a loud full stop with his pencil. He flipped his notebook closed and rose to go. 'I see,' he said. It was evident he suspected another cover-up. The family was running round in circles to protect what looked like the black sheep, Robert. He bid the old man and Annie a curt goodbye and went straight back to Union Street to consult with his sergeant.

'Right!' Annie said, as soon as she'd shut the front door on him. 'That bleeding does it! Who's he think he is, bleeding Sherlock Holmes?'

Duke wheezed and coughed. 'Ain't that just our luck

these days? To have some fresh young bobby on the case.'
He shook his head, going over what he'd let drop, to see
how he might possibly have further incriminated Rob.

'You wait here,' Annie ordered. She went for her hat and
coat, then called back in, 'Keep yourself warm, Duke. I'll
send Katie to check on you.'

'Where are you off to?'

'To find Rob and sort this lot out once and for all!'

Annie ran through the fog up Duke Street, spotted Rob's
parked taxicab and dragged him from his lunch-time break
at Henshaws' eating house.

'Hold your horses, Annie, where are we off to?' He
managed to gobble his meat pie and swallow a mouthful of
tea. Then he followed her small, determined figure out on
to the street.

'In the car, Rob. Hop in. We're gonna take a drive, you
and me.' She ran to the passenger door and sat in the seat,
willing him to hurry and start up the engine.

It fired, he climbed in and leaned forward to wipe the
windscreen. Outside, he could see about ten or fifteen yards
ahead. 'Where to?'

'Up the river, under the arches, wherever them dossers
hang around on a day like this.'

He looked quizzically at her. 'What's this about?'

'Wiggin. We're gonna find who done him in.'

'We are?' Rob pulled away from the kerb, half-amused,
half-anxious. 'We ain't gonna do nothing stupid, are we,
Annie?'

'Just what the coppers ain't been able to do all these past
weeks,' she told him. 'What do you reckon, Rob? Them old
tramps, they ain't got nowhere else to go. They hang

around the same old places, day in, day out. One of them must have seen or heard something the night Wiggin ended up in the water.'

Rob had to go along with it. There was no stopping Annie in this mood. 'Aye, aye, cap'n,' he said.

'It's getting your pa down.' Annie sat bolt upright as they drove along. 'We still got Wiggin slung round our necks like a bleeding albatross. We gotta get rid of him and give Duke a chance to pick up, otherwise I don't think he can last the winter.' Her voice choked and died, as Rob steered, almost blind, through the swirling fog.

At last, leaving the cab parked under a dripping tree, the two of them walked along the riverside to the sound of foghorns and the muffled chugging of steamboats heading upriver. Annie made Rob accost any bundled-up, stumbling shape who chanced to veer towards them from the wide stone steps leading to the wharves, or sitting silent on wet benches, waiting for the day to end. But her heart sank at each vacant gaze or hostile shove. Rob couldn't even get the tramps to stop and listen.

When they came to Southwark Bridge, they descended to the river bank and approached the stone arches where they knew the men and women slept out in all weathers. Sure enough, the shelter was crowded with misshapen figures, padded with newspaper and wrapped around with blankets, sacking tied around their ankles, half-drunk or crazy, starving, hostile as Rob and Annie went into their midst.

A woman's voice swore at them. Three men huddled over the embers of a fire made from driftwood and foul-smelling refuse. Another man loomed up, hand outstretched and shaking with palsy. Rob refused him and he went off cursing.

'This way.' Rob steered Annie towards the three old tramps crouching over the dying fire.

They were deep in conversation, discussing the means to get themselves a bed for the night.

'I won't stand another night of this,' the first man said. 'I'll go and smash a window, a big one, and get myself run in for a few days. Then I'll have a place to kip, and some grub.'

The two others mumbled on. 'Soaked to the skin,' one complained, his back to Rob and Annie. 'I been out three nights. One more night of this and they'll have to come along and pick me up dead.' He blew on his freezing hands.

The third, a taller, stronger-looking man than his companions, caught sight of their visitors. He turned on Rob fiercely. 'Don't never grow old, lad.'

Rob took a step back and put out an arm to protect his stepmother.

'Die when you're young,' the man went on. 'This is what you get for being old.' He cast a hand towards the huddled, starving shapes. 'We wish we was dead. It can't come too quick.'

In spite of everything, Annie's heart went out to him. He was sober, at least, and with the tough, leathery skin of a seafarer, his eyes wrinkled as if permanently staring across sunlight on the sea. 'It ain't that bad, surely,' she said quietly, still hanging on to Rob's arm for safety. To one side, the sluggish brown water slid by. Overhead, the dirty arch of the mighty bridge rose in the mist.

'Worse.' He shook his head. 'Worn out, I am, and I worked all my life. I ain't never taken charity, but I'm worn out now and on the scrapheap.'

He turned to wander off, but Annie stepped to one side of the fire and followed him, Rob close behind. 'How would you like to earn a bed for the night?' she said, direct as ever. 'Not charity, mind.'

'And pigs might fly.' He shuffled on.

Annie took a florin from her bag. 'There's this for you if you can help us.'

The tramp seized the money and bit at its edge. Rob made as if to snatch it back before he pocketed it without giving them what they wanted in return, but Annie restrained him.

'You got your money, now you gotta help us,' she ordered.

He returned a brief nod.

'Right, did you ever come across a man by the name of Wiggin?' Annie demanded. 'William Wiggin. Smaller than you, thinner, about the same age. Pretty far gone with drink.'

The tramp scratched at his wrinkled, bearded face. He sniffed, caught the phlegm in his throat, spat, then turned to go. 'He ain't here. The coppers already came poking round after him.'

'But you know him?' Annie stepped in quick. 'We know he ain't here. He died, didn't he?'

'Better off dead,' the tramp insisted. 'Yes, I knew a man called Wiggin. Him and me sailed together on more than one crossing. He ended up on the scrapheap, just like me. Only, he found a way out, lucky beggar.'

'How did he die?' Annie asked. 'Did you see?'

This time, Rob had to restrain Annie before she scared off the tramp with her eagerness.

'How?' The old man searched his memory, as unclear as these shapes huddled all around. 'How did old Wiggin die?' he muttered aside to his two companions, still clinging to the last red glow of their fire.

'Bled to death,' came the muffled answer. 'Like a stuck pig.'

The picture came back. 'That's it, Wiggin bled to death.'

'How?'

'He turned up here one night a few weeks back. Came staggering down them steps, blood everywhere. Someone tried to grab the glass in his hand, but not before he gave himself one good cut, right here.' The man pointed to his own chest, then made a stabbing motion.

Annie shuddered and clung to Rob. 'He stabbed himself?' she echoed. 'He done it to himself?'

The tramp nodded. 'He never knew what he was doing, just slashing away with the broken end of the bottle, catching himself here and here, like I said. He never felt nothing, mind, he was too far gone.'

The picture pierced Annie's mind. She put her head into her hands.

'Better off dead,' the tramp insisted. 'That's the one thing he did know. Drunk himself into oblivion, then done himself in with a broken bottle. You should've seen the look on his face when he came down them steps. You could see he was glad. Blood everywhere, and staggering about, and some idiot has to go and try to tear the bottle out of his hand, but he's done enough. He takes his last breath. We stand and watch him keel over the edge. There's a splash. They chuck the bottle in after him. That's it.'

Rob held an arm around Annie's shoulders. 'Why ain't you gone and told the coppers?'

The tramp shook his head. 'They can find out for themselves, I say.' He looked straight at Rob, as if he knew he would understand.

It cost them a couple of half-crown pieces, and took a deal of cajoling to get the tramp into the taxi and up to

Union Street. He'd never set foot inside a police station in the whole of his life, he insisted. But when Annie outlined the situation, what was left of his better nature triumphed. He considered it was a fair bargain; a few shillings for a week's kip in a seaman's hostel in return for the truth, the whole truth, and nothing but the truth.

They buried the mystery surrounding Wiggin's death at last, thanks to Annie. He'd taken his own life and put an end to his misery in the only way he knew. Rob described how Annie had gone down on to the wharf like a little grey pigeon, chest out, shoulders back, narrow boots pit-pattering down the steps, and God help anyone who stood in her way. The dossers had parted for her like the Red Sea. 'I was scared stiff myself, believe me.' Rob held Amy's hand, as they stood side by side in Annie's kitchen, telling Duke, Ernie, Hettie and Frances the full story. 'But I'm off the hook, thanks to Annie.'

Duke growled and smiled. He got up unsteadily from his chair. 'You come up trumps, like always.' He put a fond arm around her shoulder. 'But I don't want you going off no more, see. I was worried sick till you got back.'

Annie tutted. 'It weren't as bad as Rob makes out.' She smiled up at Duke, pleased to see him out of his chair and looking happy.

'Ten times worse,' Rob insisted. 'I thought I'd landed in hell, I can tell you. Them miserable blighters ain't got nowhere to go, asleep on their feet in that horrible fog; women with babes in arms . . .' Suddenly he stopped and turned to Amy. 'Bleeding cheerful charlie, ain't I?'

She squeezed his waist. 'Tell them now,' she whispered. 'Give them our bit of good news to keep them happy.'

'Tell us what?' Annie came up close and studied their secretive faces. Behind her, Duke stood with his thumbs in his waistcoat pocket, looking shrewdly at Rob.

Amy had taken Rob by surprise, as ever. He'd planned to share their news with his pa over a quiet drink, not surrounded by a gang of women who would go and spread it up and down the street. But he couldn't back out. He felt his face redden, began to fiddle with his cuffs, cleared his throat. 'Amy and me is gonna get married,' he said in a flood of embarrassment.

Annie's mouth fell open, then snapped shut. 'About bleeding time,' she said at last.

Duke came forward, wheezing, shaking his head, laughing and saying how glad he was. Frances hugged Ernie. Hettie squeezed Amy. There were smiles all round.

'You mean to say, you don't mind?' Amy was overwhelmed. She thought that, like her, they wouldn't see her as a good match for Rob. Their warmth touched her to the core.

'A wedding!' Even Frances looked genuinely pleased. 'When? When's the big day?' It seemed the news of Rob being in the clear and about to be married had lifted years off her.

'We ain't settled that yet, have we?' Details began to swamp Rob. He hung on to Amy's hand, squeezing it hard.

'Soon,' Amy promised. 'Before Christmas, I hope. We still gotta tell Ma and Pa and make the arrangements. Who's gonna be your best man, Rob?' She looked up at him, rolling her eyes in Ernie's direction.

Rob stepped forward. 'Ern, I want you as best man,' he said awkwardly, with none of his usual slick confidence. 'You gotta be there to help me through this.'

Ernie grinned and nodded. 'Best man!' he said, shaking Rob's hand, smiling at his pa and Annie.

Hettie came up to join in the laughter. 'Me and Jess will make your wedding outfit,' she said to Amy.

'Oh no!' Amy wouldn't dream of it. 'It ain't gonna be nothing posh.'

But Hettie gently insisted. 'Don't go and spoil things. If Jess and me can't make the outfit, how are we gonna feel, watching you go up the aisle in someone else's dress?'

'In that case.' Amy hesitated, Hettie cajoled, Amy accepted. 'A dress made specially!' Her face shone. She threw her arms around Rob. 'Pinch me and tell me I ain't dreaming,' she pleaded.

'You ain't.' He pinched her waist. 'And if I don't bleeding well get back to work, we ain't gonna have nothing to live on once we're hitched.' He hugged her, took his trilby hat from the table and went off whistling. Outside, the fog was thick as ever, and the street-lamps were just being lit. 'Blimey,' he said to himself, turning up his coat collar. 'Look what you just gone and did, you and your big mouth.'

Meanwhile, Amy couldn't wait to release the news to the waiting world. She dashed up the court, cock-a-hoop, to her own house. 'Ma, Rob and me's getting married,' she crowed. For once, Dolly was speechless.

... 'Me and Amy's getting hitched,' Rob told Walter glumly when the latter asked him what was the matter.

'Blimey.' Walter sat down at the desk. 'That's a bit sudden, ain't it?' ...

*

. . . 'Me and Rob's getting married!' Amy bubbled over with enthusiasm as she delivered the news to Charlie, who she found drowning his own sorrows at the Lamb and Flag.

'Better make it quick,' he commented, staring into his beer.

Amy's heartbeat quickened. Had he got wind of anything he shouldn't? Rob and she had decided to keep the news about the baby secret until the families got used to the idea of them being married. 'How's that, Charlie?'

'If you want me to be there,' he explained. With one dream of success in the cinema game shattered, he was quickly rebuilding another. 'I aim to sail for America as soon as I got the wherewithal.'

Amy gasped. 'Where did you get that idea?'

Charlie jerked his thumb towards a corner of the bar, where the sailor, Jack Allenby, sat deep in conversation with Katie O'Hagan. 'Jack says it's the land of opportunity.'

'What's he doing *here*, then?' Amy asked drily.

'Oh, he ain't gonna be hanging around much longer. Him and Katie are off to San Francisco, soon as ever they can.'

Amy stared. 'They ain't!'

'Ask them.'

'That'll be a bit of a winder for Mary, won't it?' Amy's imagination went full-tilt. She gazed at handsome Jack. 'Mind you, I could see why she'd fall for him.' She paused. 'Only, what's he see in her? She's a little mouse, ain't she?'

'Miaow,' Charlie said, with a gulp of his beer.

'I ain't jealous of Katie O'Hagan.' Amy gave him a shove and waltzed out of the pub, showering congratulations on Katie and Jack, sharing her own good news. 'Me and Rob

Parsons is getting married!' she said to whoever cared to listen . . .

. . . 'Congratulations. Amy's a decent sort.' Walter came to terms with the news and took Rob for a celebratory drink at the Flag. They'd missed Amy by just five minutes, Charlie said.

'Oh, we get on like a house on fire,' Rob assured Walter. He knocked back two quick whiskies.

'So what brought this on?' Walter suspected more. He knew Rob as a footloose, fancy-free sort as far as the girls went. He'd often envied him his flexibility in his choice of girlfriends. There was he, Walter, still stuck on Sadie, all these months after she'd gone off to live with Richie.

Rob fell into confidential mood, the whisky working its way down his gullet. 'Amy's in the cart, you know. I mean, that ain't the only reason, 'course. But I can't drop the girl now, can I? It ain't right.'

Walter drank and nodded. 'You sure, Rob?'

'What?'

'Better think it through now before it's too late. Not that I'm trying to put you off the idea, don't think that. Like I said, I like the girl.'

'But?'

'But do you love her, Rob?' Walter couldn't get it into his head that his friend was serious.

'You make it sound like bleeding prison.' Rob's laugh was shallow. 'I'm only marrying the girl.'

'And how do you know for sure that it's your kid?' Walter pushed the point home.

Rattled, Rob insisted that he was the father. 'Amy says

he's mine, and she ain't a fool. She wouldn't trick me, not over something like this.'

Again, Walter nodded. 'Sorry, Rob. It ain't none of my business.' He extended his hand. 'I hope you'll be very happy, mate.'

Rob accepted the congratulations. It wasn't second thoughts that Walter had just shoved into his head. It was third, fourth or fifth thoughts . . .

. . . 'He ain't getting cold feet?' Jess had invited Amy to the shop to go over some designs for her wedding outfit. She laid out the drawings on the table in the back workroom.

'I think he is,' Amy said, with a bright smile.

'Trust Rob,' Hettie laughed. 'He always knew how to make a girl feel wanted.'

'Anyhow, we already sent out the invites.' Amy studied the styles Jess had come up with. She needed something to disguise her thickening waist; a straight dress with a loose satin jacket and wide revers. Nothing too flimsy or revealing. Luckily Jess had come up with winter designs that would be suitable.

'The thing is, to keep the dress and jacket nice and plain, like this one, cut on the cross so the skirt hangs nice, in a heavy, smooth cream satin for the jacket, and something lighter for the dress.' Jess got caught up in her creation. 'Then we can put all the detail in the head-dress; scalloped lace with a little coronet of seed pearls and lily-of-the-valley. Very up-to-the-minute.'

Amy's eyes glowed. 'It's lovely. That's it. That's the one.'

Then it was Hettie's turn to show her some fabrics,

suggest some shoes from the shop. Edith Cooper was there to offer her congratulations. Amy smiled and said yes to this and that, taking her time to choose. Then she glanced at the time and said she must fly: Rob and she had arranged to look at some rooms to let above Powells' ironmonger's shop on Duke Street. She'd promised to meet him there at half-five.

Hettie and Jess waved her off, then went inside. 'She seems happy,' Jess commented, folding away her drawings.

''Course she's happy. And Rob's a lucky man,' said Hettie, ever generous, ever optimistic . . .

. . . 'I ain't never felt so important in my whole life.' Amy sighed. She sat with Rob in the taxi, parked just off Regent Street. She'd told him about her trip to Ealing to choose her wedding clothes, putting off the moment when she would have to kiss him goodbye and trudge up the metal staircase to the women's dormitory.

Rob caught her enthusiasm. ''Course you're important. Specially now.' He slid a hand around her waist.

'Yes, but Jess and Hettie, they make a girl feel special.' She revelled in it, allowing herself the luxury of believing in what until now had been a dream that happened to other women, not to her. It was a strange process, to strip away layers of worldliness, even cynicism which she'd built up over the years, to dare to be innocent again.

She was hoping for a happy ending with Rob. They'd taken the rooms over the shop, and Rob had told her to hand in her notice at Dickins and Jones. 'Ain't no point in you working after we're hitched,' he told her. 'You'll want to put your feet up.'

'I ain't sick,' she protested. 'I'm only having a kid.'

'Bleeding hell!' He stopped her mouth with a kiss. Passers-by might hear.

'They don't care.' Amy laughed. 'But I don't want mollycoddling, Rob. I'll have the rooms to sort out. We'll have to get the stuff from Tommy and paint that ceiling, for a start.'

They argued over who would climb ladders and where the baby would sleep. Nevertheless, Amy knew, as she finally waved Rob on his way round Oxford Circus, that the time would soon be here when they would have their own place, and that this would be one of the last times she would have to watch the taxi disappear into the traffic before she climbed the stairway to her lonely crib.

CHAPTER NINETEEN

St James's, Dolly Ogden's regular church, tucked away behind Marshalsea Road, was the venue for Amy and Rob's wedding on a cold, clear morning in late November 1924. Blackened by soot, its gothic tower a favourite pigeon haunt, nevertheless the bells rang out as the guests arrived spruce and correct in their suits and smart outfits.

Tommy O'Hagan turned up in a new pair of wide trousers and a double-breasted jacket, his mother, Mary, in a decent grey coat and hat. Katie went into the church arm-in-arm with her handsome sailor, the envy of all her friends. Even Joe sloped along to see the couple married. Not so much lapsed from the Church as gone for ever, his memories of the Catholic Mass were uncomfortably revived by the stained-glass angels and brass altar-cross.

Amy had sent out invitations to the whole of Paradise Court, to her pals from Dickins and Jones, and to her old mates on the market. She persuaded Edith Cooper to show up, just for the ceremony, she said. The other older women – Nora, Liz and the rest – had come to accept the ex-storeowner's wife and greeted her cheerfully at the doors of the church. They were all dressed up in Sunday best, with new feathers in their hats from Katie's stall, and fox furs slung around their shoulders.

Then, once the church was two-thirds full with friends and a gang of children and idlers had gathered at the gate, the families began to arrive.

Frances and Billy, quietly and nicely dressed, slipped in first, followed by a stir when Maurice and his family drew up in their new motor car and stepped out. Grace and Mo walked up to the church hand-in-hand with their mother, the little girl looking lovely in a broad-brimmed emerald velvet hat and matching coat. Mo was buttoned inside his pale camel-hair coat with its brown velvet collar, his black hair brushed across his forehead, looking serious as he held tight to his mother's gloved hand. Jess herself wore a fur-trimmed outfit in autumn gold, plain but beautifully made, with a neat cloche hat to frame her dark features. Maurice followed close behind in his dark suit, the picture of a successful businessman.

Then Hettie came up the path with George, smiling at friends, stopping to wait for Duke and Annie and able to enjoy a few moments of wintry sunshine. Opinion was that although the other sister, Jess, had plenty of style without being showy, Hettie's outfit came off best, with its pearl-grey hip-length jacket trimmed with grey fur, its slim, longer-length skirt and neat kidskin shoes. They thought she suited it and looked more relaxed, whereas Jess was smart but self-conscious. She hadn't quite carried it off, they thought.

But Annie, the stepmother of the groom, looked perfect. Without trying too hard, without being bang up-to-date, she radiated happiness from her little, upright figure. She came only up to Duke's shoulder, and her hat was as wide as she was; a square-crowned blue one with a dipping, broad brim. Her pointed face smiled from under it, she walked tall in her royal blue outfit, her arm in Duke's. The old man wore a white buttonhole in his pinstriped suit. He'd aged, they thought. Still, he looked proud and steady.

Then came the groom and the best man. They drove themselves to church, arriving in good time. Rob stopped in the porch to check details with Ernie: the order of events, the ring. Then they went nervously in.

Just time then for Dolly to arrive all in purple, with Charlie in tow, fussing over her hat, her gloves, her fur stole, Charlie's tie and glum expression. A dozen pigeons perching on a flat black tombstone took flight, clattering into the air as Dolly paused to inspect everyone, took a deep breath and plunged into the church.

On the stroke of midday, Walter drove up with Amy and Arthur, his car decked with white ribbon and gleaming in the sun. He opened the door to let out the bride; a white foot and stocking, a flowing cream skirt to the knee, a silky jacket and cascading veil. Amy clutched her lily-of-the-valley bouquet, steadied herself on her father's arm, and walked the endless path to the church, through the porch, down the aisle.

During the whole ceremony, with half of Southwark gathered behind and lifting the roof of the church with their singing; during the exchange of vows, the fumbling with the ring, the vicar's sing-song blessing and the signing of the book, Amy's terrified fear was that someone would 'find her out'. This was how she put it to herself. Lawful impediments would be produced, something would crash into her happiness and smash her apart from Rob. She trembled with superstition, with the notion that there was still time for him to change his mind, that fierce little Annie would find out about the baby and prevent the match.

Only when the register was signed and witnessed, when they walked clear of the small, fusty vestry to face the congregation and walk down the aisle together to the swelling notes of the organ, did she believe that she, Amy Ogden, was now Amy Parsons, and safely married to Rob.

The groom, still ill at ease, caught sight of Walter in the front pew. He negotiated two shallow steps into the aisle with Amy on his arm. Walter winked and nodded. Rob grinned back. The music pushed the couple down the aisle together, out into the bright sunshine. There was a photographer organizing guests into a horseshoe shape around the happy couple; endless photographs.

Amy's veil was trampled, Arthur fretted for a drink to calm his nerves. The photographer bent over his tripod and ordered them to smile. Dolly reorganized everyone, refused to stay still, insisted on at least two photographs from each angle. The photographer softly blasphemed under cover of his black velvet hood. At last they could disperse.

The wedding party trooped across the streets, down the main thoroughfares, back to Duke Street, where Dolly had got up a reception at Henshaws'.

Then the toasting and the speeches began. Arthur took copious Dutch courage before he stood up. He swayed and thanked everyone for coming. He said how proud he was of Amy, and how lovely she looked. Amy blushed. Dolly sat in her purple finery, challenging anyone to deny it. Arthur said how well matched the couple were, how the Ogdens were proud to have Parsons as in-laws, though at one time they'd hoped for Bishops.

'Pa!' Amy protested.

Arthur laboured the joke. 'One of Amy's young men, his name was Eddie Bishop,' he explained. 'Only, no need to worry, Rob, it never came to nothing.'

By this time, the guests would laugh and caw at anything. Arthur rambled on, people drank up and started to tuck in, lifting their glasses to this toast and that. Rob stood up to sit Arthur down, on Dolly's instructions. He offered more thanks, lost his way, pulled a piece of paper from his pocket. Then he screwed it up and tossed it over his shoulder. 'Ain't no need for that.' He grinned. 'Amy and me, we just want to say thanks to Dolly and Arthur for putting on this do for us, and thanks to Pa and Annie for everything they done.' He smiled broadly to left and right, ran out of people to thank and sat down.

Duke sat at the top table, Annie on one side, Ernie on the other. He brimmed with pride. It was the third wedding in the family, after Jess and Frances, and so far everything had gone smoothly. Rob, whom he never thought would settle down, had met his match in Amy. Duke expected there to be a few fireworks; neither was the placid type, and they'd have struggles over money, like everyone else. But Amy would coax Rob out of his moods when he got down, and if she was a bit loud, like her ma, it was what Rob needed to keep him steady and his nose to the grindstone.

In his turn, Rob had been brought up to take his responsibilities seriously, with a good, strong sense of his roots. And he seemed genuinely fond of the girl. Duke watched them joining hands over the tiered wedding-cake, ready to cut through the white icing. That was the funny thing about weddings, he thought; each one came along coloured by memories. He thought of earlier ones: his daughters', his friends', especially his own. His two marriages, first to Pattie, then to Annie.

Annie leaned over and broke into his reverie. 'There's just one thing I ain't happy with,' she whispered, her dark eyes dancing.

'What's that?' Duke clasped the hand she'd laid on his arm.

'I think that me and Dolly must be related by marriage now.' She pinched her mouth as if tasting a lemon. Dolly was winding up the gramophone, vigorously sending people out on to the dance-floor. Annie shook her head in dismay. 'Who'd have thought it, eh? Me, in-laws with Dolly Bleeding Ogden!'

'I heard about Sadie. Ain't it a shame?' Dolly felt it was time to let her hair down. She'd done the honours and got everyone dancing to gramophone records she'd heard earlier in the year at the Empire Exhibition over in Wembley. The Charleston had really got the young ones going: Katie O'Hagan was teaching the little girls all in a row, hands on knees, pigeon-toed. Now Dolly came and settled on to a chair next to Billy and Frances. 'Word gets round; it can't be helped.'

'She made her own choice.' Frances turned frosty. Dolly was employing her usual crafty tactic of making generalized, sympathetic noises, purely in order to extract more information. The music, breakneck and breathless, clattered on.

Dolly tapped her fingers in her broad lap. 'All the same, she ain't done nothing to deserve this.'

Frances weighed up what Dolly must be getting at. It wasn't Sadie's outright refusal of her invitation to the wedding; this was common knowledge and already discussed to death. Sadie had received the silver-edged card through the post and telephoned Hettie to say she wouldn't be able to come. No reason, no apology. At the same time, she let slip to her sister that she and Richie were expecting a baby. It was due in May, and she asked for it to be kept quiet. Hettie could pass it on to their pa, and he could choose who else to tell within the family. She'd rung off with a brittle cheerfulness. To Frances, the fact of Sadie's illegitimate pregnancy wasn't the stumbling block; it was the way she'd cut herself off from the family that hurt. After all, she could have come to see Annie and Duke to give them the news face to face.

But it was the sort of thing that seeped through the walls of Paradise Court. Not only had Sadie run off with the moody mechanic from the taxi depot, but now she was living in sin with him and having his kid. She would have nothing to do with her family since Rob had sacked her man. She was always spirited and maybe a bit spoiled. A handful at least. The myth grew of Sadie having had too much of her own way, and now she was paying the price.

Frances knew that the gossip about her sister had leaked far and wide. Only the other day, a woman had come into the chemist's shop for Andrews' Liver Salts and asked when the baby was due. She was tired of fobbing people off and telling them to mind their own business.

'I expect she'll have to pack in her job.' Dolly sighed. Her soft, purple, brimless hat had settled into a pork-pie shape on top of her head, in vivid competition with her rosy, round cheeks. The wide sleeves and high collars which still found favour with the older women made her seem trussed up like a leg of lamb, and trapped her body heat. Noisily she fanned her face with a napkin. 'I only hope she knows what she's doing, poor girl!'

'Yes, and I'll pass on your regards, Dolly.' Frances stood up to move away.

Dolly looked startled. 'You ain't never gonna dance the Charleston?' She'd taken offence. Frances was being snootily secretive as usual. Now Dolly got her own back. She glanced at the young girls bending their legs in and out like pieces of elastic, criss-crossing their skinny arms. 'This ain't your type of thing, surely?'

'There's the cake to wrap,' Frances replied. 'Your talking about Sadie just reminded me; I told her I'd take some cake over to her next time I visit. You don't mind, do you?'

Dolly was wrong-footed. 'Go ahead.' She scowled. 'Take her as much as you like. And be sure you tell her I was asking after her.'

It was Dolly's only setback of the afternoon. Straightaway she buttonholed Hettie to hear how Edith Cooper was making out in the shop. 'You've been an angel to that woman, Ett,' she told her. 'With her old man going downhill fast, and everything going to the bailiffs, your little job's just what she needs. I seen her at church, and I says to her she's looking very nice. I can tell she's happy to be there. It's hard on the poor thing, coming down in the world with a bang like that.'

Hettie smiled and nodded until Dolly ran out of steam and moved across to discuss Katie O'Hagan's plans to elope across the Atlantic with Jack Allenby.

'We ain't eloping, Dolly,' Katie laughed. 'Ma and Pa know all about it; it's all above board. We're saving up the passage money. Jack's writing to his ma and pa telling them about me.'

Dolly turned to the open-faced, well-built young sailor. Within five minutes she had his entire life story under her belt; his mother's age, his father's occupation, the jobs on offer in San Francisco for the likes of Katie. 'And what's your ma say?' she asked the girl.

Katie sighed. 'She says "good luck". She wishes she'd had the chance at my age.'

'She'll miss having you round.'

'She will, Dolly. Don't think I don't know.' Katie looked wistfully across the room at her mother, a little one on her knee, Tommy bending over her shoulder to tease the child.

'But good luck to you, I say and all!' Dolly rose, and, letting her purple sail billow in the wind, she drifted across the little square of dance floor to her next port of call.

By late evening, the music had slowed to the veleta and the waltz. The children rested tired heads against adults' shoulders. The feast of cold meats, sandwiches, pickles and pies lay in ruins. The beer barrel was empty, and the wedding cake neatly boxed. Balloons wafted between the feet of close-dancing couples, streamers came unpinned from the walls. Rob had Amy in his arms and they were dancing the last waltz, their hair sprinkled with white confetti, cheek-to-cheek in a world of their own.

'It went off well. It was a nice wedding,' Frances told Sadie. She'd called, desperate to build bridges with her youngest sister. Two small silver cardboard boxes of cake sat on the table between them in the Mile End living-room. 'We all had a good time, considering.'

'Considering what?' Sadie made the effort to be sociable. She'd tidied her hair and put on a touch of make-up for Frances's benefit. Richie had gone out, leaving the place to the two sisters.

'Considering Pa ain't been too well this winter, and we had all that worry over Rob.' She told Sadie about the clumsy police investigation into Wiggin's death. 'Trust them.' She laughed. 'They never get nothing right.'

They shuddered over how history had nearly repeated itself for the family; first Ernie, then Rob.

'But Pa's all right, ain't he?' Sadie knew the strain he'd been under. 'He ain't pining for the pub?'

'Oh, he's pining.' Frances sighed. 'We was worried he'd go under. Then we got the good news about Rob, and the wedding. That picked him up no end.'

Sadie nodded.

'Only, I wish you'd been there.' Frances leaned forward confidentially. 'I don't know, somehow it felt like there was a hole, and we was going round busy mending it all the time, talking ten to the dozen about everything except you, Sadie.'

Sadie tried to laugh it off. 'That's the first time I've ever been called a hole. That's me; a ladder in a stocking!'

'What's wrong, Sadie? Why can't you make it up with Rob? For Pa's sake, at least.' Frances had come as peacemaker. It was early December; Christmas was almost upon them. She wanted the family back together by then.

But Sadie turned serious. 'Rob's gotta make it up with me, Frances. Not the other way round. If Rob admits he was wrong and says sorry to Richie, then maybe I'll consider it.' She half turned away, her shoulders slumped, dark shadows under her eyes. 'But then again, Rob ain't never said sorry to no one.'

'You ain't sleeping well?' Frances changed the intractable subject. 'Are you sick much?'

Sadie nodded. 'Every morning. It ain't too bad though.'

'I'll bring you some herb teas next time. And some Pink Pills. You look a bit anaemic. Are you getting to the doctor?'

Sadie smiled again, and told Frances not to fuss.

'I have to fuss. What else am I for? I'm your big sister, ain't I?' She got up and hugged her tight. 'We miss you down Duke Street. And we wish we could help.'

'Talk to Rob,' Sadie said between her tears.

Frances nodded. 'But from what I heard, Richie won't think of going back in any case. Not after what Rob done. He's proud, ain't he?'

Sadie dried her eyes, settled one hand across her stomach and put on a brave face. 'Everyone's pride has a price,' she pointed out. 'Come spring, when the baby's born and there's no jobs for love nor money, I think even Richie will have to swallow his pride.'

'Don't bank on it.' Frances saw Rob and Richie as two stubborn enemies: one on his high horse about what the mechanic did to his pal, Walter; the other's resentment blinding him to compromise. She asked how Sadie and Richie would manage until spring. Sadie said they had a bit put by from her wages before she had been forced to own up to her condition at the office. Occasionally Richie managed to pick up casual dock work.

'It ain't right,' Frances insisted, getting ready to end her visit. 'You stuck here on your own like this, when you got us ready and willing to help just across the water. You should speak to Richie. One way or another, them two have got to make it up.' She slid her hands into her gloves and took her hat from the table.

'Frances!' Sadie's arms looked as if they would reach out, but she wrapped them around herself instead. 'Nothing.' She hung her head.

'Things is all right between you and Richie?'

'Fine.'

'Well, chin up, then. Give it time. Things usually work out in the end.' Frances tried to end on a cheerful note.

When she said goodbye and went down the stone steps, she looked back at Sadie, still hugging herself, pale and strained, all alone, and her heart turned over with pity.

Sadie herself watched Frances out of sight, then went

inside, quickly tidying away the two boxes containing the pieces of Rob and Amy's wedding-cake. They would only anger Richie, and send him into a black mood. The evening crawled by. Down the landing, a child cried. Sadie put a pan of broth on the stove, turned off the light to economize, tried to read by lamplight. Still no Richie. At eleven o'clock she went to bed, tired and cold, praying that Frances – someone, anyone – would be able to talk Rob round.

CHAPTER TWENTY

Christmas came and went without healing the rift between Sadie and the rest of her family. Neither Rob nor Richie could bear to hear mention of the other's name. Rob swore and struggled with the two unserviced taxicabs, up to his elbows in oil and grease over an undetected knock in the engine, worn-out brakes, a sizzling radiator. Over in Mile End, Richie tried for work as a road digger, or a porter at Liverpool Street Station. He brought home money from this casual work on maybe one or two days each week.

Sadie learned to make a decent meal out of pork rind and bones, a few potatoes. When she heard that a child in the next tenement had died of diphtheria, she sat with her head in her hands. Measles was rife throughout February, so she stopped going down to the public baths for her twice-weekly scrub and soak, for fear of coming into contact with anything infectious.

Her sisters visited her, bringing little nightgowns and socks, in preparation for the baby. She refused all offers of help for herself, would accept neither food nor money. But she took the tiny clothes, white and sweet smelling, wrapped them in tissue paper and put them in the bottom drawer of her dressing-table. Healthwise, the pregnancy was still difficult; her appetite was poor and she didn't gain the expected weight. The baby, due in May, would be undersized, the doctor predicted. As time passed, Jess, Hettie and Frances would choose the time of their visits to avoid Richie, since he made it plain they weren't welcome. They had the idea that he would get at Sadie for letting them come near, so they tried to miss him, letting Sadie keep her own counsel over their regular visits.

Occasionally they would drop Sadie's name in Rob's hearing, telling Amy how her pregnancy was progressing, how Sadie did her best under trying circumstances. 'She keeps the place neat and clean, but it ain't what you'd choose,' Jess reported. In fact, her latest visit to Mile End had shocked her. Sadie tried to keep house in the two rooms, but the floors were bare and there was no easy-chair, let alone a sideboard for her few bits of crockery. As for Sadie herself, she'd lost her quick movement and lively eye. She seemed to have faded, she looked awkward and apathetic.

Amy was quite the opposite, Jess thought. Pregnancy suited her. There was a natural, peachy bloom on her cheeks, even in the dead of winter, a glow of energy and enthusiasm. Her over-neat, regimentally waved blonde hair had been allowed to soften into a longer style that framed her face.

'Poor girl,' Amy commiserated. She sat gratefully in the midst of her own nice things: a tatted rug from Annie, spare pots and pans from Jess, a sturdy table that Frances had passed on from the Institute. She'd hung lace curtains at the big picture window, and she'd got her way over the problem of the dirty green ceiling; it was now a warm cream colour, and Rob had papered the walls to match. Both families had rejoiced when they heard the news that Rob and Amy were expecting a baby, and a tactful veil was drawn over the date of its anticipated arrival.

'Poor girl, nothing,' Rob remonstrated. 'She cooked her own goose, ain't she?' He hid his face behind his newspaper, checking the list of results for Palace's score.

'Still.' Amy sighed. She shook her head at Jess. 'You can't help being sorry.'

Jess said they thought the baby might not be strong. 'It's underweight, see. They say it's to do with how she lives. She don't get much fresh air, and she don't get out much for company, stuck way over there.' She prodded her brother's conscience as far as she safely could.

'Ain't we lucky, though?' Amy said softly. She gazed at the white woollen shawl which Jess had brought as a gift for their baby, so fine it was almost weightless, soft and warm when she held it to her cheek.

'Luck ain't nothing to do with where Sadie's landed herself,' Rob insisted. But he rattled his paper and sounded uncomfortable. 'Palace drew nil–nil,' he said by way of diversion.

Amy gave Jess a lighter glance. He was cracking. On her way out, she predicted that Rob would soon see reason.

Jess went from Amy's back to Annie's house to collect the children. There were signs of spring, even down Paradise Court: a lighter, longer feel to the afternoon, a general lifting of people's spirits. She said hello to Dolly, stopped for a proper word with Charlie, asking after his prospects. She was glad they didn't seem to hold things against her, but was still ashamed of what Maurice had done.

'I ain't sure yet what I'm gonna do,' Charlie told her. 'I've been thinking things through. There's America, the land of opportunity. I've been thinking of that.'

Down the corridor, Dolly dusted door-handles and banged vigorously about.

'Your ma don't sound too happy about that,' Jess said.

'Pie in the sky,' Dolly shouted. 'Pie in the bleeding sky!'

Jess smiled. 'What else, Charlie? If you don't get to America?' She wondered if that was what he was cut out for, the pioneer life, making his way in a foreign country.

'I been thinking of college,' he confided.

'Yes?'

'I only been thinking of it. They say they need teachers. I might go and train as one.' When he put it into words, he thought it sounded foolish; even more far-fetched than the American idea.

'Very good,' Jess nodded. 'I'd say that's more your cup of tea.'

Charlie looked surprised but pleased. 'You on the level?' He stood upright in the doorway, seeking her honest opinion.

'I am. Training as a teacher would be a good thing, I'd say. Shall I ask Frances for you? She'll know how to go about it.'

Gladly Charlie agreed. Here was someone with a bit of faith in him for a change. Both his ma and pa had scoffed at the idea of him going back to school. 'Where's the money in that?' Arthur had been quick to point out. 'Who puts the food in your mouth while you sit with your head stuck in a bleeding book?'

'Maybe there's a scholarship. Frances would know.' Jess promised to find out. She went on down the court, pleased after all to have crossed paths with the Ogdens.

Grace was on the doorstep of Annie's house, playing at marbles with Rosie O'Hagan, the second youngest girl. They rolled the coloured glass balls along the ground and chased after them with squeals and yells, encouraging them into the hole in the pavement which they'd chosen as their target. Jess watched, as a ragged boy appeared from the tenement doorway, ran pell-mell down the street, snatched a handful of the girls' marbles and leaped for the nearby street-lamp. He shinned up it in a flash, and perched on the crossbar out of reach.

Grace, hands on hips, looked at Rosie, then glared up at the boy. Then she hitched her skirt around her waist and promptly shinned up after him.

The boy waited until she grabbed hold of the iron crossbar, then cheekily swung himself down, leaving Grace stranded. But he'd reckoned without Rosie, who came at him like a whirlwind, diving for his pockets and the precious marbles. Grace swung and jumped to the ground. Between them, the two girls recovered their property and boxed the boy's ears. They saw him off, tongues out, calling derisively after him.

When it was over, Jess came quietly by, casting a look of mild disapproval at her daughter. 'That ain't very ladylike.' She frowned.

Grace pulled down her skirt. 'And he weren't no gentleman.'

Rosie giggled. ''Course not. That's my brother, Patrick!'

Jess smiled. 'Grace, don't you go far,' she warned. 'We have to get back home soon.' She knew Grace would pull a face and do her best to squeeze an extra few minutes out of the occasion. Smiling, she went inside to collect Mo and say goodbye to her pa and Annie.

Mo, too, was in seventh heaven. He lay flat on the carpet, face covered in chocolate, chugging his toy train between tracks Annie had sketched out for him on a long length of spare wallpaper. She'd drawn a station, a level-crossing, a signal-box, trees and houses. As Mo chugged the little metal train along, Duke played at station-master, signalman and passenger. He'd found a whistle in the sideboard drawer to add the right flavour to events. Mo blew it loudly while Annie stood by covering her ears.

'Thank God you're here,' she said to Jess. 'I ain't never gonna be able to stop this train otherwise. They been round and round that track till I feel dizzy.'

Mo grinned and leaped up. 'Grandpa's the fireman, I'm the driver!' He jumped clean over the railway track and landed at her feet. She picked him up to wipe his face.

'I hope he ain't been too much for you.' Jess set Mo down and began to gather her things. 'I know what he's like.'

Duke tousled the boy's hair. 'He ain't too much,' he promised.

Jess smiled at him. 'You're looking better, Pa.'

'His chest's clear now the weather's picked up.' Annie gave her bulletin. 'He's eating better, and he can sleep through the night, propped on three pillows.'

'Good, and you're getting out and about?'

Duke shrugged.

'Not enough.' Annie frowned. 'He won't go near the Duke. It's enough to upset anyone, when you see what they've gone and done to it. And, of course, you can't get far without going past the old place, so he stays cooped up here a good deal.'

Jess nodded sadly.

'Memories,' Duke explained. 'Happy memories.' Inside his head, he could play the old pianola tunes, he could hear the warm hum of conversation, the clink of glasses. In his mind, he could still reach for the wooden pump-handle and pull the best pint around.

'No one goes near, now Hill's got the place,' Annie insisted. 'They all swear it was him dropped Duke in it. Arthur and Charlie, Joe, Tommy; they all go up to the Flag.'

'Quite right.' Jess pulled on her gloves and fixed her hair under her hat. Mo made for the front door to go and find his big sister. 'Well, he can't last long, if that's the case.'

'He gets a few in from Union Street and further off. The young ones. They hear the place has been done up and they pop in to take a look. But Hill don't encourage regulars. He ain't got the knack.' Annie picked up the gossip from the market. The boycott of the pub was holding up. George had ditched his job and gone and found cellar work with the stretched landlord at the Flag. None of this did Duke much direct good, but it must hearten him to hear that Hill couldn't make a go of the place.

At last Jess was ready to leave. 'Chin up,' she told her pa. She went and prised the children away from their playmates in the court, told them to wave goodbye, then walked them briskly up Duke Street to catch the tram to the Underground station. On the journey home, Mo sat and chugged his train across his knees, Grace counted and re-counted her pocketful of shiny coloured marbles. Jess stared out of the tram window, swaying to its pitch and jolt, aware of a mounting regret as she left behind the warren of East End streets, burrowed underground, and emerged into her genteel, leafy suburb, and turned the key to her own beautiful, empty house.

Money was tight for Rob and Amy as they struggled through the winter, facing the harsh realities of married life after the artificial excitement of being engaged and married.

Amy had plenty of time to reflect on the loss of her busy daily routine in the company of her department store pals; her naturally sociable nature found it hard to adapt to long days cooking and cleaning inside her own four walls, waiting for Rob to show up at the end of his day's work, waiting for their baby to be born.

She didn't spend much time alone, however. Dolly was forever sailing through the door with news and advice, telling her how Frances Wray had fixed up for Charlie to go and see people at the Workers' Educational Institute. He wanted to apply for something called a Ruskin scholarship to go to college in the autumn. Katie O'Hagan and Jack Allenby had scraped together the money to pay for their tickets on a boat bound for America at the end of May. Bertie Hill was now trying to palm off Eden House on to some poor ignorant buyer, who didn't suspect it was riddled with dry rot from top to bottom. 'The sooner they pull it down the better.' Dolly was sick of living near the place; it harboured rats and dragged down the tone of the whole court.

'Don't let Mary O'Hagan hear you going on like that,' Amy advised. 'Where would they go if they pulled the old place down?'

'They'd get re-housed by the council,' Dolly said, with superior knowledge of the new welfare state. 'Into a brand-new place with their own bath and toilet, instead of the slum they're in now.'

'And who'd pay?' Amy couldn't see it; she'd heard of great new government building plans, but they were far away in Welwyn Garden, and impossible to imagine.

'The penny rate and the council, of course,' Dolly assured her. 'It's the latest thing. A bath of your own. A garden.'

'Hmm.' Amy wasn't immediately taken with the idea.

'And bleeding miles from anywhere and all.' She'd read in the newspaper that tenants were being shifted out there against their will, and that they kept coal in their baths, and pigeons too. 'It ain't for me.' She liked being able to walk downstairs on to the street, to the market, the shops, the pub.

Gossip with her ma kept Amy going through the early months of 1925, and the time she spent with Rob more than made up for the loss of her old, more worldly lifestyle. Pregnancy gave her a matronly air and she lost her flirtatious edge, dedicating herself instead to domestic life with a pleasant, humorous optimism that made her laugh at her husband's occasional grumpiness, and bully him into doing something to reinstate his old mechanic, so the whole family could get back into something like their old harmony.

Rob resisted. He swore it was none of her business. Sadie had chosen to slight them over the wedding invitation, and if she was having a hard time now, she had only herself to blame. He got angry. He pointed out how Walter would feel if they brought Richie back to work at the depot. He knew he couldn't find steady work, but he deserved everything he got.

'But Sadie don't,' Amy insisted. She never beat about the bush. 'She only made a mistake, Rob. It makes me miserable to think of her sticking it out without no one to help. I never thought she had it in her.'

Rob looked at his heavily pregnant wife in bed beside him. Their baby, conceived in August, amidst the chaos of Wiggin's murder, was due any day now. 'You know how to get under my skin,' he said, moved to be unusually gentle as he stroked her face and kissed her. He sighed. 'Wait till their kid arrives. Then I might go over and see her.'

Amy settled into a satisfied sleep. At two in the morning,

she woke Rob to tell him to go down and fetch Dolly. Her mother came. At eight she sent for the midwife, and at eleven a healthy baby boy was born.

Four or five weeks went by, but the weather reverted to winter on the day that Sadie's baby, Margaret, was born. A cold, north-eastern wind got up, and brought a flurry of light snow in the middle of May, so that people looked out of their windows and shivered and complained at the dark, unseasonable skies.

It was the middle of the afternoon, a Thursday, when Sadie seized the poker and hammered at the hollow chimney-back to let her neighbour, Sarah Morris, know that she needed help. The baby was early. Richie was out on what had degenerated into a regular, day-long wander through the streets without any real prospect of work. He spent hours hanging about in shop doorways, rolling thin cigarettes and longing for a drink, along with two or three pals in a similar situation. When her labour started, and Sadie hammered for help, Richie couldn't be reached. She would have to manage by herself.

Sarah came running in. She got Sadie to bed and sent for the doctor, at the younger woman's insistence. Sadie was glad of Sarah: a woman who took childbirth like a bad case of measles, a nuisance that disrupted the rhythm of everyday life and meant you got behind with your daily chores, by dint of the fact that you were flat on your back and in agony. 'Time the pains,' she advised. 'When they come bad and often, count your blessings, 'cos it'll soon be over.'

Sadie responded well. She waited for Dr McLeod and measured the pain. It was bearable. The next time, still bearable. She tried to judge how much worse it could get before she was forced to cry out. Quite a bit, she thought. She would grit her teeth and try not to make a fuss.

Sarah boiled water, great pans of it, on her own kitchen range. She asked Sadie for towels and sheets. 'That doctor had best get a move on,' she said, as if doctors were a modern invention, designed to complicate women's ability to give birth. She wiped Sadie's face. 'Else he'll be too late.'

Sadie gripped Sarah's wrist and kept her mouth clamped shut as the contractions tore through her and the groans rose to her throat.

'Her,' she managed to gasp. 'Dr McLeod, it's a woman.'

Sarah's eyes widened. 'That's a step in the right direction, any rate.'

Sadie smiled back.

'Lie with your legs crooked up, like this. Breathe deep.' Sarah was poised, ready for business.

The doctor arrived in the nick of time, with a young district nurse. The baby had presented in an awkward position, and for all Sadie's pushing and Sarah's practical encouragement, it was stuck in the birth canal, with just an ear and the side of its face evident to the doctor's experienced probe. There was the added complication of the cord possibly caught around the infant's neck. The doctor and the nurse prepared Sadie for a difficult delivery with a shot of local anaesthetic. Sarah held her hand tight.

And Sadie did scream as they cut into her and used forceps to deliver the child. They worked quickly, asked her to push, through the pain, through the panic that the baby might not survive. Sadie pushed and cried out.

'Harder,' Sarah urged. She saw the head emerge between the forceps, then the shoulders. The cord was round the neck.

Sadie wished she was dead. Tears streamed down her face, her neck ran with sweat. She pushed harder.

The doctor waited until she could grip the slippery shoulders, laid aside the forceps, and with a little twist and a final pull, the baby was born. 'Good,' she said. 'Very good.' The nurse cut the cord and released the half-strangled infant. She cleared its mouth, willed it to breathe.

'Boy or girl?' Sadie mumbled. The words rolled like heavy pebbles inside her mouth.

The doctor began to stitch. 'A little girl, Sadie. You have a little girl.'

Sadie sobbed. She wanted her baby to live.

The nurse concentrated on the tiny stained shape lying inert in her arms. Gently she tipped the infant upside down and applied the smart slap that was meant to make a child's lungs kick into action. Again; a second slap. The baby's arms shot wide, and in a surprised gasp, she drew her first breath.

The nurse smiled. She reached for a towel and wrapped the baby in it, wiping her face and head, handing her over to her mother. 'A beautiful little girl,' she said. 'And none the worse for wear.'

Sadie held the featherweight of her own child in her shaking arms. She searched her small, creased face, slid her own little finger inside her daughter's curled fist, speechless with joy.

'She's a bit on the small side,' Sarah said, bending forward for a closer look. 'But then, you're on the small side yourself.' She patted Sadie's hand.

'You did very well,' Dr McLeod told her, finishing with the stitching and trying to make her patient as comfortable as possible. She eased her legs straight and the nurse put clean sheets under her.

'Hmm.' Sarah warned them not to make the young mother's head swell. 'Tell her that in twenty years,' she advised. 'Time enough then for compliments.'

Sadie smiled and sighed. She handed the baby back to Sarah. 'There's a crib made up over there.' She pointed to the corner of the room, where she had padded and lined the bottom drawer of her dressing-table with blankets and cut-down sheets. There was a tiny lace pillow, donated by Jess. 'Bring it up close,' she pleaded, 'where I can keep an eye on her.'

Sarah did as she was asked, her heart softening at the feel and sight of the new child. 'She's got your eyes, see. What you gonna call her?'

'Margaret. Richie and me decided on that for a girl.' Sadie turned her head sideways to gaze at her daughter. 'She's beautiful, ain't she?'

'Worth it?' the nurse asked. She bustled to pack away her things.

'Yes,' Sadie sighed. She wanted to sleep. She wanted to wake up and find Richie there by the bedside, holding their litle girl.

Throughout May, Amy was too wrapped up in her baby's feeding and general needs to look outside her own little world. They called the boy Robert, after his father, but this was soon altered to Bobby by all his fond relations, who cooed over his crib and adored his round chubbiness. He had Amy's light colouring and blue eyes. They'd never seen such a bonny baby, such a contented child. Amy walked out with him in his high pram – another contribution from Jess – through the park in the warm spring weather, enjoying the blossom and the birdsong. Rob would worry about taking him out too soon into the traffic and the noise. He worked out the quietest route to the park, and rationed the time Bobby spent in other people's arms. 'He ain't a parcel you're posting.' He told her off for allowing Dolly and Annie too free an access. But Amy wallowed in the grandmothers' praise, and passed Bobby around as much as she pleased.

Straight away, Rob loved his son with a proud, exclusive fierceness. Though he didn't soften his public face, pretending a disdainful amusement when the womenfolk cooed, he would spend quiet time in the evening by the baby's crib, drinking in his sleeping features, keeping time with his light breathing, planning the very best for his future.

He would work even harder at the taxi business with Walter. They would build up savings until they could afford at least one smart new cab. Setting up a haulage division wasn't entirely out of the question in the long run. Talk of unemployment, strikes and slumps wouldn't deter him. They would undercut their rivals, they would come out on top.

In this mood of determined optimism, he drove across the water one morning in late May. He planned to get to Mile End early, to catch Richie Palmer before he set out on his day's tramp after casual work. There'd be no fuss; he'd offer Richie his old job back, tell him that Walter was behind the move, let Sadie know he was doing it for the sake of the family.

Only, when Sadie came to the door of the tenement rooms, and he saw how pale and thin she looked, how her colour and life had faded, and how she greeted him with a silent, unresponsive gaze, he felt stricken with guilt.

'I come to see the kid,' he stammered. Amy had parcelled up some clothes already too small for Bobby, and some spare blankets. He offered them to Sadie across the threshold.

Sadie motioned him in. 'Don't worry, Richie ain't here,' she said as she noticed him looking around. 'Wait while I go and fetch her.' She didn't show it, but she felt the enormity of the move Rob had made. When she came back from the bedroom with Meggie nestled in her arms, she entrusted her to him; a kind of peace offering.

Rob gazed at the baby. 'Ain't she tiny?'

Sadie nodded. 'Under six pounds when she was first born. She's gaining now, though.' She kept Meggie clean and dry and warm. She fed her on demand. She'd learnt the ropes quickly, with help from Sarah next door, and felt that every day she grew into a better mother; calmer and more confident.

Rob handed her back. 'Our Bobby's twice that size.' He told her all about his son as Sadie made him sit at the table and offered to make him tea.

He shook his head. 'I gotta be off soon. I came over to see Richie, as a matter of fact.' He looked round again, though he knew Sadie had said he wasn't in. 'Where's he got to?'

For a moment Sadie tried to brush it aside. 'He ain't here. Like I said, he's out.' She knew that Rob's unannounced visit could only mean one thing; he wanted to give Richie his job back. She gave a half-angry little laugh. 'You missed him, Rob.'

He took in the drab, bare walls and floor; Sadie's curtains and tablecloth, her early attempts to make a home. He saw how poverty had defeated her. 'When will I catch him in, then?' he asked, doubly stricken by conscience, determined to help set Sadie back up.

'You won't,' she said quietly. She felt she might as well

admit what she'd kept hidden from her sisters when they'd come visiting to see the baby.

After the birth, Sadie had fallen into an exhausted sleep, dreaming of Richie holding the baby in his arms. She'd woken to an empty room. Sarah came in and said she sent word to fetch Richie back home. They'd have to wait and be patient. Daylight faded, the time came when he would trudge up the step and fling down his cap, empty handed. It passed. The slow hours of night ticked by.

Meggie cried to be fed in the dark. Sadie held her close. Morning came, grey and pale. The sun never shone down the side of the tenement. Sarah looked in to report that no one had set eyes on Richie since he'd set off yesterday morning. She warned Sadie to prepare for the worst. 'Waiting's bad,' she said. 'It's the worst bit.'

For two days there was no news. Sadie began to see that Richie wouldn't be there to share their beautiful baby. She was given to understand that it was a deliberate choice on his part. Sarah said there was no point telling the police: she'd heard on the grapevine that Richie had gone off of his own accord. ''Course, he never knew you'd go and have the baby straight off,' she reminded her. 'Maybe he went and got a spell of work on a boat?'

But Sadie had heard that tale too often; men deserted their women and called it taking a job at sea. She remembered Annie and Wiggin. She counted the days.

Now, after she'd covered up to Jess, Hettie and Frances, she admitted the truth to Rob. 'I ain't seen Richie since Meggie was born. He's gone and left us. It's just Meggie and me; we're all on our own.'

PART THREE

The last laugh

CHAPTER TWENTY-ONE

June 1925

The pain of being abandoned by Richie struck deep at Sadie, and stunned her. Although on the surface she coped for little Meggie's sake, and held up her head in the Mile End neighbourhood, inside she felt numb. For him to leave without explanation, for him not to get in touch for news about the baby was something she refused to comprehend. How could he cut off so completely from his own flesh and blood?

'Don't take on,' Sarah Morris advised. She appeared in Sadie's doorway one morning early in June. 'You got your hands full now, girl, without bothering your head about things you can't change.' She'd caught Sadie wiping away the tears.

Sadie looked up and dried her eyes. Her neighbour's down-to-earth approach acted like a tonic. It wasn't as if she was alone in the world, like some women in her situation, she realized. Rob had heard the news about Richie and gone straight home to fetch Annie and Duke. Annie took one look at the room and swore to get her back to Duke Street. She would move heaven and earth to make it happen.

'I ain't got much money put by,' Sadie admitted. 'What I got left won't run to renting nothing posh.'

'But you want to come back?' Annie noticed Duke paying quiet attention to the baby in her makeshift crib.

Sadie nodded, not trusting herself to speak out.

'Yes, and I don't blame you.' Annie hurried on. 'What must it be like, stuck up here with no one on hand? Well, we gotta see what we can do, your pa and me.'

They'd gone off, and the whole family had rallied round with extra clothing, food and money. Her good neighbour, Sarah, kept an eye on her and Meggie, while Annie ran up and down the market on Duke Street, in and out of the shops and eating-houses, to catch word of a good room going at a low rent.

'I brought you a bite to eat.' Sarah came in now and put a bowl of mutton broth on the table. She never changed out of her drab brown dress, roughly pinned and patched. As a concession to summer, she took off the woollen headscarf and replaced it with a faded cotton one. But nothing changed her routine of scraping a living through taking in home work: mending, washing, labelling, picking, and sitting during these long evenings humming her ukelele songs, reminiscing about the days before the war.

Sadie nodded gratefully. As she sat down to eat, she returned to her usual theme. 'You ain't heard nothing?' Sarah was her eyes and ears on the outside world.

'About Richie?'

'Of course about Richie. Ain't nobody heard from him yet?'

Sarah shook her head. 'He don't do nothing by halves, that one. He takes it into his head to do something and he makes a proper job of it.'

Sadie's mind flew back to their courtship; Richie's almost silent, dogged pursuit of her.

'If he wants to drop out of sight, ain't no one better at it than Richie Palmer. Not even Chung Ling Soo, the famous vanishing Chinaman!' She got into her stride. 'That Chung Ling Soo, he came from Lancashire. Ain't no more China-man in him than in this little finger! My Harry told me that for a fact.' She rambled back through the years. 'Men like Richie, they don't know they're born, running away at the first sign of trouble. Not that little Meggie's trouble, mind, but men see babies that way. He's young and strong, ain't he? He can lift a shovel and carry a sack, not like some of them poor bleeders, the returnees. You ain't seen nothing like it. They was blinded in them trenches. They was gassed. And what did it leave them fit for, besides selling matches on a street corner?'

At last, Sadie was roused to her lover's defence.

'Richie done his bit, Sarah. He been over the top more times than he could count.'

'And he came back in one piece. He ain't been a mother of one of them kids killed in the schools by the bleeding bombing planes, has he? He ain't had to go down the Underground like a mole, waiting for the bugle all-clear.' Sarah catalogued the miseries of war. 'And you ain't one of them poor young widows sitting at home waiting for the telegram to land on your mat. No, come to think of it, your luck ain't all that bad. What's one little disappointment set alongside all that? Look at you; you're young, and you can make a decent show if you put your mind to it.' She reclaimed the empty bowl and stood up from the table. 'Comb your hair and dig out one of them fancy outfits I first saw you in. Make a bit of effort, for God's sake!'

As Sarah spoke, Sadie ran the gamut of emotions, from aching sadness, through shame, to anger. But as her decent, blunt neighbour stood with her empty dish, nodding encouragement, she laughed. 'You think combing my hair will make all the difference?'

'It's a start.' Sarah smiled back. 'And don't leave it all to that little stepmother of yours,' she warned. 'Ain't nobody going to pull you out of this mess except yourself, Sadie Parsons.'

Sadie nodded. 'Thanks, Sarah.'

'Well, get some fresh air, then. Take Meggie out for a bit.'

'I will, thanks.' Already she felt Sarah's outspoken advice like a breath of new life.

'Ain't nothing to thank me for. What's a drop of soup between us?' she pretended.

Sadie watched the raw-boned, middle-aged woman on her way along the balcony. She went to get Meggie ready for a trek across the river later that morning. She would go and look for work, as well as a better place for them both to live. But first, she wanted to write a letter.

When she left Hope Street, she would leave it with Sarah, addressed to Richie. One day he might come back and be able to read it. She took up pencil and paper.

It read:

Dear Richie,
Our little girl's name is Margaret. Meggie for short. She's got a round mouth and lots of dark hair. Her eyelashes are the longest I ever saw. She don't smile much yet, but she cries plenty, to let me know she's here. Her hands are tiny. Her face is all puckered up when she holds fast to my finger. When she's asleep, you can hardly see her breathing.

I want to tell you she's beautiful. I promise to take good care of her and to do my best not to let her come to harm.

We followed our own hearts, Richie. I ain't sorry. I'll tell

Meggie all about you, when she grows older. Your loving Sadie.

Then she put on her cream jacket and skirt, and dressed Meggie up in one of the dainty outfits donated by Amy. As she looked in the mirror, she considered she hadn't done too badly: with lip-rouge and a touch of powder, she managed to look decent again. She took the last of her coins from the dressing-table drawer and stepped outside with Meggie in her arms.

'Blimey!' Sarah said, sitting in the sun by her door.

'Now, Sarah, don't you say nothing!' She turned the key in the lock.

'A pair of bobby dazzlers, if you ask me!'

'We ain't.'

'You are too.' She smiled and waved them off. Sadie was bound to get back on her feet, looking like that. She was young and pretty. The baby gave her something to live for. Children did, until they grew up and went away. Then you sat alone at your doorstep and watched it happen all over again to the girl next door.

Katie O'Hagan had saved all through the winter. She put away every penny she could from the takings on her haberdashery stall. Spring trade in beads and braids, fringes and feathers was good, as East End girls copied the racy, slim-hipped styles of the fashion magazines. Lace was quickly going out of fashion, except on underthings, but there was a craze for sewing beading on to everything, and buttons of all shapes and sizes. Katie worked hard and dreamed of America. Jack Allenby stayed in Eden House and found work wherever he could. They were both saving for Katie's passage, planning on a summer departure. Once there, they would save all over again, this time to pay for a wedding, surrounded by Jack's family. Meanwhile, Jack's mother had written to Mary promising to keep a firm eye on the couple until the wedding knot was tied.

These days, Mary hardly recognized her own daughter. She'd grown tall and slender, studied the 'look' and achieved it with considerable success. Her small, lively features were framed by a wavy, dark bob, her eyebrows arched and shaped, her lips painted in a red bow. She wore straight tunics in shiny rayon, over a knee-length, pleated skirt. Her legs looked longer than ever in her dainty, high-heeled shoes.

When the day came to send her and Jack across the Atlantic, Mary had the sensation of saying goodbye to a beautiful stranger. She wondered from where little Katie had got all that determination and spirit of adventure. Not from her father, Joe, who had sunk into his old, moaning ways since Coopers' had closed down. Life for him was sometimes too difficult even to get out of bed.

'You'll write to us?' Mary made Katie promise. 'Rosie will read your letters to me. You'll tell us all about your new life.'

Katie squeezed her mother's hand. They'd decided to say goodbye at Waterloo, to avoid the long drawn-out business of waiting at the embarkation point at the dockside. Jack was working his passage, and Katie had bought a berth in the crowded, third-class section of the same ship. The time had really come. What had seemed like an impossible dream was coming true at last. 'I'll write, Ma, and I'll send money. Don't you worry.'

Mary shook her head. 'So long as you write and tell us you're safe.' She didn't want to let go of Katie's slim hand.

But she relinquished it to Jack as the train doors began to slam shut and the porters heaved the last bags up the steps. Steam hissed and whistles sounded. Everything hurried them towards this last goodbye. 'Good luck,' she whispered.

Katie stepped into the carriage. She turned and leaned out of the window, with Jack at her shoulder. 'Take care of yourself, Ma!' she cried. The train jolted and began to roll away. 'I'll write every week!' She saw her mother's long, pale face fade into the distance, get lost in the crowd. She knew she would stand there until the train drew out from under the giant glass arch, so she waved her handkerchief until the very end. She thought she saw Mary's raised hand still waving them off. Then she hid her face against Jack's shoulder. She was homesick and seasick for the first week, but launching out into a new future.

After Katie left, Annie decided to take on her old stall once more. 'It's not too much for my old bones yet,' she assured Duke. 'Leastways, not now that it's summer.' She convinced him that she was looking forward to getting back to work on the market. 'There's Nora and Liz to keep me company, and Ernie will be there to keep an eye on me, won't you?' She grinned as Ernie replied with a vigorous nod. 'See, it's for the best. I want to see if I can still turn my hand to earning an honest penny.'

And, sure enough, her stall was a lifeline, now that Duke's old trade had been taken away. Not to be outdone by his wife's grit and determination, Duke came to the decision that it wasn't all up with him yet either. On her first day back in business, he took a stroll up the court, 'To see how she's coping', he told Dolly on the way up. He found Annie complaining about the rickety state of her canvas canopy, and went straight back home for hammer and nails. Soon he was deep into repair work on the wooden frame.

'It's all well and good that Katie saving every penny for her new life,' Annie grumbled. 'But these young ones, they let things slip. Another month or two, a good shower of rain, and I'd have the whole bleeding thing down on my head!'

Up the stepladder, Duke hammered happily. 'We could do with sewing a patch or two on this old canvas.' He spotted a weakness and decided to take the whole thing down for repairs.

Annie tutted and shrugged at Liz. 'Bleeding hell; all I ask is for a couple of nails and five minutes of his time. Before you know it, he's stripping the whole lot bare. What am I gonna do if it rains?' she demanded, cocking her head sideways and squinting into the sun at him.

'It ain't gonna rain, Annie. You know very well.'

'Duke, when you've got a minute, you can have a look at this wobbly leg of mine!' Nora Brady called.

Tommy O'Hagan leaned over and leered. 'Now there's an offer for you!' He winked at Duke. 'Nora ain't never asked me to take a look at her wobbly leg.'

'Cheeky monkey!' Nora made as if to box his ears. She shrieked as he ran out from behind his stall and ducked down, promising to examine the offending part of her anatomy. 'Here, get him off me! Stop that!' She beat with the flat of her hands at the side of his head. 'I mean the table leg, you bleeding young idiot!'

'As if he don't know!' Liz said caustically.

'Take no notice, Nora,' Annie said. She served a customer with four yards of blue bias binding. 'Duke will be over to take a proper look just as soon as he finishes here.

He's very handy with his hammer, is Duke.' She made a grimace at Tommy, who had just escaped from Nora and was flitting by the fruit stall run by Queenie Taylor. Tommy picked a choice banana from the top of the pile.

'*Yes, we have no bananas*,' he sang jauntily as he peeled the fruit and bit into it. '*We have no bananas today!*'

'Blow me down, if someone don't clock him one soon!' Annie shook her head, but laughed in spite of herself. It was a lovely day. And to make it perfect, she spotted Sadie all spruced up, with babe-in-arms, coming right down the pavement towards them.

If Sadie was nervous treading back on home turf, she didn't let it show. In fact, she looked more or less her old self, but without the stand-offish edge. Amy leaned out of the window above Powells' to yell out a greeting. 'Sadie, don't you move, I'll be right down!' She came with Bobby straddled on her hip, running to compare offspring with Sadie. Meggie was small and delicate where Bobby was strapping; Meggie dark, Bobby fair-haired. Each admired features of the other's baby.

'He looks like you.' Sadie smiled. A crowd gathered for their first view of Meggie. Annie cut through them like a scythe, claiming grandmother's rights.

'Poor thing!' Amy blushed. 'And little Meggie looks just like you.'

'Do you think so?'

'You Parsons is all the same. It's them big brown eyes.'

Meggie had woken after the tram ride and was gazing round at a sea of faces. Annie offered to take her. 'Your arms must be killing you,' she said to Sadie. 'Here, hand her over. What brings you down here, anyway?'

'You do, Annie. And somewhere to live.'

Annie shook her head. So far, the search for a place for Sadie and Meggie to stay hadn't come up with anything. Duke Street was currently full of families clinging on to their rooms by the skin of their teeth, as landlords cranked up the rents and packed them in like sardines. Few, if any, were interested in taking in a single woman without employment and a child to tie her down. Annie had tried locally, and Frances and Hettie had tried further afield in Union Street and Bear Lane. There was nothing on offer.

'No, I thought it was high time I came looking for myself,' Sadie said. She soaked up the warm atmosphere; the smell of fish and fruit, the sound of taxis and buses, the sight of her old friends. She saw Walter drive by with a fare, glad that he hadn't spotted her. She felt ready to nod and speak with Charlie Ogden, who was filling in time on the market before going off to college in the autumn, but not to Walter. There were still too many recent might-have-beens between them.

'And you reckon you'll like this teaching lark?' Sadie asked. She'd given over Meggie to Annie and strolled into the relative quiet of the court with Charlie. They passed the Prince of Wales, oddly new and shiny, catching up on each other's news.

Charlie put his hands in his pockets and shrugged. 'I don't know about that.'

She smiled at his feigned indifference. 'What are you going into it for, then?'

'Because it's steady. I ain't cut out for the cinema no more. I had a dream once, but I let it slip by me. Maurice was right.'

She listened. 'You don't hold it against him, then?'

'Why should I? He gave me a job and he took it away. No use crying over spilt milk.'

310

'I wish Richie could hear you say that. It's good of you to see it that way, Charlie.'

They walked on, down the shady side of the street. 'Maurice won't never settle for someone who just wants to be steady,' Charlie pointed out. 'It's got to be bigger, better, newer, faster with him. That's why he's so good.'

Sadie sighed. 'Yes, he is good at his job.'

'I hear he's on to something big?'

'I never heard that, Charlie.' Sadie gave him a worried look. 'Jess ain't mentioned nothing to me.'

'Maybe it won't come off, then.' Charlie stopped outside his own house. 'I never said nothing, right? If it comes off, all well and good.' He looked directly at her. 'It's good to see you again, Sadie. We missed you.'

She smiled back. 'Good to be back, Charlie. Oh, and one other thing.' She had set off, but turned back quickly. She spoke softly. 'I think you'll make a good teacher.'

'How's that?'

''Cos you always had your head stuck in a bleeding book when you and me was walking out together!'

'More fool me.' He smiled, nodded, and went inside. Water under the bridge. He thought of himself as he was then: callow and selfish, too sensitive by half. He thought of Sadie then: careless and fancy-free, with her long plait down her back, her petticoats whirling in the wind as she rode her bike through the bluebell woods.

Sadie's stroll gathered purpose after she left Charlie. An idea entered her head that Eden House would not be the worst solution to her problem of accommodation. It had its drawbacks, it was true. It was old and run down, it held bad memories, and the landlord was Bertie Hill.

But it was on the doorstep to Duke and Annie. It would be cheap. Planning ahead, she thought she could take in typewriting work to pay the rent and make ends meet. She could put up with poky conditions, provided she was standing on her own two feet, taking good care of Meggie and feeling that she belonged. It was a step up from Mile End at least.

Gathering her courage, she entered the central doorway of the old tenement and began to ask around for the landlord.

Duke rolled up the canvas hood from Annie's stall, then went and fixed Nora's gammy leg. He could hear Dolly Ogden holding forth about the relative merits of Bobby and Meggie. She led the healthy, strapping lobby. Annie took the opposite view: round, pink cheeks were fine on a boy, and big, chubby legs, but delicacy was what everyone admired in a girl. 'Meggie will melt a few hearts before too long, you wait and see,' she promised proudly. The grandmothers agreed to differ. Amy invited Annie to bring Meggie up for tea. 'Sadie won't mind, will she?' She stopped for a moment, recalling the feud between Rob and Richie.

'Not a bit,' Annie said firmly. 'Here, Duke, you watch the stall while Amy and me goes for a chat. Tell Sadie to come and fetch Meggie when she comes back.'

Duke looked in bemusement at the hooks and eyes, the press-studs and rolls of elastic set out in neat rows along the stall. He stuck his thumbs in his waistcoat pockets and shuffled into position.

'A pint of the best, Duke!' Tommy yelled.

'And you!' he growled back.

'Tommy!' Liz warned. 'Don't you go pushing your luck,

312

you hear.' Seeing Duke out and about was good news, but seeing him trying to cope behind the stall was like watching a fish out of water.

'You gotta laugh,' Tommy told her. 'Otherwise you'd cry. He took it well, ain't he?'

'Now listen, Tommy.' Liz took him to task. 'You ain't been into Hill's place lately?' Like the other market-stall holders, she stuck rigidly to the boycott of the Prince of Wales. She worked hard to keep the young ones in line.

''Course not. What do you think I am?' Tommy glanced at his watch, wondering whether to nip off and risk a quick one at the Flag. 'Not that it'll do the old man much good in the end.'

'What you on about?' Liz came in quick and sharp.

'The brewery ain't gonna take him back in any case.' Tommy laid things out plain and simple. He kept his voice low. 'Even if Bertie Hill comes a cropper, and I ain't saying he don't deserve to, they ain't gonna give Duke his licence back, are they? He's out on his ear and there ain't nothing we can do.'

Liz shook her head. 'Don't let Annie hear you going on like that,' she warned. 'And don't go thinking of breaking the boycott because of it, you hear?'

The street was determined to force Hill out of business, come what may.

Inside the pub, word came up from the tenement that Mr Hill was wanted down the court. He left the bar to the booze-sodden care of Jack Cooper, to look after the thin trickle of lunch-time custom. It sounded like he could let another room if he went to sort it out on the spot.

But he was in no hurry as he went down. Too thick-skinned to bother about the sour looks that greeted him wherever he went, he sauntered along in the sunshine. He was taken aback, however, as he entered the tenement and found Sadie Parsons waiting for him in the grey inner court. He'd never expected to see another member of the Parsons family come looking for a room.

Sadie asked civilly if he had anything to let. Much as she resented Hill's existence, she must swallow her pride and find somewhere to live. She confined herself to the business in hand. After all, there had been other, more difficult things to swallow recently, and if Rob or anyone got on his high horse about renting a room from the 'enemy', she was prepared to defend her actions. 'I want something close to my pa,' she told Hill with dignity. 'It ain't easy to manage without family close by.' She met his inquisitive stare.

'Miss Parsons,' he began slowly, enjoying the situation. Sadie hadn't lost her looks at any rate, though by all accounts, she'd lost much else, including her reputation, her job and now her man. 'You'll excuse me for asking, but how do you propose to pay the rent? Supposing I have a room, which I don't say I have.'

'I plan to take in typewriting work, Mr Hill, and anything else that comes my way. How much do you charge for a room?'

'That all depends.' He came up, too close. The more civil and distant in manner she grew, the more familiar he became. She could smell the cigarette smoke on his clothes. 'A room at the front costs extra. If I have one available, which I don't say I do, mind.'

Sadie held his gaze. His sandy colouring showed up the redness of his complexion, which was already thickening and coarsening into middle age. His presence was arrogant and insulting, he used his strong physique with overbearing, swaggering pride. 'Do you have a room for me and my daughter, Mr Hill?'

'Well – Sadie, isn't it? – as luck would have it, I think I do.' He liked this idea; one of life's little opportunities to rub salt into the wound. And he liked the look of Sadie Parsons. The shine hadn't quite gone from her. She'd had more than her fair share of it to start with: smooth skin, pretty face, good little figure. In another five years, poverty and disappointment would have rubbed all that off for good. Meanwhile, he would enjoy watching her come and go through the tenement. He offered terms. She showed spirit in haggling him down. They agreed on a price.

She asked to see the room. Even her self-control snapped when he led her to Wiggin's old hole in the semi-basement. It had recently been vacated by the sailor the O'Hagan girl had run off with. 'Number five,' he offered, awaiting her reaction.

'No.' She backed straight out of the room. 'Not this one. If this is all you have, I'll look somewhere else.'

There was number eighteen, he told her. Up on the second storey, opposite the O'Hagans. It would be more expensive.

In the end, the bargain was made. She wanted to move in right away. Hill held out the key. His fingers rested too long in the palm of her hand as he handed it to her.

Annie grumbled, Duke shook his head. Frances admitted it would solve a problem for the time being. No one liked Sadie coming to live in Eden House except Ernie. He could pop in from Annie's house whenever he pleased. In the end, everyone concluded it would have to do as a short term measure.

Rob drove up to Mile End with Sadie to collect her few

possessions, where Sadie bade a tearful farewell to Sarah Morris. She handed over the sealed envelope addressed to Richie. 'If you hear of him, or if he ever comes back, will you give it to him for me?'

'I will,' Sarah promised. 'But don't get your hopes up. Men like Richie, they don't like no responsibility.' She hugged Sadie and wished her well, giving the envelope pride of place on her bare mantelpiece.

'Funny thing, that,' Rob observed, as he strapped the boot lid closed and started up the engine. He climbed into tha driver's seat.

'What's funny about it?' Sadie didn't feel in the mood for jokes.

'Funny peculiar, I mean. What the old girl just said. Richie ain't the kind to take responsibility.'

Sadie glanced back down Hope Street as her brother pulled away from the kerb. 'So?'

'So, that's just what I'd have said about me before now. I don't like to be tied down, you know me. I like to come and go. But look at me now.'

She gave a wan smile. 'Yes, but you're happy, Rob. You found the right person. It's me. I weren't the right one for Richie, that's all.'

'And I got little Bobby.' He headed for the river, threading through the busy streets. 'For God's sake, if you'd told me a year ago that I'd be hitched to Amy, with a kid, I'd have died laughing.'

He helped Sadie with her luggage and left her in Frances's capable hands. Frances was there to help put the room to rights while Annie minded Meggie. Little O'Hagans ran in and out, up and downstairs.

Rob went home to Amy and Bobby. The next day, when he took a break from work and went over to Mile End to collect Sadie's remaining boxes and sticks of furniture, he answered Sarah Morris's beckoning call.

'It ain't taken him long,' she whispered mysteriously from along the balcony.

'Who? Richie?' Rob frowned and went over.

She nodded. 'Who else? He heard she'd flitted and came snooping round late last night. Ain't nothing gets by him, not if he don't want it to.'

'He ain't away at sea, then?'

Sarah snorted. 'Not him. I could hear him knocking things about a bit, so I goes and knocks on the door. I tells him she's gone back to Southwark and I gives him her letter.'

Rob nodded.

'He shoves it straight in his pocket and looks daggers at me. It ain't my fault he's gone and left her in the lurch, is it? Anyhow, he says to me, "Tell her I'm in Hoxton, if she wants to know. She can find me there." But I'm telling you, Sadie would be a fool to go chasing him there.'

'Hoxton? Any address?' Rob got ready to leave.

'Care of the Queen's Head, that's all I know.' Sarah delivered the final scraps of Richie's message. 'He looked in a poor way. I think he's hit the bottle. Like I say, she'd be a fool to chase him.'

'She's a fool all right,' Rob said. 'Look where she landed up.'

'We don't cast the first stone round here,' Sarah replied. 'I thought she was a lovely girl, only a bit soft.' She followed him halfway along the balcony. 'You'll give her the message?'

Rob nodded. He was glad to put a distance between himself and Hope Street. When he got home, he took the boxes out of the taxi and took them upstairs into Eden

House. Sadie looked at him, half-expecting news of Richie, but he shook his head. 'Nothing,' he reported. 'I should forget him, if I was you. He ain't never gonna be no good for you.'

She fought to accept it, sitting over a cup of tea with Frances. She protested that she'd put Richie behind her already. Meggie was all she cared about now. But she lay in bed alone, looking out through the curtainless window at the starlit sky. The street noises died away. Meggie slept soundly.

If Richie walked in now and said he wanted them both, nothing in the world would matter except that. She would sacrifice everything all over again, she knew it for certain. The image of him filled her every waking moment and drifted into her dreams. She longed for him, and wished he would come back. Love was like slavery. It shackled her heart.

CHAPTER TWENTY-TWO

'Ma, spell "Mauretania" for me.' Grace looked up from her homework. She sucked the end of her pencil and stared out of the open french doors, up the long, sloping garden of the house in Ealing.

Jess sat at her sewing. 'M-A-U-R,' she began, then waited for Grace to catch up. '-E-T-A-N-I-A.'

'Miss Shoesmith told us the *Mauretania* was built on the River Tyne by the Swan Hunter shipyard in 1907, since when it has held the Blue Riband for the fastest crossing of the Atlantic at an average speed of 26.06 knots in 4 days, 10 hours and 41 minutes!' Grace recited, word for word.

Jess smiled. Grace liked facts. When she wasn't busy with homework, she was tuned into the wireless, on the 2LO transmitting station, listening to the news broadcasts. She gobbled up information, read every Chalet School book, and shared Maurice's enthusiasm for the latest aviation developments. When she grew up, she wanted to fly a De Havilland Moth at a top speed of ninety miles per hour.

'Rosie says her sister, Katie, sailed the Atlantic even faster than that. But I said, how could it, if the *Mauretania* still holds the Blue Riband?' Grace bent her head and scribbled on.

'And what did Rosie say?'

'She said I shouldn't call her sister a liar, and she'd tell her big brother, Patrick, and I'd better watch out.'

'Hmm. I hope you two didn't have a fight.' Jess took her pointed scissors and snipped into the curved seam. She spread the lilac crêpe-de-Chine fabric flat and took it to the ironing-board to finish. Outside, Mo swung high on the garden swing, slung from a low branch of the apple tree. 'Did she say how Katie was getting on?'

Grace frowned. 'No, she never. She says that in America the tenements are high as the sky. She says you can't walk down the streets in San Francisco 'cos they're too steep. Once, Katie started to run and ended up in the sea.'

Jess laughed. 'And they're paved with gold, I suppose?'

'I don't know about that.' Grace took it seriously. 'Pa says Hollywood is where they make the best cinema films. It's where Charlie Chaplin, the King of Comedy, made *The Kid*, and where Mary Pickford, the World's Sweetheart, lives.' She sighed.

Jess didn't reply. She wasn't sure that Maurice should feed the children so many of these sweet celluloid dreams. Grace knew every sequence in every Douglas Fairbanks film, and Jess wasn't sure that a girl her age could tell the fiction from the reality. If she ever went to Hollywood, she might be surprised to find that the men weren't all dressed in curly wigs and frilled shirts, or that the young women didn't spend all their days tied to railway tracks, awaiting rescue. Still, Maurice took Grace to Saturday matinées to see the latest releases, and she came home thrilled, strutting like Felix and humming his tune.

The evening shadows lengthened in the garden. Mo came in for something to eat, and Hettie came down from upstairs to take him into the kitchen to make him a jam sandwich. She planned a summer evening stroll with George, she told Jess. George had a night off from the Lamb and Flag. He had something he wanted to talk to Hettie about.

Jess raised her eyebrows.

'Now, it ain't nothing like that!' Hettie stood in the doorway, blushing and laughing. She held Mo's sticky hand.

'Nothing like what?'

'Ma means cuddling and stuff, don't you, Ma?' Grace giggled and made a face.

'Now, Grace,' Jess warned.

'It's got to do with work, if you must know,' Hettie protested.

'Is that why you're wearing your best dress, Auntie Ett?'

'She's incorrigible,' Jess sighed.

'In-corri-what?'

'Never mind.' She gave her daughter a firm look and said she hoped that Hettie had a good time. Then she took Mo back into the kitchen to wipe his hands.

When Maurice arrived home late that night, the house was peaceful. He knew Jess would be in the front room, working as usual. The door was open and the light on. He heard the stop-start-stop whir of the sewing-machine, and the even rhythm of the treadle. Instead of going upstairs to Grace and Mo, he went straight in to see her.

She glanced up to receive his kiss on the cheek. 'You look like the cat that got the cream.' She smiled.

Maurice unbuttoned his jacket and flung it on a chair. 'I got some good news.' He rolled up his shirt-sleeves, then came behind her to rest his arms on her shoulders. 'I got us a share in the cinema chain. I'm part-owner now. What do you think of that?'

She stood up, pleased for him, not yet seeing the significance for the family. 'You're very clever, Maurice. And I think you deserve it.'

'Ain't you over the moon?' He embraced her. 'I ain't just a manager no more. I'm a boss.'

'Of the whole thing?' She didn't see how it worked. Maurice hadn't taken her into his confidence over any of this.

'No, not the whole thing.' He smiled. 'I just bought myself into one branch, developing the chain outside London.'

'Meaning what exactly?'

'Meaning, we're branching out, Jess, across the whole country. I'll take on new cinemas, get them on their feet. We're gonna take over the whole country before we're through!' He saw white-stuccoed cinema palaces in every grimy northern town; the clean, modern façades of concrete and steel, the wide open foyers, the raking auditoria, the silver screens.

'You ain't gonna work in London no more?' The picture cleared. It seemed Maurice wanted to uproot them. 'Hold on a minute, Maurice, I ain't exactly sure what this means to us.'

He gave an exasperated sigh. 'Look, if I run new branches, of course it ain't in London. We'll move north, Jess, find a nice new house near Leeds or Manchester. I already telephoned a few people. There's plenty of nice places. It ain't all cotton mills and women in clogs and shawls.'

She shook her head. 'And this is definite?'

'Copper-bottom, all signed, sealed and delivered.' He stepped back from her and began to pace the floor.

'And when would we have to move?'

'It's up to us. Soon. Before Christmas.'

'What about schools?' Objections flooded in. She put to one side for now the overwhelming feeling that he should have discussed it with her first.

'They got schools in Manchester, don't they?'

'And what about the dress shop?' Jess felt strangely calm. Later, she knew, the emotions would rise.

'Let Hettie have it,' he advised. 'She's got Edith Cooper to help her run it now. You're off the hook as far as making dresses goes. No more slaving over a hot sewing-machine.'

'It ain't slaving, Maurice.'

He turned on her. 'Why do you have to go nit-picking, taking me up like that? All I say is, there's plenty of cash now. I'll take a share of the profits, see. It don't make no sense for you to go on working.'

She stared back at him. 'I'm sorry you think I'm nit-picking.'

There was an awkward silence. Then Maurice's temper exploded. 'Go on, poke your spiteful oar in, why don't you? You ain't normal, Jess. A normal woman would be over the moon to be able to take it easy. You can enjoy the good life and I'll take care of everything!' He strode angrily towards her.

She dodged and went to close the door, to contain the noise of raised voices. 'You're saying to me, uproot and go off without a by-your-leave. You never even stopped to think if it suited me!'

He laughed derisively. 'I'm meant to ask if you want to be rich? If you want the kids to have the best of everything? If you want to drive around the posh shops in a big car, instead of being holed up day after day in a back room making things that other women can look down their noses at? I ain't never heard nothing so bleeding stupid!'

'You ain't never heard nothing I said,' she pointed out. 'Not lately.'

'Are you saying you won't move?' He gave a direct challenge, standing over her, demanding an answer.

'I'm saying I ain't made up my mind.'

The answer rocked him. 'Oh, and when do you think you might manage to do that?' He didn't wait for a reply, but went on in a sarcastic tone, 'No, never mind. It don't make no difference to me, see. You take your time. You decide whether or not a wife should be glad for her husband and help him make his way. Ain't no rush. I'll just go ahead and find a place to rent. Manchester ain't that far, not on the train. I'll go by my bleeding self, if that's how you feel!' He slammed the door as he went out.

Jess slumped into her chair, exhausted by the effort of staying calm. In many ways he was right: she should be pleased for him, pure and simple. The family should stick together. She was a bad wife to put obstacles in his way.

Only, Maurice hadn't included her in his plans. *He* would say it was because he knew she'd say no. He wanted to make it a certainty before he gave her chance to object. Looked at in that light, his actions were reasonable.

She began to argue against herself and tear herself in two. All well and good to be ambitious, she thought, but who was Maurice trying to please? Did he imagine the children would be happier taken away from their grandparents, aunts, uncles, cousins? And why didn't he see that her own work was important? He was a man, that's why. He'd struggled out of the gutter with single-minded determination. He didn't understand family. He looked on women as inferior. It was the old way; ingrained and unshakeable.

Jess had never seen herself as forward-looking; not

compared with Frances. She had little social conscience compared with Ett, no training for modern business, like Sadie. But she felt strongly about her own ability to make her way in the world. The success of the shop had allowed her confidence to grow. She knew how to design and make clothes that were a pleasure to wear. She could cut cloth to flatter, her dresses were wearable as well as fashionable. Best of all, she loved the work. The hours spent at the cutting-table with tailor's chalk, paper and pins, were a challenge to both imagination and practical skill. She would work out a design to the last detail, construct her clothes with an architect's precision, an artist's flair. When she went out on to Ealing High Street and saw a smart woman dressed in one of her outfits, she felt a glow of pride.

And Maurice had never once taken this into consideration. As she packed away her sewing things and turned off the light, she felt the grain of stubbornness swell and grow. It wasn't straightforward. A wife need not follow the husband willy-nilly. There might be a compromise. Let Maurice go up north and set himself up in decent lodgings. He could travel south in his time off. This would see them through the first period of time. If he was determined to make big changes to their lives, at least he could let her sort things out at her own pace.

She got no chance to express these things, however. When she went upstairs to bed, she found it empty. This time, Maurice had collected blankets and taken them to the spare room.

In the morning, after a sleepless night, he announced his intention to go up to Manchester before the end of the month. 'No one can afford to hang around in this business,' he explained. 'We gotta get our foot in the door first. I want to show Kinemacolor as well as the old black and whites. I want to take Warner Brothers talkies before Gaumont snaps them up.' He said he planned to find lodgings, give Jess time to sell up and follow with the kids. 'Ain't no rush over that,' he conceded. 'I can see you need time to sort things out.' He felt magnanimous as he kissed her and took the children off to school in the car.

Sadie moved into Eden House, sobered by her bid to follow her own feelings over Richie. She was like a child whose fingers had been burnt, who none the less still finds the flames fascinating and cannot leave the fire alone. Richie cropped up in her thoughts whenever she had a moment to spare from washing, changing and feeding Meggie. Throughout July, in the close heat of the court, she rocked their baby to sleep, humming a lullaby, secretly dreaming that his desertion was temporary and, like a cinema hero, he would gallop over the horizon clutching a fistful of dollars, with a smile on his handsome face.

He would be contrite. He would say he'd come back to be a husband and a father. They would be a family. For Sadie could not believe that she'd fallen for the type of man who would use a girl and ditch her the moment she got pregnant – the old story. She remembered Richie: his hooded, passionate eyes, his unspoken vulnerability, their closeness in bed. He couldn't have pretended then that he loved her without her knowing that he was insincere. She trusted her instinct, a small, dark voice that said Richie was better than he seemed. His love for her and the baby would overcome his doubts. She did expect to see him again, if not with a bagful of money, then at least with his sleeves rolled up, ready to try again.

Work had been the problem. Or lack of it. If Rob hadn't

sacked Richie, Sadie felt that things would have worked out between them. Once out of work, his stride began to falter. He was a proud man, he hadn't liked her being the breadwinner at Swan and Edgar. He felt even worse when she had to leave her job over the pregnancy. He knew he wasn't a real man unless he could provide for her and the baby. Failure had driven him away.

This was not the general opinion on Richie Palmer down Paradise Court. Dolly Ogden denounced him as the ruination of a girl's good name. Long summer evenings gave her the space to proclaim these views among the older women who kept to the custom of sitting at their doorsteps until night fell. These were heatwave days, when dogs kept to the shady alleys, and every rat carried the danger of festering disease. Government promises to keep a hold on prices had been broken. The pound in the pocket didn't go as far. Only gossip was free.

'And you see how the poor girl has to live,' Dolly said. 'In that nasty tenement. It don't matter how many licks of paint she gives it, it won't make no difference. And Frances can bring over all the disinfectant and bleach she likes, it ain't gonna keep them rats away. Not in the long run.'

There was a shaking of heads. Edith Cooper confirmed she'd seen a rat scuttling up a stairway that morning as she set off for work.

'It ain't paint and disinfectant she needs,' Liz Sargent agreed. 'It's a good man.'

'Don't we all?' went up the general murmur.

'But from what I hear, she'd take Palmer back like a shot,' Dolly went on disapprovingly. She brushed biscuit crumbs from her broad lap on to the pavement.

'Never!'

'She wouldn't!'

'She would.' Dolly leaned confidentially forward. 'She told my Amy as much. Amy wormed it out of her last week. She reckons she still loves him.'

'Hush!' Liz saw Annie strolling up the court, eyes and ears alert. 'And how's the bonny, bouncing baby, Dolly?' She steered the subject on to safe ground.

'Blooming, ta. He's sitting up and taking notice already. We'll have him saying his first word before Christmas at this rate. Won't we, Annie? I was just saying, we got a little prince in young Bobby. He'll soon be toddling around, God bless his cotton socks!'

Annie agreed. 'He's spoilt to death, mind. Amy's gonna have to toughen up on him before too long.'

'And Rob,' Dolly reminded her.

'You'd think no one had ever had babies before.'

'Let them go ahead and spoil him rotten, Annie. It's more than some can do for their littl'uns.' She pushed towards controversy. Life was dull when everyone agreed.

'How's that?' Annie bristled. 'I hope you ain't referring to Sadie?'

Dolly protested innocence. 'I never meant nothing. How *is* Sadie, by the way?'

'Nicely, thanks.' Annie's face stayed stiff and unsmiling.

'Under the circumstances.' Dolly nodded. 'And how's little Meggie?'

'Dancing the tango and doing long multiplication sums,' Annie snapped.

Dolly's eyebrows shot up. 'No need to be like that, Annie. We're all on your side.'

Annie should have known better than to draw Dolly on, but she narrowed her eyes and folded her skinny arms. 'And what side is that, then, Dolly?'

'We all feel sorry for the poor girl. Sadie's been a bit

headstrong, we know that. But she ain't done nothing to deserve Richie Palmer. Look how he brought her down, it's a disgrace. I used to look at young Sadie and say to myself, "There's a girl that will go far!"

Annie growled back. 'Sadie's fine. She ain't feeling sorry for herself and she don't want your pity, Dolly Ogden. She's getting office work and bringing it home. Rob and Walter teamed up and bought her one of them typewriter machines from the pawnshop. She'll soon be on her feet.'

'And she won't hear of taking Palmer back?' Dolly knew she was pushing her luck.

'Don't be bleeding daft,' Annie retorted. 'Where did you hear that?'

'Nowhere.' Dolly pressed her lips together. 'Ain't no one mentioned it to me. I was just asking.'

'And I wonder you don't have nothing better to do, Dolly. Or I would if I didn't know you better, you old windbag.' Before Dolly had chance to reply, Annie nodded at Liz and Edith and marched on her way. She was going over to Ealing to visit Jess and the little ones. She saw trouble brewing in that direction. Maurice had gone and got himself work hundreds of miles away. That would put a strain on any family. Ett had said that Jess wasn't herself lately. Annie wanted to go and see for herself.

August broke with a heavy thunderstorm. Rain hammered on to the grey roofs, single slates slipped and fell. But the air was cleared. A weak sun broke through as Walter Davidson stopped his taxicab outside Eden House and raced up the stone steps in the final splattering drops.

'There's a rainbow,' he told Sadie as she opened the door.

'I ain't got time for no rainbows, Walter.'

'You can't see it from here.' He unbuttoned his jacket and drew out a sheaf of jumbled, dog-eared papers. 'I brought the accounts we want you to type up.'

She nodded. 'Come in. I'm sorry I snapped.'

He took off his cap and followed her inside. 'Ain't nothing wrong, is there?' Meggie was sitting propped in a big, soft chair, wedged around by pillows. Her eyes followed Sadie everywhere.

'No, except it's rent day,' she grumbled. She cleared the table, then offered Walter a seat. Since she'd come back to Paradise Court, he'd taken up their friendship in his old, steady way. He never tried to romance her though, and never referred to what had once been between them. She caught him looking at her with concern and a hand went to her hair to straighten it. 'Thanks for bringing me these.' She put the bundle of papers on to the table.

Walter drew money from his pocket. 'Paid in advance,' he insisted. He noticed how she held her breath, uncertain whether to accept. He placed the coins on the table. 'How about a quick cuppa?'

She smiled and nodded, and set about filling the kettle with water. 'How's things?' Walter often stopped by for a chat like this. It broke the monotony of her days and brought no pressure. He seemed to visit out of sheer kindness. She compared him with Richie, and found no likeness. Walter was patient and steady. His wavy brown hair gave his face an open, friendly look. Though he was tall and upright, his presence felt shy. Ready to smile, slow to take offence, she would even call him handsome. After all, she'd once been attracted to him, before their affair had fallen into its uneventful, companionable pattern.

Sadie listened as Walter ran through the street gossip.

Taxi business was down, as it always was in the summer. Rob and he were still a million miles away from getting their hands on new cars. The old Bullnoses creaked on. The boycott at the Duke was holding up. Rumour had it that Bertie Hill was already feeling the pressure from the brewery. 'I hear he's been forced to serve after hours every now and then, just to boost the takings.'

Sadie laughed. 'Who says so?' She couldn't imagine Hill being so careless of his licence.

'Tommy.'

'Well, then!' She dismissed the rumour. 'Tommy's a dreamer. He says he's moving into Coopers' old shop when he's ready. Swears blind he'll be a millionaire before he's thirty!'

Walter laughed and rose to go. 'I'd best be off.' He took his hat from the table.

'I'll get these accounts typed up and back to Rob or you by the weekend,' she promised.

'No rush.' He nodded and left, passing Bertie Hill on the stairs.

Sadie's door was still open and Hill strolled in without being observed. He stood watching as she worked with her back turned, lifting the sleeping Meggie from the chair and laying her gently in her crib.

When she turned, she started. She felt his eyes devour her, glanced down to straighten her blouse, walked to the far side of the room.

'It's that day already.' Hill strolled to the window and smirked. 'Rent day.' He folded his arms and continued to stare.

Sadie nodded. She had to cross near to him to fetch her purse from the mantelpiece. He stepped after her, trapping her in a small space by the empty hearth. She took out the money and handed it to him. His thick fingers turned the coins in his palm. 'Twelve shillings and sixpence,' she assured him. 'It's what we agreed.'

'You ain't heard the bad news, then?'

His casual manner nettled her further. 'No. What?'

'I put the rent up to thirteen shillings last week. To cover maintenance costs. The roof, it needs mending.'

'You ain't said nothing to me.'

'I am now.' He kept her locked in the corner, studying her figure, noticing the smoothness of her skin.

'But that ain't right.' She fumed against him. Twelve and six was what they'd agreed.

He shrugged. 'Please yourself. There's plenty of others would pay thirteen bob for a nice place like this.' He glanced round at her improvements; clean paintwork, bright tablecloth, a picture or two on the wall.

'It's a crying shame! And you ain't done nothing about the rats, like I asked. It's bad for the baby. Ain't you never heard of the Housing Act? This place ain't fit for nothing!'

Again he shrugged, but didn't move.

She stared back at him, furious.

''Course, we might be able to agree special terms,' he suggested. It seemed to him a reasonable offer he was about to make. 'If you was nice to me, I might see my way to a tidy little rent reduction.' He didn't expect her to turn it down. In his experience, women in Sadie's situation would snap his hand off.

Sadie looked at him with loathing. 'Stay away from me, you hear!' As he advanced, she began to push him off. The offer was meant to operate then and there.

Hill grabbed her by the elbow. 'Ten shillings. How does that sound? Don't that seem fair enough?' He reached to kiss her. She struggled as she felt his lips smear down her cheek on to her neck. She tried to turn away at the last second, and began to yell out. Her fists pummelled ineffectually against him.

He lashed out with his free hand and sent her staggering against the wall. Then he pinned her against it, tearing at the buttons on her white blouse, excited by her resistance. He felt her tug the back of his hair. Her body was soft and slender.

Sadie felt a wave of sick panic. She struggled to break free, but knew at once that he was too brutal and strong. She wouldn't give in, though. She cried out against him.

Walter had seen the landlord going up to Sadie's room and made nothing of it. After all, she'd told him it was rent day. But back in the taxicab, he frowned. Hill had seemed to give him a sneering look of the man-of-the-world type, as if he knew why Walter was a regular visitor to Sadie's room. Walter had shrugged off the implication. Now what he found in the car gave him cause to go back up and check in any case. He took up a loose page which had fallen from the bundle of accounts and grasped it in his hand. Sadie would need it so she could type it up with the rest. He ran back up the stairs, two at a time.

Sadie had almost blacked out from hatred and disgust. Hill had ripped the clothes from her breast and his great hands were mauling her. He held her up to stop her from sinking down, pressing her up against the wall. His mouth worked against her neck. She still fought him off, but was growing feebler.

Walter ran in through the open door. He hurled himself at the landlord, tore him away from Sadie. Then he punched at his body and head, sending him reeling backwards with a bloody nose. Sadie wept and sank to the ground, trying to cover herself.

Crazy with anger, Walter laid into the burly ex-police-man. Hill knew how to handle himself, but Walter was fitter, cleverer. His punch, developed at Milo's gym during his teenaged years, was stronger. There was only so much battering that Hill could take before he slumped to the ground. In the end, Sadie had to drag her defender away, to prevent real damage.

By the time Walter had lugged Hill from the room and watched him stagger away, Sadie too was almost senseless. Walter rushed across the landing to Mary O'Hagan, sent her in to help Sadie, then rushed for Annie. When he brought her back, they found Sadie in tears in Mary's rooms. She was begging for Richie.

Walter stopped short at the door.

Annie shot him a look. 'I'll see to things here. You go get yourself cleaned up.' There was blood trickling from the corner of Walter's mouth. His shirt collar was torn.

In a daze he went down to the taxi and drove himself to the depot. Rob took one look and demanded the full story. Walter spat it out, seeing Rob's own anger boil up. 'A girl ain't safe with Hill around. I hope you gave him a good thrashing, Walt. He bleeding deserved it!'

Walter dabbed at his sore mouth. The cut was swollen and tender. 'If she had someone to look after her, none of this would've gone on. God knows what he'd have done if I hadn't showed up again.'

Rob frowned through his cigarette smoke. 'Ain't you the one to do it, then?'

'What?'

'Look after Sadie, long-term. You know.'

Walter shook his head.

'Why not?'

'It ain't me she wants, Rob. It's Richie Palmer.'

Rob swore and protested, he called Sadie a fool, said Walter was worth ten of Richie. Walter wondered what Sadie would do next. 'She can't stay there no more. Hill will see to that. We gotta do something, Rob. Why can't we find Richie for her?'

'You're stark staring mad.' Rob took a step back and shook his head.

'It's what she wants.'

'Then she *is* a fool.' Rob thought through the new situation. Sadie's position as a single woman with a kid was open to all kinds of abuse. Men like Bertie Hill would crawl out of the woodwork wherever she turned. Driving a taxi round these courts and back streets late at night, Rob knew this all too well. He listened to Walter's account of Sadie sobbing out for Richie to come back. His conscience dug deep. 'We could put out the word.' Still he hesitated before he told Walter the full truth.

'To find Richie?'

Rob nodded. 'It ain't gonna be that hard.'

'You know something?'

'I heard he was in Hoxton,' he admitted. 'I don't know where exactly. And I don't know why I'm telling you this, Walt. We must be bleeding mad.'

Walter pressed him to go on. 'If Sadie wants to see him, you gotta let her.'

Rob gave in. 'Tell her she should try the Queen's Head. Like I say, I must be round the bleeding twist. And you need your head looking at,' he told Walter. 'You wouldn't find me giving up on a girl like that!'

CHAPTER TWENTY-THREE

Walter knew the Shoreditch and Hoxton area well enough to find his way easily to the Queen's Head on the corner of Regent Street and Turner Court. It was an old-style pub where street gangs graduated after a teenage apprenticeship of fights with belts and bottles, where the twentieth century had as yet scarcely impinged, and where assorted carmen, porters, navvies and railway workers gathered until well past midnight.

He had driven through the mean streets, the miles of brick and squalor, the long vistas of bricks and misery, to reach the pub where Richie Palmer was to be contacted. It was a stifling night, yet to his surprise, he found a group of children with enough energy to dance to the music of a barrel organ on the street corner. Two women sat on the pub steps, singing along.

One of them grinned up at him as he stepped by. Her companion jostled her, and their laughter showed their rotten teeth, their crooked smiles. Walter ignored them. He went in and ordered a pint of bitter, served by a small grey Irishman with a long, lined face, whose hangdog expression belied the phrase about the luck of the Irish. 'I'm trying to find Richie Palmer,' he told the man.

'You ain't the only one.' The beer sloshed on to the bar as he slammed the glass down.

Walter paid up. 'He ain't here, then?'

'I never said that. This is his second home, this is.'

Walter frowned and glanced around the dingy room. The bar was partitioned by wood and glass panels, giving drinkers the privacy to play cards or dominoes. Many of the partitions contained two or three men huddled over their beer, which he now discovered was flat and lukewarm due to the heat. 'He *is* here, then?' Walter felt his temper shorten as he peered round.

'*Was* here. Bought a drink ten minutes since. When I say "bought", I don't mean to say he had the wherewithal. What I mean is, he sweet-talked one of the girls into buying his beer. Richie Palmer ain't had the price of a drink way back as far as I can remember.'

The Irishman's sad face and tragic tones had a depressing effect. Realizing that he would never get a straight answer, Walter wandered away from the bar in search of the runaway.

He came across him deep in dalliance with a tousle-haired, pale girl with a shrieking laugh and a pretty, grey-eyed face. They sat in a dark corner, arms slung around each other's shoulders, though Walter got the instant impression that Richie was paying for his drink with a spot of compulsory flirting. When he saw his old employer, he leaped to his feet and pushed the girl away.

'Richie.' Walter gave a peremptory nod. 'I heard I'd find you here.'

'And what if you did?' He was defensive, resenting Walter's neatly cut tweed jacket and clean collar and tie.

'I came to ask if you'd come over to see Sadie and the kid.' Looking at Richie's patched shirt, open at the neck, his old waistcoat hanging loose, even Walter began to doubt that Sadie knew her own mind. He was unshaven and dirty, and bore all the signs of long-term poverty and unemployment. But if Sadie couldn't get him out of her head, if she was miserable and lonely without him, who was he, Walter Davidson, to stand in her way?

Richie went on viewing him suspiciously. 'What's in it for you? Who sent you? Did she?'

He shook his head. 'But she is asking for you.' He described her new situation and Hill's recent attack. 'She goes on about not wanting to make a fuss, but Annie came in and said it weren't right to leave Sadie in the tenement no more, not after what Hill done to her. She still wants her to go to the police, but Sadie won't.' It was three or four days after the event, and Sadie and Meggie were staying with Annie and Duke. After long family discussion, without Sadie's knowledge, so as not to raise her hopes, it had been decided that Richie should be contacted. 'Rob says you left word at Hope Street about where you was.'

Richie stood silent, avoiding Walter's direct gaze. For almost three months, since he'd left Sadie in the lurch, he'd drifted from one day to the next. He slept on garret floors, on the Embankment, in the parks. He'd left on the spur of the moment, after a build-up of shame about his diminishing prospects that he swiftly turned into resentment against the whole Parsons tribe. He'd even begun to watch Sadie, heavily pregnant, washing dishes or smoothing out the bedclothes, despising her small efforts towards respectability. She'd picked up her finicky ways from her family. Her eyes were the Parsons eyes: deep brown, big and dark.

He'd tried to foresee the future, after the baby was born. There'd have been no money. The sisters would have descended on Hope Street with a vengeance, sweeping him off his own hearth with advice, bits and bobs for the baby, tonics for Sadie. Sadie would have grown homesick, her feeling for him would have waned. She would put all her passion into the baby. Then she would have hankered for them to go back to Duke Street. If he'd given in and they'd gone back, every day he would have seen Rob Parsons in his taxicab, driving by in the car he, Richie, had looked after, and patched, and knew inside-out.

This was the thought that swung things for him. He took off suddenly, without explanation, thinking that Sadie's hurt would soon heal. Abandoned by his own parents, growing up detached from all deep emotion, he saw being let down in life as something to accept and spring back from. Letting people down was likewise nothing serious, not when you saw babies starve, old men drown themselves, girls of twelve walking the streets.

Walter grew uneasy with the awkward silence. 'She had a little girl, did you know?'

Richie nodded. 'She left me a note.' He'd tried through all these weeks to steer his brain away from forming a picture of little Meggie. But Sadie's written words were too graphic. He could see in his mind's eye her long, curling lashes, her rosebud mouth.

'And what shall I tell her when I go back?' He saw how Richie must be going through a silent struggle. Curious faces peered at the two of them, face to face. The pretty, shrieking girl was gossiping with the barman.

'Tell her I'll come and see her when I can,' he mumbled.

Richie came to Southwark a week later, waiting under the railway arch at the top of Duke Street, until he caught sight of Sadie chatting to Amy in the market. Both women wheeled perambulators. As Amy went to talk to Annie on her stall, Sadie turned to make her way up the street towards the park. He waylaid her without warning.

Startled, she stared at him. He was thinner, his expression unreadable as ever. His eyes were half closed, as if to keep his feelings safely dampened down.

Sadie had changed too, he thought. Her movements were slower, more careful. She didn't cry out when she saw him, though he could tell she wanted to. Her light dress, straight and simple, worn with a long row of pearly beads, showed her creamy-brown arms. Her untameable, wavy dark hair framed her face. She clung to the pram handle, but said nothing.

'Can I take a look at Meggie?' Richie took another step forward. People in the street rushed or sauntered by. The traffic roared and a train rumbled overhead.

The baby lay in her little wickerwork carriage, covered by a lacy sheet. He saw the dark hair against the white pillow, the same as Sadie's. He wondered what it was he was feeling. Disbelief. Curiosity. He glanced up at Sadie's proud face. 'Can I walk with you?'

She nodded. They went on past the shops, the chapel, the public baths, through the park gates, wandering like any young couple with their baby.

'I got your letter,' he told her.

She nodded. 'It ain't been easy.'

'I weren't good enough,' he said. The trees spread their leaves in a great, green canopy. They walked slowly through the dappled shadows.

'Don't go on. I ain't listening.' She looked stubbornly away from him, at the pigeons, the children playing. Then she turned back. 'At any rate, that ain't for you to say.'

340

'It's what they think.'

'Who?'

He pulled at white flowerheads on the rose bushes, crushing petals and scattering them on the grass. 'Frances, your pa, Rob; all of them.'

'They ain't me. Maybe I don't think the same way.' Sadie didn't want to make it too easy. She checked her pleasure in Richie's presence, forcing him to make the running as much as she could.

'I still ain't found no proper work,' he said moodily.

She looked him in the eyes again. 'You could try talking to Walter,' she suggested.

He frowned. 'What about Rob?'

'Rob was the one that told Walter where to find you.' Sadie had learned all this after Walter's successful mission to the Queen's Head. Since then her hopes had been high of bumping into Richie just like this, as if the bitter experience of being deserted had melted away.

Richie considered this. 'Bleeding hell.'

'Right,' she laughed. 'Being a stick-in-the-mud family man himself now, he might see things different, I think, especially with Amy coming down on him like a ton of bricks.'

'Amy's a decent sort,' Richie said. He sat down on a bench and waited for Sadie to put the brake on the pram.

'Who said she weren't?' Sadie and Amy were firm friends now. It was Amy's persuasive tongue that had laid the ground for offering Richie his old job back once he finally showed up to see Sadie and the baby.

'What's the use of him coming back to play the pa if he don't have no work?' she'd demanded. She'd recognized Rob's stubborn use of his newspaper as a shield. She went and tore it away. 'Now you listen to me, Rob Parsons!

341

When Richie Palmer shows his face down Paradise Court again, you gotta be man enough to let bygones be bygones, you hear?'

This was just after Walter had returned from the Queen's Head. She pinched and teased her husband until he yelled out and woke the baby. 'Get the gripewater,' she ordered, withdrawing her labour until he gave in.

Rob went and settled Bobby and fussed him back to sleep. When he got to bed, he found she'd withdrawn conjugal rights too. 'Bleeding hell,' he moaned. 'I'm married to a right bleeding battleaxe!'

'You are,' she warned. 'Until you learn how to behave.' She preached charity and forgiveness until well past midnight.

In a mixture of exhaustion and desire, he gave in. 'All right, he can have his bleeding job back, then.' He sighed, taking Amy in his arms. 'If it means I can get a bit of peace and quiet.'

'There ain't nothing peaceful about what you got in mind, Rob Parsons,' she challenged, kissing him all over his face, tickling herself with his moustache. 'I can see it in your eyes!'

So, by the end of August, Sadie's life had turned around once more. She was out of the crumbling tenement, and had converted her temporary stay at Annie's house into permanent lodgings at Edith and Jack Cooper's; an idea mooted by clear-thinking Frances. Since his meeting up with Sadie under the railway arch, Richie had scarcely been able to keep away from her and Meggie. He'd been humble to Annie and Duke, sincere in his desire to do better from now on. The final hurdle had been cleared when Rob came specially to find him at Annie's house. Keeping things formal and stiff, he offered him his old position at the depot.

They shook hands on it. Richie was due to start back on the first of next month. Sadie's cup was overflowing, but still she wouldn't be the one to suggest a full reconciliation with Richie. She would hold out until he asked.

'Happy now?' he said, after accepting Rob's offer. They took a stroll up the court, before he walked back over the river to Hoxton.

She nodded.

'And will you take me back?' He looked down at the pavement, up at the roofs, anywhere but at her.

'I thought you'd never ask!'

Her sharp answer drew his gaze. He grinned and kissed her. 'Ain't I the worst devil in Duke Street no more?' He'd caught sight of Dolly Ogden's lace curtain twitching.

'You never were.' Sadie linked arms and walked on with him. 'No, the worst devil by far is Bertie Hill.' She glanced at the open door of the Prince of Wales. 'So you can move back in with me whenever you like, never mind what Dolly says.' She had to check with Edith, smooth the way in that direction. 'She'll be glad of the extra rent, and the company.' She would talk her new landlady round by explaining that Richie was now all set to become the respectable family man. Sadie noticed Jack Cooper shambling up the street, and across into the Prince of Wales.

Richie said nothing, but he'd seen Tommy O'Hagan slip in just ahead. He asked Sadie about the boycott, and for five more minutes they stood by the pillar-box discussing Bertie Hill's worsening situation. 'George is sure the brewery won't stand the losses much longer.'

'How long will they give him?'

She shrugged. 'That depends. Tommy says he's up to Pa's old tricks, serving after hours.'

Richie laughed. 'That's why I just seen him heading in there, then?'

Sadie was incensed. 'Tommy? Bleeding traitor. I'll box his bleeding ears!' she promised.

All was back to normal. They parted, lovers once more. The next day, Richie moved into Edith Cooper's with Sadie, ready to start work at the depot on the Monday.

George Mann's courtship of Hettie went along on an altogether more sedate basis. For months since he went to work at the Flag, they'd been meeting quietly, watching family developments and worrying about the welfare of others. Hettie's work at the Salvation Army Mission and at the Ealing shop took her away from Duke Street a good deal, but she was satisfied that things were as good as they could be for Duke and Annie, now that Wiggin's influence was past. She scarcely forgave herself for her lack of charity towards the poor old drunk, however, and she redoubled her energies in the Christian hostel, soldiering for Jesus and putting her own needs way down the line. It didn't occur to her that sacrifice also affects those close to the martyr for the cause; her family lacked her gentle, affectionate presence, and George had to make do with fleeting conversations between shop and hostel, or fitted into one of Hettie's rare free days.

One Saturday in early September, he succeeded in persuading her to take time off to go and queue with him to take a boat out on to the Serpentine. The warm day made it a popular pastime with the young girls and their beaus, few things were as romantic and accessible as sculling across the flat surface in the mellow light. At last, George and Hettie came to the front of the queue, stepped into their slim wooden boat and headed into the stillness, away from the crowds.

George rowed for a while in silence. Hettie trailed her fingers in the cool water and took in the scene, guessing that he might have something special to say. She even had some warning of what it might be. He had been keeping her up-to-date on Bertie Hill's declining popularity with Mr Wakeley, the brewery manager – information gleaned from Alf Henderson, the landlord at the Flag. She waited patiently for George to speak.

'I'm in a spot of bother,' he began, lifting the oars and letting the boat drift.

'Oh?' This was unusual, not what she'd expected. She studied his broad, tanned face. 'How can I help?'

'That's just it, Ett. *You*'re the problem.'

'Oh,' she said again. The pleasantness of the day threatened to fall flat. 'What did I do?'

'Well, no, you didn't do nothing. You're not the problem; I said it wrong. Only, I got a problem over you, that's what I mean to say. I got myself tied up in knots.' He sighed.

Hettie let her hand continue to float on the water. In fact, she didn't feel George's problem, whatever it was, as such a threat after all. 'Spit it out, why don't you?' She held on to her wide-brimmed, light straw hat and smiled.

'First off,' he began again, 'you know Wakeley has got his beady eye on Hill. According to Alf, he only has to wait for him to make one false move before he gives him his marching orders.'

Hettie's eyes widened. 'Ain't that something? God forgive me, but I hope and pray they don't take too long about it. The sooner Duke Street sees the back of that man, the better.'

George nodded. 'So you see, Wakeley must be on the lookout for someone to step into his shoes.'

Hettie spied another rowing-boat cutting swiftly across their bows. She shouted, George seized the oars and swung away. 'And that someone could be you, is that it?'

'Could be.' He rowed for a while. The soft sun glinted on millions of ripples, the oars dipped and cleared the water in a steady, even rhythm. 'But here's where I get tied up. See, I could go right up and put my name down for Wakeley to keep in mind. Alf says he'd back me. I already know the old Duke like the back of my hand. I stand a good chance of being first in line for the licence.'

Hettie's smile broadened. 'It'd be a dream come true. It'd make Pa very happy.' She hardly dared to think about it: Duke free to come and go on his old stamping-ground.

'I know it would. Now, Ett, *there*'s my problem. If I get the licence, how can I ask you to marry me? If you said yes, I'd be the happiest man alive, but I'd be thinking you only said yes for your pa's sake, to get him back where he belongs through the back door, so to speak. And I'd never know if you'd said yes because you wanted me!' He blushed and let the oars rest again. 'There ain't no way round it as far as I can see.'

During the speech, one of the longest of his life, the smile faded from Hettie's face. She lifted her hand clear of the water and let it drip on to her dark green skirt. 'Hold on, George, let me get this straight. Is what I just heard a proposal of marriage?'

George looked alarmed. One oar slipped and the boat tipped sideways. 'That's the knot I can't undo, see. Now I can't never ask you to marry me, can I? Not if I go and put my name down with the brewery.'

At last Hettie broke into a laugh. 'Try me, George.'

'And you'll give a straight answer? Never mind Duke and the pub?'

'Hand across my heart and hope to die!'

He took a deep breath and steadied the boat. 'Here goes. Hettie Parsons, will you marry me?'

'Yes,' she said. 'Yes, yes, yes.'

'Blimey.' They were behaving like a couple of kids, out in the middle of the lake, with people in the distance beginning to look their way.

Hettie laughed and cried. 'I love you, George Mann. And I don't think there's a girl in the whole world could have had a nicer proposal!'

'And here's me thinking I'd messed it up good and proper.'

'Well, you ain't. And you know that problem you was on about, about you not being sure why I'd said yes? It's simple as pie!'

'It is?'

'Yes. George, watch out!' she cried, too late to stop them from careering into the willow overhanging the bank. The boat lurched to a halt. She stepped forward and put both arms around his neck. 'Simple. All we gotta do is get married straight off, with Hill still dug in there at the Duke. That way, ain't no one can think I'm doing it just for Pa!'

'Straight off? Now?' He fended her off. 'Get hitched now? You sure it ain't a bit sudden?'

Her eyes sparkled as she looked at him. 'George Mann, I'm thirty-six years old. What's sudden about that?' She lost him among the silvery leaves, her hat fell off into the water.

'If we don't hurry up and get cracking, we'll be drawing our old age pension!'

He leaned forward to hold her steady, then kissed her as she fell into his arms.

They married at Southwark Register Office on 21 September 1925. The family radiated happiness and even warmed the heart of the registrar, who'd tied the knot with less than obvious enthusiasm for most of his thirty-year-long career.

The next day, George and Hettie went along together to see Mr Wakeley. The manager saw them in a small downstairs office, amid the smell of fermenting hops and the sound of horses' hoofs stamping on the cobbled yard. As a hard-headed businessman, he gave nothing away about the present state of affairs at the Prince of Wales, but he noted with approval George's work as cellarman and said he would certainly keep him in mind. He made no connection between Hettie and the previous, unsuccessful interview with Maurice and Rob, on Duke's behalf. To him, she was Mrs Mann, a quiet, good-looking woman who seemed likely to do good service with her husband behind a respectable bar.

'Good job you ain't mentioned you're with the Army,' George joked. He tucked her hand inside his arm as they walked out through the yard.

'I know.' Hettie's pledge wasn't the ideal qualification for publican's wife. She included this dilemma in her prayers, and sought time to consult with the Mission commandant over it. She felt it was a problem they would have to solve when and if the time ever came.

*

Maurice used the occasion of Hettie's marriage to travel south and talk things over with Jess. They met up, for the first time in a month, almost as strangers, outside the Register Office, just in time for the short ceremony. He saw her from a distance, dressed in an elegant grey and silver outfit, with a neat brimmed hat tilted forward in the style of a man's trilby. Mo and Grace were kitted out for the wedding in new fawn coats and shiny black shoes. He felt proud and lonely. Jess came forward to embrace him and they went in together.

'I miss you,' he told her, short and sweet. It was later that day, after they'd toasted the bride and groom, and Annie had shed tears of happiness. George had stood up and thanked them, and promised them he would move mountains to oust Bertie Hill and get Duke back where he belonged. Jess and Maurice had finally driven home to Ealing and got the two over-excited children to bed. Now he sat on the edge of their own bed, watching Jess unpin her hair.

She went and sat down beside him. 'Yes, and the house ain't the same without you coming home at night,' she confessed. The rhythm of her day had changed, shifted out of balance. She missed the slow, unperceived build-up of expectation in the evening when she used to sit at her work, waiting for Maurice to arrive.

'You mean that?' He looked at her, his face drawn and miserable. His dark, strong features matched Jess's own rich colouring.

She stroked his cheek and nodded, 'Anyhow, you ain't got time to miss us that much. You're too busy building your blessed picture palaces.'

'Not twenty-four hours a day, I ain't.' He described his lodgings in a respectable Manchester suburb, which he shared with his landlady, Mrs Walters, her two Pekinese dogs, and her three other 'gentlemen'.

Jess frowned. Her initial anger against him for re-ordering their universe without consultation hadn't stood the test of separation. Already she was beginning to work around the obstacles, trying to talk the problem through with Hettie. But she often turned in ever-decreasing circles instead of coming up with any answers. 'Ett says I gotta make up my own mind,' she dropped into the conversation. 'Only, with her being married to George now, I don't reckon she'd want to take on the shop all by herself.'

'But you'd give it up?' he asked in surprise. He felt a surge of hope. During the lonely hours in his single bed, Maurice had convinced himself that Jess was more married to the shop than she was to him. He veered from sadness to bitterness, especially over his enforced separation from Grace and Mo. Being apart from them felt like an amputation, and he blamed Jess's selfishness. But now he began to regret his own high-handedness, as he saw her struggling to come to a decision. 'Come and live up north with me, and let's be a family again!'

'I can't, Maurice. I just can't!'

He gathered her to him and comforted her. 'This is bleeding stupid,' he whispered. He kissed her tears.

'And you don't hate me?' she implored.

'I love you, Jess. We can work this out. By Christmas, we'll have come up with something, don't you worry.'

The separation that had softened their anger sharpened their passion. They made love with uninhibited eagerness, rediscovering each intimacy afresh. He loved her softly curved breasts and hips. She clung to his broad, smooth shoulders, stroking the heel of her hand down his long, straight back.

Autumn loosened the leaves from the tree in the park and carpeted the grass golden-brown. A co-operative food and household goods department store opened on Coopers' old premises. Tommy O'Hagan fulfilled his boast by opening a paint and wallpaper section in the basement. He soon began to walk out with one of the pretty new shop girls, Moira Blackstone, attracted by her dark auburn hair and quick smile.

Dolly offered firm advice. 'Don't have nothing to do with that bleeding traitor,' she told a bewildered Moira, accosting her on the street outside the Prince of Wales. Moira stood waiting for Tommy, dressed in a soft-brimmed velvet hat and a matching dark blue coat. 'They should lock Tommy O'Hagan up and throw away the key for what he's done.'

Moira was startled. She'd only started work on the co-op cheese counter that Monday, and was immediately swept off her feet by Tommy's lively flattery. 'Why, what's he gone and done?' She clutched her coat tight to her throat and looked the length of the street for a means of escape.

Dolly got into her full stride. 'It ain't just me that says so. Annie thinks the same. He ain't fit to speak to. We all give him the cold shoulder these days; ain't no decent, self-respecting body will give him the time of day!' Her chin disappeared into folds of indignant flesh.

'He ain't gone and robbed a bank, has he?' Moira's imagination ran wild. Tommy didn't look like a bank robber, with his ready grin and sparkling grey eyes. But there must be something behind Dolly's account.

She snorted. 'Worse. He good as killed Duke Parsons!'

Moira gasped. 'Oh, my!'

'Yes. Might as well stick the knife straight in his back and get it over with.' She looked daggers at the sign over the pub door. 'I expect he'll take you in here for a quick drink before he takes you to the pictures?'

The girl shook her head. 'I ain't gonna go with him, after all. You say he as good as killed someone?' She backed away, stepping down into the gutter and searching in her bag for coins for the tram home. She feared she'd spotted Tommy leaving the co-op and heading up the street.

'That's what I call it. Helping to fill Bertie Hill's till is the same as signing Duke's death warrant. If he takes you in here for a drink, he's a dirty, rotten traitor, tell him.' Dolly seized Moira's arm and drew her on to the pavement. 'Tell him from me, if we don't get Hill out by Christmas, the old man won't make it through another winter. Just you tell him that!' She, too had spied Tommy, who whistled as he approached.

She left a breathless Moira to convey the message, refusing to lower herself to speak to him in person.

'Fancy a drop of something before we see the flick?' he suggested cheerily.

Moira stared at him. 'Here?' She pointed over her shoulder at the shiny new doors.

'No. Up at the Flag.' He linked arms, surprised by her stiffness. 'Ain't nothing wrong, is there?'

She took a deep breath. 'No. The Lamb and Flag, you say?' From what she could work out from Dolly's garbled story, visiting the Lamb and Flag didn't amount to a crime against the realm. For the minute, Tommy's treachery seemed to have receded. 'Right you are,' she agreed, relaxing into things.

But he'd lulled her suspicions with a decoy. After a drink at the Flag, they went down to the Gem to see the new Chaplin film, then Tommy brought her back up Duke Street and waltzed her straight through the doors of the Prince of Wales.

'A pint of best and a glass of port,' he ordered. He stood chatting at the bar with Jack Cooper, while Moira shrank into a corner.

There was only a handful of customers in the pub, two young lads from the tea and coffee counter at the co-op, new to the area like her, and an older, red-faced man with a stained waistcoat and a battered trilby hat. Much later a young man came in. Tommy was already on to his third drink. The young man scowled at her and went and slammed his money on to the bar. 'Give me a pint, Bert,' he ordered, without lifting his head in greeting.

She saw Tommy frown. Then he went up to the newcomer. 'How's tricks, Richie?' she heard him say.

The reply was mumbled. Soon Tommy left the bar and came to rejoin Moira. 'Bleeding cheerful charlie, he is.' He took a gulp from his glass. 'I bet he ain't mentioned to Sadie that he uses this as his watering-hole neither!'

'I don't like this place,' Moira whispered. 'It ain't friendly. Can't we go?'

Tommy ignored her. 'From what I hear, Richie and Rob still don't get on like a house on fire down at the depot. Walter's had to break up more than one row already.' He shook his head. 'Even I wouldn't have the brass neck to turn up here, not after what Hill done to Sadie, see. It don't seem right.'

'Let's go, Tommy.' Her evening was turning sour. She didn't understand what everyone had against the place: it was lovely and new, with posh electric lights and a brand-new, patterned carpet.

Tommy glanced at his watch. 'We can't. Not yet,' he replied. 'We gotta hang on a bit longer.'

Moira sat in the silent, almost empty bar, miserably sipping her port wine. This would be the last time she came out with Tommy O'Hagan, she decided. He ignored a girl's wishes, and he drank too much. She sulked as she watched him go unsteadily to the bar for his fifth pint of beer.

CHAPTER TWENTY-FOUR

Tommy's turncoat activities, relayed loud and clear to Annie by Dolly, were out of character. 'What's he up to?' Annie frowned and slapped her bread dough on to a floured board. 'It ain't like young Tommy to let the street down.'

Duke had heard the rumours too: Tommy was turning into a regular at the Prince of Wales. He seemed to prefer late-night drinking sessions there to keeping in with his old pals. But Duke didn't want to get involved. The days were drawing in, there was another long, idle winter ahead. He would fashion wooden toys for his new grandchildren and potter about the house as general handyman, while Annie braved the weather out on the market stall. 'Mr Baldwin's warning against an all-out strike.' He read the headline news in the evening paper. 'He wants to set up a royal commission on the miners, and much good may it do them.' He sniffed.

Annie thumped and pummelled her dough. The sweet, yeasty smell filled the kitchen. 'You ain't listening to a word I say. I'm telling you, Tommy O'Hagan's up to something. He's a cheeky little bleeder, always has been, but there ain't a bad bone in his body. No, if he's taken to lining Bertie Hill's pockets, it's gotta be for a good reason.' She scooped the dough back into the earthenware bowl, covered it with a linen cloth and set it by the range to rise a second time.

Still Duke ignored her. 'Here's an advertisement for an electric ignition set for motor cars. I'll let Rob know about that. Maybe he can get Richie to fit it to the old Bullnoses. And listen, if there's a general strike over the miners, what's the betting they just bring in the troops to keep things moving? The miners ain't got a chance, poor bleeders.' He grumbled on as he took a small pair of scissors and cut out the clipping to show his son.

Annie lost patience and began to clatter about at the sink. You ain't gonna make things no better by hiding your head in the sand,' she warned. 'I think you should pay some mind to what people round here do for you, trying to get shut of that nasty piece of work at the pub.'

He sighed. 'You think I ain't grateful?'

'No, I know you are.' Annie softened her tone and turned to face him. She dried her hands on a towel. 'I'm sorry for going on about it, Duke. Only, young Tommy's gone and got my goat, unless he *is* hiding something up his sleeve.'

He nodded. They were friends again, when they heard the latch of the front door open.

'That'll be Ernie calling in for his tea,' Annie said. She had the first batch of loaves in the oven, and there was a calm, warm feel to the room.

Ernie came in, his face red with cycling, the feeling of autumn wind about him, as he stuffed his cap into his pocket and came to sit by the fire. Annie swung the kettle on to the hob, cheered by Ernie's smiles.

Then there was a knock. Duke went and answered the door to George. 'You're just in time for a cuppa.' He led him into the kitchen. 'I think Annie's knocking together some scones. Come in, come in.'

The tall cellarman stooped his head as he went down into the kitchen and squeezed his large frame into a seat at the table, opposite Duke.

Annie made a great fuss of her new son-in-law. He and Hettie were just setting up nicely in rooms down Meredith Court. Because of his size and occupation, she made frequent comparisons between him and Duke at a young age; both built on a large scale, both correct in manner, but with hearts of gold. She made sure he had plenty of melting butter on his warm, home-made scones. They discussed the price of cheese at the new co-op. George told Ernie to look out for the forthcoming match between Palace and Bury. He sat there, passing the time of day, without a sign of there being anything unusual in his visit.

But, just as he picked up his cap to go, he cleared his throat and made an announcement. 'I came to give you a bit of good news,' he said quietly.

Annie, who was tapping out loaves on to a cooling tray, looked up sharply. 'Hettie ain't expecting already?'

George blushed. 'Give us a chance, Annie. No, it ain't that.' He turned to Duke, reluctant as ever to make long speeches, unsure how to deliver the news. 'We thought you'd like to know. Tommy O'Hagan brought in the coppers to the Prince of Wales last night. They caught Bertie Hill serving after hours.'

The news sank in. Ernie caught the word 'coppers' and assumed something bad had happened. He looked at Annie, who was standing face flushed, open-mouthed and speechless. Duke sat still as a statue.

'It seems Tommy reckoned the old boycott was getting

a bit long-winded. It was only grinding Hill down slowly, and Tommy wanted action. You know how he is.'

'I'll bleeding kill him!' Annie found her tongue at last. 'Leading us up the garden path, and all along he was working to get Hill out. Dolly will go spare with him.'

George was puzzled. 'You don't reckon she'll be glad to see the back of Hill?'

Annie tutted. "Course she bleeding well will. We all will. But she'll skin him alive for not letting on. You know Dolly, she likes to be in the thick of things.' She went over to Duke and put an arm around his shoulder. 'You hear that? Tommy's a bleeding hero!'

George filled the silence by explaining in detail to Ernie, 'Everything worked out fine. The police will get Hill into court for breaking the law over hours, see. Hill will be out on his ear, thanks to Tommy. He didn't let anyone in on his little plan because he didn't want the word to get back to Hill. Once he got the evidence that he was serving after hours regular, he got the coppers in. They came last night and closed the place down, no messing. And you know something? Tommy ain't breathed a word to no one about the part he played. It was Dolly. She saw the pub locked up and set about finding out from the brewery what was up. Word leaked out about an hour ago.'

Ernie nodded. His face lit up. 'Does this mean we can all go home, then?'

Annie quickly came and gave him a hug. 'No, I'm afraid it don't, Ern. It's good news to get Hill out. But it don't mean we can all go back.'

Again George cleared his throat. 'Now, don't go raising your hopes too high,' he warned. 'But Hettie and me, we got our name down with the brewery. And if we get the licence, we want you and Annie and Ernie to move right back in with us. Ett said to come over and tell you straight away. I telephoned her at the shop when I heard Hill was out. She said to tell you we was in with a chance.'

'And you let us sit here drinking tea and talking about football as if nothing had happened?' Annie advanced on George in mock outrage. 'Why, you and Tommy O'Hagan, the pair of you, I could . . . why, I don't know what I could do!' Speechless, she flung her arms around George's neck.

Slowly Duke stood up and walked to the door. He shook his head. 'Thanks, son.' There was a catch in his voice as he turned away.

George shot a look at Annie. 'I ain't upset him, have I?'

'No, you just made his dream come alive again.' Her own voice choked. 'Go and see him, George. I'll wait here with Ernie.' She blew her nose and set to, refilling the kettle at the tap. 'Come on, Ern, wash these few pots before you get back to work. Look lively.'

George followed Duke into the front parlour. Annie's aspidistra stood in its round, glazed pot in the window. The cream lace curtains hung in neat folds. A marble-cased clock ticked on the mantelpiece. Duke sat himself in an upright chair beside the polished, empty grate.

'We ain't got the place, not yet.' George stood awkwardly at the door, holding the peak of his cap in both hands. 'But we gotta be high on their list. I got experience, and I know my way around the old place. With Hill out of the way, Ett thought I should let you know how things stood.'

Duke looked across the room at him. He tried to clear his throat. 'You're a good lad, George. Thanks.'

He nodded. 'I'd best be on my way then.' He was

uncomfortable for the old man. Sometimes hope was harder to bear than defeat. 'Ett says she'll come over after she finishes at work.'

At first, Duke didn't answer. Then he made an effort to get to his feet. He came to shake hands. 'Let me tell you something, George. I don't mind telling you, there ain't much left in life for an old man like me. But if there's one thing that would make everything right before I die, it's to end my days in the old Duke of Wellington.' He clasped the younger man's hand between his own and shook it. 'Now, if it don't turn out that way, it ain't for the want of trying, and I'll die thankful for all you done. You and the whole family. The whole street.' His eyes filled up as he released George's hand.

Grudgingly Dolly had to admit that Tommy was the hero of the hour. Not a soul spared an ounce of pity for Bertie Hill, who took to his room in the tenement, having failed to persuade his ex-colleagues in the police force to let him stay open at the Prince of Wales until the case came to court. The brewery moved in quickly to sack him, and let it be known that the pub would re-open under new management just as soon as possible. They wanted to settle things quickly, before lucrative Christmas trade was lost. Now the whole of Paradise Court had to keep their fingers crossed for George Mann.

October winds tore the leaves from the trees. Yellow chrysanthemums appeared on the flower stalls in the street markets. The government awaited the commission's report on the miners. Trade was slow in the docks as winter crept in.

Perhaps it was general gloom in the country and scant

business for the taxi firm that put Rob's temper on a short fuse throughout October. Contented with family life, he tried not to present a worried face to Amy, and he doted on his son, Bobby, now six months old and thriving.

But at work it was a different story. He and Walter fought to keep trade buoyant by fixing their fares low. But it meant they had to be on call when sensible men were at home with their families, and Richie's wage, which they'd been spared throughout the summer, was hard to find.

Walter worked through thick and thin. Decent to the core, he didn't resent Richie's return. Seeing Sadie recover her old sparkling eye was enough, knowing that he, Walter, had played some part in bringing her back together with the man she loved. Every baby should have a father, he reasoned. God knew, too many didn't these days. He thought of the families torn apart by war, and the millions who never returned. When he looked at things on this big scale, he saw his own sacrifice as small.

But he worried about the grating, tense relationship between Rob and Richie. Rob's worry about business translated into a bullying attitude: he was always picking on Richie for slow or shoddy work, expecting him to put in unreasonable hours for what, after all, was a poor wage for a trained mechanic. Walter knew that it was only Sadie's continued part-time work as a typist that kept the wolf from their door. 'Leave him be,' Walter advised. 'He's a good mechanic, when all's said and done.'

But Rob was irritated by Richie's very presence. There was something about his look: the eyes, the slightly slouching posture that seemed to challenge, a take-it-or-leave-it attitude that was insulting, once picked up and taken personally. Whenever he came out of the office into the workshop, Rob would have to hold back what amounted to a loathing of Richie. Instead, he would niggle and argue over the best way of carrying out a repair, nit-picking over Richie's slapdash timekeeping, making it plain who was the boss.

For his part, Richie enjoyed getting under Rob's skin without making the slightest effort. He'd taken up the job again under sufferance, as part of the deal for getting back with Sadie. He had no regrets there: Sadie was loving, and seemingly contented with the way things had worked out. They both cared for Meggie with blind devotion. Only, Richie could not swallow his resentment against Rob, who had always held something against him and had sacked him for no good cause. He'd taken to drinking at the Prince of Wales, knowing that Rob would find out and hate him more bitterly. He admitted as much to Sadie, when, hurt and tearful, she had objected to his use of the place.

'Ain't there nowhere else you can go for your pint?' she cried.

He'd shrugged.

'Yes, and even if you're doing it to get back at Rob, can't you see what it's doing to me?'

'It's only a bleeding pub, for God's sake.'

'So why does it have to be *that* pub, then? Don't it make no difference what Hill tried to do to me?'

He felt low and sneaking, but he wouldn't back down. 'Listen,' he said. 'I'm with you now, ain't I? If Hill tried something again, I'd kill him with my bare hands. But it ain't gonna stop me drinking where I want.'

Sadie had to admit defeat, and accept that Richie was set on a course that didn't include finer feelings such as family loyalty.

*

They got through most of October, on tenterhooks for news from the brewery, sitting on the keg of gunpowder that was the relationship between the taxi boss and his mechanic.

After school on Hallowe'en, Jess brought Grace and Mo to Paradise Court with turnip lanterns, to meet up in the street with the O'Hagans. Jess herself planned a chat with Annie and Duke. Frances was to come over, with home-made toffee for the children. Hettie, Sadie and Amy were all due for tea; it was to be a great gathering of the women. By six o'clock Annie's little house was bursting at the seams, while down the next court, Richie was still hard at work fixing the brake rods on Rob's Morris.

'Ain't you finished yet?' Rob looked at his watch. He had to pick up a fare in ten minutes.

Richie, stretched full-length under the car, said it was a job that couldn't be rushed. 'These rods are rusted pretty bad,' he advised. 'And the split pin through this one is snapped clean in two, see.' He flung two pieces of metal sideways. They landed at Rob's feet.

Rob bent to pick them up. 'How long will you be?' Walter was out on another fare. 'Can't you get a move on?'

Richie eased himself clear of the car and hauled himself to his feet. 'I need the right size pin to fit back in,' he muttered. He went to search in a metal box sitting on the oily workbench.

'And a lot you bleeding care, by the look of things.' Rob was beginning to fume. 'I suppose you think tomorrow morning's soon enough?'

Richie found a pin that would do, and slid back under the car. He worked silently, watching Rob's legs and feet stalk the length of the workshop with their characteristic, heavy limp.

'Bleeding hell!' Rob threw a cigarette butt to the ground. After five more minutes, his patience was exhausted. He watched as Richie slid out from under the car for a second time. 'What now?'

Richie wiped his forehead with the back of his hand, smearing oil on to his face. 'I gotta test the brakes, don't I?' He reached for the door-handle, as if to climb in.

Exasperated, Rob caught hold of his arm. 'No time for that!'

Richie reacted as if he'd been burnt. He jerked his arm free and rounded on Rob.

Rob stepped quickly back. 'Touchy all of a sudden, ain't we?'

'Look who's talking.' Deliberately, with his face set in a sneer, Richie brushed off his sleeve where Rob had caught it.

The action felt like a slap in the face. 'You keep a civil tongue in your head,' he warned, stabbing his finger at the mechanic. 'Or you'll find yourself short of a job again.'

Richie drew air through his nostrils. 'And what'll you tell Sadie this time? That you gave me the sack 'cos I wanted to check the brakes?'

The comment rubbed salt in Rob's wound. He knew all too well that Sadie and Meggie's future rested on Richie keeping his job at the depot. He was trapped good and proper, and his reaction was to get deeper into the argument. 'You're too big for your bleeding boots!' he accused, forgetting the waiting passenger, forgetting his promises to Amy to stay calm when Richie riled him.

'And what'll you tell your lovely missus, eh?' Richie eyed him with contempt. 'Ain't many men tied to two sets of apron strings, like you, Mister Parsons.'

Rob launched himself at Richie and grabbed his open

shirt collar. His face came within inches of Richie's, saliva gathered at the corners of his mouth. 'You take that back, you hear?'

Richie would rather have died. 'I expect you think you've got it all worked out,' he sneered. 'Nice little business, nice wife, nice kid.' He outstared his opponent, gripping his wrists and wrenching Rob's hands from his collar. He pushed him back and turned away.

'What's that supposed to mean?' Rob felt his blood run cold. Richie meant something by that remark; something that Rob knew nothing about, that was going to make him look a fool in the eyes of the world.

'Nothing.'

'Yes, bleeding something!' He ran at Richie. Richie shoved him to one side, overbalancing Rob and sending the metal box clattering from the bench.

'You don't want to hear.'

'I'll break your bleeding neck.' Rob gasped with rage.

'I'm telling you, you don't want to hear.' Richie was so confident that he stuck his hands in his pockets. His desire to damage Rob went deep, but he didn't intend to do it with his fists. 'Why don't you ask your wife what I'm on about?'

Rob shook his head. 'What's Amy got to do with this?'

'Ain't she put you up to giving me my job back?' Richie's grin was insolent. He watched Rob's outrage swell and explode.

'So bleeding what?'

'So, she thought she'd better keep me sweet. She knew I knew. Stupid cow, she thought if she made up to me, I'd keep my mouth shut!'

'Knew what, for God's sake?' Beside himself, Rob grabbed a heavy spanner from the workbench and lunged again at Richie. He pinned him against the wall. 'You spit it out,' he demanded, like a man who knows he's just signed his own death warrant. He levered the spanner against Richie's throat, as if to throttle him.

Eye to eye, in bare hatred, Richie delivered the sentence. 'Amy ain't been a very good girl before she married you, Rob. She tells you you're the kid's pa, but you ain't. It's Eddie Bishop. We all enjoyed the laugh being on you. Bishop made himself scarce over the water, see. He weren't keen on being a pa, it seems. So Amy comes to you, and you fall for it!' He laughed.

Rob felt the strength drain from his body. He dropped the spanner and bent forward, leaning one hand against the wall. All the colour left his face. The pain was in his chest, his guts, from head to toe. With a yell he launched himself from the wall, pounding at Richie, feeling his fists make contact with muscles, skin and bone.

Richie defended himself. He ducked and grabbed Rob's waist, dragged him to the floor. The two men rolled and kicked. Rob lashed out with his fists: nothing mattered except to grind Richie's face to a pulp. He saw the blood, felt his own mouth begin to bleed.

CHAPTER TWENTY-FIVE

As Walter drove down Meredith Court towards the depot, he was in time to see the two men on the ground, still struggling. He ran in to separate them. Not caring who got in the way, Rob hit out in all directions, but at last Walter forced them apart and dragged them to their feet.

Rob's breath came in short, harsh gasps. Richie wiped his nose and mouth, head down, refusing to meet Walter's gaze.

'Get him out of here!' Rob yelled. 'Get him out before I do him in!' He seized a heavy pair of pliers from the bench and aimed them, ready to throw in Richie's face. 'And don't never set foot in here again, or I'll fix your dirty mouth for good I'll swing for you, Richie Palmer, I mean it! Get him out,' he gasped at Walter.

But there was no need. Wiping the blood from his face, Richie looked at them from under hooded eyes. 'Stick your bleeding job,' he told them. He left without his coat and cap, limping up Meredith Court towards the Flag.

Once he was gone, Rob collapsed forward, bent double, holding his arms tight around his stomach.

'Are you hurt?' Walter grabbed hold of him to stop him from falling.

Rob struggled for breath. 'No.' With an effort, he

straightened up. 'Collect this next fare for me, will you, Walt? I gotta go up home and have a word with Amy.'

He didn't wait for a reply, but set off, running as best he could up on to Duke Street, to catch her before she set off for tea at Annie's.

Amy had just wiped Bobby's face clean and put him into the perambulator in the downstairs hallway. She stepped out on to Duke Street, tucking the blankets well up under the baby's chin and heading briskly across the street to Paradise Court. She was already late, having waited for Bobby to finish his nap before she got him ready to go out. She was passing her mother's house when Rob headed her off.

'Oh no you don't!' He swerved the pram in towards the doorstep and hammered on the door. They heard someone come running.

'What is it, Rob? Oh my God, you look terrible.' She saw that his eyes were cut and puffy, his nose bleeding.

Charlie flung open the door and called straight away for Dolly, who ran to investigate. Rob thrust the pram handle towards her. 'Look after the kid. Amy's coming home with me!'

Amy felt herself dragged by the arm, back up the street. She ran to keep up, losing her hat, as Rob took her blindly through the traffic and back up their own stairs. He slammed the door behind them and stood facing her.

'You hurt my wrist,' she cried, sobbing from fear and frustration. 'What the bleeding hell got into you?'

'You tell me, Amy. You tell me God's honest truth. Have you lied to me about Bobby? Is Eddie Bishop his real pa? Is he?'

Amy backed off against the far wall. For a moment she struggled to make sense of what he was saying. The name,

Eddie Bishop, flew at her from nowhere. She put a hand to her mouth and sobbed.

'Tell me. Cry all you like, it don't make no difference. You gotta tell me the truth.' He stood in agony, as if his life depended on it. If it turned out to be true, that he wasn't Bobby's father after all, and that Amy had tricked him into marriage, he felt he would wreak a terrible revenge.

Amy saw what it meant. She knew in a flash what this would do to her and Rob, and quelled a rising panic. She must stay calm. As a great force swept through her, threatening to blow her apart, she held fast to the one fact that he wanted to hear. Holding her hurt wrist in the palm of her other hand, she stopped sobbing and looked him straight in the eye. 'I ain't lied to you, Rob. I don't know who's put you up to this, but there ain't a grain of truth in it.' She spoke calmly, willing him to believe.

'Sure?' Rob closed his eyes. He was shaking. 'You sure Bobby's mine?' Flesh of his flesh. His own son.

'I'm sure.' By her own calculations, it had been the night of Wiggin's disappearance. She explained it now to Rob, pinning down the time and place. 'What more can I say?' She bit her lip, waiting for him to open his eyes.

His head went down, he took a huge sigh. 'I'm his pa?' he repeated.

Amy went and took him in her arms. 'As sure as I'm standing here, Rob.' She rocked him to and fro. 'It's Richie what done this, ain't it? He's got his knife into you again. Well, don't take no notice. Bobby's your baby.'

They cried together, until Rob came round and swore to knock Richie's block off for trying to ruin Amy's name. She grinned. 'Looks like you already done that.' She went for warm water and cotton-wool to bathe his face.

A few minutes later, they recognized Dolly's knock. She

entered in full war cry, demanding to know what Rob had done to her girl, swearing that if he so much as laid a finger on her she'd see him sent down for good. She'd rushed out of the house in her carpet-slippers and apron, armed with a poker; a formidable sight.

Amy dried her eyes. She explained the whole thing. 'Ain't no real harm done,' she finished. 'Rob believes me, don't you, Rob? And he stuck up for me, see, Ma. Now put that poker down and don't take on.'

'No harm done! Don't take on!' Dolly spluttered. 'He only set out to ruin a girl's good name, that's all.'

'Well, Rob's given him the sack.' Amy led her mother to a chair.

'Wait till I tell your pa!' She was unstoppable now. 'Wait till I tell Charlie and Annie and Duke! Richie Palmer ain't gonna get away with this.' She was up and out of the room and down the stairs before they could stop her.

'Me and my big mouth.' Amy sighed. 'Now the whole bleeding street will know.' Her ma didn't recognize the word discretion.

Rob, still recovering from the battering around his heart, found it was his turn to comfort her. Amy began sobbing for the loss of her reputation. 'Mud sticks,' she cried. 'Sling it in my direction, and there's plenty round here that'll believe it.'

'And they'll answer to me if they do,' he promised. He felt strong again. Amy couldn't be lying now. The worm of doubt lay still.

By the time they went down to collect Bobby from Dolly's, the street was already awash with rumour. Liz and Nora got it straight from the horse's mouth: Dolly told them that Richie Palmer had tried to drag her girl's name into the mud, but Rob stuck up for her and gave him a good hiding. Richie was a nasty piece of work. Charlie confirmed to Tommy that Rob had a pair of black eyes, but he'd heard Richie Palmer was in an even worse state. Arthur joined the fray. If anyone dragged down the Ogden name, he said, standing at the bar of the Flag with his fist around the handle of a pint glass later that evening, they'd have him to answer to.

The episode had broken up the Hallowe'en gathering at Annie's house. When they heard, via Grace and Rosie, that the street was in uproar, Frances straight away volunteered to go up to Powells' to see if Rob's injuries needed any further attention. Hettie promised to take Sadie and Meggie home.

'She's had a shock,' Annie whispered. 'Not that we couldn't see it coming a mile off.' They'd all known how unhealthy it was for Rob and Richie to be working together, but they'd hoped it would work out, for Sadie's sake. 'Look after her. God knows when Richie will show up. I can't see no light in Edith's house, can you?' She went up and hugged an unresponsive Sadie. 'You're sure you won't stay here?'

Sadie shook her head. 'No, I'd best get back home with Meggie.' Her voice was hollow and flat. She wanted to talk to Richie before she jumped to any conclusions, but the shock of what he'd just done cut deep.

It dug beneath the false gloss she'd tried to put on her present situation, to those layers of uncertainty over Richie's treatment of her and her family. If he truly loved her, how could he carry on the feud with Rob, for a start? If he wanted to give Meggie a home and family, how could he spend so much of what he earned at the Prince of Wales? This latest row over Amy was scarcely a surprise, even to her. It seemed that Richie had a mission to destroy Rob in whatever way he could, and it didn't matter that in the process he would destroy her love for him.

Sadie stood outside Edith's house and insisted to Hettie that she would go in by herself. 'It looks like he's gone and done it this time,' she said with an empty smile. 'But don't you worry about me; Ett. I can manage.'

Hettie kissed her cold cheek. 'Annie says remember she's just across the street if you need her.'

Sadie nodded and carried a sleeping Meggie up the stairs.

She found Richie sitting alone in the dark. She started, then she went quietly next door to put Meggie into her crib. She turned on a small paraffin lamp on the living-room table and sat down, waiting for an explanation.

'I ain't gonna say I'm sorry,' he began, his voice more slurred than ever. He'd drunk himself calm at the Flag, but his mind was fuddled. He'd stumbled home to wait for Sadie.

'I never thought you would.' Sadie sat upright; staring straight ahead. Her face was lit down one side by the yellow flame. Inside she felt numb.

'That brother of yours deserves everything he gets, always picking on me, never leaving me be.'

'I expect he does.'

'What are you so bleeding cool about?' Richie turned his frustration against her. 'You heard I got the sack?'

'Yes,' she said. 'Again.' She folded her hands in her lap. 'I heard all about it from Dolly.'

'Snooty bleeding cow.'

'Keep your voice down, Richie. You'll wake Meggie.'

He took no notice. 'On your high horse. Miss High and Bleeding Mighty!'

She sighed. 'Ain't you done enough for one day?' She glanced at his swollen face, his cut hands.

'Oh yes, take *their* side, why don't you?' Incoherent guilt gnawed at him. He knew that everything lay in ruins, but he wouldn't take responsibility for it. 'Well, I'm sick up to here with you and your bleeding family!'

'So I see.' In turn, Sadie couldn't refrain from her snide little remarks. It was either this or break down in tears at the impending disaster.

'"So I see!"' he mimicked. 'Well, let them pick up the pieces, if they're so good and bleeding holy.'

'I never said they was. I never said nothing, Richie.' Slowly she looked at him. The angry, battered man sitting there in the dark was not the person she thought she loved. His sullen silences were no longer romantic, but destructive. His physical strength conveyed moral clumsiness; she thought him dishonourable. All this she realized in a single, icy moment.

Richie sprang from his chair. Instantly she cowered back. 'Oh,' he sneered, 'so now I batter my girl?'

She sat up straight again, avoiding his eyes. 'What will you do?' She knew they'd reached the point of no return.

'Go.' He was cruel, careless.

'Well, before you do, I want to say something.' She stood, only shoulder level to him, looking up at him. 'I want to say I don't believe a word of what you said against Amy, and it was a nasty thing to do.' Richie sneered again, about to interrupt, but she held up her hand. 'No, I don't want to hear no more. I think you're a fool, Richie, to throw all this away. Yes, like a spoilt child. You turn your back on Meggie and me now, you run away again and I never want to speak to you no more.

'We're better off managing by ourselves, just the two of us, and I won't stick up for you no more. Rob's worth ten of you for being man enough to give you your job back, and Walter's worth more than the pair of you put together, only I was too slow and blind to see it. Go on, Richie, hit me, why don't you?'

This time she didn't shrink as he raised his hand. Her stare beat it down. 'I done all I can, Richie, to give little Meggie a good start. But I don't call it fair when you pick rows with my family and drag Amy's name down.'

Sadie ran out of breath. She couldn't find the strength to say any more. She turned and went quietly into the bedroom. Richie was a big man, but he had no real courage. He was small in mind and deed. Quickly her contempt rose, allowing her to steel herself to the sound of the door slamming, and Richie's footsteps disappearing down the stairs. The front door banged. She sat a long time in silence.

Three boys sat on the step of the Lamb and Flag, their stuffed Guy sprawled across the pavement, a cap upturned ready to receive pennies, when Arthur Ogden stumbled out late that same night. George Mann, just going off-duty, helped him negotiate the exit and threw a halfpenny into the kids' cap.

'Watch it, Arthur,' he said cheerfully, as the older man swayed and set his own cap askew on his head. 'And mind how you go!'

The kids called after him. 'Wotch it, Arfer! Moind 'ow y'gow!'

'Cheeky monkeys!' He turned and hit out at them. They ducked and rolled away laughing. Arthur steered his own unsteady course up on to Duke Street.

George turned up his jacket collar and headed for home. Meredith Court was lit by gas-lamps. His own new lodgings were halfway down, midway between two pools of light. As he set off, he saw a shadowy figure moving ahead of him, towards the bottom of the court. He frowned as he identified it. Still unsure as he climbed his own stairs, he greeted Hettie with a preoccupied kiss. 'I think I just seen Richie Palmer heading down to the depot,' he reported.

Hettie's heart sank. 'What's he want there at this time of night?' She went to the window, parted the curtains and peered down into the dark street. 'Are you sure it was him, George?'

'I couldn't swear. I only caught a glimpse. I'm only saying it looked like him, that's all.' Uneasily he took off his jacket and warmed himself at the fire.

'Maybe he went back to get his coat,' Hettie suggested. She herself had just arrived back from Annie's house, having learnt all the details of the row between Rob and Richie from Walter Davidson.

'And pigs might fly,' he said dubiously.

She looked at him. 'That ain't like you, George. What's wrong? You think he's up to no good?'

George felt the warmth of the fire penetrate his face and hands. He sighed. Hettie came up to him and put her arms around him. They swayed in a long embrace.

'No,' he said, tempted to dismiss the shadowy figure. 'Maybe I was imagining things.' He held Hettie and kissed her. The novelty of being married, of having her to come home to, after all the years of respectable walking out, made him feel like a kid. He wrapped his arms around her and made a show of his feeling, kissing her softly and leading her towards their bedroom.

Hettie smiled, then sighed.

'What is it?' He cupped her cheek in the palm of his hand, murmuring against her.

'Sadie.' She thought of her youngest sister, and what the future held for her now. She looked up at George. 'What if Richie ain't just gone back for his belongings?' she asked uneasily.

Meanwhile, Richie hoped that he'd slipped down Meredith Court unseen. He kept to the shadowy parts of the street, using his own key to open up the outer gates of the depot, and leaving the padlock off as he stole across the yard to the workshop. What he planned to do would be the work of five minutes.

He switched on the electric light over the workbench and took hold of the heavy pair of pliers that Rob had threatened him with, then he eased himself under Rob's stationary car. No one had moved it since earlier that evening, when the final row had brewed.

Richie knew exactly what he was doing as he examined the underside of the old car. There, where the brake rods led up to the pedal, was the crucial main joint; a yoke which connected the rods to the pedal. It was held in place by a clevis pin. He got into position, then used the pliers to wrench the new split-pin from the clevis pin. It looked like a long, steel tooth with a forked root. He grunted, pocketed the pin, and edged out from under the car. The yoke wouldn't immediately fall apart. But some day soon, Rob would be driving along, he would hit a bump, the yoke would work loose. Then the brake rods would disconnect, he would put his foot on the pedal, and nothing would happen . . .

Richie slithered out. He caught sight of his own reflection, cut and bruised, in the windscreen. His rage wasn't spent yet. Taking his jacket from its hook on the workshop wall, he wrapped its thickness around his forearm and bludgeoned at the small pane of glass above the handle on the door into the tiny office. Then he freed his hand, shook out the shattered glass and reached through to take a spare key hanging inside. He used this to open the office door, then he went and took up a long screwdriver and used it to prise open the cash drawer. Inside was a handful of coins. He snatched them all.

By the time George had responded to Hettie's unease, had put on his jacket and braved the cold night air to go quietly down the court to investigate, Richie had stolen the petty cash and fled. He left the light on and the outer doors unlocked, careless about who discovered the break-in. Realizing that something was amiss, George stepped inside to survey the scene. There was a pane of broken glass in the office door, and the cash drawer had been forced open. He ran up to Powells'. He had to get Rob out of bed to bring him down to the depot to see what Richie had done.

'It's my fault,' he said, shaking his head at the missing money. 'I should've followed him down straight away.'

Rob stepped on to the glass and wrenched the empty drawer out of the desk. 'Bleeding bastard!' he swore, flinging the drawer against the wall. 'He's gone and done it this time, at any rate!'

'How much is missing?'

Rob shrugged. 'A few shillings. A couple of quid at the most.'

'Will you call the coppers?' George was worried as he studied Rob's pale, bitter face.

He shook his head. 'Good riddance,' he snapped. 'What I say is, it's cheap at the price!'

*

Sadie didn't think so. Losing Richie had cost her dearly. All her hopes of sharing the pleasure of Meggie with him, of planning for the future and feeling his love as the mainstay of her existence lay smashed. Only the necessity of feeding and caring for the baby held her together. In her despair she blamed herself. It was her fault entirely that Richie had fought with Rob and broken into the depot in his final spiteful act. It was her fault that Amy had been dragged down, her fault that she'd fallen for Richie in the first place and misread his character. She was unable to rouse herself from this self-pitying guilt, even when visitors came to the house; Frances, Walter, her pa and Annie.

'I been a fool,' she said over and over, sitting pale and drawn by the empty grate.

Annie took the poker and rattled the ashes into the pan. 'You can say that again.' She frowned at Duke and gestured for him to go and leave the two of them alone together.

'Right, I'll take Meggie out for a stroll,' he suggested, rising stiffly to his feet. 'It ain't too cold, is it?' It was four days after Richie's disappearance, and Sadie showed no sign of rallying. In fact, she seemed to be fading, day by day. She took no interest in anything, not even in the brewery's decision over the licence, which was due to be announced any day now.

'Good idea.' Annie nodded her approval. 'Give you both a bit of fresh air. Don't be long, mind. I left Nora to keep an eye on my stall, said I'd be back in half an hour.' She bustled into the bedroom and brought Meggie out, well wrapped up, looking sleepily around. She went down and laid her in the pram in the hall, then she stood in the doorway, waving Duke off up the court. She went back up to Sadie.

'Pleased as punch,' she commented. 'There he goes,

378

head up, chest out, strutting along. He was just the same with Grace when she was little. And Mo, when he came along.'

Sadie's face broke into a faint smile.

'That's more like it.' Annie went back to scooping the ashes from the hearth and brushing it clean. Then she rolled sheets of old newspaper and bent the tubes into a loose knot, laid several of these, stacked kindling against them and put a match to it all. Soon she was placing coal on to the growing flames. 'Ain't it time you tried to pull yourself together?' she said at last, looking shrewdly at Sadie from her kneeling position by the fire.

Sadie shook her head. 'I'm sorry, Annie.'

Her stepmother rose to her feet, frowning. 'Don't be. Don't be sorry. Get mad, girl. Take a swipe at something. Swear your bleeding head off. Being sorry never did no one no good. Being sorry will eat you away inside. Who are you sorry for, when all's said and done?' She pummelled at the cushion behind Sadie's back and made her sit up straight.

'Myself,' came the small reply.

'Exactly. And what for? So, Richie went and left you. Well, I ain't no Gypsy Rose Lee, but I could've told you he weren't the type to stick.'

'He said he loved me.'

'And most likely he did.' Annie refused to relent at Sadie's pitiful tone. 'Or what he called "love". With men like him, what's it mean? Wiggin said he loved me, once.'

Sadie stared. 'Richie ain't like Wiggin.'

'Not yet, he ain't,' came the firm reply. 'Look, if you have to feel sorry for someone, feel sorry for him. What's he got? He ain't got a job no more, he ain't got a baby to care for, he ain't got you to love him. And what have you got? You got Meggie and you got us.' She shook her head, stooping to look Sadie full in the face. 'It ain't nice to be left in the cart, I know that. But life ain't a bottomless pit, and sooner or later you're gonna stop falling and come to your senses. Only, let's make it sooner, eh?' She stroked Sadie's white cheek, saw her listless eyes fill with tears. 'Go ahead, you have a good cry,' she whispered.

Sadie let the tears fall. She put her head into her hands and sobbed, while Annie held her shoulders. Eventually she stopped.

'Good. Now, dry them eyes. Don't let your pa come back and catch you crying. That's right.' Annie kissed her cheek. 'That's the girl I know!'

Sadie took a deep breath and stood up to comb her hair. She washed her face in cold water. 'Right,' she said, 'what's the word from the brewery?' She began to make tea, looking out of the window for Duke and Meggie.

'Nothing yet,' Annie replied, satisfied that Sadie was over the worst. It was a long journey back to feeling she could face the world again, but she'd made a start. 'Poor George and Ett, they're on tenterhooks. And as for your pa, he can't hardly sleep nor eat for fretting about it.'

'Penny for the Guy!' The cry went up along the dark, damp streets. Bonfires took shape on patches of waste ground and in the parks all through the East End. On the morning of 5 November the rain came down relentlessly.

'Bleeding lovely,' Rob said. He peered miserably out on to the depot yard at the dancing puddles. He stepped to one side as Walter turned up his collar and pulled his woollen scarf high under his chin.

The rain dripped from the brim of his hat the moment Walter stepped out. 'I'll be back by eleven,' he called as he bent to turn the starter-handle. 'Look, Rob, I gotta take your cab while the sparking plugs on mine dry out. All right? I gotta pick up a fare from Waterloo and take it over the water.' He jumped in and slammed the car door.

Standing in the shelter of the garage arch, Rob nodded and swore that one day soon they would fit those electric ignition sets his pa went on about. No more starting up in the rain.

Inside the cab, Walter flung his sodden hat down on the passenger seat and drove out through the puddles, up Meredith Court.

There was nothing in his mind, except rain, as he negotiated Duke Street. This was the scene – the market stalls, the shops, trams rattling by, errand boys leaning their bikes against lamp-posts – that he'd known all his life. He waved at Tommy O'Hagan, stopped by Powells' and went down Paradise Court to see if there was anything Sadie wanted from the shops.

She looked up from the sink in Edith's back kitchen at the dark splashes of rain on his jacket. She gave a grateful smile. 'Ain't nothing I want that money can buy,' she said sadly.

He shrugged and promised to call in later with a treat for her tea.

'I don't deserve a treat.' She sighed, overcome by his kindness. Walter didn't know what it meant to bear a grudge. He was always steady, always kind.

'And I got a fare waiting at Waterloo.' He backed off before she got herself visibly upset. 'See you later?'

She nodded and took a deep breath. 'Thanks, Walter. For everything.'

He grinned awkwardly and went out. The rain had eased, but the pavement and gutter stood in huge, grey puddles.

Walter stepped into Rob's cab and set off, noticing the boys wheeling out their sodden Guys on home-made carts knocked up out of orange boxes and old pram wheels. He drove on in a good mood.

Sadie and he had slipped back into their old friendship since Richie had gone off for good. Apart from a few odd bruises under Rob's eyes, the whole street had managed to put the whole affair out of mind.

Though Amy lamented her 'ruined' reputation, they all knew she was tough as old boots in that respect. If anything, poor Sadie was the one who had lost most face. But even she was back on her feet, as Walter made it his business to check. He whistled as he drove, cursing the omnibuses that lurched from the kerb into the middle of the road without warning.

By the railway arch at the top of the street he turned left, nipping down side streets to miss the main traffic. He was late. When he came out on to a fairly empty stretch of Bear Lane, he put his foot down.

It happened every day; he was rushing to collect a fare, taking a few short cuts. There was nothing unusual, except perhaps the stiffer steering on Rob's car and the greasy surface of the road after rain.

A boy ran out from an alleyway. Walter saw him cut in front of a stationary taxi, and out on to the street. He wore grey braces and black, knee-length trousers. His head was shaved almost bare, and his thick boots were tied with pieces of string. He glanced sideways at Walter from under lowered brows. He was in a hurry, and no approaching taxicab would stop him from darting into the street, straight through a puddle, straight into the path of the car.

Walter slammed on the brake. Nothing happened. He pressed again. The rods flew apart and clattered to the cobbled ground. Sparks flew. The car kept on. Walter saw the boy's face, saw his hand go up to protect himself.

He swerved. The brake was useless. He tore at the handbrake, too late. He missed the boy, but the swerve took the taxi on to its two offside wheels, at a wild angle across the street. A tram rattled towards it, a steel giant, thundering along its track. Walter wrenched at the wheel, righted the car, too late to avoid the tram.

There was a crunch of metal, crumpling like paper. A moment's silence, before a woman screamed, the tram driver jumped to the ground and ran to the car. It lay upside-down, its wheels still spinning, the cab section invisible under the front end of the tram.

CHAPTER TWENTY-SIX

Doctors and nurses kept visitors at bay. The corridors of the infirmary were crowded with stretchers and wheelchairs, with silent, upright young women in starched uniforms and important-looking men with a dozen jobs to do.

They told Rob and Sadie that Walter had been badly injured in a traffic accident, that his case was an emergency, that they would have to sit quiet and wait for news.

Sadie sat with a tight band of fear around her heart as the inexorable hospital machine wheeled an invisible Walter into the operating theatre. His ribs were crushed, there were internal injuries. He had been unconscious when they pulled him from the wreck, and so far no one had been able to establish the cause of the accident.

Rob sat holding Sadie's hand. Annie had come along with Duke, to help keep an eye on Sadie, who was the most shocked of them all. They all held their silent vigil.

Outside, rain fell once more, and the wind battered against the long windows of the infirmary waiting-room. Duke recalled the time, eleven years earlier, when Rob had been sent home from the front, badly wounded. History had almost repeated itself again, except for the freak chance of it being Walter who had taken Rob's cab out in the rain.

'They say he swerved out of the path of a young lad to save his life,' Sadie told Annie more than once.

She nodded and slipped her hand into Sadie's. They must be patient and keep hoping. The afternoon ticked by, daylight faded. There was still no news.

'Mr Parsons?' A nurse came through, looking for Rob.

He got up.

'The doctor says you can see Mr Davidson now.'

Instinctively, Sadie jumped to her feet. 'Can I come?' she asked Rob, clinging to his hand. Rob glanced at the nurse.

'Just the two of you, then,' she argued with a curt nod, imagining perhaps that Sadie was the injured man's girl.

Mechanically, Rob and Sadie followed her through double doors, down a long, polished corridor. The pervading smell of disinfectant momentarily distracted Rob's attention, brought him out of his state of bewilderment. 'How is he?' he asked, walking quickly to keep up with the nurse.

'Comfortable.'

'Meaning what? Is he awake?'

'Not yet, Mr Parsons.'

'What's wrong with him, do they know?'

'You'll have to ask the doctor. I only know they've sent him on to the ward and made him comfortable.'

The nurse paused to swing to the left into a cream room with twenty or so iron beds, a central aisle, and a high ceiling, arched and raftered like a chapel. 'This way.' She did her duty coolly, efficiently, in her quaint, nun-like uniform with the starched collar and stiff head-dress. She led them to a bed at the far end of the ward and quietly left them alone with Walter.

Sadie approached the bed while Rob hung back. A wire

385

cage lifted the bedclothes clear of Walter's injured ribs, obscuring his face. She went down between his bed and the empty neighbouring one, saw his eyes closed, unprepared for stitches in his forehead, the deathly pallor of his skin. She caught her breath.

A doctor approached on the far side of the bed, standing over his patient. He was a stern, sturdy man with slicked, grey hair, immaculately parted, and a dark moustache, and was dressed in an everyday suit, a watch-chain slung neatly across his chest. He studied the wound on Walter's forehead, lifted the bedclothes to check a catheter tube directly into the chest cavity, which drained fluid from the lungs. He seemed satisfied, and stood back, hands clasped behind his back, rocking on to his heels.

'He's gonna be all right, ain't he?' Sadie pleaded for the right answer.

'It's too soon to say. We'll do all we can.' Another cool, professional voice refused to get involved.

'Why, what's the matter with him?'

'Crushed ribs, punctured left lung. Perhaps abdominal injuries. We don't know yet.'

'What's that mean?' She wanted a plain answer. 'He ain't gonna die, is he?'

There was no eye contact with the reply. 'As I said, it's too soon to tell. First of all, we must drain the fluid from his lungs, wait for him to regain consciousness, before we can really assesss the damage.'

The answer crushed her. Her head went down, tears came.

The doctor went and called the nurse, who drew up a chair for Sadie at the bedside, told her she could sit for ten minutes and advised Rob to take a seat beside her. Then she went off.

Sadie gazed at Walter through her tears. Only the scar across his forehead, the pale skin made him look different. He could be sleeping, one brown lock of hair falling forwards over his brow, dark lashes fringing his eyes, a small pulse flickering at the corner of his jaw. Soon he would open his eyes and smile to see her there.

'Walter,' Sadie whispered. Gently she pushed the stray lock back into place. 'Don't leave us, Walt.' She wanted him back down the court, bringing home the treat for her tea.

She watched the shallow, difficult breaths, glanced with horror at the tube feeding under the bedclothes, between the ribs of the wire cage.

'Time to go.' The nurse came back at last. 'You can come and see him again tomorrow, if you like. But there's no more you can do here now.' She took Sadie by the elbow and led her and Rob away, out of the ward, up the long corridor. Without the nurse's support, Sadie felt she would swoon away into nothingness.

'Take her home, look after her,' the nurse told Rob. 'It's hit her pretty hard. I wouldn't leave her by herself tonight if I was you. You can come again tomorrow.'

They left the hospital; Duke and Annie, Rob and Sadie. News went up and down Paradise Court: Walter Davidson was in a bad way. His brakes had failed and he hit a tram. He was unconscious in the infirmary. They reckoned his chances were fifty-fifty.

'He's strong and he's a fighter. He'll pull through,' some said.

Others shook their heads. 'You never saw the cab when they pulled it clear. Crushed like a matchbox, it was.'

Bonfires were lit for Guy Fawkes, the night sky exploded with firecrackers. In the morning, the smell of spent fireworks hung in the damp air. The police called early on Rob Parsons at the depot in Meredith Court.

Rob had spent the night in fitful dozes and sudden, chilly starts into consciousness. Unable to face breakfast, and keen to be on the spot for any news, he kissed Amy an early goodbye, went to work and sat through the grey hour of dawn on 6 November reliving Walter's parting words, 'Back by eleven . . . Waterloo.' It could so easily have been him, he thought. It *should* have been him; *his* cab, *his* accident.

When the police knocked on the yard gates at seven in the morning, he went to greet them with shaking hands.

'Any news from the hospital?' He broke the silence, turned on a few lights, invited the two bobbies into the office.

'Not that we heard.' It was Grigg, the eager constable from the Wiggin investigation, in charge now of an even younger raw recruit. 'No, we came to find out if by any chance Richie Palmer's shown his face.'

'No, why?' Rob was surprised they thought he might. Everyone was convinced they'd seen the last of him after the spiteful break-in at the depot. The coppers had all the evidence: Richie's missing cap and coat, the fact that the thief knew his way around, the clincher of George Mann seeing him sneak down the court. 'Does that mean you ain't seen hide nor hair of him neither?'

Constable Grigg shook his head. 'Bleeding Houdini. Vanished into thin air.'

'So what brings you down here, if you ain't got no news?' Rob lit up a cigarette to steady his nerves.

'We never said that.' The copper sat self-importantly in the spare office chair; Walter's chair.

Rob shot him a glance. 'What's going on?'

After much throat-clearing and settling of his helmet on

the desk, Grigg went on, 'We think there may be a link between the burglary and yesterday's accident,' he claimed. 'According to witnesses, the cab swerved into the path of the oncoming tramcar to avoid a pedestrian, a young lad called Dixie Smethurst. They couldn't understand why the cab never braked, see. They said his speed never altered. Some of them said they seen sparks fly, and when we took a look, we found loose brake rods lying in the road, some distance from the collison. Then we got an expert in to look at the cab, and he's sure the brakes had been tampered with.'

Rob sat stunned. 'You think Richie done that? Is that what you're saying?'

'We want you to help us out, sir. According to our bloke, there's meant to be a pin through a bolt that yokes all the rods together. If the pin comes loose and falls out, sooner or later that bolt, the clevis pin, comes apart, and Bob's your uncle!'

He nodded. 'That's right. And Richie just put a new split-pin in, the afternoon I went and gave him the sack.' Rob tailed off as he realized the implications. 'Oh, my God!'

The constable nodded. 'As far as we can tell, there was no split-pin holding the whole thing in place. What we're saying is, that cab was a death-trap.'

Rob stared in disbelief. 'That's *my* cab you're on about!'

'It seems like your days should've been numbered, the minute you gave Richie Palmer his marching orders. Only the plan backfired.'

'He done it on purpose?'

'You say he'd worked on the brakes?' The policeman stood up. As it happened, he didn't feel as good about delivering the result of the investigation as he expected. There was nothing wrong with the detective work: it was the effect it had on those who were innocent. He watched Rob struggling to hold himself together. 'So it looks like he made a proper job of getting his own back: breaking in here to nick the cash, *and* making a little adjustment to the brakes. That's how it looks. Only, he never guessed Mr Davidson would take the cab out that one time. He got the wrong man, as it turns out.'

Rob nodded. 'Thanks. I'll think this through.'

'We ain't got no hard and fast evidence, mind. Not till we get our hands on the suspect.' He put his hat on and pulled the strap under his chin.

Rob showed them out. 'No evidence. I got that.' He watched them up the street, two caped, uniformed figures, thinking he would have to go and tell Sadie the latest development. If she felt anything like he did, she'd straightaway see Walt's blood on her own hands for taking Richie back.

Sadie herself had been up since dawn. She tended to Meggie and left her in Edith's care for five minutes while she popped up the street to see Amy. Rob had already gone to work, Amy said. There was no news from the hospital.

Sadie nodded and returned home. Curtains were still drawn. A lad came down the court delivering milk. Safely upstairs in her own room, she checked the baby and started work on a typing task. When Rob came up and knocked on the door, she answered it quietly.

'Come in, Rob.' She was surprised, uneasy. She thought he was busy at work. 'What is it?'

'Can I sit down?' He avoided looking at her and sat at the table. He noticed she had the room tidy. A fire was already lit, small articles of clothing hung to air around the wire-mesh fire-guard.

She steeled herself, drew her own chair towards him. 'It must be something bad. You look done in.'

He nodded. 'It's Richie.'

'They ain't found him, have they?'

'No. There's no sign. But they think he's gone and done something terrible.'

'It couldn't be worse, surely.' Presentiments crowded in. She remembered sending him away with scornful, stinging words ringing in his ears.

Rob made a tight fist and thumped the table. 'Don't I wish I never told Walter he was in Hoxton!' he repented bitterly.

Sadie closed her hand over his. 'You done it for the best. I know that.'

'I should've known better.'

'So what's he done now?' She felt stretched to breaking-point, unless Rob told her soon.

'They think the accident was his fault. The brakes on my cab; they think he had a go at them. A death-trap, that's what they said it was. Richie wanted me dead, and that's a fact.'

Sadie shuddered. 'You saying he tried to do you in?' Was Richie capable of this, she wondered. Would he go so far? He was drunk. He hated Rob like poison. He deliberately smashed all he had to smithereens and left her and Meggie in a desperate state. 'Yes,' she said slowly. 'I believe he did.'

'But poor old Walter got it in the neck instead. I hope he ain't gonna die,' Rob pleaded. 'He's gonna pull through, ain't he, Sadie?'

'He is,' she breathed.

Rob got shakily to his feet. 'I wanted to come and tell you for myself, before word got round.'

She nodded. 'Thanks, Rob.'

'You'll be all right?'

Sadie stared back at him, her dark eyes blank. 'Me? Yes, I'm fine.' But she was racked by a spasm of bleak, bitter guilt. She put a hand to her mouth, turned deathly pale.

Rob caught her before she could fall. He sat her down, heard her begin to cry. She leaned against the chair. 'I'm sorry, I'm sorry!' She wept for every one of her mistakes, for Rob's narrow escape, for Walter. 'I been as bad as I could be to him, Rob! I ditched him, then I played on his good nature. Why doesn't he hate me for it?'

'He loves you,' Rob said quietly. 'He always has.'

'And I treated him rotten.' She sobbed, as if her heart would finally break. Then she looked up through her tears. 'I want him to live, Rob. Make him live!'

'He's gonna be all right, you see. Walt's like a brother to me.'

'Oh, yes,' she cried, and held on to him. 'We can't lose him, not like this, please God!'

On the afternoon of the accident Jess telephoned Maurice in Manchester, and, leaving everything under the charge of his deputy, he took the evening train down.

In spite of his reason for being there, his spirits rose as he stepped off at King's Cross, glad to be back on home turf. Grey stone instead of red brick, plain classical lines instead of the Victorian scrolls and furbelows of Manchester's master brickies. Even the Underground seemed familiar and welcoming, inviting cosy purchases of Quaker Oats, Nestlé's chocolate and Player's Navy Cut.

At home in Ealing, Jess told him the latest news on Walter. They were to visit the hospital next day, slotting in after Annie and Duke, if all went well. In his own mind, Maurice readily believed that Walter's toughness of character would see him through; a view which would hold good only until the first hospital visit brought home the frailty of the human condition.

Talking in bed together, after a gentle and loving reunion, Maurice admitted to Jess that he was feeling homesick. 'It ain't just you and Mo and Grace,' he confessed. 'It's the whole place I miss. The smell and the feel of it.'

She smiled, luxuriating in the warmth of his body. 'You ain't going soft on us, are you?' She'd never thought of him as nostalgic; only as forward-looking, thrusting into the future, feeding people their impossible celluloid dreams.

He grinned back. 'A tiny little bit maybe.'

'You ain't serious?' She put her arms around his neck, wondering where this would lead.

'Why?' Absence had worked its miracle: to him Jess seemed lovelier than ever. She'd softened into her old ways, and that evening as he'd watched her putting the children to bed, he'd realized what a good mother she was; practical and calm, ready to smile and praise, full of cuddles and goodnight promises.

''Cos I been thinking about us, Maurice.'

He unwrapped her arms from around his neck. 'Am I gonna like this?'

'I don't know. Are you?' She took a deep breath and lay back on her pillow. 'I've been thinking, the family needs to be together. I been over and over it: how can I make it happen withouut giving up the things that mean something to me; the shop, designing, taking a pride in all of that.'

He nodded, leaning on one elbow and jutting out his chin. 'Go on, hit me as hard as you like,' he invited. 'I deserve it for dropping the choice in your lap. It weren't fair.'

'Is that you saying sorry, Maurice Leigh?' She turned towards him, a smile playing around her lips. 'Well, it was a hard decision, I don't mind telling you. But I finally talked it through with Ett earlier this week, and we think we come up with the answer.' Pulling the sheets around her, she sat up and hugged her knees.

'Come on then. Spit it out.'

'Who says Ett and me only have to design and sell clothes here in London? When you think about it, why can't I do the same thing anywhere I like?'

He caught on. 'In Manchester, even?'

'Yes, or in Leeds, or Bradford. The women up there like to dress up in nice things, don't they?'

'I should say so,' he said slowly.

'Well, then, that's the idea. I'll move up to Manchester and open a new branch. Hettie will work from here, but we'll get together on the designing. We'll sell up here and buy a house in Manchester if you like, and find Mo and Grace good schools. What do you say?'

'Is that what you want?' He held his breath. No more Mrs Walters. Farewell to her travelling gentlemen and her snuffling Pekineses.

Jess smiled at him. 'You won't go on at me for opening another shop? We're not asking you for money, mind. This is something we want to do for ourselves. But I won't have no time to go to the library for you, or nothing like that. I'm gonna be busy, Maurice, I give you fair warning.'

He put up his hands in surrender. 'Anything you say, Jess.'

'Don't look so gormless, for God's sake. I ain't said we'll fly to the moon together!' She gave him a gentle push. He toppled sideways, clean out of bed. 'Maurice!' She scrambled after him towards the edge.

He pulled her down on top of him, and they lay on the floor, tangled in sheets and eiderdown.

'It's settled, then?'

'What about your pa?'

'He's got Annie and Ernie, and there's Ett and Sadie and Frances. And Rob,' she added.

That night they slept peacefully, their big decision made. They'd move north. London would be all the nicer to come home to: Duke Street and Paradise Court, with Duke in the old pub, God willing, and Walter on the mend, everything as it was, nicely in place.

Next morning Sadie had her heart set on finding Walter fully conscious and sitting up in bed. Annie, recognizing her change of heart towards her old flame, warned her not to hope for too much. Rob drove her to the hospital to keep an eye on her if Walter turned out not to be as well as she expected. He couldn't help but feel proud of his sister, walking with her head up, her wavy hair hidden under a cream cloche hat, her pretty dark face set in determined lines. They parted in the waiting-room and Sadie went on ahead, down the already familiar corridor to Walter's ward.

There were old men in here, mere skeletons, hanging on to life by a thread. There were men with mottled faces and high fevers, men with hoarse, rattling coughs and hollow eyes. Walter was not as sick as any of these, she told herself. He was ten times as strong, with everything to live for.

She approached his bed. 'He's awake,' the nurse whispered. 'And asking for Sadie.'

'That's me.' Sadie nodded and went forward. The wire cage lay in place. Walter was flat on his back, still connected to tubes.

The only piece of him that seemed alive was his face. With the rest of his body deathly still, his dark eyes slid sideways at her approach. She saw the click of recognition, checked her own distress and broke out in pleased tones, 'Walter, what have you been up to, you bleeding idiot? Giving us heart failure like this.' She bustled up and took off her hat, sat down, bent to put one hand against his pillow. 'What happened? No, don't try to talk. Tell me later. God, you ain't half given us all a shock.' She chattered on, trying to breathe life back into him. 'What have they told you, Walt? How long are you gonna have to lie there with them tube things sticking in you?'

'Sadie,' he whispered.

She put a hand on his shoulder.

'Sadie.'

'I'm here. Don't cry, Walt. I can't bear it. Listen, Annie and Duke and everyone send their love. Rob's outside waiting. He says, how's he supposed to get by without you?' Gradually her voice broke down. 'Oh, Walt, what is it? What do you want?'

'Sadie?' His eyes beseeched her. The word rolled around his mouth and seemed to fall from his lips like a heavy stone.

'I'm here, Walt. I'm here for as long as you want me to stay.'

He closed his eyes.

'Walt!' She could see he was tired, but it seemed more

than that. She was afraid he was going to slip away from her for good.

His eyes opened.

'You're gonna be all right, Walt.'

He shook his head and sighed. 'I want you to stay, you hear? Don't leave me now.' He tried to free a hand from under the bedclothes, but the vigilant nurse came and told him to lie still. 'Don't send her away,' he whispered.

Sadie looked up through her tears at the nurse.

'I don't know about that.' She looked doubtfully down the ward. 'I'll have to ask Dr Matthews.'

'Please.' Walter managed another faint sound.

The nurse nodded and went off.

It would have taken an army of doctors to shift Sadie from Walter's bedside. 'I'm still here, Walt. You sleep. I'll be here when you wake up.' She stroked his cold, clammy face, she listened to his breathing, scarcely moving a muscle in all the hours she sat there.

Matthews, the thickset doctor in the good City suit, with the gold watch-chain and the look of a prosperous merchant, reported instead to Rob. 'Your sister's still with him, Mr Parsons. He's very poorly, I'm afraid. The fluid has seeped into the chest cavity. We're doing our best to clear it, but our guess is that it's gathered around the heart and that will affect the rhythm of the heartbeat. He's a strong young man, granted, and the heart muscle's good, but it's a matter of draining off the fluid before it affects things too badly. There may be an infection too, and that can inflame the heart.' He shrugged. 'You understand what I'm saying?'

Rob nodded. 'But he ain't gonna die?'

'Touch and go, Mr Parsons. Touch and go. Try to

persuade your sister to have a rest. There's no point her wearing herself out, you know.'

'You won't prise her away from there,' Rob warned, as dogged as Sadie herself. 'Ain't no point even trying.'

During the course of the day all the Parsons family filtered in to sit for a few minutes with Sadie by Walter's bedside. No one spoke much. Sadie stroked his face and whispered to him. He woke in the early hours of next morning to find her still sitting there. 'See,' she said. 'I knew you'd wake in your own good time.'

He smiled weakly. She slipped her hand between the sheets and held on to his.

'Anyhow, Walter Davidson, just hurry up and get better and let's get you out of here. I can't stand hospitals, they make me come over all shaky.'

He gripped her hand. 'You and me, Sadie. You and me both.'

'Well, that's a good enough reason to get you out,' she promised with a brave smile.

If her willpower could do it, combined with Walter's strength and courage, they would get him home. Between them they'd pull him through, for all the doctors' shaking heads and the nice, neat nurses' cold sympathy.

CHAPTER TWENTY-SEVEN

Fever set in. The infection that the doctor had feared took hold and racked Walter's weakened frame. For days he was delirious on a nightmare sea, dredging past horrors to the surface; the whine of bullets, the stinging stench of mustard gas, the unburied dead.

He saw the faces of his young pals, smoking cigarettes, hunched up in the trenches over letters from homes that they would never see again. He stepped over them, face-down in the mud, praying that the whine of the shell with his own name written on it would never reach his terrified ears and send him reeling down into the chambers of darkest hell.

They fought to keep down the fever, tried to persuade Sadie to get some rest.

'He won't know you, even if he does come round,' they told her. 'Not at present.'

'I said I'd be here,' she said stubbornly. She turned to Walter's unconscious form. 'I will be, Walter. There ain't nothing or no one can take me away from you, never again.' She would only agree at last to give up her place at the bedside to Rob, who volunteered to sit with his friend on the third night after the accident. 'You send for me the minute he wakes up,' she made him promise.

Annie took her home to see Meggie and to persuade her to sleep.

Rob took up the vigil. A strange calm came over him as he sat at the bedside in the quiet ward. Walter's face was thin and pale but not much marked, except for the livid scar on his forehead. There was no sign of struggle; only sharp, shallow breaths and beads of sweat on his brow, which Rob sponged with a cold cloth. The night nurse passed occasionally. Far off down the ward, a man coughed and turned in his sleep.

At three o'clock, Walter opened his eyes. He turned his head towards Rob. 'Where's Sadie?' He sounded peaceful and rational.

'At home, having a rest.' Rob leaned forward so that Walter could have a clear view of him. Walter nodded and sighed. 'Know something? I think things is gonna be fine between us from now on.' He had a misty memory of Sadie leaning over him and whispering that nothing would take her away ever again.

Rob nodded. 'I said I'd sit with you for a while.'

Walter hovered on the edge of consciousness, lured by the warm, drifting haziness of sleep, alarmed by his crisp, clinical surroundings. He focused on Rob. 'What time is it?'

'Three in the morning. Don't you worry, Walt, they're taking good care of you.'

Walter sighed. 'How's Sadie?'

'Worried sick, if you must know. She don't let on though.' He thought she'd been a marvel of toughness and loyalty. It had taken the accident to do it, but her feelings for Walter were shining out strong and true.

'And little Meggie?'

'Happy as Larry.' Rob kept his voice to a whisper. He

knew the nurse was keeping an eye on them. 'What about you, pal?'

'Not so good, Rob. I'm weak as a bleeding kitten.'

'I ain't surprised.' Rob whispered an account of the accident and Walter's injuries. He took care not to upset him by mentioning Richie Palmer's probable part in the whole ugly business. 'We all knew you'd give it your best shot, though. Sadie, she won't listen to no Jeremiahs. She says you're tougher than any bleeding tramcar!'

Walter smiled.

Rob leaned forward to speak in his ear. 'I reckon she might be right. We're proud of you, Walt, for doing what you did. The kid got off without a scratch, thanks to you.' He watched his friend give a faint nod.

'I ain't done nothing special.'

'We think you have, and you gotta keep that in mind. It's a hero's welcome for you, Walt, when we get you out of here, back to the old Duke.' Rob's voice trembled.

'How's that?' Walt stared at him. Had he heard right?

'I said, back to the old Duke. That's where we'll be celebrating when you get back. Pa just got the word from Wakeley at the brewery. The licence came through for George this morning. He's taking over. It's all signed and sealed.'

Walter grasped his hand.

Rob nodded. 'We're all thrilled to bits. Ett says she'll finish with the Sally Army. Her major says it's the right thing. She says Ett's given the Army more than most already, and God won't mind her helping to run a decent, honest pub. You know Ett, she'd give her last farthing away. She's a saint.' He chatted on, knowing that the good news would help raise Walter's spirits.

'Whoa!' he protested. 'You say it's all settled?'

'Signed, sealed and delivered.'

'Blimey.'

The nurse came up at last and warned Rob not to overtire her patient. She checked his temperature. 'Going down nicely,' she reported.

When Sadie came in early the following morning, Walter was sleeping peacefully. Dr Matthews came and studied his charts, sounded his chest without waking him. He nodded briefly.

'What's he say?' Sadie demanded of another brisk, pretty nurse, as soon as the doctor had passed by.

'He says things look a lot brighter than they did this time yesterday,' she reported.

Sadie held her breath. She thought she saw the colour creep back into Walter's cheeks as he slept.

So far, since she'd realized the depth of her feelings for Walt, she'd merely managed to outstare despair, convincing herself with blind faith that he would pull through. Now she relaxed as she looked at him. His breathing was deeper, he slept soundly, without the haunted, tormented look. They said he was over the worst.

He would come back to Duke Street. She thanked God and the doctors and nurses. For the first time since the accident, she was able to think beyond Walter lying in danger on his hospital bed, to having him home safe and well.

There was a collective deep breath down Duke Street as Walter Davidson turned the corner on the road to recovery. His survival raised spirits and was seen as the triumph of courage over adversity. It made a change from short-time working, rising prices and dire warnings on the radio against the depraved new craze for Dixieland jazz. This, and the prospect of Duke returning to his pub, under the auspices of George and Hettie Mann, brought the year of 1925 to a happy close.

They likened Richie Palmer's disappearance to the famous music hall illusionist, Lafayette. He'd vanished in a puff of smoke. It was just as well: a lynching mood overtook the men of the area whenever they thought of him tampering with the brakes on Rob's car; an ugly, riotous intention which the police were glad to see dissolve, as Christmas approached. There was no trace of Palmer, either in Mile End or in Hoxton, and they made no great effort to bring him to book. People said he'd joined the restless, unhoused tramps whose shadowy figures drifted under the railway arches and along the Embankment: anonymous, faceless, hopeless men who shrugged off another layer of their humanity with each cold and bitter night they spent, numbed by drink, drifting into oblivion.

Sadie shivered when she thought of him. Richie and Wiggin began to mingle in her mind. She cried when she thought of what he might have been, decently set up in the motor trade, with a loving family. She forced her mind over what had sent him downhill on his destructive path. In the end, she saw that forces of degradation were too strong for some; for every Maurice who rose out of the bleak misery of East End poverty there were ten thousand Richies. She felt that in her own distress she had judged him too harshly. 'Poor Richie,' she thought now. 'I read him wrong, right from the start.'

As usual, Annie was the one to pull Sadie out of the past. 'Ain't no use moping, not when you've got more than enough to do already.'

'I ain't moping, Annie.' Sadie folded freshly laundered clothes for Meggie.

'You been over to see Walter lately?'

'This morning. I took Meggie along. He's nicely on the mend, he says.'

'And what about you and him?' Annie's inquisition was less sharp than it sounded. She wanted to heal the wounds for good, now that Walter had been given a date for coming home. 'We don't want no more rows over you-know-who!'

Sadie sighed. 'Over Richie. No, I ain't gonna think no more about him. Walter says I weren't the one to blame.' She ran her fingertips along her forehead. 'It's good of him, Annie, but it ain't all that easy to forgive myself.'

Annie took her up sharply. 'Oh, so you *meant* Richie to go and take them bleeding brakes to bits, did you? You meant Walter to jump right into Rob's car and have his accident? On top of getting yourself dumped with a kid and no job? It was part of your plan? Oh, very clever, I must say!'

Sadie felt her eyes smart. ''Course not.'

'Well, then.' Annie's fierce gaze drew a smile from her stepdaughter. 'Listen, girl, if Walt's forgiven you, I should say you're duty bound to let yourself off the hook, otherwise we'll all end up in the cart!'

'You're a hard-hearted woman, Annie Parsons. Can't a girl have no guilty feelings?'

Annie shook her head. 'Who did you intend to harm? That's the test.'

'No one.'

'Well, then.'

'But it ain't just the accident. I treated Walter rotten from the start.'

'Bleeding hell, if they handed out medals for feeling bad,

404

you'd be the first in line. Like I said before, did you plan it so that Walter Davidson would mope after you for the rest of his life? Or did he choose that for himself?'

Sadie shrugged. 'I never meant to hurt him, you know that. And so does he. I told him that in the hospital this morning. He's been very good.'

'More fool him, then.'

'Annie! Whose side are you on?'

'You just mind how you go, and don't go leading him on, not unless you made up your mind this time.'

Sadie was exasperated. She went through to the other room to lift Meggie and get her ready for a trip to the market. 'I thought you said not to feel bad.' Now she couldn't make head nor tail of Annie's inconsistent advice.

'Just don't take him for granted, that's all.' Annie took Meggie into her arms and smiled down at her. 'Dress up nice for his homecoming. He'd like that.'

Sadie grinned. She saw that Annie wasn't beyond a spot of matchmaking. They went downstairs together and walked up the court, Annie still carrying Meggie. They paused on the corner to watch the workmen restore the old pub name. Down came the Prince of Wales, up went the Duke of Wellington, in traditional gold letters against a beautiful green background. Annie beamed and nodded. 'Prince of Bleeding Wales!' she chuntered, handing Meggie over to Sadie, shaking her head and trudging back up to her haberdashery stall.

Walter came home from hospital on 12 December. Rob drove him down an empty Duke Street. It was half past five. The traders had packed up their market stalls and the street-lamps were already lit. Walter noticed the lights on in

Cooper's old place. The co-op was already well stocked for Christmas, with game-birds hanging in windows piled high with cheeses, tins, pies, cakes, nuts and dates. There was a buzz of activity. Shop boys mopped the floors and shook out the doormats. Girls wiped down the counters. Blinds came down and lights went off as they closed up for the day.

'Good to be back?' Rob grinned. He held open the door for Walt to step on to the pavement outside the Duke.

Walter stared up at the old building. The name felt right. He wasn't so sure about the electric lights as he stepped inside. Gas ones had been good enough before Bertie Hill came and upset the applecart.

Sadie came out on to the front step to greet him, dressed in a lovely, soft dress of pale blue wool. She held out both arms. For a moment he clasped her to him.

'Come on, you two love birds, get a move on!' Rob stood on the pavement in the icy wind.

Sadie ignored him. 'I love you, Walter Davidson,' she said. 'And I don't care who knows it.'

'At this rate, that's the whole bleeding world,' Rob grumbled. He pushed past the embracing couple and swung open the doors into the crowded bar.

Inside, Tommy led the rousing cheer of greeting. He stood there grinning like a Cheshire cat, a pint in his hand. Walter released Sadie at last and went up to shake his free hand warmly. He let the noise die down before he walked across to the bar, leaned both elbows on the copper top and waited for Duke to come up and serve him.

Duke slung a teatowel over one shoulder. He stuck his thumbs in his waistcoat pockets and took his time. He winked at Annie. 'What'll it be?' he inquired.

'A pint of best, please, Duke.' Walter enjoyed every

syllable. He watched the action of the pump handle as the old man drew the clear, amber liquid from the barrel.

'It's on the house,' Duke said, 'and a Happy Christmas to you.'

'Down the hatch.' Walter grinned.

There was another cheer. Grace darted out of the crowd and began to dance around the guest of honour. Soon Rosie O'Hagan followed, and the formality of the welcoming group broke up. Walter found his hand shaken right, left and centre. All the regulars were there: Joe and Arthur, Tommy with another new girl, Charlie talking ten to the dozen about his college course. There were newcomers from the co-op swelling the crowd, and ever more customers walked in off the street at the sound of cheerful celebration.

George and Duke worked as a team, serving pint after pint. Ernie put in a marathon washing-up stint, while Annie and Hettie went round clearing empties. Dolly insisted on music.

'Scott Joplin!' one of the girls from Dickins and Jones cried out.

'Scott who?' Dolly dug deep into the box of pianola rolls.

'No, the hokey-cokey!'

'Ta-ra-ra-boom-de-ay!'

'Give a girl a chance,' Dolly muttered. 'How about this one, "Abide With Me"?'

'God save us!' Annie came and turfed her to one side. She delved into the box. '"Tipperary", "Sister Susie".' One by one, the wartime favourites were discarded.

'"Ragtime Infantry"!' Tommy leaned across and pulled out the roll he wanted. Before anyone could stop him, he slotted it into position and set the pianola playing. He began to march in and out of the tables, followed by Mo, Grace and Rosie, leading them in a raucous chorus, with the pianola thumping out the tune in the background.

'We are Fred Karno's Army, the ragtime infantry,
We cannot fight, we cannot march, what bleeding good
are we?'

'Tommy!' Jess stood up to protest, but Maurice grinned and held her back.

'And when we get to Berlin, the Kaiser he will say,
Hoch, hoch, mein Gott, what a bloody rotten lot
Are the ragtime infantry!'

'That ain't nice, Tommy!' Dolly pretended to be shocked. 'You little ones, you cover up your ears, you hear!'

Mo clapped both hands to his head and marched on. '*Hoch, hoch, mein Gott,*' he chanted, while Grace and Mo filled in the rest.

New music soon took over. Sadie, Amy and Frances brought down food on large wooden trays: cheese-straws, sandwiches, pies. The party was in full swing. Soon Walter drifted across to chat to Sadie. She slid her arm around his waist and gave his cheek a kiss, bold as anything. Walter blushed, but he looked like a man whose dreams had come true.

Looking on from across the room, Rob thought that Sadie seemed different; less cocksure somehow, and more gentle. She was still pretty enough to turn heads, though.

He turned to Amy. 'Is Bobby asleep?'

She nodded. 'In Sadie's old room, with Meggie. They've

got their heads on the pillow like two little angels. Come up and take a look.' She could tell he wanted to.

They crept upstairs hand-in-hand to view the sleeping children, and afterwards stayed in the old living-room, listening to the laughter and music rise.

Duke had taken his eyes off Walter and Sadie for a moment to watch Rob and Amy go upstairs. He glanced round the bar at the joking, laughing crowd, caught sight of Frances and Billy sitting talking to Edith Cooper. He spotted Jess, and remembered the family would soon have to bear another split when Maurice took them off to Manchester, and good luck to them. Sadie caught his eye and smiled. She passed more empty glasses to Ernie. 'Here,' Annie said, shoving Ernie along. 'Let a dog see the rabbit.' Soon she was up to her elbows in soap suds, helping him get through the work.

George went down and tapped two new barrels. He rolled the old ones off the gantry and stood them on end. At this rate they'd need to re-order before the end of the week. He came up from the cellar and grinned at Duke.

'You seen the time, Duke?' Annie finished at the sink and glanced at the clock above the till. 'Time for last orders.'

'Let's give them just a few more minutes,' he suggested, reluctant to break things up. The music was still in full swing, the party at its height.

'Duke Parsons!' Annie gave him the full force of her most severe stare. 'If you don't go and put them towels over them pumps, I'll do it myself!'

He grumbled, but he knew she was right. 'Time, gentlemen, please!' he called in his gravelly voice.

Slowly they drank up and wished Duke and George goodnight. 'Never thought we'd live to see the day.' Arthur shook Duke's hand and slapped his shoulder.

'O ye of little faith!' Dolly quoted. She pulled him from the bar. 'Bleeding limpet,' she complained. Then she hooked her arm through Arthur's and turned for a final say. 'We all knew you'd get back where you belong, Duke!'

He turned and thanked them. 'Come along now. Time, gents!'

The noise died. The doors swung and closed until the pub stood empty. The family left Duke to lock up and went upstairs. He slotted the bolts into position, taking a moment to look around the old place, hearing last orders echo down the years.